AGE OF CONQUEST

RISE OF MANKIND 8

JEZ CAJIAO

Published through MAH Publishings Ltd
Editing by Michelle Dunbar
Editing by Faith Williams
Cover by Marko Drazic
Typography by May Dawney Designs
Formatting and additional editing by Christine Cajiao

CONTENTS

THANKS

Hi everyone! Well, another book done! This is book 8 of the Rise of Mankind series, and while I'm going to be jumping to the UnderVerse next for a few books, I'll be returning soon to finish this series off, don't worry. As always, I genuinely enjoy Matt's adventures, so it really won't be too long!

Now then, I've spoke about Chrissy, my wife, and about my eldest, Max, but this time around I'm going to talk about my youngest, my spicy, mad little bugger, *Alexander*.

Xander—as he's normally known—is a wild, affectionate and wonderful little man, and when I say 'little'? Its only in terms of his age, not his size, and certainly not his heart.

Now neither I nor Chrissy are small people, but Xander? Well, as a hint, I tend to call him 'Gigantor', because he's going to be huge. Like 'Reacher' levels of huge.

He's kind and caring, sweet and smart, and damn, I'm so proud of him. There'll never be a day when I don't smile, thinking of him and his brother, and even now, knowing that the nights when I get to tuck them in are limited and always counting down, I know I'm truly a lucky man.

Xander, I hope that should you one day read this, you'll know that I love you, that you're wonderful, and that in time you experience this love for your own little ones, be they mad or furry, grown or small.

You and your brother will always be, the best part of me.

Thank you.

-Daddy (Jez)
10/02/2025

PROLOGUE

"Are you fuckin' mad?" Petey hissed to his brother as the pair followed the obviously exhausted soldier through the houses. "Keep back!"

"Shut it!" Dave snapped in response. "Keep it down or he'll hear us!"

The pair had spent the past few weeks in their "hidey-hole," but after what the last few days had shown them…well, it'd been clear they couldn't just stay there anymore, that was for sure.

Peter and David Booth were both in their mid to late thirties, and although they'd never been angels exactly, they'd not been what you'd call "bad lads" either. Or at least not so's they'd admit.

Sure, they'd been arrested a few times—sometimes a few times a week—but who hadn't, right? They liked a drink, they liked a party and the footy, and occasionally they got a bit rowdy.

Nothing new or unusual about that.

The pair had a bit of a reputation as troublemakers, though—completely unreasonably, of course—but after that little incident where Dave had headbutted his manager? Well, they'd given up on office jobs.

In Britain's modern "customer service" economy, that meant that with most of the jobs being either minimum wage, or basically shite, sitting around being told what to do all the time, they'd been pretty limited in work.

Mainly because after Dave's little "Glasgow Kiss" incident, word had gotten around that you didn't want them working in your office.

After that, they'd had to register for a government training program, and they'd been furious when they'd found out they actually had to even go to it as well, just in order to keep their state unemployment benefit coming.

They'd been surprised to find that when it came to basic joinery, electrical work, and plumbing, they both had a significant aptitude for it. And it'd almost surprised their trainers and friends as much as it had them.

The pair had never previously been able to last at a job more than six weeks in their entire lives, but after a solid year of taking every training course the local government had offered, they'd taken a small start-up state loan, and they'd begun servicing their local area.

Electrical hook-ups, plumbing, sheds being erected—all of it, they'd found it surprisingly easy to turn their hand to it. And then along came the big one.

After the pandemic, all those posh buggers from the big cities and the idiots in their cushy office jobs all wanted to work from home, didn't they?

Well, if you didn't have a spare room to make into a home office—and most didn't—then people started buying Do-It-Yourself home offices. Mostly, they were the kind that you could put up in the garden.

Sure, there were plenty of big expensive ones that you could pay through the arse for—if you had the money—but for most people? A cheap little one was all they could afford.

Of course, "cheap" in this case wasn't exactly cheap. A basic one, three meters by five, was being sold for around five thousand quid!

Five thousand quid for essentially a few days of their time to knock up a simple timber frame, a base, and cut the roofing sections to the right shape.

It wasn't hard to take a manual someone else had made to build one, and just cut and paste the bits you needed into a new document, then slap their own new logo on it.

Sure, the locals were a bit unsure; they knew the brothers and their habits when it came to cutting corners. Put it on the internet, though? Idiots up and down the country were lining up to give them money!

They'd paid a pair out in the Philippines to do their customer service and handle complaints, with the understanding that if a complaint never made it to their door, then they'd pay a bonus.

Life had been good—no, *great* even.

They'd been raking it in, telling everyone to go fuck themselves with their dragging up old shite, and the pair had been loving it. They'd been saving up to buy a boat, one of those fancy ones with the big engines, when suddenly it'd all gone Pete Tong.

The power went out. At first, they'd not been bothered. Sure, it was a pain as they had orders to fill, but no power meant no complaining customers over little things like wonky walls and nails that hadn't been hammered all the way in.

Instead, they'd taken it as a holiday, and they'd started day-drinking. The next day when the power still wasn't on? Well, the beer down at the local boozer wasn't cold anymore, sure, but the pressure in the kegs meant it still poured, and the pub knocked a few quid off the bill, which wasn't bad.

As the days mounted, and they ran out of cash to pay? Well, the pubs were running out of booze anyway.

The supermarkets had closed at first, saying that the tills didn't work so they couldn't sell anything, but after a day, people had started kicking off. After three, the first riots had started. Although the bigger supermarkets had these massive shutters and security gates and grates, the smaller ones didn't.

The police were stretched too thin before this happened, and with not so much as a car working, they were dropping out of sight as well.

It wasn't long before people started to break into the shops, looting. And in a small town? Well, everyone knew everyone else, didn't they? When you see the local copper grabbing armfuls of baby powder, you stopped worrying whether he was going to come after you for grabbing a few little essentials like a case of whiskey and a dozen tablet computers.

The brothers had realized one thing right then: if people were hitting the smaller supermarkets, it'd not be long before they started making the tools they needed to loot the biggest one in the area.

When that was done, when it was all gone? Food would start being worth more than gold. And whoever had that food? They'd make a killing.

Add to that, the most secure place in the area here wasn't the local army base on the outskirts of the town. No. After all the ram-raids in the nineties, the biggest supermarket in the area was also the one place that'd hold off an army.

For a while, at least.

The brothers had taken less than a day to figure it all out, and then they'd set to work. Their power tools were all out of action, but they still had the old-school gear. And with the help of some stolen scaffolding, a lot of swearing, and a lot of alcohol, they managed to muscle the panels and everything they needed up onto the roof of the supermarket and out of sight.

For whatever reason, the building had been made with a raised, peaked roof that ran around the outside of the massive square building. The inside? That was where it was weird, as it dipped down into a protected square that was both out of sight and out of the worst of the weather.

It'd been covered in solar panels and air conditioning units, but it was protected from the worst of the wind. Sure, it was exposed to the elements from above, but the brothers had been building offices designed to survive the weather anyway.

Admittedly, now that they were building it for themselves, they put a bit more effort in than they did for anyone else's orders. But that just meant that it got the all-star treatment.

It took three days to build the main section of the hidey-hole, and at the end of day two, they'd broken through into the supermarket from the roof access, and had started looting.

The original plan was that they just beat everyone else to the "good stuff" and stash it on the roof, hidden from anyone who might come looking, but where they didn't have to really move it anywhere.

As they filled the space, though, they'd quickly realized that the scaffolding left them vulnerable. Given that the ten-meter-by-two-meter structure they'd originally planned for was rapidly getting filled, they decided to expand.

The building underwent a rapid redesign, including them stripping their nearby stockpile of building materials and then looting a DIY warehouse as well.

Then, with everything they needed on the roof with them, they'd taken the scaffolding down, and had climbed back up a rope they'd left ready for just this moment.

The scaffolding connectors were taken with them as well, so that if anyone got the bright idea about trying the same thing they'd done…well, they'd have a hard time of it. Then, without much more to it, the brothers had moved into their new home.

A week passed while they built, continued to hide, looted the store below them, and partied.

Then came the day that the main gates were breached, and a few hundred people swarmed the supermarket.

By this point, the brothers had taken to thinking of the entire building as "theirs," and their fury at the thieves below knew no bounds.

Not content with taking a little, like them—they conveniently overlooked that literally hundreds of thousands of pounds of alcohol, food, and electronics had been squirreled away behind them—the people below were just stripping away anything and everything they wanted.

It was obscene!

They watched, furious as people fought in the baby and new mother aisles over powdered formula—while behind them an entire pallet, utterly unneeded, sat secure—and they went to work.

The next few days were frantic ones, and they began as soon as most of the people left.

They climbed down, beat anyone who hadn't left, secured and resecured the gates, the doors, and the staff entrances and exits. And then they started to make traps.

Cans of paint fell to brain unwary intruders. Planks were set in darkened doorways, nails hammered through and left exposed, driving through soft-soled sneakers as unsuspecting people battered and broke their way in again and again.

Screams filled the air as the pair, hidden in the roof, watched their handiwork claim lives and cripple those seeking to steal "their" treasure.

The supermarket was quickly avoided by all but the more ardent looter, and the brothers celebrated their triumph, arguing that their methods were justified as it was "every man for himself."

Out beyond their walls, that had certainly become true.

Fights were a regular occurrence, and as they hid and watched, they saw more and more murders—and worse—committed.

Gangs rose and fell as the weeks passed. The local army base was abandoned almost at day one, the troops recalled to London. When people built up the courage, they looted it, too.

Some were disappointed—the most valuable and dangerous equipment was either taken with the soldiers or secured in an armory that was practically as secure as a bank vault. But, here and there, were other toys that could be taken.

The area fell into total anarchy as weeks passed. And that wasn't even counting when the monsters came sniffing.

The brothers had seen nothing like the creatures that began to hunt the local area. Fortunately, as vicious as they were, it was clear there was something about the area they didn't like.

They hunted by day or night, depending on their kind, but each time the brothers built up the nerve to watch them, they roamed the area only a little, then moved off.

By the time the undead came, the brothers were practically alone in the town. Those who could had either moved northward, heading for some kind of perceived safety in London, or had moved east and west along the coast.

Some had headed for Dover, looking for the sustainability and safety of the moored boats. Those who did were glad to find that that the older ones, with their minimal electrics and solid diesel engines, still worked, and yet… The brothers watched through binoculars and a stolen telescope as boat after boat was attacked by either sea-borne beasts or enterprising pirates.

Nowhere was there safety. That was made clear when the dead began to rise. Dave began cursing that it was true what the old priest used to say—that they'd come to a bad end.

Apparently, there was something called the rapture, and that meant that all the good-un's would be taken to heaven, and the rest would be left to fight it out.

It didn't make much sense to the pair, but considering there'd not been any point they'd noticed where hundreds of people were all fucked off into the sky meant that they weren't the only ones who weren't welcome, presumably.

Anyway, the sight of the undead roaming was taken to mean that all bets were off, and it was the end of days. No more fried chicken, cold beer, and—unfortunately, paid for—blowjobs. It was just them until they died. They'd set to, planning to make sure that when they went, it was due to having too much good food and booze that did them in.

Then came the lights in the sky—gunfire…what looked like magic in the distance.

There wasn't much that the brothers could see from where they were. The slope of the land meant that although they could see out to sea from their little home, when they looked northward between the trees, the rising hill, and the surrounding buildings, they couldn't see much in that direction.

It'd seemed to come from the Channel Tunnel, though, what they'd renamed the Euro Tunnel at some point. Although they'd been curious and wanted to see what was going on…there'd also been a veritable army of the dead streaming in from all sides.

Literally.

They'd watched in horrified silence as huge, rotting, and bow-backed creatures had streamed up into the shallow water off the coast, turning about slowly as hundreds of smaller figures stepped over the side, plunging into the sea.

Then, they'd walked up and out, water streaming out of holes in their bodies. Tens of thousands of dead from both the sea and the land had marched past in an unending flow. The sight was horrific enough, but the smell was worse, rising from corpses that were from mere hours old to rotting cadavers, all the way to gleaming bones that had long been picked clean.

The real thing, though, had been the solid knowledge that no matter what they did, there was no escape for the pair. There was no way they could escape the undead. They were passing shoulder to shoulder in the nearby streets, and that was just the regular ones.

Others flew past, drifting like evil thoughts given form. They hunted, and it was only pure luck that kept the brothers safe, as a pair of the flying half-men, all hissing fury and maniacal laughter, claws and glowing green fire, were seemingly summoned up the hill just before it seemed certain they'd be caught.

Instead, the undead had gone past in a great wave; then, a storm the like of which neither brother had ever seen had risen. All at once, it'd come out of nowhere, tearing the sky apart, and great blasts of light had lit the sky from horizon to horizon.

Explosions, screams, flaming balls, and the sound of heavy gunfire had filled the air. They'd cowered, with barely enough sense to drag themselves into their hideout.

Those flashing screens that kept popping up showed that there'd been a war—between actual *gods*, if you could believe it—and that had been the final straw.

When things had calmed down, they'd looked out and had seen the tens of thousands of corpses that covered the town. The undead that had been still marching up to join the fight—the war, if that was right—had just collapsed in place at some point.

Their strings cut, they'd clattered to the ground in a great rattle of bones and cloth, meat and metal. Since then, they'd just laid there, and the brothers had looked at each other as the sun rose over the remains of their little town.

"Fuck this place," Dave said to Petey, and his brother nodded firmly. It was time to get the hell out of Dodge.

They'd packed up everything they thought they needed, got their tools, and they'd climbed down from the roof, navigated their traps, and headed north by northeast.

They were determined to pass around the scene of the battle, but also nosey enough that there was no way they were passing up a chance to see what had happened.

On climbing the closest hill to the crest—it'd been known in the area as Caesar's Camp forever—they'd stared in horrified wonder at the devastation revealed below.

To the west of the hill was the entrance to the Euro Tunnel and its attendant compound. They'd seen it often enough, and they'd even used it, once.

France had been a shithole, they'd decided—expensive drinks and none of the hot foreign women they'd been expecting waiting for two handsome British lads—so they'd come back after a few days and had vowed to never again leave these hallowed grounds.

Now, they looked out over the sea of the dead, watching as tens of thousands of bones vanished skyward, collapsing into great waves of light.

That light lifted, as if determined to follow the tale of the rapture, only to twist and stream down again, collected into bulging constructions that were dotted here and there across the battlefield.

In the distance was the army as well—or something like it, anyway: a hundred or so of them all drawn up, armed to the teeth and arguing with a bunch of others who were dressed like some kind of larping lunatics.

There were monsters—literally, great big lizard-like buggers—all dressed in the same armor, cat people, and fuck knew what else. But they were everywhere, marching about and doing jobs.

The pair had stared, wide-eyed, as the two groups argued and shouted, until Dave spotted just what they needed.

A single soldier—on his own, looking like he was on his last legs through sheer exhaustion and distracted, wearing a mixture of the armor the larpers wore and with a rifle—headed through the trees to the north. He was just disappearing into the forest. Best of all, not only did he have all his gear on him…he was *alone*.

The pair hadn't been bad lads when the world had been normal, not really, and they weren't now. No, they were just taking what they were due. After all, if the army had done what they were supposed to do, they'd have protected them all and sorted this shit right out, wouldn't they?

It didn't matter that to anyone watching that was an obvious conclusion to draw from the undead all being really dead again and the army being in sight. No. That wasn't important.

What was important was that the undead were all gone—or at least no longer moving—the brothers were still alive, and that bugger right there? Well, he had what they needed, and he owed them, didn't he? They all did.

Dave and Petey had set straight off after the vanishing figure, being careful to move cautiously, like wolves stalking a deer through the forest, and then across the following fields.

There were a bunch of posh, rich bugger houses on the far side of the fields to the left, and then beyond them, the new build estates that the brothers had been selling their work to for a while. Until their reputations caught up with them, anyway.

They lost the soldier twice, only picking him up in the distance thanks to their natural skill and amazing abilities. Then they'd sprinted, each telling the other to shut up, to be quiet, and that they were too loud.

It wasn't until the soldier vanished again, in the damn housing estate, that they realized where he was headed.

They broke into a house, then climbed the stairs and found the rear windows, looking out over the area that had once been an old RAF base.

It was all overgrown now, long since abandoned.

At one end was the Battle of Britain museum, with a bunch of the old war planes still there, decommissioned, and charging people just to come look at them.

That must be where the soldier was heading, though, because he was struggling through the muddy field as fast as he could.

"Here, Davey!" Petey called, grinning at his brother as Dave turned, then rolled his eyes. "You seen the size of this? Wish she was around still, eh!"

His brother had been rummaging through the drawers and now had a bra on his head, his entire head squashed into one cup, while he waved some lacy underwear in one hand and the other trailed thin golden chains he'd grabbed from a nearby nightstand.

"It'll be costume crap. Man, you remember when we tried to sell all that stuff we nicked ages ago and got a kickin'?" Dave, the brighter of the two, snapped, exasperated. "And get yer head outta there. She were probably old and ugly anyway!"

"Ah, fuck it, man. Might as well have some fun." Petey snorted, yanking the bra off his head and tossing it aside, before stomping back out of the room and down the stairs after his brother, the filthy, mud-covered footprints they'd left behind uncared for.

Clearly the soldier wasn't a local, as he'd not known that there was an easier way to the museum. The pair set off jogging, clattering fit to wake the dead as they "stealthily" ran to cut off their quarry.

A few minutes later, they turned off Pannell Drive and ran across the sodden field, as yet another blustery rainfall began, barely making it to the parking lot of the museum before the rain really set in.

Once there, though, they paused, looking at each other.

"What do we do now?" Petey asked Dave, who shrugged.

"We find 'im an' scrag 'im," he said, uncaring. "Get what e's got an' we fuck off for pastures new. Who knows…might be we find us somewhere nice!"

With that, as Petey nodded encouragingly, the pair turned and headed for the museum, guessing that if the lone soldier wasn't inside yet, he would be soon.

***

Andre shook his head in disgust from where he hid behind a nearby wall, before letting loose a low whistle, getting Saros's attention.

"We kill them?" she asked, and he nodded grimly.

"We've seen enough," he spat, lifting a hammer and giving it an appraising swing. "Stupid fuckers never once looked back," he pointed out disgustedly.

The Scepiniir scout nodded in agreement.

They'd been late getting to Jimmy, and he'd set off, well aware that after the undead incursion there wasn't likely to be anything in the area that was any kind of a risk to them now.

They'd reached the trees in time to see the pair of idiots slogging after Jimmy. While Andre had stayed on them, occasionally having to pause and wait while they caught their breath and found the obvious trail again, Saros had circled them and caught up to Jimmy.

He'd been aware of them as well, and had decided to give them a chance, making it obvious where he was headed. That way, he figured, they could get ahead if they wanted to and talk.

Instead, they'd decided to lay a trap, apparently, and that wasn't going to end well for the pair.

He swung the hammer through the air, liking the whistle as it passed, and nodding to himself.

No, they weren't going to like what was coming.

CHAPTER ONE — WHAT HAD BEEN...

I launched myself into the air, traveling back up the path of the storm even as the clouds above faltered. The power of the storm was ripped free of it, channeled down my sword and into me, building and scouring me from the inside out. I felt cored, like an apple, and yet filled to bursting as more and more mana flooded me than I could hope to contain.

Always in the past—heh, those many, many times I'd done this—I'd fed the power into the dungeon, using it.

Now, instead, the storm had been supercharged by the dungeon. I'd been filled with mana that was perfectly attuned to integrate with me, the dungeon's lord.

The clouds on all sides began to unravel. The wind slackened as mana continued to stream into me, feeding me, making my form tingle as more mana than I could ever expect to constrain tore along my mana channels. Then even more power continued to stream through the connection as I screamed, my body heating to the point that my skin and bones should already be turning to ash.

Balthazar hung there. He'd been speaking, staring down at Kaatachi as he hefted his shield, determined to protect Akuba, his love. The sudden cacophony of the storm had silenced his gloating, his evil villain monologuing, as the bursts of rising sunlight shone through what had been cloud cover.

I rose, staring at him in abject fury over all that he'd done to me and mine, and what he'd planned to do next. I distantly felt others as that furry little shit-biscuit guided them somehow as well.

The mana slackened off, and for a split second, the balance was disrupted. A pillar of pure Fire mana was unleashed by Dante into the air, rocketing it upward in a fountain of brilliant power.

On the far side of the battlefield, his opposite knelt, one arm wrapped around a deep wound in his stomach, holding his entrails in, even as Kilo unleashed everything he had into the sky in a burst of coordinated Ice mana.

Both streams twisted and joined the storm, pouring into me, forming a connection between me and their mortal casters. I dragged the mana down; the spark that flared within coalesced into a fresh neutron star.

He stared at me, as I flashed through the air toward him. My eyes glowed so bright, it was as though I'd become the soul of light itself.

He snarled, thrusting both hands out, glaring at me as he switched his target, throwing a great gout of necrotic black and yellow energy from his left, and sickly green fire from his right.

They raced toward me, obscuring him from sight, and I stared, my resolve forming into an iron-hard ball of determination in my gut.

"No," I said simply.

I made no gesture, cast no spell—I simply refused to allow this. His spells were failures. They were corruptions of the mana that I, too, could use. Their

Unlife was made of Life and Death; their necrotic fire was Fire and Death; they traveled through my Air. They used my heat. They drew on my Water to create the life that they perverted into this form. The clouds around me petered out, even as below me, Dante dug deeper.

His form flashed from a human wielding fire into a physical personification of the element of fire itself. He burst into living flames, raising his hands and sending that fire streaming up in greater and greater quantities.

Kilo saw him, saw what he was doing, and he dug deeper as well, grabbing something within him and pushing past it, breaking a barrier that he'd never known had even existed.

As the streams of Fire and Ice rose behind me, pouring inward, meeting the Air that surrounded me, the Water that even now cascaded in its last run from the shredded clouds overhead, I dragged in a deep breath, and I *knew*.

The incoming spells from the Lord of Unlife simply…failed, as for the first time, I formed a Dominion. I knew it instinctively, even as I knew that all around me, this land was mine.

The component forms of mana broke free. The unusable mass of mana scattered while that which could be used—the Life, the Death, the Water, the Fire, the Air—it all streamed forward to feed me.

As the spells collapsed, the sneering form of the lord of liches beyond them was revealed. And that sneer poured off his face as he saw that instead of being destroyed by his attack, I was being fed by his mana.

I opened my mouth and dragged in a deep breath.

Twisting, he tried to dive aside, fleeing as he saw that something had changed, and failed.

The beam of lightning that I unleashed was different from anything I'd ever channeled before. The sound that accompanied it was like a void in space. As the blast hit him, he shrieked, lifting both hands and trying to conjure a shield between him and me—one that, again, simply…unraveled.

The blast punched its way through the still-forming shield, then into him, boring into and through his forehead with a power that I'd never felt.

The life that had been animating him was ripped free and snuffed out—and the force that he'd granted to all his creations vanished at the same time.

His body fell, slowly at first, then with growing speed. He came apart; everything from the lower jaw down was now lifeless and crumbling to dust. And from the jaw up?

It seemed to have been erased from existence.

On all sides, the crash as thousands of boney creations simply collapsed was incredible. But it was nothing compared to the chime that shook me, balls to bones.

WORLDWIDE ANNOUNCEMENT!

THE FIRST LORD OF THE STORM HAS DESTROYED HIS OPPONENT THE FIRST LORD OF UNLIFE IN A PITCHED BATTLE, ROUTING HIS FORCES AND CASTING DOWN ALL OPPOSITION!

KNOW THIS! THE ONLY LIMIT ON YOU IS THAT WHICH YOU PLACE UPON YOURSELVES. GROW, ADVANCE, *LEAD*!

It was only the first of the announcements, and a shitload of decisions would still have to be made, but for now, it was done. I batted it aside, fighting to see through the fucking things as they blinded me.

The next immediately replaced it, and I couldn't help but stare at it and the flickers that indicated updates being made to the notification, as others added their surrender.

Congratulations, First Lord of the Storm!

You have eliminated the majority of your enemies' forces, annihilated two of its chief lieutenants and its primary intended source of reinforcements, as well as destroying utterly the opposing god, Balthazar, First Lord of the Pantheon of Unlife.

The remaining forces of the Pantheon wish to sue for peace. What say you?

Will you accept their vassalage, or continue this war, to the knife?

All enemy forces save one—Petr, Lord of Darkness, his Dungeon Fairy Sin, and their bonded Dungeon #91—have added their unconditional surrender.

Petr offers conditional surr—

"No. They all surrender unconditionally, or they die," I whispered hollowly, staring out across the fields of the dead. "No negotiation. They obey, they kneel, or I'll come for them."

VERY WELL, DUNGEON WARMANCER, FIRST LORD OF THE STORM, AND OVERLORD.

YOUR VASSALS AWAIT YOUR ORDERS. CONGRATULATIONS ON YOUR ASCENSION. BE READY FOR UPGRADE IN 3... 2... 1...

The notifications went mental, and the world flared like the white rabbit had been caught with its dick in the plug socket.

As it all came crashing in, I'd had a split second to think, "Well, at least I've gotten through the fight without being rendered unconscious." And then the mana that had been powering my flight, my abilities, and more, was suddenly turned on me, flashing through my body and beginning my new "upgrade" as the system decreed it.

Minor issue—I was forty meters in the air at that point.

"MOTHERFUCKERS!" I screeched and fell, tumbling from the air. The divot I plowed in the bones that covered the field was the least painful of the changes I was encountering.

The world around me screamed and exploded; the storm above us all was long gone and yet, inside? I felt like it had only just begun. The rings that compressed and contained my mana, speeding up the cycle as it streaked along those pathways, were shaking now fit to burst, and so was the mana that I still held.

I stared inwardly, horrified, as I saw it, the tightly constrained power that even now fought to escape, and yet…and yet I knew that I couldn't release it.

The shuddering grew worse by the second. Despite the power that I'd just unleashed, I was already approaching terminal failure.

Desperately, I cast about for the damn cat, knowing in my heart that he'd already be off somewhere, having a nap or licking his bollocks.

No, I was right. There was no sign of him here, and as I stared, panic rising, a fresh notification bloomed.

Congratulations, Dungeon Warmancer!

Through your mastery of the Dungeon, your access to its reserves, and your dominance of the twin forms of mana [Storm] and [Lightning], you have established your first Dominion!

A Dominion may be formed when the resident entity controls more than 70% of all mana in the area, and although only one may be active at a time, the benefits far outweigh the costs…for that singular individual.

<u>Effects:</u>

- All Storm-aspected mana within your Dominion will be amplified

- Foreign spells cast within your domain will be weakened

- You may freely manipulate ambient mana to reinforce Storm energies

Warning: While your Storm Dominion is active, all non-Storm mana aspects will be naturally suppressed, making other forms of magic more costly and less effective within your territory.

That was what I'd done to help kill that undead fucker, I realized, and it was because my dungeon was all around me, and the others—Emma, Kaatachi, and Akuba—had all been helping to spread the reach of the storm.

I'd just made this whole area ground zero for Storm mana as a training area, I was sure. But considering it was a weaker area for mana already, and the mass of Unlife mana already loose?

I panted, trying to calm my heart rate, to get control of the changes roiling through me, even as I realized that this dominion had to have been something that came from my ascension as well.

It was providing me with an incredible amount of mana right now, breaking down the local forms at a ridiculous rate. But the side effects? First of all, I was drowning in mana! I was literally fucking shaking, I was absorbing so much of it. And I couldn't figure out how to slow it, never mind stop it!

Secondly, that bit about other forms of mana being suppressed? That wasn't good. Fuck, that really wasn't good, especially considering how many people I had in the area who were going to need healing.

I…

I shook it off.

Sure, I needed to figure this out, but if I exploded or whatever because I lost control of my mana, then all bets were off. No, I'd have to fix this myself, because that fluffy turd was gone again. Looking inward, I concentrated on a single gate, braced on my hands and knees.

The gate shuddered and shook even as I watched, growing, lengthening, and moving to cover more of the mana channels in one go. I stared, torn between hope and horror as more and more of them did so. The ring became a tunnel as it seemed to stretch outward along the stream. In desperation, I moved, quickly heading for the next gate.

It, too, was larger and longer. They weren't growing outward in size, increasing the dimension of my channels. Instead, they were *lengthening*, covering more and more of them. There was a long way to go like this—*miles*, if I were to look at it as following the entire path of the channels.

The mana in those same channels started to spin as it passed through each gate. No longer content with flowing like a river, now it began to spiral, twisting tighter and tighter even as the pressure climbed higher.

The increasing power could be felt throughout my body and my fingers shook. I drew down shuddering breaths, trying desperately to regain control even as more and more notifications flashed in my vision.

I was panting, I suddenly realized. I blinked, finding my vision twinned. Overlaid over the mana channel was the sight that came from my eyes, the world all around me, and I twisted my head, looking at the bones as they began to move.

I swallowed hard, moving incredibly slowly and carefully as my body fought me. The power that filled me—already picking up speed and being drawn in twisting, dancing streams toward my core—made my entire body shake with each breath.

The bones around me blurred, they were moving that fast. I tensed, desperately trying to regain control. If the undead somehow were rising again, then I needed to be up. I needed to defend myself. I needed to…

No, they weren't moving! They weren't moving to *reform*, as I'd first feared. No, the undead weren't rising again…

The bones on all sides were instead shuddering and quaking from the power that was bleeding free of me! The bones on all sides moved from a slight shiver, to a shudder, to bouncing wildly!

The wind rose; drifting bones clattered as they were shoved backward, the epicenter focused squarely upon me. I could hear the grinding, grating sound of bone against bone as they began to clatter, before being sucked into the air.

As they went, the bones suddenly began to sparkle. A glimmer of the reflecting light of the dawn spread along their length, then became clearly more.

Lights, like fireflies given purpose, spread along them, and the bones began to fail. Breaking down into mana—mana that instead of being drawn into my dungeon, my dominion was altering and feeding straight into me!

A vortex of power built, one that was changing from being all elements and none, into Storm. I gasped, my heart racing.

"Brave cub!" came a distant voice.

My eyes frantically darted from side to side, but I couldn't make the furry little bastard out!

"You seek to become a tiger—this is good!"

"No..." I groaned, as pain racked me. My stomach twisted like I was about to vomit again.

Instead of vomit, though, I felt... I felt... I felt fucking horrible! I had no words to describe it!

I felt like a snake that was shedding its skin. A shivering, shuddering pain flooded me, as my mana reached its peak speed. But instead of the racing mana pouring out into the ocean of mana that surrounded my divine core...it was boring its way directly across my chest and burning a fresh connection!

Below my heart, where the core always seemed to be located to my inner eye, there was now a bypass growing, one that burned and burrowed, melting and reforming my insides as it created a bridge.

Mana hammered into it...not content to empty out, not content to flood my core. It rejected that path. Instead, I saw a growing bright blue-white light that seemed familiar and yet alien.

It started as a spark in my core, one that rode upward, soaring through the starry blackness. In seconds, it reached the bypass, hitting the thundering mass and being carried across the gulf by its pressure washer-like drive.

Hitting the hole, the fresh channel that was being bored, it dragged a wet wheeze from me, as blood and something foul suddenly burst free in my lungs.

"I have helped." Thor sounded inordinately proud as I desperately tried to regain some kind of control, before vomiting spectacularly everywhere.

The sludge I was bringing up, that seemed almost to be fighting to retreat down my throat as I forced it out, stank like an opened grave. No, it was worse than that: a sewer that had been sealed for millennia and the flatulent ghost of a phaal curry mixed with ducks' eggs rose around me. The smell—well, that was nothing compared to the taste.

The mana around me grew denser, dragged inward as more and more of the bones fragmented apart, draining into my channels and being forced through.

The channel that was being burrowed by the sheer, ferocious force suddenly burst, breaking into an earlier section in the loop of my mana. Instead of the relief that I'd hoped, the pressure only grew worse.

My mana picked up speed. As it increased the spin, it drew more and more mana in—more than I could control and then double that. It was just too much!

The shaking grew worse. A sound, like the humming of a bell, rose, starting deep within my channels. I whimpered, realizing that whatever was happening, the shaking that I was feeling was this same note, one that had been too deep for me to identify before.

My mind screamed in joined agony and desperate, panicked need to find a solution. To stop this, this runaway thing!

"Good! You hold on tight!" came that furry little turd's voice.

I gagged, before forcing out the words. "Wha... what's ha...appen...ing!" I coughed and vomited, glad that I'd managed to take my helmet off before I'd killed that fucker, but horrified at the mess that I brought up.

It was black and oily, stinking...and *bits* floated in it. Bits that wriggled and fought to break free, before bubbling and breaking up, being torn into the spinning maelstrom of mana on all sides.

"What's happening!" I wailed, then vomited again.

"Ascension," Thor sent proudly. ***"A brave cub to try this so soon!"***

"I don't know… urk… what that… *oh gods*… means!" I managed to get out, and I felt as much as heard the sniff of dismissal.

"Then you learn now, young Cyclone."

Cyclone? That word… Oh gods, the world around me shook so hard, it seemed as if it'd explode at any second. The word—no, the *title*—Cyclone sparked a sudden change as more and more of the world around me spun, the frantic building, the summoning of ambient mana into such a vortex.

The world fell away beneath me, but this time as I felt myself sent hurtling into the heavens, it wasn't by my will. In fact, I had no clue how I was rising as my power, rather than diminishing—being drawn upon to fuel my flight—was instead building at a horrific rate.

I started to spiral, being dragged by the force of the mana. The remaining bones that rose alongside me were whipped around, being hurled this way and that.

As they crashed into one another, shattering and filling the air with fragments of broken bone, cloth, and old flesh, before erupting into light, I lifted my head and looked desperately toward the heavens.

I couldn't help but see the circular cone that extended above me and into the mass of mana.

The humming rose in pitch, climbing until it was so loud that I knew that glass would be shattering, that dogs would be howling, and that my insides were desperately attempting to become my outsides through my butthole and mouth.

My skin flaked, peeling off, as black and oily masses were extracted.

It was as if every pore of my body was suddenly, desperately purging every gram of fat, every processed carbon molecule, every food additive and man-made crappy fragment of food that had ever passed my lips.

It all streamed free, whipping away from me, collapsing into the mana-laden air as it was absorbed, broken down into its constituent atoms. And still the power climbed higher.

"Brave! Hold on!"

That furry little fucker congratulated me, and I roared in pain and distress, shaking. My head whipped back and forth as power surged through me and the mana seeped free of the channels that could no longer contain it.

It rampaged through my body now, with a feeling like every single cell was being torn apart and rebuilt. My bones rang as one, the mana climbing with the note that now resounded from a hum to a chime, one that shook the heavens. A new announcement appeared before me, blinding me with its golden gleam and the triumphant echo of trumpets.

WORLDWIDE ANNOUNCEMENT!

THE FIRST LORD OF THE STORM HAS REACHED A NEW PLATEAU! AS THE FIRST CYCLONE IN THIS SECTOR OF THE GALAXY, HE RECEIVES BONUSES. TWICE MORE SHALL SUCH BONUSES BE GRANTED, BEFORE ALL OTHERS MUST FIGHT TO CLIMB HIGHER.

AS A UNIQUE REWARD, AS THE FIRST TO ASCEND TO THE THIRD TIER OF HIS EVOLUTIONARY PATH, HE RECEIVES A GREATER BOON: THE EYE OF AMALTHUS!

KNOW THIS! THE ONLY LIMIT ON YOU IS THAT WHICH YOU PLACE UPON YOURSELVES. GROW, ADVANCE, *LEAD*!

I shuddered and shook. The rising chime drove blood from my ears, making my heart pound intermittently. My head thundered like the worst migraine I'd ever felt, as Thor spoke again.

"Beware, cub!" he hissed. ***"Impure forms cannot ascend further! Cease!"***

"HOW?!" I screamed at him, and at the world in general. For a split second, I felt it—a sudden confusion that radiated from him—before it finally gave way to annoyance and disgust.

"Idiot cub," he hissed. ***"Again, you disappoint."*** And with that, and a mental image of the little bastard flicking his tail in outrage and marching off, the mana that had been filling me suddenly jerked aside.

A single channel was forced open wider as the mana that desperately circled with ever increasing speed was guided around toward my hands, and I gasped, as I understood.

I reached out desperately, trying to hold it back, trying to hold onto it long enough for the Storm converter I frantically ordered be created from the dungeon, right before me, trying to give the mana back to the dungeon, to not waste it…

I *failed.*

The mana screamed from me in a great torrent, slamming into the real world and exploding with power. The converters in the area were overloaded in a second, as more and more mana exploded free. Finally, I fell.

Crashing to the ground and bouncing, I rolled until I came to a stop, staring up at the gradually brightening sky, panting with both pain and panic, relief and—frankly—terror at how close I'd come to turning myself into a bomb and painting the surrounding area.

I eventually managed to speak, taking in the cold, bright-blue sky as it was revealed high overhead.

"I hate that fucking cat," I whispered, meaning every damn word.

CHAPTER TWO

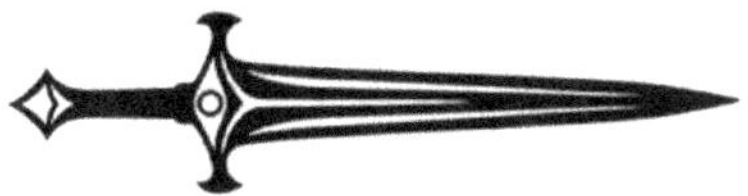

"Do I look like a goddamn idiot?" I forced out a short while later, sitting slumped in an uncomfortable chair and tiredly rubbing at my face. "I mean, seriously, do you want to have a word with yourself and then come back?"

I sat at a table in a small room near the top of the cube, our little citadel. With me were Mike and Dante, and across the table were Brigadier Peterbilt, the commander of the local forces for the British Army that had been sent to assist us in "our" fight, and two of his officers who he'd neglected to introduce.

That they both wore MP or military police armbands and glared at us the entire time made it even more clear that this wasn't going to be a friendly conversation.

Mind you, I wasn't looking for one. I'd barely gotten some clean pants on, never mind had five minutes to myself since I'd been carried into the fortress.

"The agreement was that we provide an armed force to assist you in your battle, and in return you provide an unsecured, open, and available nascent dungeon. We upheld our end of the bargain," Brigadier Peterbilt snapped.

I pulled my hand from my face, glaring at him, before glancing at Mike. "Mike, did they, and I fuckin' quote, 'bring their entire army'?" I asked him, and he shook his head. "I mean, that was the deal, right?"

"They brought less than a quarter of the available soldiers they had in the base when I was there," Mike said. "That's not including the FOBs, the supply chain, or their forces out on patrol…just the soldiers who were in and around the base while I was there."

"Don't be ridiculous," Peterbilt snarled. "We cannot leave London undefended."

"No, and you've already explained that," I replied with a cold smile. "You couldn't strip your entire garrisons, you couldn't empty the forward operating bases, and you couldn't pull in the patrols. No time to do it, right?"

"Of course not. It's ridiculous to assume—" the brigadier started, nodding and clearly thinking I was in agreement.

I slammed my fist into the table before me. "BULLSHIT!" I roared. "You had three fuckin' days! Three days in which we lost people. Three days in which you could have managed that easily! We made it four hundred fucking miles in less than that time, and you didn't even bring half of the forces you had sitting around with their thumbs up their fuckin' arses!"

He glared at me and took a visible breath before responding as calmly as he could, speaking as if to a petulant child. "Clearly this is a trying time for you. And yes, I understand the stress that you are under. Command, after all, isn't for everyone." The sneer as he said that was clear. "The stresses and strains are often enough to drive lesser men to failure."

I glowered at him.

He went on. "For many, the loss of a soldier is more than they can bear, but an *experienced* officer understands that in war, there are losses. For those unsuited to command, however, the desire to lash out and punish others for their own failings is common."

"Oh, believe me." I shook my head. "I understand that you lose people in a fucking war. What I don't understand is why the hell you think you deserve a dungeon core, something that is incredibly rare and powerful, in exchange for you showing up two days late and with a fraction of the agreed-upon force."

"There was an agreement made, in your name, through a serving NCO of the British Army." Peterbilt smiled. "That agreement was that we would provide our forces as soon as was feasible, and that we would aid you in *your* war. We did that. Now, the bill has come due, sir. Release the core to us, and we can discuss future transactions with good grace. Or admit that you never intended to be fair, and we'll take the appropriate steps."

"I *really* wouldn't do that if I was you." Mike snorted, glancing from the glaring brigadier to his two companions, and back. "Sir, threats are not going to end well for you in this situation. The agreement was, as I stated, that you bring all your forces—"

"Less those who were unable to be feasibly recalled in time, and less those required to mount a successful minimum defense of the capital," Peterbilt quoted with a sigh. "Sub-section one-thirty-seven, chapter fifteen, paragraph three, item C."

"What the…" Mike scowled, before grabbing his go-bag from under the table, pulling out the contract that had been foisted on him at the last second as the soldiers had started to move and slapping it down on the table between us. "That's not in here!"

"It's in the appendix," Peterbilt assured him, gesturing to one of the companions who pulled out a second, much thicker document and set it down lightly, before smiling coldly.

"You're fucking kidding me, right?" Mike growled, looking from the document he had to the one that they were demonstrating.

"No, *Sergeant*, I am not, and I expect you to remember your place!" the brigadier snapped. "You and I will be discussing this on our return to London."

I glared at him, noting the reference to Mike's former rank and the disregard of my promotion of him.

"Oh, I'm not going to London…" Mike started, only to have the brigadier make a gesture to one of his companions; he stepped forward in response.

"At ease, Captain," he said firmly, before turning back to me, and smiling an oily little smile. "Now, I presume you have never served your country in any official capacity, Matt…?" He paused, clearly expecting me to provide my surname.

"No, I haven't," I ground out through gritted teeth, trying to maintain my calm as this dickhead pushed.

"Well, as the former sergeant appears to have forgotten, when you enlist, you agree to abide by certain laws. He appears to have forgotten that such laws exist, and that he signed up in the full understanding of his place and the punishments should he refuse lawful orders. Captain Munroe here is a member of the military police, and he's here for the express purpose of ensuring *our* forces return to the fold. As you clearly require the realities of our positions be demonstrated—

Jefferson, this is your last chance. Will you submit to my lawful orders and return to London under my command?"

"I'd sooner burn in hell than serve under you again, Peterbilt, and you damn well know it," Mike ground out. "You got a lot of good people killed and—"

"Captain, please do your duty." Peterbilt smiled coldly as he sat back and waved at one of his subordinates.

"Yessir," the captain said in grimly formal tones. He stood, then stepped around the table and faced Mike. "Sergeant Michael Jefferson. You are under arrest for disobeying lawful orders and potential desertion. You have the right to remain silent. Anything you say can and will be used against you in a court-martial. You have the right to speak to an advocate and have them present during questioning. If you cannot afford an advocate, one will be appointed for you. Do you understand these rights as I have read them to you?"

"Hold the fuck up," I growled as Mike surged to his feet and stepped back, glaring at the captain, even as the MP reached for his arm, pulling a set of handcuffs from his belt. "Hold, I said!"

In seconds, everyone else was standing as well. And to his credit, it was Dante who stopped them, not me.

The pillar of fire that rose, crackling, from his right hand as he held it palm up, bathed the entire room in a sudden heat, making the MP freeze as Dante spoke.

"Touch him, and I swear you'll regret it for the rest of your life. Both seconds of it," he said, clearly not liking the confrontation, and just as clearly ready to back his friends, even against the British Army.

Damn, I was proud of the lad then.

"Sir?" The MP swallowed hard.

"Control your man, 'Dungeon Lord,' or I'll take action." Peterbilt sneered.

"Are…are you for real?" I paused, genuinely surprised at the utter lack of fear in his eyes. "You're seeing this the same way I am, right?"

"Why don't you enlighten me?" He smiled coldly.

"You've just tried to arrest a friend of mine on a bullshit charge, and one of my other friends is inches away from reducing you and your people to charcoal briquettes. You can't win this fight, so why the hell are you provoking it?" I asked, curiously.

"Can't I?" He smiled, then jerked his hand to the right in a cutting motion. As he did it, Dante's flames cut off like a switch had been pulled, and he grunted in shock.

I glanced at him, then back to Peterbilt.

"Stand down your people and sit, young man." The brigadier sneered. "I'm here to collect on a debt to the British Army, and the nation. There's two ways this plays out. First and foremost, and to be clear, I would much prefer this end bloodlessly. But, if you choose to make this into a confrontation, I have been authorized to do whatever is necessary to ensure I return with the dungeon core intact."

"Bullshit," I said with forced calm, sitting as he indicated as I frantically tried to figure out what the hell he'd just done. "You've come here deliberately looking for a goddamn confrontation, but go on."

"The deal that was made with the former sergeant was that you, as his interim commander, would provide a dungeon core in exchange for the assistance of the British Army. We provided the assistance, and now it's time to pay the piper. You can either choose to do so willingly, and we can then move forward from this situation in a hopefully respectful manner, or you can choose not to, and we'll be forced to resort to violence."

"Again, you won't win this fight," I said.

"Matt..." Dante whispered, looking sick as he stared at his hands.

"Listen to your friend," the brigadier suggested smugly.

"Dante?" I looked at him.

"I'm cut off from my mana," he whispered, horrified. "I can feel it there, but I can't use it."

"That's a very accurate description, actually." Peterbilt smirked. "One of the abilities of my class enables me to restrict the powers of those around me. Any focusing of mana that I choose to suppress, I can."

"And the range?" My icy horror was followed by a building rage. "Can you do this at range or against multiple targets?"

"I don't see that the details are any of your business." Peterbilt sneered. "It's enough that I can, indeed, do this, and yes, I can do this for all of you."

"Can you?"

"Oh, yes. Do you really want to push this yourself?" he gloated. "I assure you, I'm quite capable of cutting you all off from your talents, no matter how you struggle."

I stared at him, fury rising in me as the last battle replayed over and over in my mind. Had I had someone with this power? I'd have cut that fucking undead bastard off and stomped his face into dust in seconds!

No. No, I realized that wasn't right. No matter how he was presenting this, it couldn't be accurate. He'd managed to cut Dante off, yeah, but if he had the power to do this for long, or at range, he'd have been able to make himself totally invaluable in the battle.

He could have done it—cut the enemy off as a demonstration—and hell to the yes, I'd have been a lot more respectful of him in our meeting. He'd have gotten the core in seconds, and he had to know that.

That meant that at least in part he was bluffing.

"Last chance to resolve this without bloodshed," I offered softly, before reaching out with a mental flexing of my will.

The light that sparked up from the floor on all sides of the table was bright, like a thousand fireflies being disturbed and launching skyward all at once from a darkened field.

In this case, though, as they lifted and drifted, spiraling, they left behind the feet, then ankles, shins, then knees and more of a quartet of heavily armed orcs. The light faded as the orcs were "printed" into existence, and the army trio were caught in differing reactions.

He'd not managed to cut me off from the dungeon—though when I reached for my own mana, my own spells, I could feel something there, between me and my magic.

I pressed against what felt like a wall, but it was one that moved as I pushed. As I glared at him, I already knew he had to be weakening. This power was too much, too complete to be this easily used, and especially by someone who had been sent out to be such an asshole.

No, if he was really as powerful as he seemed, this conversation, the fight before—hell, the entire situation—would have been very, very different.

He had to be bluffing. He *had* to be.

A single bead of sweat rolled down his forehead, ignored by him as he seemingly felt me exploring whatever he'd done, and we glared at each other.

Whatever he'd done, it felt like a gossamer-thin strand between me and my mana—thin, but stretching. The more I pushed, slowly increasing the pressure, not willing to let him see me panicking, the more the edges frayed.

I could force my way through this, I was sure, and between us, if Dante and I both pushed... I glanced to the others, trying to decide the next move. Did I incinerate them both, taking out the armed guards, or did I go for the head of the snake...?

The MPs both looked stunned and horrified. Peterbilt? He forced a smile and nodded as if either of us believed he was in control here.

This was riding the fucking tiger's back, and we both had to know it. He swallowed hard, then stood slowly, turning his back on me as if I were beneath his notice as he started to examine my orcs.

"Oh yes, this will do nicely," he declared, staring at the nearest orc. "They appear to be dumb brutes. Is that accurate?"

"You're about to find out," I assured him flatly, before switching to address the quartet. "If by the time I count to three, he's not on his knees and fucking apologizing to me..."

"Matt!" Dante gasped, clutching at his chest in horror and sagging sideways, his face suddenly grey as he struggled to breathe. "No..."

"Dante?" I grabbed him as he collapsed, before looking up at Peterbilt. "What the fuck did you just...?"

"Don't you do it!" Mike snarled, glaring at the pair of MPs. His hand rested on the holstered butt of his handgun. "Don't you fuckin' move, lads. You know how this'll end..."

"What you felt at first was the light touch," he gloated. "I can do that—let you see your mana but not touch it. Or, as that was *clearly* not enough to teach you some respect, instead I can remove his ability to ever feel the mana of the world again," he replied smugly. "Him and any of you." He nodded, leaning forward and pressing his knuckles to the table between us, apparently seeing something in my eyes. "That's right, I can strip your ability from you, both your lightning powers and the access to the dungeon. But I've restrained myself so far, despite your rudeness."

"Bullshit," I growled, pressing Dante into his chair as all around the room, the orcs, picking up on my anger, growled as well. "Release him, now!"

"Boy, if I have to make an example of your companion to prove myself, I will. But be warned—once I do this, he'll never channel his mana again. No matter what you do—" The look in his eyes made it abundantly clear, regardless of what he might be saying, he was actually overjoyed to get the opportunity to do this.

I, though, I felt fear...hot and sharp. The realization that if he could honestly do this? I was our best chance to protect our people. *If he could somehow do this, if he could cut me off from the dungeon, then what else was I missing? What else could he do? Could he take it? Throw Kelly and the others out? Rip control from us?*

The possibilities raced through my mind. Right behind the fear and the exhaustion of the last fight and everything that had come with it came the anger.

He was cut off as a blade was suddenly pressed to his throat from behind, his hair grabbed roughly by a green-skinned fist. His eyes widened in fear, before narrowing in anger. "Fine, you want—"

"Last chance!" I snarled as Mike, the MPs, and the other orcs all squared off. I desperately tried to come up with a way to de-escalate this. Failing that, I knew what was about to happen, what *had* to happen.

"Fuck you!" He sneered. "You just dug your own grave, you and all your freaks—"

Before he could finish his sentence, unbidden, the orc drove the serrated dagger through the brigadier's throat. Blood sprayed as he shoved it upward into the idiot's brain.

The brigadier's eyes shot open in horror. For a split second, everyone froze. Then, as one, the MPs both went for their guns. Before they could even touch them, they were doubling over as the orcs on either side of them drove daggers into their stomachs and backs, falling on them.

"Fuck!" I shouted, surging to my feet and frantically shoving the command out even as I clamped down on them through the dungeon sense. "STOP!" I roared.

It was too late, though, as the brigadier fell, dead beyond any chance of saving him. The orcs, surprised at my orders, ripped their daggers free, the serrated backs doing more damage on the way out than they had on the way in.

"Get Jo in here!" I roared. A nearby orc shoved the door to the corridor open in response to my unstated desire, allowing my voice to carry to those out there.

This was *not* how I'd wanted our relationship with the army to start.

Mike was already moving. The highest strength healing potion we had access to coalesced into his hand with a thought, even as I rounded the table, my right hand opening instinctively, then closing on an exact copy as it formed at my call.

The orcs were confused as hell, but they dropped down and pinned the struggling MPs at a thought, giving us access to them to pour the potions into the wound first, and then to force it down the soldiers' throats as they fought us in their panic.

Though it probably only took Jo all of two minutes to reach us, they were long ones. And through it all, all I could think was that my being pissed off, and this guy trying to throw his weight around, might have just started a fresh war.

Why the hell did everyone in authority I met these days have to be a fucking asshole?

CHAPTER THREE

"It's not good," Jo said to me without preamble, half an hour later, as I sat with Kelly, Mike, and Aly in the dungeon sense.

"How bad?" I asked grimly.

She shook her head. "They'll live…"

"That's a relief." Aly sighed.

"You know, no." Jo cut her off. "No, it's not. They're both convinced we were the aggressor, and that their brigadier was entirely within his rights. I've tried talking to them, and I can see it in their eyes. They're both waiting for an excuse, any chance, to try to make a break for freedom. They had to be restrained the entire time I was dealing with them."

"We're trying to heal them, though," Aly responded, shaking her head. "They can go whenever they want. They just need to…"

"Not right now they can't. I've sedated them both," Jo said grimly, holding a hand up to prevent any more interruptions. "I *had* to. They tried to fight the orcs, they tried to fight the kobolds, and when one got the chance, he tried to take me hostage."

"What?" I growled.

"They claim we started it. Like I said, they think we're the aggressors, and they've just seen their commander cut down before their eyes. They won't listen to reason, and they're determined to fight their way free to their forces," she explained. "If we let them go, they're going to either attack us straightaway, or they're going to run. To take their forces back to London and then turn around and come right back with their real army!"

"Fuck's sake, Matt," Mike whispered, rubbing at his eyes. "Why the hell did you have to summon orcs? You know they're dickbags!"

"I wanted to make an impression—"

"Oh, you did that, all right!" he snapped. "Matt, you just started a war!"

"No!" I snapped back. "*He* did, or he tried to! Aly, Kelly, you were there, right?" I asked, having been so focused on the idiot before me when he'd demanded a meeting "right now" that I'd barely paid attention.

The battle with the undead had been over less than an hour. Everyone was exhausted, bloody, and frankly, on the ragged edge of delirium, with the twins sent off on a make-work job to keep them out of the way as Jo fought to save both Emma and Griffiths, who had both been unconscious. Jenn was working the hospital as well, and the rest of the team—those who had survived, anyway—were all on triage duties. And yeah, just to make shit harder, their mana was fighting them as they tried to use it, and I'd yet to find a way to take down my domain.

Andre and Jimmy had been getting underfoot in the makeshift hospital, and when the brigadier and his pair of dragging bollocks had come stomping in and demanding a meeting, Andre had nearly swung for him out of pure reflex.

Griffiths was barely alive and currently unconscious. His injuries were severe enough that a simple healing spell was only going to do more damage until the foreign matter was removed and his body needed to be… well, "un-pulped" wasn't really a word until now, as far as I knew, but it fit his condition.

He'd had half of the bones in his body reduced to fragments and splinters, and the only way he'd lasted this long was by being healed.

That, however, was when the reality of life had struck home. Less talented healers had simply hit him over and over with spells. Those spells had healed sections, but they weren't powerful enough to regrow limbs. So half his body was now entirely malformed, and the rest had fragments of foreign matter embedded and healed around that were already fighting to kill him from the infection alone.

The undead weren't sterile things, and the effect on him, when I'd seen him? I honestly didn't know how he'd survived this long.

So, with Griffiths unconscious and barely clinging to life, command of our forces had fallen back to Mike, who was doing his best.

That meant that although he knew the brigadier, as he'd both come here with him from London and had dealt with him in the past as well—he'd been a captain before all of this had kicked off—his relationship with him hadn't included anything good. Mike also didn't have the formal training in negotiation and basically handling officers as one of their own that Griffiths did.

For a career NCO, officers were put into two clear categories, I'd been told.

The first was that they were dumb as shit and actively dangerous to those around and under them, and should be patted on the head and assured that yes, they were a good boy and everyone liked them. This was despite the evidence that almost everyone around them who wasn't a fellow "Rupert"—slang for a useless, and usually rich officer—like them, really didn't.

This essentially kept them out of the way long enough that they could be shuffled into a position where they could do no real harm, or they grew up and became the second kind.

The second kind was what the officers were *supposed* to be. They were skilled commanders, occasionally experienced but when they weren't, they knew to listen to those who were. They didn't risk the lives of those under them needlessly, and they understood that an ego was a bad thing in 99.9% of situations.

The goal was to deal with the *problem*—or, as Arend-Jan had put it on one of our infrequent conversations, to get "as much milk, for the minimum of moo, as possible."

In contrast, Peterbilt was all fuckin' ego. He'd come in spoiling for a fight at the worst possible time. And clearly, I'd also handled the entire thing in exactly the wrong way.

"Matt, I need to return to my patients. Griffiths is touch and go still, and Emma…" She shook her head. "I don't know if she's going to wake up, if I'm honest. I need to be there."

"Go. Our people are our priority," I said. "Sorry to have dragged you away from them."

"It's my job." She smiled tiredly, before vanishing from the dungeon sense.

"What the hell do we do?" I carefully asked the remaining group, trying to contain my anger at myself for it all getting out of control, and my surety that I'd just made a massive fuck-up. Not to mention that regardless of anything else, Peterbilt had been a dick, sure, but now he was dead, and it was my fault for letting him goad me.

All because, as I started to realize, the orcs were actually easier to communicate with through the dungeon than the kobolds or any other race I'd summoned so far.

The one that had killed him had stabbed up in *exactly* the way I'd been thinking was the best was to remove the threat. I'd not commanded them to do it, but I'd certainly *thought* that. I'd felt rising fear, anger, and desperation, I'd been exhausted, and I'd just wanted the fucker gone. He was playing silly fuckers with Dante, and that had been the way I'd thought about dealing with him in that split second.

"I'll go and find the officers I met before this," Mike suggested, after a moment's thought. "I was warned by some of the others that Peterbilt was a dick and that he was out of his depth in a puddle. Maybe I can explain this to them, and prepare them for what's happened but…"

He shook his head, and I knew exactly what he meant. Peterbilt had been angling for the dungeon as a personal prize, but I didn't doubt that someone had genuinely started out planning to do the bare minimum to get a dungeon from us, and he'd been in on it. Mike had said that the contract—which he'd still not read all of—had been foisted on him just as they were ready to leave. He'd read over it as fast as he could, but that there were a hundred and forty-four pages of legal mumbo-jumbo and that his friends were dying meant that he'd just made sure it wasn't magical in any way and then he'd signed it.

Until the meeting just now, he'd had no clue that there was a second bloody document that was referenced in the first as an "appendix."

He'd believed that it'd all be okay, mainly on the grounds that with everything that was going on, there was no way they would actually be playing silly fuckers. And even if they were, there had to be a lawyer involved somewhere, and once we'd killed them, things would go a lot easier in sorting out the fallout.

"We're going to need to give them a core. You know this, right?" Kelly said suddenly.

I stifled a curse, before groaning and rubbing my face again. "Yeah," I admitted, tiredly. "I know."

It was true. They were getting what they wanted out of this one way or another, because as aggressive as that idiot had been, now we were only left with two options. Either we gave them a core and hoped to fix all this short of a war, or we refused. After killing their brigadier and injuring his guards, and refusing to pay up the fee that we'd offered and they'd demanded. That way led to most likely a war.

This day sucked.

"Matt," Aly said, and she waited until I looked at her. "I don't agree. We need to give the core up—yes, eventually, but I don't think we give it up just like that," she said. "They started this—they were blatantly pushing, and overly aggressive. So, what if Mike goes to the soldiers he knows, he tells them what happened?

What if he explains that the brigadier struck first, then he tells them to send back to their base for someone to come here and explain this?"

"Explain it how?" I asked.

"That's not for us to decide." She shrugged. "We make it clear that the brigadier attacked your advisor—it was Dante, but I know, I *was* there—and threatened you and your companions. Mike plays all furious and warns them you want an explanation, and we keep the pair of MPs drugged and basically in jail for now.

"What he doesn't do is go in with the 'we're so sorry, but this happened' route. Instead, he goes in all angry and demands an explanation. We make it clear that the dead idiot started this, which, honestly, Matt, he did with the provocation. Yes, you summoning the orcs was incredibly bloody stupid, and they instantly did pretty much what we all knew they were capable of.

"But they and *you* were put in that position because of his actions. We don't apologize to them. We tell them what happened, namely that their leader used an ability on the members of the group when his threats weren't working, and the orc guards killed him in retaliation. We're sad that he was killed—you'd rather have captured him, planning on questioning him to find out if this was their plan all along or if he was a rogue actor—but there wasn't time.

"When they send someone else in, they know not to fuck with us because of the consequences, and they also know that they need to try to fix this. Also, if this guy was sent along and those sending them knew he was an aggressive dick? They're going to be a lot more understanding and a lot more apologetic, wanting to hide their mistake, rather than coming looking for a fight."

"Plus, as much as this is going to sound bad but…" Mike sighed. "Look. The entire group was expendable. The *army* basically is; to achieve a goal, you obviously don't *want* to lose forces, but if you do? It's acceptable, provided you achieve the goal. In this case, getting a dungeon core is the goal. If they lost the entire army but achieved that? They'd accept it. I'm not saying there wouldn't be consequences further down the line…but honestly, if we make this clear they started it and the orcs responded to their aggression, that should cover us."

"In the future, Matt?" Kelly said softly. "No more orcs, okay?"

"I know." I nodded. "I mean, we weren't using them at all. Hell, they're the big bad, the long-term enemy, but the way they fought in that battle…"

"It just shows how good they are." Mike grimaced. "We need to up our game."

"Yeah." I sighed. "Okay, Mike, yeah, you go see what you can smooth over, but take…" I paused and thought about it for a second. "Take Dante, Kilo, and Beta. Those three can cover your arse no matter what happens."

"Is Dante okay?" Kelly asked.

I winced. "Sort of?" I hedged. "He says he is, but he really isn't. The way that the brigadier cut him off from his mana frankly terrified him, and I think he needs to do something. He's gone from the village punching bag to on top of the world—hell, somehow, he even got a hot girlfriend and gets laid—and then he grew to be a goddamn power in his own right. Then just like that…" I clicked my fingers. "He was back to powerless."

"And it freaked him out, understandably." Mike nodded. "That's the other thing as well. The idiot was suppressing our powers, sure—or Dante's and yours, at least…mine are all funneled into my weapons and abilities, so, well, no clue if that would have been affected. The inference was that he could cut us off any time he chose, but that wasn't going to stop us physically, and it certainly didn't work against the dungeon."

"That's the other reason I summoned them." I nodded. "I was terrified that he was actually able to cut me off from the dungeon and I had a split second of 'Well if we need to fight them in here with them having some kind of a trump card,' I decided it was best to have the most vicious, aggressive dungeon-born we had."

"And so we're back to why the hell was he like that," Aly said. "He was goading you, I saw that much, clearly…whether he was expecting to cause a fight and somehow come out on top, or he was just such an arrogant cockgoblin that he thought he could throw his weight around without consequences…" She sighed then, and shook her head.

"This is getting us nowhere. Mike, go talk to the army. See if you can smooth this out and make it clear their representatives were rude, abrasive, and then attacked us. We want an explanation or they don't get shit. They want to be friends and get the core we offered? This is on them to solve. Is that good with you, Matt?" she asked me, and I nodded.

"Yeah, do that, Mike. Be clearly pissed, but open to an understanding that he basically fucked around and found out. That can be the end of it, if they play their cards right…" I paused, then spoke as a thought occurred to me.

"Are they a danger to us? The army's survivors, I mean," I asked Mike bluntly.

He hesitated, then shook his head. "Honestly? No, no they're really not. We've got enough forces right now that unless they were insanely lucky, they'd not win, and that includes if they attacked us by surprise. That's why that asshole's actions made so little sense. They're outnumbered, and frankly they're under-leveled for the fight. Sure, there's some of them who would be a real handful if they kicked off, but I'd back Beta in a fight with any of them. Hell, I'd back *Dante* in a fight with most of them, and that's one-on-one in a physical scrap. With magic? Especially in that new flame form of his, they'd not stand a chance."

"Flame form." I grunted. "Yeah, I need to talk to him about that, and Kilo and—" I broke off, groaning at all the things I needed to do.

"Matt, you look terrible." Kelly reached out a hand to me.

I forced a grin. "Hey, I love you too," I joked, before forcing myself to relax. "I know, but I can rest when all this shit is sorted. So, they're not a threat, not really?"

"They could do us some damage, but we've got enough mana now that there's just no sense in them attacking us," Aly said. "Just in case, though, I'll summon a few dozen more advanced dungeon-born, and have them on hand, and obviously armed, okay?"

"Yeah, just in case," I agreed.

"Always glad to have extra backup," Mike said, clearly about to leave. He hesitated. "Uh, if you're going to do what I think you're going to do? Be subtle?" he suggested, glancing at his wife.

She grinned.

He sighed the sigh of a long-suffering husband and vanished.

"What's this?" I asked.

"We were discussing it during the meeting and before," Kelly admitted. "We could see it was going badly, but before that, with the dungeon core settled here, and the Tunnel being right there through to the continent, it's pretty obvious that we need to keep this as a fortress at the very least, right?"

"Yeah," I agreed, glad to concentrate on anything else besides that fucking mess that the meeting had ended up as.

"Well, if we're to keep this as a fortress, it needs to be a *fortress*, not just what we had time to make it into. To do that, we need actual mana converters in the area, a steady stream that can support the site, and we need to build a real fortress, secure the Tunnel, and, well, flatten the area."

"Talk to me." I sighed, sitting back, rubbing at my eyes again, "Distract me from my goddamn migraine with plans."

"No," Kelly replied firmly, squeezing my hand. "Matt…no, honey. I'm sorry, but you're running on empty. The reason that meeting went as badly as it did isn't entirely on their side. Yes, they forced a confrontation and they did it deliberately right after the battle had ended. But you were…unstable. Not in a bad way," she hastened to assure me.

"There's a good way to be unstable?" I snorted, leaning forward with my elbows on the table.

"Matt, you've been fighting round the clock or studying magic for what? Two days straight? Three? More?"

"I had a sleep…" I tried to reassure her, then I frowned. "Might have been yesterday?"

"It was at *least* two days ago," Kelly replied. "You're also not the only one. None of us have been sleeping, and as much as now isn't the ideal time to do it, it has to be done. It's time to bring in the changes we discussed over the last week or more. I want us to move to a two-, and eventually, three-shift system. Matt, I'm sorry but genuinely I think it needs to be done *now*."

I hesitated, the feeling of losing control not one I liked, but then I took a deep breath and said the word. "Agreed." I sighed, nodding, then lowered my face into my hands and rubbed my eyes, before blinking.

"First shift is going to be me and Aly. We're going to be the primary team, so if the shit hits the fan and we're not there, the second shift's job is to maintain things until we can take over. But the long-term strategy is that we train them to stay with us, to help in running the entire edifice."

"Right?"

"I mean that we don't just train them up and then send them on to run their own dungeons in the future," she clarified. "Instead we train them and keep them here. The other side of that is that we *will* need managers for the other dungeons as we expand, but that's a discussion for when we're not all feeling like we were face-fucked by a dragon."

"A dragon…" I started to ask, grinning despite how tired I was.

"Head-fucked, just head-fucked, regardless of who or what did it," Aly corrected, waving the distinction away. "Don't worry about it. Look, the second shift for now…we're suggesting Clarissa and Markus. They work well together, they're highly organized, and we trust them. Markus can run the military if he needs to, and Clarissa is just, well, Clarissa. She could probably run everything better than we can."

"Agreed." I sighed, straightening up and gesturing imperiously. "Make it so, Number One."

"I don't know if I should hit you for that terrible reference or applaud." Kelly smiled tiredly. "Okay, thank you, Matt. We'll talk to them and get ready for a handover. They're aware that we wanted them ready to help a lot today, and we asked that they be as rested as they could be."

"Go for it," I agreed. "Look, I'm not sure if I should—"

"Rest?" Kelly interrupted me. "Matt, you're not firing on all cylinders right now. Aly will go with Mike—through the dungeon sense, though, obviously; he's not even out of the building yet—and she'll watch over him. I'll pull Clarissa and Markus in and walk them through their new responsibilities. Then we're both hitting our beds. I want to find you in ours in ten minutes, okay? You need to rest, actually rest. Please."

"I'm fine…" I whispered, and she shook her head.

"Matt, you're not. Whatever happened out there—I mean, I saw the fight. We were there with you at the end, trying to hold it together. We could get close enough to see you, but we had no mana to spare to help, not after we'd unleashed everything through Emma like that."

"I know."

"No, you don't. We've still not spoken about what happened after that…the way that you changed, the way that the system keeps saying you're evolving. I mean, you're at the third stage of four, Matt! You're approaching real godhood, and yet—" She looked at me, leaving unsaid that I looked like absolute shite.

"I know," I repeated. "Look, we'll talk about it, okay? Just…not right now."

"Then go and rest, Matt," Kelly said softly. "Whatever you did, or whatever was done to you, you're as broken as I've ever seen you. *Please*, get some rest, and then we can help, okay?"

I opened my mouth, again feeling like I was, well…slacking, frankly. It wasn't a case of it was just me in the fight by any means. We'd *all* been fighting for days.

Hell, if I was honest, I'd been working on my magic. I'd been talking, meditating, and discussing all sorts of crap.

The others? They'd been battling it out hour after hour. If anything, having healing magic made things worse for them at times as well.

Instead of having time off from the fight to recover, they were being crippled, getting patched up, and shoved back out the door twenty minutes later.

I felt guilty as hell, and yet…I also knew that the girls were right. I couldn't just push through, because I was already making mistakes. If I continued? I'd only make more.

Plus, if the shit hit the fan? Better that I was capable after a rest, rather than on my knees through exhaustion. Because if I was honest? I really was broken. I had no clue what all that gunk had been, but I was as tired as I could ever remember being in my life, and the room swam in and out of focus as I tried to keep my brain on track.

With that cheerful thought solidly in the forefront of my mind, I thanked the pair and left the dungeon sense. I couldn't just go to bed, though, despite what I'd said. No, first I had a couple of last jobs to do, such as taking the time to check in on the medical section and make sure things were going okay there before I headed down to the gate area.

It didn't take long to reach my first stop. The medical suite was by the entrance to the cube. I vaguely noted that it wasn't like this before, but it'd now been transformed into a modern medical facility, complete with the mana-powered scanners and several doctors and nurses moving from bed to bed.

At the back was a closed section were the two surgeons who had recently joined us from the hospital in Gateshead were still working to save Griffiths.

In the fight, at some point—I was only vaguely aware of the details at the minute—the enemy had *air-dropped*, with the aid of literal banshees, a handful of corpse lords onto the roof of our citadel.

They'd wreaked havoc, including one of the massive monstrosities literally stomping on Griffiths.

He'd had one side of his hip, the top of that leg, and part of his rib cage basically reduced to paste, gritty with shattered bones.

That should have been the end of him, if not for the fact that there were healers nearby, mages who had taken the fucker on, and Beta, who'd ripped its head quite literally off it shoulders.

Of course, as the lord and master of all I bloody surveyed, I was greeted with the respect I deserved. Just inside the doors, and as soon as I stepped through them, I was hit in the face with a thankfully clean, but still damp cloth.

"OUT!" Jo snapped at me, glaring from two beds down. "Go on!"

"Jo, I—" I started, only to have her cross the small room, flapping her hands at me like she was shooing away a chicken.

"I've already spoken to Kelly and Aly, so you know you're not supposed to be here."

"Jo—" I tried again.

"Matt, you're on your knees and so am I! I've neither the time nor the energy to give you a tour and hold your hand while you worry over all you could have done differently. You kicked the god of the undead to shit and saved the world. Or fuck it, the country at least," she corrected, pushing the distinction aside as I opened my mouth to correct her.

"There were losses, and there always will be. There's people here who need my help, and nothing has changed since I spoke to you a few minutes ago. They're fine. Trust me, you've done enough."

"They fought because of my choices, Jo," I said woodenly. "The least I can do is look them in the eye and say thank you."

"They fought for you because you damn well rescued them," she rejoined. "You didn't start the war but you're fighting it for us all, so quit that shit. We all stand together or we die apart. Matt, as much as I'll deny this if you ever repeat it, you're our big dick, and we need to be able to pull you out and wave you around on occasion. We can't do that if you're unconscious. Go. Rest."

"I…you know what?" I saw the look on her face, as well as the genuine concern, making it clear that she was actually worried I'd collapse at any point. "I trust you. You know where I am. Let me know if you need anything."

"Not from you—you've earned a damn break, but if you don't get out of here soon I'll make that break your neck!" She shot it at me, in the true style of any northern woman looking after a friend.

With that ringing endorsement of my leadership, I nodded and moved on, heading for the main doors.

The interior of the cube was still in flux. Floors and rooms were added as they were needed or decided upon, making a higgledy-piggledy mess of confusion. That'd need to be addressed and soon as well, but I had one more job to do.

I stepped out into the cold air, taking a deep breath. The rain was starting *again*. I glanced about, searching for our new allies. A small contingent of them were to one side, discussing who knew what, and I started over to them.

The courtyard that we'd been fighting in, the area between the building itself and the walls, was still liberally strewn with bones, but they were vanishing steadily even as I walked over, heading to the small African contingent that had come to our rescue.

They were—*well...*

They were impressive as hell, frankly. Their leader snapped something at the rest of the group as I was spotted approaching. As one, they stood, forming up behind him in a semicircle, before smashing their fists against their chests in unison with a solid crash of high-quality metal on metal.

As I came to a halt before them, I couldn't help but stare. Kaatachi and Akuba had come through for us in the end. My God, had they—bringing their elite warriors and themselves, coming to fight by our side as we faced the main force of the undead.

Then they'd left a small contingent of those warriors, ten in number, and scarily identical in their equipment and size. Each of them was male, standing at least seven foot in height and heavily muscled, wearing armor that could have been designed by a comic book company, all tiny fish-like scales that reminded me of the panther of those selfsame comics.

My armor was much more massive, scales like those of a dragon rather than a fish. Just looking at them distractedly, I already knew that I'd need to speak to Finn about upgrades as they looked much more flexible.

Where it changed was that first of all, their armor covered them neck to foot, like in the movies. But a solid mask that was carved into a tribal face sat atop that. Instead of all the armor being only scales, like mine, they'd gone for plate armor reinforcing set atop it, covering their chest, groin, forearms, shoulders, and thighs.

Thick boots that ended with claws covered their feet. And their weapons? They fought in pairs, one with a shield and the other a spear bearer, and both were trained in magic.

They'd proved that in the fight to devastating effect.

I blinked as a memory came to me. The group that had come through first—it'd only been Akuba and Kaatachi that had been like this, a spear and a shield separate, hadn't it? I thought the ones I'd seen come through the gate were all spear wielders?

"You are the Dungeon Lord Matt?" the leader asked in a heavy African accent.

I nodded, dismissing the thought. Either I'd find out the details later or I wouldn't.

"I am, thank you," I greeted him. "And you are...?"

"I am Kofi, the leader of this troop. We were ordered to remain behind until you were secure."

"Secure?" I asked. "And thank you, both for your help and for coming in the first place."

"It was demanded by honor. We are to remain until you are secure." He gestured once, a quick stab outward in a circular motion with the spear tip that was clearly meant to encompass the local area. "Our lord and lady were not sure if you needed help. But they could not stay. There is much to do in our territory."

"I understand," I said. "There might be another fight here, and soon, but probably not for a few days…"

"We are allies." He nodded. "We are here."

"Can you stay and help, or are you needed?" I asked after a brief pause; he cocked his head to one side, clearly assessing me as I went on. "I don't think there's much chance of a fight in the short term, so if we need you, would it be better for us to call? Then you could return?" I changed my request, and he nodded once.

"We left one war to come to your aid. That war was won, but there was much damage," he admitted. "Our people need us."

"And yet you're still here?"

"Our lord and lady told us to remain until you declared we were free to return." He jerked his head in the direction of the wall. "You have new forces, though, and the enemy is dead. Perhaps yes, you call us if needed? Release us for now?"

"Yes," I agreed. "You can return to your homes, with my thanks, and that of my dungeon. Please tell your lord and lady that I'll come and visit them soon, to thank them properly for their help."

"We will." He bowed his head again, then said something in a language I didn't speak. Then the entire group was streaming past me, heading for the gate in seconds.

Clearly they'd been waiting for any chance to get going, and they weren't hanging around and risking me changing my mind.

If it wasn't for our ability to summon more forces here, I'd not have released them so happily. But after we'd defeated literally hundreds of thousands of the undead yesterday, we now had matter and therefore mana to spare, even with what I'd used up transforming myself.

That matter was in the form of the bones that were hip-deep out beyond the wall in places, and several meters deep in others. They were being reduced to mana by the second, powering the changing of the area.

I wanted to look at it. I wanted to see what changes they'd come up with and to oversee them, to guide them to what I felt was the best. But again, Kelly and Aly were right.

I waited until the African contingent had connected the gate to their home and passed through, before stepping up and using my own access to the dungeon to link a gate from here to the Newcastle dungeon.

I paused, watching the way that the swirling field of stars appeared in the gate before me, the event horizon that seemed to be both a bubble that could burst at any second and a pit of infinite depth.

Taking a deep breath, I let it out slowly. I glanced around to make sure everything was okay still, and then, shoving down the feeling that I was abandoning my people to work while I lazed about, I stepped through.

CHAPTER FOUR

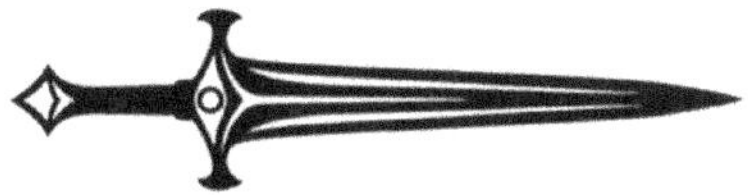

I woke early the next morning, having slept for almost an entire day, barely stirring in all that time. As I blinked back to the real world, a dream vanishing into memory, I shifted slowly, stretching.

The bed was warm, the room was cool, and Kelly was fast asleep by my side. The warmth she radiated almost made up for the fact that, as normal, she'd stolen the majority of the blankets.

Half of me was out of the covering, and blinking tiredly, I slid gently and quietly out entirely, heading to the toilet and performing the necessary ablutions.

Those done, I was tempted to go back to bed, and I almost tried to wake Kelly up for some fun on instinct. But for some reason, I just felt off. It was a mixture of sad and deflated, mainly because of the losses we'd suffered, I was sure, as well as the sheer ongoing weight of the war. But also because I was just so damn *tired.*

I wanted to go back to *sleep.*

I *wanted* to just climb into bed and ignore the world, but that wasn't a response the Dungeon Lord could have to the situation, and so, I stepped into the shower instead.

Clearly it was set to Kelly's tastes as the last user, because I almost had my skin boiled off before I could reduce the temperature to something that wouldn't instantly cook a lobster.

By the time I was finished and back out, I was surprised to see that Kelly was still out for the count, snoring in a very unladylike way that she swore up and down she didn't do. So, I dressed as quietly and quickly as I could, before slipping out into the hall and padding down to the small private area that the original group of us had shared for so long.

I found Aly prodding Amy along, telling her to keep the noise down, before the pair greeted me, giving me a hug each. They vanished again, Aly apparently taking Amy to school.

Sitting on the nearest battered couch, I pulled my boots on and yawned, before heading upstairs to the main cafeteria and scooping up a little breakfast, then sitting in a shadowed nook as far from everyone else as possible.

I'd grabbed a fry-up from the trays automatically—beans, bacon, sausages, hash browns, fried eggs and toast, an energy drink. Then, as I worked my way through the lot mechanically, I slid into the dungeon sense and started to work.

It wasn't effortless, though. I'd barely managed to do this while working out, and the motions there were much more repetitive. But the more I could do this while doing tasks, the better, I guessed.

My first stop was easy, though I suspected I'd have heard if anything had changed. I flitted to the southern dungeon and found Mike. He was calmly eating with a few others in a new cafeteria that had been recently built there.

I reached out and tried to reach him, but got no response. Then I thought better of it and left him to enjoy his food, slipping myself through a wall and out to check the area, and headed straight to the army encampment as a first step.

The remains of the force that had been sent from London, some five hundred strong, had been cut down to less than a hundred in the end. Seemingly half of them had been dispatched back to London for orders after the incident, I guessed.

It wasn't a difficult guess, judging from the tracks and the lack of so many people, but I resolved to get confirmation later. I also noticed that we weren't exactly being subtle in the whole "We don't trust you fuck nuggets" sense, because there were almost as many of our dungeon-born close by to them, ready to go, as there were survivors of the army contingent.

I accepted that we were as safe as we could be, especially considering we had the cube to retreat to and could summon more if we needed, and a protective wall around it as well.

Next was the medical suite, and I winced as soon as I entered. Griffiths was still on what had to be a respirator.

There'd clearly been a lot of medical research done over the last few days, judging from the new machinery and the mana signature that it emitted. But as I stared at it, I couldn't help but feel it was a bad sign.

I'd had so many injuries healed simply by basic healing spells now that it felt wrong, him not being healed the same way. But I trusted Jo, and I accepted that she would be doing all that she could.

I moved across to Emma and her sister Jenn, who was slumped in a chair by her side. I stared in dismay.

Jenn was exhausted, great rings under her eyes, her hair lank and unkempt, her clothes clearly slept in; she just looked a mess. Worse than when she and her sister had first come to us from the park.

It was Emma's situation that really got my attention, though.

Emma looked outwardly fine. If you had no sensitivity to mana, you'd be able to look at her and her sister and wonder why the healthy one was in the bed. But if you had any kind of a mana sense? It was *very* clear that something was incredibly wrong.

I reached out, but from here and through the dungeon sense, there was little I could tell beyond that she was in a hell of a state. She seemed to radiate mana, but not in a way that any of us should.

We all drew in, purified, and made use of mana…all of us, all the time, and so did she. The issue became that what we normally did was draw it in, and our mana channels collected, guided, and converted it. Instead of her doing that—being like all the rest of us, a void that dragged in—she was constantly giving off sparking, fractured fragments. They seemed to be falling from her body as regularly as she breathed, which made absolutely no damn sense at all. And laid over her stomach was the furry shitbag himself.

Thor, the Raiju.

I stared at him, forcing myself to tamp down my anger and irritation, wanting to punt the little bastard off her. My immediate thought was that he'd just found a body that wasn't moving and was making the most of it.

Then he opened his eyes and stared right at me.

I was in the dungeon sense; I wasn't there physically. And sure, Thor was a dungeon-born, a creature of the dungeon, but the way he always acted? The way he showed himself to always be more than the others?

I stared back at him, and the pair of us watched each other for a long moment.

That was when I realized something, something that had escaped me until right that very minute. I was *furious* with the furry little turd.

He'd shown up at the last minute, he'd swanned around, and he'd dropped a few little fucking confusing hints—then he'd buggered off all over again! Now he was having a nice little nap and…

He closed his eyes and settled back down, wrapping his tail around himself and starting to purr.

He was fucking purring?!

I nearly reached out then and there to absorb the fucker back into the dungeon. Literally, I stopped myself a hairsbreadth away from killing the furry little bastard. And that was when Jenn reached out to stroke him, mumbling tiredly about what a "good kitty" he was.

He deserved to be shaved bald and punted up the arse into the nearest snowdrift! He wasn't a good kitty. He was a—

"Matt!"

I jerked at the shout, blinking out of the dungeon sense.

Aly stared worriedly at me, standing a good two meters away from my table. "What's wrong?"

"Nothing," I snapped. A small collection of the people who had been nearby now stared at me from behind ornamental flourishes, tables, and counters, all staying well clear for some reason.

"Nothing?" she repeated, clearly in disbelief, before gesturing around me.

I frowned, glancing, then staring in shock. My plate was shattered. The food that had been atop it? The food I was fairly sure I'd barely eaten any of was a charred mess of carbon.

The table itself was an old and heavy thing—thick wooden planks, black painted rivets, and heavy steel fittings—and it was charred to buggery. Much of the paint on the metal flaked free.

The solid brickwork walls that surrounded me in the little alcove I'd retreated to was marred by age and peeling—this section had apparently been uncovered to add a "feature wall"—and now looked as if someone had taken a jackhammer to it.

The more I looked, the more I cursed.

Even the floor and ceiling showed signs of damage. And all of it, all of it had been because of that little…

I choked the anger off as fresh sparks crackled from my fingertips, dancing across the table. Clearly, I'd found out how the damage had been done, I realized, staring down. I forced myself to release the lightning and the rising mana I felt picking up speed. Making myself to get a good grip of everything I'd been feeling, I looked at it; then I took a deep breath and I looked at myself…and I didn't like what I saw.

I was shifting the blame for everything that had gone wrong onto the cat. Yes, I wasn't happy with the little...with Thor. Yes, I felt he could have done a lot more than he did.

He wasn't a cat, though. He wasn't even entirely a dungeon-born creature, which annoyed me as well. Unlike the rest of the creatures I summoned, I couldn't sense or summon him at will.

I felt that I couldn't control him nor bend him to my will, and I wasn't even entirely sure I could get rid of him if I wanted to. I was also fairly sure he was more powerful than me, and certainly more knowledgeable in terms of magic.

What had taken me weeks of painstaking work to reconstruct my mana gates, he managed to create in the first place in a matter of minutes. When I was doing it myself, I was repairing the work he'd done originally.

Was he annoying? Yes. Was he—

"Matt?" Aly prodded again, and I sighed.

"I'm sorry." I banished the thoughts and made myself let go of the anger I felt toward him. I focused, and the table, the walls, ceiling, and floor around me all blurred, before fixing again. "You joining me?" I nodded toward the chair and she slid into it, forcing a smile that was clearly for the benefit of those watching at a distance.

"I will if you get some damn control, Matt," she hissed through her fixed smile.

"How bad was it?" I asked grimly.

"You trashed the immediate area, and you weren't listening when I tried to talk to you, until I shouted," she said. "Kelly's already on her way."

"Kelly!" I cursed. "Dammit, she was asleep! You didn't have to wake her and—"

"And you were covered in lightning that was burning half the room apart!" Aly snapped, before closing her eyes and taking a deep breath, plastering a smile on her face again. "Matt, get more food and eat it," she advised in as calm a voice as she could manage. "Kelly is coming. She's worried, but I'll let her know it's under control. You get the food, and make sure everyone can see you're okay."

"Am I?" I grunted, but I waved away the look that she gave me. Instead, I absorbed the charred mess and summoned the same again, not bothering this time to go to the trays. Then I sat there as the table was consumed in a flare of light, then dimmed back to reality, the formerly charred table now topped with normal food.

Aly closed her eyes, clearly communicating with Kelly, before blinking and looking at me again.

"Matt..." She prompted after a few seconds. "The food?"

"Yeah," I muttered, before starting to eat. The food tasted like ashes in my mouth as I tried to get my head straight again. I could feel the anger there, the disappointment, the frustration... I wasn't used to this.

I wasn't a man given to bouts of introspection, despite it all. I mean, I meditated, but generally that was just for the mana side of things, and to improve my abilities.

Maybe it was that? That I was just pushing too hard? I didn't know, but what I did know was that I was starting to react with more violence and with less of a reason each time.

"Matt."

This time when I blinked, it was to the sight of Kelly sliding onto the bench seat next to me, resting one hand on my arm and kissing my cheek.

"You okay?" she asked carefully.

I nodded. "I'm fine." It came out a little harsher than I intended, and I sighed at the way she flinched and how Aly was staring at me. "I'm sorry," I said softly, setting my fork down and realizing that, again, I'd barely touched the food.

"Don't be sorry," Kelly whispered, taking my hand and holding it under the table. "What's wrong?"

"I'm just…" I drew a deep breath. "I don't know," I admitted.

"Talk to us," Aly suggested. "Matt, we're friends…you can talk to us, you know."

"I know," I acknowledged. "I'm just a bit… I don't know." I shook my head. "I spend half my time fighting to survive—literally, fighting with everything on the line, and all around us our friends, our people, they're all falling, and then I looked at Thor. He's on Emma's bed in the medical facility."

"I know. Thank God we've got him," Aly agreed, spearing a bit of sausage, then freezing at the look on my face. "What…?" she asked, confused.

"*Thank God*?" I repeated her words as calmly as I could.

"Yeah?" She glanced from me to Kelly, then back again. "Jo said he's really helping Emma, that he's doing something that's stopped her deterioration, and she seems to be starting to heal now?"

I stared at her. Anger and frustration warred with relief that she was getting better, and most of all, the knowledge that Thor knew exactly what I'd been feeling toward him, and he'd even given me that look, one designed to piss me off as much as possible.

"I didn't know that," I forced myself to say in as even a tone as possible. "I didn't know he was helping."

"Yeah, he is. What's the problem, Matt?" Kelly asked.

I attempted to explain it. "It's that he's so fucking smug!" I eventually exploded after a few seconds of struggling to articulate it. "He's just so goddamn happy with himself and he only ever helps when he feels like it!"

"Is this about during the fight?" Kelly asked.

I nodded. "All that time, all the days before, he could have been helping and instead, where was he?"

"He was here," she said softly. "He was roaming the dungeon while we waited to open the gate. And when we managed it, he went through and was helping at the fortress."

"I never saw him until the end!" I groaned, covering my face with one hand. "I… I just feel like there's so much he could teach us, that he could teach me, and yet he just turns up when he feels like it! He's never there except…"

"Except when you need him the most," Kelly finished for me.

"Exactly!" I snapped. "And that boils my piss because…" I floundered.

"Matt, you know you're not making much sense right now, right?" she asked. "Are you…is there more to this?"

"No!" I snapped, then sighed. "I'm not the right person to do this," I whispered. As the words slipped out, all the anger and worry seemed to go with them. "I'm not the one who should be in charge of all of this, and I certainly shouldn't be having meetings with people like that brigadier tosspot."

"Maybe not," Kelly said after a long pause, and I looked at her, shocked. "Maybe you're right, Matt." She shrugged. "Do you want to hand the dungeon over to someone else? What are you going to do?"

"I…no, I mean…" I felt like my legs had been cut out from under me.

"So, you don't want to hand the dungeon over?" she asked. I shook my head, and she smiled. "Matt, seriously, honey, you're exhausted. You're making mistakes, sure. We all are, though, I promise you. What's brought this on?"

"I don't know," I whispered, feeling conflicted as all hell. I didn't want to give all of this up, not really. Sure, there were plenty of days where I just wanted to toss it all aside and just chill with Kelly, but, really? Half the time, sure, I was scared out of my mind, but the rest? If I wasn't running from job to job, I was having the time of my life. I didn't know where this was coming from any more than she did.

"I think I know," Aly said slowly. "Matt, these feelings, what do you want to do, right now? Not what do you think you *should* be doing, or should want to be doing but what do you actually, honestly want to do?"

"I… I want to go to bed," I admitted after a few seconds' thought.

"Alone?" she prodded.

I forced a smile. "Well, you know…" I started to joke, before dropping it when I saw the serious looks on both of their faces. "Yeah." I felt like I was letting Kelly down, like I was rejecting her somehow with that statement.

"I think it's burnout," Aly said.

"What?"

"Burnout," she repeated. "I've seen it in Mike. I've seen it in a load of our people, and considering everything that's been happening, I'm not at all surprised I'm seeing it in you as well. Hell, after everything that you do and that we pile on your shoulders? It was stupid of me not to see this before now."

"Okay, so how do we fix it?" Relief filled me that she knew what was going on, and then it vanished as she shook her head.

"There's no cure, Matt. No pill or spell that'll fix it."

"Well, fuck," I muttered. My heart dropped.

"You're not the only one," she repeated. "Matt, more than half of the population has it. More, I'd imagine—the gung-ho idiots like you are just the ones who have been pushing the hardest, and you're all starting to get hit with it at the same time. Mike is struggling with it."

"Mike?" I asked, stunned.

"Matt, what do you think burnout *is*?" she asked.

I shrugged. "No clue really. Just being tired out?" I tried.

"Matt, what do you think you should be told, to deal with this?" Kelly asked me shrewdly.

"Well, to 'man up' and pull my finger out my arse, and get on with things, I guess?" I winced as I saw the anger in both the ladies' faces at that.

"God, I *hate* that comment," Aly spat. "To say 'man up,' like you're being pathetic about it."

"Well…yeah, I know, but it's not like it's a real thing, right? Like an injury or man-flu."

“Mental health is still health.” Kelly took my hand back, holding it tightly. “And I think this is the problem. We’re all working our asses off, and I know in the north, this is a big thing, that we have entire generations that were raised on the belief that therapy is something shameful, and that you have to be a failure to need it. You don’t.”

I wanted to say that I didn’t need therapy, that it was all bullshit, but the more they spoke, the more I agreed with their words.

That wasn’t to say I thought I needed a couch to lie on and an “I love me” jacket with the long sleeves that enforced a special cuddle from me to me, either. But still, I listened to them.

“I don’t think there’s a good way to say this, so I’ll just say it, Matt. I think you’re building to a nervous breakdown,” Aly said.

I blinked in shock. “Nah, I’m fine.” I shook my head, a nervous laugh escaping.

“No, you’re not, and you’re not the only one,” Aly said. “Matt, you need to listen, not just push this away. You’re not fine; neither is Mike. Neither are more than half the people in the dungeon. We’re all on the ragged edge. The frustrations, the snappiness—all of it are signs of a bigger problem, and it’s one we need to face.”

“We’re all taught to just make do and soldier on, and especially given the current situation—” Kelly started.

“The end of the world,” I added helpfully.

“Yeah, that,” she said flatly, glaring at me.

I shut up as quickly as I’d spoken.

“Matt, we’ve talked a few times about the need for downtime, and frankly it’s becoming a serious issue,” Kelly said. “Aly is right. As things are, you’re headed for a breakdown, and so are at least half of the dungeon. Probably all of us.”

“So what’s the solution?” I asked, and she hesitated. “You’ve got something,” I pointed out. “Want to share it with the class?”

“Relaxation.” She shrugged.

“Well, yeah, it’d be lovely.” I waved it off. “Seriously, though?”

“I’m being deadly serious, Matt,” she said. “You ever wonder why the military, who isn’t exactly known for being big on the touchy-feely side of things, insists their troops get regular rest and relaxation? Think about those majors and generals, who you know don’t give two shits about their men, and yet insist that they give their people time off for holidays as soon as a deployment is over?”

“Not really,” I admitted. “I just… I don’t know.” I thought about all the movies, all the books and more that I’d read, and they all had the common theme that when the heroes were back from the fight, they were given time off. “I always thought it was just what you did, but…”

“They enforce R&R because they don’t think of them as people but investments.” Aly took over the conversation. “An investment that just costs you money isn’t a good one, so the cold, hard logic is that you push them hard, but then you give them time off as well, or else you end up with broken soldiers. It’s one of the theories behind the state of people after the First and Second World Wars. Why, when they came back, they were so absolutely broken that they were unable to reintegrate into society.

"Part of it was their experiences—yes, of course it was. An entire generation was lost, fathers burying sons, seeing them dying from mustard gas or worse—but at least one of the contributing factors was that they just never stopped. They were thrown into the fight over and over again until they died, they won, or they broke mentally. They could still fight, but that was all they'd been reduced to—unthinking and unstable weapons. As much as they desperately wanted to go home, to be with those they loved, to return to their old lives, they just couldn't.

"That's the extreme, of course. I know that they saw things that were far worse than anything we're dealing with, but they were also different people and they needed different things. For us? We're seeing the signs of serious decline in at least half of our population, and we need to start dealing with it before the damage becomes permanent."

"So you're saying we need time off?" I asked. "I mean, I'm not against it, but—"

"Matt, for most of the dungeon, yes, that's all they need…even just a couple of days here and there. Maybe we start a weekday and weekend rotation as well. Maybe we run everyone on four days on, two days off. Or maybe we have a monthly holiday or something. I don't know, but we need to start working toward downtime for everyone, and that includes you."

"I'll take time off when I can…" I agreed dubiously. "But it's not going to work that I take set times."

"No, that won't work for us, not in the leadership cadre, but what will work is that we start working as a team. You've said that you want to build more dungeons, right?"

"Yeah?"

"Well, I'm suggesting that we build a dungeon somewhere we can relax," she suggested.

"Are you for—?" I broke off, barely, before I could say something I'd regret. "A holiday dungeon?" I asked in disbelief.

"A dungeon," she agreed. "A dungeon in Crete or somewhere like that."

"That's madness," I said. "It's also wasteful as hell and—"

"How?" she asked.

I looked at Kelly, my head cocked to one side. "To build a dungeon somewhere like that instead of here?" I threw my arms up. "Instead of a major city where we could save a load of lives?"

"You think the islands in the Med didn't have populations?" she countered. "Matt, I'm saying we look to build a dungeon in the Mediterranean. No, it's not just for partying and shit—that would be ridiculous. We try to save the people who are just as likely to be on a major island down there or one of the coastal cities. We build there and we follow exactly the same process we're following right now: we strip the surrounding area, we develop the base, and save people.

"The only real difference is that we do it in a damn place that we can send our people to relax with a nexus gate, somewhere that has a nice pool and blue skies. I know it sounds ridiculous—I *know* it does…it feels it as I say it, but it's also desperately needed."

Kelly hesitated, then smiled. "You know, we—you and us, I mean—and those in the leadership cadre, we could do a lot of what we do around a pool. We could swap for a week, even to a one-on, one-off rotation. We could work alternate days. Fuck's sake, Matt, we could even work our arses off all day and then take the evenings to sit and relax. It doesn't matter how we do it, just that we do. We need our people to rest and recuperate."

"Okay..." I sighed. "Well, maybe we could look at if we were to—"

"Matt?" Aly interrupted me.

I glanced at her. "Yeah?"

"I've got an alternative, but before you shoot this idea down, think about it first, okay?"

"Yeah, I will," I promised.

"What if we *didn't* set up a dungeon?" she said softly.

I frowned. "You just said..."

She shook her head. "What if instead of taking a dungeon core and setting it up, we captured one of those that are already there?"

"What, we just start conquering others?" I snorted.

"No, well, yeah..." Kelly admitted. "But, I mean, wasn't there a few that had declared for the other side?" she asked. "I mean, they surrendered, right?"

"I...oh, now there's a thought." The potential ran through my mind. "There's two other dungeons that had declared for the Unlife team, and they surrendered, or one of them did. The other refused, I think? They were trying to add conditions, but..." I bit my lip, then sighed and nodded.

"All right, give me a few minutes, because I've got a hell of a lot of notifications to check." I settled back, damn well hoping.

CHAPTER FIVE

Needless to say, it wasn't as easy as that. First of all, as soon as I opened the backlog of notifications, I was hammered with them.

The first few were useless, general skill upgrades, a bunch of kill notifications…loads of minor shit like that. They were important, don't get me wrong, but they were nothing compared to what I was looking for.

A few were a hell of a nice surprise, though.

Congratulations! Area Event Conquered!

Due to the large numbers of undead in the area, a naturally occurring event was spawned, and subsequently completed!

The Lord of Unlife was drawing closer to his fated battle with the Lord of Storms, and in doing so, due to the higher than normal concentrations of Unlife mana his forces generated, a runaway reaction was formed.

All undead in the area, out to a two-hundred-mile radius, were drawn inexorably inward to join his forces, like a lodestone draws iron, and for the remainder of said event, he received additional free reinforcements.

That situation has now passed, however, and due to your survival, you now receive the following rewards:

- +3 to top three Attributes
- +1 Class Skill point to allocate
- 25,000 XP

First Lord of the Storm, you have reached the third evolutionary Plateau in your Evolution from Terrestrial Local Variant Human to Storm Titan. Your specific evolutionary path stands thus:

~~Tempest~~ > ~~Thunderstorm~~ > Cyclone > Storm Titan

Your current evolutionary position is:

Cyclone: 1%

Increase your capacity to reach the next level of Evolution.

As a [Lord of the Storm], you no longer gain [+9 points] to distribute at each level; instead, you now receive:

- [+15 Points] to distribute

Congratulations!

You have reached the next stage of your ascension, and as such, your formerly human body has undergone a considerable transformation.

The metrics that governed your old body are no longer suitable for the powerhouse that you are becoming, neither are the simple measurements that once decreed your limits.

These are for lesser beings; the only limits placed on the ascendant gods are those that they inflict upon themselves.

Your Character Sheet will be adjusted over the next five cycles to reflect your new physical form.

Fifteen…*fifteen* fucking points?! And my sheet was going to evolve along with me?

I stared in wonder, not to mention desperately wishing the fuckers were awarded retroactively. Hell, when I reached level ten, twenty, thirty, etc. I got double the usual points for hitting a threshold level. That meant I'd gain thirty goddamn points!

I couldn't believe it!

I tried to bring up my stat sheet, but before I could, still more notifications appeared before me. I hesitated before moving on with them. When I had the chance, I'd bring the sheet up and treat it, and the points I had to spend, as if the changes coming to my character sheet weren't a thing.

The main reason for that was that a shitload could happen in the next five days—I hoped the cycles were of the day/night variety and not the annual kind, but there wasn't much I could do if it wasn't—and that way, if anything did happen, at least my points were of use.

If not, well then, the changes that would come, would come regardless. Fuck it.

Congratulations, First Lord of the Storm!

You have eliminated the majority of your enemies' forces, annihilated two of its chief lieutenants and its primary intended source of reinforcements, as well as destroying utterly the opposing god, Balthazar, First Lord of the Pantheon of Unlife and his subordinate, Thierry, the Lord of Bones.

The remaining forces of the Pantheon have sued for peace, and you agreed, provided they surrendered entirely. Three of those four remaining forces agreed to your terms.

Kyd, Lord of Phantoms, new First Lord of the Pantheon of Unlife, Agrees and swears to be your vassal.

Clive, Lord of the Western Winds, his Dungeon Fairy and Wife [Identity Hidden], and their bonded Dungeon #4 Agrees and swears to be your vassal.

Petr, Lord of Darkness, his Dungeon Fairy Sin and their bonded Dungeon #91 Agrees and swears to be your vassal.

Sari, Mistress of the Ocean, Refuses your demand, and declares the war continues, unless you agree to a conditional surrender.

Terms offered:

Sari, Mistress of the Ocean, will deliver one part in three to you of all plunder gained, be that lives, resources, or mana, in exchange for her freedom to operate in the [Mediterranean Sea].

Do you accept?

"No," I said resolutely, drawing curious looks from both Kelly and Aly, but they didn't interrupt me. The war notification updated.

Do you wish to make a counteroffer?

"Unconditional surrender or a war to the knife." I felt it as the system apparently processed the offer, then it responded again.

WAR!

You have received an update to the Declaration of War from the Pantheon of Unlife…

The Pantheon of Unlife have surrendered and declare Sari, Mistress of the Ocean, as a Rogue Agent. The war is over! Congratulations, Cyclone!

Due to the outstanding nature of the single rogue agent, the war screen remains active, with a link between yourself and the Mistress of the Ocean available to both sides.

The Rogue Agent Sari sends this message:

This is foolishness! We can either be allies, and I can pay you tribute, or not. That's your choice, but before you decide, consider well that I'm the Mistress of the OCEAN, you idiot!

I and my creatures can sail the seas; you can control the land. There's no need for us to have a conflict, not now. Our spheres of influence don't overlap. I have no interest in the land, and you can't reach me on the ocean, so why force this?

Accept my conditional surrender. I have no issue with you, and bent the knee to Balthazar simply because I had to. We can resolve this and you get tribute—or we continue it and you get nothing!"

-Sari, Mistress of the Ocean

Be aware, any response to this declaration will result in a formal Link between the Pantheon of the Storm and its vassal the Pantheon of Unlife, and Sari, the Mistress of the Ocean.

I thought for a second, then responded.

"Unconditional surrender, or a war to the knife," I repeated unwaveringly, knowing something that she certainly didn't. Thanks to my plans for the dreadnought dungeon, she could run all she wished. The oceans weren't out of my reach, and I sure as shit wasn't leaving her to basically set up as a pirate queen.

The response came several seconds later.

The Rogue Agent Sari sends this message:

Fine! You want this? That's fine—I tried. Good luck trying to catch me, you goddamn idiot!

-Sari, Mistress of the Ocean

With that done, I banished the screen, slipping out of my personal notifications screen and to the dungeon sense, and then the command center, pulling up the map and checking it against the new markers flashing for me.

I'd seen and sensed them roughly before, but I now had a better sense of where Sari was, as well as the others.

Sari was just off the coast of Portugal, near the border of it and Spain. I grinned to myself as I made a mental note to make damn sure I got the dreadnought up and running as soon as I could, then moved to fuck her up.

Beyond that, I also got an update on the other three, as they were now my vassals and showed up on the map as well.

Kyd, the new First Lord of the Pantheon of Unlife, was in Maine, North America. Clive and Dungeon #4 were on the southern-most tip of the Dominican Republic. And as for Dungeon #91?

He was in Libya, on the northern coast. That wasn't a bad location, to be fair. Well, no, that wasn't right…for a dungeon, I wasn't impressed, that was for sure, from what I knew of Libya. I'd never been there, but I was familiar with the basics through the news.

None of which was good, of course. Basically, since their last major nutjob leader came down with a bad case of lead poisoning—introduced by the international community via a lot of rifles—the entire country had been in various states of civil war, famine, outbreaks, more wars…

More than half of it was abandoned before the fall, because most of their citizens had been determined to escape their war-torn home and instead move to Europe.

That meant that I couldn't see the country being in good condition to raise a dungeon, and certainly not to act as a home to try to save humanity.

WAR Notification:

As the victorious party, the bonuses previously selected [+ 10% Health Regeneration] and [+10% Ambient mana regeneration] have now been changed to permanent 10% increases. Plus, you receive the previously selected boon granted to the Unlife Pantheon [10% damage increase to Melee attacks].

I read it, decided it was a nice bonus, and moved on.

Congratulations, Cyclone! As the first of your kind to ascend to such a lofty height, you receive a bonus item, the Eye of Amalthus. The Eye of Amalthus is a powerful magical artifact, one that can aid you in establishing your Divine Core and reaching for the next level of evolution!

SYSTEM ERROR: Divine Core identified. Previous reward issued for activation ahead of projected timescales: Divine Shard: Zeus's Master Bolt.

Item [Eye of Amalthus] is no longer suitable…processing.

Solution Found:

Congratulations, Dungeon Warmancer! Due to your capacity, your greater than expected evolution in establishing your divine core in a sub-optimal stage of ascension, and your position as a Dungeon Warlord, a solution has been discovered:

You may receive your previously awarded artifact: [The Eye of Amalthus] a device created to aid in the establishment of a Divine Core, or you may choose to refuse this artifact and instead receive a [Rare] Bonus at the end of your next Trial Dungeon run.

Which do you choose?

I paused, thinking about it. I already had one of the bonuses to claim when I ran a dungeon again next—it was given to me when my dungeon became the first to reach Glass as well as a secondary nexus gate. But I had been planning to run it again anyway, if I could—mainly because the dungeon fairies that I'd fought before had been incredibly knowledgeable about the dungeon. I'd damn well planned to summon at least two or three of them and try to get them out at the end of the run, rather than summoning "blank" dungeon fairies that wouldn't have the same level of knowledge.

Sure, Drak was a bit of a dick, but he'd also proved a hell of a boon—when I could get the fucker to stop scheming for advantage or getting high and make him actually work.

Add to that, the Eye was designed to help with establishing my core, which was already established…so it wasn't really a hard choice at all.

I did consider taking the Eye of Amalthus and trading or giving it to Akuba and Kaatachi, but I was betting that I could talk them through some of what I'd done, and the path probably was different for each person.

Fuck it.

I accepted the additional "rare" bonus, and moved on.

Congratulations! As a newly formed Cyclone, freshly ascended to the third level of your evolution, you gain [+10] to all stats. Note: this increase is effective immediately, due to the nature of your ascension.

Okay, now that was nice. Very nice, in fact! Even at fifteen points a level, ten additional free points to each stat meant that I'd just gained what, seven levels' worth? A hundred points?! Also, the damn pain when I hit Cyclone just became so clear as well, as was the exhaustion. The points hadn't been held the way they usually were until you acknowledged them. Instead, they'd all hit at once, and damn. A hundred stat points assigned at once was an excruciating experience, all right.

I moved onto the next notification.

Congratulations!

You have killed the following:

- 1x Enemy God, First Lord of Unlife, Balthazar Level 37, 12,170 XP
- 1x Enemy God, Third Lord of Unlife, Thierry Level 21, 8,140 XP
- 5,114x Mindless Undead Shamblers, Level 1-19, 10,228 XP
- 37x Banshee Undead, Levels 1-11, 4,699 XP
- 1x Draconid Variant Abomination, Level 9, 2,500 XP

Total XP earned: 32,623 XP

A force under your command killed the following:

- 104,312x Undead Levels 1-22, 316,267 XP
- 315x Banshee Undead Levels 1-27, 40,005 XP
- 5x Draconid Variant Abomination, Levels 2-7, 11,250 XP
- 1x Hydra of Lerna, Level 1, 7,500 XP
- 1x The Eternal Coil, Level 1, 7,500 XP
- 1x Battlefield Colossus, Level 1, 7,500 XP

Total Party XP earned: 390,022 XP

As war leader, you receive 50% of all XP earned.
Total XP awarded 32,623+(390,022x0.5=195,011)= 227,634
Partial XP is lost to the ether.

Current XP to next level stands at 228,595/90,000

Congratulations!

You have reached Level 31 & 32!

You have 30 unspent Stat Points, and 1 unspent Skill Points.

I was practically gibbering over the point drop I was about to receive, though the change that I knew was coming…well, it was going to be painful. I pulled up my stat sheet, counting over the details, seeing where I was the most deficient and the most advanced. I noted that with the upgrade to myself with the change to Cyclone, I'd lost all the improvements that were in place as well, like where thanks to my exercise and all that, I'd almost reached another point of Endurance and so on.

Worth it, though.

Then I came to the irritating conclusion that, as much as I'd like to bang them all into my magic-improving stats, I really needed to even myself out a little, and I'd do that as soon as I read the last of my notifications.

Congratulations!

For the first time, you have passed a century threshold! Through exceeding the 100 points range in any one stat, you have gained a specific ability tied to your path.

As the relevant stat is [Intelligence], you receive a bonus:

1x [random spell]

2x modifier to Mana Generation

Aegis of Recovery: Create a protective dome of restorative energy that accelerates healing, and increases stamina and mana regeneration for you and your allies. Those within the Aegis experience rapid recovery from injuries and fatigue while being shielded from external threats. (Beware, mana cost is directly linked to the size of the field established).

Note: This spell has increasing effects depending on the area covered and potency of regeneration, ranking from 0 (5m radius, 2x recovery rate) to 5 (50m radius, 10x recovery rate).

Okay, hell yeah that was nice! That'd just doubled my mana to over twenty-two thousand points! Even without the spell, that would have been incredible, but with it?

I focused on the spell, and I got the basic details that weren't being described. As I kept the spell active, those inside the shielded area would gain health, stamina, and mana regeneration bonuses. The downside? The field cost a whopping two thousand mana per level to cast, and lasted up to an hour.

That sounded okay still, when you considered that I would recover at double my normal rate, and that even without me investing any of my thirty damn points—I loved that I got that for gaining two levels—in Wisdom, I'd gain twenty-eight hundred mana in that time.

A win-win, right?

No.

Not even close. Because that two thousand mana was the passive cost. That's what it cost to generate the field in the first place, and leave it active.

Sure, if nothing attacked, then that was a win. But if something did attack? The damn shield was tied to me for as long as it was active, and I'd not banished it.

If someone started wailing on it and pounding the shit out of it in a few places at once? I could find myself out of mana in a matter of minutes!

That's how bad it was, that I could end up drained to my limit almost before I could cut the spell free.

On the other hand, though… Even as I considered this, I rubbed at my chin in thought, before cursing. If we had mana potions, I could carry a load of them, and then essentially set up to allow the others to recover their mana in this space. I lost the cost of setting the spell up, and if the shit hit the fan and I lost the spell, I've lost my mana, but the rest of my party were fully recovered.

Then I down a few mana potions, and boom. Bob's your uncle, Fanny's your aunt. It could be worth it… I shook that thought free.

It *was* worth it, even if I never used it, because the damn spell was a freebie for hitting my century. It cost me nothing and if I never used it, it was no loss.

I went back to my screens, actually really tempted to spend all thirty points on Wisdom to boost my mana regeneration, as that was on seventy right now. If I was right, that'd result in me getting a second century bonus, as well as boosting my mana regeneration to two thousand an hour without the Aegis active. With it, I'd be on four thousand an hour.

I thought about it. I *wanted* to do it, and I knew it'd be a mistake. My body was getting incredibly lopsided in terms of my physical to mental stats allocation, so it was time to make the most of my windfall, and fix that.

So, physical stats were Agility, Constitution, Dexterity, Endurance, and Strength mainly. Perception was more borderline between physical and mental, as was Charisma, along with Intelligence and Wisdom as purely mental stats. And Luck? Well, who the fuck knew with that one.

No, thinking about it, if I needed to even things out, as much as I'd like to boost my Agility to a hundred and see what I got, it was time to be sensible and get a trailing stat boosted up higher.

Constitution was tempting, as being able to take a hit and keep rocking was getting to be ever more important. That was one to consider again.

Dexterity was important, but I wasn't really into the kind of weapons that Dexterity favored, like daggers, and I didn't craft. Sure, it'd increase my damage with melee weapons, but…not this time.

Next was Endurance. Stamina, basically, and yeah, it was important, but I was reaching the point where I could fight all day and all night, and unless I did something stupid like didn't sleep for several days, then had a pitched battle with a god, I was generally still firing on all cylinders. I was pretty much good with Endurance these days.

Strength? I almost dismissed it. I mean, I was plenty strong already, right? I wasn't a meathead, and after seeing the state of some of the guys who had hammered their Strength stat already at the cost of all the others? One guy couldn't even wipe his own arse after bulking up that much.

No clue what happened to him, but I'd imagine having a crap-coated arse probably led to his death, considering the way the world was these days.

I went over the details a few times. I had thirty points. After all, as much as my instinct was to pound them all in one place, like put them into Strength and see a massive difference, that wasn't the only way I could do it, right? I mean, I could split them up…

I went back and forth on it for a few minutes, trying to decide, then sighed.

Strength was my lowest stat at fifty-one, so I put fourteen points into that, taking it to sixty-five. That took my maximum damage to an additional hundred and forty-three points of melee damage on top of where I hit them and what I hit with.

Then I split the remaining sixteen points. Eight went into Endurance, taking that from fifty-seven to sixty-five as well.

Of the last eight points, I put five into Dexterity, taking that to sixty from fifty-five. The difference there was mainly that it took my additional melee damage that it granted from twenty-two extra to twenty-five, taking the overall to a hundred and sixty-eight. And then the last three points went two into Constitution, hitting seventy there, and one into Perception to push it to fifty-five.

I pulled up my stats and read over them, unable to wipe the satisfied smile off my face, even as my body shook, muscles twinging and cramping as the changes were carried out.

Name: Matt, First Lord of the Storm				
Host Powers: 1 (Enhanced Regeneration)				
Species: Cyclone			**Bonus**: None	
Level: 32			**Progress to next level**: 33,595/120,000	
Stat	**Current Points**	**Description**	**Effect**	**Progress to Next Level**
Agility	70	Governs dodge and movement	Heightened chance to dodge attacks 140%+24% = 164%	0/100
Charisma	53	Governs likely success to charm, seduce, or threaten	72% more likely to succeed in events that require seduction, persuasion, or threats ((43x2)+10% = 96)	0/100
Constitution	70	Governs Health and Health Regeneration	HP: 70x80 = 5,600	0/100
Dexterity	60	Governs ability with weapons and crafting	+60% Increased chance of improved result, +25 to melee damage	0/100
Endurance	65	Governs Stamina and Stamina Regeneration	Stamina: 65x70 = 4,550	0/100
Intelligence	103	Governs base manapool,	Mana: 103x110 (x2) = 22,660	0/100

		standard intellectual capacity		
Luck	61	Governs overall chance of bonuses and critical hits	+102% increased chance of positive outcome	0/100
Perception	55	Governs ranged damage and chance to spot hidden items/traps	+45 to all ranged attacks	0/100
Strength	65	Governs damage with melee weapons and carrying capacity	+143 to all damage with Melee weapons ((65*2)+10% = 143)	0/100
Wisdom	70	Governs mana regeneration	1400 mana regenerated per hour *(Arcanist class 2 boost)*	0/100

CHAPTER SIX

With the notifications all dealt with, I turned to the map on the wall.

Standing in the dungeon sense in the dungeon's command center, I let my eyes roam across the map. First checking out the country, and then expanding the field of vision until it covered the western side of Europe.

As much as it went against every instinct, and made me feel like I was taking the piss more than a bit, considering the war that was still to come, Kelly and Aly had a point.

Not about me being on the edge so much. I knew this was just a bit of a low point, and after the level-ups and the dopamine hits of the new spell and the other bonuses, I knew I was probably fine. Probably.

No, they were right about everyone else.

They needed a place to rest. They deserved it, and the people in the Med deserved help as well.

From what I understood of the dungeons so far, they were intended to be bastions to help humanity. But whoever was responsible for the contingency programming had taken the afternoon off and had phoned in the job—when they'd bothered to do it at all.

That meant that there was a good chance that any dungeons in the area weren't helping people. Or at least, if they were, then they were only just starting into that phase. I'd had interactions with about ten dungeons so far; seven, beyond my own, had been through the nexus gate.

One of those I'd met was batshit and tried to set up a confrontation, goading me. Another was filled with the undead, and a third was at the very least using humans as disposable fodder, considering the people that had been pushed through as scouts and were desperate to escape.

That left four that were reasonable, and they were…well, they were all right, let's put it that way. I'd ended up allied with one of them, after all.

The other two dungeons I'd met in without going through the gate were both set up to harvest and kill people, instead of helping them. The Gateshead one had been full-on sacrificial in its outlook, and the Oxford one wasn't much better.

Sure, they'd been looking at it as a way to jump-start the dungeon's development, but still. Human-goddamn-sacrifice.

Then there was my own, a dungeon that had crashed, losing its fairy and being left basically to get claimed by a wandering idiot.

Working through that, and having a hundred and twenty odd dungeons that were known to have been deployed, that gave me a ten percent failure rate, at a guess.

Not good, but that was at least better than the minimum twenty percent sacrificing and mass murder rate that the others were working with.

If another ten percent were slaving bastards, ten percent more were undead lunatics, and another ten were out-and-out monsters?

Well, maybe there was something to the plan to try to conquer some dungeons in the area.

I put my massively increased intelligence to the test, which was something that I did very infrequently, but was overjoyed with the ease of the math when I tried it.

If there were a hundred and twenty dungeons planned out for the world, then taking Western Europe down to the Med that gave me, by landmass, a likely breakdown of two in the UK.

Literally working out the size of the UK compared to the rest of the world, that was an easy calculation. My own dungeon wasn't supposed to have been set up here, after all, and that helped make me think that there might be something to the calculation.

Then, if I looked at Western Europe, I got three more there before you reached the Med. *Probably one in...let's see...*

I worked my way over the map, plotting out points with the two places that I knew of holding dungeons so far. I knew it was a likely inaccuracy, but I reminded myself that this had been done with a logical base, so it should be possible to predict.

I considered first that they might have been set up to lock in on population centers...then I reconsidered. London apparently didn't have one, but Gateshead and Oxford did?

I mean, I could certainly see the issue of landing a spacecraft in London. Having driven there far too many times for work, I knew that flying a spacecraft in would have three likely outcomes.

First, five minutes after it'd landed, you'd have someone trying to sell you a tour or some bullshit cheap merch that had cost them about five pence and they expected you to mortgage your grandchildren's houses for. Second, people would be clambering all over your spaceship and taking selfies, then screaming at you when you told them to get off—I'd seen this too many times with people who had luxury cars there. They parked, went to get something, and had people climbing on the car to get photos, leaving scratches and scuffs all over it; then they literally screamed abuse at the car's owner, while filming themselves for social media, for shooing them off.

Lastly, you'd try to take off and find that there were now three fines for things that hadn't been signposted, the wheels had been stolen and the ship was now on bricks, and two more people had turned up with written evidence that your spaceship had been in their family for six generations, and they were suing you for trespass.

Worst of all, the lawyers would be circling, having sniffed out a weakness and a potential to earn money from all sides.

Not that I hated the city or anything.

No, if they'd been going for population centers, they'd have hit London without a doubt. And as much as I was pissed with the army and their handling of the latest debacle, I didn't doubt that had there been a dungeon in the middle of London—the magical kind and not the sex kind—then they'd have known about it.

That meant that unless it was down to ley lines or some shit that I didn't have access to, then it had to be general locations to cover as much ground as possible.

If they'd been setting up in areas of high mana concentration, after all, the Gateshead one would have set up in Otterburn instead, and it was close enough that they could have made a tiny correction on entry and landed there instead of Gateshead, so yeah.

I was guessing physical distance and laid out across the landmasses to get a dungeon roughly spread out evenly across the world.

I decided landmasses instead of across the entire world, because we knew that the Cinthians mainly wanted us as intergalactic shock troops, so wasting two-thirds of the dungeons by putting them at the bottom of the oceans? Unlikely.

Using the map, I plotted two points in the UK as they were, then added in Akuba and Kaatachi's dungeon in the Congo and the Darkness dungeon by the coast in Libya.

With those as examples, I quickly came up with a likely location for a dungeon in the Pyrenees mountains, separating France and Spain. Another was likely in Germany or Denmark, and one in the Alps, around Switzerland or Greece.

It was literally guesswork, but until I had any more information to work off, it was the best I had.

Now, if those were anywhere near accurate, and we extended that map, let's see...

I shifted the map around, trying to pinpoint additional likely spots, then shook my head as too many places caught my eye. There were literally thousands of variations I could see that might move a dungeon here or there. I stopped, scratching at my cheek as I thought, then decided to approach the problem from another direction.

If there were a hundred and twenty or so dungeons, then logically, with the size of landmasses, there was a good chance that they'd be spread out, with say…

Thirty to forty in Asia, twenty-five to thirty in Africa…North America would be…twenty? Maybe twenty-five depending on the logic. Fifteen to twenty in South America; five to ten in Australia. I was guessing that although Antarctica was a big place, the fact that it was basically inhabited by penguins made it unlikely as a dungeon location.

I could be wrong—totally wrong, in fact…the whole thing might be worked out by totally different shit than I was thinking here—but the truth was I had to start somewhere.

I plotted out a few more positions, based on what I knew, then cursed and started again.

And again.

On the sixth attempt, I suddenly found Kelly by my side, staring at the map, and I jerked back in shock, then grinned ruefully.

"Sorry," I said, and I meant it. If she'd come looking for me, I'd clearly been distracted longer than I thought, considering I'd told her and Aly that I'd be a few minutes while I dealt with my notifications.

"What's this?" She gestured at the map, and I grunted.

"I'm looking at plotting out the dungeons in western and southern Europe," I admitted. "I was thinking if one of the dungeons that had surrendered was somewhere useful, then we could have taken it over and started making it into this resort dungeon. But I'm thinking northern Libya isn't a real winner for us, as that's the only one we can reach easily.

"The other dungeon is in the Dominican Republic, and while yeah—I see that look." I grinned at her, seeing the "hell yes" look as I told her the location. I went on quickly. "While I totally agree, I would love to set up in the Dominican Republic…getting there? It's going to be an absolute ballache, not to mention that to set the dungeon up, there's not much in the way of sacrificial infrastructure.

"If we set one up in say, Athens, or one of the Greek islands, then great. We can keep the nicer, older buildings, absorb all the crap, and have a dungeon that can support itself fairly quickly. We're also likely to be able to draw in survivors in the area. And knowing the Greeks, they'll have an incredible fishing culture going already.

"In the Dominican Republic, as much as I'd love it, there's just not enough there that we can set up as easily. If we chew the area up to generate the mana we'd need, we'd end up with a completely ruined location, while in Greece, there's an extra thousand years plus of habitation to tear down," I finished.

"There's likely to have been a lot more people there in the first place as well." Kelly sighed. "Damn, I could have done with a Dominican holiday, though."

"I'd not say no," I agreed. "And maybe, once things are going a little smoother and we've got transport? Sure, we can do it. But for now, it's a hell of an ask." I smiled, letting her see that I genuinely meant it, even as I tried to dismiss the momentary thought of chasing her, bare-ass naked, down a white sandy beach.

Damn.

"Unfortunately, this means that we need to tread lightly with regard to the surrendered dungeons as well…for now. Once they realize that we can't reach them easily, they're more likely to rebel and start doing whatever they want again. So I think we need to let them think we've forgotten about them, and hope they don't want to draw our attention, I guess."

"You're right." She squared her shoulders. "Okay, are you done with this? Aly is still waiting, and we both finished breakfast a while ago. I mean, we can just move over here and work, if you want? I'm just thinking of the way it looks right now."

"Looks?" I asked, then nodded. "Of course, we're still sitting around in the cafeteria…"

"Oh, well, yeah, there's that, but Chris came over and drew something on your forehead while you were distracted as well," she said offhandedly. "You're getting a lot of looks right now…"

"Motherfu—" I snarled, exiting the dungeon sense and jerking upright. I twisted around, looking for him, before summoning a mirror to my hand and squinting suspiciously at it.

I couldn't see anything. *But maybe it was off to the side or…* I shifted it this way and that, stopping only when I heard Aly's words.

"Really, Matt? I'm sorry, honey, but you're just not pretty enough to be this vain."

I glanced at her, then at the grinning Kelly, and groaned.

"Okay, you got me." I congratulated her as she started to chortle, explaining to Aly what she'd said. "I'm totally going to get you back later for that, though."

"Promises, promises!" she managed to get out, still laughing.

I sighed. "Okay, let's take this to the control center and get things back on track. I need to figure out what the hell is going on, and—"

"And you need to focus on a rest and recovery plan," Aly said. "We won the war, Matt. Yes, there's a hell of a lot of fighting still to come, but this is the time that we expand, reconsolidate, and then expand again. We need to make the most of the situation before the next phase."

"Aly, genuinely I want to, and I agree there's a damn good reason to get a place that our people can relax up and running. But the war is still coming and we have to make that our focus, so—"

"Matt." She cut me off. "You said that you used to game a lot, right? One of the games you'd mentioned ages ago was a civilization builder?"

"Yeah," I agreed, wondering where the hell this was going now.

"Okay, so with that, would you just build one city, or even two or three, or would you try to get as many as possible?"

I shook my head. "You try to get as many as possible to claim the resources," I agreed. "But that's not the point here. We don't need to grab the iron or saltpeter. We can just make it all…" I trailed off.

"We can make it through mana," she agreed. "Mana that we generate through draining an area, be that the ambient mana, the structures, or from the bleed off from the people who live in it."

"The people," I mused. My mind now set off on another track as I thought about the Life generators that were constantly ticking along as they fed on the mana all living beings generated and released into the air.

"And if we have multiple cities, or in this case dungeons, and they're all feeding their spare mana into crystals, crystals that we can stockpile…" She left it hanging.

"Then we're ready for the fight when it comes." I nodded. "I get what you're saying. And yeah, you're right…if we can survive long enough, get a load of dungeons up and running, then the mana we can generate becomes an exponential growth curve."

"So what's the problem?" Kelly asked. "And why is it a problem specifically when we're talking about the dungeon in the Med?"

"It's an issue because in the short term, we're crippling ourselves. In the game you were talking about, Aly, there were three paths I could follow, generally to victory. First, I could build a single city, and then start churning out warriors. Literally just do that—get eight or ten of them, get a few bonuses like a boost to flanking, and then use them to attack everyone else fast.

"While most people are building infrastructure, I could overwhelm their paltry defenses and get enough cities in short order that I would secure the area and get enough of a boost that nobody could catch me. Or, you know, kill them all."

"Right?" she said.

"Well, the issue with that was, if I came up against someone with city walls, or even a few tech advancements that were geared for defense, I was fucked. I'd lose everything, and then I'd be defenseless as they counterattacked."

"I don't see the problem."

I nodded. "I'm getting to it," I assured her. "But that's an option. We could have done that with the dungeon, and that's what the Gateshead dungeon was doing before we took it out, remember? Sending out waves of goblins to capture and bring back resources, essentially. That's the first path to power, but it's risky as hell. The second path to power is to aim for bonuses to building cities, and then do minimum defenses, put in place the infrastructure and let the cities grow as fast as possible.

"Once they're up to a certain point, if you've done your research and infrastructure right, you can steamroller everyone around you. There's just no way they can win, because they're using spearmen and cavalry, and you're using infantry and tanks."

"Right?" Aly repeated, still not getting it.

"Well, that's the way a lot of people play. They do the whole 'Let's be nice, and we don't need risk' playbook, right up until they're unbeatable, and then they roll out and crush their enemies. It's safer, it gives you long-term bonuses, and it means you generally win, but it can be boring and I basically didn't have the patience for it. The third path, the one I generally took?

"It's a mixture of the two. Build the infrastructure, build the defenses, and get a level or two higher than everyone else nearby with your tech. Then steamroll them, before pulling back. Secure the cities you wanted and the resources they had access to, and then start all over again: put in the infrastructure, build their defenses, expand."

"That sounds like the same thing," Kelly said.

"It's similar," I agreed. "The thing is, it's about mitigating risk. Expand, consolidate, then expand again, rather than an ever-expanding wave. If you have a lot of cities, and they're all building at once, then you get a period of time when you're basically able to do fuck all, because they're all making granaries and shit. When all the low-level stuff is done, though? That's when you can go all in, because the cities are ready to build. And because they've all got the infrastructure already, they expand and build much faster."

"Right…" Aly said for the third time. "I don't get the point of all of this?"

"You started by asking me about the games!" I snorted. "That game? That was how you won it. The risks that I took there didn't come with actual lives lost, though. In real life? Yeah, I was focusing on our singular dungeon a lot, getting things in place, but I agree, we have reached the exponential growth curve point. How much mana do we have access to?"

"You mean right now or daily?" Aly asked me, and I nodded.

"Both."

"We've got about six hundred thousand in the tank currently, with perhaps two million in bones on all sides, ready to be rendered down," she mused. "Another ten million or so in the airport. Going off the things that Mike said, they need to be broken down and changed into crystals, as the mobile dungeon—"

"Dreadnought," I corrected.

"The *mobile dungeon* only has a limited space for storage." She sniffed.

I grinned, knowing that she was playing and didn't really disagree with the name for the dungeon, not now that she knew the plan. Though, as it stood currently—a glorified truck and trailer—meant that "dreadnought" was a bit pretentious.

"So if there's limited space for storage, the main bottleneck is converting the mass into mana and then into crystals which can be transported?" I asked, making sure I understood the issue.

"Basically, yeah," she agreed. "The northern dungeon is expanding solidly, and while it's producing more than it should need, and by a lot, it's currently spending all of it and more on Arend-Jan's side projects."

"I thought we'd agreed that he would fund that himself?" I frowned. "He could do whatever he wanted…so long as he could produce the mana, he could invest it?"

"He is," she said. "The northern dungeon is expanding rapidly, but for the next week, it'll need all it can produce. At that point, he's going to switch from expansion to production, he said, and then it should start making a profit in mana of at least a million a day."

"Well, that's all right then, but it's—" I started.

"That's a million a day, sustainably," she interrupted. "No draining the area of its mana. Instead, if anything, the mana concentration will get *higher*."

"What?" I frowned again. "Look, someone said that he'd figured out how to do that, but it doesn't make sense. There's no such thing as a free lunch."

"There is if you know how to set it up, apparently." Kelly snorted. "Look, he's been testing on a small scale, and we gave him the go-ahead to scale it up, because it genuinely seems to work."

"Explain," I said.

"Let's talk about it on the way," Kelly suggested, glancing around at the rising buzz of conversation in the cafeteria, before focusing and reabsorbing what was left of her breakfast and drinks into the dungeon.

I nodded. Aly did the same, and I wiped mine free too. The flash of light as the food, crockery, and empty drinks containers vanished into the dungeon was by now so commonplace that it was utterly ignored.

We rose and filed out, pausing briefly when people stopped me, offering congratulations or to ask questions.

The only one who didn't just get a general "Wow, thanks; hey, we did it together" kind of an answer was when a young and particularly earnest man asked me for details on religion, and when I'd be holding the first service "for the faithful."

I stared at him for long seconds in disbelief, wondering whether he was trying to take the piss out of me, before deciding he was sincere, which was even worse.

"Talk to my Paladin, Robin," I suggested, wincing even as I said it. He beamed and nodded, backing away, as we made a break for the door, heading into the hallway and down the stairs.

I kept my mouth shut until we were definitely out of earshot, before asking the question.

"What the fuck was that all about?" I groaned.

"The religion?" Kelly quirked an eyebrow.

"No, his tie and suspender belt combination," I replied sarcastically. "Of course the bloody religion!"

"What did you think was going to happen?" Kelly replied, and I glared at her. "Seriously, Matt—you can fly, you've been declared a god by the system that's integrated into everyone's lives now, and you're leading the fight to retake control of the world. You're saving people, and you do things like explode into lightning and kill monsters and other gods. You have your own Paladin, and don't get me started on that mess. What did you actually think was going to happen?"

"I thought…I thought that people would get over this shit!" I exploded. "I'm just *me*, for fuck's sake! The system could have named me a cheese sandwich just as easily as a god—it doesn't mean I'm a damn cheese sandwich!"

"Matt, it doesn't matter if the system calls you a god or not—you're right," Aly said. "What does matter is that there's bonuses being offered by the system for calling you this, and it's not just the physical or magical powers.

"People are talking about how we're being led by a 'god.' People compare you to Thor, the Norse god of thunder. They believe that if the shit hits the fan? You'll fix it. Sure, you might fuck it up, you might be late, or things might happen and people die before you can get involved—"

"Fuck, is this supposed to be a pep talk?" I asked grimly. "Because I'm telling you, it needs work."

"It is and you'll damn well listen, Matt!" she snapped at me, making me look at her in surprise at the genuine anger both in her tone and on her face. "They believe that if you're not there, then it's because you're busy doing something equally heroic for others! They think of you as a literal demigod. You're not expected to be omnipotent, but you *are* more than human. You are, and you damn well know you are. As such, more and more people are coming to this point of view, so you need to accept it. But they think that you're their best chance. You're someone they can rely on to kick arse and take names, to fight for them, and if you can't protect them, to avenge them."

"Aly…" I said quietly. "You know I'm not—"

"I know no such thing!" she shot at me. "Matt, the only one who's confused about who and what you are these days is *you*. Since the beginning, you've been saving people. You created a safe place for everyone. You raise them up and you give them power. You provide food, training, a home!

"Then you go out and you conquer their enemies. You kill anything that threatens us! You get blown up, stabbed, shot—you're fighting fucking *gods*, Matt! One-on-one, you fight them and *win*. You might not think of yourself as a god. If you're looking at the modern version of a god, something that's all-powerful across the cosmos, creating all life and weighing suns in the palm of their hand?

"Then no, all right, you're not a god. If you're looking at a Norse-style deity, though? Back when they understood that the world was a shitty place that was out to fuck them up given half a chance? Seriously, what the fuck, Matt? You *are* that! You control storms. You fight to protect the innocent, and you bring them food and plenty. You defend the people against the things they can't fight. Sure, it's not against frost giants, but that's only because we've not found any yet!

"You think you're not a god because you've got it in your head that you're not the kind of a being that sits on an ivory throne and judges souls? Well, good! We don't need one of those. What we need is a warrior god…a demigod, if you want to claim you're 'only' that powerful. We need someone who's more than another man or woman to look up to. The system declared you a god? Fine. No stress. That's a great title, and it'll give some people peace and hope. Sure, we can use it, but the thing that I'm saying we need to be focusing on isn't what you're thinking.

"What I say we need to focus on is that people are given hope by this. You're developing real powers, powers that can be shared out to the Paladins and the priesthood. You say you don't want to be some asshole on a throne? Great! You say you don't want a bunch of Priests and Paladins? Well, tough titty, because you need to grow up, Matt." She shook her head in disbelief.

"Wow, thanks for the tough love." I snorted.

"I mean it, Matt. You're thinking that these people shouldn't be viewing you like this. That you're just an average guy. We all know that's bullshit, but that's not the point. Regardless of how you look at it, regardless of how you might want it to be, or how much of a ballache, or how embarrassed you might feel about it, you're missing the biggest point. You gave Robin powers that meant at a low level she could go toe-to-toe with a literal ogre that was the leader of a gang of murderers and rapists.

"She smashed in the face of her personal demon that had been responsible for killing kids. She did that with barely any levels because she believed in you, so what the hell could someone like Chris, who you know trusts you with his life, do with that kind of power?

"Stop thinking about what you want and what you feel, and start thinking about reality. This is a *tool*. We need to be using it. For all we know, the Priest class could banish the undead. All that shit we just went through down at the southern dungeon? You could have had a dozen guys just wave a hand and turn them into dust to float into the ocean."

"I don't think it would have been that easy…" I tried to interject as we walked around the outdoor pool, ignoring the drizzle that immediately started soaking us all, as she went on.

"No, no, it probably wouldn't have been," she agreed. "But you know what? WE. DON'T. KNOW." She turned to me and jabbed me in the shoulder with one finger. "We don't! For all we know, these could be amazing powers, or they could be utterly shit. We don't know, but what we do know is that—"

Her tirade was cut off as a new announcement suddenly rolled out, flaring in everyone's vision and staying until it was acknowledged, regardless of the settings each user had in place.

CHAPTER SEVEN

WORLDWIDE ANNOUNCEMENT!

THE FIRST LADY OF THE FOREST HAS PUBLICALLY ACCEPTED HER FIRST PRIEST, RAISING UP A NEW CLASS OF WORSHIPPER AND BEQUEATHING HER ESSENCE TO THOSE SHE LEADS!

KNOW THIS! THE ONLY LIMIT ON YOU IS THAT WHICH YOU PLACE UPON YOURSELVES. GROW, ADVANCE, *LEAD*!

"GODDAMMIT!" Aly shouted, before spinning and glaring at me. "That's exactly what I was saying! Someone else just beat us to it, to the bonus of raising up the first Priests!"

"Aly, we don't know if there was a bonus," Kelly interjected calmly, and Aly shook her head.

"No, no, we don't, but there might have been. What if it was a fifty percent boost to mana regen or healing spells or—" She broke off, seeing the way we were both looking at her, and she visibly tried to calm herself.

"Look, I'm sorry. For what it's worth, I wouldn't want a load of mentally unstable people following me around either, and regardless of the religion, there's always a lot of them in their ranks. What we need to do, though, is utilize every single possible advantage we have. If we ignore the path of religion because of the connotations we're all leery of? Like the whole 'altar boy monthly' side of things? We're just weakening ourselves.

"This is a chance to do what religion could do, and *should* do, Matt. It could empower people. It could bring them hope, and make sure they're safe to learn and grow. It doesn't have to be a parasite preying on society, or even a gentle and well-meaning thing; it could be a weapon. It could be a protector…it could be anything you want it to be." She chewed on her lip as she clearly tried to find the words, and Kelly took over.

"She's right," she said. "We agreed that we needed to try to figure this all out, and we really do need to. I know 'we' said we'd try to figure it out, but this is all on you, Matt. As much as I'd love to help, this is literally on you. Just think about it, okay? Because there's going to be perks—there always are. And for all we know, the biggest perk with all of this is that every follower gets a hundred extra health, or a healing spell, or an offensive one. This religion could be the difference between people living and dying, so you need to take it seriously."

"I…I know," I admitted, hanging my head as we trooped up to the entrance to the Parthenon. "I know and I'm sorry. Yeah, I've been avoiding even thinking about it."

"Because it feels ridiculous and that this isn't something that should be centered on you?" Kelly asked gently, and I nodded. "Okay then, well, why not fix that?"

"What?" I held the door for her and Aly to pass through and entered the warm foyer beyond. A newly placed plush sheepskin rug by the entrance caught the dirt and water from our shoes in only a few short strides, before shimmering back to perfect condition behind us as soon as we stepped off it.

I smiled my thanks to an older lady in a high-backed chair to the left with a small child on her knee, and she smiled back. Clearly she'd chosen to read to the tousle-headed child right where she had, just so she could do this.

A good dozen adults were around the large marble area already, and at least triple that number of children. The older ones were corralled and led through clear lessons in the distance, while nearby, a handful of little ones, each no older than three, were being led in a nursery rhyme by a pair of smiling elderly ladies.

No matter how many times I saw this, I couldn't help but be lifted by it all—the way that the kids were kept safe, taught, and looked after by the older generations, and the way that those people in turn were generally over the moon to be able to contribute again.

"Kelly, hold that thought. Quick question first," I interrupted her.

She frowned, looking at me. "What's wrong?"

I shook my head. "Nothing's 'wrong.' Well, nothing about this. I just wondered, Amy was off to school this morning, right?" I directed it at Aly, and she nodded. "Well, where is it?" I asked.

"The school?" Aly asked, and I nodded. "Here. There's not that many kids in the main dungeon, so there's a handful of classes going on in the rooms back there for those who are older, mainly things like math, English, sciences, and history."

She gestured toward the rooms further along, on the ground floor. "The day is still pretty much split evenly between play and work, though we have a few teachers who have come forward and are putting together more comprehensive lesson plans now. They're mainly at the park. Frankly, I didn't want to send a load of kids there each morning and expose them to the risk.

"Some of the helpers here are ex-teachers as well. Sure, there's a lot of advances in technology and discoveries in science that they're a bit behind with since they retired. The other things? They're better with. Melissa, or as the kids all call her, 'Mrs. B,' who was sitting by the door?

"They take turns teaching, and she was a teacher in a private school for forty years. There's not much she can't teach, and the kids, especially the little ones, worship her."

"It just wasn't something I was really up to date on," I admitted. "So we're running a real school in the park?"

"We are, and one here too," Aly said as we headed up the stairs. "The majority of stuff you learn in the lower schools is simple stuff by rote, and the reason it takes all day is that kids' attention wanders so much. With the smaller classes, because we've got so few kids, it means that their lessons are much more efficient. For the kids in 'real' school, they're in classes of six to ten, with a teacher and an assistant. That's three to five kids per adult, so they get personalized attention, much like they did at the best private schools before all of this.

"We've dropped the things that just don't make sense for the world as it is—other languages, computers, design and tech, business…all that kind of thing.

Instead, they get a solid day a week where they study art and making things with Finn and one of his volunteers.

“They’re in seven days a week, but it’s lessons built around play for now, and they’re learning a hell of a lot. Sure, we need to do a lot more, like the fact that for now we’ve just scrapped all the languages entirely. Long term, that’s not good, as languages are great for neural flexibility. For now, though? We need a basic lesson plan and to move forward, and that’s what we’re doing. The new world is very different, and we’re going to come up with better plans as soon as we can. Most likely, we’ll set up a central ‘school’ at one of the sites once we’ve got more gates available, and then have everyone go there. It’ll make things a hell of a lot easier to arrange and to defend.”

“Sounds good. I’m sorry to derail us, again, Kelly, Aly. I just realized that I had no clue what was happening, that’s all. So, you said I could have the religion, without the religion?” I prompted Kelly as we reached the top of the stairs and headed back along the hall to the command center.

“Yes and no,” she hedged, and I groaned. “What I mean is that you don’t have to be the heart of the religion on your own, not if you don’t want to.”

“Go on,” I prompted, having little hope that it was going to go well, but knowing that we did, indeed, need to find any win we could out of this.

“So, first of all, yes, you are a major part of the religion, and that’s not going to change, okay?” she asked, and I nodded. “Glad you accept that. Now, if we take that as a given, the next point is that we…you…whatever…we have a *pantheon*! That’s what people keep forgetting. There’s a pantheon of gods, and now that both Kaatachi and Akuba have ascended as well, they’re starting to grow in power too.

“You need to help them establish their divine cores, and to teach them to spread their power out, but you can each cover a different aspect of the Storm. That’s what I just realized we were missing. You’re a Storm lord, and a Lightning god, right?”

“Yeah?”

“Well, the others are going to be ascending and changing their species as well, becoming Storm lords like you, but they became the Lady of Monsoon and the Lord of Dust. They’re totally different aspects of the Storm. What if what we started to push people toward was the worship of a symbol?”

“Like a cross or whatever?” I frowned.

“No, more like we pick a symbol—it could be anything, but we need it to be something with no prior connections. Then we build the worship around the symbol for the group, and around the basis of the Storm. Not the individual too much? That way, you’re not going to be as freaked out by them and—”

“It wouldn’t work.” I shook my head.

“What?” Kelly asked.

“Splitting it up like that, it wouldn’t work…not entirely,” I explained. “As much as I’d rather that personally, as near as I can tell, it’s just not going to work. The power has to come from one of us, and it also needs to go to one of us through the worship side. We feed it out to people directly, so it’s not like a pool that we can all draw upon. If we encouraged Akuba, for example, to run the system and to develop all our joint followers as priests, then all of the priests would be able to draw against her only.

"Similarly, if we all agree to have a single shared and outwardly identical Priest group, and we call them, I don't know, Priests of the Storm, and everyone gets used to them performing miracles like healing through divine power, that's great. It spreads the word about us and builds the belief structure, right up until one of us runs out of power and the priests can't heal any more. You'd have priests side by side who might not be able to heal, while another had a shitload of divine essence available. That'd confuse people and ruin the belief and trust that we'd built so carefully real quick, wouldn't it. I—" I broke off. "Fuck, I'm sorry…I'm not explaining this very well, am I?"

"Not really," Aly agreed. "So, first off, you accept that we need to develop the religion side of things, right? No argument on that?"

"No, we need to do it and it could save people, so there's no argument on that," I agreed.

"Right. Secondly, you're not explaining it well, you're right, but that's usually, in my experience, when you're explaining something that you know but don't know how you know. Matt, is this all something you know, no explanation—you just know it—or something you're guessing at?"

"I know it," I admitted. "I can't explain how, I just…"

"Then it's probably the bleed-through of knowledge from the system. Don't worry about it. But it does mean that we need to do it the other way, where you end up as the head of a church, I'm sorry to say."

"Not as damn sorry as I am," I muttered.

"Hey, at least you've got a formal role." Kelly snorted. "I wonder what my title would be? Actually, don't answer that." She glared at me.

"Head priestess?" I suggested, and she frowned at me.

"Seriously, you'd be the head priestess!" I assured her.

"Okay…" She drew the word out, waiting.

"And then people, when they ask who the head priestess is, would be told, 'It's her, the one with the dirty robe, because she's always on her knees'…" I managed to back away two steps before she hit me. I burst out laughing, but it was worth it for the joke.

We took our seats around the central table of the command center. Clarissa and Markus were already there, looking at us in a mixture of amusement and cheerful disbelief at our antics.

"Morning, children." Clarissa sighed, smiling.

"Morning!" Aly said, and we all chorused the same, as the pair started to sit upright.

I deliberately didn't say anything about the way that the pair had moved their chairs to be much closer together, nor that the seemingly much older Clarissa now looked to be younger and healthier.

Clearly the constant time she spent around the Life converter was helping her.

"Anything to report?" I asked, and they shook their heads.

"The northern dungeon is on track. Arend-Jan will be arriving mid-morning to go over the changes he's instituted there, as I've asked him to explain them to Starr and to help us with the farms we have on the upper floors here as well," Clarissa started.

"Then we have the resource teams here. I've shifted them around some of the older buildings but kept them tearing down the more modern buildings and the housing units. The influence generators with the converter facility inbuilt are proving to be a much more efficient way of working. If we slide them along the floor as the group works, it costs a little mana but keeps the input side close enough that it's maintaining the highest efficiency in absorption," she went on.

"And it's also still pushing out the dungeon's influence." Markus smiled. "I'd like to get the research done to increase them to the next level, if that's doable, Aly?"

"Certainly is," she agreed. "It was on my list to do anyway, but if that's helping, then I'll bump it up."

"Thank you," he said.

"So, the local area is doing well, but Starr has asked to have a meeting with you when you have the chance, Aly. He has apparently made great strides in the Alchemical field, but he's asking that we start focusing on dungeon runs for Alchemical components, and that we set up a specific section of the training dungeon to develop and grow ingredients."

"Why?" I asked bluntly. "I mean, he can summon the ingredients, and I thought he wanted to grow them, so that we didn't end up with just ten thousand copies of identical herbs?"

"He and Drak were talking, and it seems…"

"Bloody Drak!" I groaned. "I swear, he's like a plague!"

"A hard one to make work, but his knowledge is useful," she agreed, before going on. "So, Drak has confirmed that the dungeons that are set as 'trial dungeons' aren't set by the same rules as the others. If you get a set area that's designed to be a herbalist garden, for example, then once the dungeon is completed, it continues to be accessible to others who want to run it."

"And?"

"And that location frequently spawns herbs that we don't have," she finished. "The trial dungeon was heavily damaged before you completed it, thanks to the army assault. Due to the situation after, nobody entered it again for over a week. When a small party attempted to run it as a training experience, they found several small growths of herbs in the dryad's garden that we'd never seen before."

"Wait—the trial dungeon, the one that trapped me inside it?" I asked.

Aly nodded absently. "We reopened it after you confirmed that they could back out if they got offered a trial. So far, nothing has gone badly with the runs that people have done, but they've also not said anything to me about the herbs before this."

"You were aware that it is still locked to the layout that young Matt experienced on his 'run,' however?" Clarissa asked.

Aly and Kelly both nodded.

"No," I said quickly. "Hell no, it's locked?"

"Yes and no," Kelly said. "We can change it, but the layout stayed as it was after you completed it. Apparently, it's randomized when a new trial starts. But I didn't know people were getting much out of there with herbs?"

"It was more the crystal mine," Clarissa said grimly. "Apparently, some of the crafters and mages had heard about the mana crystal mine, and they were paying the small number of adventurers we had available to take them to it, or to mine it and bring the crystals back to them."

"Why?" Kelly asked, clearly as confused as I was.

"Because the rule is that they get to keep what they loot and this was classed as looting it. If it's a spellbook or an artifact, they have to hand it over, but the raw materials? They're much easier to mine than to spend hours breaking down rocks or anything else to earn enough mana to create them."

"And yet they cost us to produce," I said flatly. "So people have been going on and stripping them out, and the dungeon has been drawing in the mana to replace them? Dammit."

"They've not been doing anything wrong," Kelly said. "If anything, them finding this loophole is a good thing, right, Aly?"

"It is, actually." Aly nodded. "First off, we've not missed the mana, so it's not like the amount of mana we've been earning there is down. It seems that the dungeon has been siphoning a tiny amount off and using that to regenerate the 'stock' of the training dungeon. Secondly, they're using this stuff to level their skills and to improve on their creations. And thirdly, they're paying people to go in and essentially train.

"We had hardly anyone we could send to help with the fight down south, Matt, because so many had been either injured or killed by the coronaughts. That's why you ended up with a small number of soldiers. And then, when you had the gates open, we sent those who had recovered through.

"The training regimen is starting again, and if people know that they can harvest while they're in there? It just makes sense that they'll do it. The fighters will take in miners and harvesting teams and guard them while they work, which gets them all levels. It's a clear win for us."

"Great," I muttered, then I sighed and nodded. "No, you're right. It's just another thing that makes it clear we're missing so many little tricks, that's all."

"Well, we made an alliance, so now I guess it's time to make the most of that," Aly said. "Kelly wanted to go and visit them, and she's got a lot of questions to ask, so maybe that's something we should do sooner rather than later?"

"Definitely," I agreed. "Okay, sorry for interrupting the handover," I said to Clarissa, who smiled and continued.

"It's fine, Matt, and congratulations on your victory again. So, as I was saying, Arend-Jan is coming today to discuss the setup for the farms with Starr, and Starr has asked that we try to expand the growth area of the dungeon with the herb garden in it. According to Drak, as it's set up, it'll grow the usual herbs that it has, but if we increase it in size and set up some dryads with orders to maintain the place, that will help tremendously.

"They'll have to be told that they are neutral, to prevent them going on the offensive automatically, but apparently they can be set that way, provided they're low level enough to be unaware. Or, if they're actually aware, then they can be directly ordered by a high-ranking member of the dungeon and they will obey.

"Minor point on that side of things—they need to be neutral, not protective, or however it would be explained. Basically, that way, they'll let people harvest a little, and then move them on, so that they can't deplete the area. But then, if the harvesting teams cross the line, they have to be fought. That way, it lets the lower levels get something, while the higher levels get a better reward if they can fight the dryads and survive."

"Better to leave the dryads be." I glanced at Aly and Kelly, who looked like they were thinking the same. "That way, there's a better chance of them growing and becoming aware, not to mention they cost us less."

"No fighting the dryads." Clarissa made a note. "That's fine. Moving on, the park is going well. No major incidents to report, though there was another fight over drugs again. John arrested both sides and confiscated their supply. There's a lot less available, meaning that the price is climbing significantly. But he's concerned that we thought we'd cleaned most of it out, and there's now a new supply coming from somewhere. He wants us to make cutting that off a priority, so that people can start healing."

"Sounds good. It shouldn't be hard to cut that off now. It's not like we're going to be getting smugglers anymore. When the supply is gone, it's gone," I agreed, summoning a drink and getting comfortable. I then noticed that Kelly and Aly were exchanging looks on the drug issue.

"Moving to the southern dungeon, there's been some improvement there. We excavated a large cave under the site and created both Darkness and Earth converters down there. They're both creating reasonable numbers for mana, just so that there's always a bit of secure income for the dungeon. There's a small rolling cost as the converters are being 'slid' across the ground there, heading out to both the northeast and the southeast, aiming for the local towns. The resource teams are already absorbing the buildings as they go."

"Speaking of which, I know we discussed this before, Matt, but there's a World War Two aircraft museum not far from the dungeon—" Markus started, only to be cut off by Clarissa.

"If you don't mind, I'll finish my report. Then it's bed for me," she said firmly, and he colored.

"Of course. My apologies, dear lady," he said quickly.

"It's fine. I'm just tired." She smiled at him, and I again noted that there was a lot of warmth in that smile… "So, the buildings are being absorbed, and a secondary fractal pattern has been worked out for the influence generators, with one being spun up and pushed on by a skeletal resource team every six hours.

"That gives us the best expansion rate that we can manage, with the lowest cost, and it should result in a significant portion of the town of Folkstone being under our control in less than a week.

"There are also two teams working to expand to the southern coast, and due east to the high mana zone in that direction. Once they reach them, they'll lay infrastructure conduits and start to generate much higher levels of mana. That should have the southern dungeon up and running, self-sufficient in around three weeks, with Arend-Jan—again, that poor man never stops—helping to set up the farms nearby."

She took a deep breath, then smiled, seeing we were all waiting. "That's it. Report done."

"Thank you," I said. "It's a relief to have you both."

"It's our honor, lad." Markus shook off my comment. With a smile at Clarissa as she stood and headed for the door, he started to give his own report.

CHAPTER EIGHT

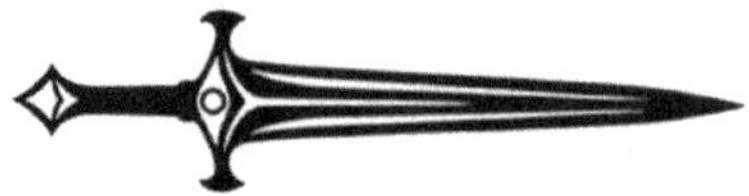

"Okay, well, sounds like it's my turn then..." Markus scratched at his beard. "Well, first and foremost, the army is doing well. I know that's my focus, so before I get on to the more fun things, let's go over that.

"The majority of the armed forces that joined us in Otterburn are now beginning to recover. They're going to be cleared for duty over the next week. But to be clear, for most, it's still light duty only. Two-thirds of them were infected right back at the beginning. Where people like Mike had the advantage of a heavily leveled body to aid in their recovery, these were at most level four or five, and frequently level one or two.

"As such, their bodies are much weaker, and their longer infection time has meant that they need significant recovery time. From the results we're getting from the doctors and the training team? We're looking at around a month before they're ready for any kind of 'real' duties.

"After previously speaking with Griffiths and with Rhodes just now, I'm expecting that they genuinely will need to go through our new version of 'basic training' again and certainly the physical conditioning parts. The majority are just that physically reduced. There are small numbers, such as those who were raised to fight and sent down south with you before, but others—anyway...." He shook his head.

"As such, we have a lot of walking wounded, and very few viable fighters currently. That being said, this is the army, not the navy, so they're used to doing what they have to with the least available resources. They have the base secure, and between the soldiers who are able to operate for short periods and the freshly summoned Scepiniir, the base is protected.

"An additional benefit that's come out of this is that the soldiers and Scepiniir are growing closer. Both groups are learning a lot from one another. And there's a team of goblin Luminaires that are rotating through, casting their...dammit, what was it called?" He checked a note and nodded. "Ah yes. Their Radiant Burst spell apparently helps in a lot of ways—not least is morale. They cast that on a regular basis next to the most wounded and around those who are suffering the most. It seems the effect isn't purely physical. There's been reports of it being a much more effective treatment for dealing with the mental side effects of the coronaughts' legacy for many."

"Damn, I didn't even consider that," I admitted. "Who did?"

"That was Kelly," Aly said proudly when her sister-in-law looked a little embarrassed. "We heard that there were a rising number of suicides in the survivors. There's a lot we can offer our people physically, but there's very little mentally we can do."

"Well, there's only so many puppies you can give out," Kelly said a little defensively.

"Puppies?" I asked curiously.

"She set up a guide dog housing area at the base, and asked certain people to help get them used to humans again, ready for being given to the blind," Aly said, a twinkle in her eye.

"The blind?" I asked. "I didn't know we had any…"

"We don't," Aly said, smiling widely. "There was one person who was blind in the survivors of the Hillsong Church, and Jo cured him. But either the soldiers didn't think about the effect of healing spells on conditions like that, or they just don't care. As such, we've got around a hundred Labrador puppies running pretty much wild at the barracks now."

"Wow…" I shook my head. "And nobody considered that they're being summoned?"

"Nope, they're just happy to have them, I think. I mean, they are gorgeous as well." Kelly grinned. "Ask no questions, receive no answers!"

"And there's only been one suicide since the Luminaires and puppy teams were deployed, and that was someone we couldn't find to include in the program," Aly said. "It's working…though, for some, no matter what we do, we can't help them. Too many have lost their families, with no hope of seeing them again."

"Griffiths…" I nodded. "We need to get him and his people home, even if it's just so that they know for sure."

"Very much so," Kelly said. "Before we discuss his condition and that, though, anything else to report, Markus?"

"Most definitely." He smiled. "So, the northern dungeon is secure, as is here. We have more of 'our' adventurer teams that had been captured by the coronaughts back up and running again. As I said, they had higher levels when they were captured, so are correspondingly quicker to recover. They're now clamoring to get into the dungeon. The limit on entry of once per day, and a new limit on an hour per run, upsets those who want to push harder. But without the time limit, people were staying for hours and monopolizing the dungeon.

"There's been a lot of requests to expand it, and as this one has resources that can be mined or collected over and over, it's now become the main draw for a lot of people over the training dungeon in Gateshead." He paused to look at me. "I know when the dungeon became a trial dungeon, specifically for you, it was a significant threat, but…"

"But can I do it again, and do it with the other dungeon?" I finished for him.

"Yes…" He sighed. "I don't ask lightly, Matt, but the dungeon is a major resource. And when we've tried placing similar layouts in the training dungeon…the crystals, for example? They don't recover."

"But this one does," I agreed. "Honestly, as much as I don't like the idea in a lot of ways, there's a lot of merit in it."

"Matt…!" Kelly interrupted, and I shook my head.

"No, there's a good reason for me to do it again, and it's not that I like fighting, I promise. Instead, it's since then that I've gained two more rewards, rewards that I can only claim at the end of the trial dungeon, and they're 'rare' quality. That's the same level of reward as the bag of holding. You know how incredibly useful that is, and we're only scratching the surface with it. Now that we're going to have to look at moving further afield? It means that our people can take entire camping setups with them in a simple pouch…ammunition, resources, food…and that's a single reward. Things like the skill boost…"

Kelly nodded, clearly unhappy. "We'll talk about the glassblowing project in a minute too," she assured me, and I went on.

"Okay, good point. So, it's worth it, but the main resource we can get from the trial dungeon is survivors. If I summon a group of fairies or any other creature in there to aid me—not the bloody Tuatha De Danann to be clear…the fairies, sure, but not those overdressed wankers." I glared at nobody, just annoyed even thinking about how much of a pain those buggers had been. "Anyway, if I summoned the fairies and managed to keep them alive until the end of the dungeon, we get people, people with memories of the greater galaxy and a reason to help us, as well as skilled magic users. If I run the trial dungeon again, I can increase my skills, I can gain loot—I hope—and a new self-replenishing resource as well as fairies that are worth a damn."

"We could try summoning regular fairies," Kelly suggested with a wince, and I nodded.

"We could, and we can," I agreed. "We can do that, and see what we get. If they're useful, then great. If they're dicks, then at least they're small enough we can crush them easily."

"That's a bit harsh," Aly pointed out.

I snorted. "One was about to core my brain out using a needle last time I saw them, but then she became sort of a friend by the end, so they're a bit…unstable," I pointed out.

"And that's who you want to recruit?" Kelly groaned, dropping her head into her hands. "I mean, look at Drak—he's a pain."

"He is, but he's also helping with potion production, right?" I commented.

"Yeah…" Kelly drew the word out, before shaking her head as she looked up. "And by 'yeah,' I mean 'no.' He refused the job to take over potion production. He's just interested in making his own personal supply. He realized that if he was in charge of producing it all, then he couldn't sell it to us still."

"What?"

"I mean it. He agreed to it, then he helped with the defenses at the southern dungeon, before coming back to me and refusing the job. Said he needed time to himself to figure things out. As he's not really a frontline fighter, and he'd made it obvious he wasn't willing to go there and fight directly, we thought nothing else of it. I was annoyed, but fine, it's his life. Then Starr came to see me yesterday," Kelly said, clearly annoyed.

The ladies exchanged a look, and I groaned, knowing this wasn't going to be good as she went on.

"Starr had found most of the more powerful ingredients for potions he had been developing were gone," Kelly said. "We couldn't figure out where they were, but it was all the naturally grown ones, not those that could be summoned. So rather than just replacing them, I got John and he tracked them down, and we found Drak at the same time. He apparently decided we were going to lose, and had probably been stockpiling for a while. His quarters were full of the remains of similar things and a full alchemy set…and he was unconscious, drugged up to the eyeballs."

"On healing potions?" I asked, confused. First, they weren't something that should have that kind of an effect, surely, and second, they were valuable as hell!

"On healing potions, and we think…cocaine."

"WHAT?!"

"So…there's been a few, though steadily rising number of ingredients going missing, according to Starr. He assumed they'd been lost to experimentation, because why steal what can be summoned, right? Well, we think it's because the summoned ingredients can be traced through the system. John had asked him to try to come up with a healing potion that would cure an addiction, and Drak asked for permission to take some of the cocaine to work with so that he'd know what he was dealing with, and when I went looking…" Aly sighed.

"We found it's possible with the recent core upgrades to get records of things that have been created, and while some things are very obvious, others aren't. When it comes to cocaine, that's another of those things, of course. It's classified by the system in three ways: first as a chemical compound, second as a sugar replacement—that's how they were creating it originally, if you remember—and now as a poison. Between those three descriptions, we found that Drak had been creating himself a *lot* of it, spread across the various versions, and then using healing potions to clean himself of the side effects before anyone saw him."

"Is it possible that it's a genuine attempt to do research?" I asked after a few seconds of stewing, hoping to find any kind of a ray of goddamn sunlight in all of this. "That he's been stupid, but until this time, he'd been actually experimenting with it in his lab, not just up the nose?"

"It's possible, but if that's the case, why hide it?" Kelly said disgustedly. "No, Matt, he's an addict, and it's no longer just to healing potions."

"Fucking hell, Drak!" I groaned, covering my eyes with a hand and rubbing at the bridge of my nose. "What the hell!"

"Exactly. Now, there's the second problem on top of that as well," Kelly said, and I looked at her. "John thinks that the reason he's been unable to find where the limited amount of cocaine in circulation is coming from…might be because it's coming from Drak."

"What?!" I gaped. "Are you sure?"

"No, he's not, and we can't make it stick because nobody is talking. The fight last night was between two rival suppliers. One had no coke to sell, and the other suddenly had a new source. It's not like we can check for a maker's mark on the coke, but if we could, I'm betting we'd find it was manufactured in the dungeon."

"Markus." I looked at him, and he straightened. "You know I'm no saint. I've done plenty of things over the years and that includes coke, but this is the end of the goddamn world. We're fighting a battle every day to preserve life on this fucking planet, and knowing that someone is selling coke? If it was a small amount that was used in the privacy of their own homes? I don't like it, and yeah, we said publicly it was banned, but I wasn't going to make a thing of it. If it's controlled and responsible, then I don't give two shits. It's when people are unable to function because of it…that seems to be the state that Drak was in. And that it's driving people to fighting? This ends now.

"You deal primarily with the military, while Clarissa deals with the day-to-day running of the dungeon on the second shift, right? Do you have time to deal with this as well?"

"In what way?" he asked me. "I mean, yes, I'm happy to take it on, but what am I doing?"

"You're working with John. The two of you need to get on the ball with the crime and punishment side. Actually, what time are you coming back on tonight?"

"On shift?" he asked, and I nodded. "Around ten?" He shrugged. "We don't need to be in back-to-back, so generally—"

"We've been working from about eight in the morning until around five or six at night," Aly interjected. "Then we have a few hours where things are ticking over and we're monitoring while we do things like have dinner and relax, then Clarissa and Markus start around ten or eleven at night and we sort of sign off."

"You're doing long shifts?" I asked him, and he shrugged. "Ten last night until now, I mean…"

"I'm old, lad. I don't tend to need that much sleep, and it's not like monitoring the systems and doing the jobs we're doing now are hard. Clarissa and I spend at least half the night talking and reminiscing about the past as it is while we work."

"Fair enough. But if you feel it's unfair, I want you to tell me," I said. "Now, what I was thinking is that we need to get you and John to discuss this and see what you can figure out…" I paused; then I nodded and went on. "And it's time to take care of the problem of Merriman, Gerald, and Sharon."

"Oh?" he said softly, sitting back. "I thought they were being dealt with by internment in prison?"

"They were being held because we were too busy to deal with it all, and I wanted to be both sure that what I was doing wasn't because I was just angry with them, and because I wanted to secure my hold on the new people to the dungeon. That time is past. We're at war. I'm not going to waste the time of a guard each day to watch over them when that guard could be improving themselves and saving lives. Tomorrow, we deal with them."

"Can I ask how?" Markus asked.

"Death."

"That's…a final solution," he said after a few seconds.

I nodded. "It is, and it's what I said they'd face if they tried to return to the dungeon, when I put them out. They didn't try to return—instead, they deliberately incited an attack on us by a group that should have been our allies from the start. They cost lives, and frankly, I should have dealt with this before now. Tomorrow, I'll take care of it personally."

"Matt…" Kelly said softly. "You don't have to."

"I know," I agreed. "But in this case, it should be me. I'm not going to ask anyone else. And if what you meant was that I didn't have to deal with them at all, that we could leave them in the makeshift prison for good? That's just putting off dealing with things for the long term."

"I agree." Surprisingly, it was Markus who spoke up. The older man nodded to me as I looked at him curiously. "Don't get me wrong, lad—I don't like it. There's too many easy ways for a society like ours to slide into barbarism, even with the technological aspects, and enacting the death penalty isn't something that should be done lightly in any situation.

"But, as you say, there were warnings, there were chances given, and even now, the only one among them who has shown any understanding that they were in the wrong is Gerald, and he still went through with it all, believing it would lead to personal power. No, the only options are that you do this and release them into the wilderness—which, unless you provide them with equipment, guards, and more is a death sentence as well…just out of sight. That or they'd do exactly what they already did, and I don't see that as a risk worth taking.

"Or, you keep them locked up for the rest of their lives, and frankly, that's a waste of resources and cruel to them as well. No, I agree on the death penalty, and you'd probably be surprised how many others will also. My question was because I wanted to be sure that you were aware of this, and why you're doing it. It's a hard thing to end a life like this, in cold blood."

"It needs to be done, and I'd not burden another with it," I said grimly. "Kelly, Aly, any objections?"

"No," Kelly said after a brief struggle with it. "It has to be done, and they do deserve it. It's just not an easy thing to do, that's all."

"They do deserve it, and as much as I don't like it, Mike and I have already discussed this, and it was on the list of things for us to talk about today, in fact," Aly admitted.

"Oh?" I looked at her curiously.

"Mike was going to speak to you and offer to carry out the sentence, if you needed him to, but, *and I did not say this…*" She looked at all of us to make sure we understood before going on. "But he was really hoping that you wouldn't ask him to do it."

"As I said, I'll do it." I scratched my chin. "So, thank you for the offer, but it's my place to deal with it. Now, Markus, you have anything else to tell us?"

"A few things," the older man said. "So, the army, as I say, are more or less on the road to recovery, but they're very battered and worn out. We have small adventuring teams, and they're ready, but again, they're not up to full strength or capacity yet. We need to set up better facilities for them.

"Moving on from them, we have the mercenaries, and the defenses to go over…" he said. "Now, the mercenaries, the Scepiniir clan that you dealt with, they're asking for their pay, which was apparently a dozen 'boxer' vehicles, and—"

"It was one." I snorted. "Or, more accurately, it was the one that I was in at the time, which I later ended up crashing and leaving abandoned. Fine, though—they came through when we needed them and they fought damn hard. I'd say give them two boxers. Maybe recover and repair the one that I had to leave in the field on the way in, and then build them one from scratch."

"I can sort that." He hesitated. "They are good, though, and they appear honorable. It might be worth trying to make a more permanent connection."

"Honorable? This is the fourth claim I've heard they've made, and one of them included that the dungeon there was to be theirs." Aly scoffed. "They're not honorable at all."

"It actually feels like haggling with someone in the Turkish bazaars." I grinned. "They always viewed trying to get the best deal as only honorable, and if you were stupid not to deal, then that was your problem and they didn't respect you for it. I think they're trying to bargain constantly, but if we can get a price out of them to be scouts, and to train with our people, it might be worth it. They put Saros to shame in how fast and agile they were, and they know London, at the very least. I'm happy to give them more than the original cost just to end it on good terms with them. If we could recruit them? I'm interested. Hell, just getting them to be a raid party on the British Museum for bones would be worth it."

"I'll see what I can do." He nodded. "As to the defenses, I wanted to raise with you that the army is likely to have a great many high-explosive weapons, and the walls of the southern dungeon aren't that high, or strong. They were designed to deal with the undead. So I'd like to put aside a percentage of the mana coming in to turn that into a much more fortified location."

"Ladies?" I asked, aware that although I'd jumped back in during this update, I had handed these things over to them.

"Ten percent?" Aly asked Kelly, who nodded.

"Ten percent of all mana coming in to be diverted to defenses," Kelly agreed. "There's twenty percent being diverted to resource gathering and expansion now, but that investment's starting to come back in real terms, as well as offering increased security."

"Make it so." I grinned as Kelly rolled her eyes. "Anything else?" I asked Markus as he sat waiting, rather than going as I'd expected.

"Oh yes, the best bit." He grinned. "So, Matt, how would you feel about making the dreadnought into a *real* mobile platform?"

CHAPTER NINE

"Wow, I mean, I knew it was here, but that…" I whispered, shaking my head as I looked at the list of equipment that Markus had provided.

"There's three more or less complete Supermarine Spitfires, a Hawker Hurricane, then there's a lot of other parts and sections as examples. But the best bit of it all is the Junkers Ju-52."

He passed the details over for the plane that had been recovered from the museum, and I stared at it in wonder.

Most of the planes, and indeed the equipment, was scrap—not in the "it's just trash" mentality…more that it was either dependent on systems that weren't viable anymore like electricity, or they were made out of materials that we'd surpassed and the technology we had was just more advanced.

The German-made bomber was indeed the best of the bunch, and the short description that sat alongside it in the brochure that had been recovered and fed into the dungeon made that clear.

The Junkers Ju-52, apparently called the "Iron Annie" for some reason, was basically big enough that we could fit the dreadnought dungeon into it with only minor reworking. It was also both designed for a short takeoff and landing, which was massively preferred to a long airfield being needed every time and it had only minor electrical systems compared to a more modern airliner.

The layout of the plane in the glossy museum brochure was clear, and I nodded to myself as I read it over. Sure, it wasn't as large as I'd like—you know, such as a commercial liner, with a nice first-class area and possibly some stewardesses available as well—but *damn.*

If we could integrate the design into the dungeon, get the teams working on upgrading it, and then start the next stage of construction from there with that as a base?

We had massive advantages over traditional construction methods, and not just because we could copy and repair anything we needed to. We could design the new frame in the research field of the dungeon sense and then test it in there, before using the dungeon research systems to research anything we couldn't figure out ourselves.

Add to that, we could create the newer version out of anything we had access to. Titanium covered in polished diamond? Yup, totally doable, provided we were willing to spend the amount of mana that would cost.

It seemed a bit of a waste, in one way, because we could do all of this and then the design would be obsolete in a damn week. As soon as we researched "real" aircraft, we'd be off in those instead, not to mention spacecraft as quickly as we could. But this would potentially save us weeks of traveling, both physically running and driving over damaged roads and through cities.

We could hit…I don't know, *Paris* for example, in only a few hours from here, rather than several days, as we'd have had to march through the Tunnel, and then navigate our way across France, dealing with their roads and whatever vehicles were left in place.

That decided it, I realized.

There weren't any parked and abandoned cars, left smoldering in the sky and blocking the path, after all. And once we had viable long-range transport, we were a definite entire level ahead of everyone else.

Long term, I still wanted my destroyer design in place, both because they always struck me as being insanely cool, and because any other fans of the Wars in the Stars series that suddenly saw them in the sky overshadowing their cities would really freak out and be confused to all hell.

Yeah, I could be a dick, I knew.

"So?" Markus prompted after a minute.

I glanced at him. "Sorry, what?"

He snorted. "Matt, I asked what you wanted to do." He smiled. "I take it you see the potential?"

"Definitely," I agreed fervently. "Aly?"

"Already expanding in that direction as it is," she said. "The museum is in the next town to the northeast, and we were aiming for the town as a resource area to strip. I'll make the museum a priority. But, to be clear, what do you want me to do with it once I get the teams there?"

"We need flight capability," I said. "If we can get this…uh." I checked the details. "The Ju-52. If we can get that design in the dungeon, then use it as a basic version, take what we know is a viable and working system already—"

"It'll not be that." She interrupted. "At best, it'll be at least sixty, and probably eighty years since it's been used properly. Everything from the tires and landing gear to the engines will be scrap. The controls will be in place to show them off, but they won't work. Nothing will."

"Then repair it," I said. "Take the mana you need and repair it fully. Get it up to perfect condition. Then, when the dungeon has a perfect copy stored, we start the redesign. Best to start from what we know is a working base." I paused, thinking, and she took over.

"I just wanted you to accept that there wouldn't be one of these available in a week, that's all, Matt," she said. "Right, so we'd need to replace the engines with something mana-based, regardless. I don't know what the fuel composition they used in the forties was, but I guarantee we don't have any of it. Also, it just makes sense—after all, there's no point in lugging all the fuel with us when we can instead put Air mana converters on the wings, then have it refuel its mana containers during the flight." She tapped on the brochure as she spoke now, thinking fast.

"Then we're going to need a better control system, communications, definitely a larger bay for transport…hmmm, maybe we increase the main dimensions by, say, forty percent?"

Aly was already miles away with the new project, and I grinned at her, before adding in two details.

"Aly?"

"Hmmm?" she responded distractedly.

"Just be ready to upgrade this over and over, okay? Modular design," I prompted. "And remember, the aim of the platform is to act as a transport for the dungeon. This way, we can fly the dungeon into an airport, set up and strip the airport, pass the mana crystals through the nexus gate, then fly on to the next target."

"Why not make it into the new dungeon shell then? Instead of a truck body for the transport, I mean?" she asked.

I nodded. "I see what you mean, but that won't work. It'd be easier in some respects—that was my first thought, in fact. But if we land at, say, Paris? I want to be able to drive the dungeon into the city and strip as much as we can as we go. Think locust style—land, loot, strip, and move on. That way, we can be ready to set up smaller outposts in the major cities as well if there's nobody in place already."

"And there's no room for the wings and more in city streets." She sighed. "Shame. That would have been incredible."

"You can still do it, just do it further down the line, as until we don't need a landing strip, it's not going to work."

"That raises an interesting idea, though," Markus pointed out. "The Spitfires are there…what about rebuilding one of those and putting a new dungeon core in it, then have a pilot who can fly wherever, set down, and start a new dungeon up?"

"Cost," I said. "Cost, risk, and timescale. Not even starting with the whole 'we have no pilots yet.' But if there's a pilot, and he or she flies to a city, lands and sets up, they can only do so much in a short period of time, as the growth of a dungeon is an exponential one. Believe me, when I started letting others into the dungeon, it massively increased the speed the dungeon grew.

"Alone, you're significantly slower. I'd expect them to take at least a week to make anything bigger than a house into the dungeon. If they instead set up a full dungeon, one that we fly the dreadnought in and set up with a full team? They'll be able to set up much quicker as we essentially jump-start them over and over again. And we get to make sure each one is set up the way we want, rather than training up a pilot, then sending them off and hoping they do as we've asked. No risk of them taking the new dungeon, flying off, and maybe vanishing."

"And the cost because at a million mana a core, they're not cheap, even when we're at the point of the dungeon recouping that quickly in comparison now," Kelly added distractedly as she worked through details. "Okay, Aly is on with this now. Is there anything else we need from Markus, or can we let him get some rest?"

"You go, mate, and thank you," I said to him. "I'll have a chat with John later and get back to you about the justice system."

"Thank you." Markus smiled. "And again, lad, I'm not exactly rushed off my feet. Feel free to call me in when I'm needed."

"Will do, mate." I smiled as the older man climbed to his feet, bid the ladies goodbye, then moved off.

"So," Kelly said once he was gone. "What now then?"

"My question exactly," I agreed. "I mean, I was planning on upgrading the dreadnought regardless, but this feels a little like two birds and one stone, right?"

"How do you figure that?" she asked me suspiciously.

"The mobile dungeon?" I prompted, confused. "We upgrade it, focus it on stripping the area, and we make a new version of the Ju-52. Then we fly that to wherever we need to be. We roll out and convert the city, somewhere like Crete, or Athens, right? That way, we get the location for a dungeon that's viable in the Med, it's somewhere that we can rotate people out of so that they get some downtime, and it's also somewhere that we can recruit the locals if we find them?"

"That's a relief." She sighed. "Knowing you, I was half expecting you to plan to make a flying *trial* dungeon."

"Hey, that's unfair," I complained, before ostentatiously rubbing at my chin. "Although, if we *were* to put wings on a building, maybe we could..."

"Dammit, Kel, you know better than to give him ideas! You know it's me who'll have to figure this shit out," Aly theatrically groused, before grinning at me. "Ah, all right, I was only joking. Okay, I've set the wheels in motion to get the museum under our control as soon as possible. What's the next step?"

"I was considering hitting the dungeons that had surrendered to us," I admitted. "As in, I was thinking of hitting them directly—start heading in the direction of the nearest one and aim to take it over. They surrendered to me unconditionally, so probably take the leadership out and then bind the core to us somehow."

"Kill them?" Kelly eyed me.

I shook my head. "Not if I can avoid it," I said. "Ideally just give them a pack and some gear, then send them on their way with one of our people put in command. They surrendered already, after all, but they did declare war when they knew jack shit about us. That doesn't scream 'trustworthy' to me, moving forward."

"It'd be a good idea to remove them, if we can," Kelly agreed, but Aly shook her head.

"I don't think you'll be able to," she said. "Not you *shouldn't*...more, *can you*? My concern is the mechanics...not the emotional side, to be very clear. I mean, what are you going to do?"

"Well, I wasn't planning to send them a 'Dear John' text and ask them to turn the lights out as they leave, put it that way." I snorted. "I was thinking we take a team to the dungeon, and then we tell the fairy this is how it is. We already know from the incident on the Nexus platform that a fairy can boot a human easily enough. Given the choice between 'we core you out and kill you now,' or they keep their word about surrendering? I don't see a big issue."

"Maybe not, but how were you planning on getting to them?" Aly asked, and I shrugged.

"That's why I was checking where they were, and the notifications. The distance for most of them means that's out of the window, but now?" I cleared my throat, then grinned at the look Kelly gave me. "Okay, yeah, so there was a thought that I could gather a team of fliers and set off, head straight to the North African dungeon, this Petr and his Darkness dungeon in Libya."

"But you're thinking better of that idea now, right?" she asked, her tone dangerous.

"Of course!" I assured her quickly. "It barely crossed my mind as an option before I dismissed it!"

"Bullshit," she said bluntly. "What was your justification for taking a bunch of creatures and going alone? Just so I know before I start hurting you?"

"That I could take the dungeon, set up a nexus gate, and then we didn't have to fight our way across a third of the world," I admitted. "If it's any consolation, I did realize that it wasn't a realistic plan…it was just a thought."

"We'll see," she grumbled. "For the next few days, you're recovering, okay? We all are. And while Aly and I, and the others, are focusing on the dungeon and all the various moving parts, you're not to do that, or at least not to the same level. Remember, we handle day-to-day operations, and you do the overview, then you go train, evolve, and do whatever you need to."

"I don't deserve you," I said, and the annoyed look on her face softened.

"You do, and more." She reached out, taking my hand in hers. "Matt, you were *right*. When you said that you needed to rest and to learn, to work on things besides the dungeon. That last fight just proved this. You literally channeled the storm into a weapon. Hell, using it as a method to recharge and develop the dungeon is insane enough, but internalizing and using an entire storm's worth of power? You used that to blast Balthazar, killing a literal god. Could you have done that without the time you spent in magical research?"

"No."

"No," she repeated. "So had we not done what you asked, we'd have all been fucked, right? And now, you need to do that again. We spend today getting the various systems in place and planning the next stage, then you go and start your classes or navel-gazing or whatever you need to do. And Matt?"

"Yeah?"

"Anything you need, just tell us, and Aly and I will do it, okay?" Then she smiled as Aly spoke up.

"Just to be clear, any *reasonable* request—not wearing yoga pants and bending over to touch my toes or anything," she said dryly.

"Ah, okay," I agreed seriously. "No pants at all. Got it."

"I swear, one day I'm going to kill him," Aly said conversationally to Kelly.

"Oh, that's fine," she assured her friend and sister-in-law. "I plan his murder at least twice a day. But let's wait until he's killed everything else we need him to first. Then we can get rid of them both, get ourselves some new boy-toys and relax on a beach somewhere."

"Good point," Aly agreed. "Matt, dear? Make a Caribbean or Fiji dungeon a priority, would you? I'll even lie and promise to wear a bikini all day if that helps to hurry you along?"

"I hate you all," I muttered. But we all knew it was just a joke. "So, what's next then?"

"The dungeon generally is running smoothly," Kelly admitted. "It's what happens when we have you out of the way." She shot me a look, and I grinned as she went on. "But, you need to go over the progress of the crafting teams, and specifically the glassblowing section. Then I'd suggest you check in with Starr and Arend-Jan. Beyond that? Sort things with John, and keep your ears open. When we have any news from our allies, be that Kaatachi and Akuba or potential ones like the London lot, I'll let you know."

"Thank you," I said. "Okay, I'm alive, though, so what I need to do, if there's nothing that has to be dealt with right this very minute, is go to the southern dungeon, and check in on Emma and Griffiths, and—"

Finn suddenly popped into the room, glanced around, then sighed. "Hey, I'm sorry to interrupt, and congratulations on the win, Matt." He clearly forced a smile, before it dropped from his face.

"What's up?" I frowned.

"I can't find Patrick," he said morosely. "I…"

"I can look—" Kelly started before he shook his head and cut her off.

"No, it's okay. We had a stupid argument, and he went for a run, then off to work in the southern dungeon last night. I know he's just staying out of the way while he cools off, but I'm starting to get worried, that's all."

"Do you want us to look?" I offered, and he shook his head.

"No, he'll come home when he's ready. He'll have lost himself in a project, I'm sure." He sighed, then forced another smile, apologized for interrupting, and vanished again before anyone could get a word in edgeways.

"Well, if I see him, I'll let him know Finn is looking for him, I guess." I shrugged. "Then I need to hit the medical suite and have it out with Emma, considering everything."

"Damn, yes." Kelly winced. "That's a good point."

"Then I need to speak to both Kilo and Dante as well about that shit they pulled, see if I can guide them a little and figure out how we use that more." I sighed. "After that, well…I have a trip to the Congo in my near future and London to deal with." I shrugged, then I winced.

"Then, I'll get onto the crafting and the priesthood, teaching and more. Fuck, I hate being the boss at times," I finished, getting a knowing look from Kelly.

"It's crap, I know, Matt, but for now, how about you focus on our injured? Then see John and face that. Set some time aside for tomorrow, say, maybe two hours to talk to Robin and anyone she's gotten interested. Set aside a place and a time and then tell her; then she can gather up those who want to be involved. And don't do anything else for the rest of the day.

"This gets the religion and the law details off your plate, and then tomorrow you can deal with it properly. Do the lessons with Dante and Kilo and the others after that, and…"

"And then I'll have a session in the gym, maybe head up to the northern dungeon and try a workout with their gear…show my face around there a bit. Maybe meet with Arend-Jan and Starr after that," I mused. "It's a lot of jumping around, but it's also getting things dealt with as quickly and cleanly as possible. I'll do the crafting on the morning of the day after."

"And around that, and between those jobs…rest, Matt. Meditate or do whatever else you need to do, but do it somewhere that you're not going to be pestered, and focus on those priorities. We can deal with the rest," Kelly finished, and I nodded, before climbing to my feet and kissing her cheek.

"I will, and thank you." I shot Aly a smile, and headed for the door.

It felt a little like I was running and hiding, abandoning the jobs or putting them off until later, when what I really needed to do was power through them all in a day and get my plate clean of such things…but Kelly was right.

I needed to rest, to recover, and I needed to deal with the lesser details.

One of which I'd not told them yet, because I wasn't sure how it'd work. But I'd noticed a new "feeling" since I accepted the dungeons' surrender.

It felt a little like when you knew someone was behind you, having a conversation, possibly when you were going down a flight of stairs, and their voices were almost, but not quite, hidden by the scuffing of your feet.

It wasn't a feeling of threat or anything like that, just of others almost close enough to hear and speak to.

I was fairly sure that I could force a connection to the other dungeons using it. But, again, I chose not to mention it, nor speak of it, as I got the distinct feeling that once I did make that connection, then they'd be able to connect to me and mine as well.

As such, I was planning on a little conversation with the fairy of Kaatachi and Akuba's dungeon, Onyx. As both an ally and a fairy, I was betting she'd be the best placed to give a little advice.

With all of that settled in my head, though, I got my ass in gear and set off jogging down the hall, down the stairs, and then finally out into the light drizzle that was now practically tradition for the area.

It was colder than a witch's tit, but thanks to the nearby pool we had in the Newcastle dungeon, the sleet and snow that was falling was hitting a warm front that turned it to mere freezing bloody rain by the time it hit the ground.

It was also filling the entire dungeon with fog, so there was definitely going to have to be a solution found to this, and soon.

I continued my jog to the nexus gate, passing between a handful of armed kobolds standing around in their new armor, with Beta apparently in the middle of beating them into shape.

Then I powered the gate and stepped through, coming face-to-face with a bloody orc that glared at me, slapping the head of its "weapon" into its opposite palm, as I arrived at the southern dungeon.

CHAPTER TEN

"You better be fucking glad to see me, considering that thing." I snorted as I locked eyes on it, instantly feeling the connection and recognition of one of my own dungeon-born, and seeing the lack of any threat in it.

The orc dropped to one knee in the snow—its weapon left a frankly traumatizing pattern in it—before I told it to stand up.

The orc was one of ten arrayed around the gate. I blinked, before realizing that clearly this was why the kobolds were around the gate back in the Newcastle site.

They were there as guards.

I shook my head, gesturing for the orc to rise. His companions that had maintained their position on either side of the gate bowed their heads as I looked at them as well.

"What's going on here?" I asked the one that had greeted me, and he ducked his head again.

"Guard nexus gate," he grunted, before lifting his weapon hopefully and waggling it.

"Please don't wave that at me." I closed my eyes for a long heartbeat. "What's wrong?"

"Master, we ask for new weapons?" he asked.

I glanced from him to the others, noting that his skin and that of his kin, usually a mixture of greens that ranged from deep forest all the way to practically yellow, was currently pale as hell and they were all shaking.

"And armor?"

"Why the hell are you…?" I started, then shook my head. "Fuck's sake."

They'd been presumably summoned by someone who was in a hurry and they wanted a guard force around the gate. That was totally understandable—a good plan, even. The issue, though, was that they'd used the original "standard" template, and they'd clearly not looked at it first. The standard template for the advanced kobolds must have been updated to include their current loadout. The armor, for example, was now heat regulating, making them no longer as useful as tits on a bull when it snowed.

The standard template for the orcs, on the other hand, had presumably not been updated, as all they came with was the super-sized suction cup-ended dildo, and a loincloth.

That was it.

It was snowing, with at least three inches of snow on the ground. And considering the state of the orcs? Well…someone had fucked up, and they were just putting up with it. Two of them looked to have the gleam of intelligence and awareness in their eyes as well—the leader on the ground and one to my left—while the rest stared on in gormless idiocy.

"Here." I focused and pulled up the dungeon menu, before shifting through a few options until I had a basic suit of armor that was suitable.

They'd been summoned with a standardized setup during the fight as well, and that was different, but I couldn't find it now so just summoned a collection of armor that *should* fit them, and some mixed weapons.

They picked them up, showing a lot of enthusiasm, especially as they dressed, and I noted the difference in the "aware" orcs compared to the dumb ones.

The dumb ones gave the aware plenty of room, and the aware…they directed the others and seemed a lot less aggressive and combative. If anything, they almost seemed resigned to just getting through, if the look in their eyes and the way they directed their less aware brethren was anything to go by.

"Anything else you need?" I asked. They seemed confused by the question, so I dropped it. "Okay, is there anything to report? Anyone used the gate who shouldn't… You know what, you just guard it," I finished, as I saw the utter look of confusion in their eyes at that question as well. "Do you have a name?" I asked the most vocal among them.

He seemed to think on it for a while, and just as I was about to give up, he replied.

"Grokmar?" he asked me.

"Is that your name?" I asked back.

"Grokmar," he repeated, with a little more surety.

"Okay, good chat." I sighed. "Nice meeting you, mate."

I moved through the small group. The area beyond had changed a little, with the walls around the structure being added to and pushed back a bit, giving a sort of larger cleared courtyard around the cube fortress than had been before.

Glancing around, I noted that there were only two humans in sight: one atop the wall directly opposite the gate, and another who was hurrying down from the first's position, in what looked like full cold weather gear, heading to meet me.

I took the hint and jogged over. The iron-grey of the sky overhead and the heavy clouds made it clear that there was plenty of snow to come yet.

"Sir!" Zac came to a halt and attempted a damn pitiful salute.

"Zac." I greeted him, remembering him from several of the earlier parties that had gone through the dungeon training program and the adventuring parties. He was a survivor of the battle against the undead legion in Bents Park, and the coronaught queen, so to see him here again? It was good.

Unfortunately, there were precious few who had survived so many fights now besides my own high-leveled party, and that just drilled home to me how effective the higher levels made you.

"Yessir!" He beamed at being recognized, and I nodded, smiling.

"So, what's going on?" I gestured with a thumb over my shoulder between the orcs behind me and the post he and his companion had been occupying when I arrived.

"Standard watch," he told me. "Mike said we were to maintain a watch, and ordered me to summon the orcs and have them around the gate just in case anyone arrived and tried to come through who shouldn't."

"And that they're practically naked?" I frowned.

"Oh yeah!" He grinned, and I blinked at that.

"*Why* are they practically naked?" I clarified.

"Well, they're the enemy, right, boss?" he asked, clearly confused. "I mean, that's what I heard, that the orcs are the main enemy, and that one day we'd need to fight a load of them?"

"Right. There's a sub-race of them…well, an evolution actually…but these? You—wait, did you summon them like that deliberately? In a loincloth in the snow and with a dildo?" I squinted at him.

He hesitated, before nodding. "Well, yeah?" he admitted. "I guessed that if they didn't have armor, then if they went mad and attacked us, then they'd be easier to kill, and if they didn't have a real weapon, it was less of a risk?"

"But they were also less bloody useful as guards though, right?" I pointed out, and he shrugged.

"Sure, but I mean, they're orcs, right? We're just going to use them as cannon fodder anyway, so what's the risk? They're just there to hold the line and soak up the damage until we can get someone who matters into the fight."

I stared at him, and he went on, clearly trying to explain.

"I mean, I used the design that the Dungeon Mistress used for the dungeons for training, that was all. Was that wrong?"

I saw on his face he genuinely wasn't being a dick. He thought that was fine.

It was *fine* to use a possibly sentient race as disposable meat shields, because their cousins were our enemies.

Worst of all, the look on the orcs' faces—those two I guessed were either fully or at least partially sentient—showed that they knew it.

"Yeah…" I said slowly, "I get it, Zac, I really do. But in the future, summon them with clothes and armor at least. They're not your enemy, and they need to be able to survive." I left unsaid that this was probably building even more of a hatred for us from the orcs than anything else.

Were they pushed to rebel and start the war through people treating them like dicks like this? I wondered, before shaking it off and moving on.

The two that were aware, more or less, were unusual, as the majority that I'd summoned so far in the past, at the common level, hadn't been.

Mind you…

They were also a bit bigger and considerably less wild-looking.

I paused, then reversed course and headed back to the orcs. I got an uncertain salute from them again as I Examined the seeming leader of the group.

Orcan Warrior	**Dungeon Creature**
Orcan, or as they are more commonly known, orcs, are a muscular, thick-skinned race. Similar to the goblinoid races in that they share a highly polymorphic tendency, resulting in as many versions of the Orcan as there are worlds, the gift of life to Orcans is a costly and highly risky decision that few Dungeons are willing to make lightly. Uncommon Dungeon Orcs have a greater chance to become self-aware and understand their traditional role as disposable troops. They are frequently used as the first line of defense, a meat shield to buy time for others. They will fight ferociously and will not hesitate to sacrifice themselves to ensure the survival of the clan.	

Rage: A berserker orc gains increased strength and pain resistance when its health is below 50%. Weaknesses: Death, Fire, and Air magics HP: 250/250 Stamina: 250/250 Mana: 0/0 Speed 6/10 Level: 6	
HP: 250/250	**Special Abilities**: 1/1

I stared at the details and then checked the dungeon system. Uncommon, not common. They'd been upgraded after all. I vaguely remembered a conversation about it, but… I looked into the eyes of the orc, and saw it there beyond any doubt. He was aware. And at level six, that meant that he was almost certainly a survivor of the battle as well.

I glanced from him to the others, seeing that they were all now dressed. The more open-jawed and dull-eyed were slightly smaller and certainly more brutish of features than he was. And now that I was looking for the differences, I noticed that the majority of the lower-leveled orcs had a duller grey and green or yellow cast to their skin, while the uncommon pair—both the fully aware and possibly aware one—were a deeper, richer color.

"What happened here?" I asked the orc.

He hesitated, before gesturing at himself and the others, as well as hefting the hand axe he now had as if to remind me. "The clothes and weapons you granted? We wear them. Is this…not good?"

"It's fine. That's what I gave you them for," I assured him. "No, I meant, give me a description of what you see here. What happened as far back as you can remember?"

He paused, then seemingly thought on it. His brow furrowed before he started to speak.

"I fight. All I know is fight. Enemy there, here. Everywhere. I fight with holy gift. It is…" He glanced at a dildo sticking out of a pile of them close by, and he clearly struggled with what he needed to say.

"It's a crap weapon?" I offered, and he nodded.

"It bounce. Damage, but not enough. This better." He hefted the axe.

"There was a good reason your people were given those weapons," I said. "Others of your people attacked the weaker dungeon creatures that are your allies. When you couldn't be trusted with better weapons, you were given them, and then a mistake was made, and you were all given them automatically. I'm sorry."

"We…we fight?" he asked.

"You fight if there's enemies that come," I agreed.

"No, we fight for rank?"

"I don't understand."

"Rank," he repeated. "Command."

"You…wait—you want permission to fight for your own ranks?" I asked.

He nodded. "On guard duty, no fight here. Needed here. After?"

"How long have you been on guard duty?" I asked him, and he shrugged. "When were you all summoned?" I asked, seeing he didn't understand the question.

"For battle."

"And after the battle, what have you done since then?"

"This."

"You've been on guard duty, since the battle?!" I gasped. "In a fucking loincloth, here?"

"Yes." He tilted his head to one side and corrected himself. "After others pass gate, then we told be here. Before, we on wall."

"Fuck's sake." I groaned. "Right, I'll make sure there's a shift rotation sorted. For now, keep guarding the gate, and no, no fighting for rank, yet. I'll sort out a place you can."

He just grunted.

I paused. Then, seeing that there was nothing he felt he needed to say, and knowing that he probably honestly didn't give a shit, I left them.

I moved inside. A human guard waiting by the door—on the inside, out of the weather—nodded to me, and I clapped him on the shoulder as I passed him. I knew him, but didn't remember his name. It felt a little wrong to use an ability for that. Like I was checking his personal shit.

It didn't take long to make my way to the medical suite. As soon as I stepped inside, a mix of relief and irritation washed through me. The first person I saw was Emma—sitting upright in a hospital-style gown with a blanket over her, the bed literally half lost behind a mass of flowers—and in her typical style, she was already tearing a strip off someone. In this case, it was her husband, Andre.

"They make him sneeze!" she finished, before bodily shoving some lilies away with one hand, all the while stroking that furry little turd Thor's back.

"I didn't know!" Andre complained. "How would I know? He's a damn cat!"

"Look!" She crooned, half lifting the furball and wrinkling her nose as she spoke to him in a singsong voice. "He doesn't like them, do you? No, you don't!"

I snorted in disgust, walking over and nodding to Andre as he and his brother started going through the flowers and selectively absorbing some of them, leaving others.

"Hey, boss." Andre sighed, before smiling at me in greeting apparently not holding any grudge for the condition his wife ended up in during the battle.

"Andre," I greeted him, then nodded to the others, before settling on Emma, and ignoring Thor for now. "How are you?" I asked her bluntly.

"Better." She smiled ruefully. "I see what you mean about needing to increase my affinities."

"I bet," I agreed. "You learn more from burning your hand than you do being told not to touch the pretty flames."

"Well, yeah." She sighed. "Look, about the fight…"

"You learn from it?" I asked her, and she hesitated, then nodded. "You increase your affinities?"

"Yeah," she admitted in an ashamed voice, picking at the side of the blanket she still lay under, her other hand pausing in stroking the cat.

"Well, that's something at least." I blew out a breath, before looking at the others. "Guys, give us a few minutes, please."

They looked at each other, then Emma. As they stood, she nodded to them, looking ashamed and worried, but gesturing to them that it was okay and to go.

"We need to talk." I summoned a wooden wall around the bed, floor to ceiling. As it appeared, I adjusted the design on the fly, the outside and inside covered in acoustic dampening tiles that I'd seen added into the dungeon's database at some point.

It wasn't a cheap thing to do, over a thousand mana it cost in total, and it'd be getting absorbed again in a minute, but it was needed, as this was better dealt with right now before it could fester any longer. That done, I summoned a chair and sat in it, leaning back and watching her for a long minute, before starting to speak.

"Look, Emma, you made a choice based on your gut and I get it—seriously, I do. We get the affinities we get for a reason, often a damn deep-seated one.

"It took me months to get over my aversion to Water mana, but the more I do, the more I grow. And now? Well, I need every aspect of my mana to be in harmony as I ascend," I explained. "You chose to follow your gut. In other situations, I'd have totally agreed that it was both your right and reasonable. *But*…in this one? You knew what we needed. You knew how you could best help in the fight, and you still went your own way."

"I know," she said slowly. "Look, I just…I don't know, I needed to…" She shook her head, before trying again. "I felt that it was the right thing to do, and that it'd give me, and us all, more power in the future."

"Yeah, 'in the future,'" I quoted back to her. "You knew it wasn't a solution for there and then, when we were fucking well *under siege and might all die*, and you still made that choice."

"I know," she said softly. "As soon as I made it, I regretted it, but I still did it. I've been thinking about it…" She took a deep breath, before going on. "And I'd do it again."

I opened my mouth; then, struggling to hang onto my calm, I shut it, staring at her, before folding my arms over my chest and waiting. "Explain that, please," I said, proud that I didn't respond by shouting "Are you fucking kidding me?"

"Look, I know you're not happy, okay? But…" She paused again.

"Oh, don't you worry," I assured her. "'Not happy' is way, way away from where I am right now. But please, *do* go on."

"I get bonuses from my Bloodwytch class, okay? And one of them is the Crimson Spark, a lightning spell that's unique to the class that brings a bleed effect as well as doing direct damage that I have access to. I know you wanted me to focus on my storm abilities, but this…"

She shuffled her bum more up the bed, moving from half reclining on it, to sitting upright as she gestured animatedly with one hand. Her other returned to the furry turd as he hit her in the face with his tail to remind her of her duties.

"The spells I have access to synergize with the storm already, and Thor said that I can still help. He said that he was guiding me as best as he could from the distance, but that as a Bloodwytch, I could bring strength and depth to the team!" She stared at me, her eyes shining as she went on.

"That was why I felt it so strongly, and now that I've raised my affinities, I can see why he guided me to stick with it. You always say that we need to be guided by our instincts to get the best potential match of classes. That's what I did—I did what was best for me and the team, despite the risk."

"Thor…spoke to you?" I asked slowly, struggling to contain my building rage.

"Yeah!" She nodded. "He doesn't all the time, just a little now and then. But right before I made my choice, I could feel him, you know? And I know that he's a Raiju, not just a cat, no matter what body he likes to use. And the way he helped with my rings?"

"The rings," I said flatly, switching from her to look at the now purring, self-satisfied, little fucking bastard.

"He helped to guide me during the storm, made my rings, and he bonded to me…said that it'd help my ascension, though he won't tell me what to or why. He said…" She paused, looking at me then biting her lip.

"He said that he was helping me to help you, but, it wasn't exactly like that," she admitted.

"What did he say?" I asked with brittle calm.

"He said that 'the biggest cub is the stupidest,' and something about you burying your nose in a ground-wasp den."

"I'm foolish?" I asked Thor slowly, smiling at him. "I think you and I are going to have a little chat soon, you furry fuck." He just flicked his tail at me, and I bit back the need to grab him and see whether I could drop-kick him to the moon or not.

Images flickered through my mind, and I knew instinctively they were being sent by him as I saw what looked to be a particularly stupid version of me lumbering around. Dammit, I looked like I couldn't string two words together. And then I started digging my face into a big pit? No, not a pit, I realized—a fucking anthill!

I focused and sent back an image to him in return, one of me pinning the little shit down and shaving him bald! He turned his head away, dismissing me, then rolled onto his back and offered his belly to Emma to scratch!

That little…!

"Matt…look, I know you're mad at me, but it turned out okay in the end, right?" Emma asked, and I shifted my glare to her. "So it's okay."

"It 'turned out okay'?" I mused. The anger that filled me right now grew colder instead of hotter. A strange feeling of disconnection built, like I was observing the entire discussion from somewhere behind us all. "No, Emma," I said after several seconds. "It didn't 'turn out okay.'"

"But we won, so that's all that matters." Her gaze switched from one of my eyes to the other before flinching as I forced down the sudden crackles of lightning that began to dance across my fingers.

"We did," I agreed as calmly as I could, before sitting forward, and clasping my hands together. My fingers went white with the pressure as I clenched them, trying to keep my fragile calm.

"So what's the problem?" she snapped.

"PEOPLE FUCKING DIED!" I roared as I lunged to my feet. Lightning exploded from me, crashing into the fresh walls around me. The Raiju spun and leapt to its feet, staring at me, even as Emma flinched and jerked back from the incandescent rage that was suddenly pouring off me.

"I fucking warned you, Emma! I told you, either obey my orders or don't, but fuck with me in a battle and people will die! Well, they died, Emma! I don't even know how goddamn many of them, but they died and we could have finished the fight in half the time if you'd done as you were goddamn told!"

"I… I…" she babbled, trying to get her words out as for the first time she was faced with my actual anger, rather than seeing it at a distance or when I was containing it.

Lightning thrummed and crackled all around me. The lights in the ceiling were flaring, the walls started smoking, and the cat? That goddamn furball stood on the bed, facing me and staring as a blue nimbus appeared all around it.

As a crackling stream of my lightning lifted and slammed into the nimbus, others suddenly joined it, dragged into place by the field. The light grew brighter and brighter as Thor worked to suck the power that was escaping me into himself. I tried to get control back, only to feel it being dragged from me, along with my mana.

"And this little shit?" I shouted to the room at large, gesturing to Thor. "This fucking '*Raiju*,' a spirit companion to the gods, here to help me learn to control my powers and to help in raising them? He's been hiding from me for weeks! Weeks that I could have been reaching this power level and higher. Weeks that could have made the difference in this last battle.

"He's always shown up when he wanted, relying on the fact that he's a goddamn cat in form and people, well, they just accept that, don't they? Well, fuck this shit! From now on, you're both on my shit list and you're going to learn to DO AS YOU'RE FUCKING TOLD, or I'll unsummon you…" I pointed at the cat, then turned to Emma. "And you'll get the hell out! You want that, Emma? Because you know your little family will follow you, and you've seen the kind of crap we face every day. How long before your attitude gets one of them killed? How long before Jenn's the one out there, cooling in a goddamn gutter!"

I saw the shock in her eyes, and I knew I'd hit home with that one.

"I've got to go and *face* these people, Emma! I have to stand and hold a ceremony for the dead. I need to tell their loved ones that the people we lost were heroes and there was nothing we could do to save them. And right now? I don't think that's goddamn true, do you? Because I'd *love* to hear it if you feel you did a good job!"

Silence greeted that. I saw the tears that had started to track down her cheeks. Instead of making me back off, as such things always had before, believing that I'd made my point, I kept going, my anger raging out of control.

"No? Nothing to say?" I snapped, realizing I stood now, towering over her. "Because get this through your head, Emma! You made a decision to help YOU in the future, and you tried to justify it because of something a fucking cat told you? You decided not to accept my recommendation and my request—you wasted fucking hours of my time, if not *days*, because you decided to help *yourself*! Either you're the most sociopathic and uncaring bitch I've ever met, or the luckiest, because—"

"Stop…enough," Thor snapped in my head. His nimbus flared brighter as he grew in size before me, clearly trying to overawe me.

Something snapped. For the first time, I reached out through the dungeon sense and did something on instinct that I'd guessed intellectually I *could* do, but I'd never done before, or ever intended to do either.

I reached out to the mana that sustained him, given freely by the dungeon, and I ripped every single drop I could reach out of him.

The bubble popped and the cat collapsed, his strings cut, convulsing and wheezing as if he were having a heart attack, and I glared down at him.

"Interrupt me again, and I'll damn well remove you from the dungeon *permanently,*" I whispered, before clicking my fingers. The mana connection was restored to him. He gasped for a breath, before leaping from the bed and darting down to hide on the far side, out of my sight, as I turned back to the woman who stared up at me.

"This is the last time, and believe me, if you hadn't done what you did in the end, you'd not be getting this choice. From now on, you do as you're told, or you're out. No discussion, no 'one more chance.' You'll be out. And you and I both know they'll follow you. My dungeon will be weakened, and so will you all, but I'll not have such a *selfish* piece of shit here."

"I did what I thought was best!" she snapped, struggling to her feet, yanking herself free of the connections that had been monitoring her, several of them already chiming at the changes in her vital signs.

"That's just it, Emma!" I shouted, even as lightning burst free again in response to my rage, slamming into a collection of vases and detonating them. Flowers burst into sooty flames and were hurled about the room even as the next in line detonated as well.

"Fuck's sake, I spent *days* of my time, time I could have been fighting! Time I could have focused on *my* spells alone, and I spent that helping *you*! You didn't just take that from me like some spoiled little shit—oh, no. You kept me doing that and distracted, when I could have been helping others! Every single goddamn death out there? We'll never know if they could have been avoided! Your decisions, your goddamn belief that you knew best, that trumped everything else, didn't it! Well, come on then!" I threw my arms up in frustration.

"What?" she shouted at me.

"You think you know best, right?" I snarled, jabbing a finger into her shoulder as I glared down at her. "Why don't *you* fucking take over? You think you're so smart? You take my place! You can have it all—the pressure, the fucking people who come crying and screaming because their sons and daughters, their wives, mothers, husbands and fathers, they're all dead, and it's OUR FAULT!

"You get to tell them why their siblings won't be coming home, and then you get to ask them to take up arms and fight for you, just so you can lose them in another meaningless battle where some stupid fucking mistakes cost them their lives as well. You can tell them they'll be okay, and then you get to see their kids, kids you *orphaned*!

"You can be the one who gets told you're a god, but you don't know what that means, or that a single mistake, a goddamn path of research that you didn't choose, could be the difference between the life and death of your entire species!

"There's no wiki, you know, but you won't need one, will you? Not you! Just because there's not a single person you can turn to who knows more about this than you, and yet everyone comes and asks you for answers you don't have. All they want is five more minutes of your time, just five minutes.

"It's not much to ask, is it?" I snapped savagely. All this time, my voice had been dropping, and as I collapsed back into my seat, all the rage seemed to drain out of me, all in one go, leaving me suddenly exhausted and so cold inside.

"All they want is a little bit of you, but there's so many, and every single mistake is a life lost. If you stop, if you rest for just a few seconds, if you put down the mountain? Someone else *dies*, Emma. Every single time I stop, I know that somewhere out there, another person has died because I didn't get to them fast enough."

I was whispering now, as I went on. "They used to say that there were dozens of people born every minute. Well, now that's the other way around. There's dozens dying by the minute, and we can't sustain it. We're running out of people, we've got alien 'allies' who are using our world as a fucking meat shield, and everyone who's here keeps trying to fuck each other over."

There was silence then, silence for a long time as I sat, my elbows on my knees and my face cradled in my hands. A hand rested on my shoulder, and I drew in a shuddering breath, before looking up.

"There's only us, only our dungeon, and maybe a handful of others out there who even give a shit about the species, and they're constantly under attack. At any time, it could be just us, and the orcs could arrive, and it'll all be for nothing. We'll all die, and we probably won't even stand a chance."

She stood over me, her face tear-streaked, the room behind her charred and blackened from the overload of lightning that had been escaping my fragile control. Now, her hospital gown was just a mess, both because of her own tears and something else that was smudged across it, as well as a collection of small bloody wounds caused by flying glass.

"I'm sorry," she whispered, before she leaned down and…hugged me. "I'm so sorry. I didn't know."

I swallowed hard, suddenly aware I was shaking, that I had tears streaming down my face. I dragged down a shuddering breath; I coughed and dashed the tears away with the back of my hand, before closing my eyes and accepting the hug.

I sat there. The sounds of distant shouting, as the others outside clearly tried to get our attention, faded away as it was dealt with, and I sensed a pair of familiar comforting presences by my side in the dungeon sense.

I reached out, mentally, and I felt both Aly and Kelly move in close and wrap ghostly arms around me.

I stayed there for long seconds, before I forced myself to my feet. "I'm sorry," I said to her. And then, as Thor stuck his head over the edge of the bed, I nodded and repeated it to him as well. "I'm sorry, Thor."

"It's not all on you, you know," Emma said suddenly. "And I'm sorry as well."

"It is," I said. "It is because if not me, then who? We're a team, in the dungeon, all of us pulling in the same direction. But, Emma? This can't happen again. Do you understand? If I tell you to do something, either you do it…"

"I'll do it." She shook her head. "I'm sorry. I thought Thor knew what I was supposed to do, and I—"

"He's a dungeon-born, Emma, no more and no less, and I think it's time we all remembered that," I said. "I've been relying on him for ages as well, but with me, he makes me come to it on my own, then turns up at the last second to give a nudge."

"A nudge you need." Thor's voice echoed in my mind, and I glared at him. My anger flared again, and he ducked back down.

"A nudge that I might not need if you damn well explained what the hell you were trying to teach me!" I snapped at him, before taking a deep breath and centering myself again.

"Right, Emma. Get your arse in gear. As of now, you're back on duty. You work to increase your affinity for the storm, and build your power. That furry little shit likes you a lot better than he does me, so that's fine. Thor, you stay with Emma now. You teach her and help her, because it's both of your heads on this now." I left unsaid that I was still incredibly close to unsummoning the cat.

"Okay," Emma said.

I looked at her. "You look healed—are you?" I asked bluntly.

"Mostly," she admitted. "I still feel hollowed out, but my stats say I'm healed."

"Then get to work." I reached out and absorbed the wall I'd created around us.

As the light of the dungeon working flared and dimmed, the drifting smoke that was left from the lightning strikes was suddenly released into the middle of the ward. I nodded to a worried Andre, stepping around him and moving toward the back of the ward, gesturing for Jo to follow me.

She did, falling in, even as the others—Jimmy, Jenn, and a doctor who had been nearby—got the hell out of the way and went to check on Emma.

"What was that all about?" Jo asked me, and I shook my head, refusing to speak until we were out of range of the others.

We stepped through a door at the end of the hall, coming to a halt in a shorter corridor. This section was no longer open plan with the beds dotted down on either side of a bay. Here, beyond the double doors that separated the outer area and this inner one, were four rooms on either side.

They were larger and more spacious, with three of them open and unused.

"Why was she out there instead of in one of these?" I asked Jo, and she snorted.

"Emma is a pain, and she thrives on attention. Don't get me wrong, I know what she's like and she's working on it. Whatever you said in there looks to have had an effect as well, but she wanted to be out where people could see her. Not that she'd admit that."

"And the hospital gown?" I asked her. "I've not seen anyone else wearing them."

"She summoned it herself." Jo smiled. "She wanted to look the part for Andre, I think."

"Whatever." I dismissed it. "How's Griffiths?"

"Unconscious still," she said. "He needed a lot more specialized work than anyone we've ever worked on before. Realistically, he should have died. Whatever spells that corpse lord had cast on it, they've caused merry hell with the healing."

"Spells?"

"I've spoken to a few of the others who were on the roof with him when it attacked them. It had a nimbus around it, according to a few, though most didn't notice anything."

"And?"

"And whatever wounds it inflicted, it managed to take a section of the health of those who were injured directly by it. According to my skills, it was a curse, but I can't tell any more than that. I'm hoping it's a case of just outlasting it, because no matter what we do, his health keeps dropping. As such, we've got him sedated still. We have both a permanent drip with enough sedative to kill a rhino, and a watered-down healing potion, both working on him at the same time, in two separate bags."

She led me into the fourth room, the one right before the doors that led into the final area, marked Theater, Authorized Personnel Only…then scrawled below it was So Fuck Off.

I couldn't help but smile at that, knowing that despite the doctors who were no doubt telling her she needed to be more professional and well behaved, she wasn't changing for anyone.

The room that Griffiths was laid in was a pleasant, standard boxy one. The bed was in the center, its head pressed back against the wall and arms extending out that held a bag on both sides. An IV feed line descended and slid into the sleeping form of Griffiths, while a trainee healer sat in a seat to the side of him. A clock on a small table gently ticked along.

"We heal him every hour, on the hour," Jo explained. "That deals with the majority of the injuries. And then the combination of the sedative to keep him down and the watered-down healing potion are keeping him stable. Beyond that, honestly, we're hoping that dealing with the injury as much as we are will unlock a curse-fighting class for the next of us to reach a threshold. But beyond that? It's just fight and hope."

"Will he pull through?" I asked her bluntly.

"Not sure which part of 'fight and hope' is confusing you, Matt, but honestly, I don't know," she said grimly. "As near as we can tell, he should. But *will* he? We just don't know."

"Is he improving?"

She sighed. "Matt, we think there are signs that he is, but they're so small that we just can't be sure. Half of his bones were ground into fragments, and those as well as sections of the undead were buried in him. If we could have just cut them out, it'd be for the best, but there were so many damaged sections we'd kill him before we'd cleared half of it, unfortunately.

"He also appeared to be lost in nightmares, which is another reason for the sedation. He was thrashing around and doing himself more damage. It could be a sign that he was starting to heal and awaken, but the damage he was doing to himself just couldn't be risked. As it is, we're keeping him under until we see an actual significant sign of improvement."

"You know best," I admitted. "Sorry for back there." I jerked my thumb in the direction of the main area.

She shook her head, leading me out into the corridor again and closing the door behind me before speaking.

"What happened?" she asked. "Matt, I know you, and that was… We could hear you through the barrier, you know?"

"I'm surprised Andre didn't try to break it down then."

"Honestly? He seemed to think it needed saying. He, Jimmy, and Jenn were getting worried, especially when the lightning started getting out of control. But beyond that, they waited."

"You knew there was lightning?" I asked, eyeing her.

"Matt. Do you think that lightning would be stopped by wood?" she asked instead of answering, and I sighed. "Yeah, exactly that. The tiling on the wall burned up, and we had to summon water and toss it on them before the tiles could catch fire. The lightning hit a few things—and Jimmy. But it was more of a strong taser than a blast, or so it looked when I healed him."

"Great." I closed my eyes and leaned back against the wall, bouncing my head off it as I berated myself for losing control so much.

"What's going on?" she asked me in a softer tone, and I shook my head, not wanting to discuss it. "Matt, for better or worse, I'm your doctor." She rested a hand on my shoulder. "Can I help? It'd be kept between us."

"I don't think so," I said softly. "Honestly, I think Kelly and Aly have it right. I know they're watching over me right now, so I won't have to say it again, but yeah. Burnout."

"It's hit a lot of people, and there's a lot of ways to deal with it. But the best?" She raised an eyebrow and looked at me quizzically. "You know what I'm going to recommend, right?"

"Rest?" I asked, and she nodded.

"Rest and talking to someone."

"Yeah, well, I'll make that happen as soon as I can." I pushed off the wall and forced a smile. "Thanks, Jo. I'll go and stop trashing your place now."

"You do make it look untidy," she admitted. "But there's a door on the other side of the theater, if you'd rather go out that way."

"Infection control must love that." I snorted, before heading in that direction.

"Infection control would shit a brick," she agreed. "The doctors I have here all did at first as well, but when they realized that magic exists and that there were ways of dealing with that? Well…it means they can sit out of the sight of everyone, and we have changing rooms and so on. Best of both worlds."

She led me through, letting me out of the doors at the back that were apparently coded to only accept medical passes. I nodded and left it alone, curious how they'd done that, but not caring enough to question. I knew if I needed to, I could override it, and there was no need currently.

The door closed behind me, and I paused for a few breaths, finding myself in a narrow hall that led to a few small rooms that appeared unused, and then to a set of stairs that climbed higher.

Five minutes later I was outside, standing on the roof and surrounded by converters, and I found an old friend right where I thought he'd be.

CHAPTER ELEVEN

"Kilo." I greeted the kobold cryomancer. The fucker just had to have been working his coconuts off again, because not only was he clad in new armor, but it, and he, were different from the last time I'd seen him. "New gear?"

The kobold opened his eyes slowly and blinked languidly, before smiling. "Matt."

I stared at him, seeing a difference, but not knowing exactly what it was. "What's happened?"

The smile turned into a full-on grin, one showing an obscene amount of teeth, as he gestured to himself. "You like?"

I nodded. "The armor suits you, but…holy fuck," I grunted, as he rose to his full height.

The cryomancer was big. He had awoken and grown from a standard advanced kobold base, a significantly higher-level caste than we as humans belonged to, being the common or at best uncommon variant.

Now he was a lot bigger—like "eight foot tall and imposing" where before he'd been…less?

"What the hell did you do?" I asked him, squinting.

He grinned, then opened his wings, making me stare in wonder as they extended, blocking out the sky. "I evolved."

I shook my head, unable to decide whether the details I saw were entirely new, or just incredibly boosted.

The kobolds were recognized as dragon-kin in all the games I'd played. These kobolds, although more reptilian than most of those versions, were also distantly related to that bloodline as well.

For the lower-level kobolds, they went from something closer to a humanoid raptor—all the head bobbing while they walked and tails as balance aids—up to the uncommon level, where they were closer to reptilian humans.

At advanced, they grew wings, though they were smaller and more suited to gliding than anything that could really help with flight. They were significantly more humanoid, with a shorter muzzle, more upright posture, and twin horns, as well as a crest that grew to a raised line of small spikes that ran down their back between their wings.

They looked awesome, frankly, and then when Kilo had gained the cryomancer line and skill set, he'd changed again. His scales had adjusted to follow the new line of skills, and he'd gained some kind of immunity to the cold, which had really helped, considering most of his kind had been practically catatonic with the first snows of winter rolling in.

The final change, though, had clearly been a sudden one, and as I stared at him, I realized what it was.

***Evolution: Lord of All!* The creatures of your Dungeon know their true master, and those who follow willingly can now receive arcane gifts that match their level of devotion!**

The evolution wasn't exactly earth-shattering. I'd only seen it trigger once before, but as I stared at the description, I knew that was what had happened. Beta had evolved through the use of this. Her devotion to me lifted her from an uncommon kobold to what was apparently the start of a real draconic evolution.

She steadily grew more and more incredible. And the way the other kobolds watched her as she passed them by? Clearly, in the kobold world, she'd have been a model of some kind as well.

Now, I saw a similar evolution, but it was one that took from both Kilo's cryomancer class and his advanced original level. He was almost a foot taller than Beta had been after her own change. As he turned slightly, allowing me to marvel at the changes, I couldn't help but be impressed.

His horns were larger, and the scales were more of a blue: darker as they vanished under each other, and a lighter, icy blue at the tips. No longer was he just tinted blue with the scales; instead he was blue through and through, and majestic.

His teeth were still gleaming sharp, looking like he'd just taken a polisher to them. His neck was thicker, and his shoulders bulged. And the wings? He was now clearly capable of flight, and no longer just gliding.

His tail was longer, and tipped with a spike that looked dangerous. Overall? He just reeked of lethality.

"This is my main form. I have not the strength to change yet, but from now on? All my points go to Constitution and Intelligence," he said proudly. "As soon as I can survive the change, I will make it!"

"The change?" I asked.

"I don't see it all," he admitted. "Don't *know*, not for sure. I sense…things. Not everything, though. Some is hidden and some I am not ready for, but soon? When I can survive the evolution, I will do it."

I questioned him some more, getting only more confused answers that showed me that as much as he wanted to share, he just didn't know more.

It also turned out that the new armor, a pristine white that covered him from head to toe, with blue plates of metal in place over the major organs, was a gift from Finn, after the old set would no longer fit him.

I couldn't help but be impressed.

"How did this happen?" I asked, and he shrugged.

"I felt your need, and I heard a voice, telling me to give of myself," he said softly, as if casting his mind back to the fight. "I gave all of my mana, but knew you needed more, so I gave of my health and soul as well. In the end, it was enough…just."

"It was," I agreed, remembering sensing him, collapsed on the battlefield, his guts half hanging out, as instead of healing himself he gave his mana to me to help with the fight.

That was the difference between him and someone like Emma. He'd done… That wasn't fair. I choked the thought off, and instead focused on Kilo and his accomplishment. He'd basically chosen to give everything he had in a wild-ass last ditch. And instead of dying, as he was obviously willing to allow, he was recognized and uplifted by the dungeon through whatever means it had at hand.

A second form wasn't clear, but I was certainly full of hope, knowing the crazy bastard before me.

"You're okay now?" I asked.

He nodded. "Better than okay." He grinned and winked, before moving his eyes in a weird way, then again when I didn't get it.

"Wait…" A horrible thought came to me, and that expression suddenly registered. "Are you trying to waggle your eyebrows?!"

"Maybe." He grinned.

"Holy shit! No—you got *laid*?!" I gasped, and he nodded. "Who?!" I asked.

He waggled his eyebrows again, or he tried to…you know, the whole "being a draconic kobold with no eyebrows" slowed him down a little.

When he didn't respond, I thought it through, then couldn't help but gasp.

"No!" I said, shocked, knowing of only one person he'd ever hinted he was interested in. "*Beta*?!"

"Shhhh!" He waved his hands, looking about and making sure nobody was within earshot. "You no tell anyone!" he insisted, and I nodded.

"Fuck, man, that's wonderful, and weird. But wonderful!" I assured him. "Wait… Chris doesn't know, right?"

"I told him, but he swear, no tell anyone," he admitted.

I burst out laughing.

"What?" He looked confused.

"Kilo, my wonderfully naïve friend, Chris will have told half the base, and be on his way to her to try to get juicy gossip on you *right now*."

"No!" He gasped, horrified.

"Run," I said firmly. "Run very, very fast."

With that, he spun and raced for the edge of the building, diving off in what might be the first flight he'd ever attempted. I watched him go fondly, feeling a whole hell of a lot better as I realized that I wasn't the only one struggling with shit.

Or at least, I wasn't the only one who would be suffering very soon. Admittedly, I'd needed to talk to him, but this was a better use of both his time and mine.

Chris or Kilo was going to regret their next moves, and after all, what friend didn't try and annoy each other? Kilo would either catch Chris before he made it to Beta, and he'd beat the crap outta him, or Chris would get there first, and Beta would see Kilo leap on him and attack, and kick both their asses.

Ah, *karma.*

I moved up to the Storm converters and laid my hands on them, sucking in a little spark of the storm and breathing it through my mana channels. I relaxed, trying to banish the shitty mood, the worries, and everything else.

After a short while, my inner self back in as much equilibrium as I could manage, I set off back into the cube again, heading down the stairs and going room to room, looking for Robin and her nutters.

I could have searched for them in the dungeon sense, but honestly, I'd find them too fast, and I was all for putting this shit off as long as possible.

It was all too soon, though, that I found the four of them. Robin, two more adoringly idiotic buggers staring up at her, and a soldier, all discussing the nature of "the divine."

"Morning all," I said with as much false optimism as I could manage. I stopped in the doorway, leaning against the frame as I looked them over. "Am I interrupting?"

"Lord!" Robin gasped, jumping to her feet; the other three idiots did the same. "No, never!" she assured me. "How can we serve?"

"I…" I paused. I had intended to tell her to gather up whatever lunatics she wanted and meet me tomorrow at the main dungeon, that we'd do it in the mage's tower. Then I dismissed that thought, instead deciding to make a start right now, and get it out of the way.

I still needed to find Dante and Chris, followed by John after this as well, I'd decided, to check on them. Chris was probably being beaten by Kilo at the minute, though, and I didn't want to interrupt that.

"Well, I caught the last bit of what you were saying as I entered, and I thought I'd listen in, if that's all right?" I suggested, figuring I might as well see what shite she was spouting.

"Of course!" she squeaked, before closing her eyes, clearing her throat and trying again. "Of course, Lord. Your guidance is always appreciated."

"So, you were saying?" I asked.

"We were discussing the nature of the divine," she said. "If humanity…"

"And the dungeon-born," one of the others added in nervously, glancing at me and away.

"Yes, and the dungeon-born," she agreed quickly. "If they can both sense the divine, as we always have, reaching for a god or gods, then surely this is for a reason? I mean, it stands to reason that this is why we've always been drawn to such things. Perhaps…"

The conversation went slowly at first. None of the others wanted to add anything in while I was there, so I spoke up once I'd gotten the gist of it all.

"So you think there have always been gods, or at least a need for them—in us, I mean?" I asked, and she nodded.

"I believe that we probably always needed them, always felt that they were real, and yet, they were beyond our understanding. Perhaps in the past there was once mana here, long ago. This would explain the mentions of magic and beasts throughout humanity's history. What if, following along this path logically, then there were gods as well?

"We as a species would have worshipped the most powerful, in exchange for protection, and as time went on, the tales of the gods would have grown, blurring together."

"And they'd have been expanded upon," another added quickly. "Like if, say, there were gods, like now—" He glanced over at me and then away, as if embarrassed or checking that I wasn't about to smite the fucker for his heresy. "Well, maybe say there were, just as an example…" He glanced at me again.

"Just spit it out." I sighed as he paused, waiting.

"Okay…" Deep breath, and then he went for it. "What if, say, ten gods all had powers…like one could make it rain, one could make the rain stop and make it sunny…another could make it warm even in winter…all those kinds of things, right? Minor things, when you consider the stuff that people expect God to be able to do now, but back then? That'd have been incredible.

"As a civilization, being able to plant your crops earlier than another group, and know, without doubt, that they'd get the best possible growing situation? That would bring about massive population booms."

"Okay…" Robin frowned. "I'm not seeing where you're going with this?"

"Well, let's say you hear about a group of gods that can do this, and word gets around that they're helping the next village over or whatever. You're going to want that kind of support, right? Support that means the difference between you and your family starving or prospering?"

"Yeah?" I agreed.

"Okay, so you start getting your friends together, and you all offer a little portion of what you make to entice that god to help you. They agree, and they send one of their people over to help, to assess it and to see what they can do, as well as to decide if you're a dick or not." He shifted around.

They sat on old, shitty-looking plastic chairs.

I snorted. I'd sat on one as well, and screw this. I summoned a recliner and a beer, then settled into it, gesturing at him to continue.

"Ummm, can I…?" he blushed, and I nodded.

"Sure, just don't take the piss." I shrugged. "The chair is a bonus for anyone in the room to be able to relax. It doesn't need to be damn well uncomfortable, after all."

That started the group summoning things and a minute later, I prompted him to continue, getting a grin as he went on.

"So, let's say his friend he's sent over to look at things likes what he sees, and the gods agree to help. They get a portion of the harvest, and anything that's made in the village, and the village does well out of it.

"Now, as time goes on, more people hear about this little group of gods, but they don't get to see them—they just meet their representatives, their priests. They occasionally might see one of the group, but after a while all the gods blur together, because it's not like the gods' friends who are doing the day-to-day gathering and checking in are going to be explaining things, is it?"

"I get where you're going with this." I nodded. "Over time, the word spreads, and the gods' powers and descriptions end up rolled into one. Maybe there's a fight and the group is killed or splits up, and the priests…well, they like the support they're getting. They keep their mouth shut and keep the tribute coming in."

"But what about when the weather turns bad because the god isn't helping them anymore?" Robin asked.

I shrugged. "They offended the god," I guessed, getting a nod from the guy who was speaking. "Okay, so let's take this a step further forward. The gods are offended, so you give extra and you build them a nice place to show you like them. You spread the word of the gods, and in the telling of the tales, well, the story grows.

"There's some things in the story which don't really help out. Maybe there's a monsoon and people think they should have been protected, so you take that out of the stories. Maybe now they're a god of growth, and the weather is separate?"

I shrugged. "Take it a little further and maybe there's a new town on the other side of the river, and some fuckers there have their own gods. Well, we can't have that. Conquering comes along, and to make things go smoother with your new conquered territory, you absorb a few of their god's facets into yours. You spread the word that the reason you won was because the old priests of that city had led people astray."

"And in a few centuries, the original message is totally lost, with a new group in charge who are just happy to keep themselves in power, nothing else," he finished for me. "That's why the majority of religions now have a single massively powerful god, rather than the older records where there were hundreds of gods."

"Interesting." I nodded. "So, where do you see me and mine fitting into all of this?"

"Ummm, I don't know?" He blinked. "I mean, I was a history major, and I did religious studies, but…"

"But you don't know where I fit in, right?"

"Not really," he admitted.

"That why you're here?"

"Basically, yeah," he said. "Look, I'm a soldier, and I sort of get the shit that's going on—most of it, anyway. But you? The system calls you a god. And the shit that you can do? It…well, it makes sense?" he said uncertainly.

"It does if we look at the gods in that tale you just told as just very powerful humans, anyway," I agreed. "Look, here's the long and short of it. I've been told I'm a god. Yeah, that's true. And now, I can empower others. Robin, for example, can share in my powers. I can grant her abilities that help her in a fight."

"He really has," she assured the others.

"Well, here's the truth of it, okay? I don't think of myself as a god. I genuinely don't. It freaks me the hell out that people think I am. BUT…" I looked at the others, making sure I had their attention before I went on. "But, I can share these powers. I get more powerful the more people believe in me, from what I understand. Think of it like a mana tithe. I think—and again, that's the important word here, I *think*—that when you focus on me, and you believe, you gift me a portion of your mana. I can then change that into divine essence, which I can then share back with you. That divine essence can be used by those I choose, like Robin, to smite our enemies.

"So, here's the deal, all right? I don't know what I'm doing, but I'm damn well learning. I've been given a quest to develop a priesthood, and to build the Paladins, as well as a few other things. Now, I'm not interested in being worshipped, and I'm sure as shit not interested in conquest and being a dick, putting all other religions to the sword and all that. My plan is that we start a religion, but we make it the kind that we'd actually want to be a part of.

"We set this up as a support structure between the dungeon and its people. You, should you want to help me with this, are going to go out and damn well help people. I'm thinking we try to build a Priest or Paladin into a person who can make a real difference. The Paladin corps will be the fighters, obviously, but they'll also serve justice and bring hope."

I was spitballing now, but it "felt" right. "Look, I'm not the kind of a guy who wants to be worshipped, but what I do want? I want to make us powerful enough that when the orcs, or anyone else comes looking for us, they back the fuck up and go somewhere else! I want to make sure our people are safe, all of them! The assholes and the great people. Not a single human gets taken out by an orc, not if we can help it. Now, I know that's not realistic, and it's sure as shit not practical, but what it is, is a goal.

"We build a priesthood around teaching people and healing them. A group that can go out and fucking help. We're not going for priests who hide in the church and wail and ask for God to help them, or fiddle with choirboys. We're going with warrior priests! Priests who are as comfortable arguing theology or pounding shit with a hammer. The kind of people who are going to be guiding people to stop being assholes and fuckheads, and protecting them."

"What about the Paladins then?" Robin asked.

"Glad you asked, Robin, because the Paladins are going to be the other side of it. When the army and the Priests can't help, the Paladins will be the last line of defense. Where we don't dare send a team of less than a hundred, we'll be sending a Paladin instead…maybe with support, maybe not. But you'll get all the support I can give you. You'll be taught to dispense justice and to reinforce the rule of law. Slavers, rapists, and all that kind? You killed them once—how'd you feel about being the right arm of the law and going out to pound the shit out of them? Put that Smite to good use? Hunt monsters for me, Robin, both the human kind and the kind that you can see a mile off."

"So this is you recruiting then?" came a voice.

I looked over my shoulder. A grizzled man in a soldier's uniform halted in the doorway, with two more just in view behind him.

"Hell yes, I am." I grinned, thinking he looked like he could handle himself and would be useful. "How much of that did you hear?"

"Enough," he said grimly. "How much of it was bullshit?"

"Honestly, it's the intention I have for the dungeon and for the religion." I frowned as I realized he wasn't one of our people. "And you are…?"

"Thomas," he grunted. "And your security is shite."

"Nice to meet you, Thomas," I said carefully, standing and turning to face him. I took in his clothing, his stance, the way that he kept one hand out of sight around the doorjamb…all of it. "Want to tell me who you are really and why you're here?"

"Let's say I'm an interested party, and leave it at that, for public consumption." He stepped back and brought his hand out to show it was empty. "Can we talk?"

"Seems we already are."

"Don't take the piss, son. I've got limited time, and this is a conversation that benefits you more than me. It took me a full goddamn day to get here, so if you're going to play silly buggers, you won't like how this turns out." He folded his arms across his chest and glared at me. "How about this? You come and talk, and I'll sweeten the deal by telling you how I got past all your security."

I nodded, before turning to the others. "Have a think about what I said, and we'll meet again tomorrow, around lunchtime, after the announcement."

"Announcement?" Robin asked. Then she glanced from Thomas to me and back again. "Do you want me to come with you, lord?"

"No, it's fine. And for the last damn time, call me Matt!" I scolded her, before looking around. "Actually, I'm going to ask you to find somewhere else to talk. It makes more sense for us to stay here."

She nodded, quickly chasing the others out.

"You do that a lot?" Thomas asked me, as he stepped in, closing the door behind him, but not fast enough that I didn't see the shadow of a figure in full combat gear taking up station outside of the door.

"Do what?" I focused and sent a sense of urgency to Kelly, as best as I could. When I got nothing in return, I sat in the chair, and gestured for him to come and sit.

"Kick people out of the room so that you can talk, rather than find a place that wasn't in use," he clarified.

I squinted at him. "Normally no, but considering I'm the Dungeon Lord, and I don't want you wandering around the building, I made a decision that they could move instead. It's the advantage of being the boss. I get to do that when I need to."

"Fair enough. It's not like those I represent are any better than you there." He sighed. "So, you want to try to sell me on joining your cause then?" He sat down and folded his arms across his chest.

"I mean, I could," I agreed, settling back, watching the way the cheap-ass plastic chair he'd chosen almost buckled under the weight. "But we both know it'd be pointless, right?"

"And why do you think that?"

"Well, let's treat it like a logic puzzle," I suggested, smiling coldly. "You came here with a team. There's some of them out in the corridor right now, and you're armed for bear. You didn't try to take me out straightaway, so you're probably not an assassin squad, but you sure as shit aren't friendly either. You look tired and annoyed, but you're still well fed, you're clean-shaven, and your gear is well looked after.

"My bet is military, probably sent by London, and you're here with orders to find out what the fuck went wrong, and try to get a dungeon core out of me. If I prove resistant, then you go down the assassin route and try to deal with my successor?" I guessed, rubbing my chin as if in deep thought, and he nodded.

"Mostly right," he agreed. "Ex-military, no longer serving, and somewhat of a private contractor."

"One that goes by the name of Thomas, and wants to offer me a deal, eh?" I shrugged. "All right, I'll bite, what's the deal?"

"Let's say that there's an interested party that would like you to honor your debt." He sat forward, then scowled. "Seriously, is this some kind of dominance maneuver or what? Because, I have to tell you, it's a shitty one."

"What's that?" I asked, confused.

"The damn chair," he growled. "I always hated these things, can barely get one arse cheek on it." With that, he stood, looking around at the other chairs, before pointing at me. "How do I make one of those like you've got?"

I grunted out a laugh. "Oh damn, you're so subtle!" I shook my head. "Seriously, you almost had me, until I saw that you'd picked the smallest chair in the room. If you wanted to know how the dungeon worked, you only have to ask."

"So, tell me how the dungeon works." He gestured for me to get on with it.

"Not until you tell me who you really are and why you're here," I countered, folding my arms across my chest. "You said I was mostly right before, so come on, spill."

"Those I represent asked me to come and sort out the bill." He shrugged. "It's not my usual skill set, but it's what you do at the end of the world when a job needs doing."

"So, what'd they tell you about this bill, and the payment terms?" I asked curiously.

"Just that you promised a dungeon core, showed off some high-tech weapons, unlimited food, and medicines, and then when our people fought and bled for you, you tried to get out of paying your side of the deal."

"Interesting." I nodded. "All right, let's make this a nice even playing field first, though. You know who I am—Matt, the Dungeon Lord. And you're Thomas—you're from London, or operating on their behalf, but that's all I know. Who's behind you, and what's the deal? I mean, are they the government, the army, what?"

"A mixture of the surviving government representatives and the armed forces." He dragged a more realistic chair over and sat in that. "The survivors of the fires, the fights, the looting, and more. You're from up north, right?"

"That's right." I nodded.

"Well, unlike you buggers up there, surrounded by farms and easy food sources, we had to impose martial law immediately. The food, weapons, and more were seized. An accounting was worked out as to the value of the goods, and the merchants offered a scrip, basically an IOU that said that when we got the power back on and so on, they'd be paid. Until then, they were just joe public, and to rest and accept it.

"Most did, some didn't, and there were some riots. They were put down, and put down hard by the joint armed forces and the police. They were generally grouped together and for the first few weeks, things were easy enough. People weren't happy, but fuck it. No mass fighting or killing, which was the main thing.

"By the end of the third week, with the power still not coming on, and more and more people getting sick and tired of the rationing, the discontent started to boil over, and the real riots began.

"It wasn't helped by the fact that the monsters had started to appear. But nobody believed people about it, or at least, not those at the top. People were going missing, and at first it was brushed off as gangs and trafficking. But it wasn't long before the first real monsters showed themselves.

"The forces were pulled in and tighter controls added. People started either working for their support, or they were told to fuck off. That's where I came in. Me and a bunch of my lads were here, between jobs, and we started hunting the monsters, getting experience and generally earning our keep.

"As time went on, more and more joined us, and eventually the setup that's in place now was worked out. The civilians are in the middle, working various jobs. The armed forces are split between the army, who protect the city and the people, and the vanguard.

"That's us, if you didn't work it out. We're separate from the army, in that we don't hide behind the walls. Instead, we go out and hunt. Be that resources or monsters. Now you know who I am, and what I'm doing here. So how about we cut the crap and you pay your debt to us? That way, me and mine can get back to dealing with the monsters, and you can do…whatever. Start a new cult or whatever that little speech was, if I don't miss my guess. And as long as you fuck off back up north to do it? There's no reason for this to turn ugly."

"And they sent you as a negotiator?" I cocked my head to the side. "Gotta say, I'm not impressed."

"That's because you were expecting someone to come and blow sunshine up your arse. Truth to tell, my boss wanted that too. Sent someone who's much better at this kinda shit than me."

"But…?"

"Snake bite." He shook his head. "No clue what kind. Hell, I'd never *seen* a wild snake in the damn country before. I knew we had them, but whatever this was—a single bite, three steps, and he was gone."

"So, I'm left with you instead of the guy who was supposed to negotiate." I nodded, and he shrugged.

"Listen, this doesn't have to get messy, but here at least, in the south, we're fucking civilized. You made a deal, and people died. Then you tried to get out of the deal, and fucking killed the soldiers sent to collect on the debt. Some people might say that we shouldn't be here asking. Some people might say that you should already be on the ground with a barrel against your head, but that's life, isn't it."

The look in his eyes made it damn clear that one of those "some people" sat across from me right now.

"Interesting," I said again. "So, just so we know exactly where we stand, I'll explain it from my side now. The deal that was struck was that your entire army came to help, not the small fucking percentage that was sent in the end, and days later than agreed.

"Had the full army made it over, then some of my people wouldn't have died, and we'd have not been left with a massive amount of them needing injuries healed, resources replaced, and of course, time fucking lost. I get it, though—you didn't want to play until you decided there was a real chance you could grab everything instead of what was offered.

"Then, despite showing up, as I said, late and fucking understrength, your representative came in here and gave it all "Billy Big Balls" threatening us, before finally attacking one of my people when the threats didn't go the way he wanted." I watched him as I spoke and noted the impassive face.

Nothing I was saying was getting through, and it was either because he didn't give two shits and was, as he said, "here to collect," or he knew all of this already.

"So, what happened from my side is that we asked for help, and we offered something in exchange for that help. You turned up late and made a half-arsed effort, before trying to attack us when we told you no, and now we're here. Had you done what was agreed? We'd have paid. Hell, I *wanted* to pay, you know that? I wanted you to have a dungeon core, because then when the shit hits the fan and the real war starts, I'd have more backup."

"So pay up," he said. "Everyone's happy."

"Not so much," I disagreed. "See, you want something for half a job. I get the deaths. I'm not fucking happy either about that, and not just because of the whole 'all lives are sacred' crap. I want them alive because we damn well need each and every fucking soldier we can lay our hands on.

"No, the issue for me is that I offered to hand over a piece of technology that can literally change reality. Something that can enable you to turn bricks into a steak dinner, and a burnt-out car from the seventies into a rail gun.

"In return, instead of acting like a possible ally and someone I could rely on, you tried to do the absolute minimum, and you also had a guy in command who came in ready for a fight, then attacked us. Maybe he was acting on his own, or—and let's be honest about this—or he had orders from someone higher up. He shows up late, but still in time to clean up, right? I mean, if both sides had worn each other down to a nub and were injured, when he turns up and kills them, who's to say if I'd died in the fighting? Maybe he takes over and there's a new Dungeon Lord in town."

That got a reaction, only a small one, but a tremor of the left eye and slight tensing.

"Now, you and I both know that was part of the plan," I said. "Thing is, I was willing to accept that it was the plan of that bag of goblin shite acting on his own, instead of a coordinated one. All that I needed for that to happen? I needed to not think that you'd all stab me in the fucking back as soon as I looked away. I could accept that he did it; he overstepped and he died for it, provided you turned up here, and were fucking contrite.

"Had you said 'whoa, sorry, mate…not our plan at all…now how do we fix this?' then I'd have had a different attitude. Instead, as things stand right now? Nada," I snapped, sitting forward.

"What?" he growled.

"No dungeon core," I said flatly. "You're asking for something that's incredibly difficult to produce, and that bonds to a user, a Dungeon Lord. If you kill that lord? You kill the dungeon—if there's not a fairy attached, anyway. You might want to make some notes, just sayin'." I gestured at him, and I settled back in my seat. "So, you try to kill me? You kill the golden goose. You piss me off? You get nothing. So here's where we start again. Right here and now, we make a new deal, and you can either pay it, or you can fuck off."

"Playin' hardball isn't going to work out well for you," he said softly.

"Think so?" I cocked my head to the side. "I'm curious, are you the one who can summon an army? Who can arm them with unlimited weapons, feed them, and more? Or are you the one who's fucked if you don't find a new line of supply?"

"I don't believe you." He smiled. "We've got our own sources, and we know if we kill you, then the core will bond to someone new. Not only that, but if you try some shit with me and mine, you know, like trying to disappear us?

"Well, that sweet little lady of yours, Kelly, is on her own back at Newcastle, isn't she? As is Aly, and her daughter, little Amy. So let me know…what do you think happens to them, when we kill your little pissant forces, and then we take the dungeon from you?"

"You're playing a dangerous game," I said slowly as my blood ran cold.

"Not from my side of the board," he disagreed, with an uncaring shrug. "From this side, it looks like the only game in town, so it's the one we've got to play. So, how about this…we do a new deal, like you say. You pay your fucking debt, and you pack up your people, then fuck off back up to whatever shithole up north you crawled out of."

He smiled at me then, and I stared back. My mind raced as I considered things on two levels. First and foremost, on blind instinct I wanted to smash his face in…just summon a hammer and pound it into him until he was reduced to pâté.

Secondarily, though, he knew too much. He knew stuff he could have only gotten from our people, from…

I kept watching him. But instead of seeing the fucker, I slipped into the dungeon sense, finding Aly and Kelly waiting, both furious, and already searching.

"We're missing Patrick and Catherine." That was the first thing Kelly said, and I glanced at her, before Aly spoke up.

"Mike's on his way, and considering the unsubtle threat that was made about Amy? He's going to teach this fucker a lesson."

"So, you think he's taken them?" I asked.

Kelly nodded. "He knows enough that he's either gotten access to detailed reports, and it's not stuff that Mike would have shared, or he's questioned someone directly. I don't see anyone sharing all the details about the dungeon, not with an outsider. They might have snatched or questioned one of the soldiers from the northern dungeon as well…" She paused, then shook her head. "I'm trying every trick I know. I'm getting nothing from Patrick or Catherine. Patrick wouldn't talk, but…"

"But anyone can be made to talk if they have them long enough," I said. "He might have spilled everything or nothing at all, as might Catherine. Hell, he might have a dozen of our people all locked up, and we're only finding out now."

I switched back to reality, facing him coldly as he smiled.

"It's pretty clear when you're in the dungeon sense, you know, rather than here? I could have stabbed you in the throat and had this all dealt with. So take that as the best gesture of goodwill you're going to get."

"Had you tried, you'd have been in for a surprise." I snorted. "All right, so you think I'm just going to bend over, do you?"

"No, I think you're going to fight. A lot of people are going to die, then you and your group are going to be labeled as terrorists and I'll end up with a mandate to hunt you all down." He smiled.

I saw in his eyes that he genuinely didn't have an issue with that. He'd accepted it and was ready.

"And you think you'll survive long enough to do that?" I asked.

He cocked his head to one side, then snorted disgustedly. "Now I see it."

"You see what?"

He pointed a finger at me. "You—that's the problem. You've made this into a fucking cult that's based around you and your abilities. You think you matter, and that's the difference here. You don't. I don't. The survival of the species is the driving imperative, so when you ask if I think I'll survive, that's obvious, because I don't care. I can die here and another of my squad will simply take my place.

"For us, it's about the survival of the human race, and specifically, our nation. As such, if we die? It doesn't matter, because we'll have saved thousands or even millions of people with our sacrifice. What could one life mean against the fate of the world?"

"So you're happy to die?"

He shook his head. "Happy or sad has nothing to do with it. It's duty, and that's something your kind will never understand. So let's cut the crap. Hand over the dungeon core, get out of here, and take your people back up north. Or better yet, get through the Tunnel and fuck off into the sunset. I don't care where you go, but unless you start moving, you're a dead man."

"Interesting," I said for the third time.

"Tick-tock, motherfucker," he said grimly, reaching down and drawing a handgun from his waist. "Are we doing this the easy way or the hard way?"

"Oh, I think we know exactly what's going to have to happen here." I forced a smile as I cursed myself for not wearing some fucking armor.

"Matt, what do we do?" Kelly asked me in the dungeon sense.

"Fuck this shit. Get ready. We need to find the others and defend ourselves, because we're about to get hit," I sent to the others.

In response, a glow started to the right of my chair, originating at the ground and then flowing slowly upward, as a goblin was printed into existence.

If it'd appeared to be any kind of a threat, I had no doubt I'd have been shot instantly. But the creature that appeared was anything but a realistic threat.

The feet came first: flappy, oversized things that even as they resolved into reality looked oily and dirty. The legs were as thin as sticks, the knobby knees were scuffed and dirty, the loincloth barely decent, and the belly protruding.

The chest was a toast-rack of ribs and yet it still managed to convey the impression it was a glutton that fed on absolutely everything, thanks to the greasy stains and marks that ran up and down it.

It wore a hooded robe, one that was too short for it. And if you were wondering why I knew it was also wearing a loincloth? It's because as soon as it finished printing, the thing had hiked up the cloth, and started rummaging around and scratching itself with clear signs of enjoyment, before stopping to sniff its claw-tipped fingers.

It somehow managed to have both an over *and* an underbite, with the mouth giving the impression of a dentally challenged octogenarian working on a toffee. Tiny, gleaming black eyes stared out, filled with malice, and the long, floppy ears were possibly a danger to it in high winds.

Overall, the goblin mageling was already fucking disgusting, and that was before it triggered its signature spell.

CHAPTER TWELVE

Disgust washed out across the room, latching onto the only viable target and doubling down.

Thomas's eyes bugged out. For a half second or so, he clearly hesitated, fighting the urge, before whipping the gun around and opening fire. The first was one in the head, and then, as the goblin flew backward, he lunged to his feet.

The gun blazed again and two more shots rang out, slamming into the goblin's chest, destroying its heart and making damn sure it was dead. Then he spun, gun coming up and zeroing in on me, until I slammed into his chest from the side.

I'd hit him with all the power I could muster. Between my legs—which were frankly well past the strength of any pre-apocalypse Olympic weightlifter and sprinter combined could have managed—and my flight?

It was a hell of a blow, and clearly one that was a lot stronger than he was expecting.

I drove him into the wall, then through it as the sheetrock collapsed and into the room beyond. We tumbled to the floor and I grappled him, lifting then slamming him down, even as he opened fire.

He'd tried to get the gun to my head, but the speed and force of the blow, combined with the wall that I just slammed him through, had it going off at an angle, tearing a furrow along my back.

I hissed in pain, smacking the arm aside. Then, thinking better of it, and instead of going for the body-blow, I gripped his right wrist with my left hand, then slapped my right over his face.

Then I released the constraints I kept on my lightning at all times, and let it flow.

The lightning that coursed through me by now was utterly attuned. It'd gotten to the point that I barely felt it. But fuck me sideways with a head of broccoli dipped in spaghetti, it was a memorable experience for him, that was for sure.

He screeched, his eyes opening wide. His face blackened and his hair caught fire. Muscles up and down his body spasmed and the handgun went off, firing randomly into the wall nearby.

That was as far as I got before I was body-checked in turn from the side, as whoever he'd had take up station beyond the door barreled into the room through the hole in the wall we'd left.

He plowed into me, bringing a modified rifle around and slamming the butt of it into the side of my head. My world filled with stars, even as he, too, screamed in pain, having caught more of my "gift" as he touched me.

I hit a table. The flimsy thing collapsed around me, falling to half cover me as I crashed to the floor, dazed.

He jerked and stumbled back before collapsing, shaking.

Forcing myself to my feet, I cursed as two more of the figures stormed in through the door. The first had his rifle raised, already aiming, and I unleashed an Incinerate to the face. He managed to get out a choked scream, ending in a hiss as he collapsed. His friend behind fired. The first shot went wide, before the second took me in the shoulder, carving a line through the T-shirt I wore and the flesh and muscle beneath.

I triggered a second Incinerate, this time into his hands and the rifle. It turned cherry red in an instant, reducing his hands to a blackened, charred mess, and taking him to the floor, screaming.

My plan had been to capture him, to keep him for questioning, until the ammunition in the magazine went off, exploding and shredding the mag itself.

Most of the bullets were caught by the metal, but a few zinged this way and that. He doubled over as he apparently caught one, going silent as he collapsed.

As I saw that, though, I heard Thomas roar, finally overcoming the shock of the tasering and forcing himself to his feet. I twisted, diving sideways as I saw the gun coming around.

He fired once, twice; the bullets slammed into the cheap, shitty table. I grabbed half of it, dragging it between us. The bullets, if not stopped, certainly slowed to the point that they did a lot less damage when they hit me than they should have.

The room and the corridor beyond was flooded in the sparkling light of dungeon-born summons now, as more and more appeared.

Thomas grabbed the table and yanked the half that had been my cover aside, leveling his gun at my face, and by instinct, I scissor-kicked his legs out from under him, bringing him down.

I wanted to kill him. I wanted to reduce his head to a charred lump, but I needed to take the fucker alive!

His handgun rammed into my chest as he turned the fall into a dive, deliberately coming down on me. I had a split second of sudden realization before it went off with a dull thump that shook through my entire body, even as my lightning raced into him again.

This time he was ready for it, and he gritted his teeth, fighting through the pain. Again, he fired, and we stared into each other's eyes. I saw the satisfaction—no, the *glee*—as he fired, only to snarl in anger as the gun jammed on the next round. Then it was discarded; his hand dipped into his battle rattle and then came back out. Something glinted.

That was when I grabbed his forearms and unleashed more lightning into him.

His muscles locked up, teeth gritting, and he made a strangling noise as he juddered and jerked in my hands. Whatever resistances he had was not enough to overcome the sheer levels of power I pumped into him. I cut it, grabbed his collar, and yanked him down into my forehead.

I was on my back now. He'd been straddling me, and that wasn't a good position to fight from, especially not when trying to deliver a Glasgow Kiss. But the tasering left him momentarily stunned, and my forehead easily broke his nose.

I hissed as pain surged from my left shoulder where he'd managed to stab me with something. I twisted my arm, breaking his grip, and smacked at a feeling of something hard in the meat of the muscle. Whatever it'd been, it was fragile, breaking as soon as I batted at it, exploding into a wisp of darkness that faded away.

Then, before he could recover, hands were grabbing him.

I saw scaled fingers drag him back, claws already digging into his throat as a hand closed over the gun, ripping it free with a sound of breaking bone and cartilage as a finger apparently decided to go with the weapon.

He tried to speak, and I frantically tried to as well, knowing just how much we damn well needed him, only to find it was already too late. Another figure was there, and a dagger slammed into his armpit with a meaty thump.

Bones broke, blood gouted, and I saw the look of shock on his face, as the kobold warrior with the dagger yanked it back out. Then another was there, and drove its dagger up through Thomas's chin and into the brain, skewering his last thoughts.

I collapsed backward as others streamed into the room. Shouts rose from all around now, and I hissed in pain, reaching down to my chest. My fingers came away bloody.

My health was dropping by the second. I swallowed hard, then pulled my lightning to me again, this time flooding myself and circulating it rather than letting it run loose and hit others.

My affinities kicked in. The lightning was absorbed and began to heal me. The blood loss slowed, but didn't stop.

A kobold dropped to his knees next to me, pressing his hands over the wounds and trying to slow the spurting blood. He hissed, jerking back as the lightning discharged into his hands.

I forced myself to pull in the mana, to reduce it and contain it again, as he poured a weak healing potion into my mouth.

My lightning was probably more suited to healing me than a damn weak level of potion, but I found I couldn't get the words out. Waves of exhaustion flowed through me, and with the choice of take the potion or kill the being who was trying to help me, I chose the potion.

Another, stronger potion suddenly appeared next to me. The flood of light as it was printed into existence made it stand out. The second kobold, the summon that had killed Thomas, grabbed the top of the bottle and yanked the cork free.

Half was poured over my chest as the other moved his hands; then the rest was poured into my mouth. I swallowed as quickly as I could, noting that the pain was…manageable, even if the still rapidly dropping HP said otherwise.

I sagged backward, looking at the ceiling. More voices rang out. The blurry forms of dozens of others suddenly crowded the room; shouts reverberated and then some more distant gunfire.

In fact, the pain was fading quickly, and…

I blinked as fresh pain ripped through me, making me gasp and shake. The room suddenly came back into sharp focus. I saw Jo's face above me, glaring down, her hands pressed to my chest as light burst from her.

"Don't you *dare* die on me!" she was shouting, before her face went fuzzy again.

I felt myself falling, down an endless dark tunnel—the light, her face and that of the others with her, seemingly at the top of a mineshaft, far above.

I wasn't going to die…not me. No, I was just tired, and the pain fading away was because she was such a good healer, that was all…

Light flared, and I was back, gasping as the pain intensified, then faded as I started falling again, then more light.

"Fuck! It's spreading too fast!" someone shouted, before another pulse of power flooded me.

This one made me jerk and suck down a gasping breath as everything came into focus, before more shouting ensued, and others were pushing in.

Someone shouted something I couldn't make out, until a ringing slap jerked my head sideways. Then another pulse washed through me.

"Heal yourself!" Jo shouted into my face. "Heal!"

I stared at her, confused. She was the healer, not me. I was the storm…*lightning*.

I sucked in the mana from all around, converting it and releasing my own blocks again, washing the mana out from my core through me. A little of the fuzziness receded.

A pulse washed through me, making me gasp again. My HP pulsed in the corner of my vision. One second, it was a deep, dark red, the numbers down to double digits as it tried to climb then sank again. My mana bar dipped as I frantically converted it to lightning which then healed me, as my health bar surged higher, then was flooded with a cancerous green and black. A notification flashed desperately.

It opened and I focused on it, pulling my lightning through me, and I saw it.

Beware: You have been poisoned!

Three-phase poison detected. Phase one in progress:

50HP lost per second for 60 seconds… 59…55…57—

The countdown was down to twelve seconds when I read it, and as my mana poured through me, converting to lightning and then being converted again a heartbeat later into healing and HP, I understood.

"Medit…ation!" I managed to gasp out, and Jo nodded.

"Meditate. We'll keep hitting you," she said grimly. "I need more people in here! Life affinities! Okay, people, if you've got a high Life affinity, get in here! If not, get out!" she yelled over her shoulder.

A fresh pulse of power flooded through me, making me groan in relief as the flood brought additional healing.

"And someone get Loren!"

I sank back, focusing and trying to add a little increase to my mana regeneration through my meditation. But between the pain and the effort of drawing on it as I tried to regenerate it, I barely managed it. The increase in my mana wasn't much, but as my own lightning had burned away the fog that had been clouding my mind, the urge to just stop and accept it—that what would be, would be—was replaced with a burning agony that now began to climb by the second.

At five seconds, I was writhing; my HP bounced like a stripper's ass as the pain ratcheted higher and higher.

As the countdown dipped, the pain became more and more incredible. I felt like my veins were tearing apart, my mind fracturing, and my bones being ground to dust. Organs? They were alternately cooking and freezing, and with each second, it only grew worse.

I lost control of my lightning, no longer able to focus even enough to channel it into my body to heal me. Instead, it arced and spat; people screamed, and it vanished.

Light flared somewhere close by, and a soft voice intruded in my personal hell as the light filled me, making me howl in pain.

"Sorry, lord! So sorry!" the voice came, but nobody I recognized, not that it mattered right now.

The light…the light poured into me, racing through my veins, through my flesh and blood.

It was like acid, burning me, scouring me clean of whatever the hell filled me. And as it passed, the pain ratcheted higher and higher, then slowly retreated, seeming to gather itself for one last attempt.

Fresh agony tore through me. My muscles turned against my bones, tendons tore as they were pushed past their breaking point, and the sound of breaking bones echoed as I screamed… I screamed until my voice was hoarse and I could no longer breathe…

Then, as suddenly as it'd come, it was gone. My wheezing scream faltered as I collapsed. My health, at two points, flashed a crimson danger pulse that filled my vision. A new face appeared above my own, staring into my eyes, then vanished as a familiar one took its place.

Emma.

She looked haggard, exhausted, and a mess. Her hair was all over the place, her lip was swelling already, and her cheek bloody. But as I stared into her eyes, my heartbeat and breathing ragged, she took a deep breath, then grabbed my head in both of her hands, and channeled lightning into my skull.

Beware: You have been poisoned!

Three-phase poison detected, phase two in progress:

50 Stamina lost per second for 600 seconds… 599…598…597—

The world exploded again, and I lost track of everything else. But this time, waves of brutal exhaustion poured through me. My health bar flickered still, but as the lightning poured into me, it ticked upward steadily. I gained enough health that, for the first time in I had no clue how long, I was actually healing properly.

I was—until my stamina flatlined, anyway. At that point, I started to roll backward. My health dipped point by point, as others stepped up and healed me again and again.

Stamina potions were brought and set up on an IV. Then, when the skin healed and the IV kept pouring across the sheets, someone was detailed to simply dribble a little into my mouth constantly, meaning until they got the hang of it, I nearly drowned on a regular basis.

As time passed, I was moved onto a gurney. A handful of kobolds with the best lightning affinity manhandled me onto it, and all the while, Emma healed me again and again as soon as she had the mana, trying to combat the drain.

Jo and more healers arrived and left, and eventually I sank into an exhausted sleep, distantly recognizing as others came and went. Noises in the hospital wing arose, as more and more things happened…but for me, all of it was distant.

Hours must have passed, because when I finally awoke fully, blinking around blearily, it was to a notification that warned the third phase was active, then that it'd finished.

Congratulations! You have survived a three-phase poison!

Three-phase poisons are highly rare and incredibly expensive to produce, with their attendant deployment tools becoming highly sought-after assassination tools.

You have gained the skill: Poison Resistance!

Your body has decided that near-death experiences are the best learning opportunities. Next time someone tries to poison you, your cells will collectively yawn and say, "Is that all you've got?"

Note: This doesn't mean you should start licking suspicious substances for fun. No responsibility is accepted for any Darwin Award-worthy decisions made by the user.

Current Poison Resistance: 1 (Clueless food-taster: "I survived, barely.")

Next level: 2 (Amateur: "I can handle licking (some) toads now.")

I read and reread it, noting that the sometimes informative, and sometimes downright fucking sarcastic tone of the system was back, before dismissing it, and the rest of the notifications.

Congratulations!

You have killed the following:

- 3x Unknown Military Contractors, various levels 870 XP

Total XP awarded: 870 XP

Current XP to next level stands at 34,465/90,000

I blew out a long breath and straightened slowly, pushing up from the bed I'd been left on. The healer who sat by my side reached out quickly, murmuring meaningless platitudes that I couldn't make out, before I waved her off.

The world around me was…wrong.

A quick check of more of the notifications revealed the source of the issues.

Beware! You have been infected by a curse from an artifact-level poisoning. For the next 48 hours, the following will be reduced by 50%:

Agility

Constitution

Dexterity

Endurance

Perception

Strength

I read it over, then snarled as I forced myself to my feet anyway. Thankfully, I was still wearing pants, and they were clean, which was a slight relief—as anyone who had woken up unexpectedly in a hospital bed was well aware of.

My top was gone, and as I'd not bothered to take any of my gear with me, well, I had nothing to collect. My boots were by the bed, and I slid them on, glancing at my stat sheet, then cursing as I saw the markers, each showing the reduction of my stats and the countdown timer.

What the hell had that fucker used on me?

I made it out of the door. My body was used to a level of grace and strength that although not hugely different—not for these kind of actions—was still different enough I felt like I'd just gotten off a cruise.

The floor seemed to tilt and shift, just slightly, but every time I put a foot down…it felt like the positioning was wrong.

I stumbled out of the private room. The healer—a trainee, I guessed—was at the other end of the main ward now, speaking quickly to Jo, who looked like shit.

The real shock, though?

The ward was *full* of people, humans mainly. The dungeon-born were here as well, or at least one or two were, but the majority were definitely human.

They were bloodied, beaten, and here and there, a body was being wrapped in a body bag. I stared at that, then stepped forward as a pair of goblins I'd not seen before moved past, carrying a body between them.

"Pardon, lord," the closest breathed, inclining her head in respect, then moving past me to a room on the right.

I took three steps after her, then stared in, seeing the bodies in there stacked like cordwood.

There were at least two dozen dead, laid one atop another. I stared in horror as the pair moved back out, bowing their heads as they passed me again.

"What the fuck?" I gasped. "What happened?!"

"We were attacked," Jo said from behind me, tiredly. "A coordinated attack, one that was ready before your conversation even got started, we think."

"Jo?" I turned to see her, the threat from before rising to my mind quickly. "Kelly and the others…?"

"They're fine," she assured me. "The other dungeons are on lockdown, only military personnel to move around, with Kelly and the others perfectly secure." She snorted. "Turns out they were prepared for a lot, but the realities of life with a dungeon wasn't one of those things. Doors that vanish and are replaced with solid walls, or bricked up from behind, really confuse them, as do the dungeon-born appearing from rooms they've cleared.

"There was a single attack on the Newcastle site—two men, and they made it less than a dozen meters. That Xanthia was watching for people entering the dungeon, and saw straight through their disguises apparently. She reported it and the undead there slaughtered them before anyone else even knew they were attacking.

"As to here, when you were attacked, that was seemingly the signal, because as soon as the first bout of gunfire rang out, people were dropping out of stealth all over the dungeon. Thankfully, they mainly focused on the dungeon-born, as they felt they were clearly the most threatening."

She held a hand up as soon as she said it.

"I know the dungeon-born are people, and they're aware now…the majority, anyway. But as much as I know it's shit, I'm still glad it was them, and not just the humans."

"I know." I nodded, my heart like lead in my chest. "I know and I feel the same, but…who did we lose?"

"Saros." She sighed. "Arend-Jan was badly injured, as was Starr. Apparently, they were both here to try to talk to you, and they were caught in an explosion. They've been sent to the north, their wounds healed. But still, while they're both capable, neither are really combat troops. Not any more for Starr, anyway, and he carried the older man in, bleeding out. He was heartbroken when he thought his friend was dying, so don't think to lecture me on the relative 'worth' of dungeon-born and their human counterparts, okay?" she snapped, before rubbing at the bridge of her nose and shaking her head.

"No, don't answer that. Sorry. You said you were the same as me on that, they're alive, and you feel as shitty as I do. Fuck, my head hurts."

"I'm sorry. Are you okay?" I asked her, frowning and stepping in close. "Jo? Wait, are we under attack right now?"

"More of 'under siege.' If there's an attack ongoing, you'll know, don't worry. There's a standard rule in place that they make us aware now, and I'm fine." She sighed, before stretching and wincing as her back clicked. "Damn, it turns out that those new stamina potions have issues if you chug a lot of them though, sorry to say. We've been in a fight for the last day, and here, it's been a lot worse. Too many people we've needed to stabilize and move on, then come back to, simply because we've got too little mana."

"And no mana potions," I agreed, before cursing myself for using the ones I'd gotten out of the dungeon all those weeks ago. That decision might have cost a hell of a lot of lives, and it definitely had cost a lot of people more pain than was reasonable.

"It's fine. Right, you're healed, I know—I checked on you half an hour ago—but you've seen the curse?"

"The fucking curse, yes—what the hell?" I asked, and she nodded.

"That asshole Thomas, seems he had an artifact, no clue where it came from, nor how it worked. It crumbled when Emma touched it. She swears she didn't destroy it, and frankly I doubt she did, but it's not like I can tell. She recognized the curse. Something about her Bloodwytch class reacted to it, and before it was put on you, she knew there was something going on.

"She dragged me out of the canteen and straight to you. It's the only reason that we were close enough to save you, so I'd say you owe her a little slack after everything."

"She knew?" I asked.

"She did, but considering it's the first time she's seen or felt an artifact like that, she didn't know what it was, just that there was something very wrong, and it felt…" She paused, biting her lip as she thought before shaking her head. "I don't remember the terms she used, but she said that it felt wrong, basically, like something was creeping through the dungeon, and she came to get me, thinking I could help her get rid of it."

"And you did." I nodded. "Thank you."

"Not me." She smiled. "And before you go looking for Emma, not her either."

"Who?"

"Loren." She gestured to one of the goblins helping with the bodies. "She was summoned in the fight against the undead, and she's a Luminary. Turns out they're a sort of counter to the curse classes."

"Damn." I sighed. "Fucking glad we have some then. I… I think I remember her?"

"She damn near killed herself to save you, pushed herself through the mana limit and drained her own health to a handful of points to keep fighting the curse. Said she needs a little more experience and then she should level, but she's currently level nine, so I'm waiting to see what she gets for the class choice."

"Me too now." I reached out, laying a hand on the shoulder of the shorter advanced goblin and smiling as I spoke to her. "I remember you, Loren. Thank you for your help. I'm not sure I'd have made it if you hadn't been here."

She looked up at me, blinking, clearly unsure what to say, so simply nodded. "I help." She then looked to Jo mutely, as if appealing to her.

"Thank you, Loren. Go on with your jobs please," Jo said, clearly taking pity on the panicking goblin, who bowed her head and scurried off before I could get a word in. "So, looks like she's a little less sanguine about you when you're awake."

"Oh?"

"She was fine around you when you were asleep. She and the other goblin, Naxos, helped with you off and on. Something about their magic helped you, and it's not like they can use it anywhere else. Once the undead were defeated, that was the end of her leveling, or so we thought. Since the fight went the way it did, though, she's been using her Radiant Burst almost constantly."

"Oh?" I asked, looking around. "I don't see…"

"We told them to stop," she clarified. "It was helping, but it also drains them a hell of a lot, and they're weak. It costs them a hundred mana to cast it once. Between their regeneration and their intelligence, I've ordered them not to use them unless they'll have more than half of their mana left after the usage."

"Just in case?" I asked, and she nodded. "Okay, makes sense. You said we're under siege, so I need to get out there." I expected an argument from her, mildly surprised when I didn't get one.

"Just be careful, and make sure you don't end up on my tables again." She smiled, though it was clearly an effort. "Matt, whatever you might think, they came here to fight. If they were asking you for something, once they'd gotten it, they'd have just upped their demands, so don't blame yourself for this."

"You've been talking to Kelly," I said dryly.

She smirked then patted me on the shoulder, having to reach up to do it. "Go on, go spread terror and dismay or whatever you do out there. Get your butt outta my medical suite. You're making it look untidy."

"One point…" I paused. "…I got a new ability recently, it helps mana and health regeneration, and it's a location specific one, so I can set it and walk away. If you need it, I could activate it here, I don't know how expensive it is, though I got a warning that means it'll cost more, the larger the area covered. Do you want me to cast it here?"

She paused, considering then shook her head.

"Honestly, as much as it would have been useful earlier, we've got things under control now, and I think we'd all feel better knowing you've got your mana available if the shit hits the fan. Thank you though, and I'll let you know if that changes. For now, you might want to go get some clothes on. "

I glanced from her to the gurneys that lined the sides of the ward. Each and every one of them had a body laid on them, many bloody or burned, and I nodded, looking from them to my exposed body.

I was stripped to the waist, and heavily muscled now, as well as clean, as someone had clearly wiped the blood away. I reached up, touching the skin over my stomach, lower left lung, and right below my heart. The memory of the holes that had been there made my fingers flinch back, even as they touched smooth, unscarred flesh.

"Go on, get!" Jo ordered with a half smile, flapping her hands like she was trying to drive a chicken from the room.

I took the hint and left, drawing a deep breath as I did. Determination filled me. Some fucker had sent Thomas, and I was going to find them and fuck them up.

CHAPTER THIRTEEN

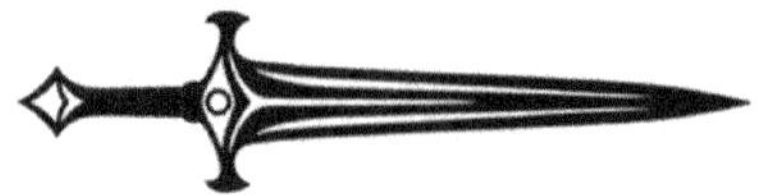

The first stop I made once I was outside of the medical wing wasn't a surprising one, not for anyone who knew me. I found the first room that had nobody in it, summoned some replacement clothes, and sank into the dungeon sense, flitting to Kelly's side, finding her hovering high above the dungeon, looking out to the north.

"Matt!" Kelly clung to me as soon as I arrived, holding tight, before leaning back and seeming to examine me. "Are you okay?"

"As good as I get," I assured her, smiling tiredly. "So, what the hell happened?"

"Did Jo tell you anything?" she countered.

I nodded. "That we were attacked, that they were in place before the meeting I had with that wanker Thomas, and that they used some kind of an artifact on me."

"Yeah. Well, that's the bare bones of it, all right. There were at least a dozen of them. They didn't seem to understand that the dungeon was an actual dungeon, but they seemed to think it was a building with just a core that could be taken. Three of our soldiers were killed when they wouldn't tell them where the core was stored."

"They knew about the core but they didn't understand?" I asked, confused.

"Shit, that really didn't make sense. Okay, let's put it another way. They knew about what a dungeon *was*, but they were questioning if there was a core here or if it was stored somewhere else. And when the dungeon-born appeared before them, they were totally unprepared for it."

"That's…weird," I said slowly.

"Very much so." She nodded. "It's also weird that the group we've been dealing with—well, it's a lot smaller than I would have expected. They've got nearly three hundred soldiers still out there, and a bunch of snipers, but the group inside the walls when the attack was launched were special forces, I think. That says they're desperate to try to take the dungeon, but the lack of knowledge and the sheer fucking stupidity of the assault? It says there's something else going on to me."

"Do we have any of them alive?" I asked. "Can we question them?"

"That's the other thing. The common soldiers? Yeah, we've captured a few of them and they're split between petrified and ranting about us being monsters, and pissed off, determined that we attacked them. The one I observed claimed we backstabbed them while they were negotiating. Yeah, the goblin I summoned when you were with Thomas there was a provocation, but it was obvious that the fight was about to kick off anyway, and that way it died instead of you.

"Beyond that, we've managed to capture four of the special forces in the last three hours. Each and every one of them had some kind of suicide device, and as soon as they couldn't escape? They used it."

"Suicide?" I stared at her. "Fuck's sake, that doesn't make much sense, unless…"

"They're fanatics," she said grimly. "Matt, we might have gotten out of the frying pan, and into the fire. We didn't think to ask—I mean, I don't even know what the hell we *could* have asked—but the way that dickhead Peterbilt acted when the fight was over, it was almost like there was no way we could possibly understand and we were the inferior ones. It's like they're a cult of some kind. And the way that Thomas acted as well, that contempt? I don't know, but what if the group in London aren't the kind of people we want to know about us?"

"If they…shit." I closed my eyes, taking a deep breath. "Okay, let's stop a minute. We don't know anything yet, so let's just deal with what we do know. Where are we with the fight—what's happening?"

"That's the weird thing." She shook her head. "They were desperate to take the wall. The forces that were inside went on a killing spree, but it was aimed at almost exclusively the dungeon-born. The special forces were happy to kill humans, but the others? It makes no sense. Some are happy to kill anything, others act like they're rescuing our people and don't understand why we're pissed.

"There was even one group that started firing on their own people, shouting that they were out of control. As soon as the special forces attacked, one of them was waiting on the roof and fired a flare into the air. That got the second group moving, before they tried to use the roof as a sniper nest. The majority of the main group then charged the wall, brought in mortars and shoulder-mounted rocket launchers.

"They took out the outer wall, but once they were inside and the only way to use them was to risk their own people? They kept using them! They used all the rest of their heavy weapons to get inside the walls, then dumped them. Once inside, they were almost 'spray and pray' rather than the way the army usually is. You know those movies where they go room to room and sweep for the enemy and they're all 'Cover me' and so on? Well, it was like a mixture of that, where they shout military-sounding things, and a bunch of idiots on an online game all doing their own thing.

"There was little coordination and almost none of them listening to one another. They just wanted to shoot the kobolds and the orcs. If a human got in the way, sure, they shot them as well, but it was like they were hopped up on something and just manic."

"Shit." I cursed. "I hate not knowing what's going on! Where are they now?"

"They're broken into two groups. There's about three hundred left, with a hundred outside the walls, sprinting like their arses are on fire, or sniping at us. They pulled back once they started losing too many. And that's another thing. They seemed totally unprepared for the dungeon to repair itself. I mean, we resummoned the walls once they weren't near them, and that freaked them out."

"And where… I see them." I cut my own question off, staring down at the small group.

They were split into two, as Kelly had said. A handful of figures currently hotfooted it across the fields and hills beyond, some of which had dumped their gear to run faster. The majority were currently holed up on the inside next to our outer curtain wall. They were trying to make a pyramid for the others to climb up, but it was obvious to anyone who looked at them that it was destined for failure.

A handful had climbed to the top of the pyramid, and rather than then helping the next in line…they climbed over the far side, making a break for it.

I glanced down, remembering what Kelly had said about a sniper. I found a smear of blood on the roof, with a body on the floor of the courtyard far below.

Replacing whoever that had been were a dozen of our own snipers, and they were taking out the enemy in the fields as they ran, focusing on those few that were returning fire.

"You got him then," I noted, seeing the body broken in the courtyard.

"Yeah," she said grimly. "Turns out there's a way to get around the limit on summoning things too close to him. I summoned a block of concrete a meter above his head just fine."

"Ouch. Well, fuck him very much," I agreed. "Have you tried talking to them?"

"Twice. They shot the messenger," she growled.

"Fuckers. Fine. That sounds like it's a job for me then."

The pyramid collapsed. The component parts broke into fighting as they realized that their fellow soldiers were taking advantage and just running for it.

"Matt, that's not a good idea," Kelly said. "You literally just got out of the medical ward."

"Just means they'll not have filled my bed yet." I grinned. "I need to get Finn. I need armor and I need to look fucking amazing. We've only got a few minutes, and it's time to make sure they surrender."

"You start getting ready with…whatever else you need," she said after a long pause, staring at me. "I'll find Finn."

That was it; we both blinked out of the air above the dungeon—me back to my body, and Kelly to search for Finn. I knew I could have summoned him, but she was sorting that, and for all I knew, he wasn't even awake currently.

"Matt, dammit, it's about time!" Finn shouted as he shoved the door open and stormed in, making me stare at him in shock.

"How the hell…?" I started.

"I was here!" he said quickly. "As soon as I heard, I came here. It was the last place anyone had seen my Patrick and now those fuckers have him!"

"I…we don't know that for sure," I said carefully, and he shook his head.

"Matt, we had a fight. That was it—an argument. We fight enough that it was just that…we were both pissed off and that was all. But I said some things I shouldn't have, so when he didn't come straight home, I thought I'd pushed him too far and he was still cooling off. If I'd not done that? He might still be at home, all right! This is all my fault!"

"No." I grabbed him by the shoulders; the smaller crafter dashed the tears away that streamed down his cheeks as he refused to meet my gaze. "Finn, this isn't your fault, but we don't have time for this. I need armor. My usual isn't going to cut it. I need to shock them. I need these people to see me as a god, one that's come to save them or punish them, I don't care which—but I need them to listen long enough to surrender. We need people to fucking question! If we kill them all, we won't find Patrick and Catherine, so help me!"

"I've got you," he whispered, wiping the tears away again, before taking a deep breath, then looking at me. "This isn't going to be cheap," he warned me.

"What? What do you want?" I asked, thinking this was a shitty time to try to extort something from me, before he shook his head and I understood—he meant the *mana* cost.

"I mean the armor!" he said quickly. "It's something I've been working on…and it should be…it should work. It's not finished yet, but for this, it should work."

"Do it," I said grimly. Then, to my goddamn shock, over two *million* points of mana, almost all the dungeon had stored, vanished from the count. "What the…" I grunted, before falling silent as the armor started to appear before me.

"I've been working on it awhile, and I had Aly give me a portion of the research budget. It's what I want to make for everyone at some point, but this level?" He cleared his throat, then went on. "The materials aren't something we had access to before. They're magically reactive, and they store and use mana. They should be able to take a portion of any incoming magic fired at you, and impacts as well. Then it'll store that power up, like kinetic energy…or at least I think so."

"That's not something that fills me with confidence."

"Matt, this is a prototype, and it cost two million mana, plus all my mana crystals I'd been saving up for a surprise for Patrick, okay? I couldn't test this. I just know what the component parts do, or should do. I had the dungeon do some of the research for me, and I still don't understand it, but this is the very best armor I can make for you, and I don't have anything else, okay! Just take it and go do what you do!"

I nodded, looking at the armor that was still being summoned into being before me. The printing by the dungeon seemingly took much longer than a regular suit.

"Matt, it's a prototype," he repeated softly. "That means this version might be incredible or useless. We won't know until it's done. But if you give me the time, this will be the base layer of a new kind of suit. One that will change the course of the war."

"I trust you," I assured him. "So, what goes on first, and what do I wear under it?"

"Here, strip to your boxers, then this goes on first…" He held out what looked like a boy's extra-small pair of fucking pants.

I cocked an eyebrow at him, and he just gestured at me again grimly.

"It'll stretch!" he assured me.

"It'll fuckin' need to," I replied, taking it and starting to strip.

The next few minutes, despite me rushing as much as I could, passed with agonizing slowness as I continued to hear distant gunfire outside. As I pulled on the base layer, I noted the scales that made this up were so small that I could barely see them.

The armor sliding across my skin felt cool, and these new sections were far more impressive than our previous armor.

The armor that materialized before me was unlike anything I had ever seen. As the final pieces assembled themselves, I stood in awe of Finn's creation.

The suit was a masterpiece of alien technology and divine inspiration. Its surface was a seamless blend of intricate, sweeping lines and sharp, angular plates that seemed to flow like liquid metal. The dark, gunmetal-grey surface had an almost organic quality, as if it were alive and shifting subtly with each movement.

The chest piece featured a glowing blue circular node at its center, pulsing with barely contained energy. Similar nodes were placed strategically across the suit—on the palms, knees, and temples of the helmet. These, I assumed, were conduits for the mana absorption and redistribution Finn had mentioned.

The helmet was a work of art in itself. It featured a T-shaped visor that glowed with the same ethereal blue light as the nodes. Two swept-back horns or antennae rose from the forehead, giving it a regal, almost crown-like appearance.

As I donned the armor, it adjusted and molded to my body; the tiny scales of the base layer became one with the larger plates. A cape-like extension flowed down from the shoulders, adding to the divine aesthetic.

"Finn," I breathed, flexing my hands in the articulated gauntlets, "this is…incredible."

The suit hummed with potential, ready to channel and amplify my storm powers, even as Finn handed me the helmet.

"Let's hope it works as good as it looks," Finn said, a mix of pride and worry in his voice. "Now go show those bastards what a real god of the storms can do."

As soon as I stepped out into the hall, the few people who were moving around jerked to a halt, staring in wonder.

I strode through the lower floor to the main doors, feeling in the dungeon sense the attention of others as they gathered around, staring at the armor. It was truly a thing of beauty, and yet, as I flexed my hands, rolled my wrists, and shrugged my shoulders, letting it all settle into place, I couldn't help but want to know what the next evolution would look like.

Finn walked by my side, speaking quickly as I headed for the door.

"It should be able to take more direct hits than the old suit, and it certainly looks the part, but be careful here and here…" He gestured to the sides of his stomach, the areas alongside his abs. "To keep it as flexible as possible, I needed to trim this, so the armor is almost down to the base layer there. A high-powered round will go through it, or at least I think it will."

"And the impacts?" I asked. "Are they dispersed or…?"

"Dispersal weave as part of the scale layer," he assured me. "You're going to have to learn to use the suit. The next version will be a hell of a lot stronger and more impressive, if things hold up in this version. I want to add in muscle improvement and twitch response stimuli as well as…"

The description rolled over me as I nodded my thanks to a nearby soldier holding the door open for me. I stepped outside, then lifted my helmet and slid it on.

The scale layer went all the way up my neck—it was actually fucking annoying there already, the tiny flexes providing gaps that snapped and yanked on the hairs of my beard as I moved—but as soon as I slid the helmet on, the scales connected to the bottom of it.

There wasn't anything like a heads-up display or a nice cooling breeze in here. It was technological only in the materials used, but damn, it felt good!

I crouched, doing a full-on show for the gathering crowd. Then I leapt upward, pushing hard with my abilities, calling the Air mana to help me, to lift me and to be able to fly with my lightning. I doubled down as soon as I was clear of them all…

And there was a crack in the air behind me as I rocketed upward at a truly horrific speed.

The world around me blurred. I shot through the drifting sleet and rain, into the clouds and, seconds later, burst free of them into the sunlight beyond.

My mana had taken a hell of a hit, I realized. Whatever the difference in the armor was that allowed me to launch myself and break the goddamn sound barrier, it'd cost me an arm and a leg in terms of mana, but *damn*.

My arc was parabolic. As soon as I stopped pushing so hard behind me, I rose a little farther, then started to slowly arc over, heading downward as the earth tightened its grasp again.

I nearly let it. The sheer shock of the difference with the armor was incredible.

As I flew, I powered it by use of my mana. I basically told the earth and its gravity field to go fuck itself, exerting enough pressure that I was able to fly through a combination of pure Air mana and the Storm and Lightning that were my primary elements.

As strong as they were, I had no issues soaring through the air normally, but now? It was almost effortless. I spun around, almost losing myself in the joy and wonder of the feeling.

Then I came to a halt, feeling my dungeon through the clouds below, and the reality of everything that had happened poured back in.

It was time to sort this fucking shit out.

I twisted around, making sure I was aligned with the right area. Then I reached out, sending lightning crackling through the clouds. The boom of thunder announced me as I fell through them, once again with my flight under my full control.

The lightning was different as well. Far less effort was needed, in fact. Reaching out, I took a deep breath, and I felt the Lightning mana all around me being sucked back into myself, as my armor blazed to life, lit from within by an unearthly blue-white glow.

The dungeon was clear through the clouds now as I bore down, as were the dozens of running figures sprinting across the fields.

Even as I looked at them, the tree line in the distance rang out with the crack of a high-powered rifle. I felt something spang off my left shoulder.

It hadn't been a solid hit, just a glancing one, but still. Even at this distance, the shock of the impact should have done a number on me. But between the plate it hit and the angle, combined with the new level of armor meant I reached up and flicked that plate like I was shooing off an annoying fly.

Then I drew in a heavy charge of lightning and replied.

The bolt that burst free of my right hand was thicker than my thigh. It tore across the distance with almost no delay, punching into the trees and being dragged from left to right across the rough areas that the shot had come from.

Trees crashed down; fires started as the overwhelming power of the lightning bolt overcame little things like sodden wood and mere snow. I didn't know for sure whether I'd gotten them; I got two kill notifications that I simply dismissed but I'd gotten two fuckers, that was for sure.

It was only as I turned and looked down at the soldiers who were below me now that I realized that it could have just as easily been where they were holding our people, and I could no longer afford indiscriminate slaughter like that.

It was time to put on a show, though. And judging by the way these people cowered below me, they were ready for it.

They were gathered around the wall still, below me and to the left, on the inside of the dungeon wall, forming a human pyramid all over again, though this time it looked like they were actually trying to help each other.

They saw that I was looking at them now, and a solid dozen or so crouched, bringing rifles up and aiming, before opening fire.

The first few hits were negligible, though as more and more managed to zero in, the pain ratcheted up, as did the level of damage. So as cool as this suit looked, it really wasn't entirely resistant to small arms fire.

That was fine, though, because I had plenty of lightning to go around.

The dozen were hit by a second bolt of lightning that I dragged from right to left, carving them apart. Flesh melted and tore; clothing burst into flames, as did hair. Metal conducted the charge, making it oh so much worse, and they all died in less time than it took to tell about it.

As I stopped the bolt, releasing the power and staring down at them, I took a deep breath. The pyramid had collapsed, as people panicked. Then I pulled in as much of the Air mana around me as I could.

It wasn't anywhere near the level of a storm here—not now, anyway. It had been literally just drifting sleet and snow mixed with rain, in that horrible "gets everywhere" kind of way that shitty weather always did.

Now, though, the wind—which hadn't been that strong to begin with—dropped like a stone.

The sudden silence as the wind vanished, then the gasps as I flexed that same Air mana to cut a curtain, visibly, through the air and send the falling crap to either side, brought a level of fear to the group below that was palpable.

"Surrender!" I called down in a grim voice as I floated closer, diverting a current of Air mana to make my cloak stream out behind me in the wind. "Or I will kill you all." Then I unleashed a thunderclap that shattered the sky, and a crackling, fractally branching pair of lightning bolts that spread outward, illuminating the world for them all.

There was barely a pause, and most of that was caused by the few people still trying to climb the wall, falling. Then the sound of the guns being tossed away resounded, and the work of dealing with this monumental fuck-up began.

CHAPTER FOURTEEN

"Explain that to me again," I growled, my anger rising, as some five hours later, I sat in the southern dungeon around a brand-new command table with Kelly, Mike, Finn, a somewhat battered and tired Patrick, as well as Chris and Jo all attending physically.

Joining us in a more ghostly sense, their bodies projected through the control room facilities, were Aly, Clarissa, Markus, Ashley and Dante. I glared at Mike, holding a can of my now de rigueur energy drink as I listened.

"They seriously did that?" I snapped.

"They brought back the noble houses and rebuilt the monarchy," he said. "It took some digging, and we're fucking lucky we managed to stun one of the dickheads who was holding Patrick and that Catherine was able to use her powers to call back the spirits of the dead as well. That's how we know as much as we do. Catherine, can you explain it, please?" Mike glanced over at the elderly-looking, yet young woman on the far side of the table.

"When people are carried away with something, they make emotional decisions based on the moment." She looked down at the table. "When they die, all of it is stripped away, and the only way they get to feel anything ever again is if someone like me either summons them, or shares a fragment of their power with them."

She sighed and shifted in her chair. She had a blanket wrapped around her shoulders and her legs were drawn up under her. A cup of untouched hot chocolate sat on the table before her, as she stared at it morosely.

"They regret it, you know? The dead? They regret the assault. There's a lot of things different once you cross the veil, and one of those things, like I say, is that the emotion is gone and that you see things more clearly in some ways. Another is that I can share information and memories, and so can they. It's not like a conversation, so much as mind-to-mind.

"I see their memories, the arguments they had, the orders they were given, and the happier times, as well as the sadness. There's annoyance, but it's a cold thing. They know that they were lied to. The majority of them, anyway. They're frustrated, and they're sort of angry, but it's more of an awareness that they *should* be angry, and a taste of regret for the life that was taken from them."

"They should fucking regret it," I muttered, and she flinched, before nodding.

"They do, sorry. Most of them, anyway. They're scared and tired and now they're all alone. They don't know what to do. But when I showed them what happened, when I shared the fight and what I knew of the discussion after that Peterbilt guy attacked you? Then they shared more. The majority had no clue about any of it."

"Start at the beginning, please," I said to her. "And Catherine? It's okay—we're all angry and stressed, but none of this is your fault. I don't hold you responsible for anything, so don't be afraid."

"Okay." She still didn't meet my gaze.

I looked at Ashley as Catherine started to speak, and she nodded, reassuring me that she was paying attention to the slight woman, and that she was working on her still.

"So, when things went well, when the end came in London, at first it was all very slow and civilized. The government stepped in and took control of the food and the utilities, as they were. Most things stopped working, but there was plenty of water in the reservoirs and in the shops, so it, like everything else, was rationed, and people were okay.

"Once it became clear that the power wasn't coming back on, though, and the food was starting to run out, things started to change. Originally the group that was in charge was all based on money. From that money came the ability to make things happen. Basically, it was the basis of the ruling class's power. They could do things, because they were so rich, so they could either make your life better or much worse, depending on what you did and they wanted.

"Now with the new way of the world, with all the electronic money gone, and the money in the banks being mainly paper, not 'real' money, as well as being mostly out of reach…well, that changed everything.

"The richest and most powerful were already the ones in charge—they'd made sure of that once things first broke down—so once they realized that the money they needed to pay everyone and stay in command was gone, they moved quickly. The way the old power groups started off in the past, and maintained control, was through powerful groups that worked together.

"That was the basis of the old noble houses—people who kept control and shared it with a limited few, always making the next generation earn their place. That's what they decided to do now. They secured the food chain, then put people they could control into positions of power in the newly reforming military. Where they needed to, for some of the new 'houses' that didn't have people they could control as easily in positions they needed, they assassinated each other instead. For a few months, that was it. A bloodbath behind closed doors, and in public it was all the stiff upper lip and a united front to keep people doing as they were told."

"They knew all of this? The dead, I mean, the majority?" I asked, scratching at my chin in thought as I listened.

"No. The one who called himself Thomas did, because he's a son of one of the houses now, but most didn't. His name used to be Major John Thomas, though he'd gone by 'Thomas' so long it was how he thought of himself. He was once in the army, but never made it to special forces. He'd tried to get into the SAS, but they refused him. The report he'd managed to get hold of through family connections said he had too many psychological issues, and I can believe it, having met his soul."

"That makes a lot more sense," I muttered. "All right, so they formed new noble houses…" I felt a twinge of warning and a sudden constriction around my chest. I snarled as I asked the next question. "The Queen…is she all right?"

"No, she died," Catherine said uncertainly, staring at me as I waved her concern off. "A heart attack it was announced as, but Thomas didn't think so. She was too hard, too firm and respected. Both her and her son Charles died within a few days of each other. Then they held a fast coronation for the son, William.

"He and his wife and children are alive, but despite the rise of the nobility again, the monarchy is still a figurehead, one that Thomas thought was being kept in place until one of the houses had enough power to take full control and kill them. There was talk that he was being kept under control with a tight leash, and a threat against his wife and young children."

"Fuck." I grunted. "Now we need to rescue them as well. Fucking oath."

"If we can," Kelly reminded me. "The oath says that we need to do all that's reasonable to rescue them and offer them safety. You don't need to plow into the army on your own."

"The phrasing is—you know what?" I cut myself off. "We'll sort it out…that's a plan to sort out later." That was enough for the oath to release the hold it'd been establishing on my heart, and I let out a breath. "Right, okay, so let's move on. You say they formed new noble houses, which is all nice for them, but is it important for us?"

"Very much so," she said in a low voice. "Sorry, I was getting to it."

"Go on." I hated how mousey and afraid she always was around me, but didn't know how to "fix" it.

"They split a lot of the city between them, and they all have certain groups and resources divided among them. They're supposed to be sharing control of the army—it's the King's force officially, after all. But they're all fighting one another out of sight for control. Thomas works for the Johnstoneites. They're the worst of the lot—or I think so, anyway. They don't care who they kill, or break, to get what they want. They just don't believe anyone else matters. Their leader, Alexander? He wants to be 'king of the world' though even his own family view him with contempt and they'd all stab him in the back to get what they want as soon as they think they can replace him."

"Great, so we've got some dickhead with delusions of grandeur," I muttered, before shutting up when Kelly elbowed me. "Sorry, go on."

"He's the one who sent the group, and they were as desperate as they were to hit us hard and fast…because most of the rest of the nobles didn't know they were being sent. They're still arguing over how they should respond—or they were when Thomas set off. This was a power grab, pure and simple. And when Thomas got here, he found the other group, the army? There were two hundred sent by another noble house that nearly beat him to us.

"He arranged a meeting with their leader to see how they should move forward, and as soon as they were alone and he'd gotten all that he needed from him? He killed their leader. His forces outnumbered the rest, so what was left of the force's leadership fell into line when they were shown what had happened. They were offered a choice.

"Only the upper officers knew the truth of the situation they were marching into. The lower ranks were all told various stories. The Johnstoneites told their people that we'd been taken prisoner by a bunch of monsters, and that they were coming to save us. The Trust Collective, the second force, were told that we reneged on a deal, and we murdered the soldiers who were sent to help us. That we were holding both a load of humans prisoners, but that we also had a stockpile of their food and medicines that we'd stolen.

"The story was they were paying us for something, though nobody knew what, and that when they'd come to make the deal, we'd taken their stuff and murdered their representative. Apparently, we were going to sell them to their enemies. No clue who their enemies are, but that's the way the Trust Collective seems to be—they're paranoid fantasists who blame any failure on imaginary dark forces and swear that what they told people last week was totally different from whatever they said. Again, this is coming mainly from Thomas. I didn't have long to interrogate him, but he had nothing but contempt for them. It's just all a mess."

"That's why neither story made any goddamn sense," Kelly said softly. "We were only getting part of the picture, and that's conflicting as well."

"Yeah, and it gets worse." Catherine took a deep breath, then went on. "The one thing most of the houses could agree upon was that the dungeon was too valuable to leave in *anyone* else's control. It was to be taken from us, and we were to either be paid for it, and offered a place of high honor and power with them, by the better nobles, or executed, to keep the secret from spreading by the others.

"Lots of them see the dungeon being a powerful tool, but Thomas thought that all the houses were making plans to take the dungeon by force, including backstabbing their allies and rivals alike if they could get it under their control. The 'common' people would never be told what it was. Instead, they would be kept working, believing that they were growing the food and so on that the dungeon was producing. That way, they'd be easier to control." She finally glanced at me. The look in her eyes made it clear that she knew exactly what that meant.

"And that, folks, is why they can't have a dungeon," I said firmly. "Even after all of this, if there was some way that they could have been reasoned with, I'd have considered it. But as it is? Fuck no. If they're planning on hiding the dungeon, then they're not going to work toward the end goal, they're not going to prepare their people, and they're not going to be allies we can rely on." I lowered my head into my hands, my mind whirling as I tried to process it. "What the fuck do we do now?" I asked myself rhetorically.

"If we don't give it to them, we're going to be looking at a war," Mike said grimly. "I don't like it, not one bit, but there's a fuckload more of them than there are us. The only way we can deal with this and come out on top is a bunch of surgical strikes. Maybe we send in teams, take out the leadership of each house, leave evidence that points to the other houses each time?"

"Then it'd lead to a civil war in London, as they all fight each other, and long term we'd still be weakened because we need humanity a lot more than we need the land." Aly shook her head. "Thousands would die…more, probably. Besides, what if you got caught?"

"That'll only start the war sooner," Clarissa agreed. "Is this a war we can win is what we should be asking ourselves. You built the new dungeon to be mobile…can we not take advantage of that? Simply pack up and move?"

"They need to be faced now…" Finn snapped, one of his hands holding Patrick's tightly. "They need to pay for what they did!"

The room broke down into a dozen arguments. Everyone had an idea of what we should do, and all were trying to offer it at the same time.

"Do they need to know?" Chris asked suddenly.

I looked up at him. The expression on his face made it clear that he knew this wasn't the time for a joke, as he held a hand up in a "just listen" gesture as we all looked at him.

"Go on," Kelly prompted, frowning at the usually jovial man.

"What if you gave them a dungeon, but it wasn't a dungeon?" he suggested.

"Make sense, Chris—I've not got the bandwidth for this shit," I said grimly.

"What if you gave them a dungeon core, one that was linked to a control panel, and you set it up with a fake core and everything. Make it clear that if they open the core, they'll break the dungeon, and that they need to use the control panel to use it. We make a simple control panel, something that they can use to buy whatever they need."

"Go on." I frowned at him, not seeing the advantage to setting up a fake dungeon.

"You block them from summoning creatures until they hit a certain level—say it's something about generating a secondary core…can't be done, too bad, so sad. They can only create items…food and so on. They need to power the dungeon, though, and the only way to do that is to provide it with mass, an absolute shitload of mass.

"We make anything they want on the system cost three or four times as much as it really does. You make a fake research screen, and then when they pay the cost, you unlock the relevant system. If it's a new thing? Great, we're getting paid to research it. If it's something we already have? Even better.

"All the time, it's one of our people working a shift behind the system—a researcher, a team of skeletal resource gatherers, the works. You build a room underground, well below the level they can reach, and you set up there. The dungeon isn't theirs, it's still ours, but we *tell* them it's theirs. Anything they notice that's weird? Well, it was built by aliens, wasn't it? Bound to be fuckin' weird."

"They can't summon creatures, and any research they do is stuff we've already done," I said slowly, thinking my way through his suggestion. "A fake core, one they have to pay for, in mass, to upgrade. Hell, we could have them pay to play…the only way they can train is to run a training dungeon and charge out the arse for that too. We could make a dungeon in the middle of their most secure area, and a nexus gate…keep it under their feet and they'd never know.

"They pay us in mass for everything they want, and we convert that mass to mana, then feed that mana through the system and make crystals. We can feed the dungeon on London's heart, and we get three-quarters of everything. Those crystals can be carried out through the nexus gate to our dungeons, and they'll have to protect it for us."

My eyes were wide now as I considered it from all angles.

"They'd also have to do all the work to develop it, invest in new mana converters…all of it. We'd need a system for them to see. Maybe we offer an advisor, but at a cost and only by remote because of their actions?" Kelly suggested. "That way, we can convince them that they need to build things the way we want, so they're not putting converters in stupid places."

"Fuck them." I laughed suddenly. "Let them! They're paying three times what the cost is for everything—we let them pay it, because all the time we can be pushing out and establishing control over the local area!" I looked at Chris and couldn't help but grin. "Oh, you sneaky bastard!" I shook my head, laughing. "You're a sneaky, sneaky fucker!"

"I do have my moments." He smiled, clearly glad to be able to help.

I nodded. Then I twisted, looking across the table. "Okay, Dante, you said that you've got some system admin type friends, right?" I leveled a finger at him, and he blinked, then nodded.

"Yeah, Clint and Gary. They'd be able to help, I'm sure…"

"Good! Because we're going to be having a meeting with them soon." I nodded to myself as my mind raced. "In fact, tell them what the general plan is. Tell them that they'll have a week, and I need a viable operating system in that time. I want a system map figured out and options."

"Can do. I mean, I think they could do this?" he hedged.

"Either of them ever build a website before?"

He nodded. "Yeah. Clint got investigated by his training course when he did his. They thought he'd hired someone to do it for him, it was that good. He's also…well, there's no nice way to say it, so I'll just say it. If you ever thought I was awkward around people? Clint's a lot worse.

"Give him something like this, though, a problem to solve and a deadline? He's in his element. Give him coffee, a broom cupboard to live in—don't ask…he likes small spaces and to be left alone—and just keep feeding him? He'll do it. Just don't expect him to be friendly to anyone who can't keep up with him."

"Sounds perfect. All he needs to do is figure out the system, that's all…make it work as a relay and a feeder for us." I nodded. "I get the feeling that the system will have options ready for us for this kinda shit."

"It should," Ashley said musingly. "I mean, if you think of traps and that kind of a setup, I can't imagine nobody has tried to create fakes that weren't at least similar."

"Well, we'll find out soon." I grinned. "Okay, so what we'll give them is sorted out. Now we just need to figure out how we do it, and why."

"Why?" Catherine frowned, then colored when she saw everyone look at her. "I mean, we're doing it to prevent a war, right?"

"We are, but people get suspicious when they get something for nothing, so they'll have to fight for it, or to bargain harshly." My good humor vanished again. "So they're going to have to fight for it, or buy it."

"If it was a fight, we'd lose a lot of people, including this dungeon," Kelly pointed out. "They'd need to take it from somewhere, after all."

"Yeah, we sell it to them," I muttered. "That or we have them get wind of a location, a transfer for the core, where it's being brought to here from the north…"

"Whoever's transporting it would die," Kelly repeated.

"They would, so we need additional research doing," I agreed, before grinning and looking at Aly. "Have you looked at the mechanist upgrades yet?"

"Oh no." She folded her arms and shook her head as she sat back, glaring at me. "You're not fucking up my schedule all over again!"

"What's this?" Finn asked, and I smiled.

"Oh, I think you'll like this," I assured him. I reached out, pulling up the details on the system. A hologram came into being and hovered before us all, along with the system description. For the first time, an image appeared alongside it.

Glassine	Dungeon-born

Techno-Arcane Construct: The Glassine are a primarily peaceful race, one that evolved through harmonious development of their technology, biology, and minds. They are a solvent-based species that have fully integrated the ability to build their own bodies, resulting in long-lived beings of exquisite beauty. Glassine reside within intricately carved and often embossed bodies crafted by master artisans.

Cost: Glassine (Advanced): 1000 Crystal, 4000 Pure Mana, 50 Control points. Maintenance is 200 mana points per day, per individual.
Current level: Advanced

Note: *Glassine are highly adaptable and can attune themselves to various energy types within the dungeon. At higher levels, they can manipulate and redirect energy flows, potentially enhancing the dungeon's overall efficiency.*

Special Traits:
Self-Sculpting: Can alter their own form for aesthetic or practical purposes.
Energy Harmonization: Can attune to and manipulate various energy types within the dungeon.
Tech-Magic Interface: Can create seamless connections between magical and technological systems.

Warning: *Although generally peaceful, Glassine may take offense to crude attempts at replication or forced evolution. Respect for their craftsmanship and autonomy is advised to maintain positive relations.*

Durability: 250/250	Abilities:?/?

The creature that hung there was…it wasn't what I was expecting, put it that way. The glassine that was shown was incredible in some ways. It appeared to be literally living, molten glass. It flowed around a workshop, the "hands" morphing into different forms to allow for intricate detail work, even as the surface of its body shifted. Patterns rose to cover the skin, like see-through tattoos, before it shifted.

The image changed, no longer one of the glassine in its own workshop. Now it strode through a forest, its hands—more like tentacles in the way that the fingers simply elongated to pluck a leaf from a tree and then brought it back to the main body—drifted around as the creature explored the wilderness.

Its body was that of amber glass, golden hued and beautiful, but it was protected inside of a constructed frame, one that was clearly mechanical in nature, though presumably made by a master craftsman, judging from the detail work on the bronze, titanium, and onyx of the frame.

The original prompt and warning appeared again, and I reread it.

Congratulations!

Due to your rare circumstances—unlocking the techno-arcane fusion path at a relatively high level of dungeon—you have received access to higher-form beings.

Beware: mistreatment of the Glassine Race is considered a crime across much of the galaxy!

Once that was done, I moved on, bringing up the details for the second creation I'd gained access to as part of the quest to bring down the mechanist dungeon.

Clockwork Crawler	**Construct**
A small, insect-like automaton powered by a combination of basic clockwork mechanics and minimal mana. Abilities: • Basic Scouting: Can explore and report on simple environmental details. • Rudimentary Repair: Can perform very basic maintenance tasks on mechanical objects. Summoning Cost: 20 mana to summon, 2 mana per day, 2 control points.	
Durability 5/5	Abilities: 2/2

This was the creature I'd been thinking of, as I figured creating a bunch of the glassine, a species that the system apparently revered to some degree, and then using them as bait probably wouldn't go down well.

The clockwork crawler was small, slightly smaller than my palm, which was tiny for a summoned creation. And yet, considering it was clearly based off an insectile design, was fuckin' huge as well.

The crawler that appeared and slowly revolved around in the air was impressive. A simple, triangular body, like a wedge of cheese, had been set down on its side. Two eyes were added to the top, and a disc to the bottom. From that disk sprouted four legs on either side, making it more arachnid than insectile I guessed, but fuck it.

The front two legs had grasping implements attached, and the other six ended with a ball. Last of all, on the back of the wedge, was a small basket, clearly for carrying anything it'd found.

"What the hell is that?" Jo squinted, then shook her head. "Nope, spiders give me the willies. I'm out."

"It's cute!" Ashley countered. "I mean, look at it—it's literally a tiny clockwork worker!"

"That's the point. It's a tiny thing. There's no way that London will believe that we'd transport this without a load of guards," Aly agreed.

"And that's why you need to research some more for us," I agreed, smiling at her evilly. "They had some seriously nasty shit in the dungeon. Most of them were destroyed, but a sample corpse was still brought back with us, I think. I know I meant to bring it anyway…" I looked to the others, and got shakes of the head.

"Nobody knows what happened to it?" I asked, and Kelly suddenly winced.

"Was it humanoid, but with a mass of cogs for a head?"

"Yeah, that's it!" I relaxed.

"I scrapped it for the mana yesterday," she admitted. "It was brought in and nobody knew what it was. I thought it was some crappy sculpture someone had welded up for their garden or something."

"Joy," I said flatly, then I sighed. "Okay, fuck it, we've got the dungeon shard still. When I integrate that with the dungeon, that should bring an upgrade or bonus as well…it did last time. Once that's in place, we'll know what we're working with, and we can start the ball rolling."

"Keep that for now." Aly shook her head. "If we can do it without using that, I want to keep it for emergencies. But we can talk about that later. So, these research paths…"

I settled back, knowing this was going to be a *long* conversation.

CHAPTER FIFTEEN

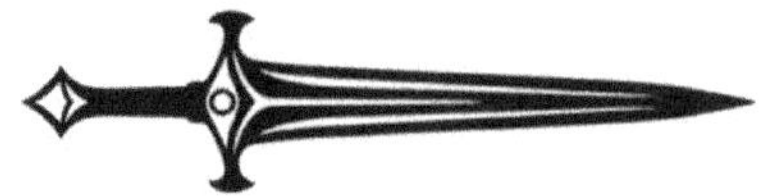

The rest of the day had been lost to the planning for the next stage, though we'd sent Catherine and Patrick to bed—separately, obviously—after another hour or so.

Catherine and Patrick had been found in the basement of a bar about twenty minutes' walk from the dungeon, once we'd started interrogating the soldiers. The ones who had been involved in that had given up the details pretty quickly.

It'd turned out that the next morning after the main battle, when I was sleeping and everyone was recovering, Catherine had sensed something nearby. She'd felt something that was very old, and guessing what it was, she'd wanted to try to communicate with some of the ancient dead.

Afterwards she'd tried to explain that something about all the masses around us on all sides had made that much harder, but she'd felt a presence and had been curious, so she'd been incredibly stupid and had followed it.

Patrick had seen her, had been curious in turn and had gone to find out what was happening. He found her in a sort of trance on the top of the local hill, called Caesar's Camp.

There was something there, a spirit that was truly ancient, she'd said, and it'd started communicating with her. Minor issue, however—the effect of communication with something that old and that long dead had knocked her out in a heartbeat. She'd been catatonic when he found her. But before he could get her back inside the dungeon's radius, a team of "local soldiers" had offered to help. He'd had no reason to be suspicious and had said yes, relieved at having others around.

Once one of them had his hands on her, a knife had been put to her throat, and Patrick was left with the option of going quietly or having her head half sawn off before he could get to her.

As she was essentially unconscious, he'd reluctantly agreed and had gone along with it, figuring he'd escape soon and tear everyone involved a new asshole.

The soldiers who had taken him and Catherine to the cellar had been part of the "special" group—it was never entirely clear whether they'd been part of the soldiers who were left behind, or whether they'd always been under Thomas—but he'd turned up and as soon as he had what he needed, they'd left them in the cellar, moving out to begin the assault.

Patrick had been chained up with some kind of metallic restraints that not only sapped his strength, but made him incredibly pliable. Although he'd planned that, as soon as he could grab her, he'd have fought his way clear, instead, once he was chained up, he simply agreed to whatever they said.

He'd been able to hold some details back, but he'd shamefacedly admitted that was mainly due to them asking shit questions rather than anything he'd done. He'd managed to not volunteer anything, but that was the best he could do.

Mike and his group simply questioned the soldiers they'd captured, and then they'd gone and got our people. Catherine, now conscious and terrified, was tied up and gagged in the corner of the cellar, and Patrick sat in a chair that was covered in the black, glistening chains, staring ahead and waiting to be told what to do next.

We'd had the pair back in the dungeon for a few hours and it'd been necessary to force Patrick to rest, almost as much as we'd had to press to have Catherine work her magic.

I'd disliked doing that a hell of a lot, considering if she wasn't watched she now tended to be drawn to whatever slumbered in the nearby hill, but we needed the information.

Now, as the second shift was taking over the dungeon, and they were hopefully resting, I stood atop the highest point of the citadel, my arms crossed on the crenelated wall that ringed the top of the cube. I stared out across the grey landscape before me.

I knew now what I needed to do: I needed to find a way to deal with London, before it derailed everything I'd damn well worked for. But I really wasn't sure about the plan we'd come up with in the end.

It made sense, but I still hated the necessity of it. Almost as much as I loved the idea of making them pay so heavily for it.

"You ready to come home yet?" Kelly walked across the rooftop from behind me, and I glanced over my shoulder at her, before smiling as I straightened.

"Yeah, sorry," I said, my voice soft. "Just thinking."

"I know." She stepped up and cuddled into me.

I wrapped my arms around her and kissed the top of her head, before staring out over the fields in front of me.

The walls had grown higher, and the citadel—because it really wasn't a cube now—was growing with them through the magic of the dungeon. Additional sections were literally summoned into being and sections were rebuilt in seconds, where they couldn't simply be extended.

The design we'd come up with before was a wall that surrounded the citadel, and then a second wall that surrounded that, creating a gated courtyard that was defensible around the base of the citadel. A space outside of that included the exit from the Euro Tunnel, making sure that anything that came out was corralled into a killing field that we controlled.

Now we were improving upon that design, extending it both higher into the air and deeper underground.

The walls were five meters-thick stone, designed to be a bitch to try to climb from both sides, extending out and overhanging the ground, and slippery as hell to prevent anyone doing as they had before—standing on one another's shoulders. Then the entrances to climb up to the top of the wall and that led up to the parapet that ran all the way around were hidden in specially designed access areas.

Those entrances could be sealed, and were moved by mechanical means, as well as purely magical, just in case. That way, anyone with the right "key" could open the passage to the top of the wall even if there wasn't enough mana to do it.

That was a real concern here, after all, as once the mana in the area had been used up, there wouldn't be much left to play with.

That was currently augmented by the crystals being brought in, and by the absorption of the thousands upon thousands of undead corpses that still littered the ground.

Once that windfall was used up, though, this dungeon was going to have issues.

That was why Clarissa and Markus were focused on increasing the dungeon's reach to the nearby towns. Once there, the resource teams could strip the buildings for mana, while a second team continued onward.

It did mean, however, that this dungeon was going to be more parasitical in nature than the others, at least at first.

There were areas a few miles away that had a much higher concentration of mana naturally occurring, and only a mile or so to the south, on the other side of the nearest town of Folkestone, was the sea, so we were focusing on extending in those directions now.

There were plans to put Water converters out there, under the ocean, replacing the now defunct sea and wind turbines of the last few years with literal water magic gatherers.

I'd finally had a conversation with Arend-Jan as well, and that, at least, was sorted.

The older man was an incredible wealth of information. According to him, everything in nature was connected in one way or another, and the magical world was the same, or so the evidence was proving now.

What he'd done in the northern dungeon had borne fruit, and then he'd replicated that in Heathrow to some degree, creating fields that essentially grew mana in direct relation to the amount inputted.

Weird as that sounded.

The mobile dungeon currently had a large secondary trailer that was to be attached, allowing its small test field to be taken with it. The next step was to be carried out as far away as possible from anyone else. Yeah, it needed a dungeon core, but for this experiment, it was worth it.

We knew that too much of a particular form of mana was bad, the delicate elemental balance needing to be kept. The shadows that had started to manifest and creep around the Newcastle dungeon, for example, when we had too many Darkness converters underground had proved that.

What he had done was start a field of converters up north, based around a single point of naturally dense mana generation.

From there, he'd set the converters out in a wheel, with Life at the northern compass point, then, moving clockwise, came Fire, Darkness, Earth, Death, Water, Light, and Air, before we were back to Life.

He'd literally made a hole at the center, where the densest possible naturally occurring mana had sparked from, and then he'd ringed it with first one of each of these, and then he'd added more.

A few meters out from the first ring, as soon as there was room, he'd created two more Life, two more Fire, Darkness, etc.

Once that ring was complete, a space was created and then three of each converter were used in the next ring. That was as far as he'd managed to go so far—the cost was insane, after all. But the plan was that after this point would come four…and it would continue out until there would be ten of each at the northern dungeon. The gaps between each ring would grow larger and larger, and then he'd start to make more converters to fill in the gaps.

Once the field was creating mana, it seemed it needed less and less input for some reason. And with only a small investment of crystals—the naturally occurring mana had started to diminish by this point, so he'd included a handful of crystals as a generation point as well—the field kept growing.

There was a lot of ambient mana around. After all, my experiments with my own mana system had proved that. The "sludge" that settled to the bottom of my mana channels as the purer elements were broken free were an example of it as well.

There was even a theory that mana had always been here, but that it was just naturally so low in purity and so bound up in shitty mixes, that the entire system had collapsed at some point in the deep past.

I called bullshit on that, but honestly? If the Tooth Fairy turned up with the Easter Bunny and started shit right now, my life couldn't get much weirder.

The mana generation seemed to be around ten percent higher than the input for the first level of the ring, and that doubled with each ring as they went onward. The exponential growth formula created a flourishing field of mana as he reached the third level of the ring.

This was fantastic, but the next stage, the one that we'd be creating far from any prying eyes?

It would start the same, but once it reached twenty of each converters in the ring, the "arms" would start.

The intention was that paths of each element would flow outward, four of the twenty would go straight ahead, then the other sixteen would twist around in a fractal pattern of four, fours. Then they would interact with the other mana forms.

Ice, as an example, would be formed and Ice converters created where the Water and Death converters flowed next to each other, and more elsewhere.

The additional growth of mana that came from the converters sucking in the ambient, free-flowing mana all around as well as the naturally generating stagnant mana, when combined with the crystals that were given as well, meant that the fields were currently generating mana at a steady rhythm, and that should only increase as time went on.

Then, the intention was that a small percentage of the overall production was rerouted back to bloom as mana crystals at the heart of the field, where it'd all began.

The theory was that due to the pattern of generation, there'd always be more mana then there had been with the last cycle, meaning that once it was established, it was self-propagating.

The best part about this was that once it was fully active, it would continue, growing until it added more mana to the world, and all of that would be sucked down to feed the heart of our dungeons.

If it worked, of course.

If it did work, though? While mobile dungeons like the dreadnought would be our battle stations, this would become the heart of our power generation.

We would be able to field great armies when we needed to, because the infrastructure was finally starting to grow at a pace that would feed it.

Arend-Jan's discovery was wonderful. It'd all come from his past as a farmer, his desire to feed the land, and to gift the crops he grew to us all, strengthening us.

They were now being nurtured by dryads, surrounded by Nature and Life converters, with Earth, Air, Fire, and Water dotted here and there in strategic locations. That created an overlapping field of beneficial effects that were, in turn, boosting the growth and efficiency of the herbs that were being grown for the dungeon.

That was where Starr had come in. The kobold was learning about cross-pollination and more from his older companion. And the Alchemical information he gained as he leveled his skills meant that they were feeding their discoveries back and forth constantly.

There were two people now who had gained classes that were helpful to this project as well—apparently, anyway. I had yet to meet them. They were a farmer and a Fire mage, weird as that last sounded.

The Fire mage had zero spells that he was willing to use offensively, but he'd always believed in razing his land at the end of the annual growing season, and his signature spell was Volcanic Regrowth.

Whatever was left on the land at the end of the year, he'd burn. And as the fallow months passed, the land would recover faster and stronger than his neighbors'.

Now, between the various mages, the dryads, and basically the magic, we had growth cycles that were almost constant, and they took around a week to pass a full season. That meant that when he took any kind of compost he could get his hands on, and spread it across the fields, before drying it out and sifting it back into the earth with his volcanic spell, he was making the fields more and more fertile each time, instead of depleting them.

I'd come up onto the roof after the meeting. Kelly and Aly had both seen the state of me, and how frustrated I was, and they'd started summoning people to get as many of the meetings out of the way in one fell swoop as possible.

Inside of an hour, I'd seen Arend-Jan and Starr, and then I'd seen Rhodes, who gave a very firm and almost abrupt breakdown of the military capacity for the dungeons. That had included a request that we find out what the hell had happened to the soldiers' families "*right fuckin' now*" or we'd be facing a mutiny. Then she'd told me I looked like shit, and that as of tomorrow, unless I had a damn good excuse, she was taking over my training again, before she'd buggered off.

Next was Alison, as apparently Sierra didn't *want* to report. Alison was our resident Sand mage, and Sierra the glassblower, and they were "having some issues."

First and foremost was that Alison wanted to find the *perfect* sand. She'd found a shitload of sand so far, ranging from builders' sand to kiddies' playpark sand and all the way to freshly broken-down sand at the coast, though that had come mixed with a load of sediment as well.

She had an affinity for sand that was frankly concerning, given that she was prone to losing herself for hours playing with the damn stuff. But there had been two bonuses for her finding her place with us.

First and foremost, as a Sand mage, even a baby one who had almost no control over her element, she could find sand like nobody's business.

Every single place that she'd pointed out in the local area that she'd loved before the fall came? A little searching—and some wading and digging by our creatures—revealed high-quality sand.

Secondly, I'd also given her the job of sorting out the gathering room. It was a production-style facility that was basic, with a small number of collection points and their attendant drones.

In this case, there were four, and I'd set them to search for certain things, then I'd forgotten about them and let them just keep going. Once I remembered, I'd told someone to sort it out, then let others set their priorities, and then I and most people had just forgotten about them all over again.

That and individuals had gone and gotten the thing they'd wanted to be collected, and then they'd buggered off with it without another thought.

The end result of that, as the control system—beyond when it was linked to my brain directly—was extremely simple, was that it just kept going.

There'd been some attempts to sort it out before, including boxes for the various things that were collected to be put in. And then the fights had come, and we'd lost a lot of people, and I'd not stopped running and fighting since.

That meant that when I took Alison in there, and asked her to "sort it out," it'd been a clusterfuck.

It'd also reeked, because one of my earlier orders had been for seeds, and then for chickens, thinking we could plant stuff, and either eat or trade the chickens.

Then, as we'd forgotten all about it, they'd just been brought back and dumped in there by the machines. The chickens had eaten the seeds and crapped everywhere and grown; they'd started to breed, and yeah...

It was a clusterfuck, like I said.

That was when Alison was given the job, and damn. She'd taken us all—through the dungeon sense—to the gathering facility and she'd shown what she'd done.

It was incredible.

She'd summoned a bunch of the undead and set them to work in clearing it first. When Aly had checked in on her, she'd decided some investment was required after all.

The more basic facility had been upgraded all the way to advanced, and by God, it'd been an improvement.

The advanced gathering system came with a total of sixteen rows, each with its dedicated drone, a conveyor belt that unloaded the materials, and a collection of storage options, along with a much more capable management system. Half of the drones were set to items that the dungeon needed: ammunition, foods, materials, that kinda shit; then the other half was set for people to add in requests.

Then the undead came into their own.

They stood silently on either side of the conveyor belts, and as the gatherers landed and disgorged their finds, the undead sorted them into boxes.

Those boxes were then sorted into the dungeon, and she'd made it so that any requests were made through a simple system that recorded the user's identity.

That way, the item, when found, could be sent to them or into storage and it was removed from the "find this" list.

There'd been a surprising amount of ammunition that had already been collected, though the majority was useless, having been recovered from places that the bullets weren't designed to be left in, such as puddles, and people who had apparently annoyed other people.

There'd also been a lot of sex toys, presumably requested by different people, given the sheer number of separate requests made to the system. Strangely, only a handful of people came forward to claim them, for some reason, meaning that handful had a whale of a time picking through and taking home a sex shop's worth of toys each.

Alison assured me she'd made great strides in that area—the setup and management of the gathering system…not the sex toy delivery business, I hoped—but only minor ones in her magic. So although she'd indeed started to "feel" the sand and could move it slightly, beyond sensing it and starting to be able to clean it, then sorting it by grades, she wasn't having much luck.

That, in turn, had created a problem with Sierra, as she was a very focused kobold, and particularly one that took her job *very* seriously.

She was the glassblower for the dungeon. She needed to make improvements on the glass we had, and she was experimenting, but the sand that she needed for these experiments was slow in coming, and even slower in being cleaned.

The impurities needed to be sorted through and removed before she could use it, and when she had a small pile, she'd absorbed that into the dungeon, before replicating it over and over again.

That took a shitload of time, though, and it was frustrating for the kobold who needed the sand literally by the ton.

It'd been absorbed in small quantities, so for whatever reason, the system was replicating it in those quantities. To scale that up took time, summoning more and more, remaking the piles and reabsorbing them into the dungeon each time.

That also, unfortunately, included the lingering impurities that Alison hadn't managed to purge yet, and Sierra was furious when her experiments failed due to those impurities.

The end result was that they weren't getting along at all, and as such, stayed clear of each other as much as possible. So when they'd been summoned to give a report, Alison had come, and because Alison was going, Sierra had stayed clear.

I gave some advice, then handed that particular problem right back to Clarissa and company, after finding out that so far there had been three highly limited successes, and around two dozen failures.

The successes included a potion bottle that was made of toughened glass, which was a massive improvement. A second was a single orb that could be imbued with a spell. It was generally weaker than the ones we had in the focal orbs we had the pattern for, and it only lasted in the orb for an hour.

Lastly, though, was a simple, yet cool invention: sapphire steel.

That was what we were calling it, anyway, because of the slight blue tinge to it.

Sierra had gained three levels for creating it, and she now had the pattern in the dungeon. It was essentially slightly cloudy, blue glass, with the strength of steel. The issue was that it couldn't be changed once it cooled, so there was no chance to shift it into a shape that was useful yet. Finn was working on a mold, with the intention of making a shitload of them if it worked, and taking the molten version and pouring it straight into there.

First of all, the sapphire steel was lighter than regular steel. Yeah, it was slightly see-through, so underwear was a requirement if it was made into armor, but it could in theory replace normal steel.

Secondly, once the shape was set and the mold had the new creation cracked out of it and absorbed, that could in turn be easily reproduced by the dungeon. And because it seemed harder than steel, Finn had all sorts of plans for next-generation tools.

I'd sent Alison away to study more and get herself back on track, as well as to take no shit from Sierra. If there were issues with Sierra in the future, she'd been told to take them up with Clarissa.

The older woman had no patience for that kind of crap, and with the help of Ashley was working to stomp such things out.

Next was the meeting with John, which was both a bit of a pain, and not.

It was a pain because he spent an hour going over phrasing of laws, which was an absolute pain in my ass, and not, as this time he just sighed when I mentioned the terrible trio, and nodded.

"It was coming either way," he agreed. "At first, and I'll be the first to admit it, it was something I was fighting against because we just don't have the death penalty in the UK, and it's for a good reason. There were too many miscarriages of justice over the years and the whole 'off with his head' thing is kinda final. No amount of sticky tape and superglue can fix it if you change your mind, after all."

"But you've gotten over that?" Kelly asked.

"Not fully. It still feels wrong, but it's also a case of two of them don't accept they did anything wrong at all. And the other, Gerald, is so weak and spineless, he went along with it. He thought he'd win so he took the chance, even knowing that it was wrong.

"That makes him slightly better than the other two in that he could possibly be redeemed, taught not to do that kinda shit in the future and so on, but honestly, it's not worth it. We'd need guards on him constantly, and the first opportunity that he saw, he'd stab us in the back again. No, I think it has to be either life imprisonment for them all—which is kinda cruel, both on them and the guards and so on who have to interact with them, and pointless. Why feed them for the rest of their lives, after all? They already contributed nothing, so it's a waste."

"Exactly as I feel." I nodded. "We'll do it tomorrow. No sense in prolonging it. You coming with me?" I asked him.

He nodded. "Where do you want to do it?"

"In their cell," I said. "There's no need to put it off, no need to hide it, but also no need to flaunt their punishment. Two of them have no more understanding that what they did was wrong than a rabid dog, and I'd not make a spectacle of killing a dog. Why should they get more consideration?"

"That's…cold." Aly glanced over at me.

"Maybe." I sighed. "It's right, though. I like animals and I'd regret killing a dog. Killing them? It's a cancer that needs to be cut out of the dungeon, that's all."

"Well, I hope it's as easy to forget," she said softly, and I nodded.

Inside, there was a lot more going on emotionally than I showed, and Kelly seemingly sensed it, reaching out and taking my hand again.

I didn't want to be in charge, let alone be the man deciding that for pissing me off and crossing me they should be executed. But on the other hand…it had to be done, and as I'd heard said before, "if not you, then who?"

"Fuck it," I muttered. "Anyway, onto more important details. So Drak is an addict on coke as well?"

"He is, and I think he's a supplier to the others too. I can't prove it yet, but someone is doing it, and he's been summoning a lot more than he needs, either for personal reasons or for experimentation."

"Then tomorrow, once the execution is done, we see him and deal with this. For now, revoke all access down to the minimal levels. He can use the doors and summon food, that's it."

"We think we've closed the other loopholes, but I'll watch him for the next few hours and see what he does." John sighed. "What's all this about you having more judges?"

"Who let that one out of the bag?" I asked curiously, before shaking my head. "Fuck it, doesn't matter. Okay. Here's what I'm thinking—tell me if it works for you. First of all, Markus is solid, stable, and I think we all trust him, right?" That got a general chorus of agreement.

"So, should you, as the high judge, be in charge of the criminal investigations as well as the trials and the laws?" I asked John. "I know I sort of am, ultimately, but we both know that I'm going to side with you ninety percent of the time because you'll have investigated and done your job, otherwise what's the point in having you do it."

"Definitely not," he said firmly. "Ideally, we need a team of investigators who can bring their findings to me, and I can rule on it, but that's not something we've got. Ideally, I'd like a second or third judge as well, so that we can each watch over each other, and maintain honesty."

"That's what I thought. My intention is that you're in charge of the laws, and that you're sort of the last court of appeal. You lead from a more overall legal standpoint, but that we put Markus in to deal with the general day-to-day things."

"Sounds good." He nodded. "He's got a level head and the people like and trust him. He's also respected as he trained a lot of the fighters early on."

"Glad we agree." I smiled. "Now, beyond that, I need to do something with the religious types, and we need to frankly stop wasting that opportunity. As such, my plan is that we have you wear a second hat, and have the Paladins report to you directly as well."

"Why?"

"Because I want them trained to bring law and order to the world again. I want to have Robin spread out, and as soon as she's strong enough—once I've trained her up a bit, admittedly—I want her building her own team. I'm thinking that the Paladins should be like they were designed to be in so many stories. Knights who could kick ass with the best of them, who bring law and order, and hunt and kill monsters. Both the human and more monstrous kind," I added at the end with a shrug.

"You'll lose them fast," he said. "I've seen the shit that's out there, and we barely survive."

"That's why I want them trained up. I'm going to give them some dedicated dungeon time each day. Maybe more," I suggested, glancing at Kelly and Aly, and getting a sigh from them both as they looked at each other.

"I could design something," Kelly said slowly.

"Better to get Markus to do it." I smiled. "He's good with weapons and he'll be able to create a small training dungeon for just them, I bet. Then they can run it again and again. Build their own teams up and practice. John gives them tests and teaches them daily, Markus watches over them overall, and the dungeon forges them.

"We send them on regular training missions—the simpler ones, at first—and then we send them out to bring some law back to the country. There's enough gangs out there that need stomping into the ground. And let's be honest—it'll bring us more control over the surrounding areas, and more people. The longer we leave the problem to grow, the worse it'll be."

"I don't like it," John said, then smiled and let loose a sigh. "It'll be good to not be on my own again, though, and the police that we're likely to encounter as we expand will be able to bring more skills to the table."

"You think we'll meet more?" Kelly asked.

He nodded. "I think the most likely survivors who are still out there are gangs, ex-police, and ex-soldiers. It'll be people who have had some training or who are more vicious who still live in most places, and that's going to provide lots of opportunities for Robin and her people to level-up, if nothing else."

"Glad we're on the same page. Can you put together a rough plan for tomorrow? Lunchtime or so? We'll sort them out and then have a meeting with Robin."

"Works for me," he agreed.

That had been the second-last meeting I'd had before I'd come up here for some fresh air and to clear my head.

The last one had been with Ashley.

She was our diplomat, courtesan, and spymaster all rolled into one. Lately she'd also taken over a pet project, dealing with a small contingent of ladies in the dungeon who seemed intent on reproducing the cast of *Mean Girls*, complete with cafeteria scenes of "you can't sit with us" and other traits.

One of that group had already been selling her skills in telling other people's skills and secrets. Her and her little clique had been the reason that Catherine had been basically ostracized before she was brought along with us for the mission, and Ashley was kicking their arse and forging them into a viable tool for the dungeon.

Their little leader "Xanthia"—or, as I'd found out she'd been born, *Sarah*—was following Ashley about like a puppy whenever she was given the chance now.

She'd been the ringleader of the group, and a mean little shit, who could see glimpses of the future and identify aspects of people's classes. She'd not told anyone before we started digging and found out though, and had been using her power on anyone she felt like.

As she'd been hiding the fact she'd achieved a class from those who were teaching her and using it on her fellow students, Ashley had no issue using her own powers on her, and putting her in her place.

I'd had to meet the little group before setting off to come south, and I'd done it with the oath stone in hand, binding the fuckers to the dungeon, then having them swear to obey me, Kelly, then Ashley, and those she put over them.

In one respect, that wasn't a particularly onerous task for them. Ashley had Xanthia scanning people as they came and went inside the dungeon, and she'd already proved her worth when the assassins tried to get inside the Newcastle dungeon.

She'd seen what they were there for, had reported them, and they'd been dead inside of a minute. She was also required to listen to Ashley's right- and left-hand girls, Emma and Jenn.

Jenn, being who she was, insisted that they help people, that they look out for those who needed a shoulder to cry on, and she and they were markedly helping to lower the suicide rate.

The downside—for them—was that they were also required to listen to Emma, and Emma had adopted Catherine at Ashley's and my request.

That meant that Emma's beliefs were now their guiding mantra, and one of them was that a healthy body housed a healthy mind. In Emma's case, it was also so that she could manipulate the dafter sex a lot more easily, but that wasn't the point.

As such, Xanthia and her friends were all now required to do full military-style PT every day. Ashley had been unable to keep the smile from her face when she told me about her plan to spend some time in the morning with Emma, Jenn, and Catherine, somewhere they could be easily seen by the little group, and having a version of "high tea" as they discussed their next plans.

Preferably while the trainees collapsed from exhaustion with their expensive makeup ruined with sweat.

I'd liked that. After all, "play silly games; win silly prizes" was a firmly held belief of mine at times. But still, I was glad when it was all done.

It sounded like everything was in hand at last—with the general dungeon, anyway—and I could finally get back to my favorite pastime, namely chasing Kelly around the bedroom and trying to break our bed.

CHAPTER SIXTEEN

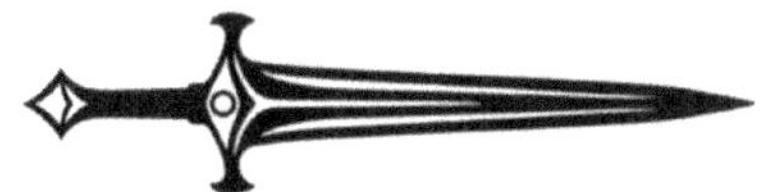

The night had gone *very* well—for me and Kelly, anyway—and when I finally woke the next morning, it was to a very hot mouth around a sensitive area.

I stared at the ceiling for a while, just enjoying it, before pulling the blanket back and appreciating the view as well as the feeling.

Then, seeing that I was awake, she moved around so that we could both enjoy ourselves and look after the other's needs, and the next two hours were spent in the best kind of a morning routine.

A kiss and a cuddle followed by a long shower, breakfast, and then I was off for a meeting with the religious nutjobs. We spent most of it thrashing out some ground rules—no fucking genuflecting was a biggie that I insisted on—and then we started with the overall plan.

It was one that Rhodes was at first pissed about, because I'd drafted her in for it, and then she, being the evil drill sergeant she was at heart, fully embraced.

There were to be two paths into the religious side of the Pantheon of the Storm, or at least my side of it. First: the priesthood.

Now, most people think of the priesthood as a bunch of guys who walk around and generally complain when anyone has been having fun things like pre-marital sex, and they dodge taxes like nobody's business.

That was certainly the impression I had of the priesthood growing up, anyway.

Our priests were to be very different. They were to be *warrior* priests, with two very firm paths open to them: they were to be healers of the sick and to work to help our people, meaning they joined forces with them and assisted as they worked. A kind of healer and union official combined. Or they were warriors entirely.

Both kinds were expected to pursue their classes, spread the word of the dungeon, which was that we're all in this shit together and to help each other, and we'd figure things out as we went, basically.

The difference between the Warriors of the Storm, as we'd be calling them, and the Priesthood of the Storm, was that the priests would be focusing on healing magic, and spending their non-fighting and training time working to help people adjust to the new world and working on theological and law issues.

The warriors would be given additional training in the dungeons, and they'd be pushed *hard*. They'd not be doing the general soldier duties though as hopefully, eventually we'd migrate and retrain the entire army up to speed. Instead, my plan was that we'd end up with a specialist warrior knighthood from that group, with them getting specific ranks that would integrate with the army as well.

The most elite of them would then be inducted into the Paladins, and the Paladins would form a sort of combined monster hunter and law-bringer class.

They'd also be available to smite the shit out of our enemies. And as they'd be slowly migrating to a traveling and exploring role, they'd bring more people to us, but be available to form the solid steel core of the army when the big fights came.

It also helped that if we could bring about this kind of a military structure, when we met other groups and the Paladins rocked up in their full-on top-level armor, smiting entire gangs singlehandedly and then moving on, it'd create a situation where once word spread, we'd have people in the thousands begging to join us.

That done, and a quick meeting with Finn later—he wanted us to make sure the glassine were summoned into the dungeon ASAP and then added to his cadre of crafters, which I didn't really give two fucks about, but agreed on the condition that he also summon a few dvorks to see what they managed as well—and then I was free, more or less.

I say more or less because all the smaller shitty jobs that I was willing to deal with myself were then out of the way, leaving only a trip to visit our allies, and to deal with London.

We'd received a messenger near the end of the conversation with Finn that a contingent from London was approaching, and they wanted to discuss the situation "before it gets out of hand."

I think, considering the whole "assaults and kidnapping" situation, that they were expecting nuclear war as an escalation, so yeah.

I agreed, and sent their messenger back—intact, though I was tempted to send just his head—with a message that they weren't to approach within one mile of the dungeon, and that I'd meet their representative at the Lord Whisky Animal Sanctuary.

It was about three miles from the dungeon, on the edge of a forest and not somewhere I'd ever visited. But when I was poring over a map, looking for somewhere that I could make them uncomfortable, and yet close enough that I could get there first, it stood out.

The forest that basically encircled it was the main reason I picked it.

They were bringing a small military force—small by the realities of the nation's former army, which meant it was a tiny force by the standards of say, the American army. But this was to be a real concerted effort by the London lot, I was guessing.

That meant that they'd be bringing *real* special forces, not the knockoff assholes who had currently tried and failed to stab us in the back.

Realistically, that meant that they'd have elites who were probably at least my equal in terms of raw lethality. But where I'd been an IT engineer before all of this, they'd been creeping through the night and slaughtering entire elite military units.

The difference between the US military and the UK one was primarily one of funding, though numbers had a quality all their own. They had a fuckload more money, which meant that if we wanted to have any elites in comparison to those much bigger nations, we had to do it on training, and sheer fucking madness.

That was why members of the SAS and similar British units often ended up as trainers to the elite military units around the world. They were small units compared to many, but by the gods, they got the job done.

That meant that if anyone was going to have that level of unit in the field, unfortunately, it was going to be the wankers I needed to face now.

As such, I could either try to compete with them on the same level, and pretty much empty the dungeon of all its best—and possibly lose them if this went badly…

Or I could be *sneaky*.

The site was picked because it was going to fuck with their heads as much as possible. The Whisky Sanctuary was on the inside of a sort of an F-shaped wood, when seen from above. The much bigger side was to the west, rising up and then curling around, with a field in the middle, the sanctuary looking out across it.

There was a second wooded area to the east of the field, and I'd given the contact strict instructions that they were not to deploy *any* of their forces into that wood, or I'd take it as an act of aggression.

Instead, we'd meet at the animal sanctuary with no more than five on their side, and we'd discuss the situation.

My plan was to go the fuck alone entirely, but with a team a mile or so to the east in the village of Elham. They were a real emergency team, and yeah, it was mainly my team that would be there, with Mike and the others, armed to the teeth and ready for bear.

The reason they were so far away was simple. I was fucking with the incoming group's heads. Telling them to stay out of that forest practically guaranteed that some of the most elite scouts would be focused there.

They'd have to know why they were being kept out of it, and when they couldn't find anything, in a world of magic, the paranoia would be fucking incredible.

That there simply wasn't anything there to be found was going to be dismissed—I hoped—as ridiculous. Why keep them out if that was the case?

Then, they'd be watching the forest all around them as well, determined that nobody would come alone to the meeting after everything that had happened unless they were mad.

Admittedly, we'd taken the time to make sure of some more mortars and shoulder-mounted rocket launchers, that they were safe to use and *should* work, and we'd armed a bunch of the undead with them.

They would be hidden in a U-shaped collection of trees between the far side of the meeting point and the small town of Elham.

That way, if they tried to jump me, the undead would pound them with long-range fire and I'd run for it back to my team.

I was hoping that all these things combined would keep the Londoners off-balance enough that they would make a deal, but there wasn't much more that I could do in the short term.

I also intended to bluff horrifically.

Needless to say, nobody *liked* my plan, but they also didn't have a better one, so we went with it in the end. The meeting was set for six hours' time. That was basically enough time for us to get our people into position, barely, so it didn't leave them much of an opportunity to scout the area out and lay any traps.

It also gave me just enough time to summon the new creations I needed, and put that dickhead Thomas in a body bag, burn his corpse a little so he was recognizable but still damaged enough for my plan.

That done, I got my arse into gear, flew in, dropped the clockwork crawlers off, and dumped him in the parking lot in the middle of the asphalt, then had a little wander around the place in my shiny new armor, looking suitably lethal and mysterious.

Catching a glimpse of myself in a reflection, I stopped and stared. The sheer otherworldly weirdness of the armor froze me in place.

The outer layer was intricate and shifted like it was almost liquid metal, and yet…it was solid.

I knew it was—the fucker was a pain in the ass to put on. I'd needed three attempts before I could set off, the layers were that complicated. They interlocked, with impact-spreading sections that were apparently inspired by crumple zones on a car.

The heaviest sections were made to collapse if enough force was used, spreading the impact through a metallic gel layer. Then they could be replaced as soon as I was back into the reach of the dungeon again.

I looked the shit, though—seriously intimidating—and as the clockwork crawlers let loose distant whistles, sounding like the local birds but going up in a set pattern, I knew my "guests" were arriving.

First came the scouts. I didn't know exactly how many, but there were at least ten from the whistles. They spread out, moving slowly through the trees.

Then, in the distance, came a monstrosity of a truck. The cab was old and the body relatively new. An accompanying small group of riders on motorcycles approached, saw me waiting, then broke off, letting a single figure draw closer, while the truck held back.

"Hello!" he called, pulling up on his bike a dozen meters away, and leaving it idling as he took his helmet off. The gravel under his boots crunched as he put the stand down, and waited. "Can you understand me?" he tried again after a few seconds.

In response, I pointed to the body bag that lay between us.

He glanced at it, then at me. He slowly got off his bike and moved over, unzipping it and opening the flap; he saw the body, then zipped it back up, before looking at me.

"Is that supposed to be someone I know?" he called, and I nodded slowly.

"Three times, we've tried to negotiate in good faith with you. The first time, your representative attacked us, and I sent his body back to you with a message to do better. The second time, that body at your feet and his friends came skulking into my base, and murdered my people.

"The first time, I gave you a chance to do better," I repeated. "The second time, you attacked my people, not only me, and we killed them all. You and your people are no longer welcome within one mile of my sites, on pain of death. This is the last time I will try to negotiate with you, so I suggest you *do better*!"

The last words came out of my mouth with a bitterness I didn't even try to hide.

"I don't know who he is, and this is the first time an official envoy of the British government has been involved. They're in the vehicle behind me. So I don't know who you've spoken with before, but they didn't attack you on the orders of the government."

"They swore they were official representatives each time, so what makes you different?" I asked.

"We're here where you wanted to meet," he called back. "Do you agree to meet with the representatives, unarmed, and swear to their safety?"

"No."

"What?"

"No, I won't be fucking unarmed. You attacked me twice when I was, and I killed your people, so no, I won't be fucking unarmed this time. They want to talk? Go get them."

I turned my back on them and walked toward the small collection of buildings behind me, shoving down my annoyance and looking for somewhere out of the gaze of snipers to have this chat.

I had no doubt there were a collection of them out there with the scouts.

He hesitated, then rode back to the truck, and had a brief conversation. Then the truck drove forward, disgorging four more people.

The five moved inside, finding me in a barn-like structure that had clearly been used to house and exercise animals at some point.

There was a lingering smell of shit, though no animals remained. I had picked it deliberately—a soldier wasn't going to give two shits about it, but any official government-type representative was probably going to hate it.

I was apparently partly right. As they entered, two in clean pressed suits looked around in dismay.

The barn wasn't that old, probably an older structure that had been redone more recently. Certainly the white-painted walls looked to be older, dressed stone, with a more recently replaced roof of painted steel and aluminum overhead.

The floor was a mixture of sand and what felt like rubber, and mixed in with it all around was horse shit, trampled in, with more sand thrown atop it, until someone had apparently given up, and the horses had escaped through a damaged gate on the far side of the building.

It meant that there was a good breeze running through, and where I stood in the middle of the room, there was no way to approach me without having to cross the shitty mixture.

It was childish, and I knew it, but they did it, coming to a halt before me and in the main walkway, staring up at me with fake smiles.

There were three men and two women. One of the men was the earlier soldier from the motorcycle, an energetic-looking mid-thirties guy with close-cropped hair showing beneath a maroon beret.

The parachute regiment then—elite, but not to the same level as the SAS. More likely to be mad than an average soldier, though, as what kind of a guy jumped out of a perfectly good plane by choice?

The next man was shorter, in his mid to late fifties, wearing a full military uniform. A collection of salad bars on his chest suggested he'd either been a military hero for most of his life…or he'd been collecting participation trophies all the way.

One look at his eyes, and the steel-hard gaze, said more likely the former than the latter. This wasn't a man to fuck with. Despite myself, I nodded in respect.

The woman was hard-faced, grim demeanor, with a short bob of blonde hair, minimal makeup and dressed in a seriously well-ironed pantsuit. Her glare as her high heels sank into the shitty mix on the ground was a thing of beauty.

Unfortunately, both she and the next in line were well-known career politicians before the fall—practically interchangeable in their backdoor deals and general untrustworthiness—and I disliked them intensely.

The man…him I distrusted most of all on sight. He was friendly, jovial, and affable. And considering I'd just greeted him with the body of one of his fucking people, I knew straightaway how much of this was an act.

He offered his help to the fifth member of the group, clearly chosen primarily for her appearance: a doe-eyed, buxom, and innocent-looking woman in a smart suit, with just enough makeup and the right outfit to stand out in any crowd.

I also felt the subtle touch of a glamour, much as Ashley had.

Examining them, I smiled behind my helmet, noting that not one of them had a clue on the details I could see, or there was no chance they'd have come before me so happily. The woman was the first, as she was the most subtle and yet clear threat.

Sarah-Jane Moffet	Human
Sarah-Jane made a career out of using her feminine wiles even before the fall, working her way up the ladder, and then up and down various bosses, until she replaced them. A believer in "come the moment, come the man," she is firmly convinced her time has come, and intends to remove all those who stand in her way. A career manipulator, she stands in the shadows, using her abilities to maintain a believable screen around her of disposable tools. HP: 250/250 Stamina: 398/400 Mana: 500/500 Fear: 3/10 Level: 14	
HP 250/250	Special Abilities:?/?

I glanced at the male politician next. He held the arm of the courtesan and helped her across the mess, despite the fact that she was clearly more stable than the older military man by his side. Examining him brought the details I knew were coming from seeing him on the TV and in election reels.

Alexander Johnstone	Human
Alexander is a career politician, with a politician's standard survivability trait: the ability to bend over backward for whoever is useful, and yet backstab them as soon as their use is ended. The only way that he stands out	

is that when he encountered any kind of moral choice, he took the one that benefited him, without even the pretense of considering the effect on others. After making it to the top of the political ladder, then falling from power due to his own incompetence, he somehow believes it is his God-given right to ascend again…this time to remain there. HP: 400/400 Stamina: 149/150 Mana: 100/100 Fear: 5/10 Level: 11	
HP 400/400	Special Abilities:?/?

Next to him, the female politician was next, and she was also easily recognized.

Elspeth Trust	Human
Where others have risen in the political world through skill, manipulation, or bribery, Elspeth is rare in that she has none of these redeeming features. Her one ability is a diamond-hard conviction in herself that only she is right, and eventually her opponents simply give in, as she believes they should. However, despite her closely held beliefs that it's because of the solid arguments she provides, it's simply a case of her opponents eventually giving up, often deciding that if she has made it this far, then there is little hope for the species. HP: 400/400 Stamina: 524/550 Mana: 80/80 Fear: 1/10 Level: 17	
HP 400/400	Special Abilities:?/?

The general was next, and although he at least seemed more human than the others, he was clearly dangerous as well.

Reginald Blackstone	Human
General Blackstone is a career military man, having climbed the ranks through a combination of strategic brilliance and political savvy. His weathered face tells the story of countless battles, both on the field and in the corridors of power.	

Although he presents a facade of honor and duty, beneath lies a cunning mind that sees people as chess pieces in a grand game of global dominance. In the post-fall world, Blackstone views himself as the last bastion of order, willing to make the hard decisions others shy away from. His unwavering belief in the greater good makes him both a formidable ally and a dangerous enemy. HP: 550/550 Stamina: 450/450 Mana: 200/200 Fear: 4/10 Level: 22	
HP 550/550	Special Abilities:?/?

The soldier was last.

James "Hawk" Hawkins	Human
Captain Hawkins earned his nickname for his keen eyesight and predatory instincts on the battlefield. A decorated veteran of multiple conflicts, he's found a new purpose in the post-fall world. Although outwardly loyal to the chain of command, Hawkins harbors a growing disillusionment with the political machinations he's witnessed. His combat experience has honed his survival instincts to a razor's edge, making him equally dangerous with or without a weapon. Though he presents as a dutiful soldier, there's a calculating mind behind those vigilant eyes, always assessing, always planning for contingencies. HP: 480/480 Stamina: 600/600 Mana: 150/150 Fear: 5/10 Level: 19	
HP 550/550	Special Abilities:?/?

Knowing that he was clearly pissed with the others, despite the impression he gave of a loyal soldier, was interesting, and I nodded to myself.

"Ah, there you are!" Alexander said cheerily. "So good of you to meet us, and such an interesting place to have the meeting! A horseman at heart, eh? I know that feeling. Loved horses myself, have a few still, and I always find comfort around them! Something about the smell that just brings back happy memories, eh?!" He was still holding Sarah-Jane's arm, but dropped it as they got close enough, reaching out a hand and clearly expecting me to take it.

Annoyingly, the instinct was ingrained deep enough that I did. The click as the fingers of my gauntlet touched, gripping his hand, rang out, and his eyes widened as he felt the cool metal.

"Marvelous craftsmanship!" He tried to turn my hand to better see and I released his, pulling back, only to have Elspeth reaching out in his place.

"Elspeth Trust," she declared, forcing a smile that was supposed to look friendly, but reminded me more of a bulldog pissing on a thistle.

"Oh!" The other chimed in, slapping his temple theatrically with one hand. "Where are my manners! Johnstone! Alexander Johnstone!"

I nodded, taking Elspeth's hand, then yanking my hand free when she, too, tried to examine my gauntlet.

Unlike Johnstone, who plastered a fake smile on his face and pretended not to notice when I'd done it to him, she scowled at me.

"General Blackstone," the general announced.

But before he could say anything else, I took his hand perfunctorily. "I'm aware. Reginald Blackstone, Sarah-Jane Moffet, and Hawk Hawkins." I nodded to them each in turn, seeing the looks on their faces as they reevaluated me.

"Well, you have us at a disadvantage, sir!" Johnstone eventually forced a smile, clearly wondering about the source of my intelligence on them.

The joke was on them, as I'd personally love to know why some targets of the Examine brought back virtually nothing and others brought back a wealth of information.

"Indeed. Are you going to share your name?" Trust asked waspishly.

"Why bother? You have it already, as well as an incomplete dossier on me." I gambled that they would have. After all, those who had come so far knew my damn name already. It wasn't like Mike hadn't told them when we were making the deal.

"Ah…ah, quite so." Johnstone forced another beaming smile to his face, then ruffled his hair, and looked around in clownish confusion. "There doesn't seem to be anywhere to sit, though, so perhaps we could go elsewhere?"

"Here is fine," I said coldly.

Before I could say anything else, Sarah-Jane stepped forward, pointing to the damaged door that was letting in a cold breeze. "Perhaps we could go…oooh!" She theatrically stumbled, reaching out to me, falling forward.

Had I not been watching for something similar, I'd have been caught out.

As it was, after a lot of conversations with Ashley, I knew that many of her abilities were touch based, and although the "glamour" worked at a distance, the really powerful abilities, to trigger real emotions and to manipulate, came from touching the target or being close enough to force them to inhale a scent-based attack.

The one thing that Ashley had drummed into me over and over again was to never let someone with her skill set touch me.

I'd been waiting for her to make an attempt, and I stepped back smoothly, watching her dispassionately as she fell.

She hit the ground, catching herself with horseshit on her knees and right hand. For a second, I saw through the mask as naked fury filled her eyes, then she was gasping and apologizing to everyone.

Hawk was the first to her side, helping her up and glaring at me, while Trust sneered at her in contempt. The general glared at me as well, and he spoke up grimly.

"No gentleman, eh?" he declared.

"No," I agreed, looking at him. "Although I'd like to think I'd have helped if it'd been genuine. But either you know precisely what her powers are, or you're a victim of them. Either way, I'm not letting her within an arm's reach of me."

There was silence at that, and I turned back to Sarah-Jane.

"I'll make this clear. First of all, I have powerful resistances to your abilities, but I see no reason to test it. Try to touch me again or use your glamour on me, and I'll remove your head."

"Sir!" Johnstone thundered. "How dare you speak so to a lady!"

I glanced from her to his red-faced open anger and back to her again. "So, you've gotten him under your control easily enough, but that's fine. I never expected much sense from him, and he was in the papers enough for a pretty face that you must have seen him for an easy mark as well."

"Who didn't?" Trust sneered, looking at Johnstone with contempt, and shooting another evaluating glance at Sarah-Jane. "Well, you've clearly done your homework, so, shall we be serious, and dispense with the foolishness?"

"I'd always rather that," I agreed, before pointing at Johnstone. "So, the body outside in the car park is one of this man's higher-paid thugs. He led a team to assault me and my people, and destroyed the dungeon core when he couldn't get it out of my base."

That brought silence, as well as the others looking from me to Johnstone, who'd gone white.

"What?" Johnstone bluffed after a few seconds, looking around and trying to pretend he had no clue. "Destroyed the core? What does that even mean?"

"He was one of his?" Trust zeroed in on that.

"Can you prove it?" the general asked, while Hawk still stared at Sarah-Jane with a slightly dazed look on his face, until she pulled her arm free, brushing at her clothes as they watched me.

"I don't need to," I said to the general. "If you have a single nethermancer in your ranks, you'll be able to question him yourself. If not, no doubt you'll have other means. Regardless, I don't need to prove myself to you."

"Nethermancer? What's that? And what's this about a core?" Trust snapped. "Explain yourself."

"The core is what runs the dungeon. It's the heart," I said coldly. "That piece of shit tried to capture the core that I'd brought here to trade with you. Each dungeon has a core, but they can only be moved when they're inactive. Trying to move them when active results in an explosion and a lot of dead people, not to mention a dying dungeon.

"Thanks to your assault—and yes, don't try to deny it; a nethermancer, for your information is someone who can question the dead, so it was ridiculously easy to tie you to this—we now have neither a dungeon core to trade you, nor a working dungeon here." I pointed at Johnstone again.

"What?" Trust screeched. "I don't believe you!"

"I. Don't. Care," I ground out. "Again, I don't *need* to convince you. As far as I'm concerned, you're oath-breakers and murderers already. I don't care what you think."

"Perhaps we could take this back a step and discuss this as adults, without the theatrics and games?" the general suggested, and I hesitated, then nodded. "There has to have been at the very least a staffroom or canteen here. How about we adjourn to there and sit down? Then we can see how we move past this point."

"Agreed," I said after a brief pause.

"Perhaps you could help me, Captain?" Sarah-Jane suggested, looking confused, before she turned to me. "I'm sorry, sir. I don't know what you fear I've done. I'm just a governmental aide, a civil servant."

"Then why are you here?" I asked.

"To see what we could do to help you," she said earnestly. "We want to bring you and your people into the safety of the capital as soon as possible, and I studied logistics…" She blinked up at me. The look on her face as she made herself as innocent appearing as possible made me waver for a second, until I felt the tiny prickle of mana around me.

"Remember what I just told you?" I asked her almost conversationally, before reaching over my shoulder and drawing my longsword from its specially designed sheathe.

Finn had done magic with that. No matter the awesomeness of the rest of the armor, the sheath on my back was my favorite part. The sides of it folded closed on the blade when it was pressed in place like the sides of a zipper, and then folded outward when I yanked on it. The entire length opened outward like it'd been unzipped, meaning no more clumsy yanking and repositioning as I drew the sword free.

I loved it, and as I brought the blade around to rest on my hand, she backed up quickly.

"Last time offered." I said it simply. "Use those abilities around me again and I'll remove your fucking head."

She opened her mouth to say something, and I shook my own.

"No, better that you don't try to speak. In fact, get her the fuck out of here, or I'll be viewing you all for bringing her, as her allies." I looked at the general before going on.

"I'm willing to talk, but I've had all of this shit that I'll take. I've been attacked twice, and just had an inexperienced Courtesan class use her ability to try to manipulate me. If it wasn't a case of me trying to find a solution to this clusterfuck, I'd have killed you all already. So, tell me, General, am I being unreasonable, given all that has happened so far?"

"We only have your word for what has happened," he rumbled after a brief pause, reaching up and smoothing his long mustache. "But if what you've said is true, from your point of view at least, then you are showing remarkable forbearance."

"Thank you." I inclined my head, freezing as he went on.

"Of course, from my point of view, you took our aid, executed those sent to collect the payment, claimed that others who are currently unidentified were assassins, dumped their bodies and are refusing to pay again. Finally, you've threatened an unassuming member of my group…a lady, at that."

"Then we've got a lot to unpack, haven't we." I turned my back on them and strode out of the damaged doors and into the early afternoon.

It was cold. The shallow puddles that had formed out here were clearly the result of lots of passes by the large tires of farm machinery back when they were working; now they were filled with ice and hardened with frost.

I led the way to the main "homely" building, an old farmhouse with a No Entry sign on it on one side, passing through what had once been a lovingly tended little garden, and what was now an overgrown and semi-frozen mess.

The door was locked, but as high as my strength was now, there was barely a pause before it opened to my shove. The lock splintered as it broke free, and I strode in. On the right, I passed a front office. Then, left and right as I moved down the short corridor, were a small collection of rooms filled with various veterinary paraphernalia and a jam-packed room full of boxes and random rubbish. Finally, I stopped as I got to the kitchen.

It was an old farmhouse kitchen that had clearly been renovated to a more commercial standard. The stone was covered around the main working areas in a form of easily cleanable plastic sheeting, the benches were mainly steel, and the oven—an old Aga—stood silent and cold.

There was a simple wooden table in the corner, though, and six chairs around it, which at first seemed almost overly convenient…until I realized that was the standard. All the tables of a certain size I thought I'd ever seen came with six chairs. I moved to the far side, sitting down on one of the old chairs, and barely catching myself on the wall behind as it creaked, splintered, and gave way beneath my weight.

That, of course, fucked the whole aura of deadly grace I'd been carefully cultivating. But at least I'd managed to brace myself on the wall, and not fall flat on my arse.

I sighed as I stood and moved back, leaning against the wall, and gestured to the seats for the others.

"They're clearly not going to support me, so you have them," I offered.

The general, after a quick-to-vanish smile, took his seat in the middle. Johnstone unhappily took the seat on his right and Trust on his left, all three facing me.

Hawk stood in the doorway, clearly sweating and glancing from the way we'd just come to me and the others, then back again, as the Courtesan had vanished.

"It'll wear off," I said abruptly to him. "I know it probably feels weird as fuck right now, though. Let me guess, you want to help her, to do whatever makes her happy, right?"

"I…" He straightened at a glance from the general. "My apologies, General."

"Don't." I looked at the general. "Don't judge him on anything that happened around her. The abilities of those I've met before are frankly terrifying, and they play on the person you are. For him…" I glanced at Johnstone then snorted. "If the stories are anything to go by, she probably simply seduced him, or made him think that he'd managed to seduce her."

He glared at me.

"Now you wait just one minute…" he started hotly as Trust chortled in amusement.

"Truth is she probably never let him anywhere near her. Instead, she made him *think* she had, and that was it. If there was anyone else involved at all, she probably made him think it was her."

"I….what?" He broke off, confused.

"What, you think in this new world, you still have enough power to get pretty girls into your bed that easily?" I snorted. "She'd probably brought in witnesses when you were in a trance, had them all watch you. Probably made you do party tricks for the crowd."

There was a long moment as he stared at me before shaking his head and sitting up straighter, as the real man behind the act came out.

"Very good," he said slowly. "You nearly had me there."

His accent, which had been joking and a little buffoonishly slurred before, suddenly sharpened as he talked, the private school enunciation and debate lessons making their mark as he stared at me.

"I take it we've decided to drop the act then?" I asked him, and he glared at me. "Good."

"So, you made some serious accusations." The general tapped his fingers on the table to draw my attention back to him. "Would you like to start there? Then, when you've had your say, we will have ours, and we will see where the middle ground can be reached."

"That works." I laid out the basic details as they happened, including their attempts to take our vehicles when we approached the first FOB and the deal that we offered, the lateness of their arrival, and then the attack by their man Peterbilt.

Following that came the retreat of their forces, the attack by Thomas, and the deaths, adding in some bullshit about our core being attacked and destroyed, then the questioning by our nethermancer—I was careful not to name her—and then this meeting where they'd brought someone as dangerous as Sarah-Jane to try to gain an advantage over me.

"An interesting set of circumstances, and I can understand that you feel aggrieved by this, so let's look at things from another point." The general paused as I held up my hand to interrupt him.

"Just to stress one thing as well. Please don't try any bullshit about me or mine owing you anything or any kind of responsibility or debt because of the past inclusion of my lands in the United Kingdom. You and yours abandoned us when the fall came, and what we fought for and took is ours, so don't go there."

"Well. There are many points of view," he said after a brief pause. "Perhaps—"

"I disagree," Trust declared firmly. "There is a responsibility involved here. The nation must secure its heart first, as without London there is no nation. Once that had been secured, we began sending out parties to bring safety and security to our people. You might believe that you have been wronged, but as a citizen of the United Kingdom, you have benefited all your life from our actions. You cannot declare today that you're free of all obligations, especially not when you use our equipment, bought and paid for by us, and…"

"I killed the soldier who bore this gun," I said. "He was controlled by a creature called a coronaught, and was spreading an infection that turned people in their thousands into slaves, just like him. I was crushed, poisoned, burned by acid and more, and that was one fucking fight," I said coldly, straightening up and glaring at her.

"I have fought hundreds before and after that. My people and I destroyed undead armies as they rose; we fought a Roman fucking legion, and I rescued people from slavers, from being sacrificed as a source of power. I gave succor and fucking safety to people in *my* dungeon that you abandoned, and your local government assholes tried to lead a rebellion and throw me out of my own dungeon!

"You want to know where they are now? They're in my prison. And had you not turned up and interrupted my day, they'd already be executed. Once I'm done here, they will be. And no, I won't be discussing that with you. I'm telling you so that you understand, as far as I'm concerned, you're a bunch of failures and cowards.

"Everything that I've built, *everything* that I've achieved is despite you fuckers abandoning your responsibilities and abandoning the North, as you always do, so don't fucking test me, Trust. Even the army hid, staying inside their barracks while normal fucking people had to fight off the slavers.

"That I'm here *at all*, instead of totally fucking ignoring you, or leading my own forces over your walls and taking London from you should be seen as me showing incredible restraint. So be very careful what your next words are, you useless sack of shit." It'd come out in a rush. The anger that drove the words made it very clear where I stood, and the looks on their faces made it clear they knew it as well.

"The final point, before you start back on your point of view and trying to make me believe that you're the good guys and just misunderstood, is that I *know*." I glared at the two politicians. "I KNOW the Cinthians tried to negotiate with you, and you fucking stabbed them in the back and caused all of this."

Alexander looked confused at that, but Trust went white, staring back at me.

"You." I nodded grimly. "Fuck me, now it all makes sense. You were directly involved, weren't you?"

"I don't… I don't know what you're talking about," she stammered, before swallowing hard and refusing to speak any more.

"Elspeth?" Alexander asked slowly. "What is this?"

"They came and tried to negotiate first. They offered technological aid that could have raised us up, but when 'our leaders' saw what they were offering, they tried to rip them off, didn't you? You took the fucking offered toys, and you tried to look after number one, as you always do. And now *this* is the result! They inflicted the change and the fall of fucking mankind on us all, because you wouldn't help anyone but yourself. So yeah, the North is mine, as is the base I have at the Euro Tunnel. You'll keep your fucking grubby little mitts off it, or I'll detonate them before I'd let you take them."

"It seems we have a lot to discuss…" the general said slowly, before clearing his throat, and looking from Trust to me. "You said that you'd had contact with an army barracks. I wonder, have you heard anything about the Otterburn Garrison? Or Catterick?"

He said it casually, but the look in his eyes told me it was anything but.

"Yeah," I said flatly. "Catterick is lost. Something is inside and kills anything that enters. No survivors. So I'll probably have to clean that out personally at some point, as it's not like anyone else fucking will. And Otterburn? Yeah." We looked at each other for a long time before I spoke again. "We disposed of what was under that base, and cleaned the area."

There was a twitch in the eye at that, before a slight nod of the head at me not saying what we both knew I'd found. "The area is clear?" he asked. "The soldiers?"

"They're recovering," I said. "They swore allegiance to me and mine after I rescued them. They're being healed and retrained now, though they're insanely pissed at what was found, and how easily the entire area would have been lost if we hadn't done what we did."

"That's a risk, unfortunately, that was decided by those higher than myself." The general flicked his eyes at Johnstone and Trust.

"Regardless, some decisions were made by our predecessors that may be viewed as foolish, given what we know now, but we deal with the world as it is, not as we'd like it to be," Johnstone said after a few seconds of silence. "As you pointed out before, however, there were regrettable delays in our forces reaching you to offer aid—delays *we* could not do anything about—but we did offer that aid…" The emphasis on "we" had been clear as he casually threw anyone and everyone under the bus there.

"And we lost a great many of our very limited armed forces defending you, which is something that I feel we can all agree on. Is that fair?" he finished, painting a look of sadness and regret on his face. "They were brave men and women who went to fight in a battle that wasn't theirs to face, and still they gave their lives."

"It would be fair, except for a few little details that you're glossing over," I said coldly. "The fight was against the Pantheon of Unlife. They want to convert all of you to corpses, and use those corpses as they see fit. Finding London on the way past, they'd have rolled over your walls and slaughtered each and every one of you…so there alone, you should be thanking us for letting you get away with so few casualties."

"They wouldn't have been coming here if you'd not started a war with them!" Trust snarled. "We know the truth!"

"The truth?" I quirked an eyebrow that was unseen behind my helmet. "Yeah, as long as you consider that the reason I was in a war with them in the first place is that one of their members was killing people up north. We stopped their army as it was marching south! We faced them, while the army hid in its barracks." I shot the general a glare. "We, a bunch of fucking civilians and a handful of soldiers who had been passing through, faced tens of thousands of undead. We lost hundreds of our people, and because we triumphed, because we killed the shitehawk, the rest of the Pantheon declared war on us."

"So, we agree that you started this war." Trust smiled thinly, as if that was a point she'd earned.

"If that's all you got from all I said? Fuck it, I'm done with you." I sighed, shaking my head. "Look, we've barely begun, and already it's clear there's nothing but point scoring going on. We defended ourselves, and we defeated an army. Then we came down here and defeated the greatest army that's ever set foot in the nation. We did that with minimal help from you. And because that help came late and in smaller numbers than was agreed, more of our people died than needed to."

"We sent the forces that could be spared," the general said. "There are other threats in the area beyond those you have mentioned, and not all the forces that could be sent were trained military personnel. You are likely unaware of this, but one thing that we do have in large numbers is military uniforms.

"Military uniforms are hard-wearing and waterproof to a degree that the corresponding civilian attire simply isn't. As such, we have a great many non-military personnel dressed as soldiers. It may be that your representative took one look around, saw a lot of the civilians and assumed that due to their dress, they were trained members of the armed forces."

"That's…" I forced myself to calm as I nodded. "That's a fair point."

"There are also internal situations that have resulted in less forces being available than we'd like," he admitted.

"You mean the establishment of the fucking noble houses and their personal armies?" I noted the blinks and the faint starts at me knowing that. "Yeah, I know, just like I know that you sent that party to come and take over my dungeon by any means necessary." I glared at Johnstone. "Thomas was his name, Major John Thomas, and like I say, my nethermancer took his corpse and spoke to his spirit. So don't try to fucking deny it, not unless you want it all brought out here and now."

"There are perhaps situations at play here that we were unaware of before we set off." The general drew my attention back to him as he sat in the middle of the wooden table, his palms flat on the tabletop before him. "Looking at these details, and that there are clear personality clashes, I think it's likely that some restructuring will be necessary on our side. But with matters in hand as they are—first, you asked for help, and we provided it. It was later and less people than you'd have preferred, but do we all agree that the help was asked for and provided?"

"I'll agree with that," I said as the others said similar things.

"Very well. After the help was provided, a soldier in command of those forces requested the core that you promised in payment, and then was killed."

"He did, less than an hour after the conclusion of the fight, with myself and hundreds of others injured, fighting to save the lives of our people. He forced his way inside, armed, and demanded we give him 'his' core immediately. I argued over the debt, on the grounds that he showed up late, with a fraction of the forces that were requested. I'll hold my hand up and admit that I was exhausted and impatient, having fought for three days without rest at that point while we waited for your forces, only to have them turn up late and understrength, adding little to the fight." I sighed.

"Then he threatened us. Instead of offering any form of explanation, he said basically that a member of my dungeon, Mike, was a deserter, and would be taken prisoner by the MPs he'd brought with him, in some attempt to blackmail me into handing the core over. There was no explanation of your force's tardiness, no negotiation. He acted like an arsehole who was doing me a favor the entire time. And when your military police drew weapons, one of my people, a Fire mage, lit a flame in his hand in response. You drew your weapons; he drew his."

"A regrettable situation, but please go on," the general said slowly.

"That was when the leader of your team, Peterbilt, attacked him directly with his own ability, and threatened to kill us all and take the core," I said. "Some of the dungeon-born behind him saw the attack, and reacted to defend me, which is how he died."

"The dungeon-born?" Trust asked. "These beasts you use for war?"

"They're sentient beings," I told her coldly. "Sentient races that have been given to the dungeons, and as such can be created at will, provided you pay the cost in mana."

"And they fight for you?" she asked me fixedly. "You create your armies this way?"

"Yes and no. They can be summoned in such a way, but only if you're a Dungeon Lord. A core without a lord cannot summon the dungeon-born as far as I know, and it's impossible to get the class of Dungeon Lord unless you're in sole command of the dungeon already."

"So how did you manage it?" she demanded.

"None of your business," I replied rudely. "Had we been working together, I would have provided a core to you and basic advice on operating it. I'd come to you originally in the hopes of finding allies, and I came with the desire and intent to give you the core and teach you, but let's be clear. You've done nothing but wriggle out of your side of the deals, then try to stab me in the back. You think I want to give you a way to achieve unlimited power?"

"Again, perhaps we're getting a little emotional here," the general interjected. "So, from your point of view, the leader of the soldiers attacked you when you refused to pay the debt owed. From our point of view, that debt was due. As I explained before, we have a great many civilians in military equipment simply because it's waterproof and hard-wearing. Would you agree that the outcome of that meeting was regrettable?"

"Yeah." I nodded. "We were recovering from the fight, exhausted, literally surrounded by our own dead and dying, and he was pushing for 'his property' before we could even help them."

"And that is regrettable." The general nodded firmly. "As it is, he would have been receiving a very clear guidance session with his superiors, but that's not an issue now. You say that he attacked you. From our point of view, the way he went about the situation was less than optimal, nor was it good manners. But, again, he had a valid point. That soldier swore an oath, and then betrayed it. Under the terms of his enlistment, he was under our command at that point and should have been returned to barracks to await trial. That is clear in the oath and contracts of his enlistment.

"That there were less soldiers than I'd have liked to send with you, again, is not denied. Ideally, I'd have sent tens of thousands and we'd have lost a fraction of what we did, but we sent those who could be freed up at that stage. Many died, and they died aiding you. I think we can agree on that?"

"Yeah," I said flatly.

"Excellent. As such, a debt is owed. Can we agree on that?"

"If, and believe me I mean *if*, but if that debt was agreed to, there's still no fucking way to pay it," I said. "First of all, as far as I'm concerned, your people trying to fucking kill us all when we're supposed to be negotiating means all bets are off. Assassins kind of have that effect. Secondly, that dickhead"—I pointed at Johnstone—"sent goddamn assassins, and when they kidnapped, tortured, and questioned a member of my dungeon management team, and found out where the core was? They tried to steal an active core.

"What you might not understand is that an *active* core is totally different from an inactive one. It's constantly drawing and feeding mana and energy. Think of what would happen if someone ripped a hole in the side of an active nuclear reactor and then tried to run off with it through a building?"

That got a wince from Hawk by the door at least, and I went on.

"What happened was an emergency shutdown, one that badly damaged my dungeon, damaging both its own core, and destroying the one that we had for you."

"That's very convenient." Johnstone sneered.

"No—no, it fucking isn't, actually, you *knob*," I snapped. "The cores themselves are incredibly dangerous, and I'm going to have to have a replacement core for my dungeon brought down now. That means that we've lost months of work! Not even considering the lives lost, there are literally *months* of work that go into a core, and they're incredibly difficult to set up. They *have* to be set up where the mana is densest, as that's what they're harvesting, and they need to be carefully controlled and guided."

"How?" Trust asked quickly. "How are they controlled?"

"A full Dungeon Lord can control it mentally, but you'd need months before the core would even start considering one of you for it," I said. "One of you would need to be the dedicated controller for all that time. Until then, you'd need to feed the dungeon mana to allow it to establish itself. My situation was unique and almost lethal. You have no fairy—"

"Fairy?" the general asked.

I paused. "The dungeons are supposed to be controlled by a fairy that's provided with it." I figured it was better to add in as much truth as possible. "The fairy is a specialized dungeon creature and it replaces the direct need for a Dungeon Lord. In my case, the fairy was dead, and the dungeon enacted some kind of emergency protocols due to the mana fluctuations and the whole situation around the fall. If I was to provide you with a core, it'd be blank, and you'd need to use the control panel to direct it."

"So there's a control system!" Trust latched onto that. "And with that, I could control the dungeon?"

I noticed the looks the others gave her at that slip-up.

"Anyone with access to it could control the basic levels of the dungeon, but it'd take weeks for the dungeon to move beyond subsistence levels. All you'd be able to do is produce basic levels of materials and food. You'd need to do the individual research for more complicated things, like more advanced materials. You start at the Stone level of technology and have to evolve the core but—" I cut myself off.

"Fuck it—why am I even bothering to explain it?" I shook my head. "Listen, this is how it is. You did a deal with me, and…" I glared at Trust as she pulled a massive tome out of a bag and set it on the table with the air of a lawyer about to really enjoy herself. "I'm going to say this once. You foisted that on my friend when you were three days late in setting off for a fight that he was well aware his friends were dying in. If you try to use that in any court of law, they'd throw it out for coercion if nothing else. And if I ever see, hear, or even *sense* that fucking document again, the very last of my potential goodwill to you will be gone. Fucking try using that on me, and I walk *now*."

"We'd do no such thing," Johnstone said quickly, glancing at Trust. "Only a truly stupid and delusional person would even consider it. After all, what court of law is there to consider such a contract?" He smiled at her as if he'd won a point there, and she glared back at him, before slowly sliding it off the table and into her bag again.

"Right. What's going to happen here is that we need to arrange a new core to be brought from the north to repair the damage that this dickhead's men caused." I flicked a finger at Johnstone. "Once that is done, and my dungeon here is back up and running, then we'll look at a core for you, and only with very strict conditions, including a fucking price."

"We've already paid a heavy price," the general said grimly.

I nodded. "And so have we. Thanks to your actions and those of the people you sent to try to take what they should have negotiated for. So, the price is going to include the one resource we can't produce for ourselves, namely the families of our people."

"What?" he asked, surprised.

"The families of my soldiers who are from this area, from the south. You provide lists of the citizens you have, and my soldiers will check to make sure it is them; then they'll be offered a home with us. You'll help in that, and we'll consider the past deal between us paid off. Your backstabbing and the damage done, and the deaths of your people in helping us on my side.

"Then, once the core is here and active, we'll look at producing one for you. You'll have to cover the materials costs, which are fucking high, but we'll give you it for cost plus thirty percent, and a maintenance contract."

"What would that entail?" the general asked me.

"The core is finely balanced, and you're going to have a shitload of questions. Essentially, one of our management team will help you set it up, and give you advice on where to set up, due to the mana density, and how to operate it. Advice like how to avoid wasting mana on needless things."

"And the cost of that contract?" he asked.

"There'll be two costs. First, we'll take any soldiers who want to join us. But understand that they'll be examined before and any attempt to implant spies will be met with a revoking of the deal. And then the physical cost. That'll be paid in mana crystals."

"We don't have any of them," he said slowly.

"You will have." I nodded. "I'll explain the research path to develop them, and then you can use them, both to trade with us and other dungeons, and the Nexus."

"What's the—"

"I think I've given you enough for free already," I said. "If you agree to these terms, you can take your forces back to London, and we'll set up a transfer point a mile from my southern dungeon, between it and London. If you have needs—medicine, food, and so on—you can bring me high-tech materials and we'll exchange there. Our core, as I said, is now failing. Although we can create limited items, we can't supply you all, so only ask for what you *need*.

"I'll also treat you with the minimum of respect in that I'll make you aware when the replacement core is being transported around London and to us. Then you can either stay well clear, or should you want to build some goodwill with me, you'll help to clear any monsters from its path. I'll not be able to send my own guards with it, thanks to our losses, so I'll be sending a contingent of armored dungeon-born. I highly recommend you don't fuck with them, as they will kill anything that gets too close."

There, that should have given them enough chances to either do what was right, or what was wrong, I decided.

"Lastly, as a show of goodwill, I'll show you the best area to set the dungeon up in London, so that when we give you your core, as you're not going to have access to the dungeon system to detect the highest concentration of mana, you can set up in an area that won't result in the core failing and being wasted," I offered.

"That would be acceptable, I think—" the general started to say, only to be cut off by the politicians.

"We can agree to these terms," Trust said coldly, before forcing a smile onto her face. The flickering of her lips looked unnatural. "However, we'll need a demonstration of goodwill from you."

"And me letting you all live after this isn't that already?" I asked her slowly. "You do understand that I defeated the leader of the enemy pantheon in fucking combat, right?"

"The weapons your man delivered." She moved straight along, as if I'd thanked her for the opportunity instead of stared at her in disbelief. "They are prototypes, I understand, but they are impressive. As an offering of goodwill, a thousand of them, their charging facilities, and the relevant ammunition for a year, would go far toward…"

She trailed off as I burst out laughing, unable to help myself.

"A *thousand*?" I chuckled, amused at her arrogance.

"Perhaps we could discuss a slightly smaller number if needed…" Johnstone smilingly offered, back to his bumbling and genial persona.

"Perhaps you could go fuck yourself." I got my laughter under control and started to bluff, knowing that they had absolutely no understanding of costs at this point. "You have no idea what you're asking for. For a thousand of them, I'd need to convert every single high technology item that you can recover from the *entirety of London*! Add in the chargers? The charging facility is a part of my dungeon. It charges mana crystals, and they are the currency the various dungeons use. Enough to power a thousand of those weapons for a year is more mana crystals than I think are in circulation between all the dungeons on the planet!"

I'd been sort of honest about a lot of that. I mean, I didn't even have a thousand of those rail gun shotguns at this point. I had barely a few hundred and that was costing me out the ass.

Either Trust didn't believe me, though, or mere reality was unimportant to her, because she started to push for more.

"Fine, eight hundred then," she offered, as if she were making a massive concession to an inferior.

"Perhaps a slightly lower-costing item and number of them as a gesture of goodwill instead?" the general tried.

I snorted. "Send a small team along the road from London to the old Euro Tunnel site. You'll find my southern dungeon there—or what's left of it—as you know. One mile before it, there'll be a small transfer point on the road. Send a truckload of the highest tech items you can find—tablet computers, servers, all that kind of shit. When it arrives, we'll exchange its value for medicines and food. Then you can give us a list of what you *need*, and we'll set a price."

"Why the highest tech items?" the general asked.

"The dungeon can convert them into mana," I explained, knowing it was information I needed them to have anyway. "The higher the tech item, the more is converted, with a brick being worth about a fifth of a point of mana. A server could be up to several hundred, depending on the size of the server."

"And these points?" he prompted.

"You spend them on infrastructure and items. A mana converter is needed to convert the mana in the local area into a form that the dungeon can use more efficiently. A Fire converter, for example, costs a few thousand depending on the level you go for. Higher levels cost more but convert more mana in the surrounding area into usable resources. They also have a knock-on effect on the local area. So if you want Fire mages, have them sit and meditate and focus on their abilities a lot around a Fire converter and they'll learn faster."

He opened his mouth to ask another question at that point, and I held a hand up to stop him. "I'm not spending my day answering your questions and teaching you shit that you'd already know if you'd been better behaved. In the future, General, you or Hawk there are welcome to come to the transfer point and ask to speak to me; we can have a conversation. You bring either of these, or their representatives, and the conversation is over. You bring the Courtesan and the offer to discuss things and move forward is permanently over. Personally, considering what she is and what she can do, I'd suggest you don't let her travel back with you, but that would leave her around here. Take her with you definitely, but strap her to the roof with a gag in her mouth or something."

That, it turned out, was a step too far for the general. I got the glares from him, Johnstone, and Hawk again, although Trust seemed to like that.

But I was done, and the seed was planted. Now either they'd earn my trust, and maybe there'd be a way that we could move forward as allies, or they'd attack the dummy core that I was going to arrange to send past them with the next generation of clockwork fuckers.

If they did that? Well, I'd know what kind of people they were and they'd get a fake core, when I'd be running a real one under their feet and charging them an arm and a leg for the privilege.

It was time to get my ass in gear. Only one job left for the day, and that was deal with Gerald, Sharon, and Merriman.

CHAPTER SEVENTEEN

It was late by the time I made it to Newcastle in the flesh. I'd told John we'd sort it out around lunchtime, but the mess with the London lot screwed that timeline firmly.

Add on that I needed to fly back to my team and make them aware of the situation, as well as send them back to the dungeon, rather than leave them hiding, ready to back me up, and that slowed me as well.

Kelly got the deployed dungeon-born moving back to the southern dungeon, and as soon as I could make it to the north, I did.

Stepping through the gate into a noticeably colder atmosphere, despite it only being four hundred or so miles north, I launched myself into the air and flashed across to the old barracks as quickly as possible. After gently landing and jogging to a halt, I waved at a few surprised guards before tugging the door open and stepping inside.

The local soldiers who were still securing the base—it'd been mainly abandoned beyond them—all seemed desperate for news, asking both about the wider war and circumstances, and if we'd found "X" person in the south, so that delayed things a little as well.

It inevitably meant I got some comments about me running late and being unable to tell the time from John, but that was life.

When I finally made it, he was seated in a chair in one of small rooms on the ground floor, and he cocked his eyebrow as I joined him.

The chairs were clearly summoned dungeon creations, as I seriously doubted the army normally went in for padded recliners in the general office, but fuck it.

I sank into the padding and relaxed, letting out a long sigh.

"You made it then," he said absently, working through some papers he held in both hands. Some were discarded into a growing pile on the floor by the side of the chair, and a much smaller number were stacked on the table that stood beside his chair.

"Yeah, sorry. I was a bit busy," I apologized.

"And a bit late," he noted. "But hey, it's only four hours and it's not like there's anything spoiling, right?"

"Just the execution of some assholes," I agreed, feeling more uncomfortable with the idea than I had been yesterday, but also knowing there was no realistic alternative.

"Well, are we still doing it?"

I nodded.

"Are *you* still doing it?" He looked at me carefully, and I nodded again.

"I think I should," I said. "Believe me, I don't want to. I've gone through a thousand different ways to do it on the trip here. I've considered a show trial, poison, just keeping them in a solid dungeon space that would reproduce their food needs daily and nothing else, leaving them to die of old age or whatever…"

I shook my head.

"I've considered everything I think I can, and as much as I want to make this into a trial for the benefit of the people, so that they can see that there's punishment and consequences…if I'm honest with myself, it's just to put this off to another day."

"It's a hard thing to take a life," he said softly. "Harder than most know, when it's not in the heat of the moment. Cold-blooded like this, it's one of the hardest things any human will ever do, I think, unless you're the kind of person who enjoys this. And, thankfully, I don't think you are."

"No." I sighed. "No, I'm not. Let's get this over with."

"Before we go in, there's the others to deal with as well, and we need to decide how that's going to be addressed." He stopped me with an upheld hand, then slid a piece of paper across the table.

Picking it up, I read almost two dozen names I didn't recognize, and frowned. "Who are these?" I put it down.

"Five are drug dealers, arrested for various violence or intimidation issues, four more are thieves or drunks who are paying off their time, and the remaining thirteen are the people who aided in this to some degree. We've been focused on the ringleaders and the main culprits, but the others were the ones who spread the word about the movement of troops, helped encourage the celebration of the trainees so that they were out of the dungeon at the time of the attack, and that carried word of their failure to them as well. They're lesser crimes, but they all need dealing with, and they're in close enough cells that they will see and hear what's done in there."

I hesitated, then sighed. "Do you think banishment for the worst or do some of them deserve the death penalty?"

"Honestly, banishment for those who aided in the attack is my recommendation, as there's plenty of evidence that they understood only a small part of what they were doing and the knock-on effect. Many are family of Merriman and the others of his ilk who died when they were banished last time." He scratched at his short beard as he thought. "I don't think death is the right response to all offenses, so execution for those three, banishment for the worst offenders, and then a sentence for the others in the army, without the right to summon anything at all, so they have to get all their food and more from their squad leaders would be my recommendation."

He nodded at that, then indicated the names on his list that were there for minor offenses and two of the thirteen.

"These two were literally lookouts and had little clue what was happening, as near as I can tell. I'd say leave them until the end, let them shit themselves along with the thieves and the drunks, then let them go with a warning, as this will either scare them straight or scare them into running most likely," he finished.

"Then that's what we'll do, then," I agreed. "Execution for the three, service or banishment for the others, with a term of defined service dependent on their actions. If they've shown understanding of the consequences and risks that they posed to others and real regret, then they can stay with a sentence. If not, they go."

"Those three will…well, they'll be dealt with, then the others escorted out, then I'd recommend that the others serve their time." He started to circle the names, and I shook my head.

"You point them out when the time comes. I don't know the names anyway," I admitted, before climbing to my feet and gesturing to the nearby stairs. "Let's get it done."

The deed, when it came to it, was simple enough to carry out. As much as I disliked it, John opened the door to the cells, and I stepped in, standing with John as he read out the laws and that they had been given a chance to leave, to live wherever they chose and to be free, and instead they'd told the soldiers a pack of lies to get what they wanted, which was personal power and to harm us.

They, of course, denied it. Sharon screamed about us having no right to speak to her like that. I endured racist abuse, sexual slurs, claims of "you people" and "terrorist" and worse when I asked whether she had anything to say in her defense.

The room was square, with a solid stone floor and walls and solid metal bars that ran ceiling to floor. The cells were on the outside, with an area in the middle to move in and out and to bring in food and other materials, as for rather obvious reasons, those who had been arrested were banned from the dungeon's systems. John and I stood in the center of the room and stared at the trio as they ranted, occasionally reminding one another of some minor slight or details that existed only in their heads. But eventually, when Sharon finally wound down, having run out of steam and not getting the response she was wanting, I asked the other two for their responses as well.

It was the calm that probably got to them in the end, I'd decided later, as I ran the whole event over and over in my mind.

They screamed, they railed against John and me, they hurled abuse and demands, and they made accusations, before slowly moving to silence.

The entire time, the other twenty-two people in their individual cells sat as silent as possible, apparently hoping we'd forget about their part in it all.

"Your actions were made to advance your own cause and not to help anyone else," I said. "They were made in full understanding of what could happen, and the consequences for those people who would be caught in the crossfire. Dozens died because of your actions, and at a time when we should have been rescuing our injured and captured friends, we were forced to fight those who should have been our allies.

"This was on top of you being put out of the dungeon for making no meaningful contribution beyond for yourself at every opportunity. Instead of helping, you refused to work to save others and spent your time complaining and attempting to undermine me. As such, you all deserve this penalty a dozen times over, but this is how we'll be moving forward."

I turned from the three to look at the others, noting the cleanliness of the cells and that they looked brand-new. Before, the three troublemakers had been kept in a single cell, one that was essentially a small closet that they had been gas attacking each other all day long in, as I'd given them a steady diet of beans and boiled eggs for the sake of petty cruelty.

Now, as I looked around, I found I was glad that someone—probably John—had moved them into this new section to carry out the sentence.

"Any of you who are permitted to leave these cells after this, I want you to remember this," I said calmly. "The laws here are simple. I treat you as adults and that comes with adult responsibilities. I expect you to show appropriate behavior, but as of today, there are new laws coming into place, as well as more enforcers of those laws.

"As before, the highest offense will be met with death. Previously we've only had to hand out that sentence to a handful inside our walls. We'd been lucky to keep it mostly restricted to outside forces attacking us, but today that changes. After that comes banishment, a single chance, and one that you either take and fuck off, making damn sure neither I nor anyone from this dungeon ever comes across you again, or it's death. If you carry out, facilitate in any way, or aid any attack on us in the future, I will hunt you personally and make your passing a hard one," I warned them all.

"Lastly, as before, army service. Minimum terms are five years, and climb in terms relating to the severity of the offense. If you're one of the very few to be given this option, you can accept it and start your service today, or you can choose banishment. You won't get to change your mind once you've left, so think hard on it."

"Death?" Sharon screeched. "Oh, so now you think you're the law, do you! You think you can decide who lives and dies?"

"Here?" I asked. "Yeah, I do."

That took the wind out of her sails for a second. Then she drew herself up, glaring at me before starting in on a fresh thundering tirade.

"Do any of you have any last words?" I asked calmly, as the screaming and frothing at the mouth continued, before I drew my sword.

That brought silence, or at least it did once I slid it forward into her heart.

There was a sudden shocked gasp from her, wide-open stares from the other two next to her cell, and stunned horror from the others that watched on as well.

Then the realization hit home, and the screams, pleas, and begging began.

All in all, it was all dealt with, within an hour. The minor criminals were led through the nexus gate to the northern dungeon and a waiting Rhodes to begin their sentence, and the others were led to the front gates, provided with a shoulder bag of provisions and a knife, then set loose.

By that point…well, I was left feeling drained and hollow.

The entire situation had been necessary, and the outcome had never been in doubt, not after their crimes, but still.

It was a hard and terrible thing that I'd been forced to do, and I knew that the few that had been pointed out as minor crimes, commuted to a warning at John's recommendation, would now spread the word, and it'd grow in the telling.

Horrible, again, but needed.

I spent the first hour or so after the executions and banishments feeling sick inside. As I was neither good company nor able to get my head in gear after that, I decided to make my day really shit, and went to the gym.

Again, someone had spent far too long in there with cigarettes and sweating on the machines without cleaning them down. A quick pass with the dungeon's abilities changed that, though, and I changed out of my fancy armor and gear, into a much-needed workout outfit.

The armor—thanks to the wonder of the expanding neckline and its whole "I'm a magic item, bitch" abilities—was disassembled as much as I could and then stuffed into my bag of holding, then I got to work.

I started with stretches, something I'd viewed as a waste of time back when I was just an IT guy trying to look good. But now, as a literal demigod, they were essential, especially considering the weights I was about to work with.

Even the warm-up required reinforced equipment. The bench and the floor beneath it had been specially strengthened, and we'd had to modify the bars to handle the load. Still, as I finished my first set at 400kg, something felt off. Instead of my usual 20kg increase, I decided to jump up by 40kg.

The new weight provided resistance, but not nearly as much as it should have. I mean, it felt heavy—there was no question about that—but as I pushed through the twelfth rep, I realized I had a lot more in the tank than expected.

I racked the bar and sat up, moving to double-check the weights themselves. I even compared them against the dungeon's system records, wondering whether someone had been messing with them to inflate their numbers. But no, they were exactly what they claimed to be.

This left me feeling even more unsettled. My warm-up weight of 400kg was already approaching the outer limits of what I could handle before my transformation. My usual working weight had been around 500kg, and although I could push beyond that when necessary, there were supposed to be hard limits to what the human frame could handle, no matter how enhanced.

Yet here I was, pushing through sets at 600kg with the same focus I used to need for 500. Within minutes, I'd worked my way up through 650, then 700, finally stopping at 750kg. Worst of all, it wasn't because I couldn't lift more, but because I was honestly getting worried about what this meant.

I sat up, staring at the loaded bar, and pulled up my notifications, looking for anything that might explain this kind of enhancement to my physical capabilities.

Congratulations!

You have reached the next stage of your ascension, and as such, your formerly human body has undergone a considerable transformation.

The metrics that governed your old body are no longer suitable for the powerhouse that you are becoming; neither are the simple measurements that once decreed your limits.

These are for lesser beings; the only limits placed on the ascendant gods are those that they inflict upon themselves.

Your Character Sheet will be adjusted over the next five cycles to reflect your new physical form.

Five cycles—five days ago, or thereabouts, I'd gotten this, and now? I looked from the weights to the other machines in the gym, then rose slowly.

As much as this was freaking me out a little, I wasn't going to be stupid about this, I decided. I was going to get a professional and be sensible.

CHAPTER EIGHTEEN

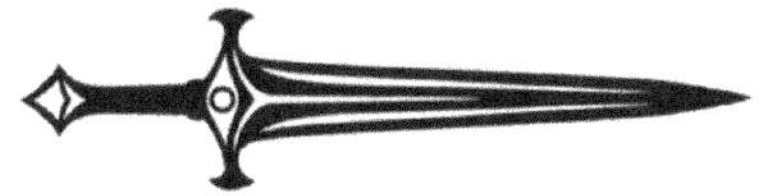

"More!" Rhodes demanded, standing there at parade rest, staring fixedly at me as I sat up, shaking with the exertion.

"Seriously?" I panted, looking from her to the weights on the bar, and back again.

It was a new bar, one that was specially built for this test, and made from a titanium alloy. The ends of the bar had been adjusted for a new locking mechanism, and the weights themselves had been changed as well.

No longer were they the rubber-coated steel of a normal gym. Instead, they were tungsten, providing a much larger weight-to-capacity ratio, and the bar had been extended even beyond the maximum previous length I'd already been using.

Now, as I took a drink and rested, catching my breath, I listened to the chatter around me.

The gym, when I'd turned up at the northern dungeon looking for Rhodes, had been quiet.

That was unusual for a military gym, no matter where it was, but in this case, it'd been in a gap between groups going on and off shift.

I'd found her and explained the issue. The next half an hour was spent in careful question and answer, and then in waiting as Rhodes vanished, before returning with the dungeon sense avatars of Kelly and Aly attached, before vanishing again.

The ladies simply assured me that this was long overdue, and a necessary expense anyway, and had started to work on the gym, changing the structure of the building in ways that they were now clearly experienced with.

The upside was that the soldiers started to stream in, in great droves, to see what the changes were.

That, and Rhodes bringing in a group of other professional utter bastards who helped with the PT for the army, plus a group of even more sergeants, meant that I was now ground zero for more betting than I'd ever known before.

The best bets weren't even for money, oh no. This was the *army*, after all. So the stakes being offered were for burpees, push-ups and pull-ups, with the numbers changing hands meaning that someone was going to be doing them until their grandchildren passed out.

For me, though, things were getting scary.

"The phrasing, what was it again?" one of the PTs asked me, and I dutifully repeated it as he wrote it down.

"These are for lesser beings; the only limits placed on the ascendant gods are those that they inflict upon themselves," he said softly. "Could that be a hint?"

"Maybe," Rhodes agreed. "Okay, Matt, that's enough of a break—back to it."

I nodded, leaning back and sliding under the bar, getting into place as four spotters took up position at various sections of the bar.

They were all advanced kobold warriors. Their strength, each in the thirties, meant that in theory, they should be able to lift anything I could, no matter how quickly it slipped.

"What's the weight?" I called out from underneath it as I put my hands in position, twisting them slightly. The chalk that one of the PTs had insisted I put on cascaded off in gentle puffs of white air as I got ready.

"Not important," Rhodes said over the hubbub as people paused to listen to the new number. "We don't need to focus on a number—just the action, soldier. Now, are you ready?"

"Yeah," I grunted, bracing myself, then taking a long breath.

"Then *lift*!" she ordered.

I pushed, hard.

The bar wobbled, but it rose into the air, to the accompanying gasps and shouts of the crowd. I continued to push it, hitting eight—my minimum permitted reps—and continuing to twelve.

"Again!" Rhodes barked to the teams on either side as they started shifting weights for me.

When I started to look, I was blocked from the view by two more PTs who moved in on either side to prevent it.

"Nothing good comes from looking, sir," one of them said. "At the end, you get to find out the numbers. For now, we're setting a new benchmark for you, so we just need you to push, and push as hard as you can."

"Fuckers," I muttered, blowing out a breath. My head hung low as I tried to move my arms. They were really starting to hurt now. The pain radiated through me, and I triggered a pulse of lightning through my body on instinct.

Fortunately, I managed to keep it contained, and not shock the people touching the apparatus. But as the pain slowly eased from my muscles, I relaxed.

"That just earned you another hour," Rhodes said.

"What?" I asked, then cursed.

"The healing…you know it resets your progress," she pointed out. "You get to heal at the end of the day, once the goal has been achieved, not before."

"Yes, boss," I groaned, before settling back and bracing myself, taking a few quick breaths, then starting as she yelled "Go!"

The next four hours were painful in a way I'd not experienced outside of combat, and even put the previous training methods to shame. But by the end of it, I was finally allowed to know what my new physical limit apparently was.

Four *thousand* and fifty-eight kilos was the point that I dropped the bar. The eight kobolds by that point that had been summoned into place to hold the bar barely stopped it before it did me serious damage.

It was, I was told, a fucking ridiculous number, as it proved that I could literally stick a pole between two cars and bench-press them if I needed to.

Although that sounded a bit insane to me, it was when Rhodes got me back on my feet and introduced me to their latest acquisition that I started to get really worried.

"What the hell is that?" I glanced from her to the machine and back. "Look, Rhodes, I know I've told you this before, but I fuckin' hate cardio…"

"Tough," she said. "This is the best that we can make to test you currently, as it's got varying resistance and it doesn't require an observer to ride a damn motorcycle to watch over you."

The machine was a treadmill, essentially. A collection of rollers with a rubberized track that ran around and around the small area. That was it. Bog standard and crap, but considering the lack of electricity, it was what it was.

"Yeah, but I mean, I've told you—" I started, only to be cut off.

"You hate cardio." She nodded. "That's nice that you've got an opinion. Now keep it to yourself or find yourself another trainer."

"I hate you," I muttered, before climbing onto the tracks and glaring at her as she grinned.

"That's a good Dungeon Lord," she praised me. "I'd pat your head and give you a cookie, but I haven't got any and I don't want to. Now run."

Still glaring at her, I pushed off. The tread moved slowly underfoot until I put more effort in. After just a few minutes, I had the rhythm down so that I could build up to a run. The treads literally flowed under me, allowing me to run in place, but the sensation was somewhat akin to running on the beach.

Sand always moved underfoot and the effort required was considerably more than you needed on asphalt.

That was when Rhodes pulled a lever, suddenly making me stumble as the resistance increased.

"Keep it up!" she barked at me. "Come on, Matt! My mother could do better, and she's dead!"

"I fuckin' hate you…" I muttered, pushing harder.

The next two hours were hard, but by the end of it, when she finally allowed me to stumble off the trainer, my legs shaking and sweat pouring down me, it was to see a group of people all doing push-ups.

"Wha…what…happened?" I gasped, shaking as I braced my hands on my knees and tried to keep from retching.

"They took the bet on your maximum speed. Apparently the treadmill doesn't look particularly fast." She smiled coldly.

"It's…not…" I agreed.

"How hard did you push?" she asked me.

I glared at her. "You said…push…hard!" I reminded her, and she nodded while waiting. "I…pushed hard!" I told her…unnecessarily, I felt.

"Over or under ninety percent of your maximum?" she asked, making a note.

"Well, yeah…about at that level," I admitted. "I pushed…hard."

"And if I told you to get back on and go again, could you?"

"Yeah?"

"Then you weren't at ninety." She snorted. "After two hours at ninety percent of your potential, you should be vomiting on the floor and crying for your mother."

"She's dead," I snapped.

"That's life. Get over it," she replied flatly. "As I was saying, this means you pushed less than ninety, so back on we go, lordling!"

"Fuck's sake!" I groaned. For a minute, I seriously considered telling her to go fuck herself and flying away. Then I remembered that she was helping me with this, and at the end of the day, the only way I was going to improve was if I pushed myself. Cursing, I did as she ordered.

Twenty minutes later, I was vomiting on the floor before her and she was making more notes, while smiling.

"That's more like it," she assured me. "A real effort at last."

"What…difference?" I asked when I could speak again, lying on my back and staring up at the infernal demon in human flesh that pretended to be Rhodes. The dungeon had thankfully cleansed the floor at a thought, and it was sweat stinging my eyes as I thought that I'd probably never be able to walk again.

I considered that, and yeah. That was it. Without me being able to move ever again, my sex life was over, and I was going to die right here and now.

"Your top speed is somewhere around the hundred and fifteen miles an hour mark, and the range of your weights suggests you could lift just over four tons of weight. That should give you, should we change up your training, the ability to kill most creatures in hand-to-hand combat no matter their level range. Considering what we've seen so far, anyway," she amended.

"Fuckin' WHAT?" I asked, stunned. I forced my shaking head up off the ground to stare at her incredulously.

"You've evolved, Dungeon Lord," she said. "Your stats have probably changed to reflect that, and we'll go over them next, but the important details are that because you believed you could push only so far, that's how hard you pushed."

I stared at her and she sighed, before gesturing for one of the others to come and help explain it.

"You have a maximum level of force that you believed you could exert without damaging yourself," he said. "We all have that, Dungeon Lord—a point that we know we can lift this, and that we can't lift that, if we try; that's the point where we injure ourselves and so we don't push past that. As Olympians train, they have to learn to push that mental limitation, to feel the physical, mechanical limit that's actually there, not what their memory and mind tells them *should* be the limit. You've heard of things like rage giving people strength? Or a mother who lifts something impossible when her child is trapped? This is how they do that.

"You've simply found that your new maximum is considerably higher than it was very recently. If we had months, you'd gradually adjust your perceived strength limits to be closer to your actual strength, which is what happens as you train naturally. But whatever you've done, however you managed it, you're starting to find the difference between a magically augmented human, and a literal demigod, sir. It means your training needs to change, and massively so, but that's not a bad thing."

"How not?" I asked, exhausted, then shook myself. "I mean, how do I need to change? I can't just spend all day in here pushing myself."

"Nossir," he agreed. "Frankly, sir, Captain Rhodes said that you had a small private gym, and it was taken over by others each time you turned around?"

"Yeah," I grumbled.

"Well, on the bright side, I don't see that happening anymore." He smiled evilly.

"Oh?" That perked me up, even broken on the floor.

"Not many humans around who are going to be able to lift the weights and machinery we're going to have to design and build for you, sir, but frankly, I like a challenge. As such, and considering the drive that a little healthy competition can give, I'd ask that we set up two gyms.

"First will be your private gym. We build that wherever you're going to be spending the majority of your time. The second one, we build here at the back." He gestured to a point that one of the other PTs was already marking out.

"That section will have what we'll refer to as the superhuman weights. It'll be a zone that you have to earn the right to enter, and that nobody below a certain threshold will be able to even move the equipment in.

"We're going to have you work out, and do it hard, and publicly. The right to use the equipment in that area will become a status symbol, as will trying to reach your level. Sure, you're a demigod, but that doesn't mean that people won't try. We'll construct an Olympic-level track as well, outside, so that the runners face real-world environments as they practice, and an indoor version for speed trials.

"That way, you come here once a week and you train, perhaps with your team, so the others can see the range of levels and physical abilities. That'll give them something to try to beat, with yourself at the top of the pyramid. One of us will be on call, twenty-four hours a day, ready to monitor you as you train, and we'll work on getting a few dungeon-born developed or trained who are capable of spotting for you, just in case, for safety.

"Between those adjustments, the training here will massively increase in drive, and so will your own. Have you checked your stats lately, sir? I know you said that it'd changed, and Captain Rhodes asked that you not monitor it until the end of the session, but I think we've reached that point?" He glanced over at her.

She nodded. "That's right. Time to share the gains, sir." She slid back into respectful soldier mode, instead of "murderbot."

I pulled up the details. The first to spring to mind was the breakdown of my new stats, and fuck me sideways with a chicken covered in jam.

Congratulations! Due to your recent ascension and notable actions, your stats have been recalculated from the baseline. As such, you have gained additional Stat Points in the following areas through constant effort.

- **+20 Agility**
- **+22 Constitution**
- **+5 Dexterity**
- **+26 Endurance**
- **+3 Intelligence**
- **+4 Luck**
- **+29 Strength**
- **+5 Wisdom**

Continue to work hard to increase these or other stats...

I stared in shock as my new stats were revealed.

Name: Matt, First Lord of the Storm
Host Powers: 1 (Enhanced Regeneration)

Species: Cyclone			**Bonus**: None	
Level: 32			**Progress to next level**: 34,465/120,000	
Stat	**Current Points**	**Description**	**Effect**	**Progress to Next Level**
Agility	90	Governs dodge and movement	Heightened chance to dodge attacks Level: Demigod	0/100
Charisma	53	Governs likely success to charm, seduce, or threaten	More likely to succeed in events that require seduction, persuasion, or threats Level: Enhanced Humanoid	41/100
Constitution	92	Governs Health and Health Regeneration	HP: 92x100 = 9,200 Level: Demigod	0/100
Dexterity	65	Governs ability with weapons and crafting	Increased chance of improved crafting result or increased melee damage Level: Enhanced Humanoid	0/100
Endurance	91	Governs Stamina and Stamina Regeneration	Stamina: 90x90 = 8,190 Level: Demigod	0/100
Intelligence	106	Governs base manapool, standard intellectual capacity	Mana: 106x110 (x2) = 23,320 Level: Godling	37/100
Luck	65	Governs overall chance of bonuses and critical hits	Increased chance of positive outcome Level: Enhanced Humanoid	17/100
Perception	55	Governs ranged damage and chance to spot hidden items/traps	+45 to all ranged attacks Level: Enhanced Humanoid	1/100
Strength	94	Governs damage with melee weapons and	Enhanced damage with Melee weapons Level: Demigod	0/100

		carrying capacity		
Wisdom	75	Governs mana regeneration	1500 mana regenerated per hour *(Arcanist class level 2 boost)*	22/100

"So," I started, then cleared my throat. "There's been a few changes…"

CHAPTER NINETEEN

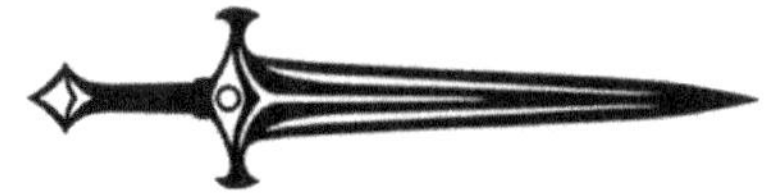

"Matt, I really don't like this," Kelly said again.

I nodded, laying my hands on her shoulders and staring into her eyes. "I know," I said. "I know, and I totally understand that, my love, but this is honestly the best way that I can see to both train my abilities and to achieve what we need. Tell me if you've got a better idea, because I'm all ears."

"You could let me and the team come with you." Chris grunted from where he stood to my right, leaning against the wall. "Fuck knows we need the practice as well."

"With your new abilities and with the team, I know," I agreed. "But that's the point, mate. I need to be able to go all out. I can only learn if I practice, and as shitty as this sounds, it's the only way that I can see to do it now."

"I know you think that, Matt, but last time you did this, you almost died and we were attacked!" Kelly snapped.

I nodded my understanding. "We were, and it was shite, but we also gained a buttload of beneficial bonuses. We need those, as well as the possible new members of the dungeon we can recruit through it."

"And, as much as I don't like it, it shows those assholes why they don't want to fuck with us." Chris sighed.

He was right, and I'd discussed it ad infinitum with Kelly and the others after Rhodes first suggested it.

It'd been her idea, after all—not mine this time—and it'd taken a week to plan out and to figure all the details, along with a second week in which we'd done the building.

A lot had changed in a fortnight. The southern dungeon's influence reached the nearby town—and tore it apart—reached the sea, and converters were installed offshore—and finally reached the nearby high mana density area.

That had given the dungeon a massive boost in terms of available mana, as had the ongoing harvesting of Heathrow Airport, followed by Gatwick—which, it turned out, was actually closer than Heathrow…I'd just not known that before. As well as sending teams from the dreadnought to the surrounding area to consume the subsidiary companies that were set up to feed into the airport.

The mobile dungeon was about halfway through the changes planned now to make it a monster of efficiency, though the flying section had been reworked three times over so far, and wasn't getting much closer.

The biggest changes had been the simplest and yet most far-reaching in design.

First, thanks to the wonder of the medical screens we'd managed to research, we now had the ability to transmit the view from something like a camera to a screen that people could watch.

It wasn't foolproof, and the texture on the larger systems was a bit shit, but it was working, and clear enough that nobody was going to be complaining.

That might not sound like that big of a deal, until you took into account that it was mainly off the back of the medical discoveries we'd already made, and that it was made for a very specific purpose.

Since we made that discovery at the gym, we'd thrown up three new facilities. The big kahuna, though, was the shiny new training arena dungeon. This bad boy was designed to be a cash cow, serving up entertainment and boosting our economy with a side of ticket sales, and to be a training facility.

Rhodes had pointed out that we'd literally gotten access to the other dungeons already—those with the nexus gates, anyway—and all they needed was a key to access this one.

We could hand out a key, keep it locked the rest of the time, but when the dungeon was in use, we could sell tickets for the masses and allow the other dungeons to use our training facility.

It wasn't just for our people to watch, either; it was for the literal masses. The other dungeons could send their people through. All they needed was a ticket, one that we'd sell for a tiny mana crystal or tech item like a phone. And if this worked, not only did they get to essentially rent our training space, they got to give their people somewhere to relax and blow off some steam.

"Picture this," she'd said. "A pressure valve for the masses, filling the gap left by footy and rugby. The thing is, footy in the UK isn't just a sport, it's a bloody religion," she'd pointed out. Matches drew crowds big enough to make economists weep with joy. Rugby's seen as football's scrappy younger brother: less popular, but tough as nails. Rugby players look at American footballers after all and snigger. Same game, they'd say, but they play it without the fancy dress.

I played rugby in school. Preferred it to footy, if I'm honest. But as Chris pointed out, that's because I had two left feet when it came to football. That fancy footwork? Miles beyond me.

But the real reason was that footy, rugby, American football—they're all cut from the same cloth. Entertainment for the unwashed masses…now that it's considered shitty to chuck Christians to the lions, anyway.

This was something to bridge the gap between "real" downtime and work, something to give us a chance to counter the burnout with a day of celebration and recovery.

That's where Rhodes's brainstorm really came into its own.

The new stadium was to be a monster, but the layout was dead simple. We started with a classic football stadium, but then flipped it on its head. Seats tiered inward and upward in a triangle formation, with the most expensive seats up at the very top. Smack in the middle of the floor below and in the center of the arena was a massive screen.

The seats formed rings, like a giant concrete doughnut with a balcony wrapping around the edge, giving the visitors a bird's-eye view of the dungeon below. The lucky bastards at the top? They got a glass floor, with the intention of making it feel like they were floating above the action, with screens placed around the inside to make it easier to see details.

The dungeon itself, though? That was the clever bit. It was built into the ground, right there in the center. The plan was to go five levels deep, maybe more if we needed to expand later. Best of all, by setting up a separate building, we'd ringed it with a wall that separated the dungeon and the stadium from each other.

We'd done that in the hope that when I went in and triggered the trial dungeon, we'd get more than a standard dungeon, and instead, like last time I'd entered, it'd be a mix of special magic and a regular layout that'd be incredible, and self-regenerating.

A colosseum for the twenty-first century, where instead of lions, we'd have monsters, and instead of gladiators, we'd have dungeon divers and their support teams. Beat that, Premier League.

The cherry on the top, as Rhodes had put it, was that I could go all out in there, and the resources would be paid for not by us, but by the ticket sales.

We could give passes as rewards to our citizens, and for the London lot? They could pay in either crystals—once they had access to them—or in high-tech items. Things like a high-end phone would cover the cost of a ticket. And considering how useless they were to the people of London currently, I was hoping it'd work well.

It'd also serve as an example.

Not only would they be able to visit and interact with us at a safe distance from the dungeon itself—this was an outpost of the dungeon after all, and as we'd told them, it was to be created with the last of the dungeon's dying strength, as there was a new core in production—but it was an advert.

It was an ad to the citizens of London that everything that they wanted could be brought back. Safety, sport, downtime, and food…hot fucking food that wasn't just subsistence. All of that would be on sale, and all the high-tech items would be funneled into the dungeon, further boosting it.

The first suggestion by Rhodes of building a stadium had been sort of waved off. It was part of the plan, we'd said, but it wasn't something we were ready to do now. Maybe in a month, maybe two or three. No, we needed to move into the conquest phase, get as much as we could conquered and people rescued, not set up damn stadiums.

That was ridiculous.

Then she'd pointed out that with the stadium built, and things like Life converters built throughout it? There was such a thing as a free lunch, because if we could get those people to come, not only would they feel healthier being around such things, but it'd feed on their life force and pour more mana into the dungeon.

There was to be a traders' station, and after we'd discussed it, and we'd done that a lot, we'd agreed.

Kelly had reached out to the other dungeons we had contact with, and she'd invited them to not only the opening event, but the traders' section. A section that they could bring what they wanted and sell it. They could trade free and easy with the others, and because they wanted to do that, to trade not only with us on a one-on-one basis, but as a real economy?

They agreed to spread the word.

After all, it wasn't as if they had to do much. Opening the gate cost mana, but once it was open, that was it—it was open. It wasn't hugely expensive to keep it that way, and the cost was in maintaining the connection, not how many passed through it. If it was five people or five hundred, it was the same cost, only expanded by the time that the connection was "live."

It was also seen as a great example for the London lot of why they shouldn't fuck with us.

I was going to go in there, after training for two weeks, and I was going to finally get to really let loose. To see what my abilities were, to see how far I could push it.

When we'd offered the chance to our friends in the other dungeons to come and watch the trial dungeon as entertainment, they'd been uncertain. After all, they were plenty busy with their own shit, and they'd be moving into our territory, which wasn't something to take lightly.

The opportunity to sell their stuff to us—well, that was interesting, especially as we'd promised to make sure the citizens who were coming from our side would have mana crystals to spend.

The real interest, though, seemed to be the opportunity to see me fight—probably in case they needed to go to war with me in the future—and to see the dungeon. A dungeon that they knew would—or we were going to be a fuckin' laughingstock—activate into a trial dungeon.

I didn't know how many—or if any of the other Dungeon Lords—had activated a trial dungeon yet. After all, it activated the first time, or so we thought, when you had a special class of reward that was waiting to be claimed.

Add in that as a dungeon lord it was clear that we received only minor XP for our kills in the dungeon, so there really wasn't an incentive for most of us to try it. So, they'd get to see the reality of the trial dungeon without them having to run the dungeon themselves.

They'd also get to see the creatures of my dungeon, as that'd be what the trial dungeon drew its inhabitants from. Once I'd run the dungeon in its entirety again, then it would be set, ready for plundering on a regular basis. And those who had seen it now would get a head start, as they'd know what they'd face in each section.

We'd provided basic details of the other trial dungeon, and more importantly, the walls next to the goblin camp that were essentially a mana crystal mine and the dryad area that grew plants that included some we'd never seen before.

They also knew that all they had to do was pay a fee, and they could use it for training their more advanced warriors, while keeping their own training dungeons as something that could be restricted to a low-level starter if they wanted to.

All in all, it was a great deal for them, and a better deal for us—provided the fuckers actually turned up and spent the mana crystals and resources, or we'd have lost an absolute shitload.

It was a risk, but when three hours ago, the very first of the London lot had started to arrive? I'd felt a knot in my stomach let go.

Thankfully, it wasn't a really bad need to use the toilet. But now that I could hear above me the roar of the stadium? I was starting to need that as well.

As it was, though, I had one last job to do, before I could go and fuck up someone else's Tuesday, and it was the thing I hated above all others.

I had to go make nice and be diplomatic with people.

The door before me was all polished oak, gleaming with an inner luster. Damn, even knowing that the others were with me, that my team had my back, I hesitated, taking a deep breath, before pushing the door open.

The room beyond was luxury personified, or at least by our standards. We'd gone all out: the deep carpets, the friggin' insanely large table, the one-way glass that covered an entire wall, looking out over the arena floor below…all of it.

In this room alone, anyone who entered could summon any kind of food or drink they wanted, no cost, and it was open to anyone who crossed the doorstep.

This was the meeting hall. The room was roughly circular, with a table in the center that could literally hold a hundred people with comfort around its perimeter. The ceiling was large, arcing overhead with rows of subdued lights that shimmered softly.

Kelly and Aly had gone all out. Finn had been involved, along with half the crafting team. The call had gone out for the most stylish and creative to help, and gods had they delivered.

Admittedly the mural on one wall that showed us fighting the undead was a bit much for me. I was depicted *waaay* too heroically, and I already knew that some mad bastard had given me perfect teeth that shone in a confident smile.

I just knew that level of hero-worship was asking for trouble, or vandalism, and I made a mental note to make sure that Chris wasn't allowed anywhere near it with a permanent marker.

Either way, though, all those bits were the minor details, because filling the room, taking up most of the seats, were the representatives of the dungeons and the various surviving power blocks who had agreed to come.

For us, the only one who we'd contacted, and yeah, that I'd sort of hoped wouldn't come, were the London lot, and they weren't happy that they'd been restricted to four members. I recognized Johnstone and Trust, and General Blackstone as well, but not the fourth player with them.

I gave the general a nod as I passed, moving around to my seat, at the head of the table, with the glass wall behind me, finding unsurprisingly, marks of drinks and food having been put down and picked up again.

Each seat that was reserved, like ours, had the chair locked into place under it and a name plate before it. Glancing down at it as I passed it, I saw finger marks around the name plate that suggested someone had even tried to lever it up to lay claim to the seat, which made me grin at the failed attempt.

"Akuba, Kaatachi." I greeted the pair who stood nearby, smiling as they nodded in greeting to me, their smiles as always bright enough to outshine the sun.

"My friend, my ally." Akuba inclined her head, and Kaatachi just smiled, before gesturing toward the window, then around at the others filling the room.

"It appears to be a success," Kaatachi said softly.

I nodded, taking a deep breath and forcing a smile. "Let's hope, eh? If we're lucky, this will all go well and the people will want to come back," I said. "I know you've met her already through the negotiations, but you both remember my partner and the lady of my dungeon, Kelly?" I introduced her, getting smiles from them. As she spoke up and they exchanged pleasantries, I noticed for the first time that the others, Chris especially, had broken off and were gathered off to one side, acting as interceptors for the randoms who were moving up, handling the crowd to let us talk to just a few people at a time.

Damn, I was a lucky man to have that kind of backup.

Ashley was there as well, working the crowd, and bringing others across to meet me. This was going to be painful, I just knew it.

"What will be, will be," Akuba said, philosophically. "Let no thought of tomorrow ruin your enjoyment of this day, for now, here, you have made your place, and by it, ours among the Dungeon Lords clear."

She gestured at the sea of Dungeon Lords who had come at our invitation, the keys left at the nexus platform having done its job well.

"We will leave you now. You must greet the others, but know that we will be watching you, and we believe in you," Kaatachi finished, before laying a hand on my arm, squeezing once in support, then moving away, as others came to take their place.

This time it was Kai and Leilani, the Chinese pair who had claimed the dungeon in the Hainan Province of China. Where she was resplendent in a full-length Chinese dress of silk and inlaid brocade, looking every inch the high court lady, he wore a simple black silk top and pants, and had a single piece of jewelry for decoration.

Admittedly, it was of a dragon made of diamond and was wrapped around his right forearm in links that were flexible, going from the elbow to finish with the dragon's head on the back of his hand, so it wasn't exactly a demonstration of "I'm just a poor boy."

I greeted them, noting the way that Leilani's companion was with them again, hovering behind: "Engineer" Zheng, as he'd been introduced.

Engineer, my arse. I glanced at him, seeing the way he stood: the ramrod-straight back, the eyes that never settled. He was a bodyguard, and clearly a fucking lethal one.

"Kai, Leilani!" I greeted them, bowing my head and expecting a smile in return, but somewhat surprised when they simply nodded cooly and moved around me, heading to speak to another.

"And fu—" I started, straightening up and about to tell them to fuck themselves as well, when Ashley stepped in close, speaking quickly.

"They and others are very cautious of you now. They think you're trying to take over their dungeons, and they don't want to appear in your camp, or against you, so be polite, and they might be able to be recovered," she said in a very fast whisper around a dazzling smile.

"I thought we were on good terms?" I muttered, smiling back at her.

"We were," she agreed, speaking aside as she ostentatiously gave Kelly a hug, moving us into place for another incoming group. "Then we formed an alliance with Akuba and Kaatachi when they were making a fortune selling them ammunition, and cut off that trade route for them."

"Fuck," I muttered.

"Exactly. Ah!" She beamed at the next person. "This is Sara. She's the representative of the Dungeon of Alaria, once known as Algeria. We were talking earlier, and she said…"

The next thirty minutes were a dizzying round of introductions, of meetings and fake smiles, kisses on cheeks and unsubtle attempts at glamour and more.

By the end of it, Ashley looked frankly exhausted, and when Kelly asked her about it, it turned out she'd been using her class abilities constantly to deflect the skills of others like her in the crowd.

I'd felt it on occasion, the most perfect woman in existence walking past and derailing my train of thought and conversation as I stared after her, lust building; then a wash of cold air and I was staring at just another pretty girl, while my partner stood by me.

It'd happened on four occasions, and clearly someone had been conducting A/B testing because each time I shrugged off an attempt, the next one was totally different: two men, two women, all of radically different styles each time.

"Those were only the most powerful of them," Ashley told us both. "The majority were easy to deflect and you wouldn't have noticed them, but those four were stronger than me, and it took a lot to protect against them."

"Any idea who they worked for?" I asked.

"Far corner, the red top, standing by the green potted plant, glass of red wine in her hand," she replied instantly.

I looked over, seeing the woman in question watching me, a small smile on her face as she stared unabashedly.

She was in her mid to late fifties, well dressed, but not standing out as incredible wealth, with five people with her: the four pretties, and a single, much larger man that just screamed out "bouncer" or "hired muscle."

"I thought the limit was four to a party?" I asked Kelly calmly, after inclining my head in acknowledgment.

"It was. How she managed six, I don't know," Kelly said grimly.

"She's reading your lips," Ashley said softly, her own smile barely budging as she spoke. "And it'll be her power. If she's built her dungeon around that skill set…"

"Let's go find out," I suggested, more curious than anything, intending to tell her to give it a rest, until both Ashley and Kelly gripped my arms.

"Not now. Wait until I can protect you more," Ashley said quickly.

"Wait until a different day," Kelly said instead. "Today's dangerous enough!"

"Also, if you think they're bad, watch the group on the left-hand side, back near the bar," Ashley said quietly, while smiling and gesturing in a totally different direction with her champagne flute.

I looked where she pointed, then glanced around, as if just looking, and saw exactly what she wanted.

Three guys, one woman, and enough leather and jewelry to make a rock concert jealous. They also looked seriously pissed, and glowered at everyone nearby.

"I'm not a hundred percent but I think they're slavers, but definitely career criminals. They've tried asking about using the gates here for 'cargo distribution' but wouldn't say what kind, and wanted to know our laws. As soon as I made it clear we'd need to know what they were moving if it was going through our territory, they cut me off and walked away."

"Joy. Do we know which dungeon they're from?" Kelly asked.

"We do, though I need some time to prepare a list of dungeons against representatives," Ashley admitted. "I've also got Xanthia working the crowd, and will add in her insights to the report once the day's done."

I glanced over and saw Xanthia, as well as two others—both men, and all extremely pretty—walking back and forth, offering drinks and so on.

"I…fine." I sighed. "Fuck it, let's get this over with. Sooner I can go kill something, the better."

I turned from the woman in the corner. Ashley glanced at Kelly, apparently seeing something I missed as she nodded and headed across the nearby mural.

Where the tower rose on one side—it'd been a fuckin' cube of a fortress, not a bloody tower but hey, artistic license and all that—there was a single metal tube that ran up the wall, looking like a piece of modern art.

She tapped it lightly at the base with a tuning fork, and it let loose a clear, shimmering note that cut across the various conversations in the room better than a bloodcurdling scream could have.

"Ladies, gentlemen, and all our distinguished visitors, if you could take your seats; the Dungeon Warmancer would appreciate a brief moment of your time," she called out into the sudden silence.

I swallowed hard as all eyes turned to me, even as they moved to sit.

"Hey," I said in what was possibly the shittiest opening to a speech ever. "Dammit. Welcome Dungeon Lords, Ladies, and your representatives!" I tried again, forcing myself not to swear when I realized I'd basically just said "fuck you" to the London lot as well by not including them in that.

"Thank you for coming to the first run of the dungeon arena. As you were made aware with your invite, after today the dungeon will be open to all of you to run personally, or to use as a training aid for your people, and to harvest, should that be your aim."

I left unsaid that I fucking hoped there would be a renewing resource available and that they would have to pay a fee. The fee had already been mentioned elsewhere, after all.

"Now, as part of accessing this gate, you have enabled a link to be forged to your own nexus gate as well, sharing your own location…"

I thought that was true, though I didn't know it for sure, not yet, but it was better to get this out ahead of any possible realizations and accusations.

"This, we believe, is the way the gates were intended to be used. But as I'm sure you all already have done, I would recommend that when you return, you set your gate to 'locked' and to chime when an access request is made, instead of simply allowing anyone to pass through. This way, you are kept safe, in case of any bad-faith actors."

I paused, noting the way a few figures around the table were looking horrified.

"If you wish to leave and check the gate settings, I'll not keep you long, don't worry," I said, smiling wryly. "So! I know you're all aware of the incoming Orakai invasion fleet, and we wanted to open this arena to all in the hopes of fostering a place that we can all meet, and build a friendship, a coordinated defense, even if not an alliance, to defend our home. Please think on that as I demonstrate the dungeon below for you all, and remember that I offer my hand in friendship. Thank you all."

That last bit was aimed squarely at the group on the far side of the table from me, where the saurian delegation glared at me.

They'd stood at the back for most of the time since they'd been admitted, taking a section of the far wall as "theirs" and glaring at anyone who came close, and not bothering to come and greet me.

Clearly the lack of a corner, in the circular room, for them to lurk in, pissed them off.

I'd held off on Examining them, knowing that if they felt my magic, it wouldn't go down well. But fuck me, I wanted to. There were three distinct races there, and even the representatives from the undead dungeon were markedly more friendly and approachable than they were.

Weirdly and distressingly, on that side note, the London lot and the undead were getting along famously, which I was going to have to do something about.

The saurian, though, had two massive, heavily muscled creatures, identical to the pair that had challenged and tried to attack me aboard the Nexus platform, then had been blasted out into vacuum as a consequence.

It looked like I'd found them again.

They were literally like someone had given a toad some sort of an uplift, then introduced them to weightlifting and leering at smaller people as a way of life. Eight foot tall, bald, with a wide but blunt face and massive lips that could have inspired a seventies or eighties singer's plastic surgeon. They had a broad stripe of bright red that ran down from their chins, vanishing below their armor.

The armor matched their flesh, in that it was scaled, and a sort of off-yellow that almost looked diseased, while their companions were apparently of two separate races again.

One was short and broad, with a wide mouth and massive eyes. Its sex was indeterminable, but it wore a huge red cape that lifted up from its shoulders and flowed out like the hood of a cobra.

The other was thinner; while the shorter figure topped out at perhaps five feet, the guards on either side towering over it, this one wore a hooded robe. It stood maybe six feet, but probably less, considering how hunched over it was. It had its fingers wrapped in layers of alternating, colored bandages. The tip of its muzzle protruded from the hood, but the eyes glimmered deep within. All that could be said of the body was that they were humanoid, though with a long tail.

They'd apparently shown a *lot* of interest in the kobolds when they'd been escorted here. And then on learning that this wasn't a kobold-only dungeon, and that, more to the point, the kobolds weren't in charge, they'd refused to speak to anyone.

As it was, we'd achieved what we wanted: we'd gotten them all to come here, and to open negotiations without any expectations. It might work out, it might not, but I had high hopes, as Kelly, Chris, and I left the room.

Ashley immediately took over as the "hostess-with-the-mostest," making friends and generally charming people, as the door closed behind us.

We wound our way through the crowds of guards who were stuck outside the room, and who were blatantly wanting to be close enough to defend their principal, without breaking the rules and causing issues.

It only took a few minutes to get down to the more private and less frequented areas, thankfully. The overall design was something like a traditional sports arena, with a hell of a lot of stairs and cold concrete.

"I mean it, Matt," Kelly said softly. "I really don't like this. You're risking your life when you don't need to."

"I know," I said, just as softly, kissing her gently, before smiling. "I know I don't need to, and I know there's a risk from this, but it's manageable. None of the creatures that can be summoned by the dungeon go beyond advanced, and my own levels now…" I shrugged. "I'm a demigod, remember?"

"It doesn't mean you can't be hurt." She stared into my eyes. "And it doesn't mean that you're invincible, remember that!"

"I will," I assured her, before straightening and rolling my shoulders. "The troops are ready?"

She nodded firmly. "Trust, but have a big hammer ready, just in case." She grinned.

"Definitely." I winked at her and kissed her again.

That'd been the insurance policy for us. When we'd agreed to all of this, to Rhodes's suggestion, it wasn't just that it was good for us—it was also that it gave us two opportunities.

If those we invited decided that this was the chance to fuck us all in the ass? Well, we'd prepared for that as well. The advantage of multiple dungeons, all stripping their respective areas like a plague of locusts, was that we'd had mana to burn.

We should have invested it wisely in the converters and in leveling up the dungeon—more than we had done, I mean. Instead, Rhodes and the others had talked us into a Hail Mary plan, as she called it.

We'd summoned a literal army, a thousand strong, underneath the dungeon. They were advanced kobolds, and they were armed to the teeth. A small number of fast, hard hits had been done over the last two weeks to strip army bases where we could find them. Most had been useless to us—already hit, or fucked up in other ways—but two had been worth the trip.

When we'd arrived at one of the sites, it'd been to find defenders who were struggling to hold off a gang, while running low on ammo. We'd arrived, and we'd essentially slaughtered their attackers.

Or, more to the point, Chris had. He'd led that one, and although the base I'd hit had yielded a shitload of arms and ammo, his had yielded nearly five hundred people.

People who were damn glad to see him, and even more so when he offered them a new home. They'd agreed after very little prompting. Their food had been at danger levels and they were literally rationing to the absolute bare minimum to keep their people going, with the gang pinning them inside as they ate the local area bare.

Chris had shown up with two hundred advanced kobolds and had basically eradicated the gang inside of twenty minutes.

Half of that had been him marching up with a contingent of twenty behind him, and telling the gang to "fuck right off or I'll tear your head off and shit down your neck."

Apparently, he'd taken a dislike to them on sight.

Once he and his team had opened fire, the remaining hundred and eighty kobolds had run out of cover, and the result had been a slaughter.

The inhabitants had asked precisely two questions once he'd explained himself and the background of the dungeon.

First of all—were humans allowed in the dungeon; second—were there really hot showers and hot food?

He'd had to call for the dreadnought and use its nexus gate to transport everyone.

Robin and her little squad of trainees had been sent on a few missions as well, though when she started preaching the good word to people, I still walked off. As much as I knew we needed to do it, it still felt entirely wrong.

Like I'd started a cult, but without the upsides of meaningless sex with lots of nubile and innocent young ladies.

I interacted with the "priests" and the Paladins. I helped to guide their training—though John had a lot of that in hand and Rhodes was dealing with the rest—and beyond that, we'd just kept working.

Now the thousand-strong kobold army hidden beneath the stadium was ready, armed with rifles we'd looted from the army bases or summoned. And with a surfeit of ammo, they were just waiting to see whether anyone tried to take advantage of the opening we'd given them.

Trust, but have a big hammer.

I'd also been forced—by my council and the ladies—to allow Johnstone and the other nobles to come to the event as well. Mainly because there was no way that they'd have allowed their people to come without them having the best seats in the house.

Also the whole "don't fuck with me because I'll tear you a new asshole" part of the presentation would be pointless if we didn't let them come.

We'd spent a lot of the last two weeks setting this up, though, and that included allowing the London lot to buy things from us at the meeting point, both medicines and other materials. From food to armor, ammunition to well…everything else.

They were buying everything with tech, and some bright spark on their side had hit upon the idea of buying mana crystals as well. It was ostensibly so that they had a stockpile, ready for when we were able to provide the dungeon that they wanted. But as they'd asked, and then pushed hard, for me to provide the location of the strongest mana fields inside of their territory, I had little doubt that they intended to let the "dungeon core" that I was transporting to my southern dungeon reach its target.

Might made right, after all, and possession was nine-tenths of the law as a lot of people saw it.

Regardless, thinking over all that had led to this stage wasn't helping me. It was just to pass the time, as I got myself ready, I knew; the others had left me alone with my thoughts as we walked down to the preparation rooms.

Chris and Kelly watched me as I checked and rechecked my gear, ready for what was to come.

"You got everything?" Chris cocked one eyebrow.

I nodded, then grinned. "Bloody hope so." I checked my weapons again.

I had my hammer on my left hip and the sword over my right shoulder. A rifle with ten mags of ammo in my bag of holding, a holster on my right hip with a Magnum Research Desert Eagle in it and ten mags for that as well, though the plan was that such weapons were a last resort only. As were the three fragmentation grenades and five large healing potions, the best that we could create—though they were still pretty average compared to my actual normal healing ability now.

Lastly was a focal orb with the healing spell in it, a load of food and water, a medicine kit and a bedroll, just in case.

Beyond that, although I could have taken a shitload more potions and so on with me, there just wasn't any point. I could heal myself better than they could, so they were for emergencies.

If I was honest with myself, at this stage and after the last few weeks, I wasn't expecting to use them at all. And there was a warning from a very nervous Drak that if I took too much gear in with me, it'd not only be a waste—I'd lose space that could have held loot—but also if I took a shitload of healing potions and so on in with me, it'd lower the risk to me, and that'd lower the rewards.

He was being *very* careful at the minute, and it turned out that the coke problem had suddenly dried up for a lot of the dungeon, mysteriously, though he was well aware he was being watched.

As it was, the dungeon wouldn't be able to entirely assess me, as at no point inside of it had I gone all out fighting since my change. But the challenges would be targeted to an appropriate level for my stats, so it was still going to be a fight.

I checked the sword in its sheath, reaching over my back and shifting it slightly, listening as the hundreds of metal arms that held it in place opened and closed. The *snick-snick* of them all sliding open at once and then closing when I held the blade in place was like the drumming of rain on a tin roof, and it relaxed me.

A gentle thrum of power flowed through the blade, and again I wondered at it. Since the power I'd flooded it with and the divine essence I'd given it as well, there'd been more to it…much more.

I could tell where the sword was at any time, I could reach out blindly and touch it, and yet when I Examined it, it gave me sod all useful details.

Enchanted Blade	**Magical Weapon**
Damage:????	**Charge:**????
This sword is enchanted with both active mana and divine essence, but has yet to reveal its true potential.	
Durability:??/??	**Rarity**:????

The hammer wasn't much bloody better either.

Enchanted Hammer	**Magical Weapon**
Damage:????	**Charge:**????
This hammer is enchanted with active mana, but has yet to reveal its true potential.	
Durability:??/??	**Rarity**:????

What made it even less fucking helpful was that I'd never actually used it in battle to a point that it showed its power. I'd used it in a handful of minor fights, but as of yet, I'd either not had the opportunity or had no need to go all out, and it'd been frustratingly elusive to pin down.

I also had a copy of my shield, the same as the last one, and yeah, again, that was telling me fuck all.

It was currently strapped to my back, and it'd stay there unless I had a real need for it.

Today was all about using my enhanced body, my new armor and showing off, while also yeah, getting some practice in.

I gave Kelly another kiss and hugged her for a minute, before she pushed off and looked up at me.

"You better be out of there by tonight," she ordered me, leveling a finger at my nose. I offered her a mock salute, grinning, before she sighed and crooked a finger.

I lowered my head, and she put her lips to my ear, whispering what I'd get to do when—there was no mention of *if*, but *when*—I managed to pull this off.

I stared straight ahead for several seconds, before coughing and nodding.

"Yeah," I agreed, straightening and nodding to her. "Yeah, that works. I'll be back tonight."

"Glad to hear it." She gave me one last kiss and headed for the door, leveling a finger at Chris as she passed him. "I know you have good hearing, Chris, but I also *know* that you didn't listen to any of that, because if I hear about what I just said from anyone else later? I'll make sure that you get blue balls for a fuckin' year!"

"I didn't hear anything," Chris said quickly, holding both hands up and shaking his head. "Absolutely nothing at all. In fact, I think I need my hearing checked."

"Good boy." She winked over her shoulder at me and stepped out, leaving me with my oldest friend in the preparation room.

"So." He moved along one wall, reaching out and gently tugging on the hooks that hung there empty and silent, ready for the teams that would later pass through to leave unneeded gear. "You still set on this?"

"You know I need to do it." I shrugged, then sat down on a bench, giving Kelly the time to make her way up to the upper floors and to meet the VIPs before all of this began.

"I know. Still doesn't mean it's a good idea though." He shrugged. "And besides, I'm your mate. I don't like letting you go off into the unknown without me."

"You're a good man." I smiled gently.

"No, I'm not." He snorted. "I'm a bastard. I drink too much, I fight too much, and I joke far too much. I spend all my time that I can eating good food, drinking good booze, and chasing Becky's arse. Doesn't mean I don't care, though. I've not seen you much of late."

"I know, and despite all of that, you're still a good man," I assured him. "Besides, you've been in the gym most days."

"Yeah, but I can't fuckin' keep up with you. Not yet."

"You will," I told him, confident in my words as I watched him moving around, avoiding meeting my gaze. "You know why I gave the bolt to Akuba and Kaatachi…" I started, and he nodded.

"It was the right call," he agreed. "Fuck, man, we discussed it and you were right to do it. And they're nowhere near your level. They want to try the gym…you hear that?"

"No?"

"Yeah, I was speaking to one of their people last night—you know, the scouts they sent through?"

"I heard they sent a few people through, and they were given access to the various sites, but I didn't know they'd been to the gym."

"Yeah. I think they were just testing to see if we'd block them from anywhere, truth be told. As it is, they basically had a look around—one guy tried to lift your barbells and then they fucked off."

"How many were there?" I asked.

"Ten, in groups of two." He shook his head. "They fuckin' freak me out, man."

"Me too," I agreed. The pair of us fell silent for a minute, reflecting on them. *That'd* been a bit of a weird discovery.

Kelly and I had gone to visit them last week as a formal thing. We'd taken Chris and Mike, Robin, Ashley, and Catherine.

Kelly and me as the bosses, Chris, Mike, and Robin as the muscle, Ashley as the diplomat she was, and Catherine…

Well, we'd taken her because over the last two weeks, she'd grown a lot.

She was now able to sense death—literally. When there'd been a mass event, like a battle, she could point to it and describe the rough details. Apparently, it was something about the Life and Death mana that was released in such an event that it left an indelible mark on the world around the site.

That was a point in favor of the theory that mana had always been here, because once she'd started to realize what she was finding, we'd trawled the local historical records, and we'd found dozens of battlefields from deep in the past as well as the more modern ones.

As it was, though, it was so that she could see whether there was anything weird about the other dungeon. I was hoping that we'd not find out that it'd been slaughtering innocents, like the Gateshead one had been—or the mechanist's one, for that matter—and thankfully she'd not sensed anything like that.

What had come out of it, though, was that most of the population of the Congo dungeon, Akuba and Kaatachi's people, were *dungeon-born.*

That wasn't that weird. I mean, there were a lot of dungeon-born in my dungeon. But no, the thing that was weird was that they were advanced *humans*.

The pair had forgone most research paths, and had instead focused on summoning and advancing the human race.

That was just too fuckin' weird for me. We were, at best, the uncommon variety, and most of us were the common level. As near as I could tell, the system viewed those lucky bastards who had won the genetic lottery as uncommon, but that was it.

You know, that one guy or girl at school who was incredibly athletic, great at their classwork, and really good-looking? They were the uncommon ones.

The rest of us were common.

Akuba and Kaatachi, though, had developed the advanced variant. And just like the kobolds that made up much of our armed forces, they'd experimented and summoned specific warrior versions.

That was why they were such fucking units, when she'd sent us her elite guards to help. She'd been sending literal *elites*, or advanced warriors anyway. That was why they were all scarily similar. Only tiny variations were permitted, much in the same way that identical twins had tiny differences that could set them apart.

We found no sign of any mass killings of the population, and the only traces of deaths that could be felt by Catherine had all been easily linked to the battles that had gone on, so we'd had that as a slight reassurance at least.

We'd lasted three hours in the Congo dungeon, explored a little, made our invites to them about coming to the stadium, and we'd had food, and then we'd hightailed it outta there, really pretty freaked out.

Mainly because, if I was honest, the thought of an advanced version of me terrified me, as I thought about where they'd start and go from there.

It also worried me, because it opened the door to conversations I wasn't ready to have. Like, should we be summoning them as well? If we did, what was their moral and legal standing? And if a fight came, would I act differently when it came to sacrificing soldiers to achieve an objective?

Honestly, I just didn't know.

Moving on from that, we'd also put out a collection of invites on the nexus platform, leaving them ready for anyone to come and collect, as well as a bunch of "keys" to be able to open that specific nexus gate when the time came.

Just to make it clear, though, we weren't overly trusting either. The nexus gate opened into a mantrap that had concrete walls sheathed in titanium. It was a box, ten meters by thirty, that gave plenty of space for people to move in; then, should we need to, we could simply seal the door and trap them in there.

You know, in case of invading armies, or the French.

We'd also made a little addition to the room: a bunch of recessed and hidden nozzles that could pump in napalm. Just in case anyone wanted to fuck around and find out.

Then, because I was the paranoid one, Kelly—and I was guessing Ashley—had taken over and redecorated, making it all look more like an expensive hotel lobby, of one of those ornate marble railway stations instead of the severe and blatant threat I'd intended it as.

There were a few more minutes of general bullshitting, some bets placed on who would do better in there, me or if I gave him my armor and sent him in for a laugh. Then the conversation went totally into left field from there, betting whether our significant others would be able to tell us apart if we wore the armor and made it identical—there was a plan to give this level of armor to all my squad—and then the conversation went absolutely nowhere that we'd ever want anyone else to hear.

I was damn glad when the chime that had been installed went off, announcing a beginning to the day's festivities, and Chris finally shut up.

The conversation had been interesting, don't get me wrong, but wondering whether we could talk our girlfriends into letting us clone them through the dungeon, and if a threesome then counted as cheating…well.

It wasn't helping anyone, and would have resulted in us both being murdered if the ladies in question ever heard it.

Besides, we both agreed that, as I'd always secretly known, any man who had more than one partner was never getting twice as much sex. He was probably getting half, and twice as many jobs.

The truth was, though, as I stood and moved to the door, that Chris, as always, had been playing the fool and working to keep us both distracted from what was to come.

"Are you ready for this?" He stepped up to stand by my side, checking my armor one last time, tugging on a hidden strap and making sure it was tight, despite us both knowing it was.

"Nope," I admitted, taking a deep breath and rolling my shoulders.

"Well, I'll be rooting for you, brother." He rested one hand on my shoulder, squeezing.

Somehow I felt it, even through the armor, even through the layers, and I knew it was because as much as he was a dick, as much as we took the piss out of each other all the live-long day…

It was as he said.

He was my brother.

I turned and grabbed him, giving him a hug that clearly surprised him, but he grabbed onto me as well, hugging me hard until I let go.

Then he stepped back and nodded to me. "You've got this."

"I've got this," I agreed, blowing out a long breath. "If anything happens…look after them, and her, all right?" I looked over at him.

He nodded. His mouth opened to say something, but the chime sounded again, and now it echoed in the empty air.

The roar of the crowds and the constant noise of thousands of people finding their seats and for the first time in forever being able to let off some steam had died away, leaving only an expectant silence.

"Fuck it." Then I stepped forward. The door slid aside, letting me into the entryway of the dungeon.

CHAPTER TWENTY

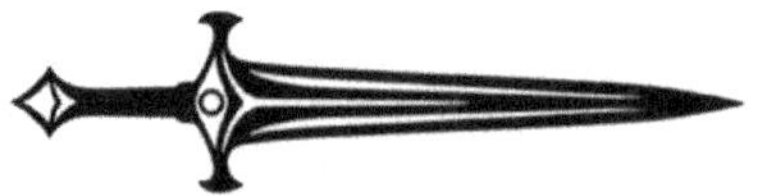

As soon as my foot crossed the boundary, the first notification rang out. As I saw it, I smiled. It'd worked.

Congratulations, Dungeon Warmancer!

You have entered the [First Glass Dungeon].

This dungeon is [Bound] and as such [cannot] be claimed.

Do you wish to continue?

*

WARNING!

Crossing the boundary will signify that you are ready and accept the risk posed to you by the inhabitants of the dungeon.

*

WARNING!

This Dungeon is set to [Advanced] and will be a lethal challenge for the unwary…

A red line appeared before me. Just like before, a light flowed across the floor, running left to right. This time, though, it wasn't across a sandy cavern floor—it slid across a floor of old flagstones. The entrance room had been created by Kelly to draw the eye, with a fountain in the center, in the vain hope that it might stay when the trial dungeon remade itself. I, being the tremendously intelligent man I am, once again immediately stepped over the line.

Congratulations, Dungeon Warmancer!

You have chosen to continue!

The dungeon has not been set beyond its most basic boundaries. Its inhabitants should be created to a level that will test your physical, mental, and magical prowess. There are currently limited options available to your dungeon to provide such beings at your level, and lower levels are obviously not appropriate for a full dive; therefore, you will face highly restricted loot.

Do you wish to face the inhabitants at this level, or, for double the chance at magical artifacts and significantly better loot, do you wish to face them at a level appropriate to your own?

That wasn't exactly a hard choice—it was what we were hoping for—but that it had acknowledged that there were few options available to set the dungeon's inhabitants was a surprise. Hopefully it wasn't about to summon a dungeon full of rare or higher opponents.

If it did? Maybe I could kill a few, and grab their corpses, and put them in my bag of holding?

Then, if they remained there, I could take them out at the end and absorb them into the dungeon. It might be a way to skip a shitload of research steps.

Mind you, that supposed I could kill them.

Minor detail, that.

And I'd still have to complete the entire dungeon each time, thanks to that 'leave it all behind' rule that kicked in at the start of the trial dungeon.

I sighed and mentally directed "higher level" at the prompt.

Excellent!

As a Dungeon Warmancer, you have entered your trial dungeon for the second time since it has grown fully active. Are you prepared to face a fresh Trial?

Yes/No...

> *Note: Although the rewards for surviving a full trial Dungeon are significant (including possible core level upgrades), the risk is also commensurately higher.*

BE AWARE — You may leave the dungeon at this time, but you will not be permitted to reenter until a fresh trial has been prepared...

I accepted it. The walls and floor shook—fuckin' violently. I grunted in shock at the drain as well. The dungeon's systems now grew opaque to me, as I was essentially locked out for the duration of the trial.

The one thing I did see, before I was locked out though, was that the drain this time wasn't a piddly little hundred and fifty-eight thousand mana—oh no, not like last time.

Three million mana was stripped from the dungeon, and I felt the shock that so much mana being torn free inflicted on the dungeon.

Weirdest of all, although it took the mana that was available—literally draining the dungeon to dangerous levels—I got the feeling that the mana it was using wasn't entirely ours.

Like last time, there had been a serious difference between the levels of mana that it'd taken, and the levels of mana that should have been required to make changes on the level that it'd done. Regardless, though, it was time to show my adoring—heh, probably bored and desperate for entertainment was more accurate—audience what they'd come to see.

Lots of death, destruction, and hopefully some seriously cool shit.

Congratulations, Dungeon Warmancer!

As you are participating in the trial dungeon, most of the high-level systems have been restricted. You have [10,0000] mana to spend to summon additional forces at any time, but this number is finite, and will not replenish.

Do you wish to access your additional forces at this time?

Yes/No

I paused, then shook my head, selecting No, as I had last time. I wanted to do as much as I could, and then summon the dungeon-born as I needed them. And, depending on the situation, with the plan of taking them out of the trial dungeon.

Except for the Daoine Sidhe, of course. They were absolute dickheads and could rot here.

Very well.

As this is the second time you have entered the trial dungeon while it is fully active, a short tutorial is available, as well as a series of recommendations. Do you wish to view them?

Yes/No…

As I'd already gone through this once, I selected No. The notifications dropped away. A final pulse overlaid my vision; the words floated in front of me, before vanishing as soon as they were read.

Then be welcome to your second Dungeon Trial, Dungeon Warmancer. The first floor, [The Verdant Cavern], awaits you…

I waited until the shaking of the floor had finished, then nodded to myself, striding forward.

The room, when I'd entered it, had been shallow and squared off, with the fountain in the corner and a bench seat. Beyond the flagstones that made up the floor and the great blocks of stone that made up the walls, that was pretty much it.

Now, the walls, ceiling, and floor gave one final shiver; dust cascaded free of them, floating downward.

The stone that was revealed beneath the previously brand-new and clean flagstones was…older. The shift had loosed a load of dust that settled gradually to the floor. Yeah, sure, that would generally make it look a lot older, but the stone was worn and battered on all sides; sand looked to be filling the gaps between the flagstones underfoot, and ancient mortar between the walls and ceiling stones.

The great doors that appeared before me on the other side of the room were wide enough that three of me could have entered abreast, and they stood at least three meters tall now. A circular motif was picked out on the stone, with the crack between the doors bisecting that motif down the center.

I reached out and put both hands flat against it, then pushed. Dust cascaded free again as with a great creak and groan the ancient-appearing doors opened…and I was hit with a blast of warm, wet air.

The passage that lay before me was dimly lit. Fitfully glowing blue mana crystals sat in sconces every five meters, giving off enough light to see by, but choked and half hidden by the tangle of vines and limbs that grew everywhere.

The passage ahead, was three meters high by five wide—a good size by anyone's imagination. But that space was mainly taken up by the growths that reached out and along toward me, filling the passage the farther I went in, until there was barely enough space for me to push through, snapping off smaller shoots and leafy tendrils as I went.

I forced myself through, stumbling when the cavern suddenly opened before me. I paused, staring wide-eyed, through the visor of my helmet at the newly revealed landscape before me.

The Verdant Cavern was a good name for it, I had to agree. The damn place had to be at least three times the size I'd been expecting as a maximum, even just considering the distance from this side to the far wall.

I was on a ledge that overlooked the cavern. The sound of burbling water was distant and muffled down to my right, a stream or river somewhere hidden from sight running that way.

There were cliffs that ran down from where I stood, and a narrow path that led down from here into the cavern below.

Hell, if it wasn't for the ceiling that I could see, literally meters away, I'd have sworn I'd somehow found myself outside, overlooking a gorge, possibly somewhere in Central America.

It had that wild, Amazonian look, with great trees covered in vines and the cliff walls coated in vibrant green mosses.

Caves dotted the walls; old, forgotten, and long-collapsed ruins in the center of the valley, and…*no*. I had to keep this straight in my mind. In the fucking *hall*!

The ruins were covered in lianas, and here and there, colorful birds fluttered. There were grassy fields that looked incredibly inviting, and even what looked—from here, anyway—like some kind of overgrown seating area.

The trees rose and fell as I looked out across the expanse before me. Where the shadows of the great canopies should have brought at least dimness, there were bioluminescent glimmers that shone invitingly.

All in all, it was a verdant paradise, and I damn well knew it was going to be a hellhole—and not only because of the seriously increased heat I was feeling…nor the smell.

It smelled like something had died in here and recently, possibly of intestinal issues. And the heat was that uncomfortably muggy kind of heat that made your back sweat like a nineties' movie producer or a priest when the police came for an unexpected visit.

No, the real reason it was going to be a hellhole was because, in addition to the monsters waiting for me down there, I'd already felt the sting of at least three mosquitos.

How the hell they'd made it through my armor, I didn't know. But it was a dungeon from hell, all right, if it was creating those little bastards.

It was also seriously concerning on another level, I realized, starting down the overgrown path along the cliffside. I had one species of vermin in my dungeon: rats.

That was it.

As far as I knew, I had no insects, nothing like this as a species that was summonable. As I moved on, trying my best to be as quiet as possible—and meaning I was making more noise than a shitting dog with a tambourine necklace in all my armor—I guessed that simply due to the sheer scale of the land we'd absorbed, and the creatures we'd killed inside the dungeon's radius by now, we had to have more templated creatures in there somewhere than I thought.

Hell. There was probably a supply of worms or whatever just from the soil we'd taken in, and yet…what the hell had possessed the dungeon to create this?

I took another step, slipped slightly on an unstable part of the ground, and kicked a stone.

It clattered against another, then fell off the side of the narrow path that I'd been following, vanishing into a low mist that was climbing up the walls around me, and clattered against something else in the distance.

There was a half second pause, before screeches and howls started up. I sighed, knowing damn well it was time to play.

I'd made it barely a quarter of the way down the side of the cavern wall, by my estimation, when the caves that were recessed into the cliff walls on all sides, as well as vanishing into the rising mist in the distance, exploded with movement.

I froze, staring and trying to track one of them. The mist interfered with my Examination, until the creature burst through it, screeching, and flew at me.

Harpy	Avian Predator
The Harpy is a large, swift, and deadly avian predator known for its vibrant plumage and razor-sharp talons. These creatures are predominantly female, with striking humanoid features that can captivate their prey. Harpies are closely tied to the elemental forces of air and storms, wielding powerful magic to control the winds and weather. Abilities: *Gale Force!* Harpies can summon powerful gusts of wind to knock back enemies or propel themselves through the air at incredible speeds. *Thunder Clap!* By infusing their wings with Storm mana, then clapping them together, Harpies can create a deafening thunderclap that stuns and disorients their prey, though this results in damage to their wings. *Storm Shroud!* Harpies can conjure a swirling vortex of storm clouds around themselves, obscuring their movements and protecting them from ranged attacks. Weaknesses: Earth, Fire, and Metal Magics HP: 120/120 Stamina: 80/80 Mana: 400/400 Speed: 9/10 Level: 6	
HP: 120/120	**Special Abilities**: 3/3

The harpy was fast-moving, and once again, the design of the creature was a serious indicator of "intelligent" design, as there was absolutely no fuckin' reason that such a creature should have had such tremendous tits under any circumstances.

That was the last thought I had time for, before a flicker of movement from my right had me jumping backward.

A second harpy had taken advantage of my distraction. I failed to get entirely out of the way in time, though it wasn't for lack of trying.

The harpy's talons raked across my armor, screeching as they left shallow scratches. I twisted, grabbing its ankle and using its momentum to drag it around and hurl it into the cliff face. There was a satisfying crunch as it hit; the indignant squawk that I'd dared to grab it was swiftly cut off by the stone of the wall partially smashing its beak in.

Keeping hold of the ankle, I dragged it down, even as it tried to claw its way free. Its other taloned foot kicked out…and did fuck all damage to my armor that I could see.

I couldn't help but grin inside my helmet, as I spoke. "Right then," I offered, reaching out with my other hand and gripping the bloody beak of the harpy. "Let's dance."

More screeches filled the air as the rest of the flock descended. I counted at least a dozen of the feathered fuckers, all with murder in their eyes and cleavage that defied gravity.

I yanked my left hand back, even as I planted my right hand on the shoulder of the harpy in front of me. The combination of the brace point, the natural movement of the neck, and yeah, my demigod level of strength didn't just serve to break the creature's neck… I nearly tore the head off.

Staring at the body as it collapsed before me, I couldn't help but grin evilly. Then the others arrived.

There was a battering of wings as at least a dozen all streamed inward, dive-bombing me at first, their clawed feet outstretched and grasping. They came from the sides, from before me and above. One even flew up from directly below—and each and every bloody one of them regretted it.

The next to arrive had tried to grasp my helmet, clearly thinking to rip it off. The second foot coming in right after the first would have probably taken out my eyes and ended the fight real fast…if not for the fact that the helmet was locked into the gorget on my throat. Instead of the harpy delivering a swift and decisive blow, it gripped onto my armor, pivoted around the fulcrum of my immobile head, and got grabbed in turn.

I used its legs as my own fulcrum, yanking it back down, then whipped it around and brought it down into the fast-flying fucker that tried to approach from the empty air over the side of the cliff and below.

There was a scream, a screech…and the pair vanished from sight in a cloud of feathers. Both were bleeding already as they fell, apparently blaming the other for the situation and determined to kill them for the affront.

Two more that had been swooping in, presumably to dive-bomb me as well, now thought better of it. They beat their wings hastily, hovering before me, as more came in.

They were weird creatures. As they stared at me now, I finally had the opportunity to see something beyond the ridiculous attention grabbers they'd been designed with.

They were covered in feathers. Even their…chests…were simply feathers, though smaller and in a ridiculous variety of plumages. Their legs ended in talons like a giant eagle's, and they had a short tail like that of a bird of prey.

Their arms and their upper legs were humanoid, if feathery, and they, too, ended in claws—though these were much smaller and tipped fingers that looked suited to gripping and tearing. The head was a perverse mixture of human in the shape of the upper skull, with feathers flowing back like hair. But where the eyes were almost humanoid, though slightly bulging, the maw wasn't.

It extended forward, looking more beak or muzzle than jaw. The shape made it clear—along with the sharp teeth that extended within—that it was a meat eater evolved for biting and tearing.

There were no chewing teeth there—nothing flat, designed to pulverize. No, these fuckers tore large sections of meat free and swallowed them whole, like a shark, and the teeth showed that.

They started casting, one at a time, demonstrating at least a rudimentary intelligence that hadn't been on show until now, as they unleashed their main attack, one after another from different directions and angles.

As I was, perched on the side of the cliff, following a narrow game trail toward the ground with cliffs all around and nothing apparently soft below to land on—besides the other two still scabbling harpies—this could have been a bad place to be caught out.

Unfortunately—for them, not me—the harpies' primary spell choice was apparently Gale Force, which was a blast of wind. I was a heavy motherfucker in my armor right now, braced with my back against the wall and feet firmly planted.

When that failed, they really made a mistake, and used Thunderclap.

It was a purely Air-based spell, which I had a high resistance and affinity for already. But combined with the fact it was a Storm-based spell?

I just started to laugh.

Then I triggered my Lightning. It coursed through me, building, and I drew my hammer. As the nearest harpy dove, I swung, connecting with a meaty thwack that sent the smaller creature tumbling free in a cloud of feathers and blood. Lightning had arced from the hammer, frying the creature on impact. It dropped like a stone, smoking slightly, and most *definitely* dead.

"Well now, you'd think you fuckers would have a high affinity to the storm. I mean, seriously?" I snorted, shaking my head as more gave up on the spells and flew in, even as others continued casting the wind spell in the hopes of unseating me.

Two more came at me from different angles, one high and one along the wall from my left. I ducked the higher. Talons whistled over my head; then I brought my hammer up in an uppercut that caught the other square in the chin. There was a cracking sound of bone and a burst of feathers as it somersaulted backward in a shower of blood, most of its head…well, gone, really, beyond the bloody mush that was raining down.

The air filled with ear-splitting screeches as the harpies unleashed their Thunderclap spell over and over, clearly not learning from the effect of it last time. My helmet dampened some of the sound, which was probably the most damaging part of it for me, but I still saw the risk they'd pose to anyone who wasn't, as I was, Storm-born. Then I saw them start to conjure their Storm Shrouds.

"You *cannot* be that stupid, right?" I growled, pouring my mana into a widespread Lightning Bolt that I channeled and tore from left to right, carving five more of them from the sky in blackened, burning bundles. Several that I'd not managed to hit with the main bolt were taken down as well as it arced and flared between the harpies, disrupting their spell. Several more plummeted to the ground far below, their fragile bodies and hollow bones shattering as they impacted the mossy stone.

As I fought, I noticed the mist below growing thicker. Squinting, I could just make out the shapes of what had to be dryads, their arms raised as they fueled the supernatural fog.

I started to make my way down the path, swatting harpies out of the air as I went. By the time I reached the bottom, half the flock was either dead or nursing broken wings.

That's when I heard it—a low, menacing growl from within the mist.

"Ah, shit, now what?" I muttered, readying my hammer as the first of the houndborn burst into view.

They were the magically augmented dogs that we'd bought the design from Leilani and Kai awhile back. And yeah, I was regretting that right now, considering the first to close with me was something like a rottweiler, the size of a small horse, with anger issues.

Oh, and it fucking glowed and breathed *fire*.

It was like fighting a pack of wolves on steroids. They came at me in waves, all teeth and claws and barely contained bloodlust. But compared to my first concerns at the aerial assault of the harpies, this was almost laughable.

The fire, which was undoubtably the most lethal aspect they had, was short range, and damaged each other when they were caught in it. It also required them to stiffen their front legs, brace themselves like a cat bringing up a hairball, and hold their mouths in just the right way or they risked burning their own faces off.

A single grab of a snout, holding the mouth of the nearest one closed induced utter panic in it, until its neck detonated in a shower of flaming gore.

Hard fail on that design, I decided, making a mental note to work on it.

The changes wreaked on my form recently meant that when I pushed hard—and I was now—I could move like greased lightning, literally blurring from side to side, dodging the snapping jaws and flashing claws, before shoving them aside with the head of my hammer or backhanding them.

The lightning that I was continually circulating through my body now meant that even these impacts at this point were like a full-on punch from Mike Tyson in his prime, combined with a taser.

I strode forward. The harpy flock above had pulled back a bit, stunned by the savagery of the assault. Now they tried again, assuming I was distracted by the houndborn.

I fell into a rhythm: swing, dodge, fire a blast of lightning upward and fry an incoming harpy, rinse and repeat. Bodies piled up around me, a mix of feathers and fur. The dryads, realizing their mist wasn't helping, started to lob what looked like exploding seed pods at me.

It was chaos, pure and simple. But with my enhanced abilities, it felt more like a workout than a life-or-death struggle. I grinned behind my helmet, feeling the rush of combat flow through me.

"Come on then!" I roared, lightning crackling around me. "Who's next?"

As the last houndborn fell and the remaining harpies finished falling, their feathers filling the air with sooty flames as the lightning set them alight, I stood amid the carnage, barely winded.

The dryads, seeing their allies fall, screamed their hatred and started to close, instead of the best thing they could have done—which was melt back into the lush greenery and hope I left them be.

The fight with the five dryads took less than a minute. The five large creatures approached me, only to find four of their number howling and collapsing to the ground, their heads charring black as I fired off four Incinerates in quick succession.

"Gotta love realistic magic," I muttered, staring at them as they fell. "Cook the brain and no matter what you are, you're dead. If this was a game, you'd have probably just lost some hit points and kept going."

The last one leapt at me, its form more "Treebeard" than "wooden woman." Its arms lengthened at the last second, questing roots and vines bursting from their fingertips to splash against my chest, then wrap in tight, squeezing and digging into my armor.

I waited as it wailed and roared in its fury, stepping in closer, before I responded by bringing the hammer up and around. It twisted, trying to dodge, but considering the stupid bastard had gone straight for the largest concentration of my armor, confident of crushing it…when it didn't work, it ended badly for it.

The flat head slammed into the side of its wooden skull and lightning discharged at the same time as the hammer landed. Given I put a lot of force into it, wanting to demonstrate the difference in my level and that of those watching, the wooden head might as well have been made of dry sticks.

Fragments of wood flew in all directions. The dryad stood for several long seconds as the vital force that animated it died away. The green light that glowed from deep within dimmed by the second, even as I tore away the limbs that were still attached to me.

Striding back, I examined the bodies, searching, until I found the last survivor—a harpy that had dragged herself into the undergrowth. Her breath whistled through a punctured lung as she tried to hide.

"Hey in there, want to surrender peacefully and serve me?" I offered, only to have her screech and—proving that she was more animal than aware—spray a load of shit out at me like a skunk.

"Wow, excuse you," I growled. The stench got noticeably worse, right up until I hit her and the area around her with a repeated dose of Incinerate to make sure it was all taken care of.

That done, and nothing else in the area that wasn't trying fucking hard not to be noticed, the first of the reliquaries appeared before me.

I rolled my shoulders, surveying the battlefield. "Well," I chuckled, "that's one way to clear a room."

Needless to say, the loot that I got from the creatures was pretty shit.

There had to be some kind of a link between the effort put in and the result, because almost everything that I got from the bodies was either healing herbs—that was the dryads—fur and leather—mainly the houndborn—and a handful of copper coins and a single silver, and some feathers from the harpies.

Lastly, after jumping up and searching the nearest harpy caves quickly, I found a pair of healing potions, a stamina one—all the lowest quality, unfortunately—and a small seedling that showed as all question marks when I picked it up. I put that in my bag of holding, and jumped from the cave to the ground, some ten meters below. Landing easily, I headed for the far side, where the door in that wall stood out, wreathed by massive vines and golden-leaved trees.

I made it halfway, before I found out that the creatures I'd fought so far weren't the extent of the inhabitants.

Fuck.

CHAPTER TWENTY-ONE

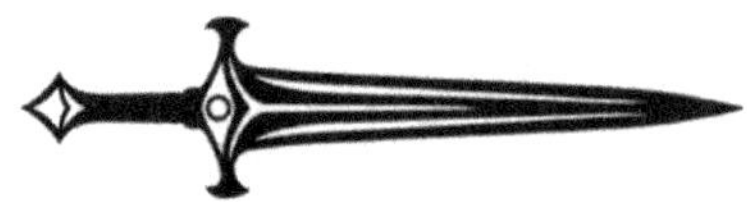

The first clue that I had was the flash that appeared in the corner of my vision. The second was the health marker that I'd gotten so used to just ignoring all day, every day, suddenly changed color from red to an off-green.

The change confused me for a few seconds. I pulled up the notification and cursed, then started looking around.

WARNING! You have been poisoned by Myconid spores. Effect reduced due to resistances

-15 HP per second for 60 seconds…59…58…

Myconids. They were the goddamn fungus thingies that I'd gotten access to before, but I was buggered if I could see them anywhere.

Mind you, they were also fuckin' mushroom people, so yeah, it wasn't a surprise that I couldn't see them. They were clearly hiding somewhere nearby, but…

A new notification flashed. I looked at it; the effect had increased and the timer had refreshed.

"What the hell?" I muttered, turning slowly. I saw a few bioluminescent patches, but when I blasted one with a lightning bolt, it just exploded, making the cloud worse. There was no kill notification, nothing of use to suggest that I'd killed something worth the effort, or even at all.

I tried again, dragging a sustained lightning bolt across the ground and back and forth nearby through some trees in the hope of at least making someone shout "Ow" but got bugger all.

There wasn't even a "You have killed a mosquito," which would have been some kind of a consolation prize at least.

Then I realized that if the spores were this strong here, nothing else was going to be alive.

Fuck.

I backed up slowly, looking around. The counter was being continually refreshed now, meaning that they had to be all around.

I checked the ground, the trees, the fuckin' air.

Nothing.

How the hell was there literally nothing anywhere nearby?

I launched myself into the air, streaming up and hopefully out of the cloud of spores…only to find that the counter was still refreshing!

How the hell had it…

Movement, at last.

I spun, staring and seeing nothing but the tree that was nearby.

I could have sworn the bastard thing had moved. But now, as I stared at it, I couldn't make anything out.

Another movement in the corner of my eye, and I spun around, then cursed and triggered my lightning, rolling it through me again and again, feeling the healing that it granted.

That was a relief, but the overall effect was up to a hundred and ten points a second now, and still refreshing—so what the hell was going on?

When I moved forward, the trees on all sides seemed to shimmer as I passed them. But looking directly at them did nothing—not up until I decided it was time to stop playing silly buggers, anyway.

There was something wrong about a tree ahead of me and to the right. It was slightly off the path between where I floated now and the exit I'd been heading for, and it looked like there was also a large clear area ahead I'd not really noticed before now.

I noticed a pattern to the shimmering, nothing I could make out, not really, and certainly nothing that was responding to my Examine spell either, but…there was definitely something there.

Checking my mana, I saw that I was eleven hundred mana down now. But considering that still left me with over twenty-two thousand mana, fuck it.

I reached out, focusing on that tree, and unleashed Atomic Furnace.

One thousand, five hundred mana vanished in an instant. The top of the tree exploded into flames, lighting the area around with flickering for all of about half a second, before I found that I'd just made what could only be described as a very big boo-boo.

First, because I'd not been sure exactly what I was aiming for, but I was well aware that the spell summoned "the heart of the sun in a designated area" that was designated as one meter. It was, however, possible to spread the area farther and farther; it just massively lessened the strength of the spell.

The thing with spreading the heart of the sun around a little, though, is that the lessened heat is a relative thing.

Even though it dropped off in effect by something like ninety percent per meter I spread it, that was still a hell of a temperature. And across the ten meters of the tree's canopy I aimed it at, it meant that the outer edge merely burst into flames, while the inner…well, the air wasn't there anymore, combusted in a fraction of a second.

As the air was eaten up, that pulled in the air around to fill that vacuum—nature abhors a vacuum, I'd been told, which seemed a bit cruel, considering it kept the house cleaner, but fuck it—and as the air rushed in, it dragged those flames with it. That spread the flames out and about even more, and the air on all sides was also pulled in to balance the loss out…

And that was when I found out that the myconid spores were, in fact, *highly* flammable.

The explosion that rolled out was close to the kind of thing a fuel air bomb created. And considering I was hurled backward across the clearing and into a wall, well, there was fuck all chance of a mushroom man surviving that, that was for sure.

I had to break myself out of the cracked and broken wall of the cliff I found myself driven into, with my health at half and my ears ringing. Blood dribbled from my ears and nostrils, as I shouldered my way free and dropped to the ground.

The formerly verdant valley before me was now a mess of burning, shattered wood, blackened vegetation, and smoldering rock, with a clear path to the far side visible as another of the great trees slowly toppled sideways with a long, drawn-out roar.

As it hit the ground—still ablaze—there came a great crash, and for the first time I saw a Myconid. Or more accurately, I saw the flaming remains of one.

Checking my notifications I found that yeah, there'd only been one, and fuck me, that made it clear just how the dungeon itself was balancing the books.

It'd put one in as a floor boss, and that fucker had to have been huge!

The vines, the lianas, the general bioluminescence…all of it—it wasn't a bunch of different creatures or plants. *It was all the top of one fuckin' mushroom man that'd been buried in the ground*!

I only knew that because notifications were flashing. The center of that clearing ahead had collapsed and was burning with a hell of a lot of enthusiasm, and right in the middle was a slowly revolving reliquary.

Given that they only appeared when you were out of danger, I brushed more of the stone free and lifted into the air, flying across the intervening distance like Superman, deliberately not looking up to see whether I could spot any of the weird alien tech that let people see me.

My armor was still covered in small burning bits, the cloak itself was tattered, and yeah, if I was honest, there was more blood dripping out of my armor than I liked.

Not that I was kinky and generally enjoyed it, but you know. Hero and all that.

I just knew that they were almost certainly watching me, though, so cool as a cucumber was the way to play this—and not as I actually wanted to go, and lob my dick out to piss on the flames while shouting about goddamn cheating mushrooms.

I *never* liked mushrooms.

I pulled up the notifications before I reached the reliquary. I only had a limited time to claim it, but I guessed that I had the time for this easily.

Congratulations!

You have killed the following:

- 1x Greater Myconid, Level 40, 5,000 XP
- 30x Harpies, Level 25, 3,000 XP
- 10x Houndborn, Level 25, 1,500 XP
- 5x Dryads, Level 20, 5,000 XP

Total XP awarded: 14,500 XP

Current XP to next level stands at 48,965/120,000

So the dungeon had leveled them all to a set place as well, which was interesting. But that the dryads had been only slightly lower in level than the grove leader I'd fought last time, or so I remembered, and yet had awarded much less XP?

Well, that fuckin' sucked.

Checking it, as I lowered myself and reached out to touch the reliquary, I found that yeah, the last time I'd fought one, I'd gotten well over double the XP and it'd only been five levels higher!

Mind you, if I was honest with myself, that fight had been hard. This one? It was taking the piss really. Looks like I was up against the old law of diminishing returns. So unless I started fighting gods and their creations more regularly, I was going to be taking a lot longer to reach the next levels.

All that annoyance—which, I had to admit, had a little hint of whiney bitch about it as well—was banished as soon as I touched the reliquary.

Thorn	**Magical Weapon**
Damage: 0-200	**Charge:** 50/50
The weapon known as "Thorn" has been wielded many times over the years since it was gifted to the dungeon collective, and yet rarely has it been wielded by one who has understood its nature. The damage Thorn wields is dependent on its wielder. Be wary, for any enchanted weapon has the potential to change a battlefield; this one, however, may just change its wielder's life… Abilities: Unknown	
Durability: 57/100	**Rarity:** Unique

I read it once, and that was all that was needed. The long, single-edged blade had a slight curve to it and patterning all along it that made me think it'd been grown rather than made.

Then add in that the handle looked like wood, felt like a living branch, and gave a solid sense of yearning for growth?

This was going to Chris, and I damn well couldn't wait to hand it over.

Sure, there was a little part of me that shouted that it was an enchanted weapon and I was the lord around these parts—it *should* be mine.

I wasn't that much of a dick, though, and it wasn't like this was the only enchanted item we had.

Hell, those goddamn Blades of T'Pau were still in storage somewhere. And just remembering that made me curse and feel incredibly stupid.

We had a load of powerful artifacts and we kept putting them aside for study, safe in the knowledge that we needed to make more of them, so that was a better use for them, rather than, you know, putting them to use stabbing people who annoyed us.

That was going to change, I silently vowed, hefting the sword and looking it over.

Thorn, as I'd noted, was a long blade, single edged, and slightly curved, making it look something like a katana, but thicker and with a pointed, sharp tip. The hilt had a basket-type guard that was formed into a pattern of leaves that seemed to roll around the hand, protecting it. When I looked closely, I could see dozens of small thorns that lay at the edges of the leaves, facing outward.

Hitting someone with the hilt of this weapon would seriously hurt!

The rest of the grip was interesting as well…some kind of leather maybe? I examined it, but couldn't make it out. The pommel stone was a black diamond the size of a hen's egg, carved to finish in a point that was sharp as sin.

All in all, when you added in the patterning of the folded Damascus-like blade and the flowing script that ran along the fuller, it was a thing of terrible beauty, and I knew my friend would love it.

I slid it into my bag of holding and moved on, floating across the field of devastation. The smoke wafted this way and that, out of my way as I headed to the doors, that even now were slowly opening wide.

The first level of the trial dungeon was complete.

I touched down at the top of a flight of stairs. The click of my boots on the stone was barely audible above the complicated destruction and burning that was all that I'd left on the last floor, and I headed downward without pause.

The stairwell was dimly lit, but this time there were no plants to fill it. The sound of the stone door behind me closing with a boom rang out, echoing down and around me. But within a few seconds, that too died away, and I was left with the clicking sound of my armored boots on the steps.

This section, like the entrance, was made up of huge and seemingly ancient stones. Dust was piled in the corners, and the occasional skeleton of a dead mouse or bits of insects were just noticeable.

I stared at a huge spider in a web that shivered as I passed it at one point, sitting in the corner where the wall met the ceiling, and I damn well watched that fucker as I went.

Instinct said to kill it, and kill it with fire, but I was being good.

For all I knew, that bloody Alexander was up there commenting loudly that I was probably afraid of spiders, and I wasn't about to give him the satisfaction.

I mean, I was, to a degree—that was just common sense, I felt—but I was also a bit freaked out by snakes, and I'd successfully kept that quiet so far.

That reminded me of a joke I'd heard about Trust and a snake, that she'd apparently stood on one when someone had been trying to get her out of office, and it'd not bitten her out of professional courtesy.

That and other inane bullshit kept my mind busy until I reached the bottom of the stairs, which definitely seemed far higher and longer than they should have been. But when I reached the door at the bottom, finally, it was a relief.

It was, however, a very short-lived relief. As soon as I opened it, there was a second door ahead of me, and a small square room between the obvious "safe zone" of the stairwell and the new area.

The goddamn door ahead of me that led to this section of the dungeon was a massive portal that just confused the hell out of me, considering it looked to have been created by dwarves on crack.

The outer edge of the door was a line of arcane-looking symbols, some kind of mixture of the weird elvish in the old stories and the kind of symbols you got around the dead pharaohs of old, all self-contained in a smooth ring of onyx that ran in a circle around the door itself.

The door was circular—obviously, circle of symbols and all that—but it clearly wasn't the kind of a door that had a cheery little floormat before it.

Oh no, it wasn't even the kind of passive-aggressive one that warned that people posting brochures were as welcome as religious nutters, which is to say not at all and to fuck right off.

No, this door was a circular mass of cogs, levers, and symbols that were set into dials and panels.

This was a fucking puzzle door. I paused, looking around the room. Vents were obvious in the walls, floor, and ceiling, and as I felt the rising heat already, I took the hint.

If I fucked this up, it wasn't going to end well for me.

The door that I'd just entered through chose that moment to give an ominous creak, and started to swing closed, giving me a brief chance to run like buggery and rethink my life, before I shrugged. My Intelligence was higher than an all-night rave at a cocaine factory, and I liked my odds.

I let the door close, then stepped up and stared at the massive gear-shaped door, wondering who the fuck designed this monstrosity. It was easily five meters across, all burnished bronze and intricate carvings. But it was the central mechanism that really caught my eye. A circular contraption that looked like the bastard love child of a clock and a Rubik's cube.

"Well, this is just peachy," I muttered and squinted through the rising heat, stepping closer to examine it. "Not a problem, though…not a problem." It also helped that I was fairly sure if the shit hit the fan, I could smash the door…eventually.

The thing was divided into four sections, each packed with gears of various sizes. They all connected to a central gear sporting a clock face, its hands stuck at high noon. Each quadrant had its own theme: Dawn, Noon, Dusk, and Midnight.

Subtle, that.

I reached out to touch one of the gears in the Dawn quadrant, running my fingers over it as I puzzled my way around it, and the whole bloody thing came to life. Gears started to spin, a low hum filled the air, and the clock in the center began to tick ominously, while steam started to rise from the various vents around the room.

"Oh, for fuck's sake," I growled, realizing this was on a timer and looking with my fingers instead of my eyes had activated it. Because why make anything easy, after all?

I focused on the Dawn quadrant first. The outermost gear had a rooster symbol, while the one closest to the center showed a rising sun. Made sense—dawn and all that. The other gears had stars and a crescent moon. The goal seemed clear: twist the dials until I'd managed to create a path from night to day.

But of course, it couldn't be that simple. Moving one gear affected the others in the quadrant. It was like trying to solve a puzzle while drunk and on a merry-go-round.

Pressing on some while I spun others let me know that there was a lot more machinery behind or inside the door than I could see, because there was no way I could just hold some in place and cheat a little, unfortunately.

That was fine, though. I was smarter than the average cookie before all this began, and I was definitely smarter now—or so I told myself.

Spinning the dials moved the others in a pattern, I could see, and with five dials, leading from the center out, I just had to figure the pattern.

There were discs in each ring, discs with small symbols that could be slid outward into the rings on either side and were clearly mixed up. So the first trick was moving the rings around and sliding the symbol from the one "full" spot on the ring, into the "empty" slot on the one that I wanted it on. That took about a minute, the solid clicking and clunking as I moved the dials and their symbols filling the air.

That done, I tried to align them in a single path from the smallest ring to the main symbol for dawn on the middle of the door.

The first dial also moved the third, so spinning those into place was simple enough. The smallest dial at the center could make three or four revolutions to a single revolution of the third wheel. The second and the fifth were linked as well, though for some reason that ratio was reversed; despite the bigger disc being, well, bigger, it took less spins to move.

I managed to align the Dawn quadrant after a few attempts, creating a path from the rooster to the sun. A soft click rewarded my efforts, and I moved on to Noon.

This one was easier—all sun symbols. I just had to create the brightest path to the center, pick the ones from slightly dim to very bright and booyah. Another click.

Dusk proved trickier. It had a mix of sun and moon symbols, and I had to create a gradual transition from light to dark. By now, the ticking of the central clock was getting louder, and sweat beaded on my forehead inside my helmet as the steam vents slid wider and wider. The air in here was hot enough and wet enough that I felt like I was going to be drinking the air soon.

Water ran down the door and walls now in rivulets, dripping from the ceiling and pooling on the floor.

"Come on, you bastard," I hissed, fingers flying over the gears.

Midnight was the real kicker. All the gears were dark, with various night sky symbols, and just sorting them out took far longer than I'd like. The thought that I should pull out my hammer and start smashing shit reared its head time and time again.

I had to align them to create the darkest path to the center, which was about as easy as finding a black cat in a coal cellar.

The clock ticked faster, the sound drilling into my skull, and in the back of my mind the music from the damn TV show 'Countdown' started playing just to annoy me further. My armor was starting to burn my skin now; steam fountained from vents around the doorframe. I blinked sweat clear, staring hard at the symbols as I moved them one after another, the dials clicking as I locked them into place.

Clearly, failure wasn't an option…unless I fancied being parboiled.

With seconds to spare, I aligned the last gear. There was a moment of tense silence, then a series of loud clicks as all four quadrants locked into place. The central clock gear began to spin wildly, hands whirling around its face.

The door shuddered…then slowly began to open with a groan of metal. The air around me whirled like someone had opened the door to a sauna, before the wet heat that had been so unpleasant a second ago was boiled away in a heartbeat by what lay beyond.

I stepped back, wiping sweat from my brow and grinning despite myself as I made the mistake of thinking I'd gotten the hardest part out of the way.

As the door swung fully open, the steam billowing free and evaporating to reveal the mechanical nightmare beyond, I couldn't help but wonder what other delights this floor had in store.

Instantly, I was filled with both elation and dread.

Elation because Finn and his people were going to go fucking nuts to get in here. Dread because not only was this perfect for them, but it was heavily populated, and there was no way the current inhabitants were going to take kindly to me rocking up and interrupting their day.

CHAPTER TWENTY-TWO

As I stepped through the doorway, the heat from the puzzle room gave way to a cacophony of sound and motion. The forge stretched out before me, a vast chamber of whirring gears, hissing steam, and clanking machinery. The air was thick with the smell of hot metal and oil, and literal rivers of glowing steel were being funneled into molds.

I barely had time to take in the spectacle before movement caught my eye. As the last of the steam vanished, a new, far higher temperature washed over me and made the water that had been covering my armor start to sizzle as the metal continued to heat even further.

The walls were a mixture of stone, veined with various metals, and solid steel plating. Pipes ran everywhere, with small vents in their sides, presumably as safety valves to bleed off heat, and damn, they were busy.

A huge clockwork mechanism dominated the center, its presses raising and lowering, and welding torches flashing from mechanical arms that juddered and slid out, illuminating the room.

A swarm of what could only be clockwork crawlers skittered across the floor toward me, their metal legs clicking against the stone. Unlike the original versions that we'd gained access to, each was about the size of a large dog, with six legs and two arms ending in various tools.

I had a brief pause as I noted that although the hammers they carried weren't exactly happy-making, at least they were tools, and not weapons. Then they changed.

The front limbs split in half, rotating, and a blade came into sight. Then the limb closed again, leaving a fucking sword at the end of each forward left arm, instead of the grasping pincers that had been there.

"Well, shit," I muttered, raising my hands as lightning crackled to life and flowed between my fingers. I unleashed a blast at the incoming swarm, taking the foremost in the head. The impact smashed it from its feet; bits flew in all directions and the arc jumped from one crawler to the next. Several exploded in showers of sparks and twisted metal before the charge died, but more kept coming.

They were faster than I expected, but the massive surge in power I'd received since my ascendence meant that although there was always a risk, it was a manageable one.

I lunged and my hammer came down on the head of the nearest as it scuttled forward. The hammer tore through the head, shattering it in a spray of metallic components, crystals, and cogs that flew in all directions.

A blade flashed out from the next in line, angled for my wrist where I gripped the hammer. I yanked the hammer back fast. The blade clanged off the head, and then I unleashed a blast of lightning into the attacker's face.

Its crystal eyes, glaring out from under a triangular prow, exploded. The body shuddered and quivered as the entire thing locked up, secondary flares of lightning dancing into the nearby metal monsters. I kicked it, sending its body staggering. I crouched, fixing their form in my mind as insectile. The body behind the head was split into two sections, a thorax and a… I forgot the word, but a butt, basically.

The butt was open to the air from above, clearly designed for transporting things. Some had a stone tank, presumably ready for metal to be poured in, while others had a basket or a collection of parts.

The one thing they all had in common—besides being scary-looking mofos—was that they were clearly not here to get me cake and cookies.

I took to the air, using my flight ability to gain a better vantage point, while almost absently throwing more lightning down toward the now confused clockwork monstrosities. From up here, I could see the entire layout of the forge. A massive central clockwork mechanism dominated the room, its gears turning ponderously.

Three narrow rivers of what looked to be liquid metal poured forward, heading into channels that in turn slid into and around the mechanism. I watched a mechanical press lower into a pool; a lower section rose to meet it as unneeded metal flowed free, the angles slowly increasing to aid runoff.

A great cloud of gasses escaped as the top and bottom met, and a screech of pressure increased. The two sections clanked free again, a now perfectly formed breastplate revealed…if a giant needed a fuckin' breastplate, anyway.

The damn thing was at least two meters across! I shook my head, and quickly returned to scanning the rest of the room, making sure I knew what I was facing.

To my left, I spotted a group of squat, muscular figures hammering away at anvils near a pool of molten metal. Those had to be the dvorks.

A glint of movement near the control room caught my attention. Translucent, crystalline beings that I assumed were the glassine were manipulating levers and dials. As I watched, the floor beneath me began to shift, panels rotating to reveal new hazards.

"Oh, you bastards," I growled, diving to avoid a sudden jet of steam that erupted from a nearby pipe. I needed to take out those glassine fast, or this whole room was going to turn into one big death trap.

Another movement drew my eye then. I cursed again, as a trio of crawlers appeared. These were much more like the cannon-turtles that I remembered from Simon and Marchioness's dungeon, though more graceful and refined.

They were much the same as the standard design. But instead of the carry-all in the butt, these had an arm and a massive crossbow, and that was even now being winched back by a clockwork mechanism.

The three paused, braced their legs, and aligned themselves with me as the loading arm slid an arrow the length of my thigh into place.

I slid to the right, unleashing a new blast of lightning at the fuckers and channeling it, as I dragged the lightning from left to right.

The first and second exploded before they got a shot off. The third managed to fire, but missed as I slid back toward the left…and that was when I was hit by two of the three I *hadn't* seen on the far side that had been obscured by more jets of gasses.

The unexpected first arrow was the worst. It slammed into my back on the right side, and the head punched through the armor where it was weakest, at a lucky flex point below my ribs and to the right and above my kidney.

I hissed in pain. The second glanced off my right pauldron, having hit where my head had been a second before. And the third skipped past to slam into the wall.

I looked down, seeing the heads of the arrows that were clattering to the ground, and let out a pained hiss of relief; they were sharp, obviously, but not barbed. I could remove them.

I swapped my hammer to my left hand and reached back as I spun, flashing to the right, then up and down, then right again, moving in unpredictable ways as I stared at the fuckers, getting a good grip on it, before ripping the bolt out of my back.

"Holy…" I clamped down in the shout, gritting my teeth. Then I pulled the arrow around where I could see it. The gleaming tip was bent and twisted, its bronze metal covered in glistening blood. I glared down at the fuckers. "Oh right, now it's fucking on, you little bastards!"

I flashed forward, dropping down low, skidding as the next set of bolts passed harmlessly overhead. The elevation cogs clicked feverishly as they tried to track me.

It was too late, though. I darted left and right, skating across the floor, before dipping my shoulder and slamming into the middle one. It went flying; one of its legs caught on the lip of the river of molten metal behind it and somersaulted over, before splashing down.

The one to my right was moving fast, skittering backward, trying to bring the crossbow to bear. But I flung the hammer behind me, aimed loosely at the head of the third crawler, and grabbed onto the second one by the head.

Its blade and hammer had been replaced with longer legs at the front, clearly intended to let it move and adjust its aim easier, and yet that just let me get in closer, faster.

I braced my feet on the ground and yanked backward. One hand gripped the junction point between the front left leg and the torso, and the other clamped on the back of the neck. Then I heaved.

In fairness to me, I wasn't trying to show off—genuinely, I wasn't at that point. Sure, it was my intention overall to scare the London lot and instill a "whatever you do, don't fuck with us" mentality, but I was angry, hurting, and I lost my temper.

That was my excuse, anyway, for spinning the machine that was about the size of a Great Dane around and flinging it across the room like it weighed nothing.

With hindsight, it would have been cooler if I'd managed to hit the other crawlers, the melee variants that were even now skittering forward and closing on me.

Also, with hindsight, it would have been better to, you know, *aim*.

Unfortunately, the nature of hindsight meant that I'd already fucked up, when these things occurred to me.

The roar of fury and the way that the crawler was flung sideways back across the room to shatter against the wall made it clear that I'd just hit one of the previously apparently uncaring dvorks with my little impromptu missile, and he wasn't taking it well.

A second's blast of steam vented close by, and I jumped backward, before darting sideways. I spotted another vent smoothly rotating nearby, a second before it, too, erupted in clouds of boiling gasses.

I surged toward the control room, but my path was cut off by a massive hammer swung by the unamused dvork. I barely managed to dodge, feeling the wind of its passage as it flashed past my face.

"Right then." I grinned despite the danger. "Let's dance."

I feinted left, then dove right, hitting the ground and rolling, coming to my feet and unleashing another lightning bolt at the dvork. It connected, making the creature scream and then lock up. That was when I slammed my fist into the underside of its chin—an uppercut with a hell of a lot of force behind it that sent the dvork staggering, blood spraying free of a damaged jaw.

I'd not gone all out. I wanted to train, after all, not just slaughter, and these fuckers seemed perfect for that.

Mind you, I'd put in enough force unthinkingly that a human would have entirely lost their head, so they really were tough fuckers.

Starting a fight with one of their own clearly crossed a line, though. The rest of them, a dozen in all, quit whatever they were doing, grabbed weapons and tools, and headed in for me.

"Let's play, fuckers." I grinned.

I had a handful of seconds before the dvorks could reach me, coming as they were from all across the room, and I used them to spin and charge the crawlers.

There were seven of them left. Their long, spidery limbs clacked as they closed on me, weapons raised. Should I let them get to me and the dvorks all at the same time, it wasn't going to go well.

I used my flight to hurl myself into the approaching pack. Lightning flared up in me, but was held ready, rather than unleashed.

I'd done some martial arts over the years, and I'd had more training since then, courtesy of Patrick and a few others. Although I was fair with it, I wasn't great.

That meant that I could either try to hide that now, and later, use my magic and my weapons, or I could use this situation to improve.

That was what I decided to do, spinning myself around and bringing a flying kick—charged with lightning—into the face of the first to reach me.

It hurtled back; clockwork parts flew as the air was filled by an echoing boom. The hammer glanced off the armored plate on my left thigh and the blade skittered across my armor in a shower of sparks before it was hurled free.

I landed, braced and lunged forward, taking the incoming blade of another on my left forearm, raised to block, and punching hard into the head of the crawler with my right fist.

The head crumpled. The crystal eyes—six of them, which I'd not noticed until now that I was in close—exploded free. The lightning that flowed through me cascaded through delicate internal workings and ruined them as the crawler died.

I used my flight now more to grease the floor and provide movement, as I experimented, adjusting on the fly as I leapt and kicked, spun and punched. I slid across the metal floor. The grates that let heat from somewhere below rise in terrible waves and the solid plates alike felt more like I was ice-skating instead of running.

I grabbed the last of them—the others had died in seconds—and I ripped its front limbs off, tossing them aside before bringing my right hand down in a hammer fist atop the head.

It tore loose; the top dented in before the neck gave way, and it crashed into the floor with a sound like a bell being rung.

Then I clamped my hands onto its back, braced and lifted, before spinning and hurling it at the figures that I'd seen sprinting in from my right.

The clockwork crawler was batted aside by the dvork.

I grinned and launched myself at him, before throwing myself down and kicking out. I skidded across the floor on my back, his hammer whistling past overhead.

My right boot slammed into the inside of his knee with far more force than I'd have been capable of even a month ago. But this time, he barely grunted, staggering as I jumped back up.

He tried to bring the hammer back, but I wrapped my left arm around his, bringing my fist up under his arm and locking it into a full extension. I grabbed him by the throat and twisted, bringing him around to intercept a hammer that someone else had graciously provided.

I'd seen movement, that was it, and I'd spun, but damn. That'd been a close one.

I let go as he fell, his skull crushed and blood and brains leaking out of his ears, nose, and mouth, his eyes bulging out. I took a quick step backward, then another before jumping to the right.

The dvorks weren't that fast, but damn, their blows just kept coming.

I grabbed the haft of a hammer as its head clanged into the floor by my foot, leaving a deep dent. The dvork—a woman this time, I guessed—glared at me and yanked hard on the hammer, and swung a punch at my head at the same time.

I blocked the punch, deflecting it with my left arm, unleashing more lightning into her. She grimaced, before tugging harder on the hammer's haft and starting a sort of tug-of-war.

I lasted only a second, though, before I stumbled back, another having hit me from the left and clamping a set of massive tongs around that arm. I tried to yank my arm free, letting go of the hammer, and unleashed a snap kick into his belly, only to see again that these things were tougher than they looked. The newcomer shook off the attack and came at me again, joined by two more of his fellows.

I weaved between them, using my superior speed and agility to stay just out of reach. Each time I saw an opening, I struck with quick jabs and kicks, unleashing a blast of lightning. Slowly but surely, I wore them down. The combination of speed and their own muscles locking up meant that although they were great for training, it was also more than manageable without going all out.

That was when I found that I couldn't focus solely on the dvorks, of course, because that would have been too easy. The second wave of the clockwork crawlers swarmed in then, trying to overwhelm me with sheer numbers. I had to keep moving, using the environment to my advantage. I darted to the side, then leapt over a literal river of sluggishly flowing metal—the heat was already incredible—soaring directly over the stream.

As I landed on the far side and spun, I channeled my lightning and kept it coming from both hands this time, sweeping left and right, tearing a group of the crawlers apart and focusing in on the dvorks.

They started to fall, their hair and beards aflame, flesh blackening and burning through. I leapt onto one of the massive gears of the central mechanism, using it as a platform to rain down attacks on my pursuers.

As I fought, I kept one eye on the control room. The glassine were still busy. The effects of their manipulations became apparent as the massive gear I stood atop suddenly jerked into motion and moved, bringing me around toward another gear that'd probably reduce me to jam if I wasn't paying attention.

Conveyor belts activated as well, trying to drag unwary combatants toward more crushing gears and panels in the floor that periodically crackled with green lightning or unleashed hellish blasts of steam.

I needed to end this fast. Taking a deep breath, I focused my energy and unleashed a massive chain lightning attack. It arced from enemy to enemy, frying clockwork crawlers and stunning dvorks. In the chaos that followed, I made my move.

Launching myself down, I slid my sword free and stabbed out, driving the tip up under a convulsing chin of a dvork. The blade punched cleanly through the roof of the mouth and into the brain, quickly ending their struggles.

Thirty seconds of stabbing and a few more blasts of lightning later, and I straightened, then launched myself into the air.

I shot toward the control room like a bullet, crashing through the glass window. The glassine turned to face me, their crystalline bodies glinting in the harsh light. They moved with surprising speed, but I was ready.

With a series of quick, precise strikes, I shattered two of their bodies before they could react. The third managed to land a glancing blow; its crystalline arm left a deep gash in my armor. I gritted my teeth against the pain and pressed my attack, kicking one of its legs out from under it and sending it crashing to the floor. Then I swung the blade around, aiming for the head…only to see it smile and lie back, clearly not afraid, waiting.

Dungeon Warmancer!

The Glassine Controllers offer you their surrender, and congratulate you on your successful attack. Do you accept?

Yes/No…

Reminder: Although generally peaceful, Glassine may take offense to crude attempts at replication or forced evolution. Respect for their craftsmanship and autonomy is advised to maintain positive relations.

I blinked, then squinted, before moving the screen to the side. The other two that I'd damaged and thrown down, that I'd been expecting to have to kill once I had this one out of the way, were waiting as well.

Fuck it. I accepted their surrender, and saw them nod, seemingly bearing no ill will, despite everything. I paused, half suspecting a trick; then I quickly moved to the control panel.

As I turned back to survey the room, I saw that the remaining enemies were regrouping. The last handful of dvorks formed a defensive line while the presses on the right-hand side, that before had been hidden from view by my position, were now disgorging more clockwork crawlers, the entire lot massing for another assault.

I grinned, cracking my knuckles. “My turn, you bastards.” I started to push and pull at the levers before me.

Needless to say, I managed very little that was good or even slightly effective, until the nearest glassine stood up and limped over to me, reaching out in question. I frowned, and it gestured to the controls, then to itself; I nodded slowly, stepping clear, holding my sword ready…

It reached out, starting to operate the panel. For the first time, I had the chance to really look at it.

The glassine were solvent-based, the description had said when I got access to them, and yeah, I could sort of see that, now that I was looking.

If you remembered that glass was a solvent, that is.

The creature before me was a sort of amber color, and humanoid, roughly—two arms and two legs. The hands had six fingers and the legs ended in feet that were…weird.

Triangular bases, more than feet, with a long section, like a double-length finger, stretching out and spaced equidistantly around the base. A set of three shorter fingers extended out in the spaces between the longer ones, and then a stretched panel spread between those points, almost like webbing.

It looked weird, but I could see it offered more stability than a normal foot, which was sort of cool. But as my gaze roamed upward, I noted that the glass part of the creature was basically wrapped around, and being contained within, a support and armor combined.

It was ornate, and as I glanced at the other two glassine that had come to their feet and were now watching with interest, it also appeared to be unique.

There were sections of brass and steel, embossed and filigreed, carved and works of art. They made it clear more than anything else that the glassine were artisans, not warriors.

Although that’d been fucking clear in the fight, both seconds of it.

One had already produced a tool from a nearby counter and was absently working on repairing their armor, as the first glassine turned to me and smiled.

“Greetings, Dungeon Warmancer. Please press here.” It gestured to the control panel, and I hesitated, then pressed it as asked.

A series of clangs sounded as the mechanism in the center sealed itself up. On hearing that, and seeing the section that started to move again, sliding into place above the rivers of molten metal, the dvorks screamed and ran, clearly trying to make it to the control room.

“Now this one please,” the glassine asked.

I obliged, pulling a lever. There was a click, a clatter, and then a shield slid down to close off the control room from the rest of the level.

“And lastly, this button.”

I pressed it, noting the whole “big red button” for doomsday shit was clearly universal.

A distant warning clanged from the other side of what I now realized was a fucking blast shield, and then an explosion shook the floor.

“What the hell was that?” I looked at my new companion.

“An emergency purge,” it explained placidly. “A frozen coolant is released into the molten metal. The resultant energetic release sends molten metal across the entire floor, and eliminates any intruders.”

"Molten…" I stared at the placid fucker, wide-eyed. "That could have killed me!"

"Very much so," it agreed. "However, once you had taken the control room, it was the most effective way to ensure the floor completed with minimal damage."

"Minimal damage?" I gaped. "That didn't sound very fuckin' minimal!"

"Using the crawlers and their repair functions, the floor can be repaired easily, and the materials repurposed. Was this not your intention?"

"Well, yeah…?" I admitted. "Just didn't expect you to be so blasé about it, though!"

"We are glassine, and aware. They are not," it said simply.

I stared at it.

"Fuck me, you're a cold one," I muttered. "Wait, you mean you don't give a shit because they're not aware, or because they're not glassine?"

"Aware," it clarified.

I was relieved, considering as they were alive still, I was guessing that I'd be able to take them out of the dungeon now if I could complete it.

"That's a relief," I admitted. "So, you're aware…does that mean you were a criminal back home?"

"Yes."

"And?"

"And what?"

"What were you convicted of?" I asked.

"Ah. Improper use of resources."

"Right… What did you do?"

"I destroyed a sun."

"WHAT?" I practically screamed.

"I jest."

"I fucking hope so! What did you do?"

"We were volunteers," it said. "Thirty cycles of awareness for access to the dungeons and a chance at dozens of new lives lived. It has been an experience."

"Yeah, I bet," I muttered. "You been killed many times?"

"Several." It didn't seem bothered by that. "Some of our fellow aware beings have taken exception to our actions, and several cycles were spent with them hunting us."

"How the hell does that work?" I asked.

"Should a Dungeon Lord fail their trial and perish, the dungeon often reverts to a more feral state and a new lord is raised. In that time, many attempt to plunder the dungeon, and on occasion, our sections of the dungeon have lasted for considerable passages of time. Traditionally, when this happens, the inhabitants fall back on a more monarchist structure, with the dungeon evolving and growing. On occasion, we have been hunted and destroyed. On others, we have ascended and taken power."

"Have you been released at the end? Or when you take over, did you get to be free?"

"On occasion." It nodded. "It is all an experience, however."

"Right… So, if I finish the trial and offer you the chance to exit the dungeon and join me?"

"We shall be honored." It inclined its head, and so did its companions. "Do you wish us to take action currently?"

"Uh…what?" I asked, still freaked out by the way it was acting.

"Do you wish us to remain here until the culmination of the dungeon run, or join you?"

"Wait here," I said. First of all, I didn't trust the fuckers right behind me. Secondly, I knew that I'd get a better bonus if I did the trial without spending the points I'd been given and summoning help.

That being said, though…

I sighed, and reminded myself that one of the main reasons for running the dungeon was to get more sentients that could bring us information about skills, situations, and the wider galaxy.

As such, these three were basically bonus free gifts, but I'd need to summon some others soon.

I'd give it a thought when I'd seen what the next floor was like. That reminded me, though…

"Goddammit!" I cursed. "I can't get through there, can I?"

"There?" The glassine indicated the blast shields that were still in place. "It is possible to open them. However, the result would be terminal."

"Dammit!" I groaned, clenching my fist. "My damn hammer is through there still, and so's all the loot!"

"Ah, this is incorrect."

"What?"

"Not all loot is contained beyond this location. There is also the reward for capturing the control room and completing the floor," it assured me, making me stare.

"Okay, where is it and what is it?" Hope surged in me.

"We are the reward," it told me happily.

I glared at it.

"There is also the chest," one of the others commented offhandedly.

I looked at it in question, seeing it was the one that was already engrossed in its own repairs.

"Correct. There is a second reward—the chest. However, it has been confirmed by sapiens in the past that the true prize is access to our kind."

It said it in all seriousness, and I squinted at it, trying to decide whether it was fucking with me.

"I've got access to you already," I pointed out. "I got the blueprints."

"Excellent. It will be satisfying to add to our number once again, and without sacrificing one of our trio, this is even better."

"Where's the chest?" I asked the more helpful and less self-satisfied one, who reached out and pressed a button on the control panel. A side panel in the wall opened and revealed a small wooden chest in a secure alcove.

I walked over, reaching for it, before Mr. Helpful spoke up again.

"Do you wish the traps deactivated?"

I froze, then turned slowly. "Why yes…" I ground out through gritted teeth, "I would like the traps deactivated!"

"As you wish," it said, unconcerned, before it pressed another button, then went back to its repairs.

"Is it safe to touch now?" I asked grimly. "Are there any more traps?"

"All of existence is a risk," the third, and so far, only one not to speak replied helpfully.

I growled to myself, before reaching out and yanking the chest free of the recess. I was so sending these fuckers to Finn, I decided. And maybe I'd have one of them go to London as well…

My irritation faded as I slid the simple latch across and opened the chest, staring at the revealed loot.

There were a collection of gold, silver, and copper coins, and three crystals, that when I picked them up felt slightly soft in my hand, making me wonder about them.

Glassine Crystal	**Crafting Material**
Damage: N/A	**Charge:** 100/100
Glassine Crystals are said to be the solidified remains of Glassine. They are highly prized by artificers and enchanters for their unique magical properties and ability to store and amplify arcane energies. **Warning:** Handle with care. Prolonged direct skin contact may induce vivid hallucinations or temporary phasing effects.	
Durability: 100/100	**Rarity:** Rare

There were also two other prizes: a blueprint and what looked like a friggin' metal rod with carvings all over it and glowing green lines.

Repair Drone	**Blueprint**
Damage: N/A	**Charge:** 1/1
This single-use blueprint provides access to create a small, spherical device about the size of a grapefruit. When constructed, its brass exterior is etched with intricate gears and arcane symbols. On activation, panels slide open to reveal an array of delicate tools and appendages. To activate, wind the key on its back clockwise for 30 seconds. Give it a verbal command or point it toward the item needing repair. The drone will hover to the target and begin its work. Note: Repair tasks are limited to low and medium grade magical artifacts; no responsibility is accepted for any damages incurred.	
Durability: 5/5	**Rarity:** Rare

Dvork Multitool	**Tool**
Damage: N/A	**Charge:** 50/50
Created by the legendary dvork artificer, Grimna Gearspark, this multitool is said to contain a fragment of her innovative spirit. Only a	

handful are known to exist, each slightly different based on its primary user's needs and personality. **Warning:** Extremely valuable and coveted. Possession may attract unwanted attention from thieves, collectors, and artificers.	
Durability: 50/50	**Rarity:**????

I stared at the descriptions for the three items, stunned at their potential. The glassine crystals were crafting components that could be reproduced, making them both a resource and a possible trade good. The repair drone?

That opened the door to a facility like the gathering one, just with a bunch of these little fuckers in it! Thinking about it like that…a car or a truck, with a deployment system on the back for these? That could be incredible, especially as it marked them as friggin' clockwork powered!

I couldn't imagine how the hell a clockwork bug could repair a magical artifact, but hey, magic and all that. I didn't need to understand all of it, just enough to survive and thrive.

The last one, though, was the coolest.

The rod thingy was an alien tool that looked to be, yeah, a replacement for the Swiss army knife, but usable in crafting? That there were only a handful of them known to exist just made it even more valuable and…and…

"What? How the hell does that work?" I asked aloud, before turning to the glassine. "This says it's one of only a handful, but it's also given out by a dungeon, so there could be more, right?"

"Correct."

"Great. Well, one-word answers aren't very helpful. Come on, people, help me out a little here," I prompted, making them look at each other before the helpful one finally spoke.

"Is it possible that you are unaware of the realities of dungeon creation?" It cocked its head to one side quizzically, and I glared at it.

"Maybe I am," I said coldly. "So feel free to explain."

"There are two possibilities. First, this was one of only a handful, when it was absorbed into the dungeon and the description was set. There may now be many thousands of these available, all linked to the same description."

"Makes sense, though it's a bit shit the description isn't updated. What's the other option?" I asked.

"This item is likely a fake."

"A fake?" I stared at it. "What the hell do you mean, a fake?"

"There is an enchantment at work to conceal the rarity from low-grade Examination. This suggests a fake, as the real creation would have no need to conceal such a thing."

"How the hell do I find out the real level of the item then?" I asked. "And how do I level my Examination?"

"Repetition, to answer your second question, and you ask, for the first."

"I ask?"

"Correct."

"I…do you have a high enough grade Examine ability or spell to see the grade on this?" I reminded myself silently that I couldn't smash it with my hammer, because my hammer was currently stuck in that fucking room and probably melting.

"Yes."

"Can you use it, please," I ground out.

"I have," it replied placidly.

"And?" I asked after a few seconds as it returned to working on its arm.

"This item is likely a fake. The grade is common," it said after a few seconds, apparently considering what I could be asking for. "May I use it?"

"Fuck's sake!" I growled. "Here!" I tossed it to it.

It caught it out of the air, twisted the narrow rod, and nodded to itself as a nozzle on the end extended and sputtered to life, an uneven flame of blue and green jetting out of the end.

"It is a low-grade copy," the glassine stated unequivocally. "Note the uneven mana conversion and activation. May I keep it?"

"No," I said after a second. "We can still copy it and see if we can improve on it…though why would you want to keep it?"

"While faulty and low level in comparison to the original, it is also a copy of a highly sought-after artifact. Even faulty, it can be useful."

"Unless it loses containment and ignites a runaway conversion," the first of them noted.

"Correct." The second nodded easily. "That would be sub-optimal."

"Runaway conversion?" I asked carefully. "What would that be like?"

"Uncertain." It shrugged. "The most likely consequence is a simple failure, possibly with a detonation event."

"And the worst?" I asked.

"The worst-case scenario would result in the ignition of the atmosphere of this world and the extinction of all life."

"This would, however, be an extremely valuable experience to observe." It continued to work on its arm, until I held my hand out.

"Gimmie," I said, and it handed the tool over unconcernedly. "This is going away for now, and maybe, *maybe* when I'm not busy and someone I trust has had a look at it, you can have a copy. Once it's fixed," I hedged.

"You have companions who are at the artifact level of crafting? How impressive. We shall look forward to questioning them."

"Artifact…ah, shit." I shook my head, and dumped the tool in my bag, resolving that nobody was going to be playing with it until we'd figured out more about it. If I ever found out who was selling knockoff tools that could accidentally set light to a planet's atmosphere, I'd kick their teeth in.

All of that being done, the coins and other loot was poured into my bag of holding, and I headed for the door at the back of the control room, well aware that the last dungeon started off easy as well.

CHAPTER TWENTY-THREE

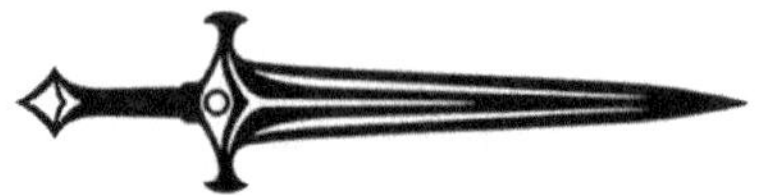

I stepped through the door at the back of the control room, half expecting another puzzle or trap at the end of a series of stairs, and instead… I found myself on a small platform suspended in…nothing?

The void stretched out before me. A sea of swirling purples, blues, and blacks hurt my eyes if I stared too long in any one direction. As I turned, looking back at the control room, the door I'd just stepped through slid shut, then vanished, making me curse.

"What the actual fuck?" I growled, inching closer to the edge and peering down. There was no floor, just an endless abyss that made my stomach lurch. I'd seen some weird shit since this all began, but this took the cake. I mean, I could *fly* and still the feeling of standing on the edge of this cliff was freaking me out.

Mind you, that could have been because besides the swirling clouds, there was literally nothing below me, or on any side, bar one.

A translucent bridge stretched out from my platform, connecting to a larger floating island about twenty to twenty-five meters away. It looked solid enough, but something about its shimmering, semi-transparent nature made me nervous about leaving the seemingly very real island I stood on.

The…floating island.

I looked at the ground again, noting the battered grass, the patchy dirt that suggested many feet had passed through here before. Then I got down on my hands and knees and stuck my head over the edge of the island, looking down and underneath.

That gave me the willies as I stared at a random section of the ground that had seemingly been freshly ripped free and catapulted into the air.

The island was maybe a foot deep, that was it, and then there was nothing. Nothing holding it, nothing beneath it, and even though, again, I could fly, that really freaked me out.

"Right then," I said to myself, standing and silently reminding myself that I was being watched at all times. "Time to see just what kind of shit's waiting for me." I started to lift into the air, refusing to play their games…and paused, as a hard rumble suddenly started from all around.

Pressure was building, and the air began to move faster, as what looked to be a fucking tornado spun up in the distance.

"Okay…" I started to say, before swallowing hard as a second, and then third appeared. Light glinted in each of them, crackling like lightning…but in reds and greens.

It also felt oppressive, not welcoming as the storm generally did for me. I landed, watching to think about this, to pick the best way through the clouds…and as soon as my feet hit the ground, the wind died away.

"What the f—" I growled, lifting into the air. The same thing happened again.

Land, walk around, and it was fine. Fly? Nope, that was gonna get messy. Okay, though, I could take a hint, I decided. And it wasn't like I couldn't just fly when the shit hit the fan, right?

I took a deep breath and stepped onto the bridge.

It felt like slightly soft glass, almost totally see-through, and yet solid enough that it bore my weight. As I strode out, trying my best to appear nonchalant, it held, thankfully, though the sensation of walking on air was disconcerting as hell.

As I made my way across, I got a better view of the level. It was like someone had taken a chunk of countryside, smashed it into pieces, and scattered the fragments across the void. Fifteen to twenty islands of various sizes floated at different heights. Some slowly drifted in patterns I couldn't quite grasp; two slowly spiraled around each other. I stared at them, my brain shuddering as I tried to make sense of this fucking place being inside the goddamn stadium!

The centerpiece as I quickly moved from the next island to another, squinting through the drifting clouds, was a massive floating island, easily twenty-five meters across. It seemed to glow with an inner light. I paused, watching the way it bobbed and drifted, other bridges connecting to it. I shook my head. Even from here, I could see veins of crystal pulsing with energy. That had to be the mana crystal mine the floor description had mentioned.

"Okay, big glowy island in the middle. Probably where I need to go, which means it's also probably where all the nasty shit is waiting," I mused.

Movement caught my eye. What could only be described as a ghostly horse galloped through the air between two of the smaller islands. A phantomsteed, if I remembered the creature list correctly. As it passed, I noticed a small, winged figure perched on its back.

"Great, flying horses and fairies. What's next, unicorns shitting rainbows? Also, how come *they* get to fly?" I grumbled to myself, reaching the end of the bridge and stepping onto another island, feeling my stress levels lower as soon as I was on solid…well, *relatively* solid ground.

No sooner had my feet touched the island than I felt a shift in the air. I spun around just in time to see the bridge I'd crossed vanish, reappearing between two completely different islands.

"Oh, you've got to be fucking kidding me," I growled. This was going to be a right pain in the arse.

I took a moment to survey my immediate surroundings. The island I was on was about ten meters across, covered in soft, luminescent grass that seemed to respond to my footsteps with gentle pulses of light. At its center was a small pedestal with glowing runes etched into its surface.

As I approached the pedestal, movement in the corner of my eye made me freeze. I turned slowly, coming face-to-face with what had to be a magewhisker. It was like someone had taken a cat, stretched it out, given it an extra pair of legs, and decided, "You know what this needs? Tentacles."

Spoiler. They were wrong. It *really* didn't need the goddamn tentacles. Although this version was a bit different from the ones that we already had in the dungeon, it was still looking at me like every cat always damn well did.

Like a furry turd that just wanted to ruin my day.

The creature's six eyes blinked at me in sequence, and I could have sworn it looked…amused? Before I could react, it darted forward with surprising speed. I braced for an attack, but instead, it brushed past me, heading straight for the runed pedestal.

"Oi!" I shouted, spinning around. "Get away from that, you tentacled twat!"

The magewhisker ignored me, placing one of its paws on the pedestal. The runes flared to life, and suddenly the entire island lurched. I stumbled, nearly losing my footing as the chunk of earth began to move, floating toward another island.

"Right," I muttered, steadying myself. "Magical puzzle bullshit it is, then."

I glanced back at the magewhisker, which now sat, watching me with what I could only describe as smug satisfaction. "Don't suppose you'd be willing to give me a hint, eh?"

In response, the creature's tentacles began to glow, and the hairs on the back of my neck stood up. *Magic. Of-fucking-course.*

"Have it your way," I growled. Lightning crackled between my fingers. "Let's dance, you overgrown calamari cat."

As I squared off against the magewhisker, I couldn't help but wonder what other delights this floor had in store. Flying horses, reality-warping zones, and now this tentacled monstrosity. One thing was for sure—I was going to take great pleasure in beating that smug fucking look off its face.

"This one's for Thor," I muttered, before grinning, as the cat hunched down, bracing itself, then leapt.

The magewhisker launched itself at me, its tentacles writhing and glowing with an eerie light. I sidestepped, barely avoiding its initial lunge, and the air crackled with magical energy as it passed.

"Missed me, you fuzzy bastard," I taunted, electricity dancing between my fingers.

The creature landed gracefully on the other side of the pedestal, its six eyes narrowing as it regarded me. It was clear this wasn't going to be a straightforward fight. And because I was so naturally patient and sensible, when confronted with unknown things, I charged it. The magewhisker's tentacles began to weave complex patterns in the air, and the island beneath my feet started to tilt.

Then I was hit by a sudden blast of air from the left, just as the island tilted again, to my right this time.

"Oh, come on!" I shouted as it bounded off, skirting the outer edge of the island as I followed, struggling to maintain my balance. "That's cheating!"

I unleashed a bolt of lightning at the creature, but it nimbly dodged, leaping to the side with inhuman agility. The bolt struck the pedestal instead, causing the runes to flare brightly. Suddenly, the island jerked violently, nearly sending me tumbling off the edge.

The magewhisker dug its claws into the sod and held on, seeming to grin at me as I stumbled, mocking me as it stayed secure despite the island's erratic movement. Then it darted toward me again.

This time, its tentacles lashed out, trying to wrap around my arms and legs. I managed to grab one. The slimy appendage writhed in my grip, and I sent a surge of lightning through it, turning my body into a giant taser.

The creature yowled, a sound somewhere between a cat's screech and nails on a chalkboard. It retreated, shaking its shocked tentacles, as its eyes blazed with renewed fury.

"Yeah, not so fun when someone else does the zapping, is it?" I grinned, readying myself for its next attack.

The magewhisker's fur stood on end, crackling with its own electrical charge. It hissed, and suddenly, bolts of magical energy shot from its tentacles toward me. I dove and rolled, feeling the heat of the magical projectiles as they whizzed past.

As I came up from the roll, I noticed the pedestal's runes pulsing more rapidly. An idea struck me. If I could just get the magewhisker to hit the pedestal again…

"Hey, kitty, kitty," I called out, positioning myself in front of the pedestal. "Is that the best you've got? My gran hits harder than you, and she's been dead for twenty years!"

The creature's eyes narrowed, and it let out a low growl. It crouched, preparing to pounce. Its tentacles glowed brighter than ever. Just as it leaped, I dropped to the ground, rolling to the side.

The magewhisker sailed over me, its magical attack hitting the pedestal dead center. The runes exploded with light, and suddenly, the island began to spin rapidly. The sudden motion caught us both off guard.

I scrambled to grab onto the grass; my fingers dug into the soil as the centrifugal force threatened to fling me off into the void. The magewhisker wasn't so lucky. With a yowl of surprise, it slid across the surface, its claws scrabbling for purchase as the patch of dirt it was over came apart.

"Not so graceful now, are you, ya twat?" I shouted over the rush of wind, watching as the creature tumbled toward the edge.

At the last second, its tentacles shot out, wrapping around a protruding rock. It clung there, all six eyes wide with what looked suspiciously like fear.

I started to feel a twinge of guilt. Sure, it had attacked me, but it was just doing its job, right? Plus, I was supposed to be the good guy here. Letting it fall into the abyss didn't seem very heroic.

"Ah, fuck it," I muttered, inching my way toward the creature. "Don't make me regret this, you tentacled shitbag."

I reached out, grabbing the magewhisker by what I hoped was its scruff. It hissed and spat, but didn't attack as I hauled it back onto the more stable center of the island. As soon as its paws touched the ground, it darted away from me, crouching low and eyeing me warily.

The island's spin began to slow, and I turned my attention back to the pedestal. The runes were still glowing, but now they seemed to be forming a pattern. It looked almost like…

"A map," I realized. "It's showing us the way to the next island."

I glanced at the magewhisker, which was still watching me cautiously. "What do you say, furball? Truce? At least until we figure out how to get off this crazy merry-go-round?"

The creature blinked its six eyes in sequence, then slowly padded over to the pedestal. It placed a paw on one of the runes, and a shimmering bridge appeared, connecting our island to another nearby.

"Well, I'll be damned." I chuckled. "Looks like you're not just a pretty face after all."

I stared at the damn cat, unable to help another chuckle, before I cut myself off, swearing.

The last time I'd been here, I'd escaped with a creature of the dungeon, giving it a chance at life. Now, admittedly, that was Drak, and he'd been as much of a hinderance as he had been a help, but…either something had happened here and the dungeon's inhabitants were a lot less antagonistic toward me—possible as I'd upgraded my Lord of All skill since I was last in—or more likely, word had gotten around, somehow.

This furball was willing to fight me, but it didn't seem as dead set on murder as a lot of the creatures I'd fought before had. In fact, it seemed like it was willing to play along and help me, though I was betting it was because it wanted out of the dungeon, and some extra kitty-kibble in payment.

The issue with this—and it was a big one—was that if I did this, if I helped it and took it with me, I was going to end up with another goddamn cat in the dungeon! Thor was already the bane of my fucking existence at times, and that furry little fucker was barely bigger than this thing's head.

I groaned, straightening and twisting, keeping an eye on it, as my back clicked, and I let out a sigh.

It was already too late—I knew that in my heart.

People were watching, and I'd only just rescued tentacled-terry-the-twattish-tomcat. Beta, if nobody else, was going to insist on keeping the damn thing.

"Come on then, you." I sighed morosely. "Let's get a move on."

As we made our way across the shimmering bridge, the damn cat trotting ahead with its tail held high, I couldn't help but shake my head at the absurdity of it all. Here I was, following a six-eyed, tentacled cat across a magical bridge suspended in a void.

Just another day in the life of a Dungeon Lord, I supposed.

"You know," I called out to the creature, "if you're coming with me, you're gonna need a name. How about Cthulhu? Or maybe Lovecraft?"

The magewhisker turned its head, all six eyes blinking at me in what I could only see as contempt.

"Right, not a fan of the classics. How about Whiskers? Hairball? No? How about Fuckface?" That last one got a glare, and I grinned. "Okay, we'll work on it, especially now that I know you can understand me."

As we reached the next island, I noticed it was significantly larger than the previous one, maybe fifteen meters across. The grass here was a deep, shimmering blue that seemed to ripple like water with each step. At the center stood not one, but three pedestals, each glowing with different-colored runes.

"Well, this looks complicated," I muttered, approaching the pedestals cautiously. The magewhisker, seemingly more at ease now, padded around the island, its tentacles twitching as if sensing something in the air.

Suddenly, a high-pitched giggle echoed around us. I spun, lightning crackling at my fingertips, to see a small, winged figure darting between the pedestals.

"Oh great, the fairies are here," I grumbled. The tiny creature, no bigger than my hand, hovered in front of my face, its gossamer wings beating so fast they were almost invisible.

"Welcome, Dungeon Lord!" it chirped, its voice unnaturally loud for something so small. "Care to play a game?"

I glanced at the magewhisker, which had positioned itself between two of the pedestals, its eyes fixed on the fairy as it darted in and out of visibility. "Do I have a choice?" I asked, already knowing the answer. "Also, nice that you're talking to me this time around instead of just attacking. Want to tell me why that is?"

The fairy's grin widened, showing impossibly sharp teeth. "Of course! There's always a choice, silly… You can play…or you can *fall*!" With that, the edges of the island began to crumble away, the blue grass dissolving into mist.

"Fuck me." I sighed, turning back to the fairy. "All right then, what's the game?"

The fairy clapped its tiny hands in delight. "It's simple! Three pedestals, three runes. Activate them in the right order, and you move on. Get it wrong…" It gestured to the shrinking island.

I approached the first pedestal, studying the runes carefully. They seemed to shift and change as I looked at them, making my head spin. "Any hints?" I glanced back at the fairy.

It giggled again, a sound that was quickly becoming irritating. "The whiskers know more than they show, and the shadows hide the truth!"

"Fucking riddles," I muttered, looking over at the magewhisker. It was still positioned between two pedestals, its tentacles now glowing faintly.

That's when it hit me. The magewhisker wasn't just waiting—it was giving me a clue. Its position, the glow of its tentacles…it was trying to tell me something.

I stepped closer to the pedestals, watching how the light from the magewhisker's tentacles interacted with the runes. As the glow passed over certain symbols, they seemed to stabilize, becoming clearer and pulsing with a faint red.

"All right," I said, more to myself than anyone else. "Let's see if I've got this figured out."

I reached out toward the first pedestal, my hand hovering over the runes. The island continued to shrink, the void creeping closer with each passing second. It was now or never.

"Here goes nothing," I muttered, and pressed the first rune.

The island—probably because I'd just trusted a goddamn *cat*—immediately flipped, spinning in a short but far too fast blur. I screamed and grabbed onto the pedestal; the cat had dug its claws into the ground and lashed its tentacles around the damn thing as well. As we came to a halt, my stomach still spinning and me panting—despite the fact that, deep down, I goddamn *knew* I could still fly—I stared at the cat with wide eyes.

"What the hell was that?!" I hissed, seeing the flat glare it was giving me and reading the whole "how are you this dumb" attitude I often got from Thor as well. "Wait, was that supposed to be 'avoid these'?" I got a roll of several eyes in response—which, in a six-eyed tentacle cat, was actually fuckin' impressive-looking.

"Well, how the fuck was I supposed to know that!" I snapped at it, before trying the other runes, in the new pattern that seemed to glow.

“Lucky you are, that you made a friend!” The little fairy giggled.

As the pedestal hummed with fresh energy, the island stabilized, no longer shrinking or spinning. I let out a sigh of relief, glaring at the magewhisker.

“You could have been a bit clearer with your hints, you know,” I grumbled.

The cat just blinked its six eyes at me, looking supremely unimpressed.

The fairy zipped around us, leaving a trail of sparkling dust in its wake. “Well done, well done! But that was just the beginning. Two more pedestals to go!”

“Of course there are. All right, what’s next?” I groaned.

The second pedestal’s runes were constantly shifting, forming intricate patterns before dissolving and reforming. The fairy hovered nearby, its grin somehow even wider than before.

“For this one,” it chirped, “you must find the pattern in chaos. What seems random may not be so!”

I stared at the swirling runes, trying to make sense of them. The damn cat padded over, its tentacles waving in what seemed like a purposeful manner.

“You trying to tell me something, Tentacles?” I asked, deciding to at least give the cat a temporary name.

It shot me a look that clearly said it wasn’t impressed with my naming skills.

As I watched the cat’s tentacles, I noticed they moved in a specific rhythm. Six movements, then a pause, then repeat. I looked back at the runes and realized they were following a similar pattern—six changes before resetting.

“Right,” I muttered, “let’s try this.”

I waited for the cycle to reset, then quickly pressed six runes in succession, following the pattern I’d observed. The pedestal glowed brightly, and another section of the island solidified.

“Hah!” I exclaimed, grinning at Tentacles. “We make a good team, eh?”

The cat just yawned in response.

The fairy clapped its tiny hands. “Excellent! Just one more to go. But this one…this one is tricky!”

I approached the final pedestal with caution. Its runes weren’t glowing or moving. In fact, they seemed almost faded, barely visible against the stone.

“What’s the deal with this one?” I asked the fairy.

It giggled, a sound that was really starting to grate on my nerves. “Sometimes, what you see isn’t what’s really there. Trust your instincts, not your eyes!”

“Oh, for fuck’s sake,” I muttered. “More cryptic bullshit.” Again and again with this crap, I had to force calm on myself, which seemed ridiculous, considering my damn life.

For some strange reason, I just wanted a nice simple solution—you know, like a fight. Stab something in the face, collect the loot, and move on—not all this crap!

Mind you, if this was such a cerebral dungeon, after the last one, I had to guess that the end boss situation would be a lot less stressful than usual.

I looked at the runes, trying to figure out what the fairy meant. As I stared, I noticed something odd—a faint shimmer in the air around the pedestal, like heat haze on a hot day.

Tentacles growled softly, drawing my attention. The cat was batting at the air with its paw, as if trying to catch something invisible.

That’s when it clicked. The real runes weren’t on the pedestal—they were floating in the air around it!

I reached out, feeling rather foolish, and tried to "touch" the air where I thought I saw a shimmer. To my surprise, my finger met resistance, and a rune briefly flickered into view.

"Well, I'll be damned." I chuckled. "Invisible flying runes. Because why the hell not?"

Carefully, I started "pressing" the invisible runes, guided by the shimmers in the air and Tentacles's occasionally helpful paw swipes. It was slow going, and more than once I accidentally activated the wrong rune, causing the island to shudder ominously.

Finally, after what felt like an eternity of fumbling in the air, I hit the right combination. The pedestal erupted in light, and the entire island solidified completely.

"Congratulations!" the fairy cheered, zooming around us in dizzying circles. "You've passed the test!"

"Great," I said, trying to shake off the vertigo from watching the fairy's flight. "So, do we get a prize or something?"

The fairy's grin turned mischievous. "Oh yes, you get a prize, all right. You get…to move on to the next challenge!"

Before I could protest, the island began to move, floating toward the massive central island I'd spotted earlier. As we approached, I could see the crystal veins pulsing with energy more clearly.

"I've got a bad feeling about this," I muttered to Tentacles. The cat, surprisingly, growled in what sounded like agreement.

As our island docked with the larger one, I saw other creatures arriving—more magewhiskers, a couple of phantomsteeds with their fairy riders, and other beings I couldn't quite identify.

"Welcome," boomed a voice that seemed to come from everywhere at once, "to the mana crystal mine. Your final challenge awaits."

I looked at Tentacles, then at the assembled creatures, then at the daunting expanse of the crystal-veined island before us.

"Well," I sighed, "into the breach we go. You ready for this, furball?"

Tentacles just blinked at me, then padded toward the center of the island.

I shook my head, grinned despite myself, and followed.

"All right, let's see what this 'final challenge' is all about." I strode forward with more confidence than I felt. Whatever was coming, at least I had a six-eyed, tentacled cat on my side. That had to count for something, right?

CHAPTER TWENTY-FOUR

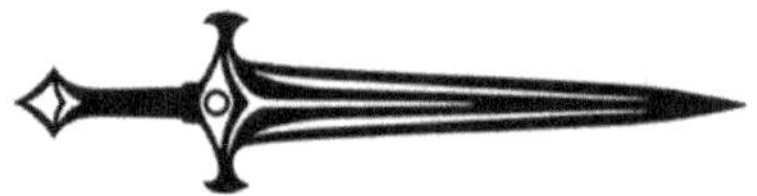

As we approached the center of the massive island, the crystal veins grew more pronounced, pulsing with an almost hypnotic rhythm. The air thrummed with magical energy.

"Welcome, Dungeon Lord, to the heart of the mana crystal mine," the booming voice announced again. Below us, in a carved hollow about three meters down from the outer ring that I stood on, a large, ornate pedestal materialized, covered in complex runes and symbols.

"Your final task is simple." A fairy, larger and more elaborately dressed than the others, fluttered down to hover near the pedestal and stare up at me. "Align the crystals to release the power within. Do so, and you shall pass this level."

I glanced at Tentacles, who eyed the fairy with suspicion as well. "Simple, huh? Now why do I doubt that?" I asked myself. In the back of my mind, I thought the voice sounded almost familiar, and definitely different from the way the fairies normally sounded.

In fact, it was making the hairs on the back of my neck stand up, but for the life of me I couldn't figure out why. Fuck it, though, because last time I checked, I was the god in these here parts, and as soon as I was finished with all of this shit and back home, I was going to be putting "these parts" into Kelly.

Time to get a move on, I decided. After all, once it all went to shit again, I'd finally get to fight something, or so I hoped.

I jumped down, not bothering with the well-worn path that led down, and circled the pedestal. The fact there was a worn path around it, but approached no closer than a meter, definitely bothered me.

Stepping up to the pedestal, I was surprised to find that it was indeed relatively straightforward. The puzzle involved rotating crystal shards to create a continuous flow of energy. After the mind-bending challenges of the previous islands, this seemed almost…easy.

As I worked on the puzzle, more creatures gathered around—mainly more magewhiskers, though these were smaller and more like the original ones—the ones that I'd gotten when we bought the design from Kai and Leilani—than Tentacles was, the big furry fucker.

Phantomsteeds were touching down around us. That whole "flying horse" thing they had going on in here was annoying, as we'd not gotten that version outside of the dungeon, but… I watched one out of the corner of my eye, and wondered whether I'd be able to fit it into the bag of holding somehow. A horse that could fly was always going to be more valuable, right?

That was when I noticed the blurs that gave away the existence of a veritable swarm of fairies alighting as well. They presumably watched in silence, their presence filling the air with an intensity that made me uneasy.

"Is it just me," I muttered to Tentacles, as he jumped down, landing near me and starting to walk counterclockwise around the pedestal, watching the fairies more than me, "or does this feel like a trap?"

The cat's tentacles twitched in agreement, its six eyes darting around warily.

I glanced up again. The horses stood almost nose to tail, forming a wall around the upper edge of the hollow center, and on their back, now visible, were dozens of fairies, all silent, sitting or standing, and staring at me with fixed expressions.

With a final twist, the last crystal clicked into place. The pedestal hummed with power; light coursed through the veins of crystal spreading out across the island.

"Excellent work!" the lead fairy exclaimed, clapping her tiny hands. "You've done it! You've unlocked the power of the mana crystal mine!"

I straightened up, a sense of accomplishment mingling with growing suspicion. "Great. So…what now?"

The fairy's smile turned predatory, sharp teeth glinting. "Now? Now we feast!"

In an instant, the atmosphere shifted. The gathered creatures surged forward, their earlier passivity replaced by murderous intent. Fairies swarmed around me. Their tiny forms belied surprising strength as they tried to overwhelm me with sheer numbers: dive-bombing down, firing off a single spell from their element, and then hitting me and biting down.

"Oh, for fuck's sake!" I roared. Lightning crackled to life around me and flowed over my skin and armor. "I knew this was too easy!"

Tentacles sprang into action, his own tentacles lashing out to swat fairies from the air, before hissing as one of the phantomsteeds leapt down at us.

Tentacles jumped at me, knocking me aside and yowling as he was hit by the discharge from my lightning, but rolled and snarled at me, before smashing another fairy from the air. I rolled to my feet, stunned as the phantomsteed impaled itself on the pedestal. Then I unleashed a blast of lightning, scattering the nearest attackers, but more kept coming.

I reached back over my shoulder, yanking the sword free, and swung it wildly around myself. I lost sight of almost everything in the flickering light of falling fairy wings, flashes of magic, and screaming tiny magical creatures.

As a weapon, a massive sword was fuck all real use against the tiny creatures. Apart from a terminally unlucky or stupid few, they spun or dove around it…but the disruption to the wave of attacks was worth it.

I slapped my left hand over the outside of my helmet and dragged it down, clenching my arm in close and rubbing it over my neck and chest as well.

The dozens of tiny fairies that had been clinging to me, biting and gnawing at my armor, gave off abrupt tiny screams, crunches, and the crackle and pop of bones, organs, ligaments and who knew what, as well as the gossamer-like tiny wings shattering under my arm. And despite every instinct telling me not to, I again dove for the ground.

Rolling over, then pushing up and turning, I grinned at the wave of broken and bleeding bodies that had been scrabbling on my armor searching for a way through…only to be hit by a magewhisker from the right.

Its maw closed over my right wrist and bit down, trying to yank my arm, and the sword I gripped, out of the way as a second bounded down the side of the bank, leaping at me.

It was intercepted by Tentacles, and the pair were suddenly rolling and spitting, as Tentacles…well, Tentacles dove down, biting into his opponent and tearing, before releasing and attacking again.

The fight was a blur, with movement on all sides. The remaining fairies, barely a quarter of the original group, hovered now. Half screamed and cried out, twisting and shrieking, but doing nothing else, apparently overcome by the loss of their friends.

The others ignored them, and unleashed spell after spell at me.

I was yanked to the right again, the damn cat still biting down on my arm, and unleashed a blast of lightning across a third of the battle, dragging it from just ahead of me, across to the left. A handful of the smaller fairies detonated before they could recover and attack me once more.

Then I flooded my body with lightning again. The cat yowled…but still kept its jaws clenched on me, even as smoke rose from its mouth and the body thrashed.

I punched it, hard on the bridge of the nose, then again, before snarling and latching my fingers over the snout. I braced and shoved down with all my might with my right arm, and pulled back with the left hand.

There was a half second of resistance, and I almost thought "I love this strength." But before I could finish the thought, the muscles and tendons popped; the top of the cat's head was ripped off and blood fountained out, covering me.

"Gah!" I shook myself, throwing the body aside as it thrashed and convulsed in its death throes, before I was hit by a new phantomsteed. This one managed to land with its front legs straight. A popping sound and a howl that started from its mouth conveyed that wasn't a good idea for a massive horse thing to jump into a pit and land like that… Then it slammed into me.

I was picked up and thrown into the grassy bank on the far side of the pedestal, before bouncing off and falling to the ground, crushing something small beneath me that wailed. I grunted, shoving myself up, before punching a leaping cat out of the air with a crunch of bones and fangs.

I roared back at them. The mass of blood, teeth, and muscles, occasional bursts of spells and the elements all combined into a chaotic rolling montage of a fight.

As I fought off the onslaught, through the mass, I caught a flicker of movement from the corner of my eye. Something—or someone—moved among the chaos, staying back and barely visible. A shimmer in the air, like heat haze, but more…purposeful. They were also mainly only visible because there was so much flying in all directions that as creatures, blood, and bits hit it, they bounced off.

"Tentacles!" I called out, before grunting, bracing myself and taking a fresh horse's charge. "You see that?" I shouted, before grunting, then lifting and suplexing the horse down, slamming it into the pedestal as well.

It screamed; the body shuddered as its spine was broken and blood fountained out.

I spun again. Tentacles bounded past, changing direction at the last second as only a cat could; a tentacle flicked my blade up into the air, flying back toward me.

I grinned, snatching the blade out of the air by the hilt and brought it around, beheading the horse, as the damn cat focused on the disturbance. It hissed suddenly, stiffening its legs and skidding to a stop, its fur standing on end.

That's when I realized that this wasn't just a random attack. There'd been a sort of a boss monster before on the other floors—the big mushroom, the glassine working as controllers to set up the fight on the last one, and now? The creatures were being controlled, manipulated by something far more powerful.

"A Daoine Sidhe," I growled as the voice finally clicked for me—the intonations, the sense of unmitigated superiority and self-belief, not to mention unlikeable utter twattishness. I remembered the lore, and the fucking last time I'd faced them. Powerful fey creatures, known for their cunning and ability to manipulate others.

I concentrated, trying to spot the near-invisible fey orchestrating this ambush. The fairies pressed their attack, their tiny claws and teeth seeking any vulnerable spot. Phantomsteeds charged, their ethereal forms now lunging through the goddamn ground to strike at me.

"Enough of this shit," I snarled. Gathering my power, I unleashed a massive pulse of lightning, creating a defensive sphere of crackling energy around me. The attacking creatures were thrown back, momentarily stunned.

In that brief respite, I caught another glimpse of the shimmer. "There!" I pointed, and Tentacles leaped, its tentacles stretching out impossibly long.

There was a shriek of surprise and pain as the cat's appendages connected with something solid. The air rippled, and suddenly a tall, ethereally beautiful figure stood before us. The Daoine Sidhe, its glamour dispelled, glared at us with eyes like swirling galaxies.

"I fucking *knew* it!" I roared, slamming my sword into the ground, point first, and cracking my knuckles as lightning danced between my fingers. "Looks like we found the puppet master. Want to surrender, or should we skip straight to the part where I kick your ass?"

The Daoine Sidhe's lips curled into a sneer as it straightened up, reaching down to tug the bottom of a fitted coat straight, somehow managing to have found fucking elegant *armor*. That wasn't fair, surely? "You understand nothing, mortal. This is but a test, a crucible to forge the worthy."

"Yeah, yeah." I rolled my eyes. "I've heard it all before. Let's dance, you pretentious prick." I grinned, thankful the bastard hadn't agreed to surrender. Frankly, I had no idea what I would have done if it had agreed. Probably stab it in the face anyway—it wasn't like I could let it live outside, after all.

As the Daoine Sidhe raised its hands, raw magical energy coalescing around it, I couldn't help but grin. Finally, a straightforward fight. This was more like it.

"Ready for this, Tentacles?" I asked my feline companion, who spat out a mangled fairy corpse onto the ground, then looked at the goddamn fey that stared back at us both with contempt clear on its elegant features.

The cat's only response was a low growl, its six eyes fixed on our opponent.

"That's what I thought." I chuckled. "Let's show this fairy tale reject what happens when you fuck with us."

With that, we charged, lightning and tentacles at the ready, straight into the heart of the magical maelstrom. The majority of the phantomsteeds were dead, or dying. The cats? Mostly in pieces or laid breathing their last. And the fairies, now apparently released from whatever control the goddamn thing had over them, streaked away in all directions.

The Daoine Sidhe moved like liquid mercury, flowing around the pedestal, keeping it between us as much as possible, then dodging my initial charge with inhuman grace. Its hands swept outward, and suddenly the air was filled with crystalline shards that sparkled and spun like deadly confetti. I covered my visor instinctively, despite the plated glass that protected me.

"Oh fuck!" I dove and rolled, as the crystals peppered my armor like machine-gun fire. A few found or made their own gaps, drawing blood, but nothing vital was hit. Tentacles was less lucky, yowling as several shards embedded themselves in his flank.

"Just another pretty light show," I snarled, channeling lightning through my body. The power arced outward, forming a shield and seeking the crystals still hanging in the air. They exploded into powder, creating a glittering cloud.

The Sidhe laughed, the sound like breaking glass. "You think your mortal magics can match the power of the Fey?" It gestured again, and the crystal dust swirled together, forming into jagged spears that launched themselves at me.

I dodged right and left, before grinning evilly as the spears flashed around and tried again. This time, I grabbed one out of the air, letting my lightning flow into it. The crystal began to glow red-hot as it bucked and twisted in my hands. "Actually, yeah, I do." I hurled it back, watching with satisfaction as the Sidhe's eyes widened in surprise.

It barely managed to dodge; the crystal spear took a few strands of its silvery hair as it passed. The projectile buried itself in the wall behind, melting into the rock with a sizzling hiss.

While the Sidhe was distracted, Tentacles made his move. The cat darted forward, tentacles lashing out like whips. The Sidhe spun away from most, but one caught its ankle. Before it could react, Tentacles braced himself and yanked hard, sending our opponent sprawling.

"Nice one!" I shouted, already moving in. The Sidhe rolled onto its back, hands glowing with power, but I was faster. My boot connected with its jaw with a satisfying crunch.

The fairy lord went flying, smashing into the pedestal hard enough to crack the stone. But instead of falling, it seemed to melt into the surface, vanishing completely.

"Oh, that's just fucking cheating," I growled, spinning around. "Where are you, you sparkly shit?"

The answer came in the form of a blast of pure force that hit me from behind, sending me staggering. I turned to see the Sidhe emerging from a nearby crystal vein, its perfect features twisted with rage.

"You dare!" it shrieked, barely able to make itself understood through the cracked jaw, all pretense of elegance gone. "You filthy mongrel, you dare to strike me?"

"Actually," I grinned, flexing my hands like claws, "I'm planning to do a lot worse than that."

The Sidhe screamed in fury, raw magic pouring off it in waves. The remaining fairies and creatures around us began to convulse; their bodies twisted and merged together into horrific new forms.

"Well, that's disturbing," I muttered, watching as what used to be a phantomsteed melded with three magewhiskers into something that looked like a nightmare had fucked a Salvador Dali painting.

The twisted mass of former dungeon creatures surged toward us, a writhing horror of limbs, wings, and tentacles. I grabbed my sword from where it was stuck in the ground, yanking it free just as the first wave hit.

"This is just wrong on so many levels," I growled, slicing through what might have once been a handful of fairies fused with half a horse's head. The thing screamed with multiple mouths as it fell, black ichor spraying from the wound. "Fuck's sake, man! You need therapy!"

Tentacles was having none of this shit. He bounded up the wall and launched himself off from it, using his own tentacles to swing clear of a former magewhisker that now had phantomsteed hooves for feet and dozens of fairy wings sprouting from its spine.

"You think your crude violence can stop this?" the Sidhe taunted, its voice echoing from multiple crystal veins at once. "Now that you've unlocked it, I'm able to power their transformation with the very heart of this mine!"

I glanced over at the pedestal and the crystals jutting through the mangled earth or dotting the ground on all sides, just waiting to be dug free. The bastard was using the pedestal's energy flow, channeling it through the crystal veins to fuel whatever fucked-up magic this was.

I also saw something else—a thin, almost invisible chain of silvery light that ran from his left ankle to the pedestal. I realized that each and every time I'd seen him appear or disappear, it'd been a very close-ranged teleport.

He was trapped in here, chained to the pedestal! As soon as I realized that, realized that the fucker was not only trying to claim the crystal mine but escape it as his apparent prison as well? Well, that made my next move ridiculously easy to decide on. There was no way this fuck was leaving. Not upright and outside of a body bag, anyway.

"Tentacles!" I shouted. "RUN!"

The cat hesitated. Then, on seeing me plant one hand on an exposed crystal vein on the floor and draw the mana from it, its eyes widened. It started sprinting, digging its claws into the dirt sides of the shallow pit and bounding out as fast as he could. I swung my blade wildly, knowing I only needed to hold off the mutated horde for a few seconds. Tentacles reached the top and spun, glaring down at me, and I grinned up at him through my helmet.

"Run, you furry fuck." I sighed, as the mutilated mass closed in on me. I reversed the flow, starting to cast a second spell, one that I needed the fucker to really not be watching for.

The mana that had been streaming into me from the crystals suddenly blasted out in all directions as I supercharged my Lightning Shield, punching it outward and expanding it as far as I could.

The Sidhe emerged again, this time right in front of me, inside my shield. "You fool! You'll destabilize the entire—"

I cut it off with a lightning-enhanced uppercut to the chin, sending him hurtling backward into the barrier of the lightning shield. "Yeah, that's kind of the point, dickhead," I spat at him, before throwing the blade at him in an underarm toss.

The fey lord blinked to the left, with glistening, bloody drool leaking from one side of his mouth. He glared at me and slashed his hands to either side, then dragged them back, as if pulling on a huge weight. The island around us shook violently.

"Either I win…" he mumbled through a broken jaw as the crystals around him started to shatter. Their gleaming mana flowed inward, forming glittering, floating spears. "Or nobody—"

"Heads, I win," I countered, dodging left and right as he threw them. Then I shoved my hand upward, unleashing the spell I'd been really focused on. "Tails, you lose… LIGHTNING STORM!"

The storm appeared out of nowhere. The cloudy atmosphere over the island gave it more than enough space to be summoned into being. And rather than the usual fifteen hundred or so mana it took, I put fifteen *thousand* into it.

That was just the joy of casting from the middle of an active mana crystal mine, I guessed.

The sudden rumble that filled the air could be felt from balls to bones. The last of the mutated monstrosities that had been trying to reach me through my shield hesitated, their will linked to that of their master, who stared upward in sudden realization and horror.

"No…you cannot!" he hissed in disbelief. The iron-grey and sea-green clouds of the storm flooded outward, the pulse of power that I both fueled and craved, building. "You fool! You'll kill us both!" he screeched. Terror and fury filled his eyes as he lunged at me, desperate to try to stop me.

Spoiler.

It didn't work.

The first of the ten blasts of lightning hammered down, punching into the ground between us. He hurtled sideways, slamming into the dirt wall; the shock apparently prevented him from jumping out.

The second and third bolts hit almost simultaneously. One punched into the pedestal itself; the other slammed into a particularly large crystal vein. The explosion of magical energies sent a shock wave through the entire shallow pit. Crystals shattered and reformed in impossible patterns, as apparently the mana helped them to reform into new layouts.

"You maniac!" the Sidhe screamed over the deafening rumble of thunder. "The containment enchantments…they're failing!"

"That's the idea!" I roared back, watching as bolts four through seven hammered down in rapid succession.

The remaining mutated monsters were dead now—whoo-boy, were they dead. My lightning shield had vanished, dismissed before it could pop like a bubble, and I watched as a smoking section of magewhisker melded with phantomsteed cartwheeled over my head in slow motion.

Each strike created a cascading effect; the released mana fed back into my storm, making it even more powerful. The chamber was now a maelstrom of lightning, crystal shards, and raw magical energy.

The Sidhe tried to teleport again. But the silver chain around its ankle flared brightly with each attempt as it apparently reached the limit of its range and jerked it back. "Stop this! You don't understand what you're unleashing!" it screeched.

"Oh, I understand perfectly." I grinned, watching the bastard's mounting panic. "You're not the only one who can use this place's power."

The eighth bolt struck the ground directly beneath the Sidhe, launching it into the air. As it fell, the ninth caught him square in the chest. Its perfect form convulsed, magic coursing through it in waves of destructive energy.

The entire island started to break apart; the void beyond seemed to press in closer. The mutated creatures were dissolving, unable to maintain their twisted forms under the magical onslaught.

"Time for the finale," I muttered, gathering what remained of my power. The tenth and final bolt was building up to be something special, feeding off the ambient energy of the completely destabilized crystal mine. But unlike for fuckface over there, lightning healed me, and that meant that I could afford to stand right here in the middle of it.

The Sidhe, somehow still conscious, locked eyes with me. "Wait…please… I surr—"

"Sorry," I sneered, not sorry at all. "But I *really* fucking hate fey."

The final bolt hit with the force of a tactical nuke. The world went white, then black, then several colors I'm pretty sure hadn't existed before. I was thrown backward, my armor smoking and my ears ringing with what sounded like a thousand of those annoying wind chimes being fed through a wood chipper.

When my vision finally cleared, at least a minute later, I found myself lying on my back at the top of the pit. Tentacles was nearby, looking singed but alive, all six eyes wide as he stared down into the crater below.

I crawled to the edge and looked down. The hollow was completely transformed. Where there had been grass and earth, now there was only glass and twisted crystal formations. The pedestal was gone, vaporized along with most of the center of the island.

And there, in the middle of it all, lay what was left of the Daoine Sidhe. The once-beautiful creature now looked like a melted action figure that had been rolled in glitter and then struck by lightning. Repeatedly.

A notification popped up:

Congratulations! You have defeated the Daoine Sidhe, Master of Fey!

Bonus Hidden Floor Objective Complete: Total Destruction of Containment Structure

Reward: Sidhe's Chain of Binding (Legendary Item)

Warning: Structural integrity of floor compromised. Please proceed to exit.

"Binding chain?" I muttered, then spotted it: the silver chain that had bound the Sidhe to the pedestal, now lying innocently in the glass-lined crater. "Well, now…that might come in handy."

The island shuddered ominously.

"Right." I scooped up the chain and stuffed it in my bag of holding. "I can take a hint. Coming, Tentacles?"

The cat gave me a look that clearly said "Do I have a choice?" before padding after me.

I moved to the edge of the island, glancing around, before finally spotting what I guessed was the exit: an island below and to the right, drifting slowly, as what looked to be a dozen of the fairies streamed toward it in a panic.

I looked at the cat, wondering how I was going to get him there. From his glare, I very clearly wasn't about to be permitted to carry him.

"You gonna jump then?"

Then he turned, and ran in the opposite direction.

I stared after him, confused, as he vanished downward on the far side of the island and out of sight. I hesitated for a second then launched myself into the air, grinning to myself when the air remained clear and welcoming.

I darted after him, finding a path that led downward on that side of the island, twisting around a long tapering underside that appeared stuffed with crystals of all shapes and sizes.

Reaching out, I snagged a few of the nearby and seemingly loosest, but didn't dare risk the time it'd take to gather more. Hopefully the island would recover soon, and without any kind of long-term damage.

A new mine was always going to be useful, after all.

He sprinted across the apparent bridge that led to the exit, and I followed, flying alongside. The final stop was coming up quickly.

It was another floating island, unsurprisingly. But this one, unlike the last, had a single door standing proud and weird in the middle of it. The stone archway that surrounded it was carved with symbols and twisted as my eye tried to follow the outer line without success.

A bunch of the fairies flew in circles and helix patterns around the edge of the doorway. As we approached, their patterns collapsed in on themselves; three flew forward, with one taking the lead.

"Greetings, Dungeon Lord, looks like you did well again." Ciara smiled.

I landed next to her, smiling widely in return. My heart lifted just a little, as the genuine fear that if she'd been reborn into this dungeon again, and I'd already killed her, *again*, was banished.

Behind us, the crystalline island began to collapse, falling into the void piece by piece. Just another day in the life of a Dungeon Lord.

CHAPTER TWENTY-FIVE

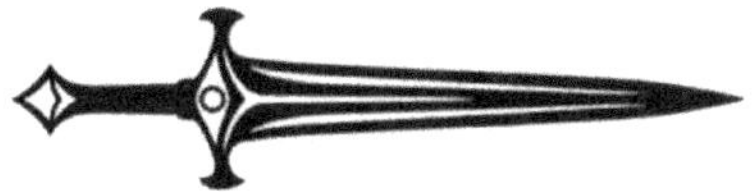

The swirling void around us shimmered and warped as we approached the door. The fairies darted ahead to circle it in an intricate pattern. As we got closer, the door opened on its own, clearly in response to my approach, and the revealed area beyond… was another door.

I paused, then nodded to myself as the fairies started to cheer.

Etched into the door in gold were familiar runes. As I looked up and around, I noted they were inlaid into the stone archway as well—the same six-pointed star in a circle that marked safe rooms in the previous trial dungeon.

"Well, look at that." I grinned at Ciara. "A proper rest stop. Don't suppose there's a vending machine in there? I could murder a beer and some chocolate right about now."

Ciara rolled her eyes. "Ever the optimist. Though there should be supplies inside, and you should be able to summon anything else you need, assuming you haven't managed to break that part of the dungeon too." She glanced meaningfully back at the disintegrating crystal mine.

"Hey, that was tactical destruction," I protested as she fell in beside me and we reached the doorway. "Very precise. Surgical, even."

Tentacles hissed, padding past me to examine the door, making it clear that he, at least, had some issues with that statement.

"Unbelievable," I groaned. "Another smart-ass cat. Because that's exactly what I needed in my life."

The door swung open at our approach, revealing a familiar sight—a well-appointed rest chamber with comfortable seating, a fountain, and what looked suspiciously like actual beds along one wall. The remaining fairies zipped inside, clearly eager for a break.

"Now this is more like it." I sighed, already reaching up to unfasten my helmet. The room had that same peculiar quality I remembered from the last trial dungeon—a sense of being somehow removed from the chaos outside, like stepping into the eye of a storm.

"You should check your rewards before you get too comfortable," Ciara advised, settling onto one of the smaller chairs clearly sized for her kind. "The trial dungeon's structure has been…altered by what you did back there."

"Altered how?" I asked, though I was already reaching for my stat screen to see what I'd actually managed to win from that mess.

"Well, for one thing," she gestured at the door we'd entered through, which was slowly dissolving into mist, "I don't think we'll be going back that way."

"Fair enough." I finally got my helmet off, setting it aside and running a hand through my sweat-soaked hair. "Though, honestly, after that light show back there, I'm not sure there's much left to go back to."

Tentacles had claimed one of the larger cushions, arranging himself with feline precision as another of the fairies spoke up.

"Perhaps you should focus less on what you've destroyed and more on what you've gained. The Chain of Binding alone is worth the chaos."

"You saw that, huh?" I nodded, before hesitating and turning to Ciara. "Ciara, the last dungeon run…"

"Hush, it's all a game." She gestured that it didn't matter.

I paused, remembering that comment, and the way that both her and Drak had used it last time we'd been together. That's what they'd been told—that all of this was just a game, and that although their deaths and the events surrounding them could be horrific, that once their deaths had been earned out, they'd be released from the dungeon again, set free and their crimes expunged from their record.

I shook my head and spoke up. "No. No, it's not a game, and you died to save me."

"It's my role," she said softly. "It was another death off my debt, that's all."

"You saved me," I repeated. "You did it, knowing that you would die, and you still damn well did it, so thank you. You're one of the reasons I came back here."

"What?" she asked, confused. "Why?"

"I owe a debt too," I said. "I said I'd try to free you, so here I am."

She stared at me, before looking over to one of her friends, then back.

I realized that the constant low hum of conversation in the background had now died away entirely.

"You came back…for me?" she said wonderingly, tilting her head to one side.

"I mean…" I colored, then went on quickly. "Not just for you. I mean, I needed the prizes as well, but yeah. That was one of the reasons I came, to try to free you. It was *a* reason, not the only one, but…"

I broke off, not sure why the hell I was trying to justify that I wasn't a nice guy, but still. It was important that she didn't think I'd only done it for that reason.

"Still, thank you," she said. "It is a surprise, and a welcome one. Did Drak escape as well? As we explained before, our only news is that which we share between ourselves, and I have not seen him yet."

"Yeah," I grunted, frowning.

"Ah. And he has been less than helpful?" she guessed, cocking her head to one side in question.

"Absolute bare minimum, and has been getting others addicted to drugs, or so we think." I sighed. "Dammit, shouldn't have said that, I suppose."

"I—" She shook her head. "I cannot speak for him, but this fits with my experiences. He was on his best behavior on our run, clearly hoping that you'd free him, and now that he's been released, I suspect you're seeing the real him." She glanced around; the others sat calmly, listening, and she turned back to me.

"It does raise a point, though…" she said carefully.

"Can you leave with me now?" I asked her bluntly. "If we complete the dungeon, can I take you all out with me, or have I lost the chance at taking you out because I didn't summon you personally?"

"We cannot travel to the entrance with you and be released," she admitted. "If you were to complete the dungeon again, then yes, there we would be able to exit, but only if bound to you, as we were summoned by the dungeon, not you directly."

"Okay, how do we do that?" I asked her, and she smiled, before asking her own question.

"Do you still have any points?" she queried. "The summoning points that you were given on entry?"

"Ten thousand," I admitted.

"Then yes, you can." She smiled an almost feral smile. "Provided you bind yourself to us and we to you."

"That sounds problematic, considering I'm bound to a dungeon," I said carefully. "Not that I think you're going to try to access the dungeon through me and supplant me, of course…"

"No, lord!" Another dungeon fairy suddenly spoke up. "Not like that!"

I glanced from her to Ciara, and the older fairy sighed.

"What Mirabelle means is that we don't need to be bound to you in that way. Honestly, most of us wouldn't want that. There are warnings in the deep past from others that have accepted such bindings."

"Oh?"

"It results in a very deep bond, one that can quickly become…inappropriate."

"Uh…"

"Sexual," another of the group chimed in. "We would be bound to your mind, and any such desires would imprint upon us. As we are without hormones or sexuality of our own in the way that you are, the result can be messy."

I had a sudden vision of a free-for-all with all the fairies changing size and shape, picking out whatever they decided I fancied at that point and jumping me.

There was a brief pause as I stared at them, my mind working. I mean, yeah, I love Kelly, but a little thought of a dozen of more incredibly hot women mobbing me for sex?

"Oh dear. We've broken him." One of the fairies sighed. "Males are so easily distracted. How do we fix it?"

"I heard that sticking your arm up its—" One of the others spoke up cheerfully, and I jerked, speaking quickly, before it could get any more out.

"No!" I shouted, then closed my eyes and ignored the conversation that started up to one side.

"That woke him up! Where do you stick your arm?"

"I heard it goes up his—"

"RIGHT!" I went on quickly. "Right, so what do I need to do, and to be very clear, so that you *don't* get bonded to me in that way?"

"We'd need to be bound to the dungeon," Ciara said, clearly amused. "It'd mean that we'd be essentially dungeon-born and in thrall to you, so we'd like an agreement that we'd be set free before you require certain things of us. We are free-thinking beings, after all…"

"Free?" another asked her friend to one side.

"Thinking?" the other replied.

I glanced at the cat, Tentacles, who let out a long-suffering sigh, and then glanced at me and nodded.

"You as well?" I asked, and he nodded again. "Okay. So the standard deal I guess…" I scratched at my chin, focusing and trying to remember the oath that I had given our people on the oath stone, and that they'd given me back, then remembering the version that Kelly had written out for me and I'd put in my bag of holding.

Pulling it out, I read my section aloud, before passing the paper over to Ciara, who glanced at it and shrugged.

"I, Matt, Dungeon Lord of Newcastle, hereby solemnly swear on my honor and life to uphold the following oath to the brave soldiers of Otterburn Camp and Newcastle, and the civilians who have agreed to integrate into my dungeon and serve as part of its defensive forces or regular citizenry, for a year and a day:

"I pledge to lead these people with integrity, fairness, and respect, always considering their well-being and valuing their lives as I would my own, and any of my citizens.

"I vow to make every honest effort to rescue and protect the royal family, understanding the importance of this mission to the soldiers and the kingdom they served.

"I promise to utilize these new citizens' skills and bravery wisely in defense of the dungeon and in our expeditions, never wasting their lives needlessly or recklessly.

"I will strive to provide for the citizens' needs to the best of my ability, ensuring they have adequate shelter, sustenance, and equipment to fulfill their duties and maintain their morale.

"As we venture to the south, I will always consider the search for the citizens' families, understanding the importance of reuniting them and providing safety for their loved ones.

"I will lead the expedition with courage, strategic thinking, and a commitment to minimizing casualties, considering peaceful resolutions when possible but standing ready to fight when necessary.

"I acknowledge that this oath is valid for a year and a day, during which time I will serve my new citizens to the best of my ability, and they will serve me in return.

"By my power and word, I hereby bind myself to this sacred oath, promising to lead and serve with honor, loyalty, and dedication. May our alliance be strong, our cause just, and our victory certain."

Then, as the others looked from me to her, Ciara, still looking down at the page, began to read it aloud.

"We, the surviving soldiers of Otterburn Camp and Newcastle, and the civilians who have agreed to integrate into the dungeon solemnly swear on our honor and lives to uphold the following oath to Matt, Dungeon Lord of Newcastle, who has sworn to lead us with integrity, to protect the royal family, and to prioritize our well-being, for a year and a day:

"We pledge our loyalty and service to the Dungeon Lord, integrating ourselves into the dungeon's defensive forces and obeying the commands given to us, as long as they align with the Dungeon Lord's oath to us.

"We will fight bravely and skillfully in defense of the dungeon and on our expeditions, or how so ever we can best serve, always striving to protect our comrades and fulfill our missions to the best of our ability.

"We will respect the hierarchy and structure of the dungeon's forces, working with our new allies to ensure the safety and success of our collective goals, and to protect our families.

"We will maintain our discipline, honor, and commitment to the values that define us as soldiers and citizens, even as we adapt to our new circumstances and roles within the dungeon.

"We will trust in the Dungeon Lord's leadership and strategic decisions, providing our input and expertise when appropriate but ultimately following the orders given to us, trusting in him, and those he places over us.

"We agree that this oath is valid for a year and a day, during which time we will serve the Dungeon Lord and those he places over us to the best of our ability, and they will serve us in return.

"We make this oath freely and willingly, understanding the gravity of our commitment and the importance of the tasks before us.

"By our words and deeds, we hereby bind ourselves to this sacred oath, promising to serve with courage, loyalty, and honor. May our alliance with the Dungeon Lord be strong, our cause just, and our victory certain."

"What do you think?" I asked her as she fell silent.

"Well, considering that there's no contingency for a free dungeon-born in here, or for us being freed if we swear and you do something, I'd say it needs work, but I'd be willing to extend a little faith, provided you make some changes…"

That started nearly an hour of the various fairies weighing in with suggestions and demands. Most were reasonable. All the sugar they could eat, for example, wasn't a biggie; as dungeon-born, they'd have access to summon whatever food they wanted at any time inside the boundaries. And outside, they could either subsist on mana or food, as they wanted and it was available.

Another that was fine was that they wanted clothes, and an option to choose their own image. Sure, go wild.

One that wasn't so much, was that one of them demanded their own mounts. Several were looking at Tentacles, and he let loose a warning growl; that was clearly who they were hoping to have.

A wage of ten mana crystals an hour per fairy was asked for as well by one. And the way that everyone turned to look at that one, who then grinned and said "Hey, you can't blame me for trying" made it clear that both sides viewed that as unreasonable.

"Look, you set us free of the dungeon, and we'll become dungeon-born in service to you, okay?" Ciara sighed eventually. "You expect nothing of us that you don't ask of your other people, and we gain full citizenship. In exchange, we'll help you get out. Though, there is one last thing…"

"Oh?" I asked, seeing the feral grin on her face.

"I get to be in charge of all your negotiations with Drak from now on."

"There's a damn good chance he's going to be jailed," I said. "If I find proof he's been doing what I think…"

"He's a survivor. If there's proof you could find, he'd be gone already," she pointed out. "No, I want him to have to come through me for anything, that's all."

"You know what…" I paused, then nodded. "Fuck it, yeah. His outstanding arrangements stay in place, but he's just refused to take over the alchemy side and help anyone but himself, so yeah. You have fun, on the condition that you run it all through Kelly, my partner and the Dungeon Mistress of Minions first."

"I can accept that. Now, it'll cost you about two hundred mana each to bind us to the dungeon as dungeon-born, and I'll need Soosta to guide us…" She turned and an older, white-haired fairy drifted forward.

Unlike most of the others, she didn't appear so much as a tiny Tinkerbell-style fairy, as a cross between one of them and a grey alien from the TV.

Her face was almost featureless, her eyes huge and black, oval and slightly tilted, with a large cranium and tiny jaw, with slits for a nose. Her thin, almost reedy arms and legs hung limp.

She floated forward, her wings buzzing like a hummingbird's, and the group watched her respectfully.

She didn't speak—no clue whether she could or not at all. Instead, I felt a little tug at the corner of my mind, and as I focused on her, she led me through the steps.

It was weird, more a mental exercise than anything I'd equate to magic, but then I connected to the dungeon with my mind, so I guess it made sense.

Ten minutes later, they were all bound to me, along with Cerin. The fucking tentacle cat had a name that he'd not bothered to share before now. The fairies could speak some of his language apparently and even weirder, the fucker wasn't even a magewhisker.

He was a voidcat, whatever that was. When I asked him about it, or how the hell he was there as I sure as shit didn't have access to his template, he just closed his eyes and went to sleep.

Prick.

There were discussions for the next half an hour as we all rested a bit, and I learned that what Ciara or Drak had said on the previous run about there not being a chatroom for all the dungeon sentients wasn't entirely true.

I mean, there wasn't a staffroom with tea and cookies, admittedly. That'd have been ridiculous, though the image of a bunch of tentacled horrors and goblins, orcs and fairies sitting around some cheap-ass table and bitching about adventurers at the end of a shift did make me grin.

No, there was a sort of disseminated information network that existed between the souls, that updated with certain details, like a successful dungeon run had been achieved, and that one of their number had even been released. Notably, Ciara hadn't been sure whether it was Drak and me, or a totally different run that she'd not been spawned for.

That was great news, as that gave them all hope that maybe they'd be summoned and released. It was designed to share that, but it neglected to share the important secondary details, like was it recent, and who it'd been.

That meant that for this run at least, as the various souls were freshly summoned and awakened with the information that a run was recently won, they had hope, and some were therefore more likely to swap sides.

The downside was, for all they knew, they'd been in storage for three thousand years, so the person they were considering changing sides for and having penalization deaths added to their tally for…had nothing to do with the last successful dungeon run.

In the end, the deal was struck, though. The fairies would help me in the next section, and I even had some mana left, enough to summon a single being, along with some change, provided I agree to Ciara's request that it not be "one of those asshole kobolds."

I chose not to point out that they were the majority of my dungeon-born outside. I took her advice, getting a flat glare from Cerin, the fucking cat, when I announced that the new addition to our team would be a Scepiniir warrior.

Before I did that, though, I pulled up my kill notification, getting that fucker out of the way.

Congratulations!

You have killed the following:

- **12x Clockwork Crawler [Uncommon], Level 10-15, 1,440 XP**
- **6x Clockwork Crawler [Advanced], Level 20-22, 1,800 XP**
- **8x Dvork [Advanced], Level 20-25, 2,400 XP**
- **6x Magewhisker [Advanced], Level 21-23, 1,800 XP**
- **8x Phantomsteed [Advanced], Level 22-25, 2,800 XP**
- **40x Dungeon Fairy [Uncommon], Level 10-15, 4,000 XP**
- **12x Mutated Creature [Advanced], Level 22-25, 4,800 XP**
- **1x Daoine Sidhe [Boss], Level 26, 8,500 XP**

Special Rewards:

- **Hidden Objective: Total Destruction of Containment Structure = 5,000 XP**

Total XP awarded: 32,540 XP
Current XP to next level stands at 81,505/120,000

I summoned the Scepiniir warrior, losing six thousand and change of my remaining seven thousand two hundred, and watched as the light coalesced into a towering figure of muscle and grace. Unlike the treacherous bastard I'd fought the last time I'd been in a dungeon, this one appeared more…focused. Her feline features were set in an expression of calm assessment as she looked around the safe room.

"Greetings, Dungeon Warmancer," she rumbled, dropping to one knee. "I am Rathaharn of the Southern Cliffs."

I couldn't help but be impressed.

Most of the Scepiniir I'd seen so far had been those I'd summoned, and the ones I'd met that were "naturally occurring"—which still seemed weird and wrong to me—had been scouts and fast-moving ranger kind of classes.

This was an out-and-out warrior and damn, I could tell the difference.

It was like a cereal company said "Hey, let's give Tony a serious 'roid addiction and get him into pro wrestling and medieval mixed martial arts, and see what happens."

Rathaharn was seriously stacked, and I mean with muscle.

Her shoulders bulged beneath the armored pauldrons. Although her coloring seemed to be mainly black and red, there were hints around the eyes that there were lighter colors to her fur as well.

They were only hints, though, because she wore heavier armor than Robin, our own Paladin, did, and the flail and shield combination that she wielded just looked nasty to face off against.

"You have finished your appraisal, yes?" she asked cooly.

I coughed, then nodded. "Yes, sorry. I haven't met many of your kind that were self-aware, and those that I have, they were scouts."

"Ah, the cowards." She purred.

"Cowards?" I cocked an eyebrow. "Takes some serious balls to hunt around in enemy territory, especially in light armor and alone, if you ask me."

"If they cannot stand and fight, then they are useless."

I stared at her before snorting my disgust at that statement. "Well, that's fucking bullshit, but whatever. We're not here to argue comparative theology an' shite. We're here to go fuck up someone's Tuesday, and with that in mind, lead the way."

"As you command." Rathaharn rose smoothly, moving with that fluid grace that marked her kind.

Ciara fluttered over, landing on my shoulder. "Not bad. At least this one seems less prone to monologuing about our inevitable doom or trying to kill us."

"That's a low bar," I muttered, checking my gear one final time. The healing potions I'd summoned earlier were secure, my weapons were ready, and my armor had mostly recovered from the crystal mine's abuse. "Everyone ready?"

Cerin gave me what I could only interpret as a withering look before padding toward the door that would lead to the next floor. The fairies gathered in formation, with Ciara taking point among them.

"Just remember," Ciara said as we approached the door, "whatever's through there, we have no way to know until we see it. The dungeon's been…creative so far."

"That's one word for it," I agreed, reaching for the handle. "All right, team, let's see what fresh hell awaits us."

I pushed open the door, and we stepped through into a small hall. Another burst of heat radiated from the doors in front of us…doors that Rathaharn strode up to and shoved at with all her might, before snarling and trying again.

"I'm tempted to let her keep trying," Ciara said softly in my ear, before she lifted her voice and called to our Scepiniir companion.

"Rathaharn dear, they're floor doors, locked to each floor to prevent us from leaving our assigned area without permission. Any strength you put into trying to open them is being redirected back into them. You can't open them. Only a Dungeon Lord can."

Rathaharn snarled something over her shoulder and tried again, eliciting a sigh and a "what can you do" look from Ciara that drew a chuckle from me as we walked up to stand by her side.

"I'd open the door if I was you," Ciara said after another half a minute of watching the big cat struggle. "She's Scepiniir, so incapable of admitting that she can't do something."

"Ciara's right," a voice came.

I glanced back. A playful little fairy sat atop Cerin's head, kicking her legs cheerily and beaming round at the change of scenery. It was also the fairy who I'd been fairly sure was advocating getting me out of my shock by sticking her entire arm up my bum before—I didn't know who the hell wouldn't be pushed *out* of shock by an unexpected assault on their rear—but the innocent look on her face and the way that she seemed totally oblivious to Cerin's mounting annoyance suggested she wasn't long for this world anyway.

Thankfully.

I made a mental note to watch her, should she ever be anywhere near me when I was planning to sleep.

I stepped forward, laying my hand on the massive doors, feeling the familiar tingle of connection as the dungeon recognized me. The doors swung open silently with a gentle push, revealing…

Heat. That was the first sensation that hit us, along with a blast of incredibly dry air from the right, even as a wave of moisture rolled in from the left. The massive chamber beyond was like nothing I'd seen in a dungeon before—or hell, anywhere!

"Well, shit," I muttered, staring at the vast expanse before us. "This is new."

The chamber stretched out impossibly far, clearly larger than should have been possible within the stadium above, at which point I just gave up on the whole scale thing. I mean, the last dungeon? Small changes, slightly larger than it should have been…that was it. Here?

It was like someone had taken the spatial rule book out, wiped their arse with it, and then flushed it away.

It was divided into four distinct sections, each one a perfect representation of an elemental domain. To our right, waves of heat distorted the air above rivers of lava that wound through obsidian formations. To our left, waterfalls cascaded down crystal walls into deep pools that seemed to glow from within.

"The elements," Ciara breathed from my shoulder. "All four of them. This is…this is not good. Any chance I can renegotiate, boss?"

"Why not?" I watched as the fairies spread out slightly, maintaining a close formation but clearly scanning the room. Cerin had moved to my left side, all six eyes fixed on something in the distance as, most concerningly, Rathaharn grinned, seemingly elated.

"Because often those bound to pure elements are creatures of incredible power," Rathaharn growled happily, her flail already in hand. "And that"—she pointed with her shield to where all four sections seemed to meet in the center—"is a nexus point. The elements should never mix like that."

The center of the room was chaos incarnate. A swirling mass of energy where Fire met Water, Earth met Air, and reality seemed to twist in on itself. Even from here, I could feel the raw power emanating from it.

"Right then." I straightened my shoulders. "Anyone want to place bets on whether we need to go through that to get out?"

A distant roar echoed through the chamber, followed by what sounded like rushing water, then a rumble of earth moving.

"Primordials," Ciara hissed. "They're here. Of course they're here. This just keeps getting better."

"What's a primordial?" I asked, already knowing I wouldn't like the answer.

"Think of them as the living embodiment of their element," she explained quickly. "Incredibly powerful, nearly impossible to hurt with their own element, and absolutely territorial about their domains."

"So we've got four super-powered elemental beings that are going to try to kill us," I summarized. "While we try to navigate their territories and probably solve some kind of puzzle involving that death-tornado in the middle."

“That’s about the size of it,” Ciara agreed.

“Wonderful.” I drew my sword, its familiar weight somehow reassuring despite everything. “Anyone else getting the feeling this is going to hurt?”

Cerin’s tail twitched in what I chose to interpret as agreement, while Rathaharn simply growled, a sound of excited anticipation rather than fear.

“All right, team,” I said as cheerfully as I could manage, trying to pick the least lethal-looking path forward. “Let’s go make some new friends…and kill them.”

CHAPTER TWENTY-SIX

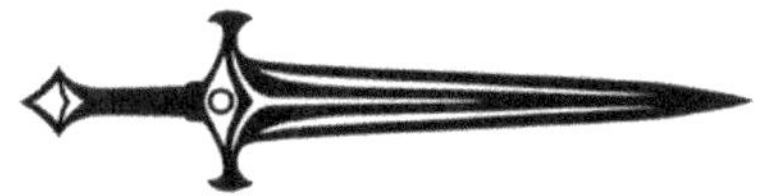

"Hold up a second." Ciara raised her hand as Rathaharn started to move forward, her eagerness to charge into battle practically radiating off her. "Before we go running in there, let's think this through."

"Think?" she growled, her tail lashing. "They are there. We are here. The path is clear."

"Yeah, that's what worries me," I agreed, despite the growing urgency I felt to just damn well fight the last floors and get the hell out. I squinted, studying the layout more carefully. The four sections were clearly defined, but the borders between them were...odd. Narrow paths that seemed to shift and blur, where elements mixed unpredictably.

Ciara lifted off my shoulder, flying up a few meters to get a better view. "The Air quadrant might be our best bet," she called down. "At least we can see what we're dealing with there."

She had a point. While the Fire section was literally glowing with danger and the Water quadrant looked deep enough to drown a giant, the Air section seemed to consist mainly of floating platforms and swirling mists. Relatively straightforward, if you didn't mind heights.

"What about those?" I pointed to what looked like crystalline formations scattered throughout each section. They pulsed with different colors, changing seemingly at random.

"Resource nodes," one of the other fairies—I thought it was the one who'd been tormenting Cerin earlier—piped up. "They'll be part of whatever puzzle we need to solve." I squinted at her, putting together that she was also the one that wanted to shove her arm up me and use me as a sock puppet, and had been asking for a fuck load of mana crystals.

I was going to be keeping an eye on her, I decided.

"Wonderful." I sighed eventually. "So not only do we have to navigate through four deadly elements while avoiding their pissed-off avatars, we also need to collect...what? Magic crystals?"

"Elemental essence, most likely," Ciara corrected. "Though I wouldn't touch them without figuring out the pattern first. Last time I saw something like this, touching the wrong one at the wrong time...well, let's just say it wasn't pretty."

I was about to ask for details when a massive shape rose from the lava river to our right. It was vaguely humanoid, if you considered "being on fire" a human trait, and it seemed to be looking right at us.

"Time's up," I announced, backing away from the Fire section. "Air quadrant it is. Everyone stay close and—"

The Fire primordial roared, surging higher and higher, topping out at around six or seven meters in height and constantly shifting in shape. Arms flowed like deceptively slow-moving lava, around and down, to scoop up a ball of glowing rock, before compressing it into a tighter ball, all the while glaring at us. Striated patterns of red, yellow, and black flowed across it and made it almost impossible to make out individual features.

It made another sound like an erupting volcano, then hurled the compressed missile at us—only now the fucker glowed with a bright-white light and looked like a small sun.

"MOVE!"

We scattered as the ball of plasma slammed into the ground. The heat alone was enough to make my armor creak in protest. Rathaharn bounded left, her shield raised, while Cerin simply vanished, though I caught a blur of movement headed toward the Air quadrant.

I glanced back at the burned and molten stretch of dirt that was all that was left of the area we'd been standing on, and for a split second I wished that Dante was here to try to calm it down…

Then I wished Kilo was here instead to help kick its ass.

The fairies split into clearly practiced formations, most following Ciara as she darted high and right, looking like a flight of geese in the damn V formation, while two broke off to circle around behind us, watching our backs.

"We can heal!" one of the ones that took up station behind me called out, and I nodded that I'd heard.

"Focus on the others. I can heal myself," I called back, wishing I'd thought to ask the goddamn fairies that had *magical goddamn powers* what those powers were!

"To me!" I shouted, sprinting for the nearest floating platform. If we were going to do this, might as well commit. "Ciara, any chance that thing can follow us into the Air section?" I yelled up at her.

"Technically, no!" she called back. "But—"

Another roar cut her off. This one was different—more like a hurricane compressed into a single sound. A vaguely humanoid shape composed of swirling storm winds and crackling lightning emerged from the mists ahead.

"But that's why!" Ciara finished, as the Air primordial fixed its gaze on us.

"Fuck me, they're territorial!" I remembered someone saying, skidding to a stop as the two primordials faced off. "Like cats with gardens!"

"Did you just compare primordial elementals to housecats?" Ciara demanded, dodging a stray lightning bolt.

"Focus!" Rathaharn snarled, her flail already spinning. "We need to reach that first platform!"

She was right. We were stuck in the neutral ground between sections, and that was rapidly becoming the worst place to be. The Fire primordial launched another attack, but this time at its Air counterpart.

A shield of crackling lightning and formed air like a roiling stormfront rose up, catching the blast. The resulting explosion sent waves of superheated wind rolling across us.

"Right," I gritted my teeth, gathering my lightning, "new plan. Rathaharn, with me. Ciara, get your people ready to run interference. Cerin…" I looked around. "Where the hell is the cat?"

A yowl from above drew our attention. Somehow, the sneaky bastard had already made it to the first platform and was looking down at us with what I swear was disappointment.

"Show-off," I muttered. "Okay, on my mark, we—"

The ground shuddered as two more figures emerged: one rising from the earth like a mountain deciding to take a stroll, the other flowing up from the water like a liquid sculpture.

"Oh, you have got to be kidding me," I groaned. All four primordials were now awake, aware, and looking mighty pissed off about our presence in their domains, even if the two newcomers were just standing, glaring. Their attitude was vaguely reminiscent of my American cousin's description of the "Karens" who ran their housing association.

"Your mark?" Rathaharn prompted, tension clear in her voice.

I took a deep breath, watching as the primordials turned to face one another. Ancient rivalries clearly trumped their immediate annoyance with us.

"NOW!"

We surged forward as one, racing for the first platform even as chaos erupted around us. The Fire primordial unleashed another sun-like projectile, but this time at the Air being, which responded with a wall of concentrated storm winds that would have made a hurricane look gentle.

The floating islands of the Air section drifted in the sky, scattered about at different altitudes, but clearly tethered together by the collection of narrow bridges that ran from one to another, looking like those narrow bloody stupid rope bridges that you got in a kids' playground, the ones designed to make sure that someone fell off and every parent lived in fear.

I was halfway to the first platform when I noticed something odd. Despite the Air primordial's fierce defense against the Fire elemental, it wasn't making any move to stop us from entering its territory. In fact…

Lightning crackled between my fingers and across my armor as I launched myself upward. The Air primordial's form shifted, winds spinning faster as arcs of electricity began to dance through its form in a pattern that mirrored my own.

"Well, that's interesting." I grinned, landing on the platform beside Cerin. The Air primordial was still engaged with its fiery counterpart, but I could feel its attention partly on me, like recognition passing between distant kin.

"My lord," Ciara called down, her formation of fairies maintaining a defensive screen around us, "the essence nodes are starting to pulse in sequence. We should—"

"Fuck the puzzle," I interrupted, a plan forming as I watched the elementals clash. Steam exploded outward where fire met wind; the other two primordials started to move in, drawn by the conflict. "I've got a better idea."

"What?" Ciara demanded, dodging a spray of superheated steam. "But we need the essences to—"

"To open the way forward, yeah." I grinned, lightning dancing across my armor as the Air primordial's power resonated with my own. "And what better way to get elemental essence than straight from the source?"

Rathaharn's laugh was downright predatory as she caught my meaning. "You mean to help it fight?"

"Better than that." I watched as the Earth primordial launched its first attack: a barrage of stone spears that the Air being deflected with contemptuous ease. "I mean to help it win, then take them all down."

"You're insane," Ciara declared, but I could hear the smile in her voice. "Though I suppose that's why we like you."

The Water primordial chose that moment to join the fray, sending a tidal wave of freezing water toward the Fire being from behind. *Perfect.*

"Rathaharn, get ready to move on my signal. Ciara, get your people in position to run interference. Time to show these elementals why they shouldn't play with lightning."

I gathered my power, building it as the Air primordial's attention focused more fully on me. Oh yeah, this was just what I needed!

I unleashed my lightning—not at the primordials directly, but at the freezing wave that was about to crash into the Fire creature's back. The water lit up like a Christmas tree. Electricity arced through it in a devastating chain reaction that tore in both directions— back along the conduit connecting the wave to the Water elemental and into the back of the Fire one—as it caught both elementals.

The Fire primordial screamed as its form destabilized, while the Water being writhed, its liquid form conducting the energy perfectly. The Air primordial paused in its attack, and I felt a surge of…was that amusement?

Its form condensed, lightning crackling through the wind in patterns that matched my own. The massive being twisted to fully face me, and I felt power building in the air around us.

"Incoming!" Rathaharn shouted as the Earth primordial launched another barrage, this time aimed at the platform we stood on.

The Air primordial moved faster than thought. A wall of compressed air deflected the stone spears while simultaneously launching a counterattack that sent the Earth being staggering. Lightning and wind combined into a devastating force that shattered chunks of its rocky form.

"Right then," I called out, already moving to the next platform. The rope bridge swayed dangerously beneath my feet, but I kept my balance. "Ciara, take your group high—keep the Water one busy! Rathaharn, you're with me. Let's go introduce Fire to some real heat!"

The Air primordial surged up and outward. Its form lost the humanoid shape and instead became a massive whirling storm cloud, lit from within by furious, dancing lightning. It expanded to fill the space between platforms. Lightning crackled between us; its power reached out, probing, and instead of an attack, I felt…invitation?

Wait, was this fucker actually offering to combine with me? To let me…

Oh, this was going to be *fun.*

I reached out with my own power, accepting the Air primordial's offer. Lightning surged between us, and suddenly I could *feel* the air currents, the way they moved and twisted through the space. The being's satisfaction was palpable as our powers merged.

The Fire primordial recovered first, launching a barrage of plasma balls at both of us. I dove left across another rope bridge while the Air being simply…wasn't there anymore, dissolving into the wind only to reform behind its attacker, no longer in its own zone, but between the Fire creation and its place of power.

"Now that's just showing off," I muttered then grunted.

The Water creature switched from attacking the Fire, and instead raced forward, its humanoid body converting into a frothing, churning tidal wave—one that dragged not only more and more water from its own territory, but a collection of random shite as well.

The flotsam and jetsam that was carried by it crashed along. Tree branches, smaller rocks, and general debris bounced higher and higher, flipping this way and that, and I just knew it was intended as a gift for us, one it was looking forward to delivering to our faces.

I grinned, though, because I too had a little treat for it. As the Water elemental crossed the metal bridge that served to connect each of the elemental's territories, I channeled lightning up from my core and sent it screaming through the air and into the bridge's supports. The metal cables conducted beautifully, creating a web of electricity that caught the Water primordial as it tried to surge toward us.

Steam exploded upward as the electricity boiled its form. Ciara's fairies dove through the cloud, their small size letting them dart in close to pepper the elemental with spells that seemed to freeze sections of its liquid body.

"Your left!" Rathaharn shouted. Her flail smashed aside a chunk of stone that the Earth primordial had launched at my head. She kept pace despite the precarious footing, moving as if the bridges were solid ground.

The Air primordial struck then, its attack coordinating perfectly with mine. While it drove the Fire creature back with a concentrated blast of storm winds, I unleashed everything I had into the Water primordial. Lightning exploded outward; chain reactions turned the entire quadrant into a light show that would have made Zeus jealous.

The Water being's screech of pain cut off abruptly as its form literally exploded. Droplets of charged water rained down across the platforms. Where they landed, they crystallized into pure elemental essence.

"One down!" I called out, already moving to the next target. "Anyone else want to see what happens when—FUCK!"

The Earth primordial had apparently decided that if it couldn't hit us directly, it would destroy our footing instead. The platform I'd just left jerked, then crumbled as a massive stone spear punched through it from below.

"You just gonna take that?" I asked my new elemental friend, and the Air primordial responded instantly. Winds caught Rathaharn and me, lifting us to the next platform along as an unseen spike slammed into the bottom of the island I'd just reached. Then it launched a counterattack that caught the Earth being in what looked like a localized tornado.

"The Fire one's retreating!" Ciara shouted from somewhere above. "It's trying to reach its own territory!"

"Oh no, you don't." I grinned, lightning crackling between my fingers. "Ready for something stupid?"

The Air primordial's form rippled with what felt like anticipation.

"Let's show them what a real storm looks like."

I reached deep into my core, drawing on every scrap of power I had, as the Air primordial did the same. Our energies twisted together, and suddenly I wasn't just channeling lightning—I *was* the storm.

For a long second, I reveled in it. This was a fragment of the power I was learning to wield as a Storm Titan; once I'd fully ascended, this…this power that

I was using to fucking smash elementals into the middle of next Tuesday…would be minor in comparison to my own.

The Fire primordial had almost reached its sanctuary when we struck. The combined force of our attack hit it like an angry god's hammer. Lightning and wind formed a cyclone of such intensity that the very air began to ionize.

But we weren't done. As the Fire being staggered, its form flickering and destabilizing, the Earth primordial launched another attack, this time a wave of stone that rose up like a tsunami.

"Perfect." I grinned, feeling the Air primordial's agreement. We let the wave come, drawing power from the very conflict between elements. Where earth met air, where fire struggled against wind, we fed on the chaos.

The Fire creature staggered, its flames whipped to new heights, but the fuel it needed was torn free…

I dug deeper, committing half of my mana to the Air elemental, and feeling the twist as it took the offered power. It created a siphon, and latched onto the now lifeless waters of the Water section, pulling hard.

It was like a firehose had been attached, dragging Fire's antithesis up and around…then slamming it into the failing creature.

"My lord!" Ciara's voice seemed distant through the rush of power. "The nexus! It's responding to the elemental conflict!"

She was right. The central point where all four territories met began to pulse with energy, the swirling maelstrom of elements growing stronger with each clash.

"Rathaharn!" I called out. "Think you can piss off Rocky a bit more?"

Her answering laugh was nearly lost in the howling wind. She charged forward, leaping from the lower island she'd been on, hitting the bridge and rolling, before bounding to her feet.

She raced forward as I continued to batter the burning fucknut with wind and wave, and her flail swept out to smash chunks from the Earth primordial's form.

It roared in fury, having been ignoring her in favor of my growing pact with the Air primordial and gloating over the fall of its hated rival, Fire. Now its attention slammed back on its own territory, locking in on the smaller figure and glaring down, before a series of stone spikes lanced up from underneath the warrior.

Rathaharn dove sideways, rolling to her feet, then dodged back, taking a lance that was thrown at her on the shield. Its stone fragmented into dozens of fléchette-like fragments…

Before seeing that it was a diversion. As soon as she'd braced to take the hit, a fresh set of spikes lanced upward, most deflected by her armor. But the clangs and dents that appeared made it clear that they'd not be denied their pound of flesh for long.

The pained roar that rang out from the Scepiniir as one hit the inside of her ankle made it clear that the bone was bruised, if not broken. She staggered backward, and the elemental turned, focused entirely on her.

The Fire being made one last desperate counterattack, and this time we didn't dodge. Instead, we caught its plasma ball in a cocoon of wind, compressed it, and hurled it around, slamming it into the back of Earth's head.

Earth screamed in fury, spinning, leaving Rathaharn and lifting its hands into the air. The elemental was stocky: thick legs, a short torso and long arms, heavy shoulders and an almost triangular head, a pugnaciously jutting jaw. But as it roared, it suddenly lost weight; stone from its body was suddenly covered in cracks, then shattered and fell loose, floating free into a swirling mass of shards, one that quickly reformed into a trio of giant lances.

It hurled them all at the dying Fire, and the elemental's scream as its attack tore through it was like a volcano dying.

"Two down!" I shouted, watching as Fire crystallized into pure essence. "Fuckin' come *on*!"

The Earth primordial's answer was to tear free its entire section of territory, raising a floating island of stone that rivaled our platforms in size.

"Show-off," I muttered, then reached deeper into the storm. "Let's see how well that rock flies."

The Earth primordial's floating island blocked out what passed for sky in this floor, casting everything below in shadow. Massive chunks of stone and crystal orbited the main mass like angry planets around a furious sun.

"You know," I called out to the Air primordial as we hovered before the impressive display, "I'm starting to think Rocky up there is compensating for something."

The elemental didn't get the joke, but was apparently amused by the sheer fucking arrogance of me saying it, while watching such a creature get ever more clearly pissed at my temerity.

A pulse of pleasure rippled through our connection as wind patterns shifted. Through our merged awareness, I could feel the air currents mapping every surface and crevice of the floating mountain. More importantly, I could feel the strain as the Earth creature fought against its own nature to keep the mass airborne.

"Ciara!" I shouted, already gathering power. "Get your people clear and ready to attack from a distance or heal. This is gonna get messy!"

The fairy barked orders, her formation scattering into little glittering trios. Below, Rathaharn had taken shelter on one of the few remaining stable platforms. Her injured ankle prevented her from doing much more than providing covering fire with a crossbow, though two fairies orbited her, and a third prodded at her lower leg.

The Earth primordial struck first, hurling one of its orbiting boulders at us with devastating force. I twisted aside, letting it pass harmlessly by as the Air being caught it in a cyclone, spinning it faster and faster before launching it back.

The projectile shattered against the main island, but did little, merely sending a fractal pattern of cracks radiating outward. That was fine, though, considering that was just cover for our attack.

Lightning roared out, slamming into the cracked rocks and burrowing deeper. Fragments and chips flew, and I cursed as the blast died away. It was working, but it'd not done a huge amount of damage.

Rocky lances rose and hurtled free, a few aimed at the fairies. But given that they simply slipped aside in the air, barely even bothering to move, they were quickly dismissed as a viable target.

Those aimed at me were easily dodged at first, but as soon as it gave up on the fairies, it apparently decided to focus on me. More and more flew, and it got harder and harder to dodge them as the elemental learned my patterns.

I checked my mana. I was down to almost the dregs of it now. The combination of flight, casting spells, and supercharging that last attack of the elemental had taken more than I thought. I slapped my sword back into my shoulder sheath, before pulling out a pair of mana crystals that I'd taken from the mine earlier.

One was larger than the other, about the size of my palm, and jagged on one side—that refilled me to half. The other, about the size of my thumb, was tugged free of my grasp before I could drain it.

I stared after it as it rocketed toward the Air elemental. I shrugged, accepting that I should have offered it, anyway. Good manners cost nothing, even in a duel with elemental spirits in a dungeon.

As the second crystal shattered, the stored mana poured free to invigorate the storm.

Earth changed tactics then. The spears broke up to form a hundred smaller spikes…then fired them all at Rathaharn.

She dove to the side, screaming as her apparently broken ankle made its disapproval known. Although she managed to dodge most of the barrage, or catch them on her shield, not everyone was so lucky.

The fairy that had been examining her was hit from behind and shredded. One of the fliers lost a wing and cried out as she fell as well, while the third unleashed possibly the smallest and cutest magic missile in the world.

It even made a "pop" when it impacted Earth instead of a bang.

"What the hell—is that a *kid*?!" I shouted into the winds as I noticed the smaller size and weaker spell.

"Petal is strong with the arcane force!" Ciara shouted, barely being heard over the wind, as the rocky elemental lifted more smaller rocks into the air, having found it was more effective than the giant spikes.

"Fucking get her out of there!" I roared, drinking deep from my lightning mana. Lightning arced joyously from my hands, conducted through the humid air still heavy with Water essence from our previous fight. The punishing power drilled in deeper and found every metal vein, every crystal deposit in the floating mass, setting up resonant frequencies that made the whole island shudder.

"Having trouble staying up?" I taunted as cracks started to appear in the island's surface. "Here, let me help with that!"

The Air primordial caught my intention and responded with enthusiasm. We split apart, circling the struggling Earth being from opposite sides. Where I went high, trailing lightning like a comet's tail, my elemental partner went low, gathering speed.

The Earth primordial roared, trying to track both threats at once. It launched a barrage of stone darts and bullets in all directions but beyond the threat to our people—several of which were hurt, but the healers were already moving—that only served our purpose better. Each projectile disrupted the air, creating new currents, new paths for our building storm as our people hid.

"NOW!" I bellowed, diving straight for the island's peak as the Air being surged up from below. We hit simultaneously. The storm lightning combined with its winds to create a devastating cyclone that tore into the floating mountain's heart.

The effect was catastrophic. Already strained from defying gravity, already weakened by our previous attacks, the island began to break apart. But the Earth primordial wasn't done yet. As its platform disintegrated, it gathered the fragments around itself like armor, condensing into a more concentrated form.

"Oh, *now* you want to play?" I grinned, launching myself back into the air and holding there as the Earth primordial rose from the ground again, standing tall.

It crashed its rocky fists together, before slamming them against its chest and roaring a challenge to the air. The rock it stood atop fractured then resealed, crumbling. Its attention was split between holding the giant rock together, and holding its physical form ready.

Fine by me, though…just meant that the stupid bastard was less ready for the fight in his arrogance.

Of course, minor point, a year ago, my life consisted of asking entitled idiots why they thought "p@55w0rd" was a great password, and explaining calmly that no, as their company's IT support, I wasn't going to be debugging and rebuilding their ten-year-old home computer, just because they wanted to be able to check their emails on it.

The difference between that individual and the man I was now, calling a literal primordial personification of living rock arrogant, when I was about to try to punch it to death, wasn't lost on me.

I landed on the rapidly fragmenting platform. It shifted and buckled beneath my feet. The Earth primordial loomed over me, its form now compressed into something that looked like a cross between a mountain troll and a crystal golem. Lightning crackled between my fingers as I sized up my opponent.

"You know," I called out, circling slowly. "Most people would take the hint after watching their friends get turned into fancy paperweights."

The being's only response was to slam its fists into the ground. The platform shuddered as spikes of stone erupted in a wave headed straight for me. I leapt over the first wave, letting the Air primordial's winds boost me higher than strictly necessary.

"Missed me!" I taunted, then winced and twisted in midair as the spikes suddenly reversed direction, shooting upward. "Oh, that's clever…"

Lightning poured from my hands, shattering the stone projectiles, but that was just cover for the primordial's real attack. Its massive fist caught me in the side. The feeling of bones cracking under the impact made me grunt as I was sent flying. I managed to right myself before I fell over the side, grinning despite the pain.

"Finally!" I twisted and felt the dented-in side of the metal, before nodding in grudging respect. "Someone who knows how to throw a proper punch!"

The Earth primordial charged. Each step left craters in the remaining platform. I met its charge head-on, lightning wreathing my form as I ducked under another massive swing. My own punch, enhanced by Storm-Strike, hit it square in the gut.

Cracks spread from the impact point, but the being simply roared and reformed; the damaged section filled in with fresh crystal that served to solidify the stone. It brought both hands down hard, slamming them into the ground with a boom that shattered the already fragmenting island more. I was already moving, though, having used my Air affinity and flight capability to throw myself sideways, sliding between its legs and coming up behind it.

"My turn," I growled, unleashing another blast of lightning directly into its back. The Air primordial joined in, its winds tearing at the being's form, trying to strip away the outer layer of its rocky armor.

The Earth primordial spun with surprising speed. One arm elongated into a blade of crystalline stone. I barely managed to dodge, feeling it slice through the air where my head had been.

"Whoa, Mr. Feisty!" I laughed, before coughing and tasting blood. The massive form was still considerably slower than I was, as I twisted and let it scrape past again, this time digging into the ground and tearing a great line of the earth free. "Now, now, how about you just give in and…die easily, eh?" I coughed again as I suggested, firing off a pair of Incinerates at its head, focusing on the internals, followed by five more when that had bugger all effect.

This time, though, they were all aimed at the joint of the shoulder. As it started to glow, the maximum heat for the rock was surpassed as one after another of the Incinerate spells built on the last.

I dodged back, then limbo-ed backward as the arm slashed at me a final time. And, in my defense, had the fucking shoulder not chosen that exact time to fail, the arm coming crashing down atop me when in exactly the least load-bearing position possible…well, I'd have looked incredibly cool.

As it was, though, the shoulder came loose, the heated end hitting me in the chest. And as molten rock tends to do on encountering a cooler item, it stuck.

The arm was around two tons in weight, and although I could bench-press twice that now, again, the limbo-bench-press was yet to be made an Olympic sport for a very good reason.

I crashed to the ground. The arm half rolled off me, before the partially molten shoulder solidified enough to stick hard. That was when the big bastard stepped forward, a grin on its face, as it raised one foot and brought it down hard atop the arm I'd just grabbed and was lifting off me.

Or trying to, anyway.

"Well, shit," I grunted, straining against the weight as the Earth primordial leaned more of its considerable mass onto its raised foot. The arm was cooling rapidly now, fusing to my armor. "This is…oh, fuuuck off!" I shoved hard, lifting the elemental slightly, gritting my teeth as it shifted to bring more of its weight to bear as my arms shook violently.

Above me, stone fragments lifted, gathered and began spinning, forming into wickedly sharp spears that hung in the air like the world's most lethal game of pick-up sticks. The being's previously expressionless face shifted; the stone melted and ran together. As the crystal flowed, the new crystalline face twisted into what might have been a smile.

There was a momentary break as it looked up. A trio of missiles slammed into its face, bringing a snarl, followed by more.

I gritted my teeth, pushing as hard as I could, but it was no good. Not only was the arm no longer lifting, the building pain told me any second there was going to be a snap, and it wasn't going to be the rock.

"Oh, come on," I growled, channeling lightning through my body in an attempt to heat the rock enough to break free. "Not…gonna die…to a fuckin'…rock!"

There were more flashes, and a roar from the goddamn walking rock as the fairies streaked past. The impromptu bombing run distracted it even more as I roared, putting everything I had into the lift…

The spears plunged downward, and I had just enough time to think that Kelly was going to be seriously pissed about this…when the Air primordial struck. Winds howled through the chamber, catching the projectiles, deflecting them just enough to make them slam into the rocky ground all around my head. They shattered and peppered me with sharpened fragments of flint and who knew what else.

Air slammed into the massive figure then, wrapping around it and forming a spiraling tornado focused on a single point. I snarled, heaving for all I was worth as I felt a minute lessening on the weight above me.

But Earth had apparently learned from watching its fellows fall. As the winds intensified, the being's form began to change, becoming denser, more compact. The foot pressing down on me grew heavier as more and more mass was pulled in. The rock around me failed even more, and was no longer being repaired as it flashed to the foot over me instead.

"Trying…to…crush me?" I managed through gritted teeth. "That's…fucking…RUDE!"

I triggered Storm-Strike, not through my limbs this time but through my entire body at once. Lightning exploded outward, superheating the air around me. The rapidly expanding gasses created a shock wave that sent chunks of the Earth primordial's foot flying.

It staggered back, off-balance for the first time, snatched at by the tornado as well, and I seized my chance. With a roar of effort, I ripped myself free of the now-brittle rock—leaving chunks of my armor's outer layer still fused to it—and launched myself out, barely managing to clear the foot before it crashed down, sinking into the earth.

"Right…then…" I panted, straightening up despite the protests from my ribs. "How about two outta three? No?"

The Earth primordial roared its hatred. I grinned up at it. Despite the helmet hiding my face, I knew it knew.

"Well, fuck you very much then!" I growled, reaching deep.

The Air primordial's approval hummed through our connection as I gathered my remaining power.

Time to show this overgrown paperweight what happens when you piss off a Storm Titan in training. Again, I sacrificed health for mana.

Lightning crackled across my armor as I rose into the air. The Air primordial's power merged with mine once again. The Earth being roared, its remaining arm reforming into a massive hammer as it tried to anchor itself more firmly to what remained of the platform, even as the second arm began to regrow.

"You know what your problem is?" I called down to it, gathering power. "You think bigger means better." Thunder rolled through my words as storm clouds formed around us. "But sometimes…"

I dove, quicker than it could track, coming in low and fast. Its hammer swung, but I was already past it, sliding through its guard. "Sometimes you need to think *small.*"

Lightning erupted from my hands—not in a massive blast this time, but in a dozen precise, surgical strikes. Each bolt found a crack, a flaw in the being's crystalline structure, and *burrowed.* The Air primordial's winds followed, pressing into those same weaknesses, widening them fraction by fraction.

The Earth primordial's roar became one of pain as lightning coursed through its internal structure. It tried to reform, to compress further, but that only drove our attack deeper. Cracks spread across its surface like a spiderweb, glowing with contained power.

"NOW!" I bellowed, surging upward as the Air being responded. Our combined power formed a spiraling vortex of wind and lightning that caught the struggling Earth primordial and lifted it off its feet.

"Let's see how *you* like flying!"

Higher and higher we carried it. Its form started to break apart as we stripped away layer after layer. I spun around it in the spiraling winds, firing again and again, slamming short bolts—not channeled at all, just fast and fuckin' furious—in from every angle. Its attempts to reform grew weaker as we separated it from its element, from the ground that gave it power.

Then, at the apex of our ascent, we simply…let go.

The Earth primordial tumbled free. Its massive form twisted as it frantically tried to reform. I watched it plummet, then turned to the Air being with a grin.

"Care to do the honors?"

The elemental's response was immediate and devastating. A blast of concentrated wind caught the falling fragments, compressing them into a tight ball, while picking up speed, pushing harder and harder toward the ground.

Just as it was about to hit, I unleashed every last scrap of lightning I had left. The resulting explosion lit up the entire chamber.

When the dust settled, all that remained was a pile of crystallized elemental essence scattered across what was left of the platform. I landed heavily, my legs shaking from exhaustion, and gave a tired thumbs-up to Ciara and her fairies.

"And that," I panted, "is why you don't fuck with the weather." Then I collapsed onto a knee, before sagging backward and falling, landing stretched out on my back, as the Air primordial reveled in its now uncontested personal domain.

I lay there recovering, watching the clouds dance overhead as my body screamed at me about all the abuse I'd just put it through. The Air Primordial's satisfaction rippled through our connection as it played with its newfound dominance of the realm.

"Anyone dead?" I called out wearily.

"Most are just tired," Ciara responded sadly, floating down to land on my chest plate. "But yes, we lost three of the younger ones, but the rest are recovering. Petal's wing will need time to heal as well. The healers are out of mana."

"Speaking of healing…" Rathaharn's voice drifted over, tight with pain. "A little assistance would not go amiss."

"Damn. Yeah, get over here." I winced at the way she was limping, clearly having massive issues with her mobility. "Is that broken still?" I frowned, before the furry bastard Cerin appeared, seemingly stepping out of the air and pausing by her side, letting Rathaharn brace herself on the voidcat. "And where the hell did you get to, you twat!" I snapped at the big cat, getting a flat look in reply.

"Yeah, yeah, all right," I grunted, admitting—to myself at least—that as the cat's main weapons were claws, teeth, and the tentacles, there wasn't much that he could have added to a fight against the Primordials of Water, Air, Fire, or Earth, besides being drowned, flung away, burned, or losing claws and being squashed.

"Glad you survived," I admitted. "Can you wait a minute?" I asked Rathaharn. "I've got bugger all mana to heal you with at the minute, but I'll sort it as soon as we all have some." I groaned, closing my eyes and focusing inward. Lightning mana began trickling back into me, but as soon as the mana arrived, it was automatically diverted to healing the worst of my injuries.

It really pissed me off that I'd gained the ability to create a healing area of effect recently that boosted mana recovery as well, and yet I needed bloody mana to use it, so by the time I'd recovered enough mana to cast it… nobody was going to need it any more. Instead it was going to be down to…

"Damn, here!" I dipped a hand into my bag of holding and plucked free two of the healing potions.

I tossed one to Rathaharn, who caught it, while Ciara took the other and worked the cork free. It looked more like it was going to be a mud—or healing potion—wrestling session, considering the size of the flask to the size of the fairies.

The smaller ones could literally bathe in it.

"I will need…more than a potion," Rathaharn admitted, clearly not liking the show of weakness as she saw it.

When I glanced at the greave where it ended over her ankle, I winced.

It was dented in; blood, bright red and glistening, ran in rivulets out from underneath the metal. And the way she moved made it apparent that the very best we could hope for was that the armor came away cleanly, because there was no way that the potion could do anything while any breaks were kept mangled by the dented metal.

I forced myself up, and she limped over, twisting around and showing me the back of the greave, where the clasps and latches lay.

At first, it was a nightmare. The metal was dented to the point that the clasps were buckling, making it almost impossible to twist them free, until a friendly twist of air slid in, then hardened, forming a semi-visible bar of force.

I reached out, feeling it, feeling the weirdness of it, before sliding it forward.

With the primordial's help to make small adjustments, the bar changed, allowing me to get it between two bits, levering them apart, as I ignored the hisses of pain from the big Scepiniir.

Eventually, the clasp released with a solid *boing* of metal. It opened, allowing me to slip two fingers in and flick the others, tugging the metal free.

As soon as it was off, Rathaharn let loose a groan of relief, followed by a gasp of pain. She lowered herself to sit, biting down on the cork and spitting it out, then chugged half of the potion and poured the other half on her lower leg.

The matted fur and bloody flesh was washed clear by the potion; the red blood dripped free as the liquid absorbed itself into the wound at an incredible rate.

I silently produced another potion, and she took it, nodding her thanks and chugging all of this one.

The change, when it came, some six seconds later, was incredible.

The bones suddenly ground their way back into alignment as she snarled and grunted. The popping and cracking sounds made it clear, when combined with the expression on her face, that the potion had no pain-dampening qualities.

All in all it was damn lucky that the situation hadn't been worse, considering the shit that Griffiths was going through.

The Air primordial's presence brushed against my consciousness, offering…something. I opened my eyes again, glancing up. A portion of its essence coalesced into crystalline form, freely given rather than torn away in combat, and floated down to me.

"Well, that's handy," I muttered, pushing myself to my feet and bowing to the massive primordial spirit. "Thank you."

Around us, the battlefield was littered with elemental essence—some still glowing with residual power. The Water primordial's essence had formed into perfect spheres of frozen energy, while the Fire's had crystallized into angular shards that still radiated heat. The Earth essence was perhaps the most impressive, forming into geometrically perfect crystals that seemed to contain entire mountain ranges in miniature.

"We need about a third of each type," Ciara explained, directing her remaining fairies to begin gathering the essence. "The rest is yours to claim."

I nodded, watching as the Air primordial's freely given essence drifted toward what remained of the central nexus. "And that opens the way forward?"

"Once we've gathered enough, yes." She paused, then added with a small smile, "Though perhaps we should rest first? You look like you could use it, and for all we know, the next section opens straight into a fight."

"I was hoping for a safe zone," I admitted, before sighing and laying back, closing my eyes and starting to meditate. A thought occurred to me.

"Did…we get anything besides essence from them?" I asked.

Ciara shook her head. "The essence is rare enough. To get this much? The fight was clearly supposed to be a difficult one, though had the puzzle survived, I think there was a way to get the essence without fighting."

"Where's the fun in that?" I asked myself, returning to my meditation.

Now I just had to hope the next level wouldn't be quite so…ele-*mental.*

It should have taken a day or more to top off my mana reserves again, had I not been surrounded by fairies. But given that I was, and that half of the surviving nine fairies had a support class, it was a lot quicker than that.

Between meditation increasing my recovery by a serious percentage, and two fairies both aiding as well with their Hearthfire and Blessings of the Benevolent Wind spells, I was done in two hours. Not topped off—that would have been ridiculous—but I had enough that I felt I could take whatever was left, considering I had a group at my back, and a single floor left to go.

I stood with the others, all of us gathering up and moving to the artifact in the center of the floor: a large fountain, one with four sides that each featured a stretching figure, imploringly reaching for the elemental focus at the four corners of the floor.

In the middle of the tinkling water rose a single spire, standing three meters or so in the air, with an empty bowl atop it. I squinted, then nodded. It wasn't empty; if I looked just right, I could make out a single spike that rose from it, ready.

That was the Air essence, I knew, feeling it as much as seeing it. I reached out, pulling the other essence crystals free of the bag and feeling the gentle tugging from them as I moved closer to the artifact.

I let go. The crystals floated, seeming almost to fall inward, twisting around to the figure that represented them, landing on the outstretched hand. As soon as they landed, the essence fragmented, shifting from a crystalline structure to a gaseous liquid, flowing inward.

The Earth one was before me now. The brown and beige mess flowed along the arm, up and across the chest, rising up the neck, before pouring in through the mouth, eyes, and ears of the statue.

"Fuck me, that's not happy-making," I muttered. The statue seemed to pulse, before seemingly awakening, then turning, completely ignoring us.

It turned its back on us all, crossing its arms over its chest and going to one knee, before pressing its hands to the rim of the fountain.

As soon as it touched the rim, a pulse of light and color washed out, rippling through the stone, then flooded inward.

The spire rose higher as each of the elements were added. Another spike grew out of the bowl atop it until it was clear that they weren't four separate spikes, but four sides of the same one.

As the fourth elemental essence was added, the spire pulsed once, then collapsed. The mixed essences hit the bowl below, which promptly lost cohesion, along with the rest of the fountain.

It fell, as though the entire mass had been turned to water, as gravity asserted its claim in the mixture. It splashed down hard, before being sucked away into the floor with a newly revealed grate left behind.

It was circular, sitting in the center of what had been the fountain. As the grate split into four equal pieces, they slid apart. The sections vanished into individual recesses, leaving stone steps dimly visible that led down into darkness.

"Well, that was goddamn freaky. Impressive, though," I muttered, before sighing. "Everyone ready?"

I got some nods, then led the way down into a dark spiral staircase.

CHAPTER TWENTY-SEVEN

It was dark in there, as I walked onward and onward. The fairies glimmered softly, bringing some light to the darkness, but the general shadows, the movement, and the constant twist as we apparently climbed ever downward in a tight spiral was enough that by the time we all reached the bottom, it was a hell of a relief.

Everyone was dizzy, and before I could say it, Ciara insisted we wait and recover from it, before opening the door in front of us.

I grumbled at the delay, but agreed. A sliver of light was visible, peeking from around the door.

A few minutes later, our stomachs and inner ears had settled, and mana topped off a little further by what had to have been ten bloody minutes of climbing down. I laid my hand against the door.

The door swung open silently, revealing…magnificence.

"Holy shit," I breathed, stepping through into what had to be the largest indoor space I'd ever seen. The circular arena sprawled out before us, easily large enough to host any pre-fall megastar's huge concert with room to spare.

Above us, the domed ceiling soared upward, decorated with intricate frescos depicting epic battles.

All around us was a smooth sandy floor, and fifty meters ahead of us, on all sides, rose the walls that led to the spectator stands.

Whatever weird spatial magic this place used, it allowed me to see the thousands of observers who I knew were actually seated in our own arena, standing and gaping alike, as they stared down at us from what seemed to be the stone stands that surrounded us.

"The Colosseum of the Champion," Rathaharn whispered reverently as we strode out. "Never thought I'd get to see it from this angle."

"You know this place?" I scanned the grand arena. Elevated platforms dotted the battlefield like islands, while in the center rose the column that we'd just climbed down to this floor inside.

Various stone barriers and pillars were scattered throughout, providing potential cover—or ammunition, depending on one's perspective.

"Every dungeon has the potential for one," she explained. "Or tries to. Most never achieve this level of…completion."

Movement caught my eye, figures positioned around the arena's perimeter. The guards stood motionless, their armor gleaming in the strange light that seemed to come from everywhere and nowhere at once. But it was the figure on the raised northern platform that drew my attention.

The Scepiniir champion was…well, impressive didn't quite cover it. Where Rathaharn was tall and powerful, this being was something else entirely. Two meters plus tall, it just exuded power and danger. My stomach twisted as I locked eyes on it; the helmet nodded in acknowledgment of my gaze, once.

Its armor seemed to be made of living metal, shifting and flowing with each slight movement. Multiple weapons hung from their belt and back, each radiating power.

"Well," I muttered, "at least we know where we're supposed to go."

"My lord." Rathaharn's voice was tight with…was that anticipation? "That is Warmaster Kh'aan. He was legendary among our people, before…"

"Before what?"

"Before he volunteered for the dungeons." She flexed her newly healed leg; the lower section of her greave armor was missing as we'd been unable to fix the dent well enough that she could put it back on. "They say he grew tired of easy victories."

"Great." I sighed, checking my remaining mana and eyeing the conspicuous lack of anything resembling a safe zone around us, besides the column that led back up to the floor above. "Anyone else think we should take a minute to prepare before—"

A horn blast cut through the air, deep and resonant. The champion raised one massive hand in greeting—or challenge—as circles of power began to gleam across the arena floor, and behind us, the stairwell sealed itself.

"Oh, come on," I groaned. "We just damn well arrived. Surely five minutes to prepare isn't—"

Then the first wave of summoning circles flared to life. I cursed. The damn guards weren't all we were going to have to face in here.

The summoning circles pulsed with familiar energy and light, and suddenly we had company. A dozen goblin magelings materialized, blinking in confusion, before snarling, nodding, and in one case, lifting a leg and letting rip. Clearly these fuckers were only common grade.

Their hands already began to glow with power as they summoned spells. Behind them, the unmistakable forms of several ghasts—and not the "lesser" breed—shimmered into existence, their spectral forms more solid and menacing than before. Then they bounded forward, blurring to vanish from sight.

"Right," I growled, lightning crackling between my fingers. "Because why make anything simple?"

"Formation!" Ciara barked. Her remaining fairies spread out in a surprisingly professional defensive screen. "They're trying to pin us against the column!"

She was right. The summoned creatures were spreading out in a rough semicircle, pushing us back toward the massive central pillar. Above us, the guards had drawn their weapons but hadn't moved yet, content to watch the show.

The Scepiniir champion—Kh'aan—remained on his platform, arms crossed, radiating an aura of amused anticipation.

"Suggestions?" I kept my voice low as we backed up slowly. "Because I'm counting at least twenty incoming, and that's just the first wave."

"The platforms." Rathaharn nodded toward the nearest elevated area. "Better position, though they'll likely try to collapse them."

I glanced at the stone platform surrounded by sand. A slope led up to the top, which in turn stood about five meters high, offering a decent vantage point…but also making us very obvious targets. Still, better than being surrounded at ground level.

"Ciara, can your people…" I started to ask, but she was already moving, her formation breaking into smaller groups.

They streaked outward, headed toward the platform, but splitting into two groups to circle around it, spells charging as they went.

"We'll keep them busy," she called back. "Just don't take too long getting up there!"

I nodded, as we ran after them. Cerin was already changing course to intercept a blur he'd apparently noticed, and Rathaharn and I slogged through the sand.

I could have left her, flown ahead, but if I did, she'd be hit from all sides by the ghasts and slaughtered, I had no doubt.

The ghasts had all vanished, their forms blurring as they activated their stealth abilities. The goblin magelings weaved their spells, the air crackling with poorly controlled elemental energy.

"Watch the shadows!" I shouted as we ran, already tracking the slight distortions in the air that betrayed some of the now-vanished ghasts' positions. "They're trying to—"

A blur of movement was my only warning as one of the ghasts materialized directly in front of me, bone spurs already slashing for my throat. I triggered Storm-Strike through my gauntlet as I blocked, and electricity arced through the creature's body. It screamed, its stealth failing; it staggered back, before its skull was smashed inward as I punched it.

Clearly, in my stress, and getting more used to my new strength, I'd used a little more than was needed, because my armored gauntlet literally smashed straight through the creature's skull, killing it instantly.

Rathaharn was already drawing ahead, her bare leg not slowing her as she charged toward the platform. A volley of mismatched spells from the goblin magelings—everything from fireballs to ice shards—forced her to dodge and weave, though.

"Covering fire would be good, yes?" she yelled over her shoulder, clearly annoyed at its lack, before ducking under what looked like a particularly unstable lightning bolt.

"Bit busy!" I replied, spinning to avoid another ghast's attack while simultaneously blasting a goblin that had gotten too cocky—literally—flashing its cock at me. The lightning bolt slammed into its member. The shout of contempt and challenge changed to a screech of pain, before it tumbled from sight. Clearly it was already dead, or wished it was.

A second nearby yelled something, and I changed to it, firing again even as I ripped the sword free of the sheath over my shoulder and slashed sideways, relieving another blur of its head. The goblin went flying; its half-formed spell exploded between its clawed hands as my own punched straight through.

Ciara's fairies were doing their best, but they were seriously outnumbered. They focused on disrupting the goblins' spellcasting or backing me up, darting in to break concentration at crucial moments. One particularly brave fairy dive-bombed a ghast's face as it leapt from the side to try to take me down, which bought me precious seconds to dispatch another and free my sword as two more jumped at me.

The fight had blurred into a mixture of in-close teeth and claws, slavering jaws, and flashing chameleon scales…and glowing spells, goblins shrieking, and blasts that screamed inward.

I tried dodging—genuinely, I did; I wasn't so stupid as to try to tank the fuckers all outright—but it did precious little good.

The lightning that hit me helped, even as poorly structured as the spell was. I sucked down a breath as healing rippled through my body, even as it was immediately used up on the collection of incoming spells.

Most of them weren't that big a concern. The firebolts were almost laughably weak, and the icebolts...well, they were dangerous, sure, but they were also slower moving than the fire, and being that it was goblins that were firing them off, at least half had missed.

The other half...well.

There were two ghasts very visible now and screaming from friendly fire.

I started flash-firing off Incinerate spells. I didn't want to burn through a load of mana, but at a hundred a pop, they were worth it—especially when they were locked onto a goblin head and released.

Five died in almost as much time as it took to lock my eyes with them; then I was fighting again. Ducking down, I slashed my sword around in a full arc, crouching low; then I rose and repeated in a second spiral that took out four more of the ghasts.

The others were firing as well. Magic missiles slammed into vulnerable spots, and once, a full roaring vertical waterfall of fire leapt up on my left, taking a ghast in mid-flight from below and firing it upward, literally cremated by the time it crashed back down.

Crossbow bolts fired left and right from Rathaharn, and the fight, now breaking down into almost an instinctual level, blurred for me.

I only realized I'd pulled my shield around from my back when the reverberation from my left arm let me know that the ghast I'd just smashed it into wasn't going to be jumping anywhere for a while.

I twisted, whipping the sword around as I turned, lopping its head off as it bounced up from the sand, stunned; then I saw the warmaster before me, still standing atop the wall and looking down. I slapped the blade against my shield, unthinkingly challenging the warmaster as I found nothing immediately around me, and he laughed aloud at my sheer ballsyness.

"Good! You're ready to begin, and we can consider the warm-up over!" he shouted, his voice magically amplified.

I winced.

Ciara, who was flying nearby, spun to give me a "what the fuck were you thinking?" look.

The ground began to ripple and crack as a fresh summoning circle rose, pushing its way through the sand. Then, as soon as it slid to a halt, a slight reverberation shaking sand free, a deep gong rang out again. This time, orcs started to emerge—because of course they did.

These weren't the usual brutes, though; their armor was ornate, their weapons gleaming with enchantments. A quick glance at those weapons and I had to admit I was damn relieved that they had hand axes and shields instead of their "normal" dungeon weapons.

That would have added a whole new dimension of terror to the proceedings.

"Elite guards," Rathaharn spat, as I finally reached the platform. "Kill them and it'll only get worse, with Kh'aan's personal troops still to come!"

"Wonderful," I muttered, gathering power as I saw a few last blurs moving stealthily nearby. "Everyone get in or get clear!" I dragged my blade around the edge of the platform, clearing a line in the sand, and nodded to Ciara as she led her fairies up in a fast burst of speed.

Lightning exploded outward from me in a dome, appearing just beyond Rathaharn's reach, a half second after Cerin landed inside the circle and buying us precious seconds as the last of the ghasts were stunned or forced back.

I used the brief moment to check my mana—three and a half thousand plus change, I noted—already scanning for the next threat.

The orcs were moving now—only six of them, but damn.

They were each taller than those I'd seen before. They came in pairs: two had green-enameled armor, two black, and two red. As they ran upward, they made it clear they were the elites that the dungeon could bring, considering not only that they were in such nice armor, but that the weapons glowed with minor enchantments.

How did I know they were minor? Well, I cut my shield, knowing that keeping it active would just drain me of all mana, and we were still fucking alive after the first few seconds.

I caught an axe blow on my shield, flicked my sword out and around, rolling my wrist to bring the blade up in a vertical cut that should have lopped the fucker's hand off.

Instead, it was caught by the vambrace. He grunted, shaking his arm and backing off, and glared at me through the visor of his helm.

The others slogged up the hill behind him. Rathaharn faced his partner, when the orc nodded in seeming respect, then darted forward.

I pulled the blade back and then stabbed out. He caught it on his shield and deflected it to pass harmlessly by his side, then hooked the beard of his axe over the top of my shield and pulled.

I pulled back, thinking I wasn't falling for that, only to find he'd been planning for it. Instead of a sort of tug-of-war, he came with the axe, planting a foot on my right knee and jumped, flipping over me in a forward roll that left me gobsmacked. I turned instinctively to follow him…

And was hit from behind as the one that Rathaharn had been facing switched targets and leapt at me.

It was only their shield that hit me, but unprepared and from behind, I staggered forward, surprised.

The orc before me ducked down and angled his shield up, catching me. Then he rose and pushed off explosively, sending me flying. His roar as he shoved and lifted turned into a scream as Cerin landed on him from the side.

They rolled; Cerin's tentacles stabbed in and out, latching onto breaks in the armor, bearing down with the savage jaws that tipped them, then wrenched free…over and over.

I crashed down on the side of the platform, though, then rolled, unable to stop. As I slid down, I kicked to get myself turned around before launching into the air.

I'd done it on instinct, but fuck me, a flash was all I saw before another axe slammed into my breastplate. A cascade of sparks flew as it took the blow that had been intended for my neck.

A flash of magic tore past me, and howls of pain rang out as the fairies swarmed in, followed by a scream. I arced around, my shield strapped to my left arm, sword in the right, and I saw a fairy batted from the sky by a well-aimed shield.

She tumbled to the ground, rolling in the sand…

"No!" I shouted, already casting a spell. Incinerate flared to life inside the orc's skull, but not in time to stop the foot that came down hard atop the tiny being.

There was a brief shriek and a crunch of tiny bones that was almost lost in the din of the fight, if I'd not been listening for it.

Cries rose, as the others focused in on the suddenly stock-still orc, launching their spells.

"No, he's already dead!" I called out. But it was too late. Any offensive spells the fairies had they used, slamming into the figure over and over as it slowly twisted, falling to the ground with a crash of armor.

The healers, two of their number, landed by the tiny body, but I already knew there was nothing they could do.

Instead, I boosted my flight, throwing myself through the air at the orc's partner. She stood, shield raised and ready.

Bracing my own shield, I unleashed an Incinerate again, this time at the back of the head of one of the two orcs that were now facing Rathaharn—with one dead at her feet—then I hit.

The force was magnified by the speed I was traveling, the weight of my armor, and the weight of my gear. That was enough to shove the orc back a half meter, grunting as our shields filled the air with the resounding crash of metal on metal.

I jumped back, landing on my feet and glaring at the orc, finding not ravening bloodlust as I expected, but a flat, determined glare—a look that said "I'll not fall without a fight" more than "raaaar, me kill," which I was used to from these creatures.

She still leapt at me, though, axe swinging low and shield braced.

I stabbed out, thinking to slide in behind the axe swing. My footwork already adjusted to keep my legs clear of the blow, and aimed my sword at her knee.

She spun her axe expertly, and locked the beard of the head around my blade, locking both weapons in close as she slammed her shield into mine.

This time, though, I was braced and ready.

I took the blow, then put all my strength into a return bash. I hurled her backward, stunned, before firing off an Incinerate into her right hand.

She screamed, writhing, and snarled at me as if I'd cheated. Then she stiffened as I drove my sword in through the underside of her helm as she tried to get up.

A twist of the blade, and she fell dead.

I was breathing heavily as I turned, checking first that Rathaharn was okay—she had the last orc on the ropes, her footwork incredible as she twisted and spun, guiding them around, while Cerin prowled up behind them, ready to pounce—then I checked on the fairies.

More had fallen than I liked. Hell, I'd rather none had fallen, for obvious reasons, and not just that I wasn't a complete total and utter bastard.

We were down to five, including Ciara and the two healers, and that wasn't many to help in the fight.

Glancing back at Rathaharn, I nodded as she dispatched her target. The orc's attention was stolen by a tentacle being simultaneously wrapped around his visor and another his neck, yanking him off-balance at just the wrong time.

Rathaharn used her flail and shield combo, and damn, it was effective.

I'd always considered those things a menace more than a "real" weapon, especially when you were new to that kind of shit. Rathaharn's weapon was a three-tailed "morning star flail," she'd said when we were resting at one point, and it just looked to be more of a danger to the wielder than the target to me.

The handle was perhaps twelve to fifteen inches long. Then there were three chains, each with a spiked ball as the head at the end. She had to spin it up to get it ready. Without the chains already in motion, it was a lot less effective. And to do things like fire her crossbow, she had to drop the thing and swap over, then start spinning it up again as she needed it.

For me? It reminded me of those idiots with nunchucks you used to see on camcorder videos, injuring themselves while trying to look cool.

Seeing her use it, though?

She wrapped it around the axe, then yanked, disarming her opponent as he stumbled. Then, with a simple shake and twist of her wrist, the axe was flung aside; she whirled it again, before smashing all three heads into her opponent's left knee, one after the other.

There was an audible crunch and clang, the knee well and truly fucked, as the orc fell and rolled. Cerin released and leapt backward as Rathaharn spun up a third time. As the orc turned, looking up as they pushed off the ground, a dagger drawn…

He looked full into the face of the incoming three heads as they came down into his helm.

A sickening crunch and clang again, and Rathaharn was bracing a foot on the dead orc's shoulder to lever one of the spiked heads free of the crushed-in metal helm.

The champion's laughter echoed across the arena. "Good!" his voice boomed. "Excellent effort. But let us see what else our challengers can handle!"

Four summoning circles blazed to life, these ones larger and more elaborate than before. From them emerged towering figures in flowing cloaks and ornate armor: more Scepiniir, but these were clearly different from the guards above. Where Kh'aan's armor seemed alive, theirs pulsed with contained power. Each warrior carried weapons that would have made most armies pause.

"This one thinks perhaps we should have prepared better," Rathaharn growled. Her tail lashed as she sized up the new threats. "These are his Dawn Guard, the elite among elite."

I tracked the new arrivals as they spread out, noting how the other creatures gave them a wide berth. "Any particular weaknesses I should know about?"

"They have none that this one knows of." She bared her fangs in what might have been a grin. "But neither are they as strong as they believe."

The ghasts and other challengers were all dead now. But there were still twelve fully armored figures on plinths that ran around the outside of the arena, watching us, and the main man himself in addition to the Dawn Guard, whatever the fuck they were.

"Ciara!" I called out. "Think your people can fall back and keep us topped off on healing?"

"On it!" she shouted back, clearly relieved that she wasn't being sent in to fight against them alone.

One of the Scepiniir warriors raised his weapon—a glaive that crackled with barely contained energy—and charged. The others followed suit, each choosing a different approach angle.

"This one suggests we do not let them surround us," Rathaharn said dryly, dropping into a fighting stance.

"You don't say," I muttered, gathering power. "Got any other helpful tips?"

"Yes." Her tail twitched in anticipation. "Try not to die."

The first of the Dawn Guard reached us. His glaive swept in a crackling arc that forced me to duck and roll. These weren't like the orcs—there was no wasted movements, no rage-fueled openings to exploit.

The second was already flanking, her twin swords humming with contained power as she tested Rathaharn's defense. The Scepiniir warrior moved like liquid mercury, each attack flowing into the next.

"This one suggests you watch the weapon trails!" Rathaharn called out. Her flail spun up to speed as she backed away. "They leave traces in the air that—"

She cut off, diving aside as the third guard's massive hammer crashed down where she'd been standing. The platform shuddered under the impact, and cracks spread through the stone.

"They're trying to collapse our footing," I realized, launching myself to the right to avoid another glaive strike. Lightning crackled between my fingers as I gathered power. "Cerin! Keep them from—"

The fourth Dawn Guard emerged from seemingly nowhere. His glaive's blade nearly took my head off as I desperately twisted desperately. *How the hell had he moved so fast?*

"The weapons enhance their abilities!" Ciara shouted from above. "Each one is different!"

"Now she tells us," I muttered, parrying another strike that sent vibrations up my arm. The glaive wielder backed off, his weapon leaving trails of energy in the air that were starting to form patterns. "Rathaharn! They're setting something up!"

"This one sees it!" She managed to drive her opponent back with a particularly vicious flail combo. "But is also somewhat occupied!"

The patterns grew more complex; the energy trails started to pulse in sync. Whatever they were planning, I really didn't want to find out what it did when completed.

Time to change the game.

"Everyone brace!" I shouted, gathering a big portion of my remaining power: five hundred mana all in a single strike. The Dawn Guard must have sensed what was coming; they all started to move at once, but it was too late.

Lightning, amplified through my entire body, met the energy patterns they'd been weaving. The resulting explosion lit up the entire arena, throwing us all backward.

I crashed to the sandy floor a dozen meters or more away. Cerin screeched; apparently the discharge on his side had set his fur alight—that was gonna be a bad one to explain later. But the fairies were on their way already, as they'd been outside of the blast radius.

The Scepiniir climbed to their feet again, and Rathaharn…well, she looked seriously pissed as she did the same. She looked over at me, and then them, as if unsure who she wanted to fight more.

"I couldn't let them finish their spell!" I shouted, running at the nearest figure, hoping that, because they were freshly summoned, they hadn't seen me fly yet.

My target was the glaive wielder. He spun it around in a great arc, building momentum and coming in on my left side, head angled so that I could either catch it on my shield, or have it punch into me.

I'd seen that trick before, though. Markus had warned me of it in training, as had others, because the head of the weapon had a beard on it, a hook that could be angled around.

If he got that behind the shield, it was coming off my arm, or my arm was breaking. If he managed to land it in front? The same. Slam it into my arm at full speed with the advantage of the weapon's insane reach?

The damn thing was what, ten foot, maybe twelve long? Even as strong as I was, that was going to cause serious issues. But…the one thing that I had going for me in all these fights was that they had been reduced from whatever their "real" levels had been, to be no more than a handful above my own.

The dungeon was making this as a trial. A trial to force me to improve and evolve, not just as a murder dungeon to kill me.

My levels were impressive, sure, but the real advantage I had?

I was *ascending*.

I leapt into the air at the last second, pushing hard with my flight ability and my leg muscles. I literally flipped over the weapon rather than flying, though; I twisted in the air and landed inside the weapon's reach, before throwing myself into the Scepiniir with all the momentum I had.

I slammed the shield into him, bouncing off and stumbling. But I caught myself again, with the power of flight gliding me back to my feet even as my opponent was hurled from his.

He landed on his back. The momentary hesitation—should he hold onto his weapon or discard it—proved his undoing as I leapt forward again. This time, I put all my weight behind my sword and drove it into his chest as he twisted, trying to bring the weapon up to block or to get out of the way.

Instead, the glaive hit my sword, driving the tip upward from the middle of his chest, and into the seam that ran around his neck.

The blade punched through with a scream of metal on metal. It cut through his neck and into the sand below, before being driven down almost to the hilt, partially beheading him.

I rolled to the side on instinct, and a second later, a hammer slammed down into the breastplate where I'd just been. I came to my feet and backed up fast. The Scepiniir rolled his shoulders as he followed, whipping the hammer around and down again and again. The glancing blows knocked my shield aside as I tried to set it.

"Behind you!" I heard Ciara cry, as a trio of missiles flashed over my shoulder from her.

I launched into the air, twisting and rising above the hammer, in time to see the second glaive driven through the space I'd just vacated.

With both of these focusing on me, I noticed that the last of the Dawn Guard was down. Red blood drained into the sand by Rathaharn's side. But she was down as well, hands clutching at a dented-in section, hissing as the healers tried to stabilize her.

"Cerin, help her!" I yelled, before dismissing her and focusing on the pair waiting for me.

The glaive wielder had taken three magic missiles to the helmet, but besides a blackening of the armor, they were unfazed. I cursed as he lowered the glaive and pointed at me, then at my wounded, before the ground finally before them.

The meaning was obvious: "Stop fucking around and fight us, or we kill them."

As much as I cursed about it, landing a few dozen meters back and watching them stride forward, I couldn't really be pissed about it. They'd be well within their rights to have killed our injured. After all, this was a dungeon dive.

If anything, it was weird that they'd not done it.

Fuck it, though, I didn't have time to consider it. I had a shield, no sword—it was in the other guy's armor, wedged fast—no hammer—fucking *again*—and although I did have a dagger, that wasn't going to do much.

Lastly, I did have "American magic," I supposed, though was that really the way to go in this fight? They'd not seen it yet, after all, and I decided to keep it for the boss as a nice surprise.

Besides, I was *really* hoping that once I'd fought these, that was the end...not another ten rounds of shit to go.

"Fuck it," I grunted. I reached for the shield, then unfastened it, tugging it off and tossing it aside. Then I smacked a fist against my chest, then pointed at the one with the glaive.

"Come on then, let's do this! No magic, no weapons!"

"Foolish cub. You think because you lost your claws, we should lose ours? Be thankful I will face you alone," the glaive wielder called back. She gestured to what was apparently her companion—sexes were damn hard to tell in plate armor, after all—and then strode forward, glaive conspicuously still in her hand.

The last Scepiniir stepped back, resting their hammer on their shoulder, calmly waiting for their turn.

I checked my mana. The little I'd managed to regenerate meant I had enough for one of pretty much any spell, and these fuckers wouldn't enjoy a meteor shower, I was pretty certain...

Then I sighed, glancing up at the warriors that watched. Knowing the little I did of the Scepiniir, if I tried pulling some dishonorable shit like that, they'd all attack.

Nope, it was time to use my greater strength and speed to my advantage, I decided.

The glaive was spun around in an arc. Then it was sent into what was obviously a well-trained kata; the head flashed with blurring speed but I spotted a silver streamer attached to the base that I'd not noticed before.

It was a length of cloth. It hadn't really stood out, so I'd ignored it before now. But as the head blurred and she shifted her grip to the middle, the streamer spun faster and faster as well. And for the life of me, it got hard to tell which end was which.

They closed on me, and I muttered a veritable stream of curses, backing up.

The glaive was a blur of motion now; the silver streamer made it almost impossible to track which end held the deadly blade. I kept backing up, watching her footwork more than the weapon—sometimes the best way to read an attack was through the stance, I remembered Markus saying, while he'd been calmly kicking my ass with the spear in training.

"This one thinks perhaps you should have kept the shield," Rathaharn called out weakly from where the healers worked on her. I could hear the mix of pain and amusement in her voice.

"Not helping!" I shot back, ducking as the glaive whipped over my head. The Dawn Guard warrior was good—each movement flowed into the next...no wasted energy, no telegraphed attacks.

I waited for my opening, watching her pattern. The streamer was clever, I had to admit. Combined with the weapon's length and her skill, it created a defensive sphere that would be suicide to charge through...if I was limited to just physical attacks.

"The great Dungeon Lord, reduced to dancing!" she taunted, advancing steadily. "Where is your storm now?"

I grinned inside my helmet. "Oh, you want to see some lightning?"

Her step faltered—just slightly, but it was enough. I sprinted forward, channeling lightning not into an attack, but through my armor. Electricity crackled across the metal plates as I closed the distance.

The glaive swept in, but I was already sprinting forward.

I caught it—not with my hands, but by letting it strike my electrically charged armor on the shoulder with the haft. The metal weapon conducted beautifully, sending feedback up through her gauntlets.

She tried to pull back, but I had the weapon now, my gauntleted hand locked around the shaft. "Fun fact about lightning," I said conversationally, gripping tighter and yanking on the weapon. "It really doesn't play well with metal armor!"

Her response was to release the glaive entirely, dropping and rolling backward. Smart, but not quite smart enough. I spun the weapon around, familiarizing myself with its balance even as I advanced, used to a spear more than this, but hey, "when in Rome" and all that.

"Now then," I called out. "Who's fuckin' dancing?"

The Scepiniir warrior straightened, head tilted slightly. Then, to my surprise, she laughed. "Well played, young one. But let us see how you handle this..."

Her gauntlets began to glow with an inner light...and then it spread throughout her armor, making me curse.

Enchanted armor. Of fucking *course* they had enchanted armor.

On the upside, *enchanted armor*!

I just had to peel the fuckers out of it, and then it was *mine*.

I lunged forward, driving the tip of the glaive at her chest, jabbing fast and looking to drive her back, to keep her on the defensive. If she'd been able to use the armor all this time, she'd have done it, right? I just had to outlast whatever she had.

The armor's glow intensified, becoming almost blinding. I kept the glaive moving, not giving her time to fully activate whatever enchantment she was channeling. But each strike seemed to slide off her plate mail with increasing resistance or be batted aside by her hands.

"The Dawn Guard does not fall so easily," she declared, her voice taking on an odd resonance. The light pulsed outward in waves now, and the hairs on the back of my neck stood up.

My next thrust was met with her bare hand, catching the glaive's haft behind the blade like it was nothing. The weapon's metal began to heat rapidly in my grip as her armor's enchantment interfered with my own lightning; the metal glowed, the wood already charring.

"Shit," I gasped, releasing the glaive before it could melt in my hands.

She casually tossed it aside. The weapon's shaft glowed cherry red where she'd gripped it. "Now then." She rolled her shoulders, the motion rippling through her illuminated armor. "Shall we continue our dance?"

I backed up a step, staring at her, trying to figure it all out. The armor was clearly defensive in nature, probably designed to counter both physical and magical attacks. But everything had a weakness—I just had to find it before she could bring her full power to bear.

"Your lightning cannot pierce this aegis," she declared proudly, advancing. "The Dawn Guard stands as shield and sword both. We—"

I cut her off by hurling a handful of sand at her helmet's visor. She batted it aside easily with a gauntleted hand, but I was already moving, diving past her guard and grabbing her arm. The armor burned against my gauntlets, but I gritted my teeth and heaved, using her own momentum to throw her off-balance.

"You talk too much," I grunted, following up with a knee strike to her midsection. It was like kicking a furnace, but the impact still staggered her. "Let's see how well that fancy armor works when you can't keep your footing!"

Her response was to grab my leg. The metal of my greave began to smoke where she gripped it. The heat was intense enough that I could feel it through the enchanted plate. But two could play at that game.

I channeled lightning through my armor again, watching as our competing energies clashed in a shower of sparks. The sand beneath our feet began to crystallize from the heat and power being thrown off.

"Impressive," she acknowledged, releasing my leg before the feedback could overwhelm either of us. "But ultimately foolish. This armor was forged to contain forces far beyond your comprehension."

"Yeah?" I flexed my fingers, gathering power. "Then let's test those limits."

I launched myself at her, no longer trying for finesse. If her armor could withstand my lightning, maybe brute force would do the trick. I slammed into her with my full weight, driving us both across the sand.

She tried to grapple, but I twisted, letting her superheated gauntlets slide off my armor. I drove my helmet into her face. The impact rang like a bell, and the heat surged around us both.

"Crude," she grunted, "but effective." Her armor's glow pulsed brighter, and the sand beneath us started to smoke. "However, you forgot—we are not alone."

I barely had time to register her meaning before the hammer-wielding Dawn Guard's weapon crashed into my back. I was sent sprawling, rolling through the sand as my armor absorbed most of the impact.

"Fucking hell," I growled, coming to my feet. "I thought this was one-on-one?"

"You misunderstand," the first warrior said. Her armor's light was now so intense, it left afterimages in my vision. "The Dawn Guard fights as one. We are sword and shield, hammer and anvil."

The hammer wielder took position beside her; their own armor began to resonate with the same fierce glow. I could feel the power building between them, like the charge before a thunderstorm.

"Well, that's just great," I muttered, backing up to get some distance. Above us, I heard Ciara shouting something, but I couldn't spare the attention to listen. The two Dawn Guard warriors were moving in perfect sync now, their armors' lights pulsing in rhythm.

I had maybe seconds before whatever they were building to reached critical mass. Time to do something stupid.

"You want to play with power?" I called out, gathering my remaining mana. "Fine. Let's see how your armor handles this!"

I triggered Storm-Strike through my entire body at once, turning myself into a living conductor. Lightning cascaded off me in waves as I charged straight at them.

Sometimes the best way to deal with an overwhelming defense was to just hit it harder than it was ever designed to take.

The world slowed as I charged. Lightning crackled across every inch of my armor; each step left scorched footprints in the sand. The Dawn Guard warriors raised their hands in perfect unison, their combined power forming a barrier of pure energy between us.

I hit it like a battering ram.

The impact was devastating. Lightning met their defensive field in an explosion of light and sound that shook the entire arena. For a moment, we were locked in a stalemate—my Storm-Strike trying to punch through while their combined power pushed back.

Then the barrier began to crack.

"Impossible!" one of them shouted—I couldn't tell which through the maelstrom of energy. "This aegis has withstood…"

I pushed harder, converting more of my health into power through blood magic. Lightning arced wildly around us as hairline fractures spread through their shield. The sand beneath our feet had turned to glass, spreading outward in a growing circle.

"Everything breaks!" I roared over the thunderous discharge. "Even gods can fall!"

The barrier shattered.

The explosion threw us all backward. I crashed into one of the stone platforms, feeling ribs crack even through my armor. The Dawn Guard warriors were sent flying in opposite directions, their synchronized power disrupted.

I forced myself to my feet, blood trickling from my nose inside my helmet. My mana was critically low now, and my body screamed in protest, but I couldn't stop. One of them was already rising, their armor's glow flickering but still active.

"Your power…is impressive," the one on the left, the previous glaive wielder, admitted, staggering slightly. "But we are the Dawn Guard. We do not yield."

"Yeah?" I spat blood, lightning still crackling weakly across my armor. "Well, I'm the fucking Dungeon Warmancer and a God of the Storm, and I'm not done yet."

CHAPTER TWENTY-EIGHT

The glaive wielder's head snapped up at that. "A god?" Even through her helmet, I could hear the sneer. "You are no god, merely another aspiring mortal playing with powers beyond your grasp."

I laughed, the sound harsh and wet with blood. "You think I'm playing?" Lightning crawled across my armor in fits and starts as I gathered what little power remained to me, feeling a resonance—faint, but still there in the air all around me. "Want to know something interesting about storms?"

The hammer wielder was up now too, their weapon dragging furrows in the glass as they moved to flank me. The synchronized glow of their armor was rebuilding, but slower this time, more unstable.

"They feed on themselves," I continued, forcing myself to stand straighter despite the stabbing pain in my ribs. I converted more of my health into mana, recharging myself; I was risking everything, but what was the point in keeping it in the tank, if I didn't live to use it? "The more energy they release, the more they gather. And right now?" I grinned savagely inside my helmet as I understood what the resonance was, recognition and understanding combining into one. "This whole arena is charged with power."

It was true. It crackled in the air around us, residual energy from our clash seeking somewhere to ground itself. The glass beneath our feet still hummed with it. *How the hell had I never noticed this before?* The power was weakening, draining away, but still there!

"More empty boasts," the glaive wielder scoffed. But there was an edge of uncertainty in her voice now. "Your power is spent, your body failing. Accept your defeat with honor."

"You know what's funny?" I reached out to the ambient energy, drawing it in like I'd learned to do with the storm. "Everyone keeps telling me what I can't do. What my limits are." The lightning responding eagerly, far more than it should have. "But here's the thing about limits…"

The remaining fairies suddenly scattered, retreating to the highest points of the arena. Even Cerin backed away, fur standing on end.

"They're only limits until you break them."

The gathered power surged through me like a tide. This time, the force that erupted from my armor wasn't just lightning—it was pure storm, the essence of the tempest itself. The Dawn Guard warriors raised their barrier again, but they were too slow, too weakened from our last clash.

This time, I didn't just hit their defense.

I went through it.

Lightning tore into the world and thunder boomed as I crashed through their barrier like it wasn't even there. The hammer wielder tried to bring their weapon up, but I moved faster than thought, riding the storm itself. My fist connected with their chest plate; Storm-Strike discharged with enough force to send them flying backward.

The former glaive wielder lasted longer. Her armor's glow intensified as she tried to match my power. For a brief moment, we were locked together in a maelstrom of competing energies—her ancient enchantments against my raw storm as we grappled, her hands and mine interlaced.

"Impossible!" she grunted, straining against me. "No mortal can channel such power!"

"That's kind of…the point!" I grunted. I broke my right hand free and smashed a vicious punch into the side of her head once, twice, then a third time. The storm surged through me. The residual energy I'd pulled in combined with my own power now, growing stronger by the second. "I'm not a mortal anymore!"

Her armor began to crack. Hairline fractures appeared across its surface as my power overwhelmed its enchantments. Light blazed from within as the protective spells started to fail.

I broke her grip entirely, heaving and twisting, bending her elbow inward, and grabbed her gorget. The neck section of her armor formed a convenient handhold as I yanked her in close, headbutting her.

A right cross, a left jab, a knee to her stomach, then a repeat to her face as her head came down. She staggered back and I let her. The power built as more of my health left me, converting into mana which in turn converted to lightning, which started to heal me, creating a steadily growing storm.

It was one that would kill me in the end—the cost of the conversion alone would see to that. But for now, as long as I had health, I could keep this going, just draining more away with each revolution.

"You cannot—"

But I cut her off, channeling everything I had into one final blast. "Bitch, please. I already did."

I drove my right fist into the center of her armor with all my might, and the explosion that followed lit up the entire arena. Her armor shattered like glass; the pieces dissolved into motes of light as the ancient enchantments finally failed. She hurtled backward to the ground, unconscious but alive, leaving a furrow burned in the sand. The grains turned to glass and the last pulses grounded, flaring off her smoking, wounded form.

I staggered, nearly falling as the power rush faded. My vision blurred, blood now flowing freely inside my helmet. I'd pushed way too far, converting far too much health into power, but it had worked.

The hammer wielder was down, their weapon lying broken beside them. Their armor's glow had died completely, leaving only scorched metal behind.

"Holy shit," I heard Ciara whisper from somewhere above. "He actually did it."

I managed to stay on my feet, turning to face the champion's platform. Kh'aan stood unmoved, but I could feel his attention focused on me with new intensity.

"Is that"—I had to pause to spit blood—"enough of a warm-up for you?"

His answer was to draw his blade, the weapon igniting with otherworldly flame as he leapt down to face me.

"Fucking me an' my big mouth," I muttered under my breath.

All around the outside of the arena, his personal guards drew their weapons, before crashing them against their shields. For those with two swords or axes, they crashed them together. A halberd or long weapon? The butt was driven into the platform they stood atop of.

The crowd that watched on had been almost unnoticed until now, their individual voices lost to the overwhelming roar that thousands of people watching a single fight produced. But now, they dropped in volume.

There was a nervous hush, one that slowly was lost to the pounding crash of the Scepiniir honor guard's actions. And as Kh'aan strode toward me, the rhythmic crashing grew louder, more insistent.

His armor seemed to flow like quicksilver, each movement rippling through the living metal. The blade in his hand burned with ethereal flames that cast no shadows, and in his wake, the glass beneath his feet crackled and re-melted.

"You have proved yourself worthy of a true challenge." His voice carried easily over the percussion of weapons. "Few have ever broken the Dawn Guard's aegis. Fewer still lived to speak of it."

I straightened as best I could, fighting the urge to cough up more blood. "Happy to be special," I managed, trying to assess just how fucked I was. My mana was almost gone, my health dangerously low, and every breath sent daggers through my broken ribs.

They were healing, though, my lightning bringing that about as quickly as it could. And although my mana might be in the toilet right now, every single point was a crackling pulse of health that rolled through me.

I grunted as a rib that had been poking into a lung was suddenly snapped free, sliding back into position and doing more damage on the way out than it had in getting in there.

The weapon-beats reached a crescendo, then stopped abruptly. The silence that followed was deafening, as even the crowds, surprised by the sudden cessation, quieted.

"You understand," Kh'aan called, settling into a stance I didn't recognize, "that this is no longer about testing your limits?"

"Yeah?" I gathered what little power remained to me, knowing it wouldn't be nearly enough. "What's it about then?"

"Evolution." The flames along his blade intensified. "The strong survive, grow stronger. The weak perish. This is the way of all things." He raised his weapon in salute. "Show me your strength, Dungeon Warmancer. Show me if you truly are becoming what you claim."

I could barely stand, but I returned the salute with as much dignity as I could muster. "Fair warning—I'm probably about to do something really stupid."

"As you should."

Was that approval in his voice?

"Face your death with courage, or transcend it. There is no middle ground."

The honor guard crashed their weapons once more, a single unified strike that echoed through the arena.

Then he moved.

He was faster than anything I'd ever seen. One minute, he was twenty meters away; the next, his blade swept for my neck.

I barely managed to get my arm up. The flaming sword crashed against my vambrace with enough force to drive me to one knee. Several inches of sand pushed up as I was shoved back.

The impact sent shock waves through my already battered body. Where the ethereal flames touched my armor, the metal began to warp and bubble. I pushed back, trying to create space, but he was already moving again.

His second strike came from an impossible angle, somehow both above and behind me at the same time. I threw myself forward into a roll, as the heat of his blade passed through the space I'd occupied. The sand beneath turned to bubbling slag in its wake.

"Good instincts," he commented, his voice unchanged despite the speed of his movement. "But instinct alone will not save you."

I came up from the roll already moving, my lightning crackling weakly as I tried to counter with a fast punch.

He batted my strike aside almost casually. His blade left trails of fire in the air and a melted patch on my armor that burned my skin as it cooled. Each movement was precise, measured, without a hint of wasted energy.

"The Dawn Guard relied too heavily on their enchanted armor," he continued, pressing his attack. "Ancient magics, passed down through generations, and replicated but weakly here, as were they. A shadow of their former might, limited to your level to provide you a challenge. But true power…" His blade swept in again, forcing me to duck and weave. "True power comes from within."

I managed to catch his next strike on my gauntlet, lightning meeting flame in a spectacular discharge. "Hope I'm not paying extra for the philosophy lesson," I grunted through gritted teeth. "I'm a bit busy trying not to die to pay attention!"

His response was to increase his speed even further. Blade strikes came from every direction: each one potentially lethal, each one pushing my reflexes to their absolute limit. I defended purely on instinct now; my body moved before my mind could process the attacks.

My hands burned—my forearms, too—as I deflected as fast as I could. My armor melted, sections of molten metal flying free as I desperately blocked.

The armor vanished, droplet by drop, scale by scale as I was literally peeled out of it by the incredibly skilled warrior.

And somehow, impossibly, I was almost keeping up. My lightning might be weak, but with every clash, every near-miss, I could feel something changing. The storm within me responded to the challenge, growing stronger with each exchange as I used it.

Kh'aan must have sensed it too. He broke off his assault, flowing back several steps. "Yes," he said, satisfaction clear in his voice. "Now you begin to understand."

I stood, panting, my armor smoking in dozens of places. "Understand what?"

"That this is not about victory or defeat." The flames along his blade shifted, taking on new colors. "This is about transformation."

Above us, the honor guard began their rhythmic beating once more…slower this time, like a heartbeat.

Or a countdown.

The flames along his blade had shifted from reds, oranges, and yellows to blue-white, so bright it hurt to look at directly. Heat rolled off it in waves, distorting the air.

"Your armor is failing," he observed, gesturing with his free hand to my melted and pitted plate. "Soon you will have nothing between you and my blade but your own power."

He was right. My vambraces were more holes than metal now, my breastplate was a mess of warped and bubbled steel, and I could feel cool air on my skin where whole sections had simply melted away. The enchantments that had made it nearly indestructible were being systematically burned away by his otherworldly flame, as he beat and stripped section by section, when he clearly could have slipped through a gap before now.

"That's the point, isn't it?" I watched him circle. "Strip everything away until only the essence remains?"

"Perhaps you do understand."

"Fuck it. If that's the point, want to give me a minute?" I asked, desperately buying time.

"To rest and recover?" He cocked his head to the side, pausing.

"Nah, to remove this." I lifted an arm, gambling that he'd give me the chance.

"A lesson learned indeed." He nodded, then stepped back, waiting as I reached up and pulled free my helmet, tossing it aside.

I'd already known that with the damage his magical blade was doing, if he truly tried to kill me—to stab me in the head—the very best the helmet would do was melt, slowing the blade a fraction of a second.

So, better that I had more freedom to face him, to see the blow coming and to react.

I stripped to the waist. The armor came away in sections, and he nodded to my legs.

"You believe the defense is worth the weight?"

"I believe not flashing my cock at the spectators might be." I snorted. "A single flame down there and my hairs are going up. No way my pants are surviving that."

"A foolish consideration." He frowned, the disappointment clear through his visor.

I sighed, taking the time to pull them off as well, leaving myself in literally a pair of under-armor pants and a top—a top that I damn well knew was fucking useless as armor. So, a second later, that went as well.

"You are ready?"

I nodded, my mana and stamina having recovered barely enough worth noticing. He moved again, but this time I was ready.

Lightning met flame as I caught his blade between my palms, gritting my teeth against the searing heat. The lightning that I used to form my shield was now redirected, focused to cover a tiny area. My skin started to glow with an inner light.

"The Dawn Guard were a test," he continued, pressing forward. "To see if you could break through artificial power to find your own."

The pressure increased, and my knees began to buckle.

"Now show me what lies beneath all these mortal trappings."

I snarled, shoving back with everything I had. "Happy to oblige!"

The storm surged through me again, stronger this time…purer. Where I dodged a swing, the near-miss of his flames touching my exposed skin, I flared lightning in response. A half-second burst—contained, constrained, locked down to a single forearm…then a section of skin six inches across.

Four.

Two.

Each clash of power sent shock waves across the arena, and I realized that the rhythmic beating from above had synchronized with my heartbeat.

Or maybe my heart had synchronized with it.

He disengaged again, but this time there was no respite. The next attack came faster, harder. His blade left trails of white fire that hung in the air like burning brands. Yet with each strike, each near-miss, I was changing.

The pain was still there, but it seemed distant now, unimportant. What mattered was the power flowing through me, the storm answering my call with increasing strength as power seemed to seep into me from the world around.

My health was vanishing to power it, the fuel that I burned, and yet… I felt more alive than ever before. The lower my health fell, the faster my mana burned, the more in tune with the world around me I was.

I deflected another strike barehanded, my palm smoking but unburned. Kh'aan's blade swept around, slamming back down and I braced, catching the blade in my grip. The crackling lightning burned bright against the flames and he pressed down, ethereal flame meeting living lightning. For the first time, I saw his stance shift, as he had to put more effort into the blow, even if only slightly.

"Yes," he growled, approval clear in his voice. "Now we truly begin."

His blade twisted free, the ethereal flames so bright now they cast no shadows at all. The air around us shimmered with power. Waves of heat distorted everything except the space immediately around me, where the storm kept the worst at bay.

"Your connection grows stronger," he observed, launching into another series of impossibly fast attacks. "You begin to understand the price of true power."

I didn't, not really, but I sure as shit wasn't saying that.

I moved on instinct now, my bare skin alive with crackling energy. Without the armor weighing me down, I was faster, more graceful; each dodge and weave left trails of lightning in my wake. Every time his blade came close, the storm within me surged in response, and with it a sense of power, of potential.

"Price?" I laughed, the sound almost maniacal as I sacrificed more health to convert to pure power. "You mean the gift!"

The lightning exploded outward from my body, meeting his flames in a spectacular collision. The honor guard's beating grew more intense, and it resonated with both my heartbeat and the pulses of power flowing through me.

"Then show me!" He pressed forward, his blade becoming a blur of white fire. "Show me what lies beyond mortality!"

The strikes came faster now, each one trailing both flame and lightning where they met. Reality itself seemed to waver around us, the very air crackling with competing energies. The glass beneath our feet began to splinter and reform with each clash.

The change accelerated with every exchange; my connection to the storm grew stronger as my body burned through its reserves. My skin wasn't just glowing now; there were moments where you could see the lightning coursing through my veins, pure power replacing blood.

The next clash sent us both sliding backward, the impact point between us a maelstrom of flame and lightning. Above us, the honor guard's rhythm reached a crescendo, and so did the screams of the crowd.

I stepped back, digging deeper. I had eight hundred and seventeen health left, that was it, out of over nine thousand. I cursed. With these fights as they'd been, I must be close to a level, if not having hit it already. There was no point in worrying about opportunities missed, though, not now.

The health I could have gained, or the mana, didn't matter.

Either I had all that I needed, right now, or I was already dead.

When I looked at the world that way, it was almost a relief, if I was honest with myself.

The fights to get to this point, the stress, the leadership questions, the wondering whether I was good enough, whether I was doing all that I could…most of all, whether I was the right person to face all of this, to lead my little corner of humanity's fight—all of it dropped away.

Three hundred mana left. The conversions were constantly running in one direction or the other: mana to lightning, to health, to mana and round again. All of it was becoming instinctual now.

Instead, I overrode the flow, sacrificing eight hundred health in a heartbeat. The residual power of the lightning all around me, the power that was filling the arena…I dragged it all into my heart. The change roared through me—the feeling of power being bottled up, of a point that was preventing the release, grew thinner and thinner, as I gathered all that power…and *pushed*!

The barrier thinned, growing to the width of a sheet of paper, of a micron, and then…it was gone!

I screamed in terrible power as my flesh vaporized—my muscles exploding, bones detonating. The divine essence that I was filled with lit like a bonfire, spreading through this being of pure lightning, an avatar of wrath, that I had become.

"YES!" the warmaster roared. "Now FIGHT ME!" He launched himself at me, blade swinging.

I twisted and my right arm came up. I realized this was what I'd been doing before. When I'd faced the undead gods, when I'd blocked with a thought—I'd been summoning my own essence, that of a nascent lightning god, and forming it as a shield.

The lightning wasn't separate from me—it *was* me.

I was it, and now there was no separation, no weakness, no flesh unless I willed it. My own mana was all that I was, and through it, I could be anything, for truly, I was the storm's avatar.

The sword flashed toward my face, faster than ever before. But no longer slowed by the time it took nerve impulses to travel, I dodged it, slapping it aside, feeling the arc of power that buffered back the flames and metal, as I released a snap kick to his stomach.

Kh'aan laughed, slapping my blow aside.

I jumped. A faster kick snapped out from my other leg, then a stomp as I twisted in the air, pushing down with the power of flight. This time, I caught him on the inside of his knee, shoving it aside.

He rolled with it, using the momentum of the blow to go down low, spinning and bringing his sword around as I leapt upward. The blade passed beneath my feet by a scant few millimeters.

Then he was rising even as I came down, with a kick of his own. He pushed off, the spin-kick vicious enough that a mere few minutes before, he might have killed me with it alone.

Instead, I pushed back. The air below my foot became solid and aided me as I moved; his booted heel passed by my crackling chin.

Arcs of power flashed out, caressing his leg as he spun again; this time, he jumped and swung a punch, driving the pommel of his sword for my face.

I reared back instinctively, and he roared at me.

"You're not flesh!" he barked. "No chin, no face, no FORM!" I snapped out a kick and he deflected it, snarling. "LEARN! If you will not evolve, then this is all for naught!"

He came at me even faster. His own flesh burst into flame, as he began his own transformation. The sword whirled away as he cast it free, driving me back with punches and kicks that were barely within my range of perception. They scarcely seemed to move, and they were there.

We danced around, moving in a half circle until Ciara's voice rang out. "The sword!" she screamed.

I dove sideways on instinct; the blade passed through the air I'd just occupied.

It punched into Kh'aan's chest…

And passed straight through!

As it erupted from the far side of his chest, now fully flames, then simply knit back together, he roared. The blows came faster: I blocked a low punch, slapped a high aside, took a third on my cheek, feeling the sting of alien mana entering me, and…

And that had been three fists.

He'd punched me *three* times, all at the same time, or close enough.

I'd let the blow to my cheek get through, judging it was the least dangerous as I moved my head to avoid most of it. And yet, what the hell? He didn't have three fuckin' arms a minute ago!

I drifted back, staring at him, seeing that he'd not even bothered to pull back the punches; they simply vanished. A conversation with Kelly, Mike, and Aly way back when I'd first been inducting them into the dungeon came to mind as the only explanation.

"Residual self-image…" I whispered, as it all crashed in.

I wasn't human anymore.

I was an avatar of the storm, and how many storms were human-shaped, unless they chose to be?

Fuck all.

I launched myself at him. My fists appeared in the gaps in his guard; deflections came a bare instant before they were too late. A foot flashed up and smashed into his stomach. A heel passed across his chin. My fists again slammed home, as the crackling power that was the line of impact between us grew wilder and wilder.

I moved on pure instinct now, at a blur that was lessened only by the computational speed of my mind—a mind that was entirely made of lightning now.

Where flame crackled, burned, and consumed, lightning arced and danced.

I was faster than him. And it wasn't just a case of thinking it—I *knew* it!

The blows came faster and faster, harder and harder until his deflections no longer made it, until I was forcing him back and beating him!

The power that I felt, this power was incredible, and it was…

It wasn't mine.

I felt it suddenly, the shock of it as I realized that my mana should have run out *ages* ago!

My health was climbing higher; I was healing, but my HP in this form was no longer important. Instead, it was mana cohesion. But still, that number was increasing. And through it all? I was increasing in power!

I felt it, I saw it, and as I smashed home my last blow into the barrier that had built between us—a barrier composed of mana that was leaking from us both—I saw it all.

The barrier detonated, shoving us both back. And in that heartbeat, that fragment of a second, I saw the satisfaction in his eyes.

"NO!" I roared, crashing my forearms together over my chest, bracing them and digging deep, gambling it all on one roll of the dice.

I shoved outward. The flare of the lightning shield exploded and caught him as he tried to push me to the end, picking him up and throwing him backward. His form smashed into the sand, leaving a burned and melted furrow to mark his passage.

"No." I panted, my chest heaving as my lightning became flesh again.

I stood there, wisps rising from my skin, everything I was now created from the mana that I'd controlled so perfectly for such a short space of time. The instinctual control, the power slipped free. I stared at Kh'aan, as he too resumed his flesh form.

"I will not kill you," I said softly.

"You think you have a choice in this, cub?" He glared. "I am Kh'aan. You cannot leave this arena without besting me."

"You're the greatest warmaster that the Scepiniir had, and you came in here for a reason. I'm betting that it wasn't just to die."

"You know nothing of me."

"Maybe not, but I know that I learned more in that fight with you, about who and what I am, than I have in…well, I don't fucking know how much navel-gazing. You're a natural war leader, and a master trainer. You know more about my powers than I do, and I'd be fucking stupid to cut my arm off and leave it bleeding on the arena sands for the entertainment and rules of the fucking Cinthians."

"You know?" He cocked his head to one side.

"I suspect," I said carefully. "More and more…it just doesn't make sense."

He stared at me for several long seconds before apparently coming to a decision.

"Cut off your arm," he said softly. But the sound carried across the sand between us, the crowd above now silent as they hung on every word.

"What?"

"You wish for my advice? You wish for this?"

"Yes!"

"Then prove it," he said. "Prove you have the strength of will. The iron-hard discipline to do what must be done…that you do not waste my time."

We stared at each other for a long few seconds, as my mind raced.

He'd been feeding me that mana, I'd seen that; he'd literally been teaching me so that I could kill him, and yet…

If I did this, if I cut off my arm, I'd be not only weakened, but I'd be disarmed, quite literally. I'd have no chance in the fight if I was wrong and he attacked, and we both knew it.

Either I trusted in what I *thought* I knew, trusted with my life that he wasn't going to just kill me and call me a fool, or I attacked. And now? With the epiphanies I'd felt before already fading, I knew I had little chance of defeating him.

"Mind lending me your sword?" I called out.

His eyes crinkled behind his visor as he smiled, then he nodded, once.

The blade lifted from where it'd been allowed to fall at some point during the battle. Now it flew toward me, the speed alone a threat that could end me.

Instead, I reached out my right hand, palm up, and the blade flipped over, slapping into my hand with a smack that sent a flare of pain, and even a little burn damage.

"From the elbow good for you?" I held my left arm out, tapping the blade to that point. "Any higher and it's not going to be clean."

"It will suffice."

I took a deep breath, adjusted my grip on the burning blade, and drove it down hard.

The pain was indescribable. Even with my new understanding of my form, even knowing I could rebuild it, the sheer visceral agony of severing my own arm nearly dropped me to my knees. Blood sprayed, then almost instantly cauterized as the ethereal flames sealed the wound.

My left arm fell to the sand with a dull thud, the fingers twitching.

"Well done," Kh'aan said softly, approval clear in his voice. "Now you understand—true strength lies not in what we can do to others, but in what we can control of ourselves."

He strode forward. His armor flowed like liquid metal as he raised one hand, making a gesture to the guards, who immediately started to shout, bang weapons against their shields, and so on again. Though this time, it seemed to be an effort to create as discordant a layer of noise as possible, until he stood before me.

His vambrace flowed suddenly, depositing something in his hand that he then subtly slid into my remaining one, even as he recovered his sword.

"We are not meant to be enemies, Dungeon Warmancer," he whispered, closing my fingers over the crystal. "The Cinthians would have us fight to the death for their cause, but there are other battles ahead. Greater purposes."

He made sure I was paying attention, then glanced down at his left arm. I followed his gaze, and saw on the surface of the armor a single bump rise.

I frowned, opening my mouth, then saw the subtle shake of his head. I shut it with a click, then glanced back at his arm as he waited. This time, the single bump had been joined by four more; then, when he was sure I'd seen it, two more.

Then they vanished and he made sure I kept my hand tightly wrapped around the crystal. I could feel it as it thrummed with stored knowledge. Hell, I could feel it even through my pain-hazed senses.

"When you are ready," he continued. "When you truly understand what lies within, seek me out again. Earn my respect further, and perhaps…who knows. The trial dungeons cannot prevent the call."

"You're not gonna stab me in the face now, right?" I managed through gritted teeth.

"No, this fight is yours. You have learned much, cub, but remember, in here, death is merely transformation." He spread his arms wide. Flames began to engulf his form, and he inclined his head, speaking more formally. "Until we meet again, young god."

Around the arena, his honor guard began to ignite as well, their forms dissolving into pure energy. The flames consuming Kh'aan grew brighter, whiter, until I had to look away.

When I could see again, they were gone. Only motes of light remained, slowly fading as their souls returned to the dungeon's depths.

A series of notifications began to flash before my eyes, and I heard Ciara's voice from above:

"Matt…your arm…"

I looked down at the severed limb, then at my cauterized stump, and smiled. Lightning crackled as I reached out with my power, remembering what I'd learned about form and essence, even as the roars of the crowd washed over me. They'd apparently liked the end of the fight.

"Don't worry." I watched my lightning take shape. "I think I finally understand how this is supposed to work."

The lightning sparked and crackled, forming the outline of an arm from my elbow down. At first it was pure energy, unstable and shifting. But as I focused, remembering what I'd learned, it began to take shape.

"Holy shit," Ciara breathed, floating closer. "You're actually…"

"Converting pure mana to matter?" I grinned. The outline became more solid, lightning condensing into muscle and bone. "Yeah. Turns out I've been doing it backward this whole time."

The process wasn't exactly comfortable—rebuilding an arm from scratch felt like pins and needles cranked up to eleven—but it was working. Tendons formed, then muscle, then skin…each layer materializing as I understood now that my physical form was just another expression of power.

"The old bastard was right," I muttered, flexing my newly formed fingers. "It really is all about understanding what you are."

A cascade of notifications suddenly demanded my attention:

Congratulations, Dungeon Warmancer!

You have survived, and *conquered*, your second Trial Dungeon!

Your understanding of your true nature has increased dramatically. The following permanent changes have been applied:

Lightning Affinity increased to 117->135

Storm Affinity increased to 107->135

Are you ready?

Yes/Yes

The crystal in my hand pulsed, reminding me of its presence. Whatever knowledge Kh'aan had passed to me, it would have to wait until I was somewhere more private.

"Dungeon lord." Rathaharn limped over, looking battered and beaten but satisfied. "The exit has appeared."

Sure enough, a doorway had materialized in the arena wall, glowing with promise. Stairs were visible inside that looked to lead up to the main floor and where everyone else would be waiting. But first, I had some loot to collect.

As soon as I hit Yes—there were so many choices to choose from, after all…the right-hand side or the left? Such a variety of options—I was greeted with three vertical, curved screens that appeared in the air before me. Each was filled with options that flowed down from the top, with a sort of "flick" menu available. I moved my hand, gesturing and scrolling through them.

I glanced to the far right, seeing that again, it was the standard "Hey, you survived the trial dungeon—go you!" option. There were five choices, and none of them were overwhelming, especially considering three of them were identical to the last time I'd done the dungeon, which was in itself annoying.

Don't get me wrong, they were all good, just not on the level of "Oh my God, I must have this!"

The single-use defensive platform I'd been offered before was, again, a bit *meh.* Had it been something we could reproduce, sure. But as a single-use thing that was just tossed away after? I stared at it for a few seconds, thinking of the utility that we could have had with that, especially against the undead army, and I reconsidered.

When we were screwed for mana, that could have made a big difference. But ultimately, we'd found a way around it, and we needed the loot to be game-changing items.

I moved on. The next was one that I'd seen before as well. A companion fuckin' duck. It'd be a companion that was offered to everyone in the dungeon, so everyone could have their own personal pet…but it was a fucking *duck*!

Don't get me wrong, with hoisin and pancakes? I loved duck! With breakfast, their eggs could be fried and added to a full English. And of course, no matter where you were in the world, ducks with cherry or orange was a favorite. But fuck me, it was a *duck*!

A. Pet. Duck.

Hard pass.

The third in the row was new: a spirit guardian, one that was single binding, but could come back. That meant it wasn't something that I could give everyone in the dungeon, and it was clearly marked as not cloneable. But if I gave it to, say, Kelly and she activated it, she'd have a spirit guardian, one that would silently watch over her. If it was killed, it would automatically respawn in a single solar cycle, so it'd be back each day.

I didn't know how weak it would be, but it was rare, so it should be able to soak up a few hits at least. The only issue was…it was a single-use. A load of people could use it. My first thought was Kelly, you know, because I loved her, but…

I could give it to Ashley.

I knew there would be people that would think "Oh, she's hot and he's giving her gifts…wonder what he's after" but it wasn't like that. I was thinking of her role as our diplomat.

Having an invisible spirit guardian that could kick some arse and nobody knew was there until it attacked, or soaked up an attack?

That could be a lifesaver, especially as exposed as she was.

Her position in enemy territory or neutral areas, I meant.

That…I put that one aside as a possible option, and moved on. The fourth was from the last set of offerings again, and again it was shit, or at least a straight refusal.

The derish dungeon-born species I could unlock were described by the system as being opportunist murderers and excelled in "idle theft, property destruction, and low-grade terror."

They were also basically tiny four-legged devils.

Hard pass—though, for a second, for shits and giggles, I did entertain the thought of having the fuckers as the only summonable creature to deploy in the London dungeon, once we had that up and running.

Then I shook it off. As much as I disliked the fuckers, I wasn't a complete dick, and "opportunist murderers" didn't sound like something I could train to just hunt politicians or the French. Most likely, it'd go after the physically weakest in society, instead of those with the weakest moral compass.

Unfortunately, the sped-up core upgrade to the next level was gone, as that'd been something I actually looked for this time. Sod's Law.

The next rare, though…that was interesting.

"Primal evolution" was the name, and the description was, well, it was tailored to that bastard Chris, that was what it was.

It was a core, a primal one that offered a single opportunity to improve a creature on a primal level from a sample, resulting in a new dungeon creature—non-sapient—that could be summoned as needed.

At first, that didn't sound that good, until you realized that it didn't have to be a *living* creature.

I knew there was a chance that I could create a living dinosaur if I could locate enough bones for a T. rex or whatever, to get the dungeon to accept the template—I'd done it with the trikes, after all. But this? This didn't need a full skeleton; it just needed a *sample*.

I glanced at the last option: a soul nexus to forcibly compel dungeon creature obedience. And with no further hesitation, I picked the primal core. No contest.

Next was the middle screen. Four options greeted me here…all rare, which was nice.

A "mana-matrix stabilizer" was the first option. Basically, it could be deployed to an area of "abnormally high or uncontrolled mana" and it'd calm it right down.

Great. Wonderful.

Also not an issue for us so far, as areas of high mana were what we wanted, so that we could harvest it, so fuck that. Moving on…

Option two was a new fruit. Supposedly it increased Shadow resistance, but considering that it had a marker that explained it couldn't increase your affinity to it past fifty percent, it was a bit fucking useless.

Sure, if you were at minus ten or something, that'd be a great gift. You'd not be as weak against that mana aspect, but that was it…no real change. Had it been a case of "eat this and your affinity climbs by two every time," then hell yes. A hundred a day getting handed out and we all become immune to, and eventually actively healed by frickin' Shadow mana. But as it was?

Nope.

A "Mana Well Resonator" was interesting. It was basically a storage device, but one that could be constructed wherever I wanted, and provided a link that was more or less stable to store excess mana that could be drawn upon when needed.

I could take it with me into enemy territory, plonk it down and hide it, and then boom, fuck off. When I needed it—provided I was in the area—I could draw on it and refill my reserves. Damn tempting, that…except I damn well knew that I'd need to level it up a load before it could store more than a mouse's fart.

The last one was a single-use deployable workbench. It had some nice repair options, and could be used on high tech, but it was single-use. Again, we could take it into enemy territory and set it up; it could repair our armor or anything we needed, but we'd have to leave it behind when we moved on. And the enemy then got it if we lost control of the area.

Admittedly, that was the case for the mana well resonator as well. If the enemy captured it, they could probably find a way to use it. But it was a part of the dungeon, so I guessed that tapping a storage device with a ten thousand mana battery—or more; I didn't have a limit on it I could see—was going to smart a bit.

Nope, out of those four, the mana well resonator was an easy choice. I took it, then moved to the last screen.

Now, this one—well, this one was an issue. This came with a marker that it'd been upgraded due to the situation with the Eye of Amalthus being refused, and *damn.*

There were four different items, and I basically wanted them all.

First and foremost, an Alchemical primer. It was basically an idiot's guide to alchemy. Fuck, did we have a need for that—and not just because we certainly had the idiots already.

The only reason it wasn't an out-and-out "yes, please, motherfucker" was that I had no way of knowing whether the ingredients were available.

For all I knew, it had a mana potion recipe—which was what I was really wanting—but it included recipes that required the bollock hair of a derishian vampire that was only found on the planet Bumbhbum-3.

The second item was a halberd—a massive one. It was four meters long, so yeah, certainly not something that could be used in the real world outside of a Japanese RPG, and only then if I got a massive restyle so that I had suitably spiky hair and a chin that could be used as an anvil at a push.

The upside, however, was that the entire damn thing was covered in runes and it was marked as a rare-grade weapon. So, in theory, we could input it into the dungeon and then produce it to order with altered sizes.

Next was a single monocle, able to artificially boost thirty levels in up to two skills.

Now that was tempting, incredibly so, but it was the final item that really got me.

It was a blueprint for a lower-grade version of the armor that the orcs had been wearing. And now that I looked around, I saw that they'd all vanished. That made me extremely unhappy, because the best thing about the fight with those bastard Dawn Guards had been the intention of looting each and every item they'd had.

Instead, there was a reliquary that floated in the air over the patch that had held their corpse, and that was it.

I hesitated, then left the screen there. I checked each reliquary quickly in the hopes of finding some armor or items that would make up for it…

Nope.

I mean, it wasn't bad, per se. I got a ruby the size of a hen's egg, thirty-six coins, an uncommon-grade dagger, a packet of cheese and onion crisps—heh—and a lump of cheese that was both warm and stinky—that was about to be destroyed until I heard the gasp from Rathaharn. It was apparently a delicacy on her world, so that now needed to be reproduced and given out as a reward, apparently.

There were also two potions: one a high-grade healing one, so that was very nice, and the other that offered a short-term boost to Water magic affinity. It lasted thirty-seven minutes and granted a ten percent increase.

That could be good or bad, but was most likely just another thing to be added into the dungeon so that our alchemists could try to figure that shit out.

The armor blueprint was rare grade. It didn't have explanations for any of the runes attached, meaning that it wasn't going to be a sneaky shortcut to learning enchanting. And, if I was realistic, I knew it wouldn't be as good as the armor that they'd been wearing, which had been seriously top-notch shit, but…it was still armor. It was considerably better armor than the shit that we currently had the orcs in, and I had to think that the armor could be adjusted or that it could at least be learned from.

Fuck it.

I picked the armor. Then, as the screens vanished, I turned and looked up at the crowds overhead, and the stairs in the wall. It was time to get the fuck outta Dodge.

CHAPTER TWENTY-NINE

I gathered up the survivors of the fight and pulled on what was left of my armor to the waist, dumping the rest into my bag of holding as it was pretty broken and battered. We all headed in the direction of the stairs. On the way, I opened my mouth to start speaking to them all about what to expect moving forward, only to be beaten to it by Ciara.

"Lord Matt—Dungeon Warmancer, does the offer of a new life, outside the trial dungeon's confines, still stand?" she asked me formally.

I nodded, frowning at the formality.

"And the terms are the same as you offered me earlier?" She went on, again speaking over me before I could respond. "That each of us would be offered a position in the dungeon as full citizens and the oath that we agreed upon is valid?"

"Yeah," I agreed, confused until I saw the look in her eye.

She'd not been thinking anything had changed; she'd been repeating it for everyone, making sure they knew that the deal we'd struck before was still valid and that nothing had changed there.

No easy outs, and no chance for anyone to make a break for freedom and forget the debt owed.

"Yes, it is. And as you swore to serve me, so too I swear to serve you as your lord. Rathaharn, the offer is open to you as well. You can stay in here, with a dungeon win added to your tally, or you can escape and live a life outside."

"Will I be free?" she asked slowly. "Free to leave?"

"You can walk away if you want," I assured her. "But be warned, my world is recently fallen and the Orakai are coming, so I'd suggest you stay. You'll be well paid, well challenged, and yeah, the term is for a single year. Outside of that? I'd ask you agree to warn me if you're planning to leave but that's it."

"You'd permit me to leave?" She cocked one eyebrow.

I nodded. "If I can't rely on you, I'd rather you were far away," I said. "But be warned—the world is a mess."

"The challenges…they are good?"

"Oh my, fuck yes." I snorted. "What level were you before you went into the dungeon?"

"Forty-eight." She growled. "Reduced to thirty-one."

"Well, I was level zero about six months ago. So tell me, Rathaharn, how long did it take you to reach forty-eight? And how long do you think it'll take you to reach level fifty with my help?" I asked.

She hesitated, then nodded. "A year. But I warn you, I am a warrior, and will not be consigned to menial tasks," she rumbled.

"If you find yourself in a situation where you'd be asked to do something menial, it'd be for a damn good reason, like a warband that was out on deployment with everyone pulling together. How about this? I'll not ask you to do anything I wouldn't do myself?"

"An acceptable compromise," she agreed after a few seconds. I let out a long breath, before she grinned. "Plus, I must level hard, if I want to challenge the warmaster."

"Well, who knows," I muttered. "We'll sort out oaths later."

With that, I nodded my thanks to Ciara, and we trooped up the stairs for nearly fifteen goddamn minutes. Most of us became winded quickly enough, and as we reached the last section—a final switchback that ended with the light of the arena overhead falling in—and the roar and thunderous buzz of the crowds ahead, we all needed to take a short break.

The final steps seemed to take forever. The roar of the crowd grew louder with each one. My heart beat faster and faster at the thought of stepping out in front of them all…which, considering what we'd just been doing, was bloody stupid.

I emerged first, blinking in the sudden brightness. I stepped out onto the top of what had been the trial dungeon and in the center of the arena. The section we stood on was barely five meters across, a flat platform ringed by railings that hadn't been there when we'd entered.

The stadium stretched out around us in all directions. Tier upon tier of seats were filled with a mixture of faces—some I recognized, others complete strangers. The sheer number of people was staggering.

For the first time, I realized that I was surprised that they were all still there as well, considering how long the fight had to have taken.

"Impressive, isn't it?" Ciara landed on my shoulder, her wings flickering in the sunlight. "Though I'd expected more bloodthirsty screaming, given the crowd."

"Give them time," I muttered, turning to help Rathaharn up the final few steps. Her ankle was healed now. We'd all been healed, but that didn't mean that we were all "all right."

There was always the fact that our bodies had been pushed to the edge of exhaustion again and again, and then we'd climbed what felt like Mount-fuckin'-Everest to get out. I had to admit, though, she bore it with typical stoic pride. "They probably haven't processed that we survived yet."

That was when I heard it—Kelly's voice cutting through the general roar: "MATT!"

I spun around just in time to see her vaulting over the nearest railing. She hit the platform at a run and slammed into me hard enough that I staggered back a step.

"You absolute bastard!" she half-sobbed into my chest. "Do you have any idea how worried we were?"

"Sorry, love." I wrapped my arms around her, breathing in her familiar scent. "Bit tied up with the whole 'trial by combat' thing."

"You cut your own arm off!" She pulled back to glare at me as she smacked my chest with one palm. "We thought you'd lost your mind!"

"To be fair," I flexed my newly reformed limb, "I got better."

More figures made their way down now—Mike and Chris leading the charge, with Aly close behind. They'd apparently found a more conventional route, taking the stairs two at a time.

"Mate," Chris reached us first, clapping me on the shoulder, "that was fucking mental! When that big cat bastard showed up, I thought you were done for!"

"Thanks for the vote of confidence." I grinned, then turned serious. "Were there any casualties? Anything happen out here that I should know about?"

"None of ours," Mike assured me. "Though we had a few close calls when that crystal mine went up. The barriers held, though."

"Good." I nodded, relief flooding through me. Then I noticed Aly's expression. "What?"

"Oh nothing," she said airily. "Just wondering if you're planning to put some more clothes on anytime soon? Not that I'm complaining about the view, mind...and I think there's a lot of young ladies in the crowd who are probably happy right now."

I glanced down, suddenly remembering I was still basically half-naked. "Ah. Right. Probably should do something about that."

Kelly snorted, already pulling a spare top for me from her bag and slapping it against my chest. "Here. Before you scandalize anyone else."

"How about we get out of here?" Aly suggested, smiling. "Seriously, the crowds know it's all over now. The fight was won, and besides the negotiations, everything is done now."

I glanced up as I quickly dressed, noting that a lot of people still stood and stared, shouting stuff—or, in the case of one small but very enthusiastic group of young ladies who were flashing me, throwing something that looked surprisingly like their underwear.

I didn't really get the point of that. I mean, I was there with my significant other. And even if I wasn't, it wasn't like I was going to go collect a thong and try to do a Cinderella routine—find the one destined for me by the perfect fit and all.

The view from here, though, was very nice, I had to admit.

Riiiight up until I noticed the steady, unamused glare I was getting from Kelly.

"What?" I asked, quickly. "I was just surprised, that's all!"

"Uh-huh." She nodded. "I think maybe we need to have rules about taking your clothing off in the arena..." she suggested to Aly, who nodded firmly—not seeing the appreciative grins on the faces of Mike and Chris behind the ladies, who exchanged a fist bump.

We headed off the arena floor, myself and my team—Ciara, the fairies, Rathaharn, and Cerin—all giving a wave now and then, a roar, a few sparkling spells that exploded in the air or whatever.

We strode out of the main arena and into the preparation area, finding it again silent as the doors shut behind us. The roar of the crowd broke down into a distant buzz, and I let out a long sigh.

I'd not even sat down before Jo was there, slapping a hand on my shoulder, apparently examining me through whatever spell she was using these days.

"Low-grade exhaustion, a lack of a great many vitamins and minerals, and some internal bruising. Looks like burns where your lightning has interacted with impurities. Get some rest. No chopping off any heads for a week, and eat a lot of red meat—you need the iron," she proclaimed, a little smile on her lips, before she turned to the others.

"I'm Jo, resident healer for the dungeon. Do any of you have anything you need me to look at straightaway?" she asked, even as her partner John, clapped his hand over Chris's mouth.

Jo took charge of the new dungeon members, and started to check them over as more familiar faces appeared: Robin, with a pair of her wannabe Paladins and several of what I guessed were trainee priests, Ashley and Dante, the twins—both sets—even the trap maker Leighton had made it, though he looked slightly green from the height as they all trooped down into the cleared area.

"My Lord Matt." Robin bowed slightly, clearly uncomfortable and trying—again—to be formal with the Paladin hopefuls and priests with her. "That was…educational."

"That's one word for it," I agreed. "Though I hope none of you are planning to try to clear it all yourselves anytime soon."

"After watching you get carved up like that?" Chris laughed. "Think I'll stick to regular training, thanks."

I turned to introduce my companions, but Aly was already there, helping to break the ice while Jo checked Rathaharn for any residual injuries and spoke quietly with Ciara. The rest of the fairies hovered nearby, clearly uncertain about the crowd of newcomers.

"Right then." I raised my voice slightly. "For those who don't know them, these are our newest citizens. I expect everyone to make them feel welcome." I fixed Chris with a pointed look. "And no trying to recruit them for drinking contests."

"Spoilsport," he muttered, but I could see the grin he was trying to hide.

The din echoing down from the crowd above started to thin out now, though I could guess at the chatter still, all things considered after years of bloodsports not being acceptable behavior. I made a mental note to find out exactly how many people had seen the trial, and more importantly, who those people had represented, as well as how much it'd cost to carry it all out.

"We definitely need to get you all somewhere private, possibly with baths, bed, and food now. We can talk in the morning," Kelly suggested.

I nodded, then paused as something occurred to me. "Wait, how long was I in there?"

"Almost fourteen hours," Aly supplied. "Though time seemed to move differently in some of those spaces. The crystal mine section lasted about four hours from our perspective."

"Fourteen…" I shook my head, sitting down on a nearby bench. "No wonder I'm starving. Anyone else fancy some food?"

The general consensus was enthusiastically positive. And Kelly's hand found mine, squeezing gently.

"Just promise me one thing," she said softly, leaning in and wrapping her arms around me, then kissing me.

"Anything."

"Next time you decide to do something this insane? Take me with you. You've got no idea how nerve-racking it is watching it from the sidelines."

I laughed, pulling her closer and sharing a second quick kiss. "No deal. Though hopefully next time won't involve quite so much getting set on fire."

The others were already being chivvied to their feet to head toward the door, voices overlapping as they discussed what they'd seen. I could hear Chris trying to get Rathaharn to explain exactly how her flail worked and the Paladin crew hanging on her every word, while Mike was deep in conversation with Ciara about fairy magic.

It felt right, somehow. Like pieces falling into place.

Now I just had to figure out what the hell Kh'aan had given me, and why he'd been so secretive about it. But that could wait until after food.

And maybe a drink.

Or several.

That, of course, was where it all went wrong.

The door ahead opened suddenly. The magic that had apparently kept it locked to only our people either had not been reset, or the door not being closed properly by the group that had led the way.

Worst of all was the group that strode in.

The first two—well, that made it clear that the door *might* have been locked, as Akuba and Kaatachi, as our allies, had access to lock and unlock most doors.

The group behind and around them, though, most certainly did-fuckin'-not.

"Ah, a wonderful show! So brave and skilled! Yes, an incredible fight don't cha know. Makes me wish I was a bit younger. I'd bet I could take a few floors on!" Johnstone boomed, his trademarked buffoon grin in full evidence as he pushed forward as if he owned the place.

"An impressive show," Trust agreed flatly, before forcing an obviously fake smile on her face as I glanced at her, then dropping it a half second later.

"Matt, is it?" A newcomer spoke over the general I'd spoken to before—a general, I noticed, being pushed to the back.

"It is." I stood and glared at the group, before turning from them and extending a hand to Kaatachi, who stared at the group around him in irritation. "It's good to see you, my friend," I greeted him, before laughing, a little surprised as Akuba pushed forward, nearly sending Trust flying, before taking my face in her hands and noisily kissing my cheeks.

I hadn't realized that we were at that kind of a level of the relationship, but fuck it, we were allies. I grinned and hugged her, before letting go, then making the point of drawing her and Kaatachi to stand on our side, as the two groups noticeably stayed a little bit apart, a space opening up between us.

"As I say, a terrific performance, simply terrific!" Johnstone enthused stepping forward and thrusting out a hand. "Incredible…!"

He smiled widely, and I felt the jab of a thumb into my back—no doubt Kelly—before I sighed and took his hand in mine.

"Impressive technology!" He chortled, before dropping his voice to a conspiratorial whisper. "How much of it was real?"

I looked at him for a long second before breaking my hand free and sliding it into my bag of holding, turning from him and completely ignoring Trust as she tried to get my hand next.

Instead, I pulled free the blueprint for the armor and handed it over to Finn, speaking clearly enough that it could be heard by all.

"Finn, this is a blueprint for the armor that the orcs I fought were wearing. It's for you. Learn what you can from it, and improve on the armor for all our people, please."

"Got it!" he replied happily, grabbing the blueprint, grinning.

It was a rolled piece of blue parchment in the original state, seemingly tied with a black ribbon and a line of incomprehensible glyphs and runes glowing along its length.

As I'd taken it from my bag, I'd surreptitiously checked it, finding a big red X over it as I tried to absorb it into the dungeon. That made it clear, to me at least, that it was a crafter-specific blueprint that couldn't be copied.

He untied the ribbon and unrolled the scroll, before sucking in a deep breath as it burst into light, then flooded into his eyes, ears, and mouth, making him stagger, gasp, and jerk. He blinked rapidly, apparently stunned.

"Finn?" Patrick asked quickly, holding his partner. "Finn, can you hear me…?"

There were a few seconds of silence as Finn stared, unseeing, clearly still working with the magic.

I sighed, turning to Chris, figuring I might as well get on with this now. "Oi." I grunted at him, before dragging the long, slightly curved blade of Thorn out of my bag. I extended it to him, hilt first. "Don't say I never give you anything," I grudgingly said in the traditional way any northern male gives anything to those they truly care about.

"You find this on the bathroom floor and thought of me again?" He took it and looked the blade over. His eyes widened slightly before he got control of himself again. "Yeah, all right, I *suppose* I can take this off your hands."

"Good man." I shrugged the whole thing off, then grinned, as I saw the real thanks in his eyes.

"Matt, I—"

I shook my head. "No need for that, brother. You've had my back long enough I think I owe you this and a lot more," I said softly. "Thank you, Chris. There's more to come as well…"

I explained about the primal core, and the potential for it. His eyes lit up, even as the London lot practically started to salivate over it.

"Perhaps we could look at a trade…" Trust interrupted.

I glared at her. "It's a gift," I said firmly. "The kind of gift that I give to my friends, knowing damn well that they'll use it to increase our overall strength, not just wasting it, fucking hiding it away."

"What a rush…!" Finn suddenly gasped, blinking dazedly and almost collapsing as he finished integrating the scroll's knowledge. Then he grinned as Patrick helped him up. "You all…you do whatever you're doing—I need to craft!"

With that said, he edged around the crowd, and Patrick rolled his eyes, starting after him.

"Nope!" I barked. "Stop right there, you bugger!"

"But—"

"I've got more!"

"Oh?!" Finn was back, elbowing Johnstone and Trust aside quickly enough he could have been teleported. "More please?" He held his hands out hopefully, making me think of that scene from *Oliver*.

"Now this one…" I pulled the multitool out and hefted it, before yanking it back as he tried to grab it. "Ah! Down!" I snapped, as the others laughed.

"But…" He whined, his eyes tracking the multitool desperately.

“This is a copy of a fucking copy. It’s possibly highly dangerous and NOT to be used outside of controlled areas…ones that you set up in the dungeon and you have the glassine help you with, all right?” I demanded. “They warned that a side effect could be igniting the atmosphere if you fuck with it, so you be careful, and do *not* burn up my planet!”

“I’ll be good!” Finn assured me hastily, taking it a lot more gingerly, before squinting at me again. “Anything else?”

“Just this.” I handed over the chain as well and glared at him. “It’s called the Chain of Binding. I don’t know how it works, so I don’t recommend any kinky shit!”

“I make no promises,” he deadpanned. He grinned some more as I dug into my bag of tricks and pulled out the elemental essences and passed them over as well; he made a break for the exit as I sighed and waved he could go.

“I’ll keep an eye on him,” Patrick assured me, before pausing and looking down at Johnstone. “Oh, look.” He said softly, “The man who had me kidnapped and fuckin’ tortured.”

That comment brought a pool of silence that spread out as Johnstone gaped then tried to shrug the whole thing off.

“Ah, ah…a case of mistaken identity!” He laughed, awkwardly, as Patrick glared before moving off. Finn had paused by the door, reversing direction as he glared daggers at the rotund politician.

“No,” I said. “He was tortured by one of the assassins and murderers you sent to try to take over our dungeon, so here’s an idea. How about you—”

“I think we’re all a little tired right now!” Aly said loudly as Kelly gripped my hand tight and squeezed as hard as she could, even as Patrick grabbed Finn and hustled him out of the door.

“I agree,” Kelly said quickly. “Perhaps a meeting another time would be an idea?”

“No, I think a quick meeting now should result in better and more honest conversations.” The third guy smiled at the way that Johnstone was now floundering. “My name is Morris Macmillan, and I’m the Earl of Stockport.”

“Nice to meet you.” My glare made sure it was clear that not only was I fucking unimpressed, but I was lying about it being nice to meet him.

“Well, it’s certainly impressive to meet you, and I have to thank you for arranging that little spectacle out there for us all. I mean, I assume that it was arranged for us as well as the entertainment of the masses?” He quirked an eyebrow.

He, unlike Johnstone, was tall and slim, with a solidly military air, and broad shoulders. He was clearly retired, or had been before the fall, judging from the grey hair and the wrinkles. But he still managed an air of formal amusement and professionalism, despite his age.

There was also a hint that he’d be the kind of a guy who looks distinguished right up until death, rather than going to fat.

Add in that he was fairly muscled, and the ramrod-straight back… yeah, ex-military and probably spent at least an hour a day working out and watching what he ate at all times.

As soon as I locked eyes with him, I felt churlish and rude for not introducing myself properly, and for tarring him with the same brush as Johnstone.

A quick glance at Ashley—who stood to one side—and an understanding shake of the head later, and I sighed. The fucker wasn't even using an ability like hers.

He was just that firm and forthright. Fucker.

"I'm Matt." I forced a smile. "The Dungeon Lord…or Dungeon Warmancer now, anyway. Yes, the show was a bit of both."

"Interesting, Matt. And may I ask why?" He shook my hand then stepped back as the others fell silent around him.

"Because it shows you both what we can do and the rewards, and it gave our people a way to blow off some steam."

"Perhaps you could explain that a little better?" he prodded, before stepping forward and bowing slightly to Kelly. "Morris, Earl of Stockport at your service, young lady." He smiled.

That, of course, broke the ice as she smiled and introduced herself to apparently a "real" noble, not just a self-proclaimed cockwomble like Johnstone, who'd been pushed none-too-gently aside.

The next few minutes were filled with people saying their names, and I finally gave in, summoning a table in the middle of the bloody changing rooms, no less, and some seats.

Once that was done and people started to sit down, I summoned some drinks.

The drinks went down well, but more than that, the way that Aly asked each person in turn what food or drink they wanted? Well, the way that we produced them on spec and with a bare heartbeat's delay really made the point clear.

"A whisky," Johnstone proclaimed loudly, still trying to score points. "I know you won't have much to choose from, so just whatever you consider good."

"Oh, you're right," Chris chimed in. "Not much choice, really. Personally, I like the Brora 1977. It's a cheeky little number with a wonderful nose—limited now, of course. There were only a few dozen casks left in the world, you know, before all of this kicked off."

He paused to look at Johnstone before going on. "Then we got our hands on it, and now there's as much as we fuckin' want there to be," he finished.

Johnstone stared at him with that, before coughing out a laugh, clearly unsure whether it was a joke or not.

"And that brings up an interesting point," the earl said cheerfully. "Oh, and I'd love one of those, if possible?"

"Sure, mate." Chris grinned at him, deliberately speaking as colloquially as possible. "Nee bother."

"My thanks." The earl took the glass as it appeared before him, then smiled as Chris also summoned both a bowl with whisky rocks in it, and a jug of ice.

The whisky rocks were carved stones, chilled as low as possible to replace having to put ice in your drink and water it down. And the water…well, that was in case you did want to water it down. Whisky never did much for me, but I still knew the basics.

"The point?" I asked the earl, and he nodded, sipping his drink neat, before letting out a sigh of pleasure.

"Oh my boy." He shook his head. "It's been nigh on thirty years since I last treated myself to a glass of this, and knowing that the cask in my cellar is now both less unique and safe to be consumed is both a blessing and a curse." He sighed, before thanking Chris. "You've got excellent taste, young man. Thank you again."

"You're very welcome." Chris beamed, apparently deciding that the "northern barbarian" image was no longer needed, as he liked the older guy.

I noticed the way he summoned more glasses for the others, popping them in front of anyone who showed an interest, without comment, before "accidentally" making Johnstone ask again, as he'd apparently "forgotten" his drink.

I noted the amused look the earl gave us at that, before he started speaking again.

"So, as I was saying, you set this up as a demonstration, both of your personal power—a very impressive one, at that—and as a demonstration of the potential of a dungeon should we achieve gaining control over one."

"We did," I agreed.

"We felt that a demonstration of the potential value was worth the investment," Kelly said, taking over. "As an example, should you wish, you could buy access to this dungeon, both for any training teams you wished to send in, and to deploy mining and harvesting teams."

"Harvesting?" He looked at her.

"Yes, not only are the reliquaries that you may or may not have seen on the death of each creature tied to their killer—they can contain a great many items that are worth collecting, from crafting ingredients to gold, to, well…" Kelly glanced at me.

I nodded, reaching into my bag of holding to pull out a handful of coins, which I placed on the table, a packet of crisps, and then I handed Kelly the ruby, getting a grin from her as she examined it.

"My God!" Johnstone gasped, staring at the ruby that was both brilliantly polished and the size of a hen's egg.

"As I was saying…" She kissed my cheek, then offered the ruby up to be examined. "All sorts of rewards are available, including potions, spellbooks, and more. Those are taken from the reliquaries, and they offer a random item of loot each time, with the higher a ranking enemy, the higher the chance of valuable loot."

"As I didn't kill the leader of the Scepiniir—he killed himself—I didn't get loot for him or his true guards," I clarified. "These are what I claimed from the bodies of the others. Now, there's also a way for sentients to leave—"

I broke off, and Kelly glanced at me as I turned to Ciara, who sat on a pile of cushions on a chair several spaces over to my right.

"You just remembered?" she asked, and I sighed, nodding. "Want me to go get them?"

"Do you mind?" I asked.

She shook her head. "It's right that they be escorted out. And don't worry—they'll be amused, not offended."

"Thank you," I said, as she rose to her feet, before zipping from the room; the other fairies went with her. "The glassine that surrendered to me are still in the dungeon as well," I explained to everyone else.

"Ah, well, they're also a boon." Kelly nodded. "They're a race of crafters, so should any of you be able to rescue more of them—"

"They won't be able to," I said quickly. "Sorry, people, that's not a case of 'I won't let you'—it's a case of 'you can't.' Or, at least, not any of your party." I nodded to the London lot. "Only a Dungeon Lord can run the trial dungeon, and the trial dungeon is rearranged for the run each time, with sentient and sapient dungeon beings taking the place of the unthinking dungeon-born. It makes them much harder to defeat, but the rewards are higher. And if you can convince them to join you, and you have the mana and dungeon points needed to bind them, they can leave the dungeon, adding their strength and experience to your side."

We all glanced over at Rathaharn, who smiled, before inclining her head. "Rathaharn 'Tar Co-Norten, warrior," she said simply.

I grinned at the looks on the faces of the others around the room. "She brings both her skills, background, and her personal equipment, as well as her knowledge of the wider galaxy and the galactic situation with her," I pointed out, before moving on.

"The other way that you can harvest in the dungeon is things like the walls of the dvork smelter. Not sure if you could see from your position, but several of them were inlaid with precious ores, and obviously the materials like the molten metal and the presses can be used and looted."

"As can the plants, the remains of the dungeon creatures you fight, and the mana crystal mine," Aly added. "It's quite possible for you to send a team in and leave a short while later with a spellbook, enough materials for your own forge, and who knows what else. As we say, it's random."

"And the cost to take part in the dungeon 'dive,' I think you call it?" the earl asked.

"Depends on the number of entrants, if you're looking to do a trial dungeon." I glanced at Akuba and Kaatachi. "If you do that, the current configuration will be changed entirely. You'd need a Dungeon Lord to go with you, and a number of spectators. If you bring a large crowd, all paying to watch, then the individual cost will be lower as that will cover some of the expense. But you'll also understand we need to make a profit too."

"Of course." The earl nodded. "So, your plan with the spectators and the high technology items they paid with was to cover the costs of the deployment and to provide a relief for the many distressed people, is that correct?"

"It is." I nodded.

"Then, I'd suggest that you also include a section nearby where they can rest at their ease, possibly a hotel with some rooms?" he suggested. "We'd be willing to cover a portion of that cost in exchange for favorable entrance rates."

"Aly and Kelly will be best to negotiate those details." I nodded. "I tend to have a more streamlined approach to such things."

"Oh?"

"He's kept ready to kill and conquer things," Chris translated. "He's not very good at diplomacy, and he gets angry easily. We try not to let him get too worked up though, as there are so many breakable things around."

Several people nodded, and Johnstone smirked, apparently thinking I was being made out to be the muscle-bound idiot of the dungeon. A figurehead that he could work around.

"You know, like towns, cities, and nearby continents," Chris finished with an evil grin directed solely at Trust and Johnstone. "He's the Lord of Lightning, and can literally summon storms to eradicate his enemies in their thousands. Best not to piss him off any more than you already have, eh?"

"Quite," the earl said with a stifled smile. "As such, perhaps I can make our position here clear?"

"Please do," Kelly agreed.

"Capital. So, I was asked to come and speak with you personally, to make it clear that there are several factions in the city of London, and while some may have been"—he glanced at Johnstone—"less than helpful, not all are against you, nor unwilling to work together."

"Glad to hear it."

"Both sides have suffered losses, through regrettable misunderstandings, and it would behoove us to try to find a path forward. We—that is, my faction, along with a sufficiently large percentage of the Parliament—would like to move forward with an agreement to work together. To share information, resources, and to grow, mutually.

"As such, and as one of the costs you were demanding, I believe you were asking about the names and numbers of the surviving families of your soldiers?"

"We were," I said.

"Then, as a gesture of goodwill, please pass this along." He reached behind him and took a list of names and handwritten notes, passed to him by the general I'd dealt with before. "We've not approached these individuals, and the list may be, I'm sorry to say, partially out of date. Names on it were verified where possible, but some have moved on and regrettably others have taken their own lives. But it is as accurate as we can make it."

"What is it going to cost us to make contact with these people?" I asked, and he smiled.

"I'm not a monster, dear boy. If they wish to leave the safety of London and join you, they will be helped to gather at a set location, and then permitted to leave, discharged into your care, with no cost attached."

"That's very reasonable of you," I said slowly.

"They will lessen a drain upon our own resources considerably," he admitted. "Though, if you wished to reciprocate, a shipment of medical supplies or ammunition would be highly appreciated," he suggested.

I glanced at Kelly, who nodded. "We can sort that," she agreed.

"Excellent." He smiled. "Well, I feel this has been a step in the right direction. Perhaps we should leave it at that?"

"Sounds good to me," I agreed, surprised. I'd expected them to gouge us for the list, then fuck us over as we were taking "their" people.

The argument that we'd be lessening the load on their supplies was one that Aly had pointed out to me already before this; she'd been expecting to have to use it to argue with, not have it offered and then dismissed.

He stood. The others with him did the same, though they looked markedly less happy.

I did so too, offering a hand, which was shook, before he smiled one last time, having bid the rest of our side goodbye as well.

"Perhaps dinner one evening would be possible?" he suggested suddenly to me. "My lady wife is always curious about my excursions, and I know she'd be interested to meet you both?"

"That would be lovely," Kelly agreed, beaming. And just like that, a date was to be set, and they all trailed out.

Best of all, from my point of view, was the hugely pissed-off look on Johnstone and Trust's faces. But as I sat back down, the group reduced to just my people, Akuba and Kaatachi, and two of their personal guards, along with Rathaharn and Cerin, who was laid in the corner, snoring already, I couldn't help but feel that had all been too easy.

"Is it just me…" I started, then paused as Kelly raised a hand.

"No, it's not just you," she said. "That was far too easy."

"The earl seems genuine enough," Aly mused, summoning fresh drinks for everyone. "But there's definitely something else going on."

Kaatachi leaned forward. His massive frame made the simple chair creak. "They seek advantage through appearance of cooperation. A classic tactic."

"The list appears real, though," Akuba added, her eyes gleaming. "I could smell no deception there."

"That's what worries me," I admitted. "Why give us something that valuable without trying to squeeze us for everything they could get?"

Chris snorted into his whisky. "Because they're hoping we'll lower our guard? I mean, that Johnstone prick looked ready to shit himself when I mentioned the storms."

"Speaking of storms." Kelly turned to me, her expression serious. "What happened in there with Kh'aan? The way you changed at the end…"

I felt the weight of the crystal he'd given me in my pocket. "Yeah, about that. We should probably talk somewhere more private." I glanced meaningfully at our allies. "No offense."

"None taken," Kaatachi rumbled. "We have matters to discuss with our own people. The demonstration was…enlightening."

"That's one word for it." Akuba grinned. "Though I notice you didn't show everything you could do."

"Nope, though I'm happy to talk to you about it, and about the methods I've used to advance my evolution. It's not you I'm worried about right now…it's others," I admitted, smiling. "Although I'm pretty sure you've got more tricks up your sleeve than you let on."

She laughed, a sound like silver bells. "As all good allies should! Come, my love. Let us leave them to their plotting."

"I agree." Kaatachi sighed, before standing. "The offer of access to the trial dungeon to run…it still stands? Not for us, but for our teams, provided the cost is covered?"

"Of course," I said quickly.

"Excellent. Oh, and the advice on evolution?"

"Yeah?"

"We choose to decline for now."

"Oh…okay?" I frowned.

"We wish to see what we can discover on our own, then we may compare notes." Akuba smiled, her brilliant white teeth gleaming. "That way, we may both make discoveries."

"Sounds good to me." I smiled.

"Akuba, just reach out to me," Kelly said.

The ladies smiled at each other, before the pair, flanked by their guards, left the room.

As they rose to leave, Rathaharn stirred from where she'd been quietly observing. "My lord, if I may…"

"Just Matt," I corrected automatically. "And yeah?"

"This 'earl'…he reminds me of the handlers who worked with the more dangerous specimens in the menageries. Always so polite, so reasonable…right up until the cage door closed."

I considered that. "You think we're being caged?"

"I think," she said carefully, "that one does not survive long in politics by being exactly what they appear to be."

That was a cheery thought. Before I could respond, Ciara zipped back into the room, leading her fellow fairies and three crystalline figures that were clearly the glassine.

"Got them!" she announced proudly. "Though they've not stopped asking to be directed to their crafting quarters."

"That we can do." I paused, looking around the room.

"How about I take care of that?" Jo offered. "I can take them with me, and then you can all bring this mothers meeting to a close, and go take some showers, get some food, and we can talk tomorrow?"

"Yes, please!" I agreed, letting loose a sigh.

"Then that's it. Everyone else, with me!" she called out.

I smiled, before raising my voice to be heard over the scraping of chairs. "Kelly, Aly, Mike, Jo, John, Chris, Dante, and Ashley, meeting tomorrow morning in the control room after breakfast, please," I requested, and they all nodded, the others hopefully not offended at being left out. I bit my lip, and added another name. "And Robin as well, please!"

CHAPTER THIRTY

The night when we got back to the Newcastle dungeon passed far quicker than I liked, especially considering I'd been in serious need of a long shower before Kelly was going to let me anywhere near her.

I had the shower, we attempted to place in the bedroom Olympics—I got a silver, while Kelly took gold this time—and then a second shower, followed by a trip to dinner, and then the pool.

By the time we made it to the pool, we were all a bit exhausted, and I was enjoying that post-coital general goodwill-to-the-world situation, which was the only excuse for the terrible idea that occurred to me at that point.

As we already had Kelly and me in the pool, along with our closest friends, which just happened to be Aly and Mike, Chris and Becky, Dante and Ashley, the only people missing were Jo and John, and Robin.

Kelly sent them a message, a simple matter of slipping into the dungeon sense and locating the nearest dungeon-born to them, then giving them a message to send over. Soon enough, all of us were laid in the pool, enjoying the water.

Well, I certainly was, and most of us were.

Dante was still clearly highly self-conscious about the fact he was perhaps a third to half the weight, never mind the muscle mass, of any of the rest of the guys. That probably wasn't helped by Chris occasionally telling him things like he had "a real purdy mouth."

Ashley was her typical exact opposite self, barely contained by her bikini, which in turn only qualified as a bikini in description because there was no way she was wearing dental floss to the pool.

Kelly, Becky, and Aly were playing a game with us, trying to act all disgusted when Ashley bounced around in the pool and nearly beat someone unconscious with her inbuilt upgraded flotation devices, while laughing their arses off at the same time.

Jo and John were typical of the medical profession and the police, unconcerned in the slightest, and having seen more and worse things by breakfast most days than "normal" people saw in their entire lives.

Lastly, Robin stayed neck-deep in the pool, wearing a full swimsuit and apparently incredibly self-conscious about the fact that her figure lent itself more to muscle and a flatter chest than the other ladies.

"Okay, people." I sighed after a little floaty time. "Let's get the meeting brought to order."

"Damn, what do I need to beat to call for order?" Chris asked Becky. "The gravel, right? I mean, I could hit it with my 'hammer' but…"

"But nobody would notice." She sighed. "Hush, dear, the adults are talking."

"But I—"

"Look at the pretty girl." She put her hand on the top of Chris's head and turned it slowly to point him at Ashley, who promptly bounced in the water and derailed his brain, until Becky pretended outrage at him being caught looking at Ashley.

The rest of the group laughed, and Ashley took a swig of her drink, nodding sagely. "Knew I'd get him eventually," she murmured.

"Order!" I called through laughter, before shaking my head. "Okay, look, we were going to do this in the control room tomorrow, but we might as well get most of it out of the way now. There's some new people who have joined us…"

"Ciara is a wonderful addition." Jo spoke up.

"Already?" I asked, surprised.

"She's basically a mother hen to the other fairies, and they all follow her lead. She likes order and they all like chaos, so it sort of works. But starting tomorrow, she's going to be leading the fairies on tours of Saltwell Park, healing everyone she can find and essentially doing a little 'hearts and minds.'"

"Awesome." I grinned. "Oh, and ladies, she's really pissed with Drak…said she wants to deal with him as the dungeon liaison with the freed dungeon-born. That okay with you?" I winced internally, aware I'd already agreed to it.

"Oh gods, yes," Kelly grunted. "If he's off our plate, it's a bonus!"

"Well, that's a relief." I nodded. "So yeah, the voidcat I named Tentacles, though his name is apparently Cerin and—"

"Tentacles," Aly said flatly. "You called a cat with tentacles 'Tentacles'?"

"I tried other names…he ignored me. Turns out he can understand he just chooses to be a dick, he later told the fairies that his name was Cerin. Mind you, with their twisted sense of humor they might be lying about that." I shrugged. "Anyway, he's a voidcat. Means he can do stealth, he's got bitey tentacles, and he can do short-range teleports, I think…although that might not be true. I don't remember him doing them at any point…"

"Might be a talent they get further on?" Dante suggested.

"Yeah, but why do I think that?" I mused. "Fuck it. He's a hell of a hunter, and although he was useless against some of the enemies, he was fantastic against others. If he's happy to help just by patrolling the dungeon walls and hunting shit, I'm happy with that."

"Me too," Aly agreed. "There's been a marked upswing in the frequency of attacks since you took Jack away."

"What's happening with him?" Mike asked. "If you don't want him, seriously, don't leave him broken. Give him to us and we'll make the most of him on base defense, if nothing else."

"I do have a use for him," I clarified. "A hell of a use. Hopefully I'll be able to go through with it tomorrow, though be warned…" I looked at Kelly and Aly. "I'm going to need a lot of materials and mana."

"We'll see." Kelly sighed. "Behave yourself and we can talk about increasing your allowance."

"Yes, mum," I said sarcastically, then winced. "Nah, that's all kinds of wrong…*stepmom*?" I suggested waggling my eyebrows sugestively, getting a dangerous glare from her. "I mean, a little roleplay now and then is healthy…" I grinned and then shut up fast as she replied.

"Go any further down that road, and 'healthy' won't be the word used to describe anything to do with our sex lives," she warned me.

"So!" I clapped my hands together then summoned a drink, changing the subject as some of our friends laughed. "Moving quickly on…the dungeon was a success, right?"

"Very much so," Aly agreed. "The costs are still being confirmed. Some weren't clear, and there's a slight uptick in the input that might or might not have had anything to do with your actions. But overall, we're looking at a profit of around four million mana."

"And that's repeatable?" I asked.

"If anything, it'll increase." She smiled. "We won't need to build the stadium again, after all, and although the dungeon will need to be reconfigured every so often, as it is, it's massively profitable. Even if we don't allow any others to use it and just harvest the nodes as they regrow, there'd be a solid profit. Add in the teams that can challenge the dungeon, and as long as there are a minimum of a hundred visitors to watch, the costs will be entirely covered.

"Obviously, if you want to increase the level of the creatures they'll face, that'll change," Aly clarified quickly. "That's worked out on a standard level of fifteen to twenty as a maximum, and a reasonable test."

"So, as long as we do say, a monthly battle, sell tickets and so on, and hold it over an entire weekend so people can gather and come in larger numbers, then it's worth it. If we then allow the other Dungeon Lords to use it whenever it's not in use, then that'll increase its viability as well as increase our standing in the community," I suggested, getting some nods of agreement.

"Yes, and it'll help pay for the second stage," Kelly said. "As we've discussed before using the dungeon-born as group troops for battle, training to deploy armies, and so on, that'll be the next area that begins construction, with an outdoor arena that'll have separate seating and a raised area.

"Mainly thanks to the screens, we'll be able to have people sitting comfortably, while entire armies of undead—low-level ones for practice at first—are deployed."

"Sounds good. I trust you guys to work with that. It's not really my skill set, but we're desperately in need of it. So, moving on…the dungeon was a success and the interaction with the London lot was a surprisingly good one. What's everyone's thoughts on that?" I asked.

"That we should bury Johnstone and Trust in a barrel of leeches up to their eyebrows, nail the lid shut, and roll it down a hill?" Chris suggested.

"Yes, I like it. I want to do it, but it's not helpful." I nodded to him, before cursing. I'd just shifted back and moved to get more comfortable, and Kelly next to me had moved at the same time. The low wave had poured over the rim of my glass and my rum now floated away in a cloud of amber.

"Let me get that." Kelly kissed my cheek and tapped my now full-of-pool-water glass. It sparkled, flashed, and there was a new one, positively two-thirds full of rum, and with barely enough Coke to change the color.

"I love you." I smiled, getting another kiss, before I took a sip and went on. "Now, who trusts the earl?"

Not a single hand rose.

"Ashley?" I asked, and she nodded, knowing what I was looking for.

"As near as I can tell, there's no ability being used at all, or at least not by him," she said seriously. "There was a weave that I could roughly sense from the back of the group, but it was focused on Trust, Johnstone, and their cronies, and appeared to be more used to keep them quiet than have any effect on us. I could be wrong, though." She took a drink from her beer, while beside her, still looking stunned by his good fortune, her boyfriend Dante drank from his fruity cocktail glass.

"So, what you're saying," Mike shifted in the water, making small waves ripple out, "is that Trust and Johnstone were being controlled?"

"Not exactly," Ashley corrected, taking another sip of her beer. "More like…muzzled. Someone didn't trust them to keep their mouths shut."

"Smart someone," Chris muttered. "Though they missed a spot with that 'impressive technology' comment."

I nodded, remembering Johnstone's attempt to dismiss what he'd seen as special effects. "The earl didn't correct him, either. Just let him make an ass of himself."

"Speaking of the earl," Kelly interjected. "What do we think about this dinner invitation?"

"Trap," Robin said immediately from her corner of the pool, before going bright red as we all looked at her. "I'm sorry…" she started, and I shook my head.

"You're here for a reason, Robin. If you want to be a Paladin, and more to the point, the leader of that group, even for now, then you need to step up and earn that spot. So, what did you mean by that?"

"Uhm…that it's a trap? Or at least, an opportunity for intelligence gathering?" she suggested, still bright red.

"On both sides," Aly agreed. "But we'd be idiots not to go. The chance to see inside their leadership structure…"

"We can have it in our territory," I said firmly. "That way, we can create whatever food they want, and we're not at risk of poison."

"Sounds good." Kelly sighed. "There's times I'd kill for a normal dinner out, though. Do you realize we never went on that date?"

"We did!" I said, shocked. "We went for drinks and…oh."

"We *met* in the bar, and then weeks later, we met again, and I just…moved in." She shrugged. "Don't get me wrong, I love you, and our life, but a real date, somewhere that neither of us is in control, would be kinda nice. You know, where you have to make small talk and have a shitty waiter who forgets half the order and still expects a tip, while trying to stare down my top."

"Oh wow, you make it sound so attractive." I snorted. "And we had a date, remember? In the aerie?"

"You know what I mean," She waved the distinction aside. "But that's what it was like. And sometimes I miss that shit, you know?"

"Being ogled by other men?" I asked.

"No! Well, it never bothered me, to be fair." She looked over at Ashley and held her drink out; they clinked them together and the pair chorused "*Free drinks*" before she went on. "I just miss the normalcy, that's all."

"Well, let's see what London holds," I agreed. "So, with London in mind, what's the plan for the core?"

"We have a full core almost ready to go with a containment jacket of mana crystals all formed around it." Aly switched to professional mode. "It's currently getting the final layer added, and will be ready for the morning. Plus, I've spoken to the Scepiniir scouts you recruited. They apparently had access to most of the city, even through the worst of the most recent fights, and their contempt for most of the guards is palpable."

"Right?" I agreed. "And that means…?"

"They're happy to escort you into the heart of the city…for a price," she clarified. "They're convinced that the section of the city we've identified as the most appropriate for the dungeon is easily reachable. Apparently, there's a lot of monsters spawning there, so the guard population is in and out a lot, but it's getting absolutely trashed on a regular basis. It should be perfect for us, if we can get in now."

"And that price is…?" I frowned.

"Manageable," she replied, clearly not thinking it was worth discussing. "Food, supplies, and permissions to roam our territory. Give me a month, and they'll be willing to swear oaths."

"Speaking of which, we need to do that again." I sighed. "There were a lot of people we've added of late and—"

"We'll sort it," Kelly said. "This is administration, Matt. Trust me, we can arrange it. And when we've looked over the oath? We don't need you involved at all. We can swear in your place."

"Oh, thank fuck for that," I muttered. "Yes, please."

"Done." She smiled at me, and I wrapped my arm around her, pulling her in tight as I kissed the side of her head.

"Then I vote we do it. Anyone else?" I glanced around. "If it all turns out later that we've been wrong, then we can hand over control or do something at that point, but for now? I think we're best off going ahead with the plan."

"I agree. We need to meet them for dinner, try to move forward. The earl seemed like a good guy, and I'd like to think it's genuine, but they're going to be sending the equivalent of a professional negotiator and someone used to dealing at that level. None of us are. So, I think let's take it as we go," Kelly agreed, lifting one hand from the warm waters that we floated in.

"I agree. Hopefully he's all that he showed, but I think we need to plan as if he isn't…then all our surprises will be nice ones. Although," Ashley added, "if they wanted to try something, they had plenty of chances today. Why wait?"

"Probably because they know from the shit they pulled already that we don't trust them," Chris suggested. "Spend some time building a relationship, then try again? Oh, and I agree."

"Possibly. Fuck it, I'm in, and vote we wait and see what happens with the dinner," Mike said.

The others voted as well, all but Robin agreeing with the plan. Eventually she lifted a hand and nodded as well.

"I don't really understand it all," she admitted nervously, "but I'm in."

The conversation drifted into speculation about London's political structure, with occasional side conversations that eventually took over the main one in critiquing their fashion choices—Trust's attempt at a smile had apparently traumatized several of our people. I let it flow around me, enjoying the normalcy of it all.

Shit-talking the other side without pause was a tradition, after all.

Eventually, Jo stretched and yawned. "Much as I hate to break this up, some of us have early shifts tomorrow."

"And some of us," John added with a meaningful look at me, "need rest to recover from having their arm chopped off."

"I got better!" I protested for the second time in a few hours.

"Still," Kelly said firmly, "we should probably call it a night. Command meeting after breakfast to discuss…other matters."

There were knowing looks from those who'd be attending, but thankfully no one pressed about what I'd been given during the trial. As people started to climb out of the pool, I caught Robin's eye.

"A moment?" I asked quietly.

She nodded, dipping deep into the water so that only her head was above it, hanging back as the others gathered their things.

"Is this about my being a Paladin?" she asked once we had some privacy.

"Partly," I admitted. "But also about what you saw today. I want your tactical assessment as well as a religious one when we talk next—you've got a different perspective than most of us."

She nodded seriously. "I'll have a full breakdown ready. Though I have to say, that flail technique was…interesting."

"Tell me about it." I grinned. "Just wait until you meet Rathaharn properly. I think you two will have a lot to talk about. And if you can induct her into the team, that'll give you a lot of experience that you're just not going to get anywhere else."

"You think she would be interested?" Robin sat up in surprise.

"I think she's a realist. Being able to bring additional power to the table is always good. And if not? She's still probably the most experienced person we're likely to be able to speak to for now in fighting in heavy armor. Honestly, I think that we need to recruit her as a heavy armor trainer for your team, if nothing else."

"That would be…well, it'd be wonderful!" Robin enthused.

"I think she's also the kind of a warrior who could bring strength and depth to your team in terms of weapons as well. I'll speak to Rhodes about…actually, no." I cut myself off. "Robin, do you want this role? To lead the Paladins, I mean. I'm sorry that I'm not involved more than I have been…there's always so much to do, though. Do you want to lead them, or do you want me to find another?"

"I want to!" she blurted, then colored, seemingly embarrassed at the declaration.

"Good. Then you need to go to Rhodes first thing in the morning and tell her about Rathaharn. Explain her potential, the skills and what you want, and ask her for help. Instead of me ordering it, you try to convince her. It'll be good experience for you, and Rhodes will help."

The thing that I left unsaid was that I was well aware that Robin liked to hide at the back of the group and was uncomfortable in her own skin at the best of times. She needed to be dragged out of that, and having someone like Rhodes helping her directly to grow would be massive.

Sure, I could order it, but it was time my Paladin started to stand on her own two feet again. She'd already begun trying to recruit, and if she hadn't included Rhodes in her training plans…well, she damn well was missing a trick there.

Kelly saw that I was done, and walked over to the nearby pool steps, towel in hand. "Coming?" she called, and I nodded.

"Yeah." I stood, and water cascaded off me. "Early start tomorrow! Think about what I said," I said to Robin, before striding out of the pool and taking the towel from Kelly. The steam that filled the air around the pool as the heated water met the icy-cold air was all-enveloping, and probably a good thing, considering the fact that I found within a few steps I could have etched glass with my nipples.

I heroically kept my eyes forward as I toweled off, getting a robe on, and didn't respond in the slightest as Chris stared past me at Ashley getting into her own robe.

Lucky as well, considering a half second later, Becky had his ear in her hand and was leading him off for a good talking-to.

As we headed back to our quarters, I felt the weight of the crystal in the pocket of my shorts, where I'd moved it for safekeeping. I'd considered leaving it in our quarters. There was definitely something important on it, so I just didn't feel comfortable leaving it yet. Tomorrow would bring its own challenges, but for now, I was content to just enjoy the peace we'd earned.

And maybe convince Kelly to go for gold again.

Spoiler: this time *I* took gold…although I won, there were definitely benefits to the various podium places that night.

CHAPTER THIRTY-ONE

Even after Jo had told me to take it easy the day before, I was up early, having slept surprisingly well, possibly because for the first time in what felt like forever, I was lighter on my feet again thanks to the Olympic try-outs.

Kelly, as always, wasn't exactly a morning person, and had grown—once again—used to having the entire bed to starfish in, so when I'd woken up, it was to her sprawled across me.

On the other hand, she was incredibly hot, blonde, and naked, so you know, waking up to that meant that I *had* to wake her in the right way. And by the time we'd finished and showered again, we'd both had a nice workout.

It probably counted as weightlifting as well when I'd picked her up and pinned her to the wall, and she'd certainly been bent into some great positions that had to qualify as yoga at various times.

Regardless, though, it meant that by the time we'd finally made it into the shower and gotten cleaned up, had breakfast in the canteen and made it to the control room, Aly, Mike, Ashley, Clarissa, and Markus were all gathered already, waiting for us.

If anything, Clarissa and Markus were about to leave, so I had to apologize for the delay.

"Morning, all!" I said cheerily. "Sorry about the delay. Jo had insisted that I rest after the whole losing my arm thing yesterday, and I slept in," I lied blatantly.

A snort came from Aly as she looked at the way her sister-in-law sat down gingerly in her seat. "Yeah, and an early morning 'exercise session' does wonders for your health, doesn't it?" she suggested, getting a slightly red-faced grin in return from Kelly. "Looking for something?" she asked, seeing me digging in a pocket.

"Yeah, that crystal..." The damn thing had gotten wedged and ripped the pocket as I pulled it out of my jeans. We all stared at the seemingly innocuous item. "Should probably figure out what was so important that Warmaster Kh'aan wanted us to know."

Kelly shifted on her seat beside me as I activated it, wincing as she pulled her legs up under herself and summoned a drink to hand.

Light spilled forth, coalescing into floating text that scrolled endlessly across a large screen that hung in the air between us all, the magic of the dungeon providing a perfectly visible screen no matter the position of the reader around the rounded table.

"*The Sacred and Inviolable Rules of Scepiniir Integration and Conduct within Dungeon Environments*," Kelly read aloud. "Well, that sounds thrilling."

"You have no idea," I muttered, scanning the first few entries. "Listen to this: '*Rule 1: No Scepiniir may be compelled to wear footwear that inhibits proper grooming of toe-claws.*'"

"Please tell me you're joking."

"*Rule 2: Dining facilities must provide adequate scratching areas within five meters of any food preparation area.*"

"They're cats," Kelly said slowly. "They're literally space cats with a honor code."

"*Rule 3: All critical combat encounters must include appropriate dramatic lighting.*" I couldn't help but laugh. "Okay, some of these have to be jokes, right?"

We spent the next few minutes reading through increasingly bizarre regulations. Everything from proper tail-grooming protocols to required nap durations was meticulously documented. By the time we reached Rule 47 ("*All final boss chambers must include at least one elevated platform for dramatic pronouncements*"), I was ready to chuck the crystal across the room.

"Are we sure this is the right crystal?" I asked Aly in shock as we stared at the information on the big screen before us.

"It's the damn one you just set down on the table. If you've got another one, feel free to replace it," she suggested.

I paused, closing my eyes and rephrasing my comment. "I mean, do you think he gave us the one he meant to give us?"

"How the hell would I know?" Aly frowned. "Fuck's sake, Matt, you're the only one who met him, and you met him in a fight. Maybe he was bored, maybe he wanted to make sure you had the rules—hell, maybe, just maybe, he's gone mad after so long in a dungeon where he only exists to fight people!"

"This is useless," I growled. "Why would Kh'aan go to so much trouble to secretly give me a rule book? And, what the fuck? I mean the rule that says that we have to provide them adequate housing and not use them for entertainment reasons isn't even in here so far, so what the hell?"

"Maybe that's the only rule that the dungeon thinks is important, while the others are guidelines?" Kelly suggested, frowning.

"More likely, that's the only one that breaking the rule will cause an issue for the relevant creators," Clarissa said musingly. "Think about the consequences. You said that you can't use them for entertainment, is that right?"

"Yeah?"

"Well, how can they be summoned into the dungeon at all then? How does the arena being set up for observers not violate that rule?"

"Shit, you think this was a way to warn us we'd fucked up?" I asked the others worriedly.

"No, I think if you'd done that, he'd have killed you all. I mean, Matt, do you think you could have taken him? In a fair fight?" Kelly asked me carefully.

"No," I admitted. "He spent more time teaching me in that battle than he did fighting, and he didn't have to do that. Shit, if he'd wanted me dead, I'd have been dead."

"Maybe you're not giving yourself enough credit," Clarissa suggested.

I glanced at Markus, who nodded.

"He could have defeated you at any point," he agreed. "The blows that I saw would have killed you, were you slower or less skilled. I suggest that he had a minimum skill level that he was willing to work with. Had you been below that level, he would have simply killed you and moved on."

"So you could have defeated him…" Clarissa repeated.

"No," both I and Markus said at the same time.

"He was teaching me, but if I'd not put in the level of effort that I had, he'd have killed me instead," I said. "He doesn't suffer fools, but—" I thought about it.

"What?" Kelly asked.

"He was there to test me, sure, but I think he was going to push me hard with one of his people and that was it. I don't think he was going to get involved at first. Then I don't know if he was bored or what, but he started teaching me while we fought. I mean, he could have killed me in seconds."

"How?" Clarissa said, confused. "I'm sorry, Matt, I genuinely don't understand."

"He gave Matt openings and attacked at a level that Matt could withstand, then gradually increased the level of his attacks," Markus explained. "Had he started at that point, simply attacked at that level from the beginning, Matt would have been killed. Instead, he gave him small gaps. You'll note that he split his sword into two copies that could fly and attack from any angle, and yet he only did that once, and further into the fight. I'd imagine if we asked Rathaharn, we'd find that two isn't the limit for him. He attacked at a speed and level of skill that Matt was hard-pressed to defend against, but always inside of his potential range."

"And his level was reduced to fight me," I pointed out as well. "Like he was broken down to face me—his stats, I mean, but his knowledge and skill levels will have been whatever they are normally. I mean, they did that with the Dawn Guard as well."

"Shit," Aly said softly. "Of course they did. They had to."

"Because if they hadn't, you'd have had to fight literally legendary-class opponents, and no matter their physical stats, if they've got years, or even centuries of fighting experience, they could beat you easily."

"Not 'easily,'" Markus disagreed. "He won fair and square against the majority, but I suspect that the Dawn Guard you faced were neutered beforehand, their armor broken down to a manageable level as well. After all, they *want* you to fight and grow, not just be slaughtered."

"Well, if he did choose to let you win, why did he do that?" Clarissa asked. "Do the Scepiniir strike you as a race that if they felt their honor had been abused would allow you to win against one of their greatest warriors, just because they wanted to share a rule book?"

"Definitely not," I said. "No, there's something in here that we need to know, and I don't know what it is. Weird that the dungeon didn't just share the full thing with us when we unlocked the species, though."

"Sounds more like they don't want you knowing some of it," Aly suggested.

Kelly frowned thoughtfully. "Was there anything else? Anything he did or said that seemed odd?"

I thought about it, going over the fight, and started to shake my head, then froze. "The bumps. On his armor—he made sure I saw them. A pattern of them."

"A pattern…" Kelly's eyes widened. "What were the bumps?"

"They appeared in a group; one, then four more to make five, then two more…" I said after a brief struggle to remember. "One, five, seven."

Kelly practically dove for the crystal, scrolling through the text rapidly. "Okay, not rule one…can't be unless it's about boots, for fuck's sake. Let's try rule five…"

"Try them all together—what's rule 157?" Clarissa suggested.

I flicked through the list, skipping loads, until I found it and leaned in to read:

"*Rule 157: If a Scepiniir's inhabitant's honor has been impugned, any unconnected Dungeon Lord may issue formal challenge for control of a dungeon through ritual combat with its appointed Champion. Victory grants legitimate claim to dungeon authority; defeat results in forfeiture of challenge rights. The Champion must be a Dungeon Lord and have a rank no higher, nor lower than the challenger.*"

"Son of a bitch," I breathed. "He wasn't just testing me. He was showing me how to take other dungeons."

"Without destroying them first," Kelly added. "If you can reach the dungeon…"

"I can challenge for control," I finished. "And with this fucking rule book? We know that any dungeon that has a single Scepiniir in it practically *has* to have broken at least one fucking rule."

"Would them not being aware of the rules be enough of an excuse?" Markus asked slowly, then he shook his head. "Of course it would…it's a law."

"Exactly." I nodded. "With this, all we need to do is make sure that the other dungeons have access to the Scepiniir species and give them a chance to summon some."

"A giveaway," Kelly said promptly. "Anyone who sends a member of their dungeon to fight in the arena, gets the sample for the Scepiniir. Then we get paid for them coming. It looks like they're getting a great deal, and we're actually giving them a Trojan horse."

"Nice," I agreed. "But what about the dungeons that don't have access to the nexus gates? I mean, we need them to go there, to get to us, right? How else do we make contact?"

"That's what we need to sort out then…"

That was the start of a hell of a discussion. But after a little arguing, a little research, and then finally me walking down and using the gate to go to the Nexus platform and just outright asking, it turned out that yes, if we chose to, we could pay the platform a crystal a day to offer anyone who went there a key that would lead to the arena, and some information, like when the gate would next open, etc.

That was a nice sneaky bonus, and as I settled back into my seat, apologizing for the time it'd taken, I found that Kelly and the others had already worked out a flyer and a plan for distribution that gave each dungeon a significant discount on their next run if they brought in another, new dungeon.

All told, it was a plan that we just knew was going to get us in the door with any dungeon that wasn't willing to work with us in the future. And for those dungeons that had surrendered to me, but that I had highly limited control over at the minute?

Well, they got to be our first test subjects.

None of them had a nexus gate yet, and Aly marked it down as one of her jobs to reach out to them and bring them into line with the rest of the civilized world, as she was going to put it.

She was essentially going to reach out through the system and play it a little dumb. First that I'd ordered her to share this technology with our allies, and she was assuming that it meant them as well, and second, that she was unaware that there was any risk from them.

That was when Ashley stepped in and asked to take it over.

"Seriously, it's no effort on my part. When they meet me, they'll see fake tits and makeup, and they'll instantly dismiss me. It'll give me a chance to hit them with my abilities and then I'll escort them around the arena. You guys get to distance yourself from the whole thing, and they'll be off-balance enough that I can assess them easily."

"And if they were stuck swearing allegiance to the undead and made an honest mistake..." Kelly nodded. "Then you get to assess them and we can extend a little trust, as opposed to the way it is now, where we just don't know what to do with them, beyond travel there and ask them nicely to step down and put someone we trust in charge."

"Exactly." Ashley smiled. "This way, if word of you taking over gets out, it's because they surrendered to you, not because we've found a way in. Because, let's face it, once word spreads, nobody is going to let any other Dungeon Lord enter their dungeon ever again."

"So, we give them the tech, give them the Scepiniir sample, and then I go visiting." I nodded. "I like it. With that in mind, though, and the bones of the plan laid out, time to move on."

"What's next?" Kelly asked, before nodding. "London."

"No, we'll come to that in a minute." I shook my head. "Markus, what's the situation with the museum?"

"Ah!" Markus smiled. "We've taken control of the museum complex. The good news is that most of the aircraft are intact, at least structurally. The Ju-52 is particularly promising—the airframe is solid aluminum and the basic mechanical systems are all there. As I suspected, anything electrical is worthless, but that's not a major concern given our mana-based alternatives."

"What about the workshop spaces?" I leaned forward. The technical facilities would be crucial for the adaptation work, as they'd have to have design details and reference manuals that could help us with understanding.

"Better than we'd hoped," he replied. "The restoration workshop is extensive. They were in the middle of rebuilding a Spitfire when everything went down. Tools, equipment, technical drawings—it's all there. The museum's reference library is also intact. We've already started inputting the technical manuals into the dungeon."

Aly pulled up a holographic display showing the museum's layout. "I've got teams cataloging everything now. The priority is the Ju-52's technical documentation. We need to understand every system before we start the adaptation work. The original had a range of about a thousand kilometers—we'll need to significantly improve on that."

"What about the materials science?" Kelly asked. "If we're rebuilding this thing with modern composites and mana-enhanced alloys, we need to make sure the structural calculations still work."

“That’s where the dungeon’s research capabilities come in,” Aly said. “We can model everything in the research field before we commit to physical construction.”

“Speaking of which—Aly, how long until we can get a complete scan of the Ju-52 into the system?” I asked.

“Give me at least another day,” she replied. “I want to absorb in at least one of every component. Once we have that baseline, we can start the redesign process. The mana-conversion engines are already being prototyped—we’re using the Spitfire’s Merlin engine as a starting point, believe it or not. The basic principles of air compression and thrust generation still apply; we’re just replacing the fuel injection systems with mana power crystals.”

“Good.” I nodded. “But let’s not get too focused on just the aircraft. We need to think about how this integrates with the dreadnought itself. The landing gear needs to support the full weight of the dungeon. The cargo capacity needs to…”

That was it, another hour and a half spent working on design, arguing over the best ways to enhance the airframe and whether titanium was a better choice than mana-infused metals, whether we should be planning the plane as a transport craft only, and the dungeon to roll out of it and along the road or whether we should make the wings slide off and lay flat along the side of the structure.

That was Aly’s choice—that or that we make the wings break down and fold away. I wanted it, but hated the idea of a nut coming loose when flying and the wings folding up again or some shit.

It went on and on, until, seeing that Markus and Clarissa were clearly exhausted, I held up a hand.

“Okay, I’m sorry, guys. You’re effectively our night shift, and it’s mid-morning now. You need your sleep. Let’s cover the next bits quickly, and let you go.”

“Thank you.” Clarissa smiled. “Normally it’s not an issue. I sleep far less than I did when I was younger, after all, but today?” She shrugged, then summoned another pot of tea and set out a cup both for her and Markus.

“So, London.” I sighed. “Aly, want to go over this?”

“It’s a simple break-in, though no doubt you’ll make it more than that by the end.” She sighed. “Essentially, we need to get you in there with the new core to set up the dungeon. You’ll use the Scepiniir mercenaries and a few of our people—just in case they decide to sell you out—and you’ll get in, find a building in the highest mana zone that works, and dig deep.”

“Probably access the sewers and go that way,” Markus suggested. “I know London has a lot of underground areas—find one of those that’s deep enough you’re confident there’s nothing beneath it, and then start claiming and remodeling.”

“Exactly. Once you’re down there, take over as much as possible, and get it set up so that once the fake core is transported around London, should they take the bait and steal it, you’ve got enough reach to link to it and make the fake look real,” Aly finished.

“That could take awhile,” I pointed out.

“It could, but the core we’ve finished for you has a lot of mana crystals attached. Take it, and some extras in your bag of holding, set up the core and use that to create a nexus gate, then link to us.” She hesitated. “Wait, can you put a core in the bag of holding? With the mana crystals around it, is it safe?”

"I mean, I did it when I went to the northern dungeon—" I shook my head. "No, actually, I didn't. It didn't have the crystals attached, so it was small, and I just put it in a pouch on my belt. I didn't risk putting it in the bag of holding."

"Then until someone else has tried it, for now we fashion something else. This one is a lot bigger with the crystals attached, so maybe a shoulder holster? We can sort that out later. What's important is that we funnel more crystals through to you and the skeletal resource teams once you're there. Then they begin claiming the area, head out as fast and hard as possible, and…"

Aly switched the view on the holographic display that had been showing an overview of London as she spoke to a blueprint of a small variation on the clockwork crawler design.

"This is a seeker," she said. "Didn't know what else to call it, so bugger it. It's literally a crawler that gives off a powerful signal, that's all. We hide this inside the fake core, and we set up a system in there—it's nearly finished, so don't you dare fuck about with it at this stage—that makes a big magical display when the core is 'activated.'

"With the seeker hidden inside, you'll be able to detect the core, so even if they choose a section of London farther outside the few streets we've recommended to them, you'll be able to find it. We set the core deployment timer on the screen as the fake core is activated to a bunch of symbols that mean nothing. That way, if you reach it quickly, great…you can take control and override. If not? It takes as long as it takes." Aly settled back in her seat and shrugged.

"And if they set it up on the far side of London?" I asked.

"Fuck it. There's a small zone there that we can tell is high mana, but it's smaller and they'd be stupid to do that. If they do that, we treat it as they broke the core and instead come up with a new plan," she suggested. "As much as this is a great opportunity for us, we need to be realistic and not waste too much time on this."

"It's about as good a plan as we can come up with, but I'll need a few days to get the core set up. So, what's the timescale we're working with?" I asked.

"Five or six days maybe?" Kelly suggested. "We set the core off from here, protected by a set of four of Aly's large clockwork transports, and we send it along the road with a bunch of low-level, unaware guards as well. We have dinner with the earl, and we warn them that the core is lethal to higher-level beings at this stage as it's an open core we need to transport or some such shit."

"That's why we won't be around such an important and valuable cargo, and we warn them to stay clear as well." I nodded. "Then if they go for it, the earl is proved to be a dodgy fuck as well. I like it."

"Yes and no," Clarissa pointed out. "If our situations were reversed, and to protect your people, would you consider stealing another's core?"

"Yeah," I said bluntly. "I've been thinking about it a lot, and if the situation was reversed, then I would. The difference is that we offer the earl, in our conversation over dinner, a core. We tell him it'll be like a month or whatever, but we're going to give them one, for a fair price. That way, he knows they're going to get one, so if they steal ours? Then he's a shitehawk. If they don't? We know that we can trust at least him in there, to this level at least."

"Fair enough." Mike nodded. "So, I'll be there with you, and we'll make sure the team is a stealthy one. If we're going to have a week from now until it gets here, how much time do you need to spend in London in a stinking sewer before the core arrives?"

"Three days at least," I said grimly. "Better if we have as long as possible, though. We'll need to convert as much of the underside as possible, and all the while we need them to have no clue we're there—so stealthy as fuck is definitely the team we need."

"Then we leave tomorrow night," he said. "You all right with that?"

"Yeah." I grunted. "But you get to tell Rhodes her punching bag is going to be busy. I know she had plans for pushing me harder and training more tomorrow."

"Dammit." Mike sighed. "Knew I should have kept my mouth shut."

"That'll learn ya!" I grinned.

"So, you leave tomorrow, but once the gate is up and running, you can come home," Kelly said. "I suggest you leave from the southern dungeon once it's dark—get the core in place overnight and make the nexus gate the main priority. If you do it right and fast, you can get—" She broke off, checking something apparently, then turned to me. "Matt, have you checked the nexus gates lately?"

"What?" I asked, confused. "What's the problem?"

"Have we not hit our limit?"

"What?"

"The limit on the gates, Matt!" she clarified. "We've got five gates in use. This will be our sixth. The upgrades you said you got before said five was the limit, right?"

"Shit!" I cursed, starting to frantically check through the details. *Five!*

She was right; it was a maximum of five gates, and…wait, was it? I pulled the details up for the Dungeon Warmancer class and checked. Yeah, five gates, but I could sense in the dungeon that there was a sixth available, so how the hell did that…

"The reward!" I gasped, feeling the relief fill me. "Fuck me, the reward we got for being the first to reach Glass!"

"Oh, thank God," Kelly whispered. "I thought that was going to derail everything."

"Nope, but it does impose a hard limit on the future," Aly pointed out. "Unless you can get more of them, and soon, we're fucked when it comes to the other dungeons. As soon as you conquer them, their gate is gonna go offline or whatever, as we'll not have a spare gate space in the network for them to take."

"Shit," I growled, before sighing. "Not that we didn't know we needed more. Fine, I'll make it a priority as soon as I'm offered any more points, though that's gonna be a painful cap on my growth if I need to keep buying them."

"What else do we need to cover?" Markus asked then, and I glanced over, seeing how tired both he and Clarissa looked.

"Honestly nothing that you're desperately needed for," I said. "We need to sort out a few things, like the Alchemical forge, but I don't think it's a good idea to put that in place until we have a solid plan for the expansion of the park. If all the crafting is going to start moving in that direction, maybe we need to build it there. As for me, I need to focus on Jack's rebuild and repair, but the London plan is pretty much done. I'll let Mike sort the details out, and I'll focus on this. Kelly and Aly can work on the others, and you two go get some sleep, with my thanks for staying up this late already."

"Thank you." He helped Clarissa to her feet.

Before they could leave, though, Clarissa paused, looking at me, and smiled. "Thank you, Matt, and you, Kelly and Aly. You've got no idea what a difference all of this has made to our lives, you know."

"The dungeon?" I asked, confused and thinking it was a pretty obvious difference, actually.

"No, being included at this level. Being given jobs to do, ways to help contribute that are more than just make-work jobs. We might be old, but we're not off to the glue factory yet, and you've given us a reason to have hope again, so thank you." With that, she turned and headed for the door, her posture proud, even as Markus strode alongside her, smiling.

"They're a hell of a pair," I said once they'd gone, having been lost for words until then.

"They are," Kelly agreed. "And we're lucky to have them. So, if you're working on Jack, then Aly and I both have jobs, such as…"

CHAPTER THIRTY-TWO

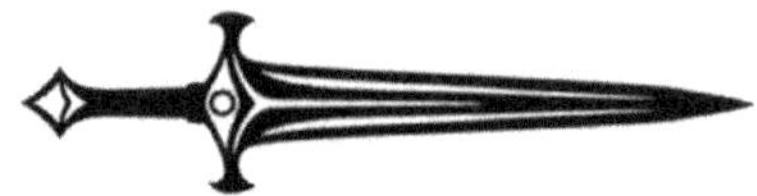

With the ladies now busy with their own jobs, I settled back and stared at the dungeon interface for a long time. I wanted to get started on Jack, but I also needed the damn notifications out of the way, as the flashing was annoying me, so I pulled them up to get it out of the way.

Congratulations!

You have killed the following:

<u>Primordial Floor Combat</u>:

- 1x Water Primordial [Ancient Boss], Level 30, 12,500 XP
- 1x Fire Primordial [Ancient Boss], Level 30, 12,500 XP
- 1x Earth Primordial [Ancient Boss], Level 30, 12,500 XP

<u>Arena Combat</u>:

- 12x Goblin Mageling [Advanced], Level 20-25, 2,400 XP
- 8x Greater Ghast [Advanced], Level 22-25, 2,000 XP
- 6x Elite Orc Guard [Advanced], Level 25, 1,800 XP
- 2x Dawn Guard [Ancient], Level 35, 10,000 XP

Total XP awarded: 53,700 XP
Current XP to next level stands at 180,205/120,000

Congratulations!

You have reached Level 33.

Current XP to next level stands at 60,205/135,000.

You have 15 unspent Stat Points and 1 unspent Skill Point.

I grinned to myself, loving the fact that I'd gained another level, but as always, one job brought another job, and in this case, it was assigning the points I'd gained, and looking over my skill increases.

I hesitated, then decided I'd put it off until tonight, there was no fight going on right now after all, and I'd gained a hell of a lot of points lately with the improvements I'd been making to my body anyway.

No, I'd save my points, and probably talk to Kelly later when I had some time to go over my options, see what she thought.

With that dealt with, and the notifications thankfully silent again—I'd blanked the skill ones for now too—I did what I'd been wanting to do for a while.

I felt terrible as I started, it being my lack of attention and fuck-ups that had resulted in Jack being lost in the first place, and so it was with a sense of guilt I began, determined to make him as damn impervious as possible this time around.

I'd looked into the system, and with a little digging, I'd found that the last version of Jack, as he was before his death, was indeed gone. But the one before, where he'd been upgraded from the panther design to the bear, meant that the dungeon had access to his core.

As such, that version of him could be brought back. But for the first time, I was no longer limited to the same small selection when it came to choosing his form.

I'd avoided looking at this section until now. As I pulled it up, like so many things, I found that the change from the Steel core to the Glass one had changed the layout, as well as the options.

Dungeon Lord Automata detected:

Automata designated as "Jack" is eligible for form [Replacement]. Do you wish to [Replace] this Automata?

Yes/No

It wasn't exactly a hard choice. He was dead, and as much as I regretted that, this way he got to live again. I selected Yes and focused on the copy of Jack that was stored in the dungeon, not the mangled remains that we had stored down at the southern dungeon now.

Kelly had arranged for the parts to be recovered, and I loved her for that thoughtfulness as much as anything else.

Please choose Automata physical form from the following:

 # Standard Forms (Glass Technology Level)

1. **Panthera (Hunter)**

- Size: Large big cat

- Focus: Stealth and pursuit

- Cost: 15,000 mana, 50 mana/day, 5 control points

- Special: Enhanced tracking capabilities

2. **Ursus (Warrior)**

- Size: Large bear

- Focus: Close combat

- Cost: 20,000 mana, 75 mana/day, 8 control points

- Special: Increased damage resistance

3. **Canis (Scout)**

- Size: Large wolf

- Focus: Reconnaissance

- Cost: 12,000 mana, 40 mana/day, 4 control points

- Special: Enhanced sensory suite

4. **Equus (Transport)**

- Size: Large horse

- Focus: Transportation

- Cost: 18,000 mana, 60 mana/day, 6 control points

- Special: Increased carrying capacity

5. **Pongo (Engineer)**

- Size: Large orangutan

- Focus: Technical tasks

- Cost: 16,000 mana, 55 mana/day, 5 control points

- Special: Enhanced Dexterity

6. **Elephas (Siege)**

- Size: Large elephant

- Focus: Heavy lifting/breaking

- Cost: 25,000 mana, 85 mana/day, 10 control points

- Special: Reinforced structure

7. **Aquila (Aerial)**

- Size: Large eagle

- Focus: Air reconnaissance

- Cost: 14,000 mana, 45 mana/day, 5 control points

- Special: Extended flight capability

8. **Serpens (Infiltrator)**

- Size: Large snake

- Focus: Infiltration

- Cost: 13,000 mana, 35 mana/day, 4 control points

- Special: Advanced flexibility

9. **Scarabaeus (Worker)**

- Size: Large beetle

- Focus: Construction

- Cost: 15,000 mana, 50 mana/day, 5 control points

- Special: Material manipulation

10. **Simia (Support)**

- Size: Large monkey

- Focus: Utility tasks

- Cost: 14,000 mana, 45 mana/day, 5 control points

- Special: Tool use proficiency

Please note, these are choices that until recently were restricted to the local species variant examples. Do you wish to access the secondary list and additional data?

Yes/No…

Again, not a hard choice, so I took it, then grinned like a fucking idiot.

Large-scale Evolution-capable Automata:

Draconid (War Machine)

- Initial Form: Mechanical Wyrmling

- Core Focus: Versatile combat and reconnaissance

- Evolution Path: Wyrmling → Drake → Dragon → Elder Dragon → World Dragon

- Special Feature: Can integrate dungeon systems when evolved

- Base Cost: 750,000 mana, 2,500 mana/day, 25 control points

Titan (Living Fortress)

- Initial Form: Humanoid construct

- Core Focus: Defense and siege warfare

- Evolution Path: Guardian → Defender → Protector → Colossus → World Titan

- Special Feature: Can create defensive fields/walls

- Base Cost: 850,000 mana, 3,000 mana/day, 30 control points

Leviathan (Aquatic Juggernaut)

- Initial Form: Serpentine construct

- Core Focus: Naval warfare and underwater operations

- Evolution Path: Serpent → Sea Drake → Ocean Lord → Deep King → World Serpent

- Special Feature: Can manipulate water currents

- Base Cost: 700,000 mana, 2,250 mana/day, 20 control points

Phoenix (Aerial Sovereign)

- Initial Form: Mechanical bird

- Core Focus: Air superiority and reconnaissance

- Evolution Path: Ember → Flame → Inferno → Solar → World Phoenix

- Special Feature: Can harness and redirect energy

- Base Cost: 650,000 mana, 2,000 mana/day, 15 control points

Golem (City Heart)

- Initial Form: Crystalline humanoid

- Core Focus: Construction and infrastructure

- Evolution Path: Builder → Shaper → Architect → Master → World Core

- Special Feature: Can create and control smaller constructs

- Base Cost: 800,000 mana, 2,750 mana/day, 28 control points

Medium-scale Evolution-capable Automata:

 # Chimera (Adaptive Hunter)

- **Initial Form: Multi-form construct**
- **Core Focus: Adaptable combat and reconnaissance**
- **Evolution Path: Basic → Advanced → Elite → Perfect → Legendary**
- **Special Feature: Can reconfigure form between different beast aspects**
- **Base Cost: 100,000 mana, 500 mana/day, 12 control points**

 # Sentinel (Defensive Guardian)

- **Initial Form: Humanoid construct**
- **Core Focus: Area control and defense**
- **Evolution Path: Watcher → Guardian → Protector → Defender → Champion**
- **Special Feature: Can create defensive barriers and control zones**
- **Base Cost: 125,000 mana, 600 mana/day, 15 control points**

 # Behemoth (War Pla…

I read over the options. I mean, I forced myself to, but it wasn't like the secondary ones were even seriously getting a look in. I read the first page of them and then dismissed them all, even as the second through one hundred and fortieth pages were being populated.

There was absolutely no need to spend a week reading through increasingly weird-ass options when I damn well knew what I wanted was going to be in the first large-scale ones.

The golem evolving form was interesting, and I forced myself to consider it. It was designed to be the heart of a city and grow over time, so that could be cool, and it could control smaller constructs. But Kelly already did that, and they were what we had already, so no need for change. Cool, but not that cool. Dismissed.

Phoenix? Sure, that was tempting. I mean, the size of a small plane and flight capable…sure, I liked that. Who the fuck wouldn't? And it was also able to carry out air superiority missions? The flying fucks around Saltwell Park were going to be absolutely fucked up by that, for sure. Beyond that, though, once it was on the ground, very limited use, I bet.

Leviathan? Interesting, sure. It'd secure the waters around the country, no doubt, and I could go hunt down that pirate lunatic, but…no. I'd never spent much time at sea, and it still freaked me out. Hard pass.

Titan? Interesting again. It could create its own walls and defensive structures. It could protect our people, but only up to a certain point. We could already create walls, so it was intriguing, but that was it.

Plus, there was already one titan in residence, or I was working toward it. Daddy didn't need the competition.

No, with them dismissed and the other hundred and forty pages not interesting enough for me to even bother with, I felt I'd done my due diligence. Or at least as much as I was going to be doing, because…

Jack was coming back as a mother-fuckin' *dragon*!

I hit Confirm on the draconid option and watched as the dungeon interface shifted to display an intricate diagram of the mechanical dragon's base form. The wireframe schematic slowly rotated, highlighting different aspects of the design—the articulated wings, the reinforced spine, the modular weapon hardpoints.

WARNING: Converting existing automata core. Previous personality matrix and memory fragments will be integrated into new form. Due to significant structural differences, behavioral adjustments may occur. Do you wish to proceed?

I paused, my finger hovering over the confirmation. Jack had been my friend, my protector. The thought that this transformation might change who he was made me hesitate. But then I remembered his final moments, how he'd sacrificed himself without hesitation to protect us. That was who Jack was at his core, and no physical form would change that.

"Yes," I confirmed, and the interface lit up with streams of data as the conversion began, along with a hell of a dip in the mana of the dungeon as it began providing mass.

INITIATING DRACONID CONVERSION

- ***Core matrix stabilization… Complete***
- ***Memory integration… Complete***
- ***Behavioral template mapping… Complete***
- ***Physical form generation… In Progress***

Estimated completion time: 6 hours

I leaned back in my chair, watching the progress bar slowly advance. The schematic continued its rotation, but now I could see the framework being filled in, layer by layer, system by system. The basic skeletal structure came first, followed by the internal mechanisms, then the outer armor plating.

In the past he'd always been built from all the scrap we'd had, as mana had been in short supply. Now instead he was getting the best we could provide, and damn, I could see the difference already.

"How's it going?" Kelly came up behind me and rested her hands on my shoulders. "Holy shit, is that going to be Jack?"

I blinked, seeing the screen before us all.

Until now, I'd been working on it silently in my head. Now though, as if sensing that I'd want to show him off, the screen that had been blank before me had updated, showing Jack's new form in all its holographic glory.

"It's…different than I expected," I admitted. "The system's being really careful about preserving his core personality. I think… I think he'll still be Jack, just with some upgrades."

"Good." She squeezed my shoulders. "He deserves this. And honestly? I think he'd love being a dragon."

I laughed. "Yeah, he probably would. Look at this…" I pointed to one of the specification readouts. "Base form is already the size of a small house, and that's just the starting point. By the time he reaches Elder Dragon stage…" I whistled.

"Just don't let it go to his head." Kelly grinned. "Though I suppose technically he'll have earned the right to be a bit smug."

"Or Smaug," I replied without thought, loving her all the more when she laughed, having got the reference.

We watched together as more details emerged. The wings were a masterpiece of engineering, layers of overlapping plates that could fold completely flat against his body or extend to their full span. The tail was segmented and could be used as both a weapon and a stabilizer. And throughout the entire frame ran channels for mana circulation, allowing him to integrate directly with dungeon systems.

"Six hours, though." I sighed. "That's a long wait."

"Then let's use the time productively," Kelly suggested. "We still need to finalize the London infiltration team. Mike would probably be happy to have your opinion on it, and I want your input on—"

A soft chime from the interface interrupted her. We both turned to look at the display, where a new message flashed:

ATTENTION: Core consciousness achieving stability. Initial activation available in: 47 minutes

"Or maybe not six hours." I straightened up. "Looks like Jack's eager to wake up."

The timer changed a lot over the next hour and a half, updating to be a few minutes from now for him, then rolling back further, then updating, then rolling back, until Mike—as both he and Aly had been made aware of the build now and what he was referring to as "The return of the Jack"—pointed out a minor detail.

"Where's he being assembled?" Mike asked.

I blinked, then slapped my forehead. "Not in here!" I groaned. "Fuck me, how the hell did we miss that? There's no room for his last form in here, never mind the new one. So…where the hell is he? I mean, I don't want to have to tear the place apart to get him out!"

A little frantic searching ensued, and we eventually found he was being constructed in a clearing to the north, beside the building that housed the ship that had brought the dungeon to Earth in the first place.

As we trooped out, we joined a host of other curious buggers who had seen the light of a dungeon summoning…and had come to see what the hell was going on when it lasted more than a few seconds.

I took up station with the others, standing at what I guessed was going to be the head end.

Then, a short while later I moved when I realized we were all staring wonderingly at what was apparently going to be his ass, as the tail began to form over it.

Once standing at the head end, I had to stare in wonder at the magnificence that was the new Jack, even as I marveled at the trio that had taken up station around him.

"What the hell are they doing here?" I asked Finn, who shook his head, staring as well.

He spoke to me with a note of distraction in his voice. "They just got up and hurried out. I followed them, and now we're here?" The crafter shrugged, splitting his attention between the trio of glassine and the steadily appearing Jack as much as I was.

The dragon taking shape before us was a masterwork of mechanical artistry. His primary frame was fashioned from polished bronze plates that caught the morning light, each scale individually crafted with subtle variations in texture that created an almost organic flow across his body. The bronze wasn't the uniform color you'd expect from modern manufacturing, either. Instead, it had the depth and character of traditional metalwork, with hints of copper and gold emerging where the light struck at different angles.

Layered over the bronze, key structural elements were reinforced with brushed silver alloy that looked like it had been hand-hammered by a master smith. These silver segments traced elegant lines down his neck and spine, forming natural armor that protected vital systems while adding to the overall craftsman look.

The effect was particularly striking along his wing struts, where the silver webbing between the bronze support structures caught the light like stained glass.

But it was the onyx elements that truly took the design from merely beautiful to awe-inspiring. Geometric plates of the black stone were inlaid with precise attention to detail, creating striking contrast against the metalwork. These weren't just decorative, I somehow knew, still linked to his systems as they were adjusted. They housed his sensor arrays and what would one day be his weapons systems, the crystalline structure perfect for channeling and focusing mana. The largest onyx placement was his chest plate, which seemed to pulse with a deep inner light as his core spun up to full power.

"Fuck a duck!" Mike whispered beside me. "He looks like something that should be in an art museum, not a war machine."

He wasn't wrong. Every joint and connection point had been given the same attention to detail as the most expensive custom jewelry. The segmented plates of his neck riffled like liquid metal as the final calibrations ran through his systems. His tail, now fully formed, was a masterpiece of articulation, each segment flowing seamlessly into the next.

His head was the last element to fully manifest, and damn was it the most impressive. The basic shape was draconic, but the level of skill was breathtaking. Onyx swept back from his brow in elegant horns, while bronze and silver plates interlocked to form a face that somehow managed to look both regal and deadly. His eyes, when they finally illuminated, glowed with a deep amber light.

This wasn't just a mechanical dragon—this was Jack reimagined as a work of art, every element of his new form reflecting both power and craftsmanship. He looked as though he had been crafted by Victorian artisans who somehow had access to advanced technology, managing to merge steampunk aesthetics with modern function.

As the last elements clicked into place, his new form settled, and those eyes focused directly on me. I stepped forward, a sudden "Fuck, I hope he's not pissed over me letting his last version get chopped up" running through my mind as I came to a stop.

"Jack, you in there?" I asked. The dragon, the goddamn massive friggin' dragon, stared at me for a few seconds—long enough to make me start to shit myself—then lowered his head and gently butted at me, pushing me back a step. I started to laugh.

"Yeah, you're in there, all right," I said softly as those amber eyes met mine. There was no verbal response, but I felt it; through the connection that tied every part of my dungeon to me, I felt Jack's presence. It was stronger than before—more complex, but undeniably him.

A wave of relief and welcome washed over me through our link, followed by something deeper: an iron determination, a promise to never fall again, to be stronger this time.

I reached out and placed my hand on his snout. The warmth of his core radiated through the metalwork. The metal was smooth beneath my palm, and the subtle thrum of power coursed through him. Through our connection, I sensed his satisfaction with the new form, his eagerness to prove himself worthy of it.

The moment was interrupted by movement from the three glassine figures. They had been standing motionless around Jack during his formation, but now they approached in perfect synchronization. I tensed, but Jack remained calm, his massive head turning to regard them with evident curiosity.

"The craft-born recognize this one," the first glassine announced in that oddly melodic voice they all shared. "The transition is acceptable."

"The form honors the traditions," the second added.

"The core remains true," the third concluded.

Then, as suddenly as they had appeared, they turned and walked away, leaving us staring after them.

"Well, that was weird as fuck," I muttered. Jack's amusement rippled through our connection, along with a hint of confusion about the glassine's interest in him.

He experimentally stretched his wings; the span of them cast shadows over the gathered crowd. Through our link, I felt his wonder at the new sensations—the way he could sense mana flows now, the power thrumming through his enhanced frame, the sheer potential of what he'd become.

Kelly stepped forward then, reaching up to pat his neck. "Just don't let it go to your head. You're still our Jack, even if you are a bit more, well…draconic now."

His affection for Kelly pulsed through our connection, along with what could only be described as a mental eye roll at the suggestion he might get full of himself.

"Speaking of which," Mike cut in, "maybe we should test out those new capabilities before we head to London? Make sure everything's working properly?"

"London?" I whispered, before grinning up at the massive form. "Oh, I think London's in for a surprise, all right."

"No, man…please, fuckin' no!" Mike growled. "I spent most of the goddamn day working on that plan—don't fuck it up the arse without at least buying it dinner and a drink first!"

Jack's head swiveled toward Mike, and I felt his eager anticipation at the prospect of testing his new form. But that enthusiasm suddenly shifted to intense focus as his attention turned toward the hangar housing the alien ship. Through our connection, I felt his surprise and curiosity. Something about his new form was resonating with the technology in there.

"You feeling that too?" I asked him quietly, receiving a pulse of confirmation. Whatever was happening between Jack and the ship, it felt important, and powerful.

"Aly?" I called out, not taking my eyes off Jack. "You getting any readings from the ship?"

"Already on it," she replied. Her eyes grew distant as she leaned on Mike, focusing into the dungeon sense. "There's definitely some kind of energy signature… It's like the ship's systems are powering up, but only partially. Shit, I didn't even realize it still *had* a power core. It's almost like it's responding to—" She blinked free of the thousand-yard stare and saw me again. "Matt, the ship's power signature? It's adjusting to match Jack's core frequency."

Through our connection, I felt Jack's fascination deepen. He took a step toward the hangar, his movements surprisingly graceful for something his size, each bronze plate flowing smoothly into the next. The crowd parted before him—some backing away nervously, others watching in silent awe.

"Should we be worried about this?" Kelly moved up beside me. "I mean, the last time that ship had power, it was bringing a core and a fairy here…"

"No," I said firmly, feeling Jack's agreement resonate through our link. "This is different. It's not like before. It feels more like…invitation?"

Jack had reached the side of the structure now, and with a thought, I reached out, focusing, and created a new entrance, before wincing as his massive form barely fit through the hole I'd just made.

I hurried after him, as did everyone else.

Inside, the alien ship sat here as it had for weeks, dark and dormant. But as Jack approached, lines of light began to trace their way across its hull, forming patterns that seemed to mirror the geometric designs on his onyx plating.

"Bloody hell," Mike breathed. "Look at the writing."

The alien script that covered portions of the ship's hull was illuminating, but not in its usual blue-white. Instead, it glowed with the same deep amber as Jack's eyes. Through our connection, I felt a sudden surge of…something. Not quite understanding, but a sense of rightness, of pieces clicking into place.

"The ship…it was waiting," I said slowly, the realization coming as I felt what Jack was experiencing. "All this time, it wasn't just broken or dormant. It was waiting for something specific. Something that could interface with it properly."

"A draconid form?" Aly asked, confused as she went back to studying her readings. "Matt, these energy patterns…they're almost identical to some of the ship's original systems. It's like…"

"Like whoever built that ship," Kelly finished, "had something like Jack in mind when they designed it. Holy shit. Matt, you said he could be upgraded, right?"

"Yeah?" I asked absently, lost in the details I was seeing.

Through our connection, I felt Jack's excitement building, tempered by caution but thrumming with potential. He wasn't just sensing the ship anymore. He was beginning to understand it, in ways that even I hadn't been able to. This wasn't just a random resonance. This was planned. This was meant to happen.

"Right then." I squared my shoulders. "I guess we need to—"

A new voice cut through the air, making us all jump. It came from the ship itself, speaking in that same melodic tone as the glassine, but deeper, more formal:

"Primary interface detected. Initiating synchronization protocol…connected. Upgrade protocol active. Potential target identified… accessing… assessing… Target set."

"What the fuck?" I asked aloud, staring in wonder, before the ship itself started to shudder.

"Current status: Damaged. Assessment: Unable to perform complete system upgrade. Solution: Partial upgrade available. Dungeon creation system accessed, assessed: Grade insufficient for full repair."

Along with the monotonous drone of system techno-babble came a data dump that, as the Dungeon Warmancer, seemed to be specially designated for me.

I clutched at my head for long seconds as I tried to focus. The data dump practically fried my fucking mind. And yet, when it went, when it finally died down? I sucked down a long breath and blinked at the options hovering before me.

SYSTEM ALERT: Partial Upgrade Package Available

Target: Draconid War Machine Designation "Jack"

Current Configuration: Base Form

Available Upgrade: Weapons System Beta-7

Primary: Enhanced Plasma Generation

Secondary: Projectile Modification

Note: Full weapons suite unavailable due to insufficient power/grade

WARNING: Proceeding will result in permanent integration of transport ship components. Continue? Y/N

I felt Jack's eager acceptance through our link even as I read the alert. This was right—this was meant to be. "Do it," I confirmed, both through the interface and aloud.

The ship's surface began to shift, plates lifting and separating with precision. It wasn't breaking apart—it was transforming, components detaching and reforming. The process was beautiful in its complexity. Each piece moved with purpose toward Jack's waiting form as he stepped forward, inserting himself into the shifting mechanical morass.

Through our connection, I felt Jack's mild discomfort as the first components began to integrate with his frame. The ship's amber-glowing components merged seamlessly with his onyx plates; the geometric patterns aligned and connected as if they were always meant to fit together.

"Holy shit," Aly whispered, her eyes distant as she processed the data through the dungeon sense. "The ship isn't just upgrading him—it's teaching him. The weapon systems are being integrated directly into his core programming."

I could feel it too. Jack's understanding of his new capabilities grew by the second. The basic plasma generation he'd had as part of his draconid form was being enhanced, refined. Where before he could only project a stream of plasma fire, now…

"Projectile formation protocols integrated," the ship's voice announced, as the systems meshed. "Plasma compression and containment systems online. Testing recommended in controlled environment."

More and more of the ship was broken down. The greater frame, the literal superstructure was left behind, and entire sections that had been damaged were left as well. But practically everything else?

The tech that had survived until now integrated with him. Connections slithered across his chest; open panels clicked and whirred to the left and right, sliding aside to allow more to be inserted, and then they folded back down.

The last pieces of the ship settled into place, the glow of the alien script fading as the integration completed. Jack looked…different. Not dramatically so, but the onyx plates across his chest and along his neck now bore intricate patterns that pulsed with amber light. His throat structure had been subtly altered, and I could feel the new potential humming through our connection.

"Matt," Kelly said carefully, "please tell me we're going to test this somewhere far away from any buildings."

I grinned, feeling Jack's eagerness to try out his new capabilities. "Oh *yeah.* Hey, Mike, about that training session you mentioned…"

Through our link, I felt Jack's satisfaction, and something else—a deeper connection to the dungeon itself, as if the ship's integration had somehow strengthened his role as a defender.

He was more than "just" a mechanical dragon now. He was carrying a piece of the same technology that had brought the dungeon to Earth in the first place.

More than that? The techno-babble data dump that I'd received? It was, among other things, a list of all the possible upgrades that he could receive, and holy cannoli.

I knew instinctively that there were "upgrades" that just weren't upgrades: they were things that would make him better suited to work in deep space, to work in the clouds of gas giants, to enable him to do things that at this point were absolutely no fucking use whatsoever. But eventually?

I reached out to the dungeon, taking a deep breath, then accessed the data that I knew had been dumped there as well. Data that was so far beyond me at this point that I felt like a monkey dancing around the obelisk, staring up at the gleaming form and wondering whether I should paint my shit across it.

I could see the basics, though. Everything that I'd been planning for the dreadnought was not only possible, it was available. Only it wasn't in the way I'd been planning.

Oh no, I needed to find any and all of the remains of the ships that were out there still. Anything and everything I could salvage, I needed! First, though? I needed to know Jack's true capabilities.

"All right," I said, already planning where we could safely test plasma fireballs. "Let's see what you can do."

CHAPTER THIRTY-THREE

The wind whipped past my face as Jack banked lazily to the left. His massive wings caught the morning thermals with an instinctive grace that shouldn't have been possible for something so recently assembled.

Below us, the patchwork of abandoned towns and overgrown fields stretched out toward the ancient city of Durham's skyline.

I'd gotten better at flying myself over the past few months, but this…this was something else entirely.

Jack flew as though he was always created for it, flowing through the air. Every movement was fluid, natural, and the connection between us meant I could feel his joy at finally being able to truly stretch his wings. Every beat, every adjustment, every subtle shift in altitude came through our link with crystal clarity.

"Let's get a closer look at the city," I suggested, though with our connection, I didn't really have to say it out loud.

Jack banked again, beginning a wide spiral that would take us over Durham's historic center. I stared down, remembering it as it had been, and never would be again.

It was a beautiful city, once, and old in a way that few cities were. Because of the ancient walls, the cathedral, the castle, all on a small rocky promontory, it meant that the buildings that surrounded it couldn't expand. The city, farther out? Sure, that was normal, a mixture of old and new and nothing special.

In the heart, though? It was still all cobbled streets and tiny, winding buildings. There were stone sections that were literally polished by a thousand years and more of arses sitting on them, and wonderful little backstreet bars and cafes.

I'd loved my time in Durham, both in younger days working in shitty catering jobs, drinking and exploring, and later on working in IT and taking ladies on dates there.

The devastation became clearer as we descended. A great fire had torn its way through much of the city center and damn, it'd left its mark.

Blackened ruins stretched from the marketplace all the way to the river. The iconic Durham Cathedral, which had stood watch over the city for nearly a thousand goddamn years, was now a gutted shell. Its once-proud towers were broken, and even from here I could see movement in the ruins, creatures that had made their home in the ancient stone.

But it was Durham Castle that got my attention. Unlike the cathedral, portions of the old Norman fortress still stood defiant. And there—along the northern bailey, a section I'd damn well worked in with Chris when we'd been moonlighting in catering jobs, feeding the rich bastards who used it as a university halls of residence—I could see clear signs of fortification.

Makeshift barriers had been erected along the walls, and what looked like a vegetable garden had been established in one of the courtyards.

"There," I directed, and Jack's attention shifted to match my focus. Through our link, I felt his systems coming online. New information swelled up as he performed a fast targeting test—the castle's defensive position was solid, but there were multiple creatures moving through the surrounding ruins. Most avoided the castle itself, but a handful of larger forms prowled closer than comfort would allow.

Jack's new combat systems came online with a subtle hum I could feel through our connection. The amber patterns along his neck began to pulse as he targeted the nearest threat, something that looked a bit like a six-legged bear, but was now twisted by whatever force had changed so much of the local wildlife.

Not that a fucking bear had roamed this country in a long-ass time, but Jack seemed to take a personal affront to him not having been the only bear-like thing to pass this area in the last few centuries.

The plasma bolt that erupted from Jack's maw was a thing of beauty. A concentrated sphere of energy that lanced down as we passed overhead to strike the creature with devastating precision. The monster barely had time to register the threat before it was simply…gone, leaving only a scorched crater behind, one that was surrounded by melting stone.

The remaining creatures scattered, but one—larger and apparently dumber than its fellows—decided to blame the locals, and smashed its way out of a hidden underground parking garage to charge the castle walls instead. Jack's second shot demonstrated that he was already learning to modulate the power of his new weapon. This blast didn't vaporize the target, but rather knocked it back and down, leaving it wounded but alive enough to flee back into the ruins…until he adjusted again, and slammed a blast into it that tore it a new arsehole.

One that led from its upper chest out the far end, and left the rest of the body aflame as it collapsed.

"Nice shooting." I grinned, feeling his satisfaction through our link. "Think you can clear us a landing zone?"

Jack's response was to launch a rapid series of smaller plasma bolts, driving back the few remaining creatures that had been lurking near the castle's main gate. As they fled, I spotted movement along the walls—people, armed but cautious, hiding and watching our approach.

"Time to introduce ourselves," I said. "You okay to hold position here?"

His acknowledgment came through our link, and I grinned. Then I stood up, making sure that the observers could see me, before I stepped off into empty air and plummeted like a meteor.

As I descended toward the castle walls, Jack maintained his position overhead, his presence both reassuring and, I had to admit, impressively intimidating.

Time to see who'd managed to survive all these months in one of Britain's oldest fortresses…

I slammed into the stone of the courtyard, pushing outward with my mana, creating a safe zone in the middle where I impacted—doing a three-point "superhero landing" I might add, thank you *very* much—but surrounding myself in a secondary ring of air that both cracked the ancient stones and sent a blast of air out that cleared the courtyard of any debris.

I rose smoothly and looked about. The sections that I'd seen people huddling in were now conspicuously empty, and I sighed. *Had I overdone it? Man, it had to have looked so freakin' cool, though! I* had *to do it. Fuck, I hope they didn't hide before they saw it. It wasn't like you got to make two entrances like that...*

Reaching up, I tugged off my helmet. Finn had already made me a replacement armor set for the one I'd worn before, though it was, he had to admit, tweaked using the new information he had, and was now an even more exceedingly expensive prototype. I'd argued that the whole thing about being covered in "runes that we don't know what they do" was a bad thing, but it was also pointed out that I was getting to the point where I was the ideal crash test dummy as well.

Kelly had also insisted I go out dressed and ready for war as apparently I couldn't be trusted to "go for a walk without stumbling over a lost fuckin' civilization or something."

I felt that was a bit harsh, all things considered. But, I had to admit, the gleaming metal of the armor made me appear even more a God of the Storm to anyone watching. I settled the helmet under one arm, and smiled, before raising my voice and calling out to the locals.

"It's all right." I kept my voice steady and calm. "I know the whole 'arriving on a dragon' thing might be a bit much, but we're here to help. My name's Matt. I'm from up Newcastle way, and we've been clearing out cities and helping survivors."

A head cautiously peeked over one of the barricades, an older woman in a heavy coat with her steel-grey hair pulled back in a severe bun. She studied me for a long moment before responding.

"You'll forgive our caution," she said finally, her voice carrying the crisp accent of an academic. "The last group who claimed to be here to help tried to take everything we'd managed to preserve."

Through our link, I felt Jack's attention shift; he'd spotted movement in one of the castle's towers. Armed figures, trying to stay out of sight while getting into position. Smart of them, but probably bloody foolish given the plasma-breathing dragon currently hovering overhead.

"Fair enough." I nodded. "How about this? I'll stay right here, you can keep whatever weapons you've got trained on me, and we can have a chat about what you need? Because I've got to tell you, that garden you've got going is impressive, especially considering the frost on it all, but it's not going to be enough to feed any of you."

I meant it. I'd seen it as I landed, a little farther over in a separate section of the castle. They'd managed to either dig through the stone, which was mad, or cart enough earth up and into the courtyard to make a garden, and then they were clearly looking after it as best they could. It even had a glass roof, I'd noticed, as I'd nearly aimed for a landing there until I considered that trashing their attempt at gardening might go down poorly.

That got her attention. She conferred briefly with someone I couldn't see, then straightened up.

"I'm Professor Marshall. Department head of Medieval Studies. Or at least I was." A bitter smile crossed her face. "Though I suppose that expertise has become rather more practical these days."

"The castle's defenses certainly seem to be holding up well," I offered, genuinely impressed. "Norman architecture for the win, yeah?"

That earned me a surprised laugh. "Indeed. Though I suspect William the Conqueror never planned for…whatever those things were that your dragon just dispatched."

Speaking of which… Jack's warning pulsed through our link just as I heard it: movement from the cathedral ruins. Something big was coming, drawn perhaps by the commotion or the death of its fellow monsters.

"Professor," my tone shifted to firm, "I suggest you get your people under cover. We've got incoming, and Jack's about to demonstrate why having a dragon on your side is pretty damn useful."

Jack was already climbing as I spoke, arcing around. His excitement built in me as well, even as someone high in the castle on the far side, presumably able to see more from their vantage point, started to ring a bell frantically.

The thing that emerged from the cathedral's broken walls was massive: a chimeric horror that looked like someone had tried to combine a bull, a bear, and way too many legs into one creature.

Jack's attack run was perfect. A linked system in my HUD appeared with a connection request, and once I approved it, Jack somehow shared his vision with me, making me grin as I saw the creature outlined. A sort of question was asked—no words, but I understood what he wanted, and what he was offering. I designated target points, thanking him for letting me play as well.

Then Jack was off. A series of plasma bolts hammered into it from multiple angles as he screamed past three times in fast succession.

The creature was bigger than Jack, perhaps thirty meters long by twenty wide, and ten tall. And as much as Jack could have toasted it with a single pass, he was experimenting with his abilities and I had to admit that this was the perfect time.

I couldn't help but grin again as I watched through his eyes. Time to show these folks exactly what we could offer in terms of protection.

The chimeric monster roared in pain and fury as Jack's plasma bolts struck home. Through our link, I could feel his targeting systems working—not complex tactical analysis, but basic threat assessment. Each salvo took several seconds to charge and fire, the amber patterns along his neck building to a crescendo before each release.

"Remarkable," Professor Marshall called down, watching the display through one of the old arrow slits in the outer wall. "Is it like you? Armored, I mean? Or mechanical? Ummmm, you are human, aren't you?" she asked breathlessly, staring wide-eyed as he turned for another pass.

"That's Jack," I said, choosing to answer only some of that barrage. "And yeah, he's mechanical, but he's also family."

"Impressive! Can they be mass-produced?" she asked excitedly.

I frowned at her, before shaking my head. "No, he's one of a kind, so far as I know."

The creature was getting pissed now. The first round of impacts had been one after the other, aimed for the mass of legs and in different levels of power, going from mild burns all the way up to vaporization levels.

Clearly it wasn't how fights normally went for this predator. It dashed back and forth, staggering and screaming, slashing at the sky and bellowing something that was presumably "*come down here and fight fair*."

After the third pass, it made one final, desperate lunge toward the castle walls. Having been drawn out onto the bridge that led up to the main gate, it was ridiculously exposed and seemed to realize that far too late.

Jack's response was slower this time. I could feel him charging up for a single shot instead of a salvo, the energy building as his targeting systems locked on. When the blast finally came, it caught the monster square in the chest. The plasma bolt burned clean through its center mass. The thing crashed into the rubble at the base of the walls, its massive form popping and crackling as the plasma continued to cook it from the inside out.

As Jack roared his triumph, arcing around to perform a draconic version of a barrel roll, before returning to take up station overhead, I turned back to the professor.

"So, about that chat? Because I wasn't kidding about the garden. We've got resources, food, and proper medical supplies. And more importantly, we've got safe territory where you don't have to worry about things like that showing up. Mainly because when they do, well, that's what happens to them."

More survivors emerged now, drawn by the spectacle. I counted at least thirty people, ranging from presumably former students to staff, all bearing the lean, hardened look of those who'd survived months of siege conditions.

"And what would you want in return?" a new voice asked. A man stepped forward from a side door—older, weathered face, with a shotgun held carefully at rest, his finger ostentatiously away from the trigger, but close enough it'd not be for long. "Nobody offers help for free these days," he pointed out grimly.

"Information, mainly," I replied honestly. "We're trying to map out surviving populations, figure out what's happening in different areas. Plus, I won't lie, having someone with expertise in medieval fortifications could be bloody useful these days."

Through our link, Jack sent another warning of movement in the ruins. Not complex tactical data, unfortunately, but I was confident that with a few upgrades, we'd be able to get that as well. No, this was just a basic warning of potential threats, as well as a marking of their types. The mana they gave off was tentatively identified as similar to the big one, just a lot weaker. Unsurprisingly, his presence alone seemed to be keeping them at bay for now.

"There's something else," Professor Marshall said slowly. "The way you move, that armor? What are you? How did you get that? And him?"

I nodded. No point hiding it. "Yeah, there's a lot of things that you'll need to be brought up to date on, but for now, I'm just a bloke from Newcastle who's trying to help people survive whatever the hell's happened to our world. The powers? They're just tools to help make that happen."

She studied me for another long moment, then turned to the man with the shotgun. "Jason?"

He adjusted his grip on the weapon, considering. "We've lost six people trying to secure food in the last month alone. The garden's helping, but…" He shrugged. "Way I see it, Professor, we don't have much choice. Winter's coming, and we're not ready for it."

"I'm not sure…" another of the group said slowly. "You want us to leave the safety of these walls? They've protected us this long!"

"They'd not be protecting us against him if he'd decided to attack," Jason pointed out, before shrugging. "Nor that big bugger from the cathedral neither.

Last time we saw it off, we had to use all the cooking oil. If that's what you've just faced that easily…"

"Big bugger?" I asked. "Lots of legs?"

"Yeah, that one your creature just fought."

"Ah, right. Yeah, it's toast." I shrugged.

"And just like that, the power differential is made clear." Another of the crowd spoke up. His scruffy tweed jacket and dirty, threadbare shirt made it clear that whatever he'd been before the fall, it wasn't a natural athlete and warrior.

Professor Marshall turned back to me. "We'll need to discuss this with everyone, but…perhaps you'd like to come inside? The Great Hall's still intact, mostly, and I believe we have some tea left…"

I grinned. "Tea would be brilliant. Mind if Jack lands in the outer bailey? He's still learning his new form, but he'll keep watch while we talk."

Through our link, I felt Jack's simple contentment, just the satisfaction of having protected his charge and the basic instinct to guard. He was still new to this form, still learning, but the potential was there. With time and upgrades, I just knew he'd grow into something fucking terrifying.

As we headed toward the Great Hall, I kept one eye on Jack through our link as he carefully maneuvered into the outer bailey. His landing was cautious, almost delicate for something his size. He was clearly still getting used to managing his new mass, but he managed it, and the ancient stones creaked under his weight, but held firm.

"This way." Professor Marshall gestured, leading us through a series of corridors whose style I vaguely remembered from my catering days. The castle's interior was different now, though, from those drunken days of being invited back for parties. Instead of drunken young lads and lasses and music, there were makeshift barriers at strategic points, supplies stacked along walls, and the unmistakable signs of long-term occupation.

"How many people have you got here?" I asked, noting the sleeping bags rolled up in what had once been a student common room.

"Forty-three at last count," Jason answered from behind me, his shotgun now slung but still readily accessible. "Started with nearly three hundred and seventy."

"The first few months were…difficult," Professor Marshall added quietly. "We lost many before we properly organized ourselves. The students who stayed…well. Medieval studies suddenly became rather practical, as did engineering. Though I suspect Professor Williams never imagined his expertise in medieval agriculture would be quite so vital."

The tweed-jacketed man I'd noticed earlier nodded eagerly at that. "Rather puts a new perspective on all those years studying crop rotation patterns, doesn't it, Sarah?"

We emerged into the Great Hall, and I had to pause for a moment. The last time I'd been here, it had been set up for a fancy dinner. All white tablecloths and crystal glasses. Now it was clearly their living space, with tables pushed together for communal meals, basic cooking facilities set up near the old fireplace, and what looked like a small classroom area in one corner.

"What the hell is going on?" I frowned. "The castle is huge. I mean, why are you all in here?"

"Strength in numbers." One of the former students nearby shrugged, his skin dirty, clothes looking stiff enough with dirt that they could probably stand up without him, and a few months' worth of a very patchy beard. "If we're all in here, nothing can pick off the weaker ones."

"Weaker ones?" I frowned at the professors and Jason as it clicked. "Wait, you mean there's something inside the castle?"

"There's things that appear and vanish, like walking shadows," Jason admitted. "They don't like the light, but we're low on supplies of burnable material. So we keep everyone in one room."

"Walking shadows?" I asked.

"They literally look like that, like tall people, all black, and they let off glowing gas from their mouth." Someone, a young woman, spoke up.

"Ah, fuck…baubas?" I shook my head in disgust. "They go up like a flash if they catch fire?"

"Ah, we've not tried to set fire to them," the crop rotation professor admitted. "We didn't want to antagonize them. As it is, they've been growing more and more aggressive since we bunched up here and deprived them of their prey."

"Fuck's sake." I sighed, covering my eyes. "Okay, new plan. Any of you got any levels? Classes?"

"I'm the highest level here," Jason admitted.

"Excellent, and you are?"

"Level four."

"Well, fuck me sideways with a lit Roman candle," I said. "Well, shit, you've all got a shock coming to your systems, let's just say that."

"Right then." Professor Marshall gestured to a chair at what had probably been the high table in better days. "Let's discuss exactly what kind of help you're offering then, and what you mean about 'safe territory.'"

Through our link, I felt Jack settling into his guard position, his basic systems already establishing a perimeter scan. Not complex, but reliable. As I sat down, accepting a chipped mug of what smelled like actual tea—even if it was so weak it barely changed the color of the water in it—I couldn't help but smile as I shook my head. These people had survived, adapted, made something work in impossible circumstances.

They'd also done it while evidently trying to remain pacifists and not piss off any of the things that were feeding on them, apparently practically nightly.

I directed Jack to search any of the castle he could for mana signatures, describing as best I could what I was expecting the baubas to look like.

"Right." I set down the tea. "First things first. We need to deal with your shadow problem. Baubas are nasty little shits, but they're not actually that tough once you know how to handle them."

"You've encountered these creatures before?" Professor Marshall leaned forward with interest.

"Encountered, killed, and catalogued." I nodded. "They're ranked as a low threat, but they're dangerous because they hunt in packs and prey on the weak. And you've basically been serving yourselves up to them like an all-you-can-eat buffet by clustering everyone together. Hell, I'm betting they've got a nest under us in the bowels of the castle."

"We had no choice," Jason protested. "We lost twelve people in the first week when they were sleeping alone or in small groups."

"Because you didn't fight back," I pointed out. "Look, I get it. You were trying to be careful, scientific even. But these things? They're not interested in science, or communication. They're predators, and they've been treating you like livestock."

Through our link, I felt Jack's alert ping. He'd detected movement in the shadows of the castle's lower levels. Even his basic sensors could pick up the characteristic mana signature of the baubas as dozens of them roamed down there, now that he knew what to look for.

I squinted at that, holding a hand up for silence as I examined the signature, using a combination of the senses he was sharing with me and my own mana sight that the dungeon had given me when I'd first bonded with it.

It was rare I used it, honestly, and I didn't think I'd ever used it to anywhere near its real possible limit, but until recently it'd been more of a curiosity than anything usable.

Seeing the way that Jack examined the mana at a distance, and then picked out the various strands, then matched them to a creature, though? That could be incredibly useful, but it'd need some practice first.

I made a mental note to explore that as soon as I got a chance, and then promptly got the hell on with fucking some shit up.

"How many rooms can you light up properly?" I asked, already forming a plan.

"We've got enough fuel for maybe three hours of bright light in this hall," Professor Williams offered. "The garden has its own solar setup, but we've been unable to get that working and…"

"Right then." I sighed. "So, first of all, I need a volunteer, just one of you, as I want to be sure I can keep them safe, and yet show you what the real goddamn world is like. No! Not you!" I said quickly, pointing at Jason as he opened his mouth. "You stay with the rest and then you know they're safe and they have you in case anything goes wrong…"

I turned slowly, assessing the group, before picking a guy at the back who looked as if he could barely lift the crossbow he was clutching. "Perfect! Well volunteered," I told him, getting a panicked look from him as he took a step back.

"I didn't… I mean, I haven't… I…" he babbled.

I ignored him, turning to the woman apparently more or less in charge of the situation. "Professor Marshall, I need a full layout of the castle—every room, every passage."

I rubbed at my chin, trying to remember the layout that I'd seen of the castle before, and came up with a rough mental map. "I think it's time to take your home back. It should take us about three hours, if my guess at the castle's size is right."

"Might we ask how you came to that conclusion?" she asked weakly, and I nodded.

"That's less time than it'd take to clear a real nest, which I know this couldn't be classed as, because you're all alive still. I flew here from Newcastle in about twenty minutes, and there's no way this is going to take me longer than it'd take me to run back on foot."

"I don't…" the boy was still stammering.

I sighed and strode over to him. The professor followed, but the others drew back as I dropped my voice low and spoke quickly, but confidently.

"What's your name?" I asked. "Come on, lad, speak up."

"Red."

I quirked an eyebrow in question.

"Redin, but everyone calls me Red," he clarified.

Judging from the terrible complexion and the rail-thin appearance under the filthy clothes, I could see why. Those spots would have been an issue for anyone, but for a guy whose face was dominated by an enormous nose already, and appeared to have been streamlined by nature to be used as an arrow by anyone else, combined with them? Yeah, he was going to need all the help he could get.

"Trust me on this, Red," I said. "Listen to my orders, do as I say, and I guarantee you will not only survive, but you'll be power-leveled by me in here personally. I'm Matt, the Dungeon Warmancer of Newcastle, the God of Lightning and First Lord of the Storm. There is nothing here that I can't tear apart with my bare hands. Follow me, *trust* in me, and be my example to the others. Let me show them what they can achieve."

"I…" He blinked, then looked sideways to where a group of girls sat.

I couldn't help but smile. "The levels you'll get will come with points that you can spend however you like," I assured him. "And just in case…" I reached into the bag of holding and withdrew a ruby-red healing potion that glimmered softly in the light of multiple fires. "This healing potion will restore more health than I'm willing to bet you've ever had. Trust me, mate. I'll keep you safe."

"Red, you don't have to do this," the professor said carefully, waiting until he looked at her, and she went on. "Perhaps I could take a weapon and go with you?" she suggested to me.

I shook my head. "They need you here, and they'll need you to vouch for him as being him when he comes back."

"As being him?" She frowned.

"If there are only a handful of baubas in the castle, I'd be surprised. Most likely it's a nest and they're the reason your other monsters in the area haven't overran you already. They're keeping you as an easy access emergency larder, and feeding on the monsters as a regular meal. That means I should be able to easily get him a few levels at least. Each level gives five points for a human. So say he gets five levels, puts them all into Strength, Constitution, and Charisma—that's not advice, by the way…just as a point of discussion—then he'll be almost unrecognizable when he comes back. He'd be literally twice the man he is, for a start."

"A man's worth is not defined by his muscles." The professor sounded faintly disapproving, and I nodded.

"And I agree. Should he be that way inclined, we have researchers, magical and normal, farmers, doctors, teachers, and mages, though the buggers like to be called mancers for some reason," I finished with a shrug. "My point stands. If he spends those points down there, you might no longer recognize him, so I'd ask you wait until we return here and then you assign your points where people can see, is that okay?" I asked him.

He opened his mouth and flapped it a little, unable to speak.

"Ah, great…overcome with excitement!" I declared, clamping a hand on his shoulder. "Where's that map?"

"Red knows the layout of the castle, better than anyone," a girl in the group he'd been looking to said suddenly, and I grinned.

"Great! He can direct." With that, I dragged him along toward the nearest door, before pausing as I spotted an hourglass sitting to one side. "Perfect! Set that going, and let's see how long this takes, eh?"

With that, I dragged Red out of the room and into the corridor beyond, slamming the door behind me. People stared after us, probably unsure whether I was their savior, a knight in literally shining armor, or whether I'd just kidnapped one of their number.

Having managed to get this far on simply not giving Red a chance to chicken out, I decided to keep going with that as my modus operandi.

"Right then!" I declared, practically dragging Red along the darkened corridor. "First lesson in monster hunting—always keep moving! Baubas like to ambush stationary targets."

"I… I don't…" Red stammered. His crossbow shook in his hands as he grabbed the bolt and just managed to keep it from falling out.

"Mate, if you finish that sentence with 'know about this' or 'think I can,' I swear I'll shoot my next lightning bolt at you instead," I warned cheerily. "Now, you see anything moving in the shadows, you shoot it. Don't think, don't hesitate—just shoot. I'll handle the rest."

Through our link, I felt Jack's amusement at my teaching style, along with a ping indicating movement below us. The castle's lower levels were practically crawling with the bastards.

"B-but what if I hit you?" Red's voice cracked.

"Then I'll be very impressed with your aim. But honestly, I don't care. It's a risk I'm happy to run because I'm going to be in front of you the whole time." I grinned. "Besides, I'm wearing actual armor. You're not going to—there! Three o'clock!"

A shadow detached itself from a distant alcove—pitch-black, shadowy claws extending toward us. Red yelped but, to his credit, actually fired. The bolt went wide, admittedly, clattering off the stone wall, but it was a start.

"Good! You actually shot!" I called out cheerfully, even as I casually strode forward and backhanded the baubas with my gauntlet; a single blow that tore its head clear off. "That's progress! Now, next time try hitting the thing, yeah?"

"That…that was—" Red stared at the collapsing remains.

"That was one down, probably about fifty to go." I cut him off. "Keep moving, keep shooting. Think you can handle that?"

Before he could answer, two more shadows emerged from the darkness ahead. I reached over, gripping the crossbow and ignoring his attempt at winding the crank, and instead dragged the string into place with pure muscle, then handed it back.

He barely managed to get the bolt into position, his hand was shaking so much. Red's next shot was still shaky, but it actually clipped one of them, causing it to screech in pain.

"Now that's more like it!" I laughed, before throwing my hand outward and unleashing a lightning bolt that screamed down the passage and blasted into, then through the pair, leaving nothing but scorched stone and the smell of ozone. "See? You wound 'em, I end 'em. Simple!"

"But…how…you just…" he babbled, terror and awe filling him.

"Less stammering, more shooting!" I called out, moving on and scooping up one of the crossbow bolts from the floor, examining it. "Damaged, never mind!" I tossed it aside and dragged him around a corner. "Besides, you just gained some XP from that lot. How's it feel? And check your notifications as we go okay?"

Red blinked, probably seeing the notification in his own HUD. "I… I gained a level?"

"Welcome to the real world, mate. Remember, no cheating and assigning points yet." I grinned. "Now, come on. I can hear more of them below us. Time to go dungeon diving in your own bloody castle!"

The look of terrified confusion on his face was priceless.

"Another one!" Red yelped almost as soon as we were out of the stairwell. His crossbow bolt actually caught this baubas in what passed for its throat. The creature staggered, red vapor hissing from its shark-like mouth.

"See? You're getting better already!" I called out proudly, casually backhanding it into the wall. "Though, honestly, mate, you could probably just punch them at this point. You've gone up what, two levels, three?"

Red was breathing hard, but there was a new light in his eyes as he checked his status. "Three!"

"Doing well then! Okay, when we get you back to the others, then you can spend the points, okay—not before! I want them to be able to see the effects, but for now, let's keep hunting!"

A growl echoed from the darkness ahead, and I grinned as Red actually stepped forward instead of back this time.

"That's more like it! Getting cocky now, eh?" I laughed, striding forward. "Right then, time for some advanced tactics. You know what happens when you hit them in the mouth with that bolt of yours?"

"They…they can't bite us?" Red ventured, already frantically cranking his crossbow.

"Exactly! Ten points to Gryffindor!" I declared. "Though, really, Durham's more of a Ravenclaw, if we're honest. Now, there's probably a whole nest of the bastards down in the underneath…the undercroft? Fuck it, the basement! Ready to clear them out?"

A screech echoed up from below, followed by several more. Red's grip on his crossbow tightened, but I noticed his hands weren't shaking anymore.

"That's the spirit!" I grinned. "Remember when these things had you all huddled in one room? Now watch this…" I stuck my head down the next stairwell and bellowed: "Oi! Fuckfaces! Two heroes here, coming down to ruin your day!"

"Should…should we really be alerting them?" Red asked nervously, checking his bolt supply.

"Course we should! More targets means more XP for you. Besides…" I paused as five baubas emerged from the shadows below, their red eyes glowing malevolently. "These things are like bullies—they only pick on the weak. Show them you're not afraid and—hey! Well done!"

Red's bolt had taken the lead creature right in its grotesque mouth, actually pinning its jaws together. The thing thrashed, trying to dislodge the projectile, while its companions hissed in fury.

"Now that's just showing off." I laughed, before unleashing a channeled lightning bolt that reduced all five to ash. "Though, really, who keeps this many murderous shadow monsters in their wine cellar? Proper health code violation, that is. Come on, time to clear out your basement."

Through our link, I felt Jack's amusement, along with a warning ping about more movement below. Good. The more the merrier.

"Oh, and Red?" I added as we descended. "If you throw up when we find their nest, I'm counting that as a forfeit and we start over—go straight out and find another monster nest. So no pressure!"

The look he gave me was brilliant—somewhere between determination not to vomit and wondering whether I was insane.

I was actually enjoying myself tremendously as we strode along. "Come on, mate, try to pick up the pace. I know I said three, but I want to be back in there inside the hour, all the job done and ready for the next step!" I called over my shoulder as my armor jingled, each step down the ancient stone ringing the dinner bell for the fuckers below.

"Next step?" Red panted, trying to keep up while reloading. "What next step?"

"Well, once we've cleared out your basement, we need to deal with the situation in the cathedral," I said lightheartedly. "You know, the thing Jack blew a hole through earlier? Sure, it's dead, but I'm pretty sure it's got friends."

A chorus of hisses erupted from the darkness below, and I grinned as Red actually managed to loose another bolt before I could even point out the targets. This one caught a baubas right in its glowing red eye.

"Now you're getting it!" I laughed, unleashing another lightning bolt that cleared the stairwell. "Though you might want to save some bolts. Based on the noise, I'd say we're getting close to—ah! There it is!"

We emerged into what had probably been a proper medieval storage chamber once upon a time. Then it'd been redecorated and done up to fit in with the whole "ancient castle turned into fucking student accommodation," which meant shitty carpeting and white-washing everything, then adding a load of attempts at art and a pool table.

"How the hell did they get that down here?" I asked, genuinely surprised.

"The far end, there's a ramp up and then cellar doors that lead out on the next floor," he said quickly, torn between wanting to answer a question, and desperately wanting to remain silent and unnoticed.

It'd probably once been part of the overall student lifestyle, a meeting point and playground combined, filled with alcohol, hipsters, and poor social choices. Probably reeking of Axe body spray. Now, the walls were covered in some kind of black, oily residue that seemed to pulse in the light of my armor's glow.

"Oh, that's just disgusting," I commented cheerfully. "Look at that—they've basically turned your wine cellar into a shadow-creature spawning pit. Bet that plays hell with the vintage."

There was a student bar here, a small one, and the grates had been broken at some point, opened up so that people could presumably loot it when the world had ended. And now, there was just a fucking mess of black spidery-like webbing that covered far too much of the place for me to be comfortable stepping in.

Red made a sound somewhere between a laugh and a retch as dozens of red eyes opened in the darkness. The baubas began emerging from every shadow, their shark-like mouths opening in unison.

"Right then!" I declared, cracking my knuckles. "New lesson. When faced with overwhelming odds, what do you do?"

"Run?" Red suggested, backing up a step.

"Nope! I'm taking three points off your score for that, mate. You go absolutely mental and show them why picking this fight was the worst mistake they've ever made. Watch this!"

I thrust both hands forward, channeling enough power to light up the entire chamber. The lightning bolts that erupted from my hands were probably a bit excessive, but hey, you've got to make an impression on your first proper student.

I channeled my power into them, sweeping them from one side to the other, dragging the crackling, cleansing light across the floor and up the walls, ensuring that nothing escaped my wrath.

Through our link, I felt Jack's amusement turn to concern at the power usage. But as low level as these were compared to me now, it was just a joke. Also, how often do you get to dramatically clear out an entire nest of shadow monsters while teaching someone the proper way to dungeon dive?

We strode across the floor, passing the ashen remains of dozens of baubas. But before I reached the door into the next area, I paused, then grinned.

"Have you been offered any quests before?" I asked Red suddenly, and he gulped and nodded. "Great. Got one for this yet?" I asked.

"Well, yes, but I turned it down?"

"What?" I asked, astonished and horrified, turning to face him. "Why the hell would you do that?"

"The professor…she told us to. We had a meeting and a vote. Nothing good came out of the quests that people were offered. They always died, so we agreed as a group to decline the quests, to always just say no."

"Are you fucking with me?" I asked him after a few seconds of silence. "That's it, right? You're fuckin' with me?"

"N…no?" he whispered, clearly seeing anger in my eyes for the first time.

"FUCK'S SAKE!" I roared. On the other side of the doors, an answering screech rang out as whatever was left clearly decided I was challenging it. "And you can fuck off as well!" I shouted in its direction.

"But the quests are traps…" Red tried to explain. "If you try them, you die. Everyone always does."

"Bollocks," I snapped before forcing myself to calm down and speak slowly, as if I were explaining things to a small child. "If you fuck up, if you fail the quest, if you try to do something you're not ready for, then you die. If you use your brain and find a way to complete it, you get a shitload more of a reward for that! Again, check your notifications as we go. Don't assign any points, not yet, but check and see if you've been offered another quest," I ordered him, hoping.

"No, nothing," he said after a few seconds.

"Fuck!" I snarled, punching the door. It cracked down its length, sagging on its hinges, and I glared at it. "Fine, fuck it. What's done is done. From now on, though? You damn well assess them and take any you can! Let's finish this."

My good mood was dramatically reduced by the sheer stupidity of refusing the quests, but the final chamber was worse. Much worse. What had probably started life as the castle's main wine cellar had been transformed into something out of a nightmare. The black, oily residue was thicker here, forming cocoon-like structures that pulsed with a sickly red glow.

"Oh fuck," I breathed, my levity vanishing as I spotted the first of the victims. Human shapes were suspended in the webbing, barely moving. "Red, how many people have you lost over the months?"

"H…hundreds?" he stammered. Then his eyes widened as he realized what he was seeing. "Are they—"

"Yeah, some of them are still alive. For now." I cut him off, my voice hardening as something massive shifted in the darkness at the far end of the chamber. "Remember what I said about not throwing up? Forget that. Just stay behind me. Try to tag as many of the enemy as you can and you'll get points for helping, but stay out of the way."

The thing that emerged was a baubas, but twisted, grown grotesque with constant feeding. Its mouth wasn't just shark-like anymore—it had split its entire head. Rows of teeth extended down what had once been its chest. Red vapor poured from between them, and the ambient temperature plummeted.

"That's…that's the queen?" Red's voice cracked, but to his credit, he was already raising his crossbow.

"Good lad," I said quietly, gathering power. "Take the shot, then get ready to start cutting people free. This is going to get messy."

Red's bolt caught the queen in one of its clusters of red eyes. The thing's screech shook the ancient stones, and suddenly the chamber was full of movement as dozens of regular baubas emerged to protect their monarch.

"Right then," I growled, lightning crackling between my hands. "Let's see how you like it when someone comes for *your* children."

The battle that followed was pure carnage, and incredibly one-sided. I strode forward, glaring at the big fucker, and as I went, I triggered Incinerate again and again. With my manapool, I could use it practically without concern…and for baubas, their greatest weakness was fire.

As they each appeared, they burst into flames and died, collapsing as they rushed me. I wanted to just flood the fucking place with the cleansing blue-white light of the storm, but there were too many bodies strung up, being fed upon. I couldn't risk them being hit as well.

The queen was tough, probably the equivalent of ten regular baubas compressed into one horror, huge and with consummate reach and lethal claws, not to mention the whole "paralyze and feed on you" thing the species had going on if you breathed in the gas they gave off. But against me? She was just a bigger target.

I wanted to go all out. Fuck, looking at the bodies around here, the struggling and desperately traumatized people who were being used as a fucking larder, a veritable snack for when the bitch was bored?

I wanted to go all out, all right, but I wanted to do it with my fists.

I wanted to grind her into paste and tear her arms off and beat her to death with them. I wanted to fold, maim, and mutilate her into a small square and then put her in an oven, and spend a week slowly increasing the goddamn temperature, a single degree at a time.

Instead, though, to save the struggling people who surrounded her, I simply lifted into the air and floated forward, staring.

She hesitated, roaring at me, before starting to back up. Apparently even her minute brain spotted that something was wrong in the way that her sneakily hidden forces had erupted into flames as soon as they appeared.

Then I pushed with my mana, and pushed *hard.*

I launched forward with the full power of my flight, drew a fist back, and smashed it through her head. The far side erupted in a spray of fluids and teeth. I dropped down, grabbing the two sides of the wound I'd just blasted through her, and heaved with all my might.

The body thrashed; gouts of blood and vapor burst into the air as I tore her literally in half, barehanded.

Then I dropped her twitching corpse to the side and shook my hands, before surrounding me in a collection of fast-lived Incinerate spells.

I dragged them out, extending the space they covered, so that I didn't injure myself. But the corpse caught fire, bursting into flames, and more and more of the ground around me joined her.

I'd been intending to just dissipate the vapor. I wasn't sure whether it would work on me, after all, not now—but I didn't want to finish the dive with me keeling over paralyzed and ruin the whole image thing.

Instead, I saw that the ground here was covered in shadowy eggs, as newborn baubas screeched and burned. I made a mental note to burn the fucking castle to the ground if I had to, once the prisoners were freed.

I turned to find Red already cutting down the first of the cocooned victims. His hands shook again, but not from fear this time.

"How long?" he asked hoarsely, cradling the head of an elderly man who was barely breathing. "How long have they been down here, being…being fed on?"

"Too long," I replied grimly, moving to help. "But they're alive. That's what matters. Get them free, get them upstairs. Your people are going to need those medical supplies I promised even more than I thought."

In the end, we found thirty-two survivors. Some had only been there days, others…others had been the queen's living larder for weeks or months. All of them would need serious help to recover, not just physically but mentally.

"Nine levels," Red said suddenly as we got the last victim free. He stared at his hands as if he didn't recognize them. "I gained nine levels killing these…these things."

"Yeah." I nodded, understanding exactly what he was feeling. I clapped a hand on his shoulder and squeezed, gently. "Welcome to the real world, mate. Sometimes the XP comes with nightmares."

Through our link, I felt Jack's acknowledgment. He'd spotted something approaching the castle. There were more of those cathedral monstrosities, though these were much smaller. Good. After what we'd just seen, I was in the mood for something I could just kill without having to stop until I'd gotten the rage out.

"Come on," I said. "Time to get these people upstairs. Then we can show your friends exactly what those levels mean."

The look he gave me wasn't confused anymore. It was determined.

Good. He was going to need that strength for what was coming.

CHAPTER THIRTY-FOUR

"Well, it's never a fuckin' dull day with you, is it?" Chris called out to me as he drove through the last of the remains of the city. The truck rolled to a halt after pushing a nearby car aside.

"About time you got here, part-timer!" I called back, striding over and clapping my old friend in a hug.

"So how bad is it?" he asked me quietly as I released him.

"Bad," I admitted. "You weren't there for the baubas fight, but you've heard me talk about them, right?"

"Yeah. Fucking nightmares, I heard."

"Basically, yeah. They're not hard to fight but insidious. And if you're weak as well…well, they're hard to overcome. Especially if you've handicapped your own side by not accepting quests."

"Seriously?" He frowned. "Why the hell would you do that?"

"Idiots," I replied. "You know academics—all intelligence, no fuckin' common sense."

"Damn, do we really have to let them in?" he asked, jokingly, and I shrugged.

"If it helps, I was thinking that Barry has more room than we do," I pointed out, then I winked.

"Oh yeah." He grinned, then nodded as the professor, Jason, and the newly minted Hunter class, Red, came over to join us.

Red had apparently invested a lot in his physical traits. Nine levels from the fight in the undercroft had been enough to get him to level eleven. Between the bonus for hitting level ten, the class bonuses, and the points he'd earned in the fight, he was almost unrecognizable.

Certainly he was physically. The entire group of girls who had been pretty uninterested in him before now stared at him in wonder. He'd put some into Strength, and more into Constitution, but Dexterity and Perception were his main skills, and he looked like the archer figure in the Marvel comics wished he could damn well look now.

Tall, practically glowing with health, and literally bulging out of his clothes, he was a hell of a sight. And he'd earned a further three levels in the time it took Chris and the others to arrive. I'd escorted him and a girl he was interested in around the city, teaching them the basics so that they could help teach the others.

Most of the creatures in the area weren't high enough leveled to be interesting to me in the slightest. A backhand or at most, a hard punch, was more than enough to end any interest they had in living. But for the lower-leveled pair, it was a gold mine.

I'd explained the realities of life to the group as well. They were caught between embarrassment at how bloody wrong they'd gotten it, and relief that I'd come…and wasn't about to take advantage of them.

Or at least that it hadn't happened yet.

"Professor, let me introduce Chris. He's my right hand and one of the best fighters we have, despite his sense of humor. Believe me when I say that unless an army attacks you between here and the park, he'll get you there in time for dinner."

"If there's an army, it might take until supper," Chris joked, before offering his hand as they introduced themselves.

"Good lord," Professor Marshall breathed, staring at the nearly silent vehicle. "But how…we couldn't get even the photo-voltaic cells to respond! How are you running these?"

Chris grinned, stepping back and popping the hood. "Want to see something cool?"

The academics practically tripped over themselves rushing forward, then stopped dead at the sight of the softly glowing crystal where the engine block should have been. Bands of metal wrapped around it in geometric patterns that pulsed with each surge of power.

"Is that…that's crystallization!" Professor Williams exclaimed, his earlier exhaustion forgotten. "The theoretical applications alone… It's a crystal—where's the power coming from? Can they be grown? And to run a vehicle such as this… Why, the energy density must be extraordinary! And the conversion rate—"

"Careful there, you're starting to sound like our Aly." I laughed. "She's the one who designed these. Wait till you see what she's done with the rest of our tech."

"The bands," Jason noted, examining them carefully. "They're reminiscent of Celtic knotwork, but more…deliberate somehow?"

"Mana channeling circuits," Chris explained, clearly enjoying their fascination and his rare opportunity to look knowledgeable. "Forms a complete loop that—"

"That maintains consistent power output while minimizing energy bleed!" Professor Marshall finished excitedly. "It's brilliant! The theoretical implications for sustainable energy alone—"

"And that's just the transport," I cut in before they could really get going.

"Wait till you see the heated showers."

I glared at Chris, wondering what the hell he was doing.

That got their attention. "Hot water?" someone in the crowd asked hopefully.

"Hot water," Chris confirmed. "Plus proper food, medical care, and best of all? Walls that actually keep the monsters out. Speaking of which…" He gestured to the three large trucks he'd brought. "Shall we? The park's about twenty minutes away, if we don't hit any trouble."

"Unless there's an army," Red quoted with a grin, helping some of the weaker survivors toward the nearest vehicle.

"In which case, supper," several voices chorused, the tension breaking as people laughed.

I caught Chris's eye as they loaded up. He nodded slightly, grinning.

"What the hell was that about 'mana channeling circuitry'?" I asked him in a low voice. "You couldn't change the time on the damn microwave before all of this, so don't tell me you've been studying that shit."

"Heard people arguing over it last night." He winked. "Made me sound smart though, right?"

"Dick."

"I have a very large one, yes." He nodded, before sighing as he glanced at the people being helped into the back of the trucks nearby. He could clearly see what the baubas had done to their prisoners. These people would need more than just physical healing. But that could wait until they were safe.

"Right then," I said, preparing to take off. "I'll scout ahead with Jack, clear any nasties off the road. Chris, try not to lose anyone this time?"

"That was one time!" he protested, picking up the joke and looking mortified. "And technically, they weren't lost. If you remember, we found most of them later. Bits were just…temporarily misplaced."

The professors exchanged worried glances at that, making both of us laugh.

"He's joking," I assured them. "Mostly. Now, if you'll excuse me…"

I lifted off the ground, fighting the urge to put one fist up and rocket away like I was in a movie. The academics' gasps of amazement followed me skyward as Jack unfurled his wings on the castle wall, leaping free as well with a great boom of displaced air. It was time to go be impressive somewhere else—I had a meeting to get to.

The flight back was a study in contrasts. Below, Chris's convoy wound its way carefully through the debris-strewn streets, while Jack and I soared overhead, occasionally diving down to deal with anything that looked threatening.

"Show-off," I muttered as Jack incinerated a pack of what looked like mutated dogs with a precisely aimed wash of plasma. Through our link, I felt his smug satisfaction. The mechanical dragon was definitely getting used to his new capabilities, and far from running all day and night to cover a small distance—in comparison to now—he was gliding easily on the thermals.

From up here, you could really see how the world had changed. Durham's surroundings were scarred by new threats: from the nests of creatures that had been happily living in the cathedral's broken towers—until this afternoon, anyway—to strange growth patterns in what had been carefully maintained gardens.

We passed over what looked to be walled compounds here and there. I saw the signs of people, of well-worn paths through mud and what must have been painstakingly cultivated gardens and small fields. I made a note to ask Jack to take Ashley out on a hearts and minds recruiting tour, and then another note that she'd need real armor for that, as well as a group on the ground to follow and back her up.

But as we approached Gateshead, there were signs of recovery too: the organized patrols around Saltwell Park, the cleared streets, the fortified positions Barry had established, high walls and the safety inside.

Hundreds of people went about their daily lives, and I saw the gleam of lights from inside the arcology, hundreds of rooms, each holding people who now had a chance to live their lives.

Kids inside the building pressed up against the glass, pointing, jumping up and down and waving; I smiled, my face unable to be seen in my helmet, but I waved. Clearly word had gotten around about the Dungeon Lord now being a dragon rider as well.

"Right, they're in sight of the park now," I told Jack as we circled one final time. Through our link, I could sense his reluctance to leave. He'd certainly taken to his guardian role with enthusiasm, and I couldn't help but smile at that. It was definitely who he was. "Come on, you great lizard. Kelly's waiting, and you know how she gets when we're late."

Jack's response was to execute a perfect barrel roll before banking toward Newcastle, clearly hoping to scare me, or make a spectacle for the kids watching. I shrugged and instead held out my hands, arms at full extension, holding on with my knees and my flight capability pressing me down into the seat that he'd graciously provided me.

He wasn't the only one who could show off, after all.

Though I had to admit, watching the sunset glint off his bronze and silver plating as we flew over the Tyne, there was something properly majestic about him now.

The dungeon appeared below us as the river fell behind, its walls gleaming and high, offering solid protection to our people. Pride surged as we arced around. I could already sense Kelly and Aly's presence in the dungeon sense as I flew overhead, and I smiled.

"Fuck it," I muttered. "Go on then, Jack—good hunting!" I called to him, before standing up and launching myself from his back. He let loose a roar of excitement, beating his wings hard as he lined up on the path we'd just followed.

I felt it through our link, the desire to clear out the nests he'd seen along the way, to slaughter any monsters that he could find roaming, and I wished him well.

For me, it was unfortunately time to look over the details for London. But once that was out of the way, things were definitely picking up in speed, as shown by how quickly and easily we'd just recruited another, what? Seventy-odd people for a day's work?

That thought rang true for me, though. For me, today had been a minor issue, barely worth the noticing. There'd certainly been little risk, that was for sure. But for them?

I'd literally saved those lives. There was no doubt in my mind, that had I not stepped in today, their life would have been measured in weeks at most.

And through it all, that was what mattered.

Today I'd saved lives, even if they were those of academics who needed a practical lesson in monster hunting.

"Well, if it isn't his lordship, finally gracing us with his presence," Kelly drawled as I strode into the control room a few minutes later. Her mock annoyance was betrayed by the way she immediately stepped over to check me for injuries and give me a kiss, a habit she'd developed that I found both irritating and endearing, respectively.

"All good. Just rescuing academics and clearing out shadow monsters. You know, Tuesday stuff," I quipped as I dropped into my chair.

Aly summoned a detailed map of London before us. The holographic overlay flickered to life, showing potential infiltration routes marked in pulsing blue lines.

"Right then," Mike began, all business. "Unlike you, I've got shit to do tonight, so let's get to it. The Scepiniir have agreed to guide us in. Apparently fighting their most revered war leader and not being instantly gutted by him has earned you a little respect. But don't worry—to me, you'll always be Potato-face and unable to tell the difference between a mag and a clip."

"That's a relief—" I started, only to be cut off.

"For a price, of course. They're fucking mercenaries, and they want better armor, weapons, and a personal chance to face you in the arena."

"Fuck that." I snorted. "I mean, I kicked their boss's arse and—"

"And I agreed, both because it'll be good for your training—no powers allowed—and I knew it'd annoy you. Know what the lesson here is?"

"What?" I glared at him.

"Don't fuck off for the majority of the day when you've told us you'll be half an hour for a test flight." He smiled at me.

"I hate you," I muttered. "Let me guess, they're not telling us how they know the area we need…?"

"Would you believe they used the excuse of shopping trips?" Kelly smirked.

"Seriously?"

"Well, they've been helping themselves to army equipment in the area, then using it to keep their people alive anyway," Mike cut in. "But, just in case and because I'm a paranoid bastard, I won't be going in alone with them. I'm taking the Karens as well as a few of our people."

I nodded at that. That was a good call. I didn't see them much—which was always a good sign in a group dedicated to stealth and assassination—but the Karens were an all-kobold sneaky-stabby-stabby team that I'd used before.

As an example, they'd snuck their way through the British Army base nearby, taking up position and ready to stab the fuckers in the back if they'd not agreed to join us when we'd had our recent slight falling-out.

Also, helpfully, they'd not been seen when things turned out well, because having been caught with them ready to slaughter everyone at the wrong time could have been a minor issue.

"The cold won't be an issue anymore as well," Aly cut in, tapping commands that brought up schematics of what looked like seriously upgraded kobold gear. "The new suits are mana-insulated. Beta's team has been training in them. They can move practically silently now, even with full equipment."

"And our fairy friends?" I noted the concerned look Kelly and Aly exchanged. "We talked about including one as a healer?"

"That's…complicated," Kelly said carefully. "They're more than willing to help, but they've got their own agenda. Something about 'maintaining balance' and 'proper succession of power,' whatever the hell that means."

"Fantastic. More cryptic bullshit. Get Ciara in and involve her," I suggested. I leaned forward, studying the map. "She won't take any crap, and if need be, remind her as the Mistress of the Minions, you outrank her. Either she comes clean, or I'll make her swear to obey you in all things and then you can ask her again. So, timeline?"

Mike pointed to several marked locations. "We move tonight. The Scepiniir will lead my team in through these service tunnels. We're heading from the southern dungeon, but should be able to make it into position—if we leave like in the next half an hour, thank you so much for taking your fuckin' time—while you and Jack wait here." He indicated a position well outside the city.

"You wait for our signal. Once we've secured the initial entry point, you move in and we get that dungeon core planted before anyone realizes what's happening.

I don't need you and your shitty stealth skills fucking this up, so you're getting air-dropped in only when the site is secure—that's it, all right?"

"Okay, that sounds good—" I started, only to have Mike hold his hand up to stop me.

"But…I don't want the fairy healer."

"All right, why?" I asked.

"They're basically fucking toddlers on a massive sugar rush, if we took the sugar away and replaced it with a straight diet of cocaine and Red Bull," he replied flatly. "In a stealth environment, that's what the military describes as a serious no-no."

"Really?" I asked. "I can just imagine you all around a table in the desert, looking for the bad guys using that 'Oh we can't do that, it's a serious no-no,'" I mimicked.

"Well, you'd be surprised the terminology we use, but fuck it, I decided that it was the closest you'd understand. You want the real phrase? I mean, I can explain how the situation really sounds to a military mind, but considering you learned any mil-speak you do have from fuckin' Hollywood, it's not going to make sense as I explain that the advance has been contra-indicated."

"English is fine," I said with a kind of massive dignity. "For ease of understanding, you understand."

"Because you're a fuckin' idiot, you mean," he replied. "Right, so we need a new healer, and we think we might need some firepower as well, as there's apparently things in that section of London that have taken to eating the Scepiniir." Then he started to smile.

"And the healer and fighter combo you want?" I asked, already dreading Mike's growing grin.

"Oh," he practically bounced in his seat, "you're going to love this, but not as much as me, considering I've already sorted it so you can't change it without looking like a dick. Remember Emma and Jenn?"

"Emma?" I blinked, then groaned. "Seriously? Bloodwytch Emma? The fucking lightning-and-blood lunatic who won't listen to orders?"

"The very same," Kelly confirmed, though she looked concerned. "She's…enthusiastic about helping. She really wants to try to prove herself."

"Enthusiastic like a puppy, or enthusiastic like that time she nearly killed us all?"

"More the second one," Aly admitted. "But Jenn's shaping up to be one of the best healers we've got, and more importantly, Emma can handle herself if things go wrong. Plus, the whole 'turn people into red mist' thing might come in handy."

I rubbed my temples. "I don't fucking like this," I growled, before sighing. "Right. Fine. But if she starts getting that look in her eye—"

"The 'everything needs to explode' look? Or the 'I know best and fuck you all' look?" Mike supplied helpfully.

"Yeah, that one. If she starts getting that look, someone tackle her. I don't care who, just…London's got enough problems without adding 'creative spell testing' to the list."

"Already covered," Kelly assured me. "Jenn's not just going as a healer. She's also there so she can keep her sister relatively stable."

"Great," I muttered, turning back to the map. "All right, so we've got space cats with mysterious shopping habits, stealth kobolds, a potentially unstable Bloodwytch, and her slightly less unstable sister. What could possibly go wrong?"

"Don't forget the twins," Aly added cheerfully.

"You better be shitting me," I growled. "Tweedle-dee and Tweedle-fuckin-dumber? They're great guys. I like them and they're good fighters, but I thought this was a stealth mission! Their idea of stealth is wearing a plant on their head and punching anyone who looks at them! And yet I'm the one told not to come in until the end because my stealth skills are shit?" I snapped, glaring at Mike.

"You want to spend the night sneaking through London with them?" he countered.

I stopped, my mouth open as I tried to come up with a counter, before shutting it slowly.

He smiled. "Exactly."

"They need the experience, and they're incredibly loyal, despite recent events. Plus, frankly, if it goes wrong, they're more likely to be useful. And once we've got the dungeon set up, you can leave them in there for a week or three. They can be the live-in security team," Kelly added.

"Aha! The truth comes out!" I leveled a finger at her. "You're fucking getting rid of them!"

"I didn't say that, just that they seem like a perfect group to leave somewhere out of sight and where they can't cause issues." She smiled again.

"You know you want them out of the way for a while as well," Aly added. "After you went a bit nuclear with her in the medical wing, she's been pestering us for a chance to prove herself with you. This…well, it gets her to stop bothering us, frankly."

"Thanks for that. Really needed the reminder, and the sacrifice." I studied the marked routes again. "You're sure about these tunnels, Mike? Because if the earl's got people watching them…"

Mike's expression hardened. "That's why we're going in heavy. If it's clear, great. If not…" He shrugged. "That's what the Karens are for."

CHAPTER THIRTY-FIVE

London sprawled beneath me, a patchwork of darkness and dim candlelight in the pre-dawn gloom. Rising smoke wreathed the area inside the walled-in compounds in a way that the city probably hadn't known in at least a few centuries.

Jack glided silently through the frigid winter air, his metallic form almost invisible against the star-filled sky. From this height, the city almost looked normal, for London—if you ignored the strange glows from what had once been Hyde Park, and the occasional movement of things that definitely weren't human.

With that in mind—yeah, perfectly fuckin' normal. It wasn't as if the monsters that would attack a young woman in the dark now were any less dangerous than they were before the fall. If anything, the knowledge that the attack would be lethal but would end there would probably be a relief to any woman caught out here.

I shook my head, forcing that thought away. The memory of a friend who had visited once, for a weekend—a single trip to the excitement of the capital for a hen do—never to return home, burned bright as I forced myself to look at my hatred of the place and deal with it.

It'd always been there, partly because I didn't like large crowds, partly because to a northerner, who was raised to be friendly—more or less—to those around them, the grim stares and shut-down attitudes of people in the city always came across as rude.

Mainly, though, it was this. My friend had been so excited to visit, her dream to move somewhere more exciting than the north, with its dreary weather and fewer opportunities.

Then she'd died, and her passing…had not been easy.

Police had found the fucker who'd done it, eventually, and it'd all come out. A half dozen homeless had vanished before her, before he'd taken someone who *mattered*, and then it was only because the tabloids had seen a pretty, fresh-faced young woman and had run with it.

They'd spun out all the gory details, newscaster warning that "the following details may distress some viewers" and they'd made their money.

It'd broken our hearts. And after that, anything that happened down here? Well, what could you expect? It was fucking London, wasn't it.

A melting pot of whackos, politicians, and worse. A place where everyone was trying to fuck you over, and made worse by the fact that it was the heart of the country's political elite, which meant that most of the taxes taken from the rest of the country were spent here.

Hardly a new thing, but as funding cuts had resulted in massive waiting lists that killed people in the north, and the transport promises were broken, it was hard to feel sorry for the south who were suffering as well, but had enjoyed so much more spending for so long.

I hated the place. But as I drifted there, staring down, seeing the terrible devastation—the streets that had been destroyed by who knew what, a sinkhole that was surrounded by blackened ruins, hundreds of houses where fires hadn't been successfully fought down, and the graves—I had to let it all go.

I had to grow up and accept that a lot of my anger and hatred of the place was from the loss of Cara, and because of the pain of that. Anything else, well…it was just heaped atop it. It was easier to hate than to accept that it could have happened anywhere just as easily…New York, Miami, Paris—fuck's sake, enough tiny villages had hidden killers over the years, through no fault of their own. No, I let it all go, as we passed over the graves again.

My God, the graves.

We'd seen them as we passed overhead, entire sections of what had been industrial land converted into mass graves, then into pyres when people realized the risk that such a thing had posed.

There were memory walls, those places where people could leave flowers, or stick up photos or write letters and leave them to those they'd lost. They surrounded entire sections of the city that smoldered even now.

Hundreds of thousands, millions in fact, had to have died here, and they were running out of flammable material to dispose of the corpses.

They couldn't bury them, not all of them. First of all, they needed the space for planting crops. Second, the dead rose when there were too many of them. As I'd drifted silently overhead, I'd seen that entire districts had already been lost to them; the signs of huge packs of the undead roaming in the recent past were clear to see.

We'd drawn them south, I realized. The fight with the Pantheon of Unlife had dragged them down there. But we'd not faced all of them. If anything…we'd probably pulled them about halfway before the fight was over and they just broke up. The draw gone, they'd have been released to wander the countryside.

I didn't dare go looking for them—I was needed here. But again, some of the shitty behaviors we'd seen from the London lot was made clear.

If they knew that the undead were currently wandering out there, it'd not be long before they drifted back inward again, and then their forces would need every bullet, every cord of wood to burn the bodies…

I shook myself free of the thoughts, deciding that maybe, just fuckin' maybe, I could extend a little trust to that earl character, and deliver some more wood. And food. And bullets.

Fuck it, medicine and blankets too, while I was at it, and…

The list was endless, and I knew it. When I was faced with politicians, I was filled with disgust and wanted the satisfaction of telling them to go fuck themselves, that they'd helped to bring us to this point. But up here? Floating overhead, staring down and seeing the houses, the thousands who worked in literal gangs to tear down house after house, repurposing their bricks to try to save people?

I couldn't do it.

I'd do better, I decided. We'd set up the dungeon, and we'd help them, one way or another.

I pulled up my notifications while we waited, partly to distract myself from the cold, partly because I just remembered that I'd bloody forgotten to assign the points I'd gained when I looked at this last time. I'd put it off thinking to talk to Kelly and maybe Aly about it later, thinking more about the dungeon management skills and possibly needing to bring my charisma stat up or something… and then I'd forgotten about it.

There were just so many damn things that always needed my attention that I kept forgetting. Instead I resolved that I'd deal with it now, and then talk to the girls later.

Congratulations!

You have killed the following:

- 1x Baubas Queen [Advanced], Level 25, 3,500 XP
- 87x Baubas [Common/Uncommon], Level 10-15, 4,350 XP
- 1x Chimeric Horror [Advanced], Level 25, 2,500 XP
- 2x Mutant Predator [Uncommon], Level 15, 600 XP

Total XP awarded: 10,950 XP
Current XP to next level stands at 71,155/135,000

Fuck's sake! I'd forgotten all about that damn skill point, I realized. I quickly brought up my skills, skipping through most of them. I'd gained a few here and there. But damn, screw all of them, because the dungeon management skill was at level nine, and I had a point to spend.

Sure, there were other places to spend it; sure, there were more sensible places where I knew what I was going to get. But that skill, even if there was no bonus for reaching level ten, had increased the efficiency of my dungeon-born by forty-friggin'-five points already!

Just in the mana that the undead harvested and the space they claimed hour by hour had massively increased through the investment in this skill. Although it wasn't leveling noticeably, it was making a hell of a difference by spending my points.

I went to spend it, and then sighed as I pulled up the skills list, taking a look. As soon as I removed the block, it was like an avalanche of notifications. I frantically toggled the block back on. The screen froze, and I cursed. Yet again, mixed in with the dross, with the "you have gained a level in climbing ladders" and summoning food, and random door fuckin'-opening, there were some good ones, *again.*

Congratulations! *You have reached level 7 in the Storm Lord's Authority skill! Through constant manifestation of your Lightning and Storm-based abilities, you have begun to master the fundamental aspects of your divine domain. This skill grants you a 1% increase in power for Storm-based abilities per level and increases the effective range of your weather manipulation by 2% per level. As your authority grows, you will gain greater control over atmospheric conditions and the ability to share portions of your power with worthy followers.*

Congratulations! *You have reached level 25 in Lightning Manipulation! Your constant practice with Lightning-based abilities has granted you unprecedented control over this element. You receive a 2% increase in lightning damage and a 1% reduction in casting time per point. Because you have gained this level in a sub-skill of Storm Magic, you have also received the requisite levels in Storm Magic, granting a 1% chance to automatically counter hostile weather effects and a 1% increased radius for Storm-based spells per point earned.*

Congratulations! *You have unlocked the Multi-Dungeon Synchronization skill! Your experience managing multiple dungeons simultaneously has given you insight into the intricate art of dungeon synchronization. You gain a 2% increase in mana transfer efficiency between connected dungeons per level and can more effectively coordinate activities across your network. At higher levels, you will unlock the ability to share resources between dungeons.*

Congratulations! *You have reached level 17 in Dungeon Mana Cultivation! Through consistent meditation and practice, you have mastered the basics of mana cultivation. Your dungeon's passive mana regeneration increases by 1% per level, and you gain a 2% bonus to mana storage capacity per level. You can now more efficiently convert ambient mana into usable forms and maintain multiple mana-intensive effects simultaneously.*

Congratulations! *You have unlocked the Divine Leadership skill! Your position as both Dungeon Lord and Storm Lord has granted you unique insights into leadership. This skill provides a 1% boost to all attributes for followers within your domain per level and increases their mana regeneration by 0.5% per level. As this skill grows, you will gain the ability to bestow temporary divine blessings and establish more permanent connections with your most devoted followers.*

"Fuck me!" I whispered, staring at the screen. The Divine Leadership alone could be incredible. Spending a point there would only slightly increase things, sure, but for *everyone* inside my dungeons!

Everyone could increase their mana regeneration rate, their attributes, their… I looked to the others and stared.

I just stared.

The Dungeon Mana Cultivation meant we could store more mana. Hell, that skill alone meant that all the storage research we'd probably done in the past had just been superseded in numbers, if nothing else.

Fuck's sake, the Multi-Dungeon Synchronization skill would let me transfer resources later on!

I stared and stared, and then cursed.

There was no point in worrying about it, though I was starting to feel like a guy in a dark room, trying to describe an elephant by grabbing bits of it. The more I felt, the more I knew there was more to learn, and specialization here was the way to go.

As much as I wanted to start digging through shit, I dismissed it all, and slid my point into the dungeon management skill instead, taking it to level ten, and getting a new bonus.

Congratulations! *You have reached level 10 in the Advanced Dungeon Management skill! Your expanded understanding of dungeon operations has deepened considerably. Your minions' efficiency in performing tasks and maintaining the dungeon increases by 50% within your sphere of influence. You can now designate specific areas within your dungeon for additional resource storage and distribution, streamlining your dungeon's operations.*

Additional Bonus! *Due to successfully managing multiple concurrent dungeon operations and reaching this milestone, you have gained the ability to create and assign Specialist roles to your dungeon-born creatures. Note: You may designate one Specialist position per two levels in this skill. Specialists provide a 10% efficiency bonus to their assigned area of expertise and can train other dungeon-born creatures in their specialization. Available specialist roles include: Resource Management, Construction Oversight, Maintenance Operations, Security Coordination, and Research Supervision.*

Just the quick read-over I did, while lazily arcing around above London, was enough to let me know two things. First, I wasn't going to be able to dismiss the points I got from quests as bonuses, not the real reward, for much longer. They were starting to become a major power play. And second?

I wasn't the person best to assign those roles.

Kelly and Aly were the ones who could assign the five spots that were available most efficiently, and I made a mental note to talk to them about it.

I sighed and moved on, pulling up my stats. I read over the kill notifications again, thinking about what I'd done and where I should focus these stat points.

"Hold steady," I murmured to Jack as I sorted through my stats, and through our link, I felt his amusement. He'd been rock-solid in this holding pattern for the last hour, barely moving except to adjust for the occasional gust of wind.

Just a glance told me that I was starting to develop serious weaknesses, not that "weakness" was really the right word for it. I had, I admit, developed a tendency to bull my way through things, relying on my power, but where I was noticing a serious deficiency was in my Charisma, my Dexterity, my Luck, and my Perception.

They weren't *weaknesses*, though. The more I thought about them, I was literally at a point that was miles beyond a standard human in those areas, but…

I was left with two choices: either enhance myself further in those areas, or accept that was why I had a team, and instead double down on the areas that were useful to me.

Charisma was covered by Ashley. Let's face it—even when I'd been spending points and she wasn't, she was more naturally charismatic and more gifted there, and it was because of her personality, not her damn tits and makeup. She *liked* people.

After years working in IT, I *really* didn't.

That was out. I'd send her in to deal with that kinda shit moving forward.

Dexterity? Crafting ability and melee damage? I needed the damage increase, but frankly, I was starting to realize that it wasn't Dexterity that was going to help me out there. Nimble fingers weren't my thing. Smashing my enemies into paste, though? Hammers were a favorite for a reason. Luck was great, but you never knew if it was working or not, so screw it. And Perception?

I hesitated, then added five points into it, deciding that it could help.

The rest, though…my other ten points? Agility, this time around. I pulled up the stat screen, reading over it, and then the notification that came after it.

Name: Matt, First Lord of the Storm				
Host Powers: 1 (Enhanced Regeneration)				
Species: Cyclone			**Bonus**: None	
Level: 32			**Progress to next level**: 34,465/120,000	
Stat	**Current Points**	**Description**	**Effect**	**Progress to Next Level**
Agility	100	Governs dodge and movement	Heightened chance to dodge attacks Level: Godling	92/100
Charisma	53	Governs likely success to charm, seduce, or threaten	More likely to succeed in events that require seduction, persuasion, or threats Level: Enhanced Humanoid	66/100
Constitution	92	Governs Health and Health Regeneration	HP: 92x100 = 9,200 Level: Demigod	99/100
Dexterity	65	Governs ability with weapons and crafting	Increased chance of improved crafting result or increased melee damage Level: Enhanced Humanoid	58/100
Endurance	91	Governs Stamina and Stamina Regeneration	Stamina: 91x90 = 8,190 Level: Demigod	83/100
Intelligence	106	Governs base manapool, standard intellectual capacity	Mana: 106x110 (x2) = 23,320 Level: Godling	92/100
Luck	65	Governs overall chance of	Increased chance of positive outcome Level: Enhanced Humanoid	56/100

		bonuses and critical hits		
Perception	60	Governs ranged damage and chance to spot hidden items/traps	+50 to all ranged attacks Level: Enhanced Humanoid	41/100
Strength	94	Governs damage with melee weapons and carrying capacity	Enhanced damage with Melee weapons Level: Demigod	87/100
Wisdom	75	Governs mana regeneration	1500 mana regenerated per hour *(Arcanist class level 2 boost)*	91/100

Congratulations! *For the second time, you have passed a century threshold. Through exceeding the 100 points range in any one stat, you have gained a specific ability tied to your path.*

As the relevant stat is [Agility], combined with your nature as the First Lord of the Storm, you receive the ability to selectively trigger a 2x modifier to Movement Speed and your nervous system has evolved to naturally channel lightning energy.

Temporal Momentum: Enter a state of heightened temporal perception where time appears to slow around you while maintaining your normal speed. Your Storm-enhanced nervous system converts ambient lightning energy into accelerated synaptic responses, creating a cascading effect where each successful dodge or evasion increases your effective speed further, allowing for extraordinary feats of mobility and reflexes. (Stamina/Lightning dependent)

Note: This ability has increasing effects depending on the duration and speed multiplier, ranking from 0 (15 seconds, 2x speed) to 5 (3 minutes, 10x speed). Each successful evasion during the effect adds a 0.1x multiplier to your speed, stacking up to 5 times. The presence of storms or electrical energy in your environment will enhance this effect.

Warning: Disconnection from an enhanced state must be managed carefully lest debuffs be triggered.

Warning: Although your evolved physiology can handle these extreme speeds, any non-Storm-enhanced allies attempting to match your pace, or remaining in the immediate area may suffer severe electrical and physical trauma.

The screen faded, and I sat, staring ahead, thinking about the new changes. The spark and fizzle of the enhanced stats arced along nerve synapses. I blinked, glancing down at Jack in annoyance.

The big fucker was jiggling me from side to side, and I was goddamn busy right now! Hell, I was focusing on important things and he was supposed to be looking out for…

"Oh, shit. Thanks, Jack. Sorry about that." I sighed, climbing to my feet and looking down at the circular disc of crackling red lightning that marked a rooftop, clearly trying to get my attention.

"I'm off." I stepped out onto his shoulder. "Keep watch until the sun starts to come up, or I call for you. But do it as high as you want—we can't risk you being seen." I paused, thinking, then shrugged. "Go searching for the undead. See if there's any large groups of them, and if there are, incinerate them, before falling back and defending the southern dungeon. Kelly and the others will—"

I broke off, then snorted, before changing what I was going to say. "Hell, why am I telling you what to do? You know the girls will give you orders if they need you. Beyond that? Go be a dragon and fuck shit up!"

With that, I stepped off from the wing and let gravity take me. I flipped over until I fell headfirst into the night, unable to wipe a grin from my face as I flew.

CHAPTER THIRTY-SIX

The night air was bitterly cold as I plummeted through it, but my insanely enhanced Constitution meant that I barely felt the chill. Below, the circle of red lightning beckoned like a target, surrounded by the skeletal remains of what had once been London's industrial heart. The contrast was stark: ancient brick kilns and chimneys stood sentinel over the melted ruins of modern factories, all of it dusted with frost that gleamed faintly in the starlight.

As I fell, I activated my mana senses to check that nothing had changed, that the area was still the best place to set this up. My God, was that the case still. The readings were stronger than any I'd seen before. Waves of raw magical energy rippled out from somewhere deep underground. No wonder this area spawned so many monsters. The concentration of wild mana here could probably power half of London if it was properly harnessed.

Perfect for our purposes. The nobles would never question why "their" dungeon was so effective in this location.

About fifty meters from the ground, I pulled up, channeling my Air abilities to slow my descent. The red circle grew larger, and I could make out Mike's position on an elevated section of the remaining roof, his rifle trained outward into the darkness. The Karens—our elite kobold assassin team—were spread out in a defensive perimeter, while the Scepiniir mercenaries prowled the shadows with practiced ease, their catlike forms barely visible in the gloom.

I touched down silently beside Emma and Jenn, who were huddled near a makeshift camp with Jimmy and Andre. Emma's eyes still held traces of that blood-red glow that marked her recent spellcasting.

"Had some visitors?" I asked quietly.

"Nothing we couldn't handle," Emma replied, smiling grimly. "Though your timing's good—the Scepiniir caught movement to the north about ten minutes ago. Might be more monsters drawn to the mana concentration."

"Speaking of which," Mike called down softly from his perch, "Jackie thinks she's found our access point. The old maintenance tunnels are flooded, but there's a secondary system that doesn't show up on any of the maps we…acquired. Looks promising."

"Jackie?" I asked, and got a wave from one of the Karens, making me snort, then I nodded. The Karens' instincts for finding hidden shit had proved invaluable once again. "Let's see it then…"

The frost crunched under our feet as the team regrouped and headed deeper into the darkened building. Time to build our dungeon-within-a-dungeon, right under the nobles' noses.

"Hold up," Mike ordered quietly as we approached the entrance. "Jackie, show him what you found."

The kobold assassin materialized from the shadows, her scaled form barely visible in the dim light. Like all her sisters, she moved with lethal grace, but there was an intelligence in her eyes that set the Karens apart from many of the regular kobolds.

"This way, Lord," she whispered, leading me past the others. Emma and her group hung back, the awkwardness between us almost tangible. I caught a glimpse of Jenn squeezing Emma's arm reassuringly before focusing on Jackie's explanation.

"The tunnel entrance is hidden behind old machines," she explained, gesturing to a massive tangle of rusted metal. "But look here..." She pointed to barely visible marks on the concrete.

They'd probably only been made visible by the burning of the coverings, as there were a shitload of obvious burns that covered this side of the wall. The combination of soot getting into every crack and then the torrential downpours that London was famous for had probably washed most of it away, leaving the marks behind that had drawn our people.

As such, now that I was looking, I couldn't imagine missing it: lines that were clear in the brickwork that were just...wrong. The soot had ended up washed into grooves and patterns that would have been missed in normal days, but right now they screamed "secret door."

"These aren't random damage patterns. Someone deliberately concealed this entrance, probably during the Cold War." Mike joined us, moving silently despite his gear. "What do you think? My best guess is that it might have been some kind of emergency bunker system. Could explain why it's not on any official maps."

I knelt, running my hand over the scored concrete. "The concentration of mana here is even stronger than I expected," I muttered, then glanced up at Mike. "Where are the Scepiniir?"

"Karen has them checking the perimeter. They're...unsettled. Saying something about this place feels wrong."

"Wrong how?"

Before Mike could answer, one of the Karens called out a soft warning. Something was moving in the darkness beyond our position.

"Shit. Okay, genius, your call. If we fight here, we risk drawing in more than just the local monsters. We already had to hide for nearly an hour when the last army patrol came through, and they were being hunted as well. I didn't like leaving them to be followed without giving a warning at the least. Either we move on, and hope whatever is coming this way fucks off, or we move inside. I don't recommend fighting," Mike said in a fast burst, his voice clipped and professional.

"We need to get this entrance open," I said after a very brief pause. "No time to fuck off and come back around. Open it now, and fuckin' quietly."

"Karen, Sharon, watch our backs," Mike ordered in a terse whisper. "Jackie, you too. Get up high and give us warning if anything gets close."

I squinted at the concealed entrance, running my fingers over the edge of the metal that blocked our way. It looked like it had been part of some kind of industrial press, now twisted and warped across the opening. Behind it, somewhere in that darkness, the mana concentration was like a beacon to my senses as the ambient mana slowly drained into the depths, drawn like a stream, vanishing through a fucking apparently solid concrete wall.

"No way to get into here but this way?" I asked tersely.

"Nope. This section is behind three other buildings. Whatever's here, they didn't want people accidentally stumbling over it."

"Stand back," I warned, drawing my sword.

Emma and her group retreated several paces, but Mike held his ground.

"You sure that's smart?" he asked. "We don't know what's down there, and that thing coming this way…"

"No choice," I replied, channeling lightning through the blade. "Whatever's approaching, it's drawn to all this mana. We need to get inside and get out of sight fast, or we'll be fighting off everything in the area."

"Movement!" Jackie called down softly from somewhere above. "Large form, maybe eight feet tall. Moving erratically, but coming this way."

"Fuck it," I muttered, then swung the sword in a precise arc. The lightning-enhanced blade sliced through the old metal of the press like butter. The severed section crashed to the floor with a thunderous clang that echoed through the empty building.

"Well, if anything didn't know we were here before…" Mike sighed, bringing his rifle up.

"I know, I know!" I snarled, sheathing my sword. I slapped it to my back, and then grabbed at the metal, heaving, and shoved it aside, only to drop it with a clatter. "Fuck me, that's heavy!" I growled.

"Shit, boss, you been juicin'?" Andre asked, wide-eyed. "What've we gotta do to get some of that shit?"

"Watch it…I hear it makes your knob shrink." Jimmy nodded. "Ain't worth it if you lose inches where it's most important."

"Shut up, you idiots!" Mike snapped, even as Jackie leapt down from above, jabbing a finger at a section of the wall.

"There!" she hissed, moving in quickly and pressing at it. She cursed and dragged a dagger free, flipping it around and driving the pommel of the hilt hard against something I'd not even noticed.

There was an audible clunk, and the wall shivered slightly, as Mike hissed out a command.

"Shoulders in!" He matched action to words as he stepped in and braced a shoulder against the wall, even as he trained his gun back on the entrance to the building.

I joined him, Jimmy, and Andre. Jackie, seeing that brute force was required, gracefully slid aside, her own rifle being shouldered as she resumed her watch on the entrance.

There was a long moment where nothing happened as we all pushed. Then a grinding noise filled the air, and the entire wall slowly pivoted backward, grating across stone fragments until there was a crunch and the wall jammed up.

There was a gap now, though—a gap that led into a solid blackness that was just large enough for us to slip through, one at a time.

"Inside, now," I ordered, kicking some of the fallen debris aside. "Emma, light!"

She hesitated for just a moment—that recent tension still evident—before raising her hand and darting through, swiftly followed by the others.

A sphere of crimson light bloomed above her palm, casting bloody shadows across the walls as she vanished inside.

"Age before beauty," Mike said from the side, backing up, but pausing by the entrance. "Fucking move it, Matt!"

"Everyone in!" I ordered, only to hear a voice from above call down.

"Too many, too many incoming. The monster is hunted! We will lead them away! Go, go now!" With that, the Scepiniir that'd been crouched above us vanished.

I froze, glancing over at Mike. *Was the mercenary going to lead them away in truth, or sell us out?*

"Karen!" Mike snapped into the darkness. "Go with them!"

"Keep Jackie with you!" Karen's voice hissed out of the darkness.

Then I sensed her withdrawing as well, as Mike turned to me.

"Fucking move it, man. I'll hide the entrance."

"Like hell you will," I growled, grabbing him and shoving him into the gap ahead of me. "The ladies would kill me if I lost you!"

"We need to—" he snapped back at me, before cutting off.

I braced against the massive slab and heaved. Spots appeared before my eyes as I forced the stone back into position, hiding the entrance, just as a scream of rage rang out from someone beyond.

"Did it," I panted, as the sound of the stone settling back into place faded. "Told you I could…"

"Yeah. Yeah, you managed to seal that off well," Mike whispered, leaning in close. "Fucking hope there's another way out and there's nothing down here we don't want to disturb, eh?"

"Shitfuck," I muttered. There were no handles on this side of the door.

The passage beyond sloped sharply downward, old concrete steps disappearing into darkness. The walls were lined with what looked like lead sheeting, which explained why it wasn't on any maps. I was sure that the belief the shit was that close to hitting the fan that we needed nuclear fallout shelters for the end of the world tended to be hidden from most people.

"Everyone shut up for a minute," I whispered, pressing my ear against the lead-lined wall. Through the thick barrier, I could barely make out muffled sounds of fighting and pursuit passing by outside.

"You know," Jimmy muttered from somewhere behind me, "when they said this mission would be an in-and-out thing…"

"Shut. Up." Mike's voice cut through the darkness like a knife.

Emma's crimson light cast weird shadows as she held it higher, illuminating more of the descending stairwell. The lead sheeting on the walls had an odd sheen to it, almost like it was sweating in the cold air. That was probably something about the mana being drawn down here. I wasn't a blacksmith, but I was fairly sure metal shouldn't do that.

"Jackie," I called softly. "You're point. Emma, keep that light steady but be ready to snuff it if needed. Andre, Jenn, watch our backs. Mike…"

"Yeah, yeah, I know my job," he replied, already scanning the walls and ceiling with practiced eyes. "But I gotta say, this setup is weird. These aren't standard fallout shelter specs."

He was right. The stairwell was too wide, the ceiling too high. And there was something else…

"The air," Jenn whispered suddenly. "It's…moving."

She was right. There was a definite draft coming up from below, carrying with it a smell that was completely out of place—something almost like ozone, but sweeter.

"Well," I said, trying to sound more confident than I felt, "we wanted somewhere hidden to set up our operation. Looks like we found it." I gestured to Jackie. "Lead on. And everyone stay alert. Something tells me we're not the first ones to find this place."

A distant metallic groan echoed up from the darkness below, as if the building itself was settling. Or something else was moving down there.

"Just remember," Mike added grimly as we started down, "whatever's down here could have been locked away since before the mana came. No telling how it might have changed things."

The crimson light seemed to dim slightly as we descended deeper, the shadows growing longer with each step.

"Stop," Jackie said suddenly, her voice uncertain. "Something…something's wrong here." Her scaled hand raised in warning.

We all froze, the only sound our quiet breathing and the soft drip of condensation from somewhere below.

"What do you hear?" Mike whispered, dropping into a crouch, his rifle already scanning the darkness beyond Emma's crimson light.

Jackie tilted her head, sniffing at the air. Like all the Karens, her senses were sharp, but she was still learning to interpret them, still growing into her skin.

"Echoes…they sound wrong?" she said, more question than statement. "The stairs go down more, but the sound comes back strange."

I shifted forward carefully, extending my mana sense. The flow of power was definitely stronger here, but it felt twisted somehow. Like the mana was being pulled in multiple directions at once, a branching in the streams of mana ahead.

"Emma," I said quietly, "can you boost that light?"

She nodded, and the crimson glow intensified. The increased illumination revealed what Jackie had sensed—about twenty feet ahead, the stairwell just stopped. The steps ended in a sheer drop into darkness.

"Well, that's not fucking ominous at all," Andre muttered.

"Smells like…dead things," Jackie added, her nose wrinkling.

Mike moved up beside her, peering down into the void. "Anyone got something we can drop? Test the depth?"

"Hold up." I drew my sword again. The lightning crackling along its length cast blue-white shadows that clashed with Emma's red glow. "Let me try something."

I channeled power into the blade, then thrust it forward. A bolt of lightning arced down into the darkness. For a split second, the shaft was illuminated.

The stairs hadn't just ended; they'd been sheared clean off, as if something had taken a giant knife and simply cut through the concrete and steel. Below, I could make out more levels, more stairs, spiraling down into the earth. And something else—what looked like claw marks scored deep into the walls.

"That's not structural damage," Mike said grimly. "That's not decay or collapse. Something did this."

"Not big marks," Jackie offered, peering at the scoring. "Small things. Many."

Great. Just what we needed. Mad shit that we didn't understand.

"Well," I sighed, "we didn't come down here expecting it to be empty. Let's just hope whatever made those marks is long gone."

A scratching sound echoed up from below, as if the universe itself wanted to prove me wrong.

"You had to fucking say it, didn't you?" Mike sighed.

"Sounds like…" Jackie paused, searching for the right words. "Like metal on stone. Lots of it, moving in patterns." She shifted uneasily, her scaled fingers tightening on her weapon.

"How far down?" I asked, but she shook her head.

"I don't know," she admitted. "Not far?"

Emma's crimson light flickered slightly, and I caught her steadying herself against the wall. The constant magic use was probably starting to drain her.

"We need to get down there anyway," Mike said quietly. "Matt, you got anything in that bag of holding that could help? Because that's a good thirty-foot drop at least."

I was already reaching into the dimensional space, fingers searching through stored equipment. "Got some rope, but nothing here to secure it to. This whole section looks like it could break away if we put too much stress on it."

"Well, good thing we've got an idiot that's far too strong for his own good who can fly." Mike grinned at me. "Get that rope around yourself, lad…time to carry us across. How many do you think you can take at a time?"

"I…dammit." It hadn't even occurred to me. Yeah, of course, it was a simple solution. "Probably all of you? It's not that long a rope, though."

"Give it here," Mike said quickly, and I pulled it from the bag, passing it over. "In the future, carry two," he told me tersely. "One like this, just a loop and the other knotted. Gives people something to hold onto."

As he said it, he started to loop the rope into a knot, leaving one about every meter and moving on. Andre tried to join in, but his pulling on the opposite end got a glare and a terse "Fuck off, you're not helping" from Mike.

A handful of minutes later, with the sound from below thankfully not getting any closer or louder, the task was done. Admittedly, the rope, knotted as it was, was both much more uncomfortable for me to loop around me, and was now shorter, but that wasn't much of a concern.

I stepped off into the gloom, hovering for a few seconds, waiting to see whether I was about to be attacked. Then, when I wasn't, I looped the rope around my shoulders with equal lengths dangling down on either side, moving close enough that people could step out onto the rope and then climb down to make room for the next.

Thankfully, as there weren't that many of us, it didn't take long. We floated down gently, finding the remains of the stairwell a little way farther down, mixed in with a collapsed section of the Tube system that served Greater London.

There were also the remains of rooms, presumably the upper sections of the building whose stairs we'd been going down before, though now that we were farther down, it became clear that underneath London, was more fuckin' London.

We landed on the shattered stone perhaps thirty meters below the point I'd stepped off. With nothing around us visible, I took a deep breath and sent out a blast of lightning. It was dangerous—it would announce our presence to anything down here—but unable to see more than a few meters in any direction, I decided it was worth it.

Obviously, that was a risk, but as soon as I saw layers of long-forgotten London, of sewers and sewage systems, of bodies and shattered cellars, I cursed.

Honestly, couldn't a guy get a break somewhere?

We were in a cave system. It probably wasn't natural, or at least if it was originally, the rest of it had been added to from our own species' stupidity.

I could see three levels that opened into tunnels that had rails hanging from them, a shattered metro that lay off to one side, and then the devastation that told of the collapse of the upper levels of this facility. Combined, it was all made clear.

If there'd been a cave here, it'd been at the bottom, and then with the constant building and digging going on overhead, a sinkhole had begun. Maybe a few grains of rock and dirt had fallen each time an overloaded metro rocketed past overhead. Given as many as hundreds of them a day would have passed this nexus point with three lines at various depths—well, the numbers were beyond me, but it was clear that there would have been a lot.

The constant movement would have taken more and more of the surrounding mass away, and the distant rush of water from somewhere below told that tale of where that rock and building material would have gone.

London was built atop the remains of London's past, after all.

Over a thousand years of the city being here, being burned down, razed, bombed and fought over, had left ample ground to build and rebuild upon, with archaeologists having the right to examine any site that was being dug up in London at pretty much any time, from what I remembered of the before.

That might not have been accurate, actually, but it seemed like every time they did any new major works, they found something ridiculous, and made a big song and dance about it. Roman occupation ruins, religious types remains, old urns full of fuck knew what—there was always something in the papers. And now, looking around, I could imagine that had this been discovered before the fall, archaeologists would have had a field day.

Mind you, considering that something had clearly eaten its way through the rock and metal around here, maybe that wasn't such a good idea after all.

"This way." Mike kept his voice down. He led the way, with Jackie by his side, across some broken building materials and into the remains of another buried building.

This one, once we'd all clambered across the shattered stone and collapsed rebar, rocks, and random bits of metal, was clearly part of the original fallout shelter. Posters on the wall looked a bit tattered and dusty, but beyond that, they offered inspiring slogans and other such crap that was popular back then.

As we moved deeper, with me holding my right hand up and channeling my lightning into it as Emma ran low on her mana, more and more of the original building was revealed.

Some sections were clearly designed for rest and relaxation. Old TVs and a full media library, for example, and a physical book library were easy to recognize. It helped with the dating as well, considering there were a mixture of LP records and cassette tapes in there.

"*War of the Worlds*," Mike muttered, having stepped over to one wall and checked for something. He grinned as he pulled it out. "Here it is, the musical version. Fuckin' classic. And no matter where you went, someone had one."

“Nice,” I agreed, before gesturing and making the light bounce as I did so. “Now, you fancy joining the party?”

“Oh, fuck off.” He snorted. “How often do you get distracted?”

“I resent that,” I said loftily. “Honestly, we need to get moving. It’s a good job Emma here is paying attention—unlike you, Mike,” I said, making the effort to try to paper over the cracks in that relationship.

“He does get distracted easily.” Emma took the figurative olive branch and moved the conversation along.

“Yeah, well, we’re in enemy territory…less of the chatter.” Mike snorted, rejoining us. With the mood just a little lifted, we continued on, moving deeper.

The rooms we passed were weird. There was no other way to describe them.

They were old, though carefully constructed and, unlike the standard government spending where it was done by the lowest bidder, there were signs here and there—like a cabinet of drinks that were apparently very good, according to Mike—that this had been a much more luxurious setting.

“You know what?” Mike said eventually, as we moved into a small room that appeared to be a central control room, or office, looking out over a silent and empty garage. “I don’t think this was a government shelter at all.”

“No?”

“I’m betting it’s one of those ones that were bought out by rich fuckers in the seventies and eighties. The old bomb shelters that they converted—there was a bomb shelter near here; it’s what we were looking for, but it was like *old*, old. And nothing like this. Plus, it was still supposed to be a few streets over.

“Want to bet someone saw it going for sale, or paid someone to lose the paperwork for it, and started their own fallout project then?”

“Damn, could be some nice loot then,” I said as we walked down the stairs, turned a corner, and nearly walked slap-bang into a dead end. “What the hell?” I grunted, staring at the wet rock wall that cut across the corridor.

“Rock?” Emma, confused, reached her hand out, only to have her wrist grabbed suddenly by Jackie, as she stared at the wall, eyes wide.

“What’s—” Emma started to say, only to be cut off as Jackie hissed a single word.

“*Alive*!”

We froze, then started backing up, the crackling of my lightning the only sound as a ripple flowed across the “wall” before us.

There was one at first, and we all stopped; then another, then a cascading ripple as the suddenly solid-seeming wall…was transformed into a mass of individual tiny bodies.

Insects…insects in their *thousands.*

Glass Scarab	**Mutated Insectoid**
Born from the volatile fusion of ambient mana and abandoned scientific apparatus, Glass Scarabs are a testament to the risks of permeating an area with excess mana, and the resultant ability of life to create and adapt from the most unexpected sources.	

Although individually fragile, they move and attack as a singular swarm. Their collective mana resonance allows them to coordinate with uncanny precision.

These crystalline insectoid creatures are a mindless form of the swarm, their transparent carapaces refracting light and powered by the mana they are drawn to. Sizes range from barely larger than a gnat to the size of small canines. Their razor-sharp mandibles and clawed limbs can burrow through stone, metal, and flesh with impressive ease.

Glass Scarabs are relentlessly drawn to sources of mana, which they consume to sustain their strange quasi-life. They will pursue magic-wielders and artifacts with tireless single-mindedness, leaving behind tunnels riddled with strange, geometrically perfect scoring marks.

Ability: *Swarm Tactics*: Glass Scarabs always attack en masse, using their numbers to overwhelm targets. Damage to individuals is less effective than area-of-effect attacks.

Ability: *Mana Sense*: Glass Scarabs can detect and home in on mana sources from a significant distance.

Weaknesses: Earth mana, Gravity mana

HP: 25/25 (per individual)

Swarm Size: Unknown

Speed: 8/10

Level: 4

HP: 25/25	**Special Abilities**: 2/2

"Oh fuck!"

CHAPTER THIRTY-SEVEN

The swarm erupted into motion. The cohesive whole that they'd formed a matter of seconds before shattered as a shimmering mass of bodies surged toward us in a wave.

In an instant, Mike's rifle was up and firing. The staccato bursts echoed deafeningly in the enclosed space. Flashes of red light joined the blue-white crackle of my lightning as Emma added her magic to the fight.

Holes were burned through the advancing wave, but they were literally that, a goddamn wave of bodies, and the only reason we were still alive was that they couldn't fly.

Instead, they moved in a mass, a surge that poured over one another, rolling toward us like a mindless multitude of glittering metal, glass, and carapace.

The swarm barely slowed. For every one shattered by bullets or burned through by our lightning, a dozen more scuttled forward, gushing over one another as we frantically backed up the stairs and away from their rising mass.

Their razor-sharp limbs scrabbled against concrete and steel, leaving deep gouges as they advanced, eating their way up the stairs, along the walls and toward us.

"Run!" I yelled, sending a wide arc of chain lightning into the leading edge of the swarm. Glass shattered and popped, but still they came on, making me feel like I was pissin' in the wind with even my own powers. I glared at them. Options rolled through my mind, but the closeness of my friends and the need to keep the location hidden constantly fucked up each option that I thought of.

Atomic Furnace? Might take out my friends in this close an environment; same for Lightning Storm. Incinerate? Lightning Bolt? Too small-scale—I'd run out of mana before I ran out of targets. Summon Demon? They'd take too long and get eaten, no doubt. Fuck!

We backed up the stairs in a fighting withdrawal, Emma's lightning and everyone else's bullets covering our retreat. But the scarabs were faster, swarming up walls and across the ceiling, aiming to cut off our escape.

Jackie cried out as a stream of them dropped on her from above, clawed limbs tearing at her scales. She vanished beneath the skittering mass for a heart-stopping moment before Andre leapt atop her,slamming the much more fragile creatures, knocking the breath out of her, but crushing them. The pair rolled, then frantically leapt upright. Jackie staggered free, blood dripping from dozens of wounds.

"Keep moving!" I ordered, bringing up a shimmering shield of my lightning to block a fresh wave. The scarabs slammed into it and were sent tumbling, stunned, but more were already scuttling around the edges.

I lunged forward; the shield slammed into them and killed them in their dozens. The way my mana flashed and dipped with each move, I knew that this *might* hold long enough. But considering we had no clue whether this was the entire swarm or just the leading edge meant I couldn't risk it.

We backed into the old control room, slamming and sealing the heavy door behind us. But I could already hear the crystalline tick and rasp of the scarabs in the walls, as they started eating a way through.

"What the fuck ARE those things?" Andre panted, frantically reloading his rifle.

"Some kind of mana mutation," I replied grimly, even as Jenn stepped up and healed a deep gash on Jackie's arm. "Individually weak, but the strength of the swarm makes them deadly."

"How do we stop them?" Jenn's voice shook slightly as she bound a wound on her own leg.

"We need a kill zone." Mike moved to check the other doors. "Someplace we can bunch them up, hit them with everything we've got."

"The garage," I decided. "It's open enough, and there's plenty of chokepoints to force them through between here and there."

A shuddering impact against the door punctuated my words. The thick metal screamed as the scarab swarm chewed its way through it.

"Won't hold them for long," Mike observed tersely. "We need to move. Now."

We burst from the room in a hasty fighting retreat. The entire wall, not just the door in it, collapsed under the onslaught of the creatures as we ran. Jackie and Andre laid down sheets of covering fire as we raced down a set of stairs on the far side, toward the garage entrance. The skittering tide of glass and chitin pursued us, scuttling over their fallen kin in a relentless advance.

As we backed into the cavernous space of the garage, I spotted our chance: a bank of old fuel drums against one wall, dusty red warning labels still bright against the rust.

"There!" I called out. "Get those drums open and spilled. We'll draw the swarm in, then run for the far side and light it up!"

Mike and Andre moved to comply, hammering at rusted bungs and valves as the rest of us formed a semicircle, pouring fire into the advancing scarabs. Their front ranks shattered under the onslaught, but still more poured forward, skittering over the twitching remains.

Then a scream like a buzz saw on ice rang out as the mass still traveling through the control room overhead decided that instead of following the rest down the stairs, they'd quite like the expedited route.

They broke through the window, pouring down the wall as we ran for it, passing Mike and Andre.

"Got it!" Mike yelled as the first black gouts of ancient fuel spurted from ruptured drums. The acrid reek of gasoline and worse flooded the garage as it sprayed across the floor. Jackie slashed at a second drum, claws puncturing the decayed metal, adding to the growing pool.

"Emma, with me!" I ordered, taking a ready stance as the first scarabs surged into the room. "Bottleneck them between us, then run! I'll light the pool once they're in!"

She nodded grimly, moving to mirror my position. We let loose with simultaneous blasts of my own clean blue-white and her glowing eldritch lighting into the leading ranks. The thunderous detonations echoed in the enclosed space. Swarms exploded and burned, but the press of crystalline bodies barely slowed.

The flow between us became a torrent, the floor beneath the swarm now slick with spilled fuel and fluids. Emma staggered back a step as the leading edge surged toward her, claws extended…

"NOW!"

At my shout, she ran.

I unleashed a handful of Incinerates at the pool of gasoline, frantically hoping they'd catch something that would spark to flame, that the fuel abandoned down here was still capable of it. I triggered a fresh Lightning Shield around us both and that…

It ignited with a throaty *whoomph.* A billowing wall of fire erupted from the floor and hurtled me backward, trailing smoke and flames, to crash into the wall. Emma impacted next to me.

The scarabs shrieked, a shrill crystalline keen, as they cooked in their hundreds, chitin blackening and warping in the heat. The stench was incredible.

Secondary explosions chased the first as ruptured drums added their payload to the inferno. Searing bursts of orange and black sent geysers of burning fuel into the heart of the swarm. They died in their thousands, swept into oblivion by the flames.

Hands grabbed us, dragging us back, as the others poured our remaining ammo into the survivors, picking off the scuttling stragglers that somehow made it through that inferno.

Backing up, I coughed and waved for the others to move farther. Then, despite the flames and the smoke, I targeted the far end of the room with Atomic Furnace, figuring, fuck it…there was a decent distance between us and there, right?

It was a goddamn garage; there was room for at least ten cars parked in here, and probably a few trucks as well.

I locked it onto the far end, where I could see some of the mass still writhing in the flames. There was movement that I could barely make out, but it was there, and I wasn't running the risk of these fuckers coming through once the flames died.

Nope. Nuclear option it was!

The Atomic Furnace was an insane spell, completely. It brought the power of the sun—that level of incredibly bad judgment—into the target I designated, and fuck me, did it deliver.

As I'd done in the dungeon before, I spread it out, aiming it over a ten-meter radius, and wow.

Three seconds later, as the flames began to gutter out, only blackened remains and oily smoke were left behind—and that was only in the areas that *hadn't* been in the radius of the furnace.

What had been inside it—well, the metal had been reduced to its gaseous state and used as fuel, so yeah. The shit that had been screwing up my day was oh *so* long gone.

Some sections of the rock and metal were left, of course. The drop-off rate for the spell was roughly ninety percent per meter that was added to it. The original spell only covered a single-meter radius, and it'd been over ten meters when I'd cast it.

The drop off was a matter of details though.

Ten meters, where the temperature achieved by nuclear fire was spread out across all of it instead of concentrated, was still an insanely toasty place. Although the metal hadn't erupted into instantly consumed gasses along all of it, it had at the center.

At the outermost edge, it'd simply run like butter encountering a blowtorch.

A long moment of stunned silence followed, broken only by the crackle of flames and our labored breathing.

"Everybody still in one piece?" I asked finally, scanning over the team. They were battered, scalded, and bleeding, but all still standing. Emma sagged against the wall, drained of magic and clearly exhausted, while Mike was having a long gash along his forearm healed by Jenn.

But we were alive.

"What. The actual. Fuck," Andre breathed out, still training his rifle on the charred remnants with twitching fingers.

"Some sort of mutation, like I said," I replied, gingerly stepping around slagged puddles of glass and chitin. "But I've never seen or heard of anything like those before."

I hesitated, thinking about triggering my area of effect spell again, speeding up everyone else's mana regeneration and healing, then cursed and dismissed it as not the right place. It was location specific and this area wasn't safe after all, so if I did it here and a new bunch of them arrived in five seconds, we'd leave it behind as we ran.

"They must've been down here for months," Mike mused, grimacing as he flexed his wounded arm. "Probably created when the fall came, and then started swarming the upper levels. Surviving and evolving off the mana concentrations ever since, roaming wild down here."

"And we just stepped into their nest like absolute fucking idiots," I cursed, anger and adrenaline still pounding through me. "We need to find another way forward. Now, that might be all of them, or it might just be the damn scouts."

As the smoke cleared, I saw a sunken vehicle ramp on the far side of the garage, leading down to a cavernous tunnel. More old metro lines, or something else entirely—there was no way to tell.

But the mana currents flowed that way just as happily as they did here, and after what we'd just faced, I wasn't going to risk doubling back the way we came.

Sooner or later, we'd need to make sure we'd gotten them all. But for now, we needed to find somewhere safe, set the core up, and get the process started.

"There's our path," I said grimly, indicating the tunnel with a wave of my hand. "We keep moving. And we stay on guard. No telling what other fun surprises this fucking place has waiting for us."

The others nodded, reloading and checking weapons with shaking hands. Emma pushed herself back to standing with visible effort, giving me a terse nod.

I took a deep breath, the sulfur reek of the flames still thick in my lungs. Then, drawing my blade again and holding it ready, I started for the ramp, down into the waiting dark. I summoned my lightning and sent it flowing around my body and then into the blade, causing it to shine bright and drive back the darkness, before absorbing it back in and around continually.

No matter the horrors, no matter the cost—we had a mission, and I'd be damned if I let anything, mutant or mundane, stand in our way.

Besides, in six days it was date night, and Kelly had insisted that she had a hell of a surprise for me, if I made it back in time.

Come hell or high friggin' water, when a man had a hot girlfriend who said something like that to him, there was no chance he was missing it.

If the armies of Sauron were waiting around the next corner, I'd kick their arses as well. Nothing was getting between me and some downright filthy sex.

The ramp descended into darkness, the acrid stench of burned fuel and melted or charred chitin still heavy in the air. My lightning-wreathed blade cast eerie shadows across soot-stained walls as we advanced, stepping carefully over rubble and debris. The mana currents tugged insistently, urging us forward into the unknown depths.

"Watch your footing," Mike cautioned from behind me, his rifle scanning the tunnel ahead. "No telling how stable any of this is after that sinkhole and all the fucking fire and shit we just added to the mix."

As if to punctuate his warning, a chunk of concrete crumbled and fell from the ceiling, shattering on the ramp mere feet in front of us. I threw up a hasty barrier, deflecting the worst of the fragments.

"Well, thank you so much for that, dude. You want to invoke the evil one, and his prophet Murphy and further piss all over the parade?" I muttered, picking up the pace. The faster we got through this death trap, the better.

"Nah, I'll let you—we don't all need to be in the range of his evil eye." He snorted, and I waved him an armor-clad middle finger in response.

The ramp eventually leveled out into a wide service tunnel. A tangle of ducts and pipes ran along the walls. An abandoned metro track stretched into the distance, the rail lines long since gone to rust. Stagnant, fetid water pooled between the ties.

"Well, this is just lovely," Emma said dryly, her boots splashing through the muck. "Post-apocalyptic metro tunnels. Classic dungeon fare, really."

"At least the murder-bugs seem to have thinned out." Jenn sounded like she was trying to convince herself as much as us. "Maybe the aboveground concentration drew most of them up?"

"Or these are just the tunnels they use to get around," I said grimly. "Spread out from wherever they're nesting. Be alert."

"Doubt it," Mike said suddenly. "Look, the metal of the tracks is right there, and it's intact."

"Point." I nodded. "Hopefully that was the last of them."

We slogged on through the tunnel, strung out in a loose formation. My lightning cast a harsh light over crumbling walls and dangling wires; the occasional scurry of unknown things in the darkness beyond set everyone further on edge.

An indeterminate time later, the monotony was broken by Jackie calling a halt. The kobold was crouched by the edge of the fetid water, peering at something intently.

"Problem?" I asked, splashing over.

She gestured at a section of wall, her expression puzzled. "Look. What are these?"

I played my lightning over the area in question. Strange gouges marred the concrete, far too regular to be battle damage or decay. They almost looked like…

"Runes, maybe?" Emma suggested suddenly from my other side, nearly scaring the shit out of me. "Those look like enchanter's runes."

"What, like magic carvings?" Andre sounded skeptical. "I thought that stuff only started working recently, with the fall?"

"Most of it, yeah," Emma replied, tracing a finger over the carvings. "But some of the mages have been experimenting, trying to see what works and what doesn't. I mean, any of the magic artifacts we've got have them, so they're not that hard to figure out. Looks like someone who was playing with them made it down here."

I frowned, an unpleasant premonition starting to form. "Just one? Alone?"

"Seems that way," Emma murmured. "See this pattern here, this cluster? I've seen them—they're to do with stealth. Something you'd use on a cloak." She glanced around the tunnel, eyes narrowed. "Or maybe, maybe they're not for a cloak…maybe they're just to conceal something?"

A long, tense silence followed her words, broken only by the soft drip of water.

"And you know this how?" I asked her again.

"Catherine." She smiled. "She's interested in them, and she was showing me. You asked us to help her get integrated into the various power factions, so I was sort of playing along, just spending time with her, and I found they kinda make sense. I like them."

"Power factions?" I frowned.

She nodded. "Different people call them different things," she replied absently. "You know, the groups."

"The girl groups who were being really bitchy?" I asked, amused.

"Well, they have the power to ruin people's lives. It's not just a *Mean Girls* 'you can't sit with us' situation. They can spread rumors, ostracize someone, and make their lives absolute hell, or they can make someone the queen of all they survey."

"Really?" I asked, still looking around. "Sounds a bit over the top."

"You came to us with Catherine," Emma said dryly. "Trust us in the way we work. Remember that the way people see someone is ninety percent of their life on social media. It was all about being seen and being respected and admired. Even if you knew you were living on cold Pot Noodles, if everyone else thought you were rich and pretty?

"You could forget your purse, or lose a card and nobody thought twice about it. Lose your phone? Can't pay for dinner? People who were rich covered the bill without a thought and then made a joke out of it, instead of you having to pay for things you couldn't afford. This is like that."

"Go on," I prompted when I saw she'd paused and was looking at me to see whether I was interested or not.

"The various groups might not seem that big or important to you—you're the 'Lord of all he bloody surveys,' after all. But to someone without that power, if there's say…three groups that are active? There are more, but let's say three for this example. If all three are filled with different groupings, different people, with a few that overlap…like me and Jenn might be in one with Ashley, and that's a leadership group, because we have access to her and you, but if we're in another group that's all centered around fashion and style—"

"Like the hairdressing group," Jenn added in.

"Yeah, like that one…the conversations are very different, and with different people. And for you, as an outsider, as a guy, you're not interested, right?"

"Yeah?" I agreed, already going back to looking around the tunnel.

"Well, let's say in our hairdressing group, we don't like Catherine—we do, this is just an example, all right?"

"Sure."

"Well, we don't like her, and we talk about her shitty fashion sense, her skin, whatever. We slag her off, and it's just a bit of fun…nothing anyone would say to her face…just, we don't like her. With me so far?"

"Sure." I sighed, not seeing where it was going, beyond that a lot of people clearly had a lot more free time than I had.

"So, now let's say there's a lot of jokes about her, and about how we don't like her. Later that night, I come home to my lad, and he asks me what we were talking about. I tell him the jokes, and he laughs—doesn't understand why we find it funny or anything; he's just being a supportive husband."

"Oh yeah." I nodded. "Been there, done that. The supportive part, anyway." I offered Andre a fist and he bumped it, knowing exactly what I meant.

"Great." She rolled her eyes, but went on. "Now Andre hasn't met Catherine before, but he knows the jokes and that we don't like her. Then he hears from another of his friends that his partner was complaining about this woman who's annoyed her, and it's Catherine again. You don't know her, you're not concerned about her, but you're already convinced that as your partner, who you trust, doesn't like her, and your friend who you trust doesn't like her, then when you come to meet her, you're already negative about her. When someone mentions her next time, when I tell a joke about her or whatever, you get it and it reinforces that. In a few days, without her doing anything wrong, just a bunch of little groups slagging her off, she's a target, and she's practically ostracized already. Do you see why we call them power groups?" Emma asked, and I shook my head.

"If they're just you and your friends, that's one thing. But for us, because we're in your team, and we're friends with Ashley, we're seen as having an inside track on things. And because of the way Ashley and we look, people always think we're dumb and easily manipulated. That means we start manipulating first.

"Most of the groups we're in aren't our friends. They're people we're monitoring for Ashley, people we're gradually making see things the way we do. And it spreads from there, all without anyone knowing how or why; they just start doing things the way we want. That's why they're power factions, factions of people and groups we're manipulating to achieve our aims." That last bit was said with air quotes as she grinned.

"I don't know about you, boss, but it fucking terrifies me when she talks like this." Jimmy sighed. "I mean, I know me and my bro here are handsome bastards, but did the girls decide we were useful, or do they actually love us?" he half joked.

"Both. You're both boy-toy and muscle," Emma replied offhandedly. "How could we not love that?"

"Well, regardless, this fucking derailed the conversation." I sighed. "So we know that they're enchanter's runes, but not much more than that."

"I've seen them, but that's it," Emma agreed.

"Okay," I said at last. "Fan out, look for more runes, carvings…anything that might tell us what our mystery enchanter was up to down here. Andre, Jackie, and Emma, you're with me. We'll push forward, see if we can pick up a trail."

The team split up. Mike took point down a side passage with Jimmy and Jenn while the three of us forged ahead. The main tunnel curved gently to the right. The enchanter's runes appeared at intervals along the walls, each cluster a little different.

"Definitely the same person," Emma said softly, running her fingers over a particularly dense grouping. "But the pattern is changing. They were learning, adapting…but sometimes, like this?" She frowned. "The others were precise and careful, but this last one is sloppy, almost like he just rushed it off."

I thought of the skittering swarms behind us, the hungry chittering in the dark. An enchanter, alone and on the run, burning mana to conceal themselves…how long could they have lasted?

The trail took an abrupt turn at an intersection, the runes leading us down a half-collapsed side tunnel. Rubble and rusted metal choked the passage, but the mana currents were stronger here, tugging us insistently onward.

"We're getting close to something," I murmured, picking my way carefully over a twisted snarl of rebar. "Stay sharp."

The tunnel opened into a small, dank chamber, the corners piled high with debris and mold climbing over at least half of it. Old metal shelves lined one wall, stocked with rusted cans and collapsed, wet cardboard boxes.

The remains of a camp were scattered across the floor, with a bedroll, a small cookstove, and a scattering of tools and books making up most of it. Then, halfway across the floor, there was a rock wall, or at least what looked to be one.

Stepping up closer to check it out, I squatted and looked at the edge of one box where it'd collapsed. The cans that had once been intended for whoever built the place to ride out the apocalypse were now covered in dirt and creeping mold.

There were three on the floor next to the remains of the box, and one that was just visible, pressed up against the edge of the cave wall…with half of it buried inside the seemingly solid stone.

I put my hand on the wall and slid it down toward the ground, feeling where the stone felt "wrong," like it was soft, instead of hard and cold stone. Then I hooked the edge of my fingernail over the edge of the can, feeling the resistance as I tugged.

It slowly moved through, though, and encouraged by that, I stood, pressing my palm against the wall, and pushed.

At first the wall felt hard, and the harder I pushed, the more solid it became, until I was grunting as I shoved against the rock… Then Emma was there.

"Maybe without the muscles?" she suggested, trying a faint smile. She pressed her hand against the wall, slowly sliding it through.

"How the hell are you doing that?" I asked, surprised, as I shoved at it again, actually bouncing off slightly.

"Redirected force," she whispered. "The carvings we kept passing—they were all about force, and hiding. If this is someone carving them, then there has to be a way to pass through. Don't shove it, because you're just giving it more energy. Instead, smooth your way through, like this."

She slid her hands across the wall as she went, almost like she was waxing her car. And as she went, the wall grew softer and softer, until, with a pop, by the time she was up to her elbows, the wall vanished.

"What the hell was that kung-fu shit all about?" I muttered in disbelief. "You going to stand on one leg and kick me in the face next?"

"Don't tempt me," she said absently. But most of her attention was on the figure that lay curled against the far wall, almost invisible behind a second shimmering curtain of runes…a human skeleton, little more than desiccated flesh and rags.

"Shit," I murmured, crouching for a closer look. "Poor bastard. Must've holed up in here, tried to make a stand."

Emma moved to join me. The runes parted like mist before her as she leaned in to examine him. Up close, I could see the skeleton wore the tattered remains of what had once been a thick red sweater, and jeans that were filthy and soiled; his head, sunken onto his chest, was half hidden in a thick hat. A wooden staff lay near one bony hand, a crystal headpiece cracked and dark.

"He must have been our enchanter, all right," Emma confirmed softly, kneeling beside me. "Wonder what happened? Why the hell did he die down here?"

My eyes fell on a scattering of loose paper near the skeleton, weighed down by chunks of masonry. Brushing away the grit and mold, I gingerly lifted a sheaf of parchment, the ink faded but still legible, even if it was a scrawl.

The line was short, and the letters, the way they overlapped and were written, made it clear that he'd written it while unable to see.

"Runes under wall, trapped!"

"There's a trap?" I cursed, twisting around to check the walls, the floor, as everyone moved back reflexively. After a few seconds of nothing happening, I heard a hiss, and glanced at Emma, who shook her head.

"It's not trapped," Emma said in horror. "He trapped himself."

"What?"

"Where the barrier was." She indicated the floor where it'd been, and there, next to scratches that were frantic and bloody, I winced as I recognized a small broken thing on the floor.

It was a fingernail. One of several. Stepping forward and crouching next to the body, I checked the hands, finding them all missing fingernails and covered in old blood.

"He was trying to get through the wall," Emma guessed. "He made a mistake and set up the wall to hide and protect him, but the runes were underneath it and he couldn't switch it off."

"But you pushed straight through it, no worries," I pointed out.

"He must have set it to have a one-way pass-through somehow, and he did it with the focus backward." She shrugged. "Fucked if I know, really. Maybe it magically opens only on Tuesdays while it's the blood moon or something. I'm guessing at this as much as you are."

"That's a relief," I admitted. "I was starting to think I was an idiot for not understanding the runes."

"Don't worry." Andre smiled as he clapped a hand on my shoulder in commiseration. "I don't understand them either, boss."

I glanced at him, then Emma, and she sighed, then smiled, clearly knowing that as much as she loved her husband, he was far from Mensa material.

Instead, I looked at the journal as Emma passed it over, the script cramped and hurried. I scanned a few lines, my frown deepening.

"Looks like our friend here was part of a group that got lost down here," I said slowly. "Some kind of exploration team, studying the new monsters and more. I guess they either found the tunnels or were dragged down here by something." I skipped through the notebook, seeing page after page covered in careful writings, then every so often a fast scrawl as it detailed discoveries about the runes.

Most of the runes I saw were vaguely familiar. I guessed that some of our artifacts and magical crap had them on as well, but here and there, I saw something new.

Emma leaned in, peering at the journal. "Does it say who else was with him, or how many?"

"Doesn't say. But it sounds like they were taken by surprise by something down here. Something that picked them off one by one, until our enchanter was the only one left." I turned a page, wincing at the increasingly frantic script. "He sealed himself in here, tried to use his magic to hide, but…"

"But something found him anyway," Andre finished grimly. He pointed at a series of gouges in the stone near the skeleton's feet, just on the other side of the barrier and unnervingly familiar. "Poor guy. Must've been a nightmare, trapped down here with no light and things hunting him."

I turned another page, hoping for some clue about what exactly had attacked the expedition…and paused, my breath catching in my throat.

There, sketched in frantic, jagged strokes of charcoal, was an all-too-familiar silhouette. Knife-edge limbs, segmented carapace, maws bristling with cruel fangs…

"Ghasts," I breathed. "Like the lesser ghasts we've got in the dungeon, but they're…different, somehow. Bigger. Meaner." I held up the sketch. The dark lines seemed to writhe in the glow of my lightning. "At least we know what the hell happened to the rest of the group."

"Shit, boss, they're nasty fuckers!" Andre shook his head, apparently not liking the thought of fighting them one bit.

Emma took the notebook from me, staring at the drawing, her face pale. "We need to warn the others."

"Let's get the hell out of here," I muttered. I searched the body quickly, murmuring a brief "Hope you find rest, mate" over the body, then picking up the staff, just in case, and sliding it into the bag of holding, even now loving the incongruity of being able to do that.

Emma pointed to a dense cluster of runes scribed along the bottom of a nearby wall, the shapes jagged with haste and fear.

"We need to come back once we know the others are safe and copy these runes," she said. "I've never seen some of them before, and they could be important."

"Fine, you feel free to come and explore later." I nodded. "The reason we're here, though, is to set the dungeon up. And the way this is looking? We need to find somewhere defensible and safe and hole the fuck up."

"Is the risk that great?" Jackie asked.

"It's not fucking good," I said. "The lesser ghasts are a pain to fight, mainly because they're ambush predators. There could be a dozen around us now in stealth—"

"There aren't," she said confidently.

"That's what I'm hoping, but are you high enough a level at stealth that you *know* that?" I asked her, getting a brief, uncomfortable shrug, before she shook her head. "Exactly. Okay, we've wasted enough time here. Let's go find the others."

With that, I gestured back along the passage we'd come from, as the rest of this storeroom—that was all I could guess it'd been—had clearly been picked clean, and was going nowhere.

The next few minutes were spent backtracking and then heading along the next passage, looking for the others. When we caught up with them, though, it wasn't to good news.

CHAPTER THIRTY-EIGHT

We found Mike's group crouched at the entrance to an enormous cavern, one that had clearly been created by a mixture of collapsing caverns and natural shaping…followed by something with more patience than skill. The walls nearby were scored with those same geometric patterns we'd seen before, but on a massive scale.

"Lights out!" Mike hissed as we approached, frantically gesturing until we understood and I cut the spell. He shook his head in relief. "Fuck's sake, I thought you'd just killed us all. We found something interesting. Have a look," Mike whispered as we joined him at the edge, gesturing for us to stay low.

I moved forward, crouching and creeping along before stopping at the edge of a pile of shattered bricks and rock. I peered over the top, doing a fast pass, left to right, trying to see everything at once. The cavern stretched at least a hundred meters across, its ceiling lost in darkness above. But it was what occupied the center that caught my attention.

A group of greater ghasts, maybe five or six of them, were engaged in a savage battle with what looked like oversized versions of those glass scarabs. These three were easily the size of small cars; their crystalline carapaces reflected the dim light as they clashed with the more familiar horror of the ghasts. And every so often, they apparently managed some kind of magical attack, given the collection of diced ghast pieces on the far side of the room.

"Well, that's new," I muttered. "How long have they been at it?"

"Few minutes," Mike replied. "But that's not the interesting part. Look over there." He pointed to a section of the far wall, partly hidden behind a fallen column.

I shifted position slightly, and that's when I saw it. A perfect circular depression in the far side of the cavern in the rock face, maybe ten meters across, surrounded by what looked like naturally formed crystalline formations.

"Crystal?" I muttered, frowning and not seeing the point.

"You can see the mana flow, right?" he prompted.

I focused, using the dungeon sense and checking…

"Holy shit," I breathed. The mana wasn't just flowing around and past there. It was spiraling inward, creating a natural focal point that would be perfect for establishing a dungeon core. "That's…"

"Exactly what we're looking for," Mike finished. "Question is, how do we get to it with the monster mosh pit between us and there?"

"You're damn right it is!" I agreed, nodding, wide-eyed, before tearing my gaze away from the crystals that were—if I was really fuckin' lucky—mana crystals.

A naturally occurring mana crystal mine!

That made me pause for a second. If that was what it was, then which came first? The heavy buildup of mana in the area, creating the mana crystal mine, or the crystals giving rise to the heavy mana concentration?

I shook the distraction loose, and focused more on the group down there now. Because it'd gone from a "do we need to know what's down here; maybe we should go elsewhere" situation into a "they need to die, and fast" deal.

I studied the ongoing battle. The ghasts held their own against the larger scarabs, but neither side seemed to be gaining a clear advantage. More importantly, they were completely focused on each other.

There was a half-collapsed passage in the far wall about ten meters from the depression that was filled with crystals, and I nodded to myself as I saw that.

"We go around," I decided. "Hug the wall, stay in the shadows and head for that passage. These bigger ones seem more interested in fighting than feeding, and the ghasts are too busy to notice us if we're careful."

"Are you crazy?" Emma snapped. "What if they *do* notice us?"

"Then we kill the fuckers," I growled. "This is the place for the new dungeon. As much as I'd have preferred a fucking smaller one, that mine there? We need that! Now, if we're lucky, we get to the passage there, and find it leads to a single room, somewhere deep in the rock and as armored as possible, because that's probably the place we set up, so that we can get some walls around us and a close enough reach to the crystals that it's reasonable.

"If we're not lucky, then we kill those fuckers, then anything else that comes looking for their friends. But regardless, we need those fucking crystals—so head down, arse up, and fucking move!"

"Now you sound like Chris." Jenn grinned at me, before patting Jimmy, her husband, on the shoulder. "The innuendo, I mean. Don't worry…he's not said anything like that to me."

"Fucker better not have," Jimmy muttered, before shooting me a quick grin. "We're with you, boss. Hope we don't have to fight them, though."

"Me too, mate, but if we do…" I patted my sword. "Then we find out if my new Temporal Momentum ability works as advertised. But let's try not to test that just yet."

The rest of the team nodded grimly. We'd all had enough fighting weird-ass shit for one day.

"Jackie, you've got point," I ordered quietly. "Mike, bring up the rear. Everyone else between us. And for fuck's sake, stay quiet."

We began our careful circuit of the cavern, pressing close to the rough wall. The sounds of battle echoed off the stone; the crystalline shriek of the scarabs mixed with the otherworldly howls of the ghasts as they tore into each other.

The first thirty meters went smoothly…too smoothly. We'd made it almost a third of the way around when one of the massive scarabs went down, a front leg ripped off a side that was already injured; the whole thing tilted over, then crashed down. Its crystalline form cracked with a sound like breaking glass played through a mike. The noise was deafening in the enclosed space, but worse was what followed.

One of the ghasts leapt upward, landing atop the collapsed creature and stabbing down, over and over with its scythe-like arms. The claws on its feet scraped along the crystal coating of the body with a sound like nails on a chalkboard.

The wounded scarab screeched. The jackhammer-like stabbings of its rider shattered more and more of the carapace, before the ghast spun and its tail lifted.

Unlike the others that I'd seen, which had a tail like a spike—more for balance than anything else—this fucker had a club like that dinosaur had on its tail, the one that was basically a fucking spiked mace.

As it brought that around and down, the armor shattered, and the ghast whipped itself around again, lunging in and stabbing ferociously.

The other ghasts, sensing victory, let loose a collective howl that made my teeth ache. It'd gone from five ghasts to three scarabs, to one that was savaging the fallen one, and two that were facing off against each of the others.

"Keep moving," I whispered urgently. "They're distracted—this is our chance!"

We picked up the pace, still hugging the wall but moving faster now. The crystal formations grew denser as we approached our target, casting strange refractions of what little light there was. Jackie suddenly froze, holding up a hand.

"Movement," she hissed. "In the crystals."

I cursed and glared ahead, before feeling my balls shriveling up. I saw something shifting among the crystalline growths. The formations weren't just geometric patterns—oh no, because that would be too *easy* for my life. No, they were cocoons or nests, pulsing with a faint inner light.

"Fuck me sideways," Mike breathed. "No wonder they're fighting over this place. It's a breeding ground."

The implications hit me hard. If this was where the glass scarabs were reproducing, using the ambient mana from the crystal mine to spawn new broods…we couldn't just set up shop here and hope for the best. We'd need to clear them out completely.

Now that we were down on the ground and moving closer, though, I was seeing something else—something that really wasn't happy-making.

The crystals that were embedded in the wall weren't the only ones. In fact, scattered around the cavern on all sides were others, hundreds of them…it was just that they were all dark and broken.

What I'd taken for rock columns, stalactites and stalagmites, were instead shattered, drained piles of crystals.

"Change of plans," I murmured, gathering the team closer. "We make for that passage, but we're going to have to come back and clean house once the dungeon is started. These things are feeding on the fucking crystals somehow. The moment we start setting up converters and anything that provides mana, they'll probably come swarming in."

"Could work in our favor," Emma suggested quietly. "If we seal ourselves in that back chamber, we could use the converters to draw them in, trap them between us and the ghasts."

I nodded. It wasn't ideal, but nothing about this mission had been so far. "First things first. Let's get to that passage without joining the all-you-can-eat buffet. Ready?"

The others nodded grimly. We'd covered about half the distance to our goal, but the next section would take us closest to the ongoing battle. And now that we knew what to look for, I could see more of those pulsing crystal formations ahead.

I was about to give the order to move when a new sound cut through the cavern: a high-pitched keening that set my teeth on edge. One of the larger scarabs had just done…*something*…to a ghast, leaving it writhing on the ground, torn up and badly bleeding. Crystalline formations began to grow from its wounds.

"Oh, that's properly fucked up," Andre muttered.

"Move," I ordered. "Now. Before they start winning again."

The next stretch was nerve-racking. Every step brought us closer to the fighting, and now we could see just how vicious these evolved forms really were. The ghast that had been crystallized was still thrashing, its movements growing more erratic as the crystal formations spread across its body like some kind of geometric cancer.

I found myself staring at that, almost as much as I was the rest of the room. Because that was either something we needed, and we'd be fucking setting up a crystal scarab farming site, where the damn thing could infect ghasts all day long and give us a shitload of crystals…or it was how these things bred, growing from crystals, in which case the crystals we were hoping to use might be their next generation and about to fucking hatch and kill us all instead.

Jackie led us through a particularly dense patch of dead crystal growths, forcing us to weave between formations that occasionally pulsed with an unsettling inner light.

Each pulse seemed to sync with the keening of the injured ghast, and I could swear the eggs or cocoons or whatever the fuck they were responded to it.

"Matt," Mike hissed from behind us. "Nine o'clock. We've got movement."

I glanced over, seeing him backing up toward us, moving with a grace and silence that I couldn't match going bloody forward. One of the remaining scarabs had just noticed something was off, though. It wasn't looking directly at us yet, but its head was swiveling our way, crystalline antennae twitching. And, of course, this was the one that only had a single ghast to face it.

"Keep going," I breathed. "Slow and steady. If it spots us…"

The ghast it had been fighting chose that moment to launch itself at the distracted scarab, its claws screeching against the crystal carapace. The scarab shrieked in response, attention torn away from us as it fought for its life, burying its mandibles into the ghast and cutting the fucker almost in half.

The ghast shrieked and frantically stabbed, its desperation showing as it beat on the mandible.

The first scarab had either stopped being an amusing chew toy for its rider, or it'd died, because as the scarab spun, releasing the dying ghast to crash to the floor in a messy heap, the rider leapt atop this new scarab and started whaling on it as well.

The air was filled with the chalkboard nails sound again as it tried to dig its claws in. But this time, there was no shattered carapace to give purchase, and the ghast was flung free as the scarab spun, fast.

The ghast landed hard, rolling and coming to its feet before leaping back into the fight, bounding left and right, then spinning and crashing its mace-like tail into a leg joint, cracking it.

The fight was hypnotic, it was moving that fast. And thanks to the limited light in the cavern—given off by a collection of glowing crystals and not an adventurer-friendly boss or whatever, just in case a human wandered down—there were entire sections of the room that would go black as the inside of a black cat on a moonless night, before being flooded by light as a scarab used some kind of ability.

We covered another twenty meters before disaster struck. I'd clearly come inside of some kind of sensory radius because the scarabs spun as if they were on a lazy Susan and locked onto me.

We all froze as they let lose a shimmering screech and started forward. And at the very same time, I felt a pulse of power from the massive bloody mana crystal collar around the dungeon core strapped to my bloody back.

"Oh shit." I grunted as I realized that yeah, of goddamn course, a bunch of creatures that were this fixated on mana would sense us. It was only sheer luck that they'd already been busy with a fight until now.

Presumably the smaller ones had been insensate or something, but who cared really.

That was when the second bit of misfortune struck.

Jenn was distracted by the whole situation at just the wrong time, and stumbled on a piece of loose rubble, catching herself against one of the crystal formations. The thing lit up like a fucking Christmas tree at her touch, and a pulse of light rippled through the surrounding crystals.

The effect was immediate. Those same crystals were now revealed to be covered in cocoons that immediately began to struggle as the scarabs within drained the pulse of power. Both the remaining scarabs snapped their heads toward us with terrifying synchronization.

Just to make the situation that little bit worse, Jenn promptly collapsed, flat out unconscious, and Emma gasped, leaping for her sister, as did Jimmy.

"Fuck subtlety—RUN!" I roared, shoving Emma ahead of me as Jimmy scooped up his wife.

The nearest scarab disengaged from its fight and skittered our way with frightening speed. The ghasts, never ones to miss an opportunity, howled in pursuit—making the most of the diversion, I hoped, because I really didn't want to fucking see whether they were going to make friends over a shared meal.

The passage entrance was maybe thirty meters ahead. Jackie had already reached it, frantically waving us on. But the scarab was closing fast, its massive form eating up the ground between us with each step of its crystalline legs.

That—because of *course* it was—was when the queen decided to make her presence felt, breaking her way free of the wall to the left of the passage we'd been aiming for, where she'd been mistaken for the fuckin' cavern!

"Shitfuck!" I heard Emma scream, before unleashing a bolt of bright-red lightning…that slammed into the queen and vanished.

"Oh, that's not good," I heard her say, before she tried again. A much heavier blast ripped out, bringing a bright-red dawn to the cavern and revealing the corpses that had lain hidden inside the crystal pillars on all sides.

We'd not found a mana mine—we'd found a joint graveyard and creche, one that Mama was not feeling like sharing!

The queen was huge. And unlike her smaller children, she appeared to have no head, nor any kind of weak spot, given that she was almost entirely made of crystal.

The collection we'd been aiming for was the central part of her body, with six legs spaced around a grouping of columns that were in turn atop the remains of whatever creature she'd started life as.

She'd been something insectoid, I guessed by the layout and the long tail that arced around, to hang high in the air, quivering.

Before I could say anything, it shot forward, the gleaming length tipped by a jagged collection of dimly glowing growths. It slammed into Andre's shield. How the wonderful bastard had made it to Emma's side so fast and gotten his shield around, I didn't know, but he'd just saved her life.

He cried out, staggering, the shield deformed and his arm had to have been at the very least bruised to all buggery by that impact, but it gave them time as the tail whipped back, shaking itself free of more of the crystals. The tinkling sound as shattered sections of crystal fell free filled the air, though it was almost lost under the roaring and screams of the other creatures.

"Run!" I yelled, shoving Andre from behind, and unleashing a blast of Incinerate into the middle of the crystal thing as well.

There was a brief flash of light that flared out from the middle of the thing as the spell activated, and my mana dipped…but that was it.

The queen shifted her position. The legs, much like those of the scarabs, were hinged and jointed as an insect's, yet gleamed and seemed entirely made of glass or crystal. The limited light reflected off them as dust that had concealed her cascaded free.

They came down, punching through dead crystals, into the rock below and into the debris that surrounded her, as I finally realized what had happened here.

The little scarabs had been marked as being something that was created between volatile mana and high-tech machinery. That was clearly only one way they were created, because if this had been birthed by something like that…

Whoever had set this place up had clearly intended to ride out the end of the world in luxury, so I was betting there'd been a massive amount of tech dumped down here. And if you had a fuckload of tech, ready for the end of the world, you weren't going to be relying on the national power grid.

If there'd been anyone expecting to use it, and I mean really use the place, then I was willing to bet that on top of the old shit we'd found upstairs, there would have been regular deliveries of modern tech, probably all set up, then powered down and ready to go.

There had to have been some kind of high-tech generator down here, and when you had a fuckload of mana, and a fuckload of high tech…this was what you got.

The queen had somehow evolved, and had been spawning the others, letting them eat their way out and bring in more and more mana for her. The crystal columns surrounded bodies, and I was willing to bet that was what had happened to the rest of that enchanter's expedition: trapped in here, turned to crystal by whatever the scarabs did to that ghast, and then converted into the smaller scarabs, which were sent out in turn to consume and convert.

Now we'd stumbled into the middle of the meat grinder, and woken her up.

Just what we needed.

I frantically ran through the spells that I had available that might help. I was fairly sure, from the brightening of the crystals both on her back and the one that Jenn had touched, that if I used spells on her directly, I was just feeding her free mana.

I couldn't get the meteors, as I was pretty sure with the overhead that they wouldn't just magically appear down here; they'd be summoned above the clouds and just pulverize some of London.

Until recently, I'd not be opposed to that on general principles, but fuck it, today was different.

I couldn't use Storm-Strike or any others directly, but maybe…

"Get through the passage!" I shouted over the sound of Mike's rifle fire. The bullets chewed up his targets as he sought to keep the incoming scarabs back, even as Jackie fired in short bursts at the queen.

Andre stumbled along. He'd lifted Jenn over his shoulder at some point, and judging from the way the shield dangled limp as he wove between the crystal columns, the other arm with the shield was useless right now.

Jimmy was by his side, rifle raised and firing in fast bursts as well, aiming for the queen's legs. Emma also backed up between the crystals, though she was muttering something and had cut her left palm, throwing blood into the air, even as more of it drained from her face, presumably, considering it flooded out of the visor and breathing holes in her helmet.

I saw it, and I swallowed hard, before shouting orders.

"Jimmy, get ready to help Emma! Mike, switch to your fucking sniper!" I barked. "Jackie, you're on stealth. Watch for any—" I didn't get to finish the sentence before she whipped around and unleashed a burst of fire into seemingly empty air, as the ghast that had been approaching, completely unseen, appeared as it was hurled from its feet.

She stepped forward, adjusted her aim, and fired a three-round burst into the head, then ejected the magazine and slammed in a replacement.

"Yeah!" I shouted at her. "You do *that*." I grinned manically, as I slapped my sword back into the sheath on my back. The sheath closed over the blade again, clicking and locking it in place. I focused, not sure how to do it, and just hoped that it'd work when I needed it.

"Temporal…MOMENTUM!" I shouted, darting forward and hoping the damn thing would trigger, even as I pulled my hammer free, sprinting at the shining creature.

I couldn't touch it with magic, but I was betting it'd have a hard time sucking the goddamn magic out of a lump of metal that I was smashing the bastard with.

The world slowed as Temporal Momentum thankfully kicked in, giving me precious fractions of seconds to decide my target as I charged. The queen's crystalline form towered above me, her legs piercing the ground like gigantic glass stakes. Behind me, Emma's blood magic was building to something, and I bet it was her Bloodwytch's Fury spell. I could feel the power crackling in the air even through my temporal distortion.

My hammer felt oddly light as I closed the distance. The enchantments on it hummed in harmony with the ability, and I just hoped that it being an imbued weapon wasn't going to backfire on me. The queen's tail whipped toward me, but with my Temporal Momentum activated, I was fast enough that I couldn't help but grin. I twisted aside, feeling the air displacement as crystal shards sprayed past me.

There was a weird booming noise as the crystal crashed into the ground, even with the sound being delayed. I whipped the hammer around, slamming the flat head into the taut length of the tail—once, twice, a third time. The cracks radiated outward.

"Matt, left!" Mike's voice seemed stretched and distorted through the temporal effect, but the warning registered. I dove and rolled as one of the massive legs crashed down where I'd been standing. The impact sent shock waves through the cavern floor around me, dislodging more crystal formations.

Using the momentum of my roll, I came up swinging, snapping the movement from my hips as much as my shoulders and arms. The hammer connected with one of the queen's leg joints with a sound like a cathedral bell being struck.

Fissures spiderwebbed through the crystalline limb, but didn't shatter it completely. More concerning was the way the impact sent feedback vibrating up my arms. This fucker was far denser than it looked.

"Focus on the joints!" I shouted, my voice sounding normal to my ears despite the time distortion. "The crystal structure is weaker there!"

Mike's sniper rifle cracked. The heavy round made its presence felt as it punched through the head of an incoming scarab.

I swung again, then dodged back and dove to the left, coming to my feet and slamming the hammer into the nearest leg three times over in fast succession.

The combined assault finally shattered the limb, sending crystalline shrapnel flying. The queen let out a keening shriek that made my teeth ache, the sound somehow managing to pierce even my altered time state.

The lower half of the leg suddenly crashed to the floor, as weak as glass, it shattered. Layers upon layers of broken glass were left for me to stumble over, even as the other half of the limb was yanked back out of reach.

I shifted my target, deciding that the damaged leg I'd been working on before was the best to aim for. But as soon as I leapt for it, she spun, slamming down her tail in a wide area around me, before yanking it tight, trying to catch me inside its loop.

I leapt into the air, barely avoiding the crushing embrace, but she wasn't done. The broken leg began to regenerate almost immediately, fresh crystal growing from the shattered stump. Worse, I could see the cocoons all around were beginning to pulse with that same inner light, as whatever they held got ready to come and play.

"We need to end this fast!" I called out. "Emma, whatever you're planning, do it now!"

Through my peripheral vision, I saw her raise her bloodied hands. Crimson droplets hung suspended in the air around her. The words she spoke seemed to echo strangely, as if coming from very far away:

"Blood of my heart, serve my will, punish…"

I missed the rest of whatever she was chanting as a cascade of smaller glass scarabs, the tiny fuckers, suddenly broke loose from a section of the roof overhead.

I dove to the left, arcing around, and unleashed a blast of channeled lightning into the mass.

At least half had died on impact. And the rest? Well, there weren't many that could have survived a blast of lightning when they were that small already. It was a senseless waste to…

I'd been dragging my lightning up the waterfall of scarabs, making sure that they weren't going to wash over our people, and I'd committed the cardinal sin.

I got distracted.

The leg that slammed into me lifted me from the air where I'd been happily arcing around, and it drove me into the nearest wall with a crash that sent dust raining free from the ceiling in a great wave.

I lost control of my Temporal Momentum at that point, and I found out the real problem with such a power. As the normal flow of time reasserted itself on my battered mind, it brought with it a debuff of minus fucking seventy percent for an hour!

I fell forward, collapsing to the floor; I shoved myself up to my feet, shaking my head and blinking. The fight before me was still ongoing, even as I tried to make sense of it all, having just had my bell rung.

That was when Emma, fortunately, unleashed her spell.

The blood that had been drained from her had gathered into a ball that was roughly the size of the end of my thumb. It'd been surrounded by her usual red lightning, and both the usual blue-white of my own, more traditional storm powers, and black lightning that I had no clue about.

Whatever it was, though, it filled the bloody ball, compressing it down, until it apparently became something closer to a fucking rail gun round. When she released it and the ball rocketed forward, it smashed through the queen's body with barely any pause, before exploding inside her.

The area around the ball, as I'd seen the last time she'd used it, was shoved outward with some kind of unstoppable force as it expanded to about the size of a beach ball. And considering it'd been inside the creature at that point, the effect was catastrophic.

The queen burst, crystals shattering and flying in all directions. The devastation was made worse by the fact that she appeared almost entirely inorganic, so there were no gaps or soft areas to absorb the damage.

Instead, the queen just…detonated.

Sections flew in all directions, and a half second later, even as bits were still in flight, Emma collapsed and got scooped up by Jimmy, who spun and raced after his brother, the pair running for the passage ahead.

Jackie ran after them, and Mike was backing up. I was already in motion as well—a little dizzy, but pushing hard, and still able to move at an Olympic athlete's top speed plus a bit more, easily enough.

Even with the seventy percent reduction in my top speed, a little effort and I was plenty fast, though as Mike opened fire and moved, I noticed that he was more of a blur than I'd seen before.

I couldn't quite follow him, and that meant…

"Down!" Mike snapped, whipping his rifle around and firing almost directly over my shoulder.

I dove for the ground, then was covered in a wash of ghast brains and blood as the unseen fucker behind me fell.

"What the hell's wrong with you?" Mike asked me, moving in and grabbing my shoulder, hauling me upright even as he one-handed his sniper rifle easily around. "Concussion?" He dragged me around and stared into my eyes.

"No…debuff!" I explained, shaking myself loose from his grasp.

"Get back there," Mike grunted, and I obeyed, surprised by the difference.

I probably shouldn't have been, though, considering that I'd been able to move at ten times the natural speed of the average human. Although I'd not noticed much of a difference, at a "mere" three times the average, I saw it now in the way the others moved.

Mike got me moving again with a shove, and I realized that, for now, I was more of a hinderance than a help.

"We'll come loot later once we know it's all clear," Mike said to me, and I nodded.

The pair of us followed the others along the passage into a small control room that was, yeah, clearly designed for the IT side of the site. The back wall had collapsed, probably when the queen became aware enough to move, and she'd dragged her bulk free, a bulk that I now recognized as made up mainly of pre-fall server infrastructure.

Regardless, though, we were through the worst of it, and the small section we were in now would have to do.

The passage that led up to it was a bit of a problem. It was open, and the doors that led into this section were wooden and pretty pathetic. Pushing the one to this room closed was pointless, as all it did was sit there with a simple lever action latch. But two of the walls were strong enough to hold, and the far one, which had presumably been intended for more important things, was a big fuck-off metal slab.

If we could have opened it, that'd be the side I'd have deployed the core on. As it was, I pulled the bugger out, set one end on the floor, and took a deep breath before I connected to it, and just hoped that there wasn't any damage from being on my back when I'd hit that wall.

CHAPTER THIRTY-NINE

The next few minutes as the crystal around the core was gradually shifted, the basic functions of the core activating slowly, were long-ass ones.

I got to the point that I had begun to believe that maybe we should back everyone else off, just in case the core went nuclear or something, when I received the first prompt.

Dungeon Seed Activated—Permeate area? — Yes/No

"Fuck no," I muttered, remembering that minor detail. It'd basically take me out of the field, then absorb everything it could reach into the core to power its birth.

That'd include killing everyone in the five-meter-by-five-meter radius.

How about no?

Confirm: Manual Permeation and expansion selection.

I approved it and moved on, picking up speed. The world around me froze again, and the collar of mana crystals that surrounded the core began to flicker as the core apparently sucked power from them.

Enhanced Creation Setup available: Continue? — Yes/No

"Fucking of course I want you to bloody continue!" I snapped at it. Thankfully, the core decided that was close enough to Yes that it was acceptable. The core floated free of me, hovering in the air as the crystal dissolved into eye-searingly bright light.

Seed Core Stabilized. Please select from the following options:

- **Form symbiotic link with parent dungeon.**
- **Form secondary associated/unassociated dungeon.**
- **Specialize dungeon core for subsidiary action.**

Yeah, again—no competition there. I selected option one, setting it up as a symbiotic dungeon that we would have full control over, as well as grinning when the mana provided was apparently more than needed for the minor task of linking:

Symbiotic link selected: Estimated time to full activation: 0 days, 1 hour, 12 minutes, 3 seconds.

Activated and fully charged Dungeon Seed housing detected. Please select from the following options:

1. **Break down and absorb Dungeon Seed housing, providing an immediate mana boost to the new core – Time limited**
2. **Store Dungeon Seed housing and begin growth of secondary Seed.**
3. **Consume Dungeon Seed housing for a one-time boost to this dungeon.**

I selected the option to feed on its seed housing. It wasn't much compared to the collar it was working with, but it all went in the right direction. That was when I found that the timer couldn't dip any further, and that the delay was a hard one, caused by construction limits.

I sensed it from the dungeon core as it continued the activation, needing a little more time to fully activate. For the first time, the dungeon core wasn't being held up by a lack of mana, and instead it was racing ahead.

Checking over the core, I found the most basic systems were beginning to unlock already. The dungeon field that it could control was already pushing out, and I worked with that, noting that the others had started to move again, the suspension of time having already expired.

Emma was checking on her sister, her husband Andre claiming that he'd be fine, even as his brother manhandled his shoulder back into its joint with a popping crunch that made my stomach turn just hearing it.

It made Andre turn practically green as well. The others weren't much better, but it was what it was. I'd been figuring on a broken bone, but he had his own healing potions, and as soon as Jenn recovered, she could check him over.

I glanced at her, finding her seemingly just out cold, and I nodded to myself, impressed.

If we could somehow copy that capability of the crystals, we'd have an anti-mage trap that was incredible.

Cover the door handles of places you wanted to protect with that and boom. No stress.

I moved on, working as quickly as I could, shoving out the line of influence toward the doorway. And then, as soon as I had control over it, I summoned in a large metal-framed door from the basic dungeon design catalog.

We'd unlocked the buggers ages ago, and we'd put these doors in all over the dungeon. They opened with a thought for anyone who was connected and who had authority over the most basic of dungeon facilities. But for anyone or any*thing* else, it might as well have been six inches of solid steel in a bank.

Nobody was getting through that without us knowing about it.

By the time the dungeon had fully activated, the symbiotic link unlocking and us connecting up to the rest of the network, I was done, and the room we were in now bore little resemblance to the one we'd first found.

As it had been, it'd been dusty, dirty, and a small rivulet of water had run constantly from the back left of the room, along the edge of the wall—which was clearly sagging slightly—to the front of the room. Then there was a shitty wooden door that had led out to the main corridor, and everywhere there were the remains of thick, armored sheaths for what I recognized as Cat7 cabling.

The cabling was gone, presumably eaten—or who knew, really—but the PVC coating that ran around the outer layer was apparently not as tasty.

Then there was the collapsed section at the back of the room: the remains of server cabinets torn apart and discarded as the queen had apparently outgrown them, the grey stone and shattered ceiling tiles, and of course, the remains of dozens of posters, folders, and half a tree of papers, all sodden and melted into an irrecoverable mess.

The right-hand side of the room had the second door in it. That was the really heavy-duty one, but considering it was opened by use of a touch pad, I bet that whoever had installed it was a moron.

There needed to be backups—backups for everything, considering this was designed for the friggin' end of days. And for the door to whatever you were keeping this safe not to have one? Well, as I said, moron.

There was no way I was getting through that without the core online. And as curious as I was, I wasn't seeing the mileage in dropping everything to push through it yet.

Instead, I'd solidified or replaced the walls, floor, and ceiling—the ceiling tiles had almost all fallen and what was left was a mess of air conditioning units and pipework that I quickly absorbed.

Once that was done, I'd changed the whole lot to marble, sheathed with steel around the outside, and then I'd absorbed the collapsed section at the back.

It took less than a minute to summon a collection of beds—bunkbeds; it wasn't like there was a lot of room—and a few sofas, a table and chairs, and a few mana crystals.

As soon as they appeared, Emma understood—I'd summoned them by her knee, after all. She hefted the first, then slid it into her sister's hand, putting one in the other hand, then had Jimmy pick her up and settle her into one of the beds.

"Thank you," she said to me, joining me in the dungeon sense, and I smiled at her.

"No worries. How is she?"

"Exhausted and drained to her dregs. Or, at least, I think that's all it is. I wish Jo was here."

"Me too," I admitted, before sighing and plowing on manfully. "Emma?"

"Yeah?" She blinked, clearly exhausted.

"Well done," I said. "There's a lot of things we're going to disagree on, I think. You and I—we're like oil and water at times—but that fight? That ability of yours is an insta-kill, and you used it well."

"Yeah, but if I miss, it's all over." She snorted. "If you'd not been keeping its attention, I'd never have got that shot off. And it takes three-quarters of my health every time as well."

"You had a health potion yet?" I asked her, and she shook her head.

"I don't like taking them," she admitted. "Knowing that you can get addicted? Let's just say that me and 'Colombian marching powder' have a history. I don't like the idea of taking anything that might be addictive."

"Hate to break it to you, kid, but the only thing that's not addictive is death." I smiled wryly. "You know a hundred percent of people who drink water die, right?"

"That's…that's fucking terrible." She sighed. "And you're like what? Two years older than me? If that? That's a dad joke all the way."

"I know, but it made you smile…nearly, anyway." I shrugged. "Seriously, the link to home should be activating any minute, and I'm going to be busy as all hell with things in there for a while. Go get some sleep and tell the others to do the same, all right?"

"Will do." She sighed. "And thanks…boss," she offered, before blinking out of the dungeon.

"Well, that was heartwarming," Kelly said from right behind me and I spun, my heart in my mouth.

"Fuck me sideways!" I hissed. "How long have you been there?"

"Just got here." She smiled, reaching out to me. "As soon as the connection went live, I reached out, that's all. Why? You trying to seduce the help now?"

"She'd rip it off and beat me with it." I snorted.

"Kinky." Kelly grinned. "Mind you, knowing that a healing potion can fix little things like that would really change the way that kinky couples do shit, I bet."

"If you think ripping my dick off and beating me with it is a 'little thing,' I don't think I want to come home after all…" I muttered, before getting a kiss.

"Oh really?" She purred. "And I've got such a surprise waiting for you in a few days as well. Are you sure about that?"

"Is it going to involve me getting my dick ripped off?" I squinted at her in mock suspicion.

"Maybe. I mean, I might try, but it won't be my hand that grips you that hard…" She whispered that into my ear in a voice that bypassed my higher brain functions entirely and hot-wired the lower regions into an instant response.

"I'llbethere!" I said in a rush.

"Good." She kissed me again, then stepped back, grinning mischievously, before looking around the room. "So this is the underside of London, eh? I thought it was mostly dodgy underground clubs and gambling."

"Yeah, I think that's Soho." I shrugged. "Fuck it, but this place is a bit of a mess as well. What we've found is…"

The next ten minutes were given over to updates, both from me about our situation and from her about the various dungeons and their progress, ending with a bit of good news.

"So the undead faction are happy to pay a premium to claim any bodies of people who fall in the dungeon arena, and while I made it clear that we will not be selling our people, those who go through the arena have to pay a fee for the privilege." She shrugged. "We can't stop people doing it, but we can make sure we make a profit on it, I guess. It makes me feel dirty, though."

"Oh?" I grinned, my brain still fizzing from her earlier comments.

"Not that kind of dirty," she clarified.

"I guessed." I sighed. "But they're using the arena?"

"Three bookings and a single run completed so far—by dungeon adventurers or trainees, I mean, not a Dungeon Lord." She nodded, smiling brilliantly. "We get our tax, which in addition to the cost of the run is that we make a copy of anything that's dropped, but they keep the original."

"Anything good?"

"Nothing yet, but the cost is negligible to most of the people. And, as we thought, the chance to not have to run a dungeon in their own limited space is very appealing to many of them. I've offered Akuba and Kaatachi a discount on their runs, as we're allies, and they agreed. They were very thankful, and Akuba said that when the pair were in London last, they visited the Museum of Natural History. They wondered if you'd considered hitting it for resources and bones?"

"Yeah." I nodded. "Fuck, we need to do that. I know Chris is going to lose his shit when we get him a raptor."

"I don't think I want to be around for that."

"You know you do," I corrected. "If anyone is going to get their junk bitten off by a monster from the dawn of time, it's that man."

"And he'd deserve it." She sighed. "Okay, count me in, as long as you can control them. I don't want a rerun of the movies."

"You ever think that John Hammond was just a necromancer who was good at hiding it?" I asked her, and the conversation went precisely nowhere after that.

Mike joined us a little while later, mainly to speak to Aly, who joined at his request via Kelly. There were a few hours of general discussion around the plans we had for the area, and then I gave in and called it a day, leaving the dungeon sense, even as Markus and Clarissa set the undead teams away on expanding our reach.

By the time I woke up the next morning, not only was it a different day, but it was also a different world.

For us, anyway.

When I woke, not only had my debuff worn off, but the air in the core room was bright and cheery. The door was open, leading into the next section, and when I got up, stretching and yawning, I found the area beyond had been transformed entirely.

Gone was the battered and shattered corridor, the gloomy passages, and the constant stink of mold and stagnant water. Instead, a short passage led to another set of five rooms, all enclosed for now—but they were the beginning of the dungeon's "real" expansion. First and foremost was the bathroom; those facilities got a visit paid to them, and a long hot shower was a damn necessity, regardless of the lack of a Kelly to help scrub my back.

I cleaned my clothes—or the dungeon did, thank you very much—and then, with the understanding that we were very much still in hostile territory, I put my armor back on, and went looking for the others.

There weren't exactly a multitude of options for the others of places to hang out, so it wasn't hard to find them.

Emma and Andre had a room to themselves under the remodel, and Jenn and Jimmy did as well, mainly because for the first week or so they were going to be the on-site security detail.

I'd also agreed when Jenn had asked offhandedly—when we were discussing this—whether she and her little family could have it just to themselves for a little while, more or less.

I'd planned to leave at least Jackie with them, for strength and depth if nothing else. But when Emma explained that if there were just the four of them, it'd be nice to be alone together, I'd suggested a compromise.

When we left, we'd leave a small team of dungeon-born here, but they'd be of a level that hopefully awoke slowly, giving them a little time at least.

I knew that Chris would have been making comments inside of ten milliseconds if it was just them alone, and yeah, a few of them occurred to me as well. But at the end of the day, they were a family, and what family didn't want a little time away from everyone else?

It wasn't like they were going to be having orgies.

The dungeon was easily accessible to anyone with the right level of clearance, after all, so that would be incredibly ill-advised—they'd have a crowd watching in minutes. But the illusion of a little family privacy to sit around and relax was hardly a big ask, and they'd earned that, though they knew that there'd need to be others as well.

The other two rooms, were, as I'd pointed out already, a bathroom and a large eating and relaxing area.

Emma and Jenn were laid half buried in massive cushion chairs when I walked into the main area. The pair sang in low voices, harmonizing incredibly. I drew to a stop, listening, while Andre and Jimmy sat at a nearby table with Mike and Jackie, cleaning their weapons.

All in all, add in the light snacks, the drinks, and the sheer fuckin' decadence of the furnishings—it looked like someone had designed an alpine lodge for royalty to visit—and it was easy to forget that just on the other side of the wall was a bunch of rotting bodies.

Or that overhead, not far away, an entire city was barely surviving.

That thought soured my good vibes in short order, and I sat with the others at the table, joining in a little light conversation while eating a fry-up.

Ten minutes later, with everything done, I stood and returned to the core room, ready to start on my job.

For Mike and the others, their job had been literally to act as security, and to help guide me in, so that I could do my job.

For me, though…I had a dungeon to get in order.

The first step, once I was settled back in the bed and then from there into the dungeon sense, was to begin mapping out the local caverns and rough area in the dungeon, then make plans for the basic layout.

The skeletal resource teams and Clarissa and Markus had been working on it all already, but they were doing the grunt work. It was on Kelly, Aly, and me to provide the overall direction and plans.

This was set to be a long-ass day.

The first job, and the most important, was to claim as much of the area as possible, while hiding the dungeon as it was. We needed to secure the entire area and make goddamn sure that if the London lot came digging and trying to set up their core here—I was still pretty sure they'd try to raid ours—then we needed to be in place to make it work.

I sort of felt a little bad about the lack of trust here, but they'd really earned it.

So, with that in mind, and given that we couldn't just seal up the tunnels that had led into this area, the first order of business was to locate them, and the areas that they were likely to try to access, and repair them.

If we arranged a cave-in at one end of the tunnel, and it was where they were planning to set up, then they were likely to go digging and then exploring.

If instead it was just a normal tunnel, though, no reason to change anything.

I'd suggested that we make it all look very clearly like if they went digging around it'd all collapse. But as Kelly pointed out, if we did that, then they were likely to not set up the one thing that was likely to save their city and power structure, right where we needed them to do it.

Instead, we first permeated as much of the area with the dungeon's influence as possible. Then we started to absorb anything that we could use or replace, before recreating tunnels and more.

It wasn't hard to reconstruct the old Tube lines as we reached them over the next few days, creating the stone and the filth that coated the walls, the general rubbish on the floors, and to even recreate a train at one end.

It was just time-consuming and basically a waste.

It had to be done, though, and so that was what we did. We created a replica of everything that we thought had been here, and we hid the entrance to the bunker, just in case.

Once that was done, we created thick walls and floors to prevent anyone digging through, sealed up the area, and started the real work.

There'd been probing attacks on the new walls overnight. I'd woken for one of them. Then, seeing that it was perfectly secure, and that Markus was monitoring it, I'd gone back to sleep.

There was a brief discussion the next day, and the decision was made that in addition to Emma and her family, when we left there'd be a dedicated dungeon security force, one that would be for now, dungeon-born. They would clear out the local area, using whatever monsters they found to level-up.

If they were outclassed, then they'd fall back and be reinforced. But as they were all to be summoned with either assault rifles and rail gun shotguns, or magic of their own, I figured that was unlikely to happen.

Plus, I wasn't planning to send them out in small numbers.

Twenty dungeon-born were summoned: a mix of five assassin kobolds, ten Scepiniir warriors, and five goblin mages. They were set to hunt out any remaining monsters, including any more ghasts, and bring their corpses back with them later that same day for integration into the dungeon.

That done, and with the basic version of the greater ghasts actually weaker than the uncommon version of the lesser ghasts we'd had already, we moved on.

Hours blurred as they marched past, with walls being smoothed, the crystals mined and protected, the scarab creatures absorbed and destroyed, removing them from the dungeon list entirely as soon as they were added. A little digging later, and I found that they were almost impossible to control without a queen. The queen cost a truly horrific amount of mana, and came with system warnings that the control methods weren't confirmed to work.

Apparently, an entire world had been lost to these things when they'd gotten out of control, and as it was one of the last dvork strongholds, it'd gotten them marked as a banned species.

By the time I finally left the dungeon sense in the early hours of the final morning nearly a week later, there was no sign of it from the outside, but the London dungeon was complete and ready for either the locals to set up, or for us to move ahead and one day open it to them.

The dungeon itself was up to a lot more rooms now, with ten sets of bedrooms—Emma and her family were told that for now they'd be the only human inhabitants, but in a week or less, they'd be returning to the fold. For now, though, they could consider this their little slice of heaven.

The other bedrooms were spares for the eventual management crew to move into and for the dungeon-born. Beyond that and the main bathroom area being reabsorbed into the bedrooms to give en suite options instead, the only other original rooms that remained were the core room and the main living area.

The other four rooms were divided into a research area—as the dungeon-born that weren't on patrol could then add to the research teams; a storage area for the undead resource team—just in case anything happened and they were cut off; an armory, and of course, the nexus gate.

The gate activated just before I went to bed. Yeah, I was seriously tempted to return home and have some time in my bed with Kelly, but I ended up staying another night as we got the place all sorted out.

By mid-morning the next day, I was confident that the area was as secure as possible, and Emma and Jenn understood that they weren't here on vacation. They were free to have some quiet downtime, but they were to help in the creation of the dungeon's future.

Lines of expansion had been laid out and would continue to be extended. Literally hours out of each day were to be spent by everyone burrowing and pushing out the dungeon's influence in all directions, randomly, in the hope that wherever the fake dungeon was set up, it'd be close enough to reach.

Most of every damn day had been spent on the mindless tasks, both increasing our active areas and adjusting the skeletal team's tracks.

Another part of each day had been even less fun, and that'd been the time I spent training my mana sense.

For months, I'd been able to see the mana in an area, mainly broken down to the color and depth of an area, and seeing little more than that. Now, as I'd discovered when I realized that Jack could see mana signatures, I'd started looking and whoo-boy was there a lot more to learn, even with this simple skill.

First of all, I was learning that once I was good with this—I refused to accept that there was any chance that I might not be a god with it, after all—I'd be able to see the mana that everything around me gave off.

That might not sound like much, but things like the baubas could be terrible, lethal predators if they were left to hunt in the dark. In the light? They were basically about as dangerous to me as a toddler with a butter knife. Sure, some of those little bastards were evil and could do real damage, but that was mainly because of them being lucky and the parents being dumb.

If I had to walk through somewhere that was pitch black, though? They could be a real threat no matter what I did. They were shadows given form, mass, and fuckin' teeth. If I could see their mana signature, though? There was no chance of them sneaking up on me.

That worked for anything that was stealthed as well: ghasts, assassins, sneaky politicians, anyone who relied on darkness or underhanded ways to hide their evil deeds would stand out just fine for me.

So would everyone else as well, which helped too, but I digress. I spent a minimum of an hour each evening when I should have been sleeping basically staring at mana so hard I gave myself a headache. But as time went on, I learned a few minor skills with it, including that I could now find the nexus gate in any area fairly easily, due to the incredible twisting of mana in the area that it enacted.

By the time I left that evening, I was exhausted simply from the tedium. But it was almost all done; only simple tasks that were mainly down to monitoring the undead resource teams were left, so I gathered the others up, and we headed for the newly completed gate.

The girls and their husbands saw us all off. Although the dungeon-born were still on site and it wasn't exactly the private time that they'd wanted, they'd agreed it was *much* better than nothing.

I arrived home, expecting a few hours to get myself sorted out, do some minor things that had been mounting up on the back burner, like checking in on the crafters, and then to get ready for date night…only to find an annoyed Kelly was already in our quarters, half dressed, and glaring when I strolled in, whistling merrily.

"What the hell, Matt!" she started, not so much as a "hi, honey" or a tickle of my bollocks before she lit into me. "We're going to be late!"

"Late?" I asked, dumbfounded. "Late for what?"

"Dinner!" she snapped, before grabbing a bra off the table and turning her back to me as she pulled it on.

"Dinner?" I repeated, confused to all hell.

"Yes!" she snapped again. "We need to make a good impression, remember?"

"No?" I said, genuinely confused. I shook my head and stepped in close, reaching out to put my hands on her shoulders and turn her around to face me.

"Oh no you don't," she said firmly, covering the lacy bra with her hands. "You're late—you don't get treats now!"

"Kelly, stop." I looked into her eyes.

"What?" She went from annoyed and rushing, to genuinely confused. "Matt, I—"

"Kelly," I repeated. "Stop."

We both did just that, stopping for a few long seconds before I spoke again.

"I don't know what's going on," I said. "The last conversation we had about tonight was I was to bust my balls to make sure everything was fixed, so that we could have a romantic dinner and some fun. That's it. I don't know anything about a deadline, so let's stop for a minute, and remember that as the Dungeon Lord and Lady, we make the schedule, and it's just us, so fuck it, we can be late."

"That's just it, Matt!" She groaned. "It's not just us! Didn't Mike tell you?"

"No, Mike ran off to see Aly and Amy as soon as we arrived," I said slowly.

"Great!" She rubbed at her eyes in dismay, then swore and threw her hands up in despair as she realized that she'd just ruined her makeup. "I'll kill that bloody brother of mine!" she snarled.

"What happened? What was he supposed to tell me?" I frowned, worried.

"He was supposed to remind you about the earl and his wife! We're having dinner with them in half an hour and they're bringing the soldiers' families!"

My stomach dropped, as I realized that all the hopes I'd had for tonight? They were fucked.

CHAPTER FORTY

"What the hell!" I groaned. "Why half an hour? Shit, I didn't even realize we'd set a date!"

"We talked about it before you went to London, remember? We set it as the end of the week for dinner, because we'd set the core off moving, and we needed the earl and his lot to know that the core was in transit, and we couldn't risk that they might have some ability to sense truth!"

"Yeah, I mean…" I struggled with my words. "I knew we were going to, but not that it was tonight, or a time. And as for the families? Fuck, I didn't even know that'd been sorted out!" I cursed, letting go of her shoulders and starting to strip off.

"That was Mike's job. When I got confirmation from the earl about the time and that they wanted to do it tonight, he was supposed to tell you, and then remind you! I'll kill him!" she fumed, before stalking off in the direction of the door to the shared area between our quarters.

"Kelly?" I called to her.

"What?" she snapped, her hand on the door handle already.

"Might want to put your top on before you go and shout at him." I grinned at her, amused despite myself. "I know Chris is about, and with that bra on, you'll give him a heart attack. Might not be what your brother needs to see either!"

"Fuck!" She sighed, turning and resting her forehead against the door, then bumping it gently. "It was supposed to be a surprise." She sighed, before turning back to me.

"Oh, believe me, it'd have been a hell of a surprise for Chris," I agreed, still grinning. "I don't know what he's done to deserve that, though!"

The bra she was wearing was less to conceal than to provide support and to really show her tits off at their very best. The fabric that would have normally covered the middle, for example, was entirely missing. I couldn't help but let out a low whistle as she walked toward me.

"Damn, you look good," I said softly.

"It was because I know you're a pervert." She smiled, stepping in close and kissing me. "I knew you'd enjoy knowing that I was wearing just this when we're having an important dinner, and that'd make you horny all night."

"Just that?" I pointed to her bra, getting a grin.

Beyond that bra, seemingly, she had literally nothing on under the long very silken skirt. The side of it was split to mid-thigh, and knowing that there was nothing there, should we be sat side by side and I chose to slide my hand across…

Yeah. She knew me well.

That was going to have me horny as fuck for the entire evening.

"Oh, now I *so* don't want to go to dinner," I whispered, reaching out for a kiss.

That was apparently the very worst thing I could say, as the reminder about dinner got her moving again. She cursed and hurried to fix her makeup, leaving me standing there, neglected.

I sighed, then stripped fully, jumping in the shower and eyeing my beard and hair.

It was too late for a proper trim, but I could tidy the beard a little, or better yet, tame it with some oil and a brush…

Twenty-two minutes later, we stepped out of our quarters. Kelly's long black skirt and sheer red silk top showed off her figure tremendously; her hair, swept up and cascading over one shoulder, completed the stunning look.

It helped the overall image that she'd had the ruby I'd won in the dungeon trial converted into a hair thingy, and now she had a polished and perfect ruby that practically glowed a deep red, nestled in her hair. Add in high heels, and she was the picture of professional elegance, especially with the specially designed cloak and hood that topped it all off to protect her outfit.

Only I knew that she was also wearing no panties, and had deliberately made sure that I knew that beyond any doubt right before we left our room.

I, on the other hand, wore a pair of black, smart trousers, a red fitted shirt, a black jacket that was already too warm for the damn night inside the dungeon, and a red cloak attached to the shoulders.

I felt entirely overdressed and ridiculous, but the look on Kelly's face as she saw me in all of it made it clear that it really did it for her.

She, however, wasn't happy that I had my bag of holding on my hip as it ruined the line of the jacket. But, as I pointed out, this way I was heavily armed still, and I wasn't going anywhere without my sword, hammer, and rifle, so either she accepted the bag, or I was putting my armor on.

That ended the argument before it began.

We paused as we were leaving the private quarters for our little group. Kelly waved to Aly, who hurried over, complimented us both, kissed Kelly's cheek and gave me a glare as she spotted the bag on my hip.

Before she could tell me anything about it ruining the outfit Kelly had planned, though, Kelly filled her in on Mike's forgetfulness.

"I'll deal with him," was all that was said, but I winced, and we hurried on.

"How do we even know the time—" I started, and Kelly gave me the look that every man has received since the beginning of time when they've questioned their boss.

I shut up, deciding it wasn't worth it.

"Would m'lady like a carry?" I grinned down at her as we stepped out into the cool night air.

She took one look at the drifting snow and smiled. I reached down to pick her up, being very careful with the skirt, as a slight mishap could result in her flashing the world as we flew.

Thirty seconds later, we were at the portal, and ten after that, we were stepping out into the southern dungeon, surrounded by orc guards in full gear as soon as we emerged. They knelt in reverence, and I nodded my respect to them, before instantly forgetting them in the bustle of hundreds, possibly thousands of people who were being drawn up into lines following Ashley and Rhodes's directions.

"Holy shit," I muttered, staring out across the sea of faces, seeing how drawn they were, the clear signs of deprivation, of hunger. I could hear hundreds of voices rising in a wild hubbub of crying children, questions, calls to stay together and the general low-level chatter that rose and rose as people tried to be heard over the noise of their neighbors.

They were being sorted into lines, and I couldn't help but shake my head at the sight. We'd been damn lucky to get through when we had, as they were being organized to be moved north now, about to be led through the gate in a great wave, presumably to the northern dungeon or to Newcastle, and from there on to the park.

"We took care of this while you were sorting the dungeon out," Kelly said, unable to keep the smile from her face. "There's accommodation already sorted for them, and yes, I know there's going to be some spies mixed in among them, but we decided it was worth the risk. Let's face it—they'll be able to spread the word about just how much better life is as one of us, and that's going to be a real kick in the teeth once word spreads."

"I like it," I said softly, enjoying both the knowledge of what these people were going to find at the other end of the portal—hot food, hot water, and a civilized life again—and that they had no real clue who I was yet.

That made a nice change, though the sullen resentment in a few faces wasn't nice. I glanced down at Kelly, who I still held, and thought about what the pair of us were wearing as well, and I couldn't blame them.

Most of them were in filthy, tattered clothes—some army issue, most all-weather and just about dirty enough to stand up without them wearing them.

I banished the instinctual annoyance to the resentment and held Kelly tighter as spoke. "Why have dinner here?" I asked Kelly.

She smiled, cuddling in as we lifted into the air, flying up and around to the top of the building, and the section that she'd literally designed for this dinner alone.

I landed on a small platform that she'd clearly intended for fliers and me, and set her down. I took her hand and led her across the last meter of the slick walkway, the snow already several inches thick.

"First, we needed the portal to get these people to their new homes. But mainly, I wanted to be able to show off the battlefield as a reminder," she admitted with a sigh. "Sod's Law, the snow makes that impossible, but the view is still impressive."

That was an understatement, I had to admit, as we stepped inside, moving from the snow-covered walkway beyond, to the red-carpeted interior.

This topmost floor of the citadel had been entirely redone since I'd last been here, as this section of the roof had been a small square that was literally used for archers and mages to bombard the enemy.

Not long since, there'd been a dozen people in it, most of them wounded, and a bunch of broken corpse lords and banshees.

Now, it was a square room. The stairs from the level below climbed up into it in one corner, and a spiral staircase led from here to the area we were supposed to have dinner.

There were two long couches and two chairs by the far wall, and a low coffee table between them. A roaring fireplace in the wall filled the place with cheery light.

That light was echoed by the candles, and the silver mirrors and various decorations around the room.

The citadel below was all intended as a fortress more than anything, but this section, Kelly had clearly gone all out on making an impression.

The couple sitting by the fire, and who had looked up as we walked in, stood. Their simple unshakable confidence and poise made it look like this was their place by right, instead of ours.

“Ah, Lady Kelly, Lord Matt.” The earl greeted us, smiling as we strode across the carpet. “So good to see you both again. May I introduce my lady wife, Sara-Ann, Countess of Stockport.”

The countess was every bit as polished as her husband: tall, elegant, and wearing what had probably been an insanely expensive dress before the fall. Her silver-streaked dark hair was swept up in an elaborate style that somehow managed to look effortless.

“A pleasure,” Kelly said warmly, stepping forward to take the countess’s offered hand. “Thank you both for coming all this way, and most of all for bringing our people’s families with you.”

“Yes, thank you. I wasn’t aware that the families were coming, and it was a wonderful surprise,” I agreed, forcing a smile. “As to the dinner and the rest of the evening, you’ll forgive me if I offend, I’m not used to formal events,” I admitted, figuring it was better to get it out in the open right at the beginning.

“Oh, no concern there, dear boy. Believe me, one of the great pleasures in my life has been watching you and Johnstone of late. I think any possible little issues can be forgotten for that entertainment alone,” the earl said, a twinkle in his eye.

“And the pleasure is ours.” Sara-Ann spoke up, smiling graciously. “Though, I must say, the journey was quite an adventure. Your escorts were most…interesting. Thank you for sending them along to protect the people.”

I caught the slight emphasis on “interesting” and had to hide a smile. No doubt Kelly had sent some impressive guards along to deliberately make an impression.

“Yes, the giant dragon that took care of a single monster we saw…well, it certainly made it clear why you felt that they were safer with you than in London,” the earl agreed.

“Jack’s impressive, I know.” I smiled. “Though, honestly? You’d be amazed by the abilities of some of our people. Beta, as an example.”

“Yes, I think that the day when she surpasses Jack isn’t far off at this rate,” Kelly agreed, smiling at the look the earl gave her. “Enough shop talk, though. We’re here to have dinner. Shall we head up?” Kelly suggested, gesturing to the spiral staircase. “The view is wonderful, even with the snow.”

“Lead the way, my dear.” The earl offered his arm to his wife.

As we climbed the stairs, I couldn’t help but notice how both of our guests took in every detail of their surroundings. The earl’s military training showed in the way his eyes tracked sight lines and defensive positions, while his wife seemed equally interested in the various magical details worked into the structure.

Like the fact that fire projected warmth and light, but had no flue and emitted no smoke.

The dining room above was Kelly’s masterpiece, though: a circular space with floor-to-ceiling windows in a dome, offering a panoramic view of the little that could be seen of the snow-covered battlefield.

Mainly it simply showed the snow falling past and the dark night sky, thick clouds overhead reflecting the limited light that shone from below.

"Are we quite safe here?" the earl asked softly, glancing over at me. "We're aware of night-time predators that have attacked sites such as this from the air."

"Believe me, if anything tries, it's in for a surprise." I snorted.

"The dome is very clear, but it's also three inches thick and armored." Kelly smiled. "Anything that tried to smash through it will get a nasty surprise."

"And Jack's out there," I finished.

"The dragon?" The earl glanced from side to side, as if hoping to catch a glimpse.

"Yeah," I smiled. "Anything that chooses to attack is going to regret it."

"Indeed," was all that the earl said. But the look that he and his wife exchanged spoke volumes.

A single round table was set for four, with elegant place settings that somehow managed to look both impressive and intentionally perfect, as if to remind everyone that we weren't limited to working with what we could salvage.

"Extraordinary," Sara-Ann breathed, moving to one of the windows. "And this was all created by the dungeon?"

"Including the food and wine." Kelly handed me her cloak and took her seat as I held out her chair. "It's possible to have individual meals still, and we do have some chefs who work in the dungeon, but they work primarily on refining their craft. Each meal they create is absorbed into the dungeon, and then reproduced perfectly, which was at first a bit of a relief..."

"Certainly was in the early days when we were getting started," I agreed, taking over at Kelly's glance. "But once we started to have a real selection, it helped to reassure people. The chefs were also a little put out, wondering what they could add once their best dishes could be reproduced effortlessly by magic at any time."

"Yes, I'm imagining that was an issue," the earl agreed.

"It was, right up until they discovered that they could access unlimited ingredients and meals. There's a dedicated hub of chefs in the park now, and they basically experiment all day, every day, creating the weirdest things."

"Very thoughtful," the earl noted, seating his wife before taking his own place. "Though, I must admit, I'm quite curious about what the dungeon can produce. The demonstration earlier was...enlightening."

"Glad you enjoyed it," I said, smiling faintly.

"Morris told me all about it." The countess smiled slightly. "He said that you battled monsters?"

She looked me over, as if unsure, given the finery, but then the juxtaposition of my size became clear as I hung both Kelly's cloak and my own jacket on hooks that sparkled into existence on the wall.

With my coat off, I was left in a fitted shirt, and as I sat, I couldn't help but note the way that the countess and the earl looked at me.

She'd never met me, but he'd seen me before in armor. Now, seeing me out of it, my height of seven feet and my build of a professional model crossed with a weightlifter was hard to ignore.

"What would you like?" Kelly reached out her right hand and smiled as a gleaming collection of firefly lights spun into existence, leaving behind a cocktail glass in her hand. The passion-fruit slice and froth made it easy to identify a Porn Star martini with just a glance.

"I'll have one of those please." The countess smiled. "It looks delightful."

"And for you?" I asked the earl, who smiled, and clearly remembering our first meeting, spoke up.

"The Brora, the 1977 vintage if you please."

His wife looked at him sharply, apparently recognizing the drink, and then blinked as I summoned a fresh bottle of it before him.

"Ah, I don't suppose you have a wine list?" the countess murmured, then smiled acceptingly as her cocktail appeared. "Oh, this will be fine…" Then she blinked again as Kelly made a little gesture, fully for the impression it gave, and the cocktail vanished.

"What would you like?" Kelly asked archly.

The next few minutes passed in a blur, mainly around "Oh have you a bottle of the…" and "I don't suppose you might have a…" until the table was full of unopened bottles.

"I'm not complaining," I noted. "But those bottles are going to be a bugger to take home with you."

"To take home?" the countess asked, then laughed. "Dear boy, you have no idea of the value of these bottles, do you?"

"Nope," I agreed.

"They represent well over half a million in pounds sterling, and you just created them all with a wave of your hand." She sighed. "What I wouldn't give to open our wine cellar to you."

"Do it." I shrugged. "Bring whatever you want, and as you're adding the bottle to our dungeon, I'll send you away with five copies for every bottle you bring us."

"That's incredibly generous, and I thank you for the offer." She said slowly, "Although, as you say, we're providing you with access to a very finite resource."

"Before you try to bargain and push the price up," I smiled, "understand that the wine is utterly meaningless to me. The resource that's being expended, on the other hand, the mana? That's valuable. Your wine being added to the dungeon is simply there as a nice bonus in case some of our citizens fancy summoning a bottle for dinner."

"For dinner…" she whispered, closing her eyes. "Your people can summon any of them, at any time, simply on a whim?"

"More or less," I agreed. "We have rules about not drinking when on duty, that kind of thing, but yeah. The bottle you have there?" I indicated the whisky. "That cost us about twenty minutes of someone's time. Let's say the average wage before the fall was what, twelve pounds an hour? Call that four pounds then."

"Unbelievable." She glanced at her husband. "The potential for an import-export business is beyond belief."

"True, if not for the fact that a little liquid and glass, in comparison to armor, is worthless," I pointed out. "We're in a war, more or less, and that's what matters, not the wine or the whisky."

"You mentioned the war." The earl settled his glass and looked at me over the top of steepled fingers. "Perhaps you could explain what you know, and how?"

"Sure," I agreed. "And you can explain what you know, because we know that shitbag Trust was involved."

"Matt!" Kelly snapped. "Language!"

"Am I wrong?" I asked the earl, and he sighed, before sitting back.

"Not entirely. There's little that anyone else has managed to glean, but from what our spies tell us, there was some form of contact attempted, from an outside source, and the government of the day made decisions that were perhaps not in the best interests of the rest of the country." He sighed as he saw the look on my face.

"Elspeth and her idiot advisors were convinced that as the alien could barely speak English, it must be stupid, and they took everything it offered, then shot it when it threatened them with consequences, should the technology not be shared."

"Because if you can't speak perfect English, then you're an idiot." I groaned. "Fuck me, aliens come with advanced tech and they still think that? How complicated is it to understand that if someone else can speak their language *and* yours, and possibly several others, they're not stupid if they can't do it perfectly.

"I grew up with this. My Italian is rough as hell, and I can barely order a drink at the bar, but Rossi, a guy I used to work with, spoke seven languages, and was a system admin for the IT company I used to work for. People still treated him like he was an idiot, though, because his English was spoken with an accent."

"Regrettably, regardless of the realities of life, many are unable to reconcile those details." The earl smiled.

"I think we could begin with dinner. Shall we?" Kelly suggested brightly, and I winced.

"Yeah, sorry, I kinda derailed the dinner already, didn't I?"

"Not at all," the countess assured me. "We're here to see if we can find a way to work together—our faction, not just us personally, you understand—and frankly, getting an accurate read on you like this is easier."

"An accurate read?" I raised an eyebrow as the first course materialized before us—a delicate seafood starter that would have been impossible to source normally, since the fall.

"Oh yes," Sara-Ann said, seemingly unfazed by the magical appearance of the food. "Morris told me you were refreshingly direct. I find I quite agree."

"What my dear wife means," the earl added, sampling the wine, "is that we're all dancing around the larger issues here. The Cinthians, the coming war, and of course, the rather delicate matter of transporting your core through London's sphere of influence."

Kelly's hand found mine under the table as I tensed slightly. "Is that going to be a problem?" she asked carefully.

"One doesn't survive in politics without developing good sources," Sara-Ann replied. "Though I must say, the news about the Cinthians was…illuminating. We had suspected something of the sort, but confirmation is always valuable."

"And your thoughts on Trust's involvement?" I asked bluntly, earning another squeeze from Kelly's hand.

The earl exchanged a glance with his wife before responding. "Let's just say that certain factions in London are becoming…increasingly problematic. Their short-sightedness may have doomed us all."

"May have?" I couldn't help but laugh. "They literally caused the apocalypse because they couldn't conceive that someone who didn't speak perfect English might be smarter than them."

"Matt," Kelly warned softly, but the countess was already nodding.

"Precisely why we're here," she said. "Some of us recognize that the old ways of thinking need to change. Rapidly. Which brings us to your core transport…"

"We'd be happy to provide whatever intelligence we can about potential threats along the route," the earl added smoothly. "Though, of course, we can't speak for all factions within London."

"Of course not," Kelly agreed diplomatically. "Though we would appreciate any…advance warning of potential complications."

I watched their faces carefully as we moved onto the main course—a perfectly cooked venison Wellington that would have made any chef proud.

They were good, I had to give them that. Nothing in their expressions gave away whether they'd pass the information about the core transport to the other factions or not.

"Tell me," Sara-Ann said after a moment. "These dungeons of yours…they're Cinthian technology, aren't they?"

The question hung in the air like smoke. Kelly's hand rested on mine again, but I decided to be direct.

"Yes," I said. "They're meant to help us survive what's coming. Which makes Trust's actions even more monumentally stupid."

"What *is* coming?" the earl asked quietly. "We've received a lot of confusing hints and oblique references, as well as some details that Trust and her allies have dropped, but little else. General Blackstone gave us a brief rundown, but a more comprehensive answer, direct from the horse's mouth as it were, would be appreciated."

I glanced at Kelly, who nodded, and I sat forward, snagging another drink as I started to explain the role of the Cinthians, the Orakai, and the other races, as well as what we'd been able to discover from the other races.

It took until the desserts were cleared away to finish. The conversation had rolled in all directions as we spoke, until at last, the earl brought it back to the core.

"So, when do you need us to gather intelligence for the core to pass?" he asked, and I looked at Kelly. "Please understand as well that to do so, we'll need to reach out to some allies, and while we'll be as careful as possible…"

"You can't guarantee anything," I finished for him. "It's fine. Anything that tries to jack our convoy won't enjoy the experience."

"It should pass at its closest point to London around sundown the day after tomorrow," Kelly said after a brief pause to check. "It's going to come down the A1M motorway to Stevenage and then break east, before crossing the Thames at Tilbury."

"That's an unusual route," the earl said diplomatically. "Are you aware of the bridges over the Thames?"

"The escort doesn't need them," she said. "The core is highly dangerous if damaged, and we're using an automated group of creations to move it, essentially a clockwork force, though there are only four of them."

"Four?" The countess gasped. "For something that valuable?"

"The four are there to keep away anything that tries to take the core. Believe me, you'd need a battalion to destroy them. And as nobody will know where it is, I think it's safe enough. Add in that for anyone to be around in a large enough number to be a threat to it, they'd be clear from a good distance and our dragon Jack and I will be checking in on it regularly, I think it's secure."

The pair exchanged a brief glance, then changed the subject, asking about the things that could be created with the dungeon, before the earl asked whether it was possible to show them the system itself.

"Unfortunately not," I said. "I'd have to add you into the system, and then you'd have a level of authority over it. Although it's possible to remove you again straight after, the pain is considerable."

"There's often mental scarring as well," Kelly lied, easily picking up the excuse. "We'd not be willing to admit you to the dungeon's systems without a very good reason, or a lot more of a relationship, as you'll understand."

"Of course," the countess gushed. "Perish the thought!"

"You mentioned negotiating for a core of our own, however?" the earl pointed out, and I nodded.

"We'd be open to it, with strict rules, and guidance from us as part of the cost."

"Oh?"

"Trust and Johnstone are to be limited to the lowest access." I grinned.

"Oh, that's a terrible shame, but I understand that being a hard line—one we'll of course do our best to argue over, but ultimately have to agree on." The earl grinned evilly at that. "Seriously, though, what would the cost be?"

"High technology items, soldiers, samples, and information," Kelly said, taking over. "You know that Trust and her allies took something from the Cinthians. We'd need access to that technology, and then we'd need any information on them you had. Museum access to study ancient records and glyphs for possible magical uses, and people, as well as a full set of bones, one from every animal you have in the natural history and all other museums. For every item we give you, there's a cost we've paid, often in blood. For you to be able to reproduce them, and to move through the core stages, you'd need advice, and that information was hard-won, so what we'd need is…"

The next half an hour was a busy one, as Kelly and I discussed logistic issues, access to technology, and more. They countered with the point that should they give us everything that they had that we wanted, they were depriving themselves of that selfsame value.

Time passed and, in the end, we'd not managed to settle on a definite price. Kelly and I made it clear that it was a "when we have the core safe here then we'll discuss it" situation.

"There's one more thing," I said slowly, hating that I needed to say it, but it was important. The thought had occurred to me, so now, if I didn't, the oath was going to punish me for that.

"Oh?" the earl asked, curiously.

"The king and the royal family," I said. "I need access to them as part of a quest."

"Interesting. Might I ask why?" he asked carefully, setting his glass down and watching me.

"I have a quest to ensure their safety," I admitted.

"They're quite safe." He chewed his lip in thought, glancing over at his wife in question.

"Are they?" I asked.

"More or less." Sara-Ann sighed. "Look, the king and his family are a delicate subject. You're aware of their constitutionally limited powers?"

"They're figureheads, and while they have power, it's pretty much a 'use it and lose it' situation. If they did something, they could do it once, and people would listen because of who they are. And then the prime minister and the republican parties would essentially strip them of any vestiges of power in punishment."

"Quite so." The earl toyed with his glass, before sighing. "The king and his family are essentially prisoners in a gilded cage, though that's been true for generations. Currently that's slightly more accurate, and disturbingly, it's also left them in a far weaker position. When Queen Elizabeth and then her son, Prince Charles, were lost in the first days of the fall, the decision was made that his son, Prince William and his family, were to be provided with round-the-clock protection."

"I thought they had that already?" I asked softly.

"They did. And against a normal creature, that would have been sufficient. Against the thing that attacked the palace, it wasn't," the earl said, though he was clearly uncomfortable with what he was saying. "There are investigations ongoing at the minute, questions being asked about the nature of the attack, but I can't say more…not yet, I'm afraid."

"William is the king, though?" I asked for confirmation, and he nodded.

"He and his family are safe. They're under heavy guard. More than that, I can't say. I'm sorry."

"If you want the core, my access to them for a private meeting will be part of the price," I warned him.

He stared at me for long seconds before answering. "I may, and I mean, *may*, be able to arrange an open meeting, but I guarantee you that a private meeting between you and the king, considering all that's happened, is off the table. I'm sorry."

"Even for a core?" I asked.

"Even for the core," he confirmed.

Kelly and I exchanged a long look. She knew exactly why I needed that meeting; then she forced a smile as she turned back to them.

"In the short term, an open meeting will be a solid start," she offered. "However, that's still down the road from now, so, if you'd like a tour?" Kelly suggested brightly, and the pair quickly took her up on the change of subject.

I stood, moving around and drawing back her chair, as I saw the earl do for his lady, and Kelly kissed me gently on the cheek.

"Do you both have cloaks?" she asked, and with a smile, summoned a pair for them when they admitted that they didn't.

It turned out that the only vehicles that the London lot had working were reworked trucks from the forties and motorcycles. The bikes weren't a good idea in the snow at all, especially without lights, and so they'd driven very bloody slowly along to get here.

We offered them a boxer to take them back, and they took us up on that quickly, as the level of comfort and protection was far higher.

The tour wasn't much—or at least, it wasn't to us.

Kelly did most of the work, explaining things as we went, and even taking them into a mocked-up room that she explained was the core, complete with a control panel that they could try to use.

It didn't respond to them, and she explained it away as them not being part of the dungeon, rather than as was the truth—that it was all a show.

The medical facilities were a hell of a shock to them, as was it when Jo, who'd been waiting at Kelly's request, took them both into a back room, and gave them an examination at Kelly's request.

The cancer that she removed from the earl's lower left lung was almost effortless. But the look on his wife's face when he agreed that it both existed and permitted it to be removed, promised a hard conversation between them when they were in private, as he'd apparently neglected to mention such a diagnosis to her, it being in the final days pre-fall.

Forty minutes later, we were back in our seats around the table upstairs, enjoying a last drink. I did my best to remain amiable and utterly engrossed in the joke that the earl was telling, when Kelly, apparently as bored as I was, took my hand from resting on her thigh under the table, to inside the skirt.

As I was reminded, there was no material there, between her and my questing fingers. She shifted, smiling at me before asking the earl a question about their wine cellar.

A subject we'd discovered was his favorite.

That was when she subtly moved her hand across and started drawing little lines atop my member with her fingernails under the table.

The pair of us lasted twenty minutes, before I just couldn't take any more and I suggested that we "get them home before it's too late."

What "too late" was taken to mean in this context, I wasn't clear on with them, but for us, it was understood to be before I lost all control and bent Kelly over the table in front of them.

Ten minutes later, the pair were inside the boxer, with an escort of a dozen kobolds and a dozen Scepiniir in full all-weather gear and atop the magewhisker cats and phantomsteeds.

The still falling snow outside had been churned into mush by the thousands of feet that had passed while we were eating. I stared out at the silent vista before us, seeing the occasional skeleton on the walls, the living having been pulled back out of the weather now.

I felt bad about the fact we'd been sitting having dinner and talking absolute bollocks while most of the rest of the dungeon had been mobilized to get everyone settled. But also?

This had come about through a conversation I'd had. In an effort to make nice with us, in another conversation, the earl had handed over the lists of people they had, and then through more conversations, Kelly had arranged the movement of all these people.

Conversations mattered, and they were more important than I liked. Arguably, Kelly and I might be able to accomplish more over a dinner than we could with me fighting from dawn 'til dusk, and that felt all kinds of wrong.

Five minutes after that…well.

Kelly had made two great discoveries with the core recently, and one of them was a version of privacy glass. That was what the dome above the citadel was covered in, providing an extra level of protection.

The other was a privacy setting that allowed a member of the dungeon to designate an area as a private one. That could be anywhere, depending on the settings, and she'd added a basic level that all bathrooms were considered private, and bedrooms as well. Beyond that, it was up to the individual.

Yeah, certain levels of access, such as myself, Kelly, and Aly and our close advisors could override that; it was basically there in case there was an issue.

A "just in case" scenario.

Kelly led me up into the dome again, locked the door to the area below us, and designated the entire room as a private zone, then pulled out my chair and told me to sit.

She removed her top, left that most interesting of bras on, as well as her skirt, then lay on her back where our meal had been until recently, and rested both her feet on my shoulders, before she produced a toy, and allowed her skirt to fall aside.

"Oh, you're cruel," I said softly, as she pressed me back in my seat, grinning evilly.

"Not really. You got me all worked up, so I'm going to just relax a little before I let you play as well. Hands flat on the table, please," she ordered, before getting started.

What came next was both incredibly frustrating, then wonderful, as we made the most of the room, the furniture, the glass, and everything else we could.

As we lay there on the floor, sticky, sated, and panting well over an hour later, I stared up at the sex swing, wondering whether it was me who had summoned it or not, it'd been that much of a blur.

"That…was just what I needed," Kelly admitted, cuddled into me, and I grinned, unable to help myself.

"Me too," I said. "Wonder if they had any clue what we were doing?"

"I think the earl guessed you were doing something at one point." She snorted.

"When you gasped?" I suggested.

"Yeah!" She punched my chest. "A little warning next time, not just straight in!"

"You were ready," I pointed out.

"Physically, sure. Mentally, with him telling us about some wine that'd been handed down through the centuries? I wasn't at *all* ready for that!"

"You started it."

"I was teasing you."

"And this is what teasing me gets you!" I said.

"Promises, promises." She sighed. "You know that the others are going to want to book turns in here next, don't you?"

"Only if they know."

"We finished the dinner meeting hours ago and enacted the privacy shield. Believe me, they know." She snorted. "Aly will have come wanting a report, seen the shield and told Mike, just to make him squirm, knowing what his little sister is doing."

"Me?" I said, and she laughed.

"Yeah, him having any clue what we were just doing would make him either shoot you, or be sick. It's fine for him to be banging Aly off the walls when we were all on vacation together, but when I went out and had some fun one night, I got a lecture from him after he'd scared the guy off the next morning."

"The three of you went away?" I frowned.

"No, well not just us, it was a big family event, *Aly's* family, before the fall and before…well—" She broke off at that point. "Let's just say that although our family is dead, Aly's is dead to her, and she'd rather ours was breathing than hers."

"That bad?"

"Worse." She pushed up, shifting around to peer down at me, where I lay on my back on the carpet. "Let's drop it, okay?"

"Sure."

"So, you think they'll make a play for the core?" she asked, changing the subject.

"Possibly." I sighed. "Honestly, they dropped that hint that they couldn't keep the route quiet pretty quickly, so my guess is that they'll try to distance themselves from it, but they'll pass the details on."

"Well, that'll end badly for them." Kelly grinned, and I had to agree.

The mental image of them fighting with themselves over the actions they'd had to take, when all the while the core was a fake, played out in my mind.

We headed home from there an hour or so later, getting to bed, and then starting again the next day a little later than usual.

The dungeons were all working well, and the expansion project was well underway, when Emma contacted us, dragging both Kelly and me into the new dungeon beneath the back streets of London, to watch as a huge group marched along under an iron-grey sky.

"What are we looking for?" I asked her, only to nod as I saw the earl and countess. To my surprise, as the orders were barked and the armed group moved out, splitting up and scouring the next few streets, checking building by building in a professional manner, it wasn't the earl giving the orders.

It wasn't until one of the soldiers turned up to give a report to her, though, that we found out why.

She might have been "just" the countess to the earl's rank—having married into the aristocracy from one of the discussions that we'd had over dinner—but that didn't mean that she'd been a pretty little thing the dashing earl had swept off her feet.

No, his rank, when he was identified by it, was major. Hers?

Field marshal.

She had to be the highest-ranking military officer left in the country, and she'd been sitting across from us the entire meal, playing the dutiful and easily impressed wife, while he distracted us with his own questions and wine cellar chatter.

We'd been duped the entire time. She was the power there, and in the streets.

CHAPTER FORTY-ONE

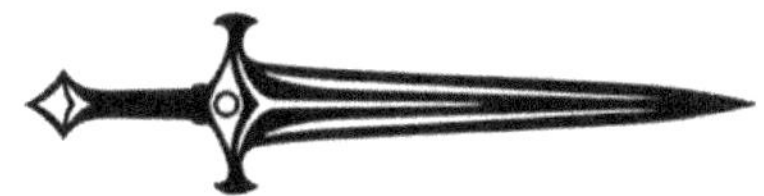

The next few hours, then the next day all passed smoothly, as the soldiers under the command of the field marshal stripped the area, ensuring first that there were no threats left alive, and then that the entire remaining civilian population was moved on.

The area was declared a "protectorate"—whatever the hell that was—and more and more, it was converted into an armed camp, with heavy defenses moved in and established.

Stockpiles were set up of the highest tech that could be found. Everything from literally crates filled with top mobile phones to boxes full of laptops and servers were assembled and kept under guard in a nearby warehouse.

The site they decided to set the dungeon core up in was picked out. The army engineers went to work, along with a good hundred press-ganged civilians, stripping nearby buildings and rebuilding others with much thicker walls.

The last straw for me was when they started to set up an area with their best workers in readiness to create as lifelike and well-hidden a copy of the core as possible.

When the countess and now field marshal described how it'd be shown to anyone who asked as the real core, while only a precious few would be permitted access to the "real" core?

That just made it as clear as possible for me. Not only was she fully intending to set up the area with a copied core to try to distract us from what she thought was going to be the real one, she was also trying to hide it from her other allies.

We pulled in Aly, Mike, Ashley and Dante, Jo, John, Clarissa and Markus to join Kelly and me in a high-level "*WTF?*" meeting at that point.

"Okay, people, we're getting hit, all right," I said. "We need to get ready for the next stage then. Kelly, what are you thinking for the first response?"

"I think it's best if you don't talk to them if they hit the convoy," Kelly said after a brief pause. "Matt, I love you, but subtle and indirect you definitely aren't. The best thing we can do is have you busy with another event, so…" She started to search through details in the dungeon sense.

I frowned. "I can be subtle."

"Matt, with the level of importance this core supposedly has for us, the only possible response if they take it is war," Mike said. "For you or me to be involved at this stage, I think war is the only real outcome they can expect. So unless that's what we're aiming for, then we need to be conspicuously busy elsewhere, and preferably with something that gives Kelly, who the earl already knows, a chance to respond instead."

"I've got something that *might* work…" Ashley said slowly. "There's been a request that you visit the saurian dungeon—personally—as apparently they want to open trade negotiations, but will only discuss things face-to-face, 'due to concerns over infiltration.'"

"Saurian?" I asked. "Those big lizard fuckers?"

"The ones that tried to pick a fight with you on sight the first time you met them on the Nexus platform, and then refused to interact at all with me at the meet and greet at the arena," she clarified.

"Now they want to talk?" I scoffed. "Seriously, I doubt they're gonna be friendly somehow."

"Exactly." Ashley snorted. "The request came in a few hours ago. You know I've been dealing with the stuff from the arena and gates, right?" She looked at me in question, and I hesitated, then shook my head.

"Honestly, no," I admitted. "I've been preoccupied with other stuff and just blanked on it. What's been happening?"

"Right, this is going to derail things a little, but you kinda need to know. Do I cover this now?" Ashley asked Kelly, looking over at her for approval.

I sighed, settling back and waiting as "the boss" nodded.

"So…I handled most of the outreach program for the dungeon, contacting the others and inviting them here, spending practically days at a time on the Nexus platform, which wasn't cheap, but was why the majority of the dungeons showed up."

"Okay, honestly I had no clue. I'm sorry," I admitted.

"I know, you've got a lot on your plate, so that's fine. But it means that for a lot of the dungeons' representatives, they met me as part of the first contact protocol on reaching the Nexus platform—you know, once they managed to unlock gate travel."

"That's a point. I'd not even considered that at first they'd have had the gate and that was it…no destinations." I grunted.

"Exactly." Ashley smiled. "So what I did—with Kelly's approval—was set up there and basically play the part of a greeter, giving out general advice and selling the idea of the arena. I made it seem like this is all part of the established package, and made it seem like they were late and we were doing them a favor by allowing them entry.

"That meant that they all knew me on arrival, and each group expected that they were the odd ones out, so they followed along with directions a lot easier. It also meant that they automatically associated us with the Nexus platform and the Nexus platform with the arena, so it was all nice and easy—'if the platform is neutral ground and safe, so must be the arena.'

"With that in mind, I also set up a little request system, one that allows anyone who arrives through the arena gates to ask to set up a meeting with anyone else, including leaving a letter for that person or dungeon, etc. with the details of where and when in it."

"Right?" I nodded. "Damn, that was a good idea, and one that's bloody useful."

"Exactly. As part of us having their spatial coordinates and their gate key, we can pass the message along that there's a letter or whatever at the arena waiting. The person dropping off the message needs to pay a small—entirely reasonable—fee to cover us using the gate to pass the message along, or they can leave it and when the next representative from the dungeon they wanted to contact comes along, the message will be handed over."

She smiled proudly. "I basically built on the image of the platform as trustworthy and safe, as well as neutral, and then decorated the arrivals area in the same style, hiding a lot of the armoring and mantrap facilities so that it looks more like a standard lobby."

"Yeah, I was betting you had a hand in that," I admitted. "And that's how we were contacted?"

"I'm getting to that." She smiled. "So, first, the fee for the letter is a single mana crystal. It's the size of a small marble, so not expensive at all, but it's a considerable profit for the mana usage of the gate to connect and pass the letter through. Basically, about a fifty percent profit, okay?"

"Right, but I mean, as the middlemen, you could have charged more than that," Mike pointed out.

"We could, but I wanted it to be a cost that nobody considers." She nodded to him. "Mainly because as soon as the letter is handed over, I have our people copy it and pass the original on, with the copy being passed to me."

"Oh, you sneaky fucker." I nodded. "Because of the speed of the dungeon in copying things, people don't have time to realize that you've done it, do they?"

"Nope. I tell them that the letter is sent out at evening, as soon as the gate closes for regular traffic, but I offer a priority option if they have to have it done right now, at triple the cost. That puts them off it generally, but some do pay it. The postage service is making a *very* nice profit, and we get to read everything that's being sent from one side to the other." She paused, then pulled out a package and set it on the table.

"We also received this. It arrived an hour ago from London. Apparently it holds a single shard of bone or tooth from a dozen different animals, and it was marked as a down payment and gesture of goodwill, following your meeting with the earl?"

I stared at her, then shook my head. "I don't get him," I said. "Genuinely, I don't. One minute, he's doing all he can to build a relationship between them and us; the next, he looks like he's pulling a fast one!"

"What is it?" Ashley asked me.

"It's for Chris. Best to get it to him as soon as possible, please. They're tokens to help him with his class, and so that he can shift into various species." Kelly then shook her head.

"What were you saying about the saurians?" I prompted.

"Okay, well, they sent a representative, and it set every alarm bell my watcher had ringing. You remember Xanthia?" she asked.

I nodded. "The Etheric Chronicler."

"Exactly. Well, I've got her sitting there with one of her friends. They act as the greeters, all pretty and in a nice new uniform that lets them stand out. They take the requests, and Xanthia makes notes about the deliverer of the message. Most of the time it's just their class. Sometimes it's more than that…concerns, hints of their future, and that kind of thing. The intention is that if they try to deliver a bomb or something, we'll maybe get a few extra seconds of warning, that's all."

"Sounds clever," I agreed.

"Can they tell what's in the missives?" John asked, and she shook her head.

"Not really. The people who are sent to deliver are generally not the people you'd tell your secrets to, so there's that angle. It's more if someone has death in their very immediate future—that's what I'm thinking of."

"Shame…might have been a good way to catch smugglers as well," he suggested. "In the dungeon generally, I mean, not in the arena, just considering the future."

"Well, her gift is unique so far, and I need her, so hands off," Ashley said firmly, and I couldn't help but smile. The courtesan turned diplomat and spymaster was definitely growing into her position.

"Just thinking aloud." John apologized. "Maybe I could borrow her for a job or two in the future, though?"

"We'll see," she temporized. "Anyway, the point is, that this is the system that we've set up, and the messages that have been passing to and from the saurians to several of the dungeons that I'm least inclined to trust—the undead and a group calling itself the Brotherhood of the Fall that I'm fairly sure is that slave trading front—were fairly quick for a day or two, then they dropped off entirely, suggesting they're now in direct contact.

"That was the day before yesterday. And today, a few hours ago, I got a request direct from the saurians that you visit them, personally, and that you take your strongest warriors along."

"Because that sounds so reasonable." I snorted. "Any reason they want our strongest people out of the arena?"

"Yeah, that's the impression I'm getting as well," she said. "I think this is another attempt to seize control. The difference is that this time around they've set up allies first, and haven't publicly declared against you first. I don't think that you're the target so much as the arena."

"Explain that, please."

"It's obvious," Mike replied, sitting forward. "The arena is the focal point for the various dungeons at the minute. The Nexus platform and the arena are the only two destinations that most of them will have. The Nexus platform can only be claimed if the other five primary accessors relinquish their claim, right?"

"Yeah." I nodded. "And I'd not want to try to take it by force."

"With a floor that can simply open out and suck you out into space if you piss it off, no, neither would I," he agreed. "That means that if you want access to everyone, and their dungeons, they need to either set up a competing platform of some kind, and then convince everyone that theirs is better, as well as that the impression of the arena being neutral ground is wrong. That instantly goes against them, because them setting up somewhere is more likely to drive everyone into doing the same."

"Or they need to capture this one." Kelly nodded. "Mike, how secure are we?"

"Very." The ex-special forces soldier grinned. "Unless someone knows something I don't about an impending attack, I don't see a way that we can be taken. I mean, the arrivals area alone is a fuckin' meat grinder. They'd have to bring heavy explosives through to blow their way out of there, and that's more likely to damage the gate and then cut them off in a small exploding box, than work."

"So what's the angle?" I asked.

"Probably that they capture you." Kelly nodded at me. "They ask you to visit; you go through with your strongest warriors and they either capture you and force you to open the gate and then let them through. Or they kill you on arrival and hope for the best. A distant third option is that they'd somehow opened a secondary portal that they're going to use to trap you, somewhere out of the fight."

"How would they kill you, though? And what's the point? I mean, I can see why they'd want the strongest out of the area so that their assault has its best chance, but if they want to just capture you, they'd be better off asking you to come alone, or to bring only your weakest guards, right?"

"Depends," I muttered, scratching at my chin as I thought. "What if the guy on the other side—or girl, sorry—isn't a fighter?"

"What difference does that make?" Ashley asked.

"I'm wondering if they're thinking that I'm a guard playing at being the Dungeon Lord as a sacrificial target and the real Dungeon Lord is Kelly?" I glanced at her. "I mean, you run most things—they could have picked up on that."

"Possibly, but I doubt it, and the notifications name you, not me. Plus, even if that was the case, the best that'd get them would be you and me through the gate."

"Where we were out of the local area and couldn't defend or help the dungeon," I pointed out. "Think about it. Let's say they got us both through there with the team…they kill me and then order you to open the gate."

"I'd tell them to go fuck themselves," she said firmly.

"Yeah, but if some of us were wounded and the only chance to save us was that?"

"I'd still say no," she said. "All they'd do is kill you and me as soon as they had what they wanted. This isn't a movie. God, I hated those scenes, where the weak idiot gives up everything and loads die, trying to save their family or whatever."

"Yeah, you'd be surprised what you'd try if it was the only chance to save your family," John said softly. "Believe me, I've seen shit you wouldn't believe in my time with the police."

"Well, regardless, I'd not do it," Kelly said. "If I did, then loads of other innocents would die, and so would my family anyway."

"That's the truth, but as I say, it's a lot harder to make that call in the heat of the moment."

"What about that possibility that there's a secondary gate that, I don't know, opens out onto a lava pit?" I asked.

"Possible, but unlikely." Ashley waggled her hand back and forth. "I mean, it's possible, but the expense of a secondary gate, and that the link we have is the one that they used to reach us? It's a hell of an expense for any dungeon. And for a dungeon that's planning an attack, I'd think they'd want to spend that mana on their forces instead of a gate that leads nowhere. Especially as you might reply and say that you're busy and send someone as a representative instead, wasting that trap."

"But either way, we're agreed this *is* a trap, right?" I asked. "So, it's really not a good idea?"

"Actually that's why I think it could be perfect." Ashley pointed out with a smile, "It gets you out of there, it sets up a reason that we'd not just start a war with London if they did this, and it also gives us a chance to start on the next part of the plan for earth."

"Which is?" I asked.

"Conquest," she replied, smiling coldly.

"Oh, right." I nodded calmly. "Of course, the bit where we become global dictators. How could I forget."

"Seriously, though, isn't that what we were going for?" She looked surprised. "Not global dictators, but capturing other dungeons?"

"Yeah, part of it," I agreed. "But it wasn't a solid 'Hey let's do this on Tuesday' plan, nor is attacking in the most expected way…directly at a target that's ready and has set a trap."

"Oh, I know that." She waved the "minor detail" away. "What I mean is, you wanted to start capturing other dungeons, and you need to do it in a way that leaves us as the good guys, which is the problem. So, what I was thinking we need to do is we start with the ones that nobody will miss, and we make it clear to the others that you've been invited to visit one of those dungeons. Maybe we set up a meeting with the Chinese delegation for right after it, and I attend with your apologies, tell them that your visit to the saurian dungeon must have overrun; then we play the whole 'Uno Reverse' and I play horrified that you've been attacked when it kicks off."

"You're scary when you're like this, you know that?" Dante said softly.

"It's just planning out stimulus and response, that's all. You do it with magic." She smiled at him. "I just do it with people."

"Yeah…" He nodded, obviously still uncomfortable with the ease that she set up such manipulations.

"So, what I'd suggest is that we set up a meeting with the saurians at their dungeon around the same time that you're moving the fake dungeon around London. That way, you're out of here, and we maybe have a situation where you offer to negotiate with the earl and his wife again, for the dungeon core. We time that to happen right when all of this is expected to go off, and you invite them, as the local representatives who will hopefully be joining the Dungeon Lords group soon, to meet Kai and Leilani maybe?"

"It might be a better idea that we make it a bigger meeting," Aly mused, rubbing her cheek as she thought. "Maybe have a few others in. Tell the earl that we're inviting him as a courtesy, and then we play it as a gesture that Matt is making just to annoy Johnstone and Trust more than anything else. It fits with the relationship and seems both irritatingly likely and embarrassing."

"Wow, thanks for the low opinion," I muttered, feeling a little hurt.

"No, this would actually be perfect." Ashley smiled. "Matt, I'm sorry, but you really made it obvious you hated the pair of them, and they really don't like you. This way, you seem less of a threat. As you're obviously a bit childish and ignorant, they'll think that, and let down their guard.

"Kelly, you play host, and you apologize that Matt is running late. We start the meeting and introduce everyone, all while keeping things as normal as possible here. If there is a trap and it's sprung, the first move the other side is likely to make—the saurian, I mean—is to cut off the gate, right?"

"That or try to hold it open so that they can go charging through," Mike pointed out.

"That's a second possibility, but that'd require them to kill or capture the entire party, and practically instantly. For me, it's more likely that they'll try to draw you away and switch the gate off. That prevents reinforcements and it gets you away from a chance at retreating."

"Okay, so what do you think happens then?" Mike asked. "On their side?"

"Most likely, if this is a coordinated attack, then each of the other dungeons involved will try to send their forces through to capture here."

"And you think that's likely?" I asked. "That in a day or two, they've managed to develop a strong enough understanding that they're willing to deploy troops?"

"Oh no. I think that, most likely, given how little we know about these groups, not one of them is really ready, and they all distrust each other. However, given the obvious covetous nature of each of them and the dislike they have of you personally, they probably think it's worth the risk, and they're planning on stabbing each other in the back and trying to take over each other's dungeons as well, given half a chance.

"Remember that these are groups that are used to keeping their people in line with threats and violence, and that have then had the power of the dungeon put at their fingertips.

"This is an opportunistic grouping of bottom-feeders, the kind of people who think they're always the brightest in the room, and so they can do things like insult you to your face, because you're clearly too stupid to realize that's what they're doing," Ashley said grimly.

"Wow, they clearly made a good impression on you then," I pointed out.

"Honestly, each and every one of them are the kind of people who, if we didn't have to deal with them for the dungeon and the future of the species, I'd very happily serve poison to at the first opportunity," she said. "You do *not* want to know the contents of some of their letters. I know that at least one of them was probably saying those things to see if we were intercepting their letters, but it's still not something I want any woman to read."

"Which one?" I asked curiously. "And how bad?"

"The most socially acceptable of them were complaints that you let your 'whores' walk around with far too many clothes on and speak to 'their betters.' And given what one of them said to me at the arena opening session, I have no doubt that any women who live in their dungeon are very, *very* unhappy."

"What the hell is wrong with people?" I groaned. "Seriously?"

"I do want to offer a counterbalance though, before anyone gets offended in general that these are the kind of people who are left after the fall." She held one hand up and looked around. "We had representatives of forty-three dungeons here that day. Of those forty-three, there are *four* that I think are seriously dangerous, two that are just weird, and the others? They're normal people who have somehow ended up in charge or are the kind of people who can at least be worked with. There's only these four out of the entire lot that I see as dangerous like this, and three of them found each other pretty quickly."

"And you think they're each setting up to attack us?" I asked.

"I think they're going to try something, and I think we should be ready to act," Ashley said. "This has the added advantage that we need an excuse as to why you wouldn't just storm in and burn half of London to the ground, and this gives us that."

"It's also a blatant trap, though," I pointed out, and that was when she grinned.

"Oh, it is," she agreed. "So what I'm suggesting isn't that you go. I'm suggesting we make them *think* you're going, and we make use of the Scepiniir situation and our much larger stockpile of resources."

"Settle in, people," I said, unable to help my grin. "Sounds like Ashley's got a plan."

"Well, it has to be better than your usual ones," Mike muttered, before summoning himself a drink. "Given that we have a very short window for all of this to happen, though, I think I'm going to need this drink."

"So, I'm going to send out some of my spies, and what we're going to do is…" Ashley pulled up the table in the middle of the room and projected a series of images.

CHAPTER FORTY-TWO

With an hour left to go to "D-day," I stood and stretched. My ass was numb, and not just because Jack had never been designed for long-distance travel. My new armor was an upgrade—again, I swear we were spending more on prototype armor than we were on dungeons these days—but it wasn't meant to be worn for extended periods of sitting, and certainly not aboard said fucking cushionless dragon.

I also had my full loadout: sword, shield, hammer, handgun and rifle, along with ten spare magazines for each in my bag of holding, twenty large mana crystals for emergencies, potions, food…everything that we thought I might need. Although, next time I was flying this far, I was including a fucking blanket and a pillow, not to mention a goddamn cushion for my ass!

The trees ahead and below whipped past at incredible speed. Jack was clearly loving the experience as much as I had been…for the first *twelve hours*.

Now, as much as I was loving the wonderful advantages that having Jack as he was gave us, I really wished that we'd either found a way to upgrade him with an in-flight lounge, or I'd thought to ask Finn to craft a goddamn saddle. As it is, I was definitely suffering, and due to the sheer speed we were going, there wasn't an option for me to get up and move around.

For a start, I'd find myself a long way behind him in seconds with this wind. And as much as I loved flying under my own power, I was a lot slower than he was.

No, this was a "suck it up" situation. That was just how this shit worked out, so I tried to shift my position as much as possible, while keeping low and clinging onto his back, watching the ruined landscape zip by almost close enough to touch.

The ruins of first southern Russia and then Georgia stretched out below us. A patchwork of ancient and much more recent destruction and nature's reclamation spoke volumes about humanity's fall. From this height, the scars were even more visible than they'd have been from the ground.

"You see that?" I called out to Jack, pointing at what had once been a major highway. Now it was little more than a snaking trail of rust—hundreds of vehicles abandoned in an endless traffic jam that would never move again. Nature was slowly claiming it back, trees and vines breaking through the concrete, but you could still make out the skeletal remains of the mass exodus that had failed.

A flash of movement caught my eye. Something metallic was using the elevated highway as a hunting ground, moving between the rusted hulks with surprising grace for its size. Even from up here, I could tell it wasn't natural. No, it was probably another of the twisted creations that the mana had spawned in the early days, like the Eidolon.

Just remembering that fucker and wondering what it would have become by now was enough to make me shiver.

Then the thought that there could be a thousand or more like that scattered around occurred to me. I hunkered down even further, hoping that we could get this fight out of the way quickly, because with that thought in mind, we desperately needed every edge we could get.

"Bank left," I directed Jack, and he complied, giving us a better view of what lay ahead, as Kelly had asked me to check it out on the way past.

The devastation around the Metsamor nuclear power plant was impossible to miss. A massive dead zone stretched for miles, the ground a sickly color that made my stomach turn. Nothing grew there, and even the mutated creatures seemed to give it a wide berth. The blast pattern told the story clearly enough: when the power had failed and the backup systems went down, the core had gone critical. The resulting explosion had left a wound in the earth that might never heal.

I felt a pulling sensation and looked in that direction, by now used to Jack's way of directing my attention as the diseased earth rumbled beneath me. His enhanced vision picked out details I'd have missed even with my own incredible vision.

The scorched earth and still-smoking wreckage of what looked like a makeshift compound stood out against the landscape. Whatever had happened down there couldn't be more than a day old. Shell casings glinted in the sun, and dark shapes that I didn't want to examine too closely lay scattered around the perimeter.

I squinted, biting my lip as I searched quickly, seeing a lot of blood, torn clothing, and the bodies of saurians…but nothing else.

"Survivors?" I asked, though I already knew the answer.

A sense of sadness and a negative rolled back to me, as Jack replied, though a touch of concern was clear as a section of blasted ground just ahead came into view.

That was the problem with flying so low: you saw things a half second before they were past. But if we flew high up, we'd be seen, be that by other predators—Jack certainly was one, after all—or if we were really unlucky, by the assholes I was on my way to visit.

I didn't doubt that the way that the saurian bodies were left behind but no human ones had been wasn't a coincidence. Hopefully they'd been captured, not killed, as it looked like the remains of a caravan that'd been hit, but it was over too fast for me to be sure either way.

So instead, we pressed on, staying low and watching as the miles fell away beneath Jack's wings as we approached the Caspian. The sun was starting to set when we finally caught our first glimpse of the port city of Baku, or what was left of it.

Jack found us a perch on what remained of a half-collapsed high-rise. The concrete creaked ominously under him; debris fell free as his metal claws and weight crushed the brickwork.

I slid off his back, hit the ground, and rolled, then rushed to the nearby wall, crouching quickly so that if anyone looked up, they'd see Jack.

If I was lucky, they'd see an apparent mana-created metal monster that was out hunting, not the mount of a particularly stupid and arrogant Dungeon Lord.

From here, we had a perfect view of the city below. I could see why the dungeon had chosen it. The once-proud capital of Azerbaijan had become a maze of broken towers and overgrown streets, perfect for anything that wanted to hide its true nature from prying eyes.

"Their gate signature is strongest near the port." I consulted the map Ashley had given me, squinting at the twisting patterns of mana that flowed through the air now. "I'm betting that there's a section with a large open area where the damn lizards can rest in the sun, considering the way the kobolds were with winter..." I mused.

Jack's head swiveled; his enhanced sensors scanned the ruins, relaying what he could see to me, and I nodded.

"Plenty of heat and mana signatures. Large ones, as well. They're not even trying to hide their presence." I scanned from one side to the other, borrowing his sensors, watching, then shook my head at the bloody obvious military buildup all around the rough area we were targeting.

"No," I repeated, musingly, watching as something decidedly reptilian moved between the buildings below. "They're not hiding at all. They're waiting for us. It's definitely a trap. Mind you, why try to hide when you think your target is going to waltz in the front door?"

I felt, rather than saw, the massive automata try to roll his eyes, apparently wishing he could either do that or just tell me how friggin' obvious it was.

"I know, I know." I grunted, stretching my still-numb legs and cursing that my arse was starting with the pins and needles now as feeling returned. "Definitely a trap. The question is, are they really stupid enough to think we didn't know that, or are they just that confident?"

The sun sank lower, casting long shadows across the ruined city. And as I stared, the obvious dungeon improvements started to stand out.

There were sections that looked completely abandoned—ruins, really—while other sections were clearly new, although a covering of fine dust seemed to cling to everything, evident even from up here.

On the far side, atop a small hill that had a wide road that led down toward the harbor, was a plaza, one that had been completely surrounded by creatures and what I was guessing had to be their warrior class, more of those big fuckers that I'd seen at the Nexus platform and the arena.

Unlike there, as Jack zoomed in on them, they were visibly heavily armed, most with oversized guns, the kind of a weapon that should have been mounted on ships in the age of sail—or so it looked to me.

They were surrounding the plaza, and with a load more inside it, clearly ready to wash over the single structure that stood forlornly in the middle: the gate.

I nodded in satisfaction; our scaly friends were certainly preparing their welcome party. I just hoped they were ready for the guest of honor to give a few surprise gifts as well.

Dozens of them scuttled around the outside of the plaza, lighting torches. More and more gathered, getting their weapons ready as last-minute additions... like a massive crossbow that was summoned into being, pointed right at the gate.

We had, by my estimation, about half an hour before it was all going to kick off. I spent most of that time worrying that there was something we'd overlooked and that shit could never actually go this smoothly, then worrying that what was to come would go badly wrong with one of the other two assaults.

That was the kicker, after all. Although it'd been Mike's suggestion, he was actually the least happy of all of us about carrying it out.

Judging from the suspicious shit that was going on, we concluded that there was a good chance that as soon as I was out of the arena, there'd most likely be an attack. Chances were, that unless they were seriously convinced they could kill me, and outright as soon as I arrived on the far side, that attack was going to include at least two dungeons.

If they wanted me out of the arena and on their territory, that gave me the saurians as the number-one threat. But it wasn't likely that they'd do all this just to make a pass at me. The most likely scenario we came up with was that as soon as I was out of commission, the slavers or the undead dungeon would attack my home, trying to capitalize on me being gone.

If not, if I was totally misjudging them, I'd need to apologize, but that was why I was here. If I had arrived and found a real welcome mat and a nice reception waiting…well, I could have marched down there and made a joke out of the whole thing. Maybe I just liked flying and it was a nice day for it, that kinda situation.

Considering that instead it looked like there was an army rocking up, ready for me, that was unlikely.

Moving forward from the "they're all dicks" playbook options, most likely as soon as I was out of the way here, one of the other two dungeons would attack the arena. Worst case, all three would.

If the three dungeons were working together to try to attack us, once we won, that was going to trigger massive paranoia mode in all the other dungeons as we'd have just taken a monumental leap forward in terms of territory and power.

That meant that given that we'd need to have witnesses and others there to see our little bit of playacting, we couldn't just lock the place down and refuse the connections because we knew what was coming.

No, instead we'd made some minor changes to the gate room, and a lot of last-minute research had been carried out—namely, to make sure that once the gate was open, it couldn't be blocked or cut off mid-connection.

That was important.

We'd hoped we could override it somehow, but it turned out to do that, you needed a gate to be established, and the other side to accept it as open. That meant a delay of five seconds while the field was established, before we could forcibly lock the gate open to traffic that could flow both ways.

That was fine, though, as it gave us a chance to deploy our little surprise as well as it giving the other side the chance to commit to a really big fuck-up.

First of all, I'd wanted to hit the undead as our second target. After all, I did have a serious case of the assholes when it came to them already, and we were good at fighting them.

The issue was, I needed the dungeon gate to be opened or kept open by one of their people for us to lock it that way. The best way we'd come up with for that was to slaughter ninety-five percent of the incoming attackers in the first six seconds.

Excessive, I know, but it was good to have a hobby. Mike had gone all in on this with the help of our resident trap maker Leighton, and it'd been impressively evil, all things considered.

The plan was that with only a handful of survivors in a few seconds of their arrival, those survivors would run for the gate and try to flee home, making sure it was open long enough for us to take control, and the Dungeon Lord on the other side would want it held open a little at least to try to get what was left of their forces back out.

That was where the issue with the undead came in. First, they weren't known for their fast reactions, and secondly, they had no reason to try to retreat. They were already dead, after all, and unless there was a new clause in the marriage documentation I wasn't aware of, they were set free of that too, so they were already living their best life, and had no fear to drive them to try to survive.

No, that left the ones that had really made Ashley's skin crawl, the ones she was sure were slavers.

The second issue was that one gate meant one connection.

There were three of them in this little cabal, after all. From what Ashley had seen, although there was little chance that any of them were seriously intending to treat each other fairly, they were also unlikely to stab each other in the back from the start.

That meant that in the short term, there was a good chance that if I went to visit the saurians, their little alliance was likely to make the most of my not being around to attack here. That was a given, and we were okay with that, but there were three of them—three dungeons that might be smaller than us, or might be hiding how big they truly are.

If they were the same size as us? We were about to have a really bad day.

Fortunately, there were the thousand kobolds that we'd already armed and prepared, their barracks buried under the gate and majority of the arena.

Secondly, there was the fact that a connection could only be open one at a time, and we knew that the Nexus platform wouldn't tolerate any funny business, so it wasn't going to be there.

If we got a connection request from any of the three dungeons on our shit list, once I'd supposedly gone through, then we knew it was game on. We let them come through, we slaughtered ninety or so percent, let the remaining group run for the exit, and as soon as the connection had been stable long enough, we locked it in place, opened up the passage, and sent our forces through to counterattack.

That gave us two options. First of all, we could accept that there was a major risk that we'd only get one of them, as they'd somehow get word to the other to call off the attack—not sure how it'd happen, but it was possible.

In that case, well, we took the dungeon that we had and we used whatever tricks we needed to, to ensure that we got the others as soon as possible.

Second, there was a chance that the enemy would find a way to break the connection while it was in progress. Unlikely, but possible. In that situation, a hundred of the kobold advanced warriors were the vanguard, and as shitty as it sounded, that was because they were replaceable.

They'd charge through, establish a beachhead, and Kelly would be able to direct them for a short time as the gate stayed active.

If the gate was solid, then Chris and his team—or Mike and his team—would cross over, followed by another two hundred kobolds, goblins, undead…the works.

The idea was that the irreplaceable humans were there more to lead and to address changes than anything else. But we all knew that if we were attacked, the other side was never going to be so stupid that they didn't have at least some defenses in place.

If that happened…well, we were only going to lose a lot of good people.

Because there were all sorts of shit that could go wrong with this plan, we were also setting ourselves up with an ace in the hole, which was the little gift that I'd received from Kh'aan.

Ashley had arranged a representative to visit each of the three dungeons with a pair of gifts: first, a crystal, one with the Scepiniir blueprints. Alongside this, their laws in a separate and helpfully printed manual, just so there was no way that they could claim they'd not been aware of the rules later.

The dungeon-born that had delivered each letter and package to the other side had reported what they'd seen, and we'd adjusted our plans.

Each of them had had a seeker clockwork crawler attached to their clothing to make damn sure that we knew exactly where the destination dungeon was, and that had provided the final nail in the coffin.

Now we just had to hope that the slavers came through with a decent chunk of their forces, and tried to attack us.

Also, that we were ready and didn't lose…that was an important point. But with that in mind, we'd made major adjustments to the entrance point of the gate, including reinforcing the chamber with three meters of lead.

Even if they somehow dropped a nuke in there, the three meters of lead that we'd sheathed it in were going to deal with a lot of it. And the solid meter of tungsten outside of that would ensure that no matter what, it was staying locked down.

The only issue was the doors, which was kinda needed, but they'd been reinforced and a tungsten plug was installed, ready to drop into place as needed.

It wasn't perfect, but it'd do in a pinch.

With me landing and cheating by not walking out of the gate here at this site, as soon as it all kicked off—we were convinced it would, after all—Mike was going to be attacking the slavers, which were the farthest away, in Cameroon. That left only one team.

Chris and Captain Rhodes, along with Robin and a handful of others, were amusingly going to be attacking the *city* of Rhodes, or close enough, anyway.

As soon as I'd dealt with this site one way or the other, I'd be back in the air with Jack, and on my way to help them. And then the entire team would be moving on to help deal with the slavers in Cameroon.

By the time the sun set tomorrow, we'd have no doubt left on our situation with London, have the three dodgiest dungeons that we knew of either under our control or on the way to it, and a massive increase in our personal power.

If we were lucky, this would catapult us into a position where we were, frankly, unassailable by the other dungeons.

That, or we'd totally misread the situation and what Jack was about to do was *really* going to end badly.

Fuck, I hated it when there were doubts like this… I drummed my fingers on the low wall next to me, squinting out over the top of it, as it ran around the top floor of the apartment block. The shattered stone gave out a crunch and some more complicated sounds of structural decay as Jack shifted slightly nearby.

I got a sense of direction, a target, and I silently wished him "good hunting" as the last seconds of the timer clicked over. We were one minute from the arrival of the volunteers, and it was time to get the party started.

Jack launched himself from the remains of the water tower atop the block. Stone fell free as he beat his wings hard, rising fast, then banked around to line up on his first target.

As he did that, I ran to the opposite side of the roof and leapt off, twisting around and heading for the ground fast, landing and darting into the nearest building.

This was a risky bit. Jack's sensors showed most of these buildings as uninhabited, but considering I was still learning to use the mana sight—and so was Jack—and the lizards were cold-blooded, there was always a chance I'd run slap-bang into the middle of a nest or whatever.

Fuck it, no plan survived contact with the enemy. None of mine did, anyway.

Jack reached the top of his climb, then leveled out. For a split second—much as you felt the need to dance along the edge of a cliff sometimes, or deliberately annoyed your partner when they were in a bad mood—I had a momentary wish that the damn thing would be too heavy for him to lift.

Just for shits and giggles.

Jack's attack when he struck was anything but subtle. The massive automaton dropped from the darkening sky like a meteor. His metal claws wrapped around one of the larger guard towers and he simply…removed it.

He tore the supports free of the ground and launched back into the air, taking the tower along with its inhabitants and massive crossbow and all with him. The screech of tearing metal and stone probably carried for miles.

As he was doing that, I hurtled across the inside of the building I was in. A mixture of my own magically enhanced flight, my insane Agility, and some parkour-style training that Rhodes and her team had put me through already fused together in a single movement method as I covered the distance at a speed that would have had sports scouts begging me to sign something.

Jack climbed hard, then banked, lined up and just dropped the whole thing—shrieking lizardmen and all—into the upturned, confused face of one of the more massive mana signatures we'd seen.

It looked something like one of the armored dinosaurs with the mace end on its tail, if you made it more or less upright instead of walking on all fours, and then added a turtle shell as additional armoring just because you wanted to make sure that if a second asteroid tried to wipe these creations free of the planet at some point, it'd need some extra goddamn effort to do the same trick again.

It was a great design, all things considered. *Or it would have been,* if not for the lightning conductor that was atop the watchtower. Because when that arrived first, with the rest of the watchtower right behind it, and it slammed directly into the face of the new dino, it really didn't matter how thick or carefully designed its shell had been.

The monstrosity died in a heartbeat. Its head split in two and the sides punched apart as the metal was driven deep into the impressive frame. As it fell, Jack simply lined up on the next monster in line, and went to say hi.

By now, the instinctive shock was falling free and more of the creatures were waking up. Cannons were aimed and fired, and although they did fuck all—most missed and their payloads were caught instead by their own warriors on the opposite side, or buildings—the speed that they'd reacted meant they weren't inexperienced or unaware.

Two more hidden crossbows on nearby roofs were uncovered and aimed, their loadout apparently a collection of massive metal spears lashed together.

Jack danced aside as I burst into the air, crossing from one building close by to another and sent him a warning. Then I was out of sight again, still hopefully unseen by the locals.

I tore through what had once been a call center, to skid to a halt when I could see more of the plaza again, barely keeping from plowing through the full glass wall of windows and out into the open air.

Jack clamped onto the next of his targets, another of the huge dino-turtles. This time, instead of fighting it, he braced himself, then launched back into the air and carried the thing with him, soaring upward as if he were a hunter that had found his dinner, all the while streaming the situation to me as I ran and leaped and flew.

That was when the dungeon gate flared to life. On all sides, the lizard warriors scrambled to change from tracking and trying to figure out Jack's attack, to dealing with the new arrivals.

The squad of orcs that stepped through looked nothing like the savages most people imagined. Their leader wore my armor—my old set, modified and polished—and it gleamed in the evening light. Grokmar, who'd jumped at the chance when I'd offered it to him, instead of ordering it, stood proud despite his obvious discomfort with the situation.

"I come. As agreed." His English was rough but clear. "For meeting of our pieces."

I almost face-palmed. He was supposed to say a "peaceful meeting," not a meeting of our fucking pieces! He was making this sound entirely fucking wrong.

A figure emerged from the mass of gathered soldiers, moving with an unnatural fluidity that made my skin crawl. His face was a nightmare of human and reptilian features, scales gleaming in the flickering light of torches.

"Ah, the great Northern Lord graces us with his presence!" His voice carried a sibilant undertone that set my teeth on edge. "Though you seem…different than described."

"I do be the lord!" Grokmar shouted back.

But something in the creature's eyes changed, a predatory gleam that told me the game was already up.

"How fascinating," the hybrid creature practically purred. "You wear his armor, carry his bearing, but…" His tongue flicked out, tasting the air. "You are not him. A clever deception, but ultimately futile."

"He comes." Grokmar shifted his weight slightly. "Soon."

The leader's laugh was like scales scraping against stone. "Oh, I think not. Your entire pathetic delegation is already here, trapped behind our lines." His head tilted, almost birdlike. "Did you really think we wouldn't recognize a diversion? While you play at being heroes here, my erstwhile allies are already moving against your precious arena. The Brotherhood of the Fall and our allies…all tied together in one glorious purpose."

“You wished for peaceful meeting?” Grokmar tried again. His hand inched toward his weapon—fortunately a massive hammer this time…not, as Aly had jokingly suggested, a massive dildo.

“Peace?” The creature’s face contorted into something between a sneer and a smile. “Peace is for mammals who fear their own extinction. We are the next step in evolution, chosen by the mana itself to rule this new world. Your lord? He’s nothing but a relic, clinging to old notions of humanity’s dominance. Even now, he scrambles to defend against attacks that are merely shadows of our true purpose!”

That’s when Jack dropped his second surprise of the evening. The massive armored beast he’d been fighting went sailing through the air to crash into what our combined minds guessed was the nearest section of the main dungeon. The impact shook the whole compound.

“Kill them all!” The leader’s composure finally cracked. “These primitive apes dare to—”

“We not primitive!” Grokmar roared, drawing his blade. “We are warriors of North! And we are…what word? Ah yes. We too is *distraction*!”

“Fucking here we go!” I snarled as I backed up three steps. I raced at the window and launched myself through it, digging deep and ignoring stealth in favor of speed. I rocketed across the intervening space, even as the orcs roared and ran at their enemies.

There were a dozen cannons being lined up on them, and as soon as I had a line of sight on them, I was unleashing a dozen Incinerates to take them out.

Of course, as soon as they all started screaming and falling, that set the entire place up in arms, including activating a shield that I slammed through in a massive eruption of magic.

Had I been a second slower, I might have bounced off. A second earlier? I’d probably have never known it was there. But as it was, it was in the middle of activation. And if I had to bet, it was there to protect against Jack, not me.

Either way, though, when I burst through it, the entire thing became visible—a great upside-down bowl that covered the dungeon and the surrounding few dozen streets. Lightning from me and some sort of greenish-white light exploded across the sky.

Given that Jack was above the shield at this point, and the sky was darkening, I was basically silhouetted in light.

I didn’t know why I even bothered attempting stealth anymore. I had meant to get into the dungeon through the massive breach Jack had just created. But considering the screams of rage that rose as I was spotted, I ducked down and dove into another of the nearby buildings instead, smashing the door open with a shoulder, then skidding to a halt along the tiled floor.

The place was exactly what you’d expect from a bunch of lizards: wood on the walls and floor with what was presumably comfortable roosting points or whatever lizards did, a shallow pool, and a couple of big fuck-off heated rocks scattered around the room.

There were also several skewers that stood in the corners with meat dangling from them, apparently ready for a hungry fuck-face to go grab a bite.

The dangling arm, complete with coagulated blood beneath it and a tattoo on the shoulder, made it clear the kind of snacks the lizards preferred.

Ducking my shoulder again, I ran at the nearest door—a wooden one, thankfully—and smashed it out, crashing into a corridor. Then I ran down it at full speed, extending my senses as far as I could.

I had one of two choices of how to play it here, and I was really hoping they'd been stupid enough to summon some Scepiniir as samples, or one of those options was fucked.

The best one, though?

I was a Dungeon Lord, and already there were messages popping up in the corner of my vision.

CHAPTER FORTY-THREE

Congratulations, Dungeon Warmancer!

You have discovered an actively hostile Dungeon! As the latest adventuring party to enter the Dungeon, in full knowledge of its potential and your own capability, you have received a Quest!

Whoever rules the Dungeon, rules the land!

As a rival Dungeon Warmancer, you have entered a hostile dungeon, triggering a maximum-level response…

The Hostile Dungeon, identified as Dungeon 104, and its Dungeon Lord are now fully aware of you and your identity—and will stop at nothing to terminate you. Should you make it through the Dungeon to the Core, however, and claim control, you would receive the following rewards!

- **1x Satellite Dungeon Facility**

OR

- **1x Dungeon Core Shard**
- **1x Additional Dungeon Core Upgrade Path**
- **1x Dungeon Perk**
- **1x Tech Upgrade (Random)**
- **1x Class Skill Point**
- **10,000 XP**

The next prompt was even more fun.

***You have received a formal Declaration of War from the Alliance of the Brotherhood of the Fall… Do you wish to Accept, Cede,* or *Negotiate*?**

Be aware, any response to this declaration will result in a formal Link between the Pantheon of the Storm and the Alliance of the Brotherhood of the Fall. Both sides will know the location of the other and will receive a [10%] or [+10 boost] to a single aspect of their choice for their forces.

Please select from the following:

- Ambient Mana Generation: Yes/No
- Mana Regeneration: Yes/No
- Health Regeneration: Yes/No

- Melee Damage: Yes/No
- Ranged Damage: Yes/No

The boosts that have been selected by both sides will be awarded to the winner of the conflict as permanent boons!

Good luck!

"You fucking shmuck!" I burst out laughing as I scanned over the details, accepting the declaration of war, knowing that the stupid bastards had just played straight into my hands.

Or, more accurately, they'd played into Kelly and Aly's, as they'd be able to use this back at the dungeon with the meeting.

I, on the other hand, selected the Ambient Mana Generation option in a fuckin' heartbeat.

Not only was that incredibly valuable already, but I'd taken it last time this shit happened. The additional ten percent boost was an insane amount now, given that we currently had four dungeons all up and running.

Ten percent increase to the mana that was generated—and could therefore be harvested—for those four? That was well over a million mana a day now, and that wasn't even considering the mana that was coming in from the harvesting teams…that was just the actual input from the generators and converters and so on.

There was no way I was passing that opportunity up. And as much as I'd love the others? Fuck no.

If I was lucky, the dumb bastards would pick something totally different and I'd get that when I won as well.

Because I *was* going to win, there was no doubt in my mind about that, even when the other two locations flared bright in my mind, as did…

"Oh, you're in for a surprise!" I growled, distracted at just the wrong time by the knowledge that Sari, Mistress of the fucking Ocean, who I already had a link to, had joined this war as well.

The problem was, I was taking a corner at that point, and I'd been distracted just enough to not notice that the wall here was sheetrock, not stone.

Instead of bouncing off it as I had done before, going slightly too fast to turn without the little bumper option, I plowed straight through it. My leg caught and I rolled, skidding across the floor of what was apparently a kitchen.

Considering the "meat" that the lizards apparently preferred, though, "slaughterhouse" was a better description.

I slapped a hand down and dug in, bracing and stopping my skid, before standing slowly. A cage was at one end of the room, full of people. Three lizards wore fucking aprons and were armed with meat cleavers, and a boy of about twelve was pinned down atop a table.

The room was set out like a commercial slaughterhouse—a place that I'd seen once and once only, and that I'd hoped to never experience again.

Whereas the hooks for hanging meat to drain and chiller units in the one I'd been in before were clearly judged superfluous here, the black iron cage, complete with waterfall above it to keep the "stock" clean, was a new innovation.

There had to be forty people in a cage that was perhaps ten by ten meters, topping out at the low roof where a continuous stream of water ran over the bedraggled inhabitants.

The floor under them was a mesh grate, like the cattle grids that marked the edge of farmers' lands back home to stop cows wandering out and still enable cars to pass.

Here it was used to clean the main course and drain away anything that might ruin the flavor.

In the main room, torsos were stacked in what looked like a modern version of an old-style mine cart on the left. On the other side of the room, on the far side of the table the child was being strapped to, was a second cart, one that was apparently for limbs, judging from the sticking out nightmare fuel. And at the end of the table?

A table on rollers, like the ones that posh restaurants used as dessert carts. Twelve heads were piled atop it. Seeing that, seeing that there were heads of all sizes and apparent ages?

Fuck me, *no.*

The pool of blood on the floor that was merrily draining away through dedicated holes and the box of limbs nearby told the story that they weren't making threats here, nor were they apparently subsisting on dungeon-summoned meat as the rest of us were.

No, these were "free range" humans they'd been prepping for the lunch run. On seeing that, and the panic on the young boy's face as one of the lizards pulled the restraint on his arm tight, reaching for a leg to strap that in next, I decided I'd seen enough.

I could have used Incinerate.

I could have used Lightning Bolt.

Fuck, I could have used anything, but seeing what they were doing? Oh, hell with that!

I threw my sword at the one standing over the boy, a straight launching of the blade to arrow forward. It took the lizard in the chest, hurling him back, even as I leapt at the next in line.

Sometimes the best option was to deal with things with your hands.

The three lizards had been positioned with one at the head of the table, where he'd been in the middle of strapping the child down; one at the far side of the table, closest to the wall, with a cleaver in hand he was sharpening, ready; and on the far side, one working on cleaning up the torsos.

The only one with a cleaver on his belt, instead of in its hand, was the one that had been securing the next victim. As my sword blurred past him to take the one sharpening his weapon in the chest, he leapt back, hissing.

That was fine; I'd not been aiming for him.

I wanted to make sure the sharpener didn't decide to kill the kid before I could get a little frustration out.

The saurian landed, his claws clicking on the tiled floor, then leapt at me. His left hand reached for my face, and his right went for the cleaver on his belt.

Unfortunately for him, I was a god, and suddenly in a *very* bad mood.

I was also ascending—slowly, sure, but I was doing it—which meant that to a creature that was low enough to not even be allowed outside to be ready to attack their enemies, and was instead kept in the kitchen, even as they planned to ambush me, I was basically a fucking unstoppable blur.

Covering the distance to it before it could even pull the cleaver free, I grabbed its outstretched arm by the wrist, then twisted as hard as I could, while snap kicking at the cleaver on the hip.

As I was rather a lot stronger than a normal being right now, and oh, so pissed off, the twin snaps of the saurian's hip being reduced to splinters and the arm being nearly ripped off rang out at practically the same time.

Given that the arm was hanging on by merely torn flesh now, I hopped into a second snap kick, alternating my feet and smashing any last vestiges of a chance at a sex life right out of the window.

At the same time, I yanked hard and ripped the arm free from the elbow joint, then threw that at the third lizard.

He batted it aside. The blood splattered across his face, then he hissed in pain and terror as I crossed the divide before he could bring the cleaver around. I grabbed his fist where it was closed around the cleaver's grip, and crushed it.

As the bones in his fingers shattered, I gripped him by the throat, ignoring his other hand, and drove my fingers in with all my might.

The eruption of blood that burst free as my questing fingers found his spinal column was impressive, admittedly.

I think, though, the impression I left as I yanked my hand back out, dropping the now uncontrollably bleeding and twitching, dying lizard to the floor, made my feelings abundantly clear.

"I should have just fucking attacked this place head-on, through the gate," I snarled, seeing just how outmatched they were in comparison to me. I stomped over and gripped the shoulder of the one I'd apparently pinned to the wall with my sword and tore him in half as I freed the blade, dropping his remains to the floor.

"Do any of you speak English?" I asked the group in the cage, as I strode over, each of them now huddling back in absolute terror.

"Little?" one of them called out, blinking against the deluge as I stalked forward.

"Wait in this room. I'll be back to take you somewhere safe soon," I ordered them. "Stay as hidden as you can. I've only just started to clean this shithole out."

I had a momentary flash of a connection with Jack, showing me that while the dome shield that had appeared over the dungeon was apparently very strong, it was also very stupid.

It was solid from the top of the walls up.

Jack had flown around and smashed his way *inside* the wall, and was now inside of the shield, a detail that should have made me pleased, and yet for some reason was only making me angrier. The fuckers were absolutely evil, and insanely incompetent, and yet here I was, wasting my fucking time dealing with them! I bit down on my rage and banished the thoughts, focusing on where I was.

I clamped my sword back in place, the *snick-snick-snick* sound of the sheath closing barely audible over the rush of the water. And to make my point about just how strong I was, I gripped the bars of the cage in one hand, the gate in the other, and yanked, hard.

If I'd been thinking, I would not have tried this. Hell, I'd have used my hammer or my sword. Iron's not a soft metal, after all, but it can be brittle. When I yanked on the cage door, the lock holding it snapped with a sharp ping. The metal clanged to the floor as I tried to soften my glare, staring in at them.

"Well?" I snapped. "Get out, find somewhere to hide, and…"

A roar of challenge came from behind me. I barely paused as I glanced over. A new saurian clambered through the wall I'd used to enter; I hurled a lightning bolt at him. His skull exploded as I put a *little* too much mana into it.

I looked back at them and sighed. "Please." I modulated my tone as much as possible. "You can get the fuck out of the cage, or stay in there. Just hide, while I go kill everything and tear the fucking walls of this place down, okay?" That last was said with what was probably too nice a tone, making me sound sarcastic. But fuck it—the way I was feeling right now, I was actively furious that none of these people were strong enough to defend themselves.

I even knew how ridiculous that was. I mean seriously, insanely ridiculous to expect them to tear their enemies a new asshole. But knowing that? Instead of calming me down, I just felt angrier.

Clearly my fury was bleeding through to Jack as I sensed him land, clamp his claws onto the head and shoulders of another of the gigantic turtle things, and bite its head off in one, ripping through the neck.

He hurled the carcass aside; blood sprayed into the air, and unleashed plasma fired across one side of the plaza where the saurians were grouped.

The lizard men had so far had less than a minute of actual fighting since everything kicked off. Although they were doing reasonably well against the orcs, they were being utterly slaughtered by the massive dragon.

Unsurprisingly.

I ripped free the strap that was securing the boy to the table, then strode past him, lifting one boot and kicking the far door out of the room open, and headed along the corridor, deeper into the dungeon.

"Yoo-hoo!" I called. "Anyone home?"

A door ahead burst open. I saw reflected light from a summoning, as a saurian rushed out, two hand axes gripped tight as it raced at me, screaming.

I started to jog as more were summoned. Doors ahead opened on either side of the long passage, and more creatures burst through, looking for a fight.

The first of them leapt at me, a stupid move in itself, considering the ceiling was barely two and a half meters here, and the saurian was two.

That in turn meant that as it screeched out its hatred and brought both axes up and around…they got caught in the ceiling, utterly ruining the whole "flying murder machine" image he was going for.

It was made even worse when I lunged forward, clamped my open hand over his face and kept going, pausing in my rush only long enough to pound the back of his skull into the face of the next in line.

With that, battle was truly joined. Seeing the levels of weapons they bore—steel hatchets and basic, though large bore guns—I didn't even bother to draw my weapons.

My armor was into its sixth or seventh iteration now, and with the blueprints that I'd given Finn, as well as the runes that several of the crafters were working with now, I had a short-range shield built into my armor, powered by a mana crystal that I could activate at any time and trust that, aside from real magic, I was pretty much unstoppable here against these.

That, in turn, only served to make me even more furious. My anger rose even higher as I raged through the incoming horde. They sprinted out of side rooms, bearing weapons that were clearly chosen to make the most of their solid size and imposing looks.

What they hadn't been designed for was common sense or fighting in restricted areas. More and more freshly summoned and unaware saurians appeared, racing out and swinging great axes, scythes, and longswords.

The hand axes would have worked, as would the daggers…if more than half the time, their own wildly swinging compatriots hadn't killed the wielders off before I could.

That was when I summoned my lightning and hurled a pair of bolts down the passage. The horrific electrical power punched through flesh, channeling through armor and dancing across the blood that seemed to surround me, even as I screamed in utter fury, driven to new heights over the sheer idiocy and waste.

By the time I'd reached the far end of the passage, I'd completely lost count of how many I'd killed, and I no longer cared about anything, bar tearing this entire dungeon down around its current inhabitants' ears.

Stalking forward, I glared right and left, searching for anyone who would challenge me…for anything I could vent this incredible anger onto, even as a tiny voice inside me screamed that something wasn't right here.

I smashed a door from its hinges, finding myself in a long, ornate room with high ceilings and arched windows that looked out into a courtyard on the right, with tiled frescos on three walls. Burners of some kind, incense maybe, hung from the ceiling, alternating with now long obsolete chandeliers filled with dead bulbs.

As I entered, a dozen warriors ran in from the far side. Their one mage led the way with a staff held high, already chanting as green, noxious smoke poured from a crystal set atop it.

I didn't bother to draw a weapon, just sneeringly clicked my fingers. Incinerate flared to life an inch behind his glowing eyes and cut his spell off with alacrity.

As he collapsed, the warriors on either side streamed past, uncaring.

Jack landed nearby, having felt my rage. He burst through the courtyard wall, dragged claws through the suddenly exposed and screaming defenders, then spun and launched himself back into the air, leaving only the dead and dying.

I ran at the injured defenders, snatching up a halberd—a fucking *halberd*—and ran the only survivor through.

I left the weapon jutting out of his body as I rampaged through the next room, then the next, hunting for anything, *anything* to fight.

Time lost all meaning and seemed to stretch out for me. I tore my way through room after room. Green blood and red flew in a deluge that blended into one until eventually, I found something that stopped my barbaric slaughter.

Unfortunately for me, it wasn't an onset of common sense or self-control.

It was a cannonball to the face.

CHAPTER FORTY-FOUR

The new armor proved its worth right there and then, as whatever structural enhancements it'd had built in lasted long enough to spread out the force and hold the helmet together. As a goddamn lucky side effect, it also drained the enchantments that held the armor active, reducing it to a much lower level.

Fortunately for me, as I slid to a halt across the floor, my head spinning, neck strained, and my bell well and truly rung, it brought a seriously needed moment of clarity.

It was like having my head dunked into a bucket of icy-cold water. The world swam back into focus, and along with the desperate memories and crushing horror at my own animalistic rage, there also came thought.

I lifted my hand muzzily, staring at it as my thoughts rearranged themselves.

The first part of which was that if there was one cannon fired at my face, there were likely others or more fire incoming.

I blinked, then rolled frantically, barely making it aside as the next cannonball crashed into the floor where I'd just laid, then ricocheted upward and hurtled off down the corridor.

The corridor.

I focused on the far end of it, finding a secured and armored point at that side, with a cannon mounted on a swivel and four of the smaller snake-like creatures that were going through the archaic "service to the cannon" rituals.

As one of them frantically shoved a bagged charge into the mouth, I unleashed a lightning bolt, aimed right at it. I missed the charge, but hit the cannon, so the joy of transference and metal with lightning kinda took care of that for me.

The secure post and its defenders detonated; the bagged charges had been clearly stacked close enough that they went up at the same time. I stared at the far end for a few seconds, before turning slowly.

Behind me, there was…utter destruction.

I suddenly felt sick to my stomach as I looked back along the corridor. Flashbacks hit me—my screaming and punching, kicking, trying to bite them, even though I was wearing a helmet. Shit.

What the hell had I been playing at?

I looked down at my hands and found them utterly covered, literally dripping with gore and blood, blood that ran upward to the goddamn shoulders and all over the front of my armor. A shift of my shoulders told me that either the inside of my armor was drenched in sweat, and I was sodden with it—which I was hoping was the case—or I'd been bathing in the blood of my enemies, quite literally.

I turned back to the passage ahead and pushed on, my limbs shaking as I took the first step.

What the hell was wrong with me? I took another step and paused, lifting a hand and staring at the way my fingers shook.

Had I been poisoned? Some kind of magical effect? No, it didn't feel like magic. How long had I been fighting? Was it exhaustion? Had I pushed past my limits somehow?

No, that couldn't be. I'd fought against the undead all day long before, literally fighting toe-to-toe with undead by the hundreds and thousands. Exhaustion didn't make sense. No, it *had* to be magic of some kind, some weirdly specific sneaky attack that—

I broke off my line of thought when I noticed the flashing icon, a handful of kill notifications, ones that I dismissed without a thought. I realized that they all dealt with individual fights, making the five of them cover a much larger degree of bloodshed than I wanted to look at.

No, the one I wanted to see was number six in line, with another kill notification for the last band of dickheads that'd formerly resided at the end of this corridor coming in seventh.

Status Modifier: Berserker — Rage 2nd level enchantment has been broken. Armor systems drained. Kill 10 more enemies to reactivate…

"Berserker…" I mumbled to myself. "Fucking berserker? Wait, my *armor?!*" It came to me in a flash. I stared at my armor, rolling my wrists and seeing the line of tiny, dimly glowing symbols that led up each side, etched into the magical steel.

Finn! That mad bastard had learned the orcish armor blueprint, and he'd used stuff he'd learned from it to improve this new iteration of my armor as well. He'd included enchantments he'd seen in there, and that had been copied over faithfully from the orcish armor blueprint onto this! If not for the cannonball to the face, I don't know what I'd have done out here, not now.

Hell, I'd been so furious with just a handful of kills, not even enough to properly activate the berserker mode, that I'd been a total dick to the prisoners back there!

The thought of what I might have done to them if I'd been full-on charged already…

Shit! He'd used it on the new armor for the others too! The rest of my team were out there fighting to take the other dungeons, wearing fucking armor that was going to drive them mad!

Was it possible? My heart said it was, that I wasn't that much of a murderous cockbag, but deep down, I was seriously worried. It was that "three a.m, it's just occurred to me and now I'm awake for the night" level of worried…

No, I had to believe I wasn't. I tried to do what was right and this was definitely *not* that! It was the rage.

I'd been so full of it, so hopped up on whatever the armor did to me that my body had responded, and that I knew, because I recognized the side effects of too much adrenaline.

I swallowed hard, knowing that was it. I knew it instantly by, of all things, the urge to cry.

It was stupid. It was incredibly unmanly, if such a thing could be said without the corresponding disbelief, considering the situation and the blood of my enemies still dripping from my fingers. But it was true, nonetheless.

The only times I'd ever felt like this before was when I'd been in fights that had been broken up. And wasn't that a stupid thing to want to cry over?

A friend had explained it once. The adrenaline hypes your system up to such a point that you're frantic. Then, without the release, it's like flipping a switch.

He said it was one of the reasons so many people who had served in the army ended up bursting into tears in strange places. For him, he'd endure a vivid flashback. Something triggered by something entirely stupid—an old car backfiring, forgetting the route home and having a sudden fight-or-flight reaction, or most of all, some young punk being all up in his face and aggressive, and his wife dragging him away because his kids were with him.

It was the surge of adrenaline and the readiness. The *need* to fight. And then the lack of that release that made the emotions surge, that sent you into an uncontrollable mess.

It was ridiculous—it certainly damn well felt that way, anyway—but fuck's sake, it was real: the jumping emotions, the feelings, the waves of bloody shaking that rolled through me.

It was that, heaped atop the enchantment…I just damn well knew it.

Distantly, I felt Jack. The confusion and hesitation that I was feeling bled through to him as well. He read my mind and we communicated mentally, after all, so it wasn't that ridiculous that he'd be feeling things and be affected by them in the same way, more or less.

Reaching out to him, I paused, resting one hand against the wall. He fed back to me a blurred collection of images, a fast burst of random things. Destruction was chief among them, but it wasn't all there was, though.

There was a brief pause while he'd also seen the prisoners from the cage trying to escape. He'd intervened there—unlike me, being too filled with rage and bloody stupidity—he'd seen them, and as much fun as he'd been having with uncomplicated destruction, he'd known enough to pause and step up for that.

Regardless, though, the day wasn't done, and I knew I couldn't afford to waste time navel-gazing. There were sounds of running feet nearby, shouts and roars, and worst of all, now that I knew the others could be in the same situation, a desperate need to get my fucking arse in gear and get to them, to make them take the armor off!

So I did what I had to do, put my big girl pants on, and I flooded my body with lightning, before chugging a low-grade healing potion. I kept my goddamn armor on, despite the mana crystal slowly absorbing ambient mana in the area and the likelihood of me going batshit again.

Was it the best choice? No. Was it a sensible choice, considering I just knew the last *however* long was going to be coming back to haunt me in dreams? No. Was it wise, considering the bloody chance of me losing my friggin' mind and going on another rampage?

Also no!

I didn't really know where I was going with all of it, beyond that I was most definitely needing to find a way through the rest of the damn fight before I worried about it anymore, though. Because running into the boss fight that I sensed was ahead in nothing but my birthday suit wasn't going to end well for anyone.

Though psychological warfare was a thing, I had to admit.

The potion and spell might be a bandage over a wound for now, but that was the best it was going to get. I damn well needed to sort this clusterfuck out.

Pushing on, and picking up the speed as I went—I had no idea how long I'd been out of it, after all—I started to run, aiming for the end of the corridor.

It didn't take long—it was barely twenty meters—but, between the potion, spell, and my own incredible Constitution, my steps smoothed out again and I picked up speed.

What was left of the doors I hit like a wrecking ball and smashed through them to burst out into a small, covered courtyard or hall beyond.

On all sides, there were signs of recent devastation, so clearly Jack had passed through already. Overhead, the once graceful arched ceiling had been punched through at one end, and the still smoldering corpse of a huge saurian creature was driven into the tiled floor.

The collection of multicolored and ornate floor tiles was covered in blood, dust, shattered rock, and the remains of that end of the hall's roof.

I headed in that direction, having picked it at random out of the two possible doors. And, of course, that proved to be the stupider choice.

I'd barely made it halfway across the courtyard, when the first attack landed. And considering it was magical, it was messy.

The first I knew of the trio of snakes with legs was when the world abruptly flipped like a table and I was smashed bodily sideways into a hitherto undamaged wall.

I shouted in shock and pain, then again when a sudden twist in the air turned into a gravitational tear.

At least that was what I'd name it later on.

Right then, I just shouted, swore violently, and fucking panicked as I was smashed from one wall into the next, then flipped over and hurtled into the ceiling, then down to tear a line through the pretty tiles on the floor, again.

I tried to aim. I tried to find them and to defend myself. I tried to figure out what the fuck was goddamn attacking me. And all of it, literally all of it, was pointless.

For the first time in this entire fight, I was in danger from more than my own stupidity, and I did what I did best when I managed to wrap my head around that "minor" detail.

I lashed out in literally all directions with lightning.

If I'd tried to throw it in a particular straight line…well, that'd have been impossible, with my inner ear doing backflips and barrel rolls. Fortunately for me, though, that just helped me to spread the love, really, and to make sure that everyone who really deserved some of my attention got it.

By the time the lightning storm had subsided, it had left scorched walls and the acrid smell of ozone in the air. To me, though, as I rolled to a halt on the floor, panting, it just tasted like home.

More importantly, it had stopped whatever the hell that gravitational attack had been. Staggering to my feet, I glanced around and nodded to myself. Yup, it was apparently hard to maintain an attack when you were being reduced to kibble.

The three bodies had been shielded from sight in an alcove, one that was hidden behind a selection of potted plants to make it look like an oasis.

The plants, the bodies, the pots and, well, let's be honest… the entire rest of the room was a blackened mess now, mainly reduced to the point of being sold at a petrol station as charcoal briquettes for a barbecue.

There was nothing in the room that had come out unscathed. In my panic and distraction, I'd apparently flooded the entire room in lightning.

Important note that, I decided, that I could do such a thing instead of the bolts I usually worked with. I mentally marked down a desperate need for more spell-slinging practice time soon. Then I launched myself up and out, through the hole in the ceiling Jack had made earlier.

The ruined rooftops beyond offered a better vantage point than stumbling around those corridors like a rat in a maze. I made the most of that as I paused, staring out across the various buildings and plotting the rough path I'd taken until now.

More than half of the dungeon had been reduced to smoking wreckage from Jack's—and my—rampages so far.

From up here, the dungeon's weird layout finally made some sense. The original buildings had appropriately fancy brickwork and decorative touches to the local style. But grafted onto it were newer sections, complete with a weird organic sheen that seemed almost alive.

The most obviously new addition was a massive onion-shaped dome about a hundred meters to the north. It dominated the skyline, golden and gaudy against the grey stone of the original architecture. Fresh growth was still creeping up its sides, the dungeon's influence literally reshaping it even as I watched. The light flared as the fireflies of dungeon creation transformed it from what had been brick and tiles—or so it seemed from a distance—to solid gold reflecting the flickering of torches.

When I'd arrived earlier, I'd seen it. But not being familiar with the architecture of the area, and having seen those weird domes in everything from pictures of Moscow to religious centers on movies, I'd just accepted it as more of the same.

"Subtle," I muttered, taking in the ostentatious display. If I were a betting man, I'd put money on finding our scaly friend in there. Nothing said "throne room" quite like a giant golden dome.

Mind you, nothing said "dickhead" quite like serving your lizards fucking human snacks as well, so I was going to need to have that out with him too.

It took ten seconds to flash across the intervening space and land atop the dome, and three more to realize that the damn thing was a very shiny trap—for Jack, presumably, as until now I'd not been flying much. But hey, I doubted the locals were going to complain at catching me instead.

As soon as I'd landed atop it, I'd noticed that it felt a little soft, then I'd promptly got on with searching around. Now, after barely enough time to focus in, I felt a strange sensation from my feet, looked down, and started to fucking swear.

The "gold" surface beneath my feet had the consistency of thick honey, but with none of the pleasant associations. As I tried to lift one foot, the material stretched like molten taffy, then snapped back, yanking my boot firmly against the dome's surface, with more of the gold sliding slowly up my calves and boots.

"Oh, you've got to be fucking kidding me," I muttered, trying to channel lightning through my boots to break free. The substance merely absorbed the energy, taking on an iridescent sheen that would have been pretty if it wasn't currently trying to trap me like a bug on flypaper.

Movement caught my eye—dozens of lizardmen emerging from concealed positions around the dome's perimeter. Each carried what looked like a hand-cannon, though "hand" was generous given their size. The weapons were basically portable bombards, medieval tech that had been upgraded just enough to be dangerous.

"Witness the might of the Brotherhood!" one of them called out. His voice carried the same sibilant undertone as their leader. "The great Northern Lord, caught like a common—"

I cut him off with a snort. "Really, dude?" I called back. "We're doing the evil henchman monologue thing? After I just slaughtered my way through half your dungeon?"

Their response was more practical this time, unfortunately, as they opened fire. The bombardment was impressive, I'll give them that. The air filled with smoke and the thunderous roar of multiple detonations as their enhanced black powder weapons unleashed hell from a dozen barrels, even as more sprinted out from under cover.

Cannonballs the size of my palm hurtled inward from all sides. I crouched on instinct, trying to present a smaller target as they crashed into the dome around me.

Two hit, one in the right shoulder—a glancing blow that made me hiss in pain, knowing it'd leave a fuckin' bruise, but that was it—and one that slammed into my right knee, hitting at just the right angle to really fucking hurt as with the bend, the way the armor had shifted, and the necessary flex points, the kneecap was dislocated.

I cried out, slapping my left hand against the side of the dome to brace myself and my right hand on the knee. Then I cursed again through gritted teeth as I realized that between crouching and that bracing hand, I was now even more stuck.

Tendrils of golden mass slid up and wrapped around sections of my armor, dragging me deeper. With the injury to my knee, this was only going to be harder to escape.

But they'd made one critical mistake, though.

Sure, I might be stuck, but I was still the First Lord of the Storm. And in coming out to stand on the rooftop, they'd just given me the perfect excuse to remind them of that.

Hidden by the drifting smoke of their black powder weapons, I raised my hands and channeled Lightning Storm, flooding the area with my mana and letting loose my fucking anger at all this shite.

I didn't go for the one, though—oh no. I dragged my right hand free of my wounded knee and slapped it against my chest, focusing and feeling the crystal in there, the one that was designed to power the armor, and that was unfortunately also powering the goddamn berserker enchantment that I could feel building.

A hundred and fifteen mana was all that it held. But between ripping that free and the mana that I already had, over fifteen thousand points still, I decided to invest a little extra and summoned not one, but three lightning storms, one atop the other for a measly four thousand five hundred mana.

Lightning answered my call—not in single bolts but in waves of crackling power that lit up the evening sky. The storm built with unnatural speed; clouds boiled into existence overhead as my fury found form. Blue-white light danced between the gathering clouds, and my strength surged as the electricity saturated the air.

Then, I decided it was about time I made the most of one of the little discoveries I'd made when I'd been practicing days before with Emma in the citadel.

I added an extra weave to the storm, one that tied it all together, and changed the clouds from being merely a byproduct of the spell, into a much more solid manifestation of my will, as a Storm Titan.

I added water, that was all, twisting the slow levels of humidity and that of the nearby Caspian Sea into the building storm, and let it begin to fall.

The lizardmen's triumphant cries turned to screams as the first bolts struck. The metal of their weapons and armor and the lead of the rooftops nearby all combined to gift me almost perfect conductors. Chains of lightning jumped from one to the next in a deadly dance. Those who dropped their weapons and tried to flee found no safety; the rain that fell was charged with power, every drop a conductor for my wrath.

My strength returned as the storm raged; the lightning healed my injuries even as it devastated my enemies. The sticky substance trying to hold me began to crystallize under the onslaught as bolt after bolt, seeking out my enemies, targeted it as well. At last, it was brittle enough for me to finally wrench free and launch myself into the air, trailing glowing light.

On all sides, dozens of smoking corpses dotted the rooftops. Beyond them, others were running, screaming and dying.

I lifted my hands out to the sides, breathing in the electrically charged air. My soul settled, even as all around me others were ripped screaming from their bodies by my might. Nearby, I felt Jack's triumphant roar of approval as much as I heard it ring out.

Through the chaos, I spotted a section of the dome's surface beginning to crack, weakened by the combination of lightning and thermal stress.

Perfect.

It was time to pay their leader a visit and discuss his dietary choices, I decided.

With a grin that probably wasn't entirely sane, I raised my hammer high, calling down one final massive bolt that ripped free of the storm. The dome shattered beneath me, and I dropped into the throne room below, electricity still crackling around my armor.

"Knock, knock, asshole."

CHAPTER FORTY-FIVE

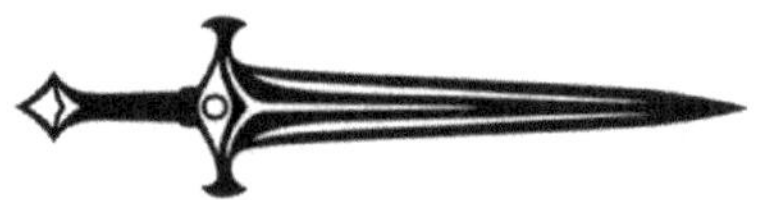

The throne room was everything I'd expected from our scaly dickhead friends: ornate, ostentatious, and lit by braziers that cast more shadows than light. Clever, that. The dim illumination would work well for creatures whose eyes were better suited to darkness than mine.

The chamber stretched at least thirty meters from end to end. Towering columns rose to support what remained of the domed ceiling, and a shitload of weird trees twisted and dripped water everywhere, adding a hell of a lot more moisture to the air in here than there was outside usually, I bet.

Well, you know, when I hadn't just summoned the mother of all storms down on their heads anyway.

Tapestries depicting various lizard folk triumphs hung between the columns, though several were now smoldering from my dramatic entrance. At a glance, I saw it had depicted handfuls of prisoners being dragged, apparently screaming, from their houses to be gutted and eaten, so setting fire to them wasn't any great loss to the artistic world, I decided.

Ten guards stood in formation around the room, each bearing a halberd that gleamed dully in the flickering light. Their scales were darker than the ones I'd fought outside, as was their armor, probably marking them as elite warriors. Behind the ornate throne, on either side, two massive shapes lurked in the shadows. Just in case, I fired off an Examine and grunted at the results I got back, absorbing the information as much as reading it.

Shadow Guard Wyvern	**Dungeon Guardian**
Shadow Guard Wyverns represent a fusion of bestial might and tactical cunning. These creatures are living weapons, their very existence a testament to the dungeon's desperate need for apex predators capable of challenging even higher-tier threats. Their scales have evolved into a dark, almost liquid-looking armor that absorbs both light and kinetic energy, making them deceptively durable for their tier. Each beast measures six meters from snout to tail, with proportionally massive wings that they use more for intimidation and combat positioning than true flight. What makes them truly dangerous isn't their raw strength, though that's considerable, but their predatory intelligence and pack tactics. In the wild, they fight with an instinctual choreographed precision, one driving prey into the other's killing zone, using the shadows of their lair to devastating effect. In pairs, they've been known to take down small dragons, though such victories typically cost at least one of the pair their life. When faced with multiple higher-tier opponents, however, they quickly find themselves outmatched due to their limited range and stamina.	

Ability: *Shadow Merge*: Can partially phase into shadows, making them difficult to detect and granting temporary damage reduction when emerging to strike.

Ability: *Synchronized Hunt*: When both wyverns target the same enemy, their attacks become increasingly precise and powerful, building up to a devastating dual strike.

Weaknesses: Light mana, Lightning mana

HP: 300/300

Speed: 8/10

Level: 12

HP: 300/300	**Special Abilities**: 2/2

Well, fuck-a-doodle-doo. I reached out mentally for Jack and found, naturally, that he was on the far side of the compound, currently guarding a group of prisoners and slaughtering some lizardmen. That he was there with the remains of the orcs I sent through earlier was a nice surprise, I had to admit, but…I'd have liked him to come crashing through the roof right now to fight those shadowy fuckers, if I was honest.

But it was the figure on the throne that really drew my attention. He—and I used that term loosely—was the same creature I'd seen hooded and monologuing at my orcs earlier when they first arrived through the portal. And now, with his hood thrown back, I could see that he was caught somewhere between human and lizard.

Scales had erupted across half his face, and one eye had transformed into a vertical slit of amber. His other eye remained human, though the madness in it was anything but.

"Welcome, Lord of Storms." His voice carried that same sibilant quality I'd heard outside. "I had hoped you would accept our invitation."

"Invitation?" I snorted. "You couldn't have made it more obvious it was a trap than if you'd sent me a bloody dagger with the invite attached."

"It served its purpose!" he hissed. "And besides, you are unworthy of more. What? Did you expect me to invite one such as you to feast with my kind?"

"That's what you call eating people these days?" I snorted. "A feast?"

He waved a hand dismissively. The gesture might have been more impressive if his fingers hadn't ended in a mixture of broken and peeling talons and fingertips. Clearly he was mid-transformation from a worm of a human into a lizard. "Mere sustenance for my warriors. The strong consume the weak. It is the way of nature, is it not?"

"Nature?" My anger built again. "Is that what you call this?" I gestured at his half-transformed state. "Looking a bit scaly there, mate."

"This?" He actually preened. "This is evolution, pure and simple. The mana has shown us the way. Humanity is weak and fragile. But dragons?" His voice took on an almost reverent tone. "Dragons are power incarnate. I will be the first in a new race, ascending beyond—"

Lightning erupted from my left hand, blasting one of the elite guards in the face. It hurtled back, its armor conducting the charge beautifully; it thrashed and curled up, dead before it could finish raising his halberd.

"Sorry," I said, not feeling sorry at all. "But I'm on a bit of a schedule today. Got two more dungeons to clear after this one, and a lot more important shit to deal with than you. So how about we skip the 'I am become death' speech and get to the part where I kill you?"

The transformed human's face contorted in rage. "You dare—"

"Yeah, yeah, I dare." I shifted into a fighting stance. "You going to nut up or shut up?"

"Kill him!" the wannabe dragon and actual turd in a robe shrieked. His human eye bulged as spittle flew from between his increasingly pointed teeth.

The remaining nine elite guards moved with practiced precision, spreading out to surround me in a loose semicircle. Their halberds gave them reach, and in this spacious throne room, unlike the corridors outside, they had room to use them properly.

I drew my longsword in a fluid motion, the blade singing as it cleared the sheath, and I snorted my contempt. "Really? The whole 'minions attack while I watch' routine?"

The first guard lunged, halberd aimed at my throat. I deflected it with a quick parry, metal screaming against metal. Two more attacked from my flanks, trying to catch me between their weapons.

Amateur hour.

Lightning crackled along my blade as I spun. The charged metal sliced through the haft of one halberd and continued into its wielder's chest. The guard's armor conducted the electricity beautifully, cooking him inside his own protection, before I ripped it free.

"That's two," I called out cheerfully. "Anyone else want to try their luck?"

They answered by attacking as one. A forest of blades descended from all sides. I dropped and rolled to the right, coming up inside their reach. Close quarters was where halberds became a liability, considering the ten foot or so length of the haft before the bit that did that damage wasn't any use, and these idiots had just given up their spacing advantage.

My sword found gaps between scales and slots in armor as I lunged to my feet close to them. The next died with a stab through the open-faced helmet… practical when you considered the faces that the helmet contained—all pointed snouts an' shit—impractical considering the point of a helmet.

Or more importantly, the point of my sword, which stabbed into the face, skewered the brain and then was ripped free. Each strike was precise, economical. These weren't mindless berserker attacks anymore—I'd learned that lesson. As the rage tried to rise, I ruthlessly crushed it, maintaining my cold focus. Three more guards fell in rapid succession; their bodies hit the floor before the last one had finished twitching.

"Four more," I announced, kicking one of the corpses toward its companions. "Come on, surely you can do better than—"

The remaining guards proved they could, actually. One feinted high while another swept my legs. I jumped the low attack but caught a glancing blow across my shoulder that sent me stumbling. These ones had apparently been paying attention.

"Finally!" I grinned, though they probably couldn't see it behind my helm. "Someone who knows what they're doing!"

I switched to my war hammer; the sword slapped onto the sheath on my back as I dragged the hammer free and hefted it. The guards hesitated for a split second at the change in armament, just long enough for me to close with the nearest one. The hammer's head crashed through his guard, powered by my ascendant strength, shattering the halberd, armored chest piece, and rib cage.

The last three tried to maintain formation, but they were rattled now. I could see it in their movements, smell it in the air. These weren't warriors who'd faced real challenges before. Although created to be elite guards, they'd gotten soft, standing around and looking intimidating.

I feinted at one, spun past another's desperate thrust, and caught my hammer's hooked beard around the haft of a halberd, using it to yank one into the path of his comrade's weapon. Then I brought the hammer down on the third's shoulder. Bone crunched, scales split, and he went down screaming. The remaining two backed away, halberds wavering.

"Run or die," I offered, genuinely curious which they'd choose.

They chose poorly.

I left their bodies cooling on the ornate floor and turned toward the throne, where the wyverns were beginning to stir in the shadows. "Now then," I rolled my shoulder where that halberd had caught me, "shall we discuss the main course?"

The wyverns emerged from the shadows like oil flowing across water. Their scales seemed to drink in what little light reached them. Everything about their movement screamed "predator," from the way they separated to flank me to how their wings remained half-spread, ready to snap forward or back as needed.

I decided right there and then that I was having them in my upgraded minion list.

"Magnificent, aren't they?" the wannabe dragon purred from his throne. "Pure killing machines, evolved far beyond their lesser kin. Perhaps seeing them in action will help you understand what I seek to become."

"Mate, the only thing I'm seeing is another pair of corpses-to-be." I shrugged as if unimpressed. "Though, I'll admit, I'm curious what my chefs are going to do with them. Chicken nuggies are old school, and I was ready for an upgrade but yeah, I can see I'm gonna need some serious dips to go with these fuckers." I kept my hammer ready but loose in my grip, watching both beasts. Their earlier examination had warned me about their synchronized hunting tactics. No way was I letting them coordinate their attacks.

The wyvern on my left struck first, a testing lunge that I easily avoided. But that simple move had shifted me two steps closer to its partner, and I realized they were already working to control the space between them.

"Clever girls," I muttered instinctively, the comment ingrained from the movie and reinforced by the narrow faces they had before I launched myself straight at the left one. It reared back, surprised by the aggressive move, while its partner let out a screech and charged.

I met the charge with a lightning-wreathed hammer blow that should have caved in its skull. Instead, the beast seemed to melt into shadow at the last second, and my weapon passed through where it had been. The attack's momentum threw me off-balance, and I felt scales scrape against my back armor as the first wyvern's counterstrike barely missed.

"Fuck me, that's annoying." I spun, trying to keep both in view, but they were already moving again, perfectly coordinated. One would emerge from shadow to strike while the other faded away, never giving me a clean shot at either.

A tail swipe caught my legs, sending me stumbling. Claws raked across my chest plate, leaving deep gouges in the metal. I responded with a wild burst of lightning that illuminated the whole chamber, but they were already gone, melted back into the darkness between the columns.

"You begin to understand," the throne-sitting shit called out. "They are the perfect hunters, and you are their—"

His gloating cut off as I hurled my hammer directly at his face. One of the wyverns materialized to intercept it, taking the blow across its wing with a satisfying crunch of bone.

But that left me weaponless as the other one emerged behind me. Its jaws closed around my shoulder and whipped me back and forth. I twisted, trying to get some leverage to punch it, before it threw me across the room. I slammed into a column hard enough to crack the stone; my armor's crystal shattered as it dumped what was left of its power into keeping itself more or less intact.

"Anytime you feel like joining in!" I snarled, reaching mentally for Jack. I pulled myself up, flooding myself with lightning, then grinned as I realized where he was.

The injured wyvern was advancing now, its broken wing dragging but its eyes still gleaming with predatory intelligence. Its partner circled around, and I could feel them building up to something big.

That's when the ceiling exploded inward, showering the room with debris as Jack burst through with a roar that shook the foundations.

When they were distracted, that was when I struck. The time I'd spent fighting with Kh'aan had changed me. It'd revealed a simple truth that I'd let slide away again, as I'd reverted to fighting in the way that I knew.

I fought with the weapons that I'd trained with, with the abilities I'd earned. But the new lightning form that I possessed? That was mine too. No, that *was* me.

I was the avatar of the storm, as Dante had shown us all the way in transforming himself into a living flame. I, too, could fight…but not constrained in my armor.

For me to fight as I could, as I had then, I needed to be free. The armor would only slow me, and as I hadn't the time to rip it off here, that left me seeking a "halfway house" of sorts, as I unleashed my lightning and reminded myself that I was no longer a human man.

I was no flesh and blood, unless I willed it.

As swift as thought, I changed my form—again, constrained by the armor, which limited my mobility—but I shifted from my flesh and blood into the lightning-that-had-mass version of myself.

I filled my armor, no longer confined by the speed of flesh and nerve impulses, of bones that could only slow down the manifestation of my will.

If there had been observers that mattered to me, they'd have seen the glow that shone from within my armor, the light that seared free, bathing the chamber in brilliant blue-white.

As it was, the only observers left were the wyverns and the dickhead lord of the dungeon, and they were momentarily blinded by my radiance.

That was when we struck, Jack and I both.

Jack slammed into the injured wyvern like a freight train made of metal and spite. His plasma breath ignited the remaining hanging tapestries and filled the chamber with harsh light. No more shadows for these bastards to hide in.

I moved in the same instant. My transformed state let me cross the chamber faster than they were ready for. The second wyvern tried to fade into the darkness even as it vanished, but it was too late, as lightning arced between my armored form and the columns, the metal decorations, even the abandoned weapons on the floor.

The wyvern barely got one foot to the only shadow within range a split second before I reached it, and it screeched as it was caught half-in and half-out of the darkness. It tried to run, then shrieked as I dragged it free of the darkness and back into the light by one scaly forelimb.

Its scales conducted electricity beautifully, explaining why it was marked as weak to lightning. I grinned evilly as I poured power into it, the metallic compounds of the scaling sparking and conducting.

It thrashed and tried to break free, but before it could do more than heave, lightning coursed through its body, cooking it from the inside out until its eyes literally exploded.

Meanwhile, Jack had gone to town on his. The first thing he'd done was strike it across the face with a claw, before slamming into it with a shoulder, hurling it into a column, then smashing it to the floor beneath him as it rebounded. Then he'd pinned his target: one massive foot stomped down, claws ripping through its remaining good wing…the other planted on its throat.

Then he'd smashed down, alternating bites and blows from clawed feet.

The wyvern's struggles grew weaker as Jack systematically dismantled it, eventually ending its life with a bite that separated head from body.

"Impossible!" our wannabe dragon friend shrieked, stumbling back from his throne. "You're just a human! You can't—"

"Really?" My voice crackled with power as I turned to face him. "Still thinking I'm human after all that?"

He fumbled with something at his belt—probably a weapon or a magical focus or device—but I was done playing games. Lightning lashed out, a directed bolt that picked him up and slammed him from standing before the throne and into the wall behind it. He screamed as electricity coursed through his body, his partially transformed flesh offering no protection before I cut the spell off, allowing him to crash to the floor.

"You know what your problem is?" I asked conversationally as I approached. "You wanted to become something greater than human. But you went about it all wrong. You didn't evolve—you *de*volved. Became something lesser. A predator, sure, but just another beast."

He writhed on the floor, his right arm constricted into a charred mess, his chest blackened, armor melted and damaged beyond repair, where the stupid fuck had been wearing it.

Jewels and burnt silks were exposed as he writhed, making it clear what his priorities had been. "Please," he gasped. "I can show you—"

"You can show me where your core is," I interrupted. "That's about all you're good for now."

His eyes—both human and reptilian—widened in fear. Then he jerked his head toward the wall nearby, right behind his throne.

Smart man. Would've been smarter to tell me sooner.

"If you spare me…" He started to say, and I ignored him as I turned away.

I ended him with a final blast of lightning; his body crumbled to carbon and melted metals. Behind me, Jack was already stomping forward, rearing up and splitting the hidden panel behind the wall apart with a single blow. One more swipe of his claws later, and there it was: the dungeon core, pulsing with sickly green light.

I strode forward, slapping my hand down atop the core, and nodded to myself as the system acknowledged the death of its former master and opened itself to me, linking up easily.

I released it, the connection made, and moved back, slumping onto the now-vacant throne, catching my breath. I let my form revert back into flesh and blood. As I flexed my fingers, my whole body felt weird about it.

It was definitely better doing that little trick without the armor, I decided.

Notifications flooded in about the dungeon's capture, and I opened them as I sat back, starting to read.

"One down," I muttered to myself, reaching out mentally to start the claiming process. "Two to go."

The core's light began to change, shifting from green to electric blue as my influence spread through the dungeon's systems. Soon this would all be mine to command, to cleanse, to rebuild into something better.

For now, though, I needed to do the bare minimum: stop the ongoing fights and fucking murders, establish control over the dungeon, then open the gate again, and bring through reinforcements I could trust, before I set off to help my friends.

I couldn't afford to leave the dungeon wide open for another to take as soon as my back was turned.

Congratulations, Dungeon Warmancer!

You have found an unguarded Dungeon Core and have completed your Quest!

Now is the time of choice. Do you wish to raise up another Dungeon Lord and cede control of this Dungeon to them, thereby creating another dungeon in your Vassal Empire? Or do you wish to fracture the Core, claiming its treasures as bonuses for your own Dungeon?

Rewards:

- ***A Satellite Dungeon***

OR

- ***1x Dungeon Core Shard***
- ***1x Additional Dungeon Core Bonus Research***
- ***1x Dungeon Perk***
- ***1x Tech Upgrade (Random)***

- ***1x Class Skill Point***
- ***10,000 XP***

I focused on it, not liking the options presented. There damn well had to be a third path to take, considering that the options when I deployed a dungeon were to set up a new dungeon and it could be linked to the others or not. So only offering a choice to give it away to someone as a vassal or fracture it were shitty options.

I'd accepted it as gospel when I fought Simon, but looking at it now? I just couldn't see that as the only options. It made no sense!

No, I wasn't having this. And as a powerful Dungeon Lord who had integrated as far as I had, I damn well knew there was something missing with this.

After a second of trying to figure it out, I blinked as a second thought flared for me, and I really searched the local area.

There'd been no mention of the dungeon fairy!

Now sure, the fucker might be another like Simon, who deposed his fairy. But that limp lizard dick had been halfway through turning himself into a house pet, and didn't seem the sharpest spoon in the drawer.

No, I was betting that had he tried to depose the fairy, it'd have fucked him up, so what the hell had happened to it? Searching around the room netted me no clues, and it wasn't as if I could ask the fucker now—which might have been a mistake, but fuck it.

Instead, I reached out to the dungeon, hoping that if I could connect it all up to mine, then we might get access to the logs, as I'd heard there were some there now that we'd reached Glass.

Either way, though, as I slid my mind into the dungeon space, reaching out, I wasn't prepared for the shitstorm that I found.

CHAPTER FORTY-SIX

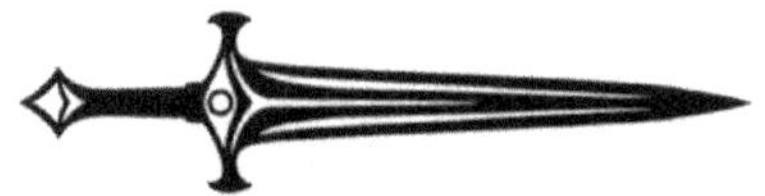

The dungeon sense was usually pretty serene. Apart from when I'd had to deal with my own highly damaged core, I'd not had a challenge in working with it. But fuck me, as soon as I connected to this one? That was turned into a fond memory.

The lack of direction in the way that the core had been layered was worse than mine had been. Some of the techs were structured in ways that left the next level of the expansion standing atop damaged pillars.

More sections were just a mess, entire areas had no support, while the next core, where the user had clearly been going all out, they had a load of different techs.

More and more as I searched, there were places that the core was failing. And touching it, even just with my mind, I felt the distant ghostly horror of the fairy that had bonded with me.

I'd never expected to feel anything from her again, but some remnant clearly remained—too little to help, too weak to communicate or lead, but enough to be horrified by the mess before me.

Regardless, though, her memory shocked me out of the frozen state of staring, and made me actually start work.

The core was open to me; it was waiting for a command, but the condition of it? Fuck me, I might shatter it by touching it. For a long moment, I considered it. *Should I shatter it intentionally? Gain another core fragment...that could bring serious upgrades to the dungeon, after all.*

No, a fragment was a waste in this situation. Not taking the entire dungeon was just stupid. Considering the area, and that there was a dungeon gate here, to fracture it was just madness. Better that I convert the whole thing into an unmanned expansionist and mana collection dungeon if nothing else...you know, if I could.

I sank into the rushing maelstrom of mana, feeling it battering me this way and that, feeling the drain on the dungeon that was coming from improperly connected conduits, broken links, and yeah, the damage to the core.

How the hell had that idiot managed to fuck the core so badly?

I dove deeper, finding that the core, at its heart, was the same as every other layer: fragmented, improperly constructed, and pushed too hard.

I had a decision to make now that I'd seen this, I knew. I could abandon it, which was probably the smartest play, or I could gamble.

If I could save the core, it'd be worth much more, not to mention establishing a foothold here, so far from home. But the risk...?

It wasn't just to me, either—it was to my friends. I couldn't see this being a fast fix, not at all. Hell, it might fail—it might explode, for all I knew. And if it did?

Not only would I be out a core, and possibly out a me, I'd be out the dungeon core shard I'd gotten from Simon's mechanist dungeon as well.

I didn't know why I'd held onto it all this time. I'd certainly not intended to. It was something I kept meaning to bloody use, but…if I used it here, there was a chance that the core material would be enough to reforge this battered POS. And if not? Well, if I was lucky, at least I'd be around to admit I'd learned something.

Worst-case scenario—because I wasn't accepting the core detonation risk; I just damn well wasn't—was that the core failed and we lost everything. In that situation, we were down a dangerous enemy, one that was a murdering fuckhead, which was a bonus.

Then, provided the entire area survived, we could fly in a new core and set up in the dungeon's place, start it from scratch and bind it to our others, or set it up as a totally fresh, unconnected dungeon and put someone I trusted in charge of it, with strict instructions.

The dungeon gate was here and that was a massive investment that had to be worth trying to save. And I'd gained other rewards, so fuck it.

I glanced back at the rewards, biting my lip, then letting out a relieved breath as the dungeon and the system, apparently sensing what I was about to try, adjusted and offered me an updated quest.

Congratulations, Dungeon Warmancer!

You have claimed and pacified an actively hostile Dungeon! As a Dungeon Warmancer, and in full knowledge of its potential and the existing damage, you have chosen to refuse the offered rewards for a chance at a greater prize! As such, you have received an updated Quest!

Save the Dungeon!

The damaged dungeon, identified as Dungeon 104, is missing both its lord—thanks to your successful attack—and its fairy, through an unknown earlier calamity. As such, the core is actively failing, and sector-clearance levels of detonation are building.

You have decided to ignore the risk, despite its clearly likely meltdown and the obvious effect: creating a new super volcano with your personage as ground zero.

Congratulations! Rarely have we seen such devotion to the dungeon expansion cause, and as such, you will receive—should you survive and succeed—consummately greater rewards:

- **1x Satellite Dungeon Facility — Linkable to your other holdings**

AND

- **1x Additional Dungeon Core Upgrade Path**
- **1x Dungeon Perk**
- **1x Tech Upgrade (Random)**
- **1x Class Skill Point**
- **100,000 XP**

I nodded to myself. Well, that was a relief, after all, that it was possible to link this to my other dungeons. But the whole "super volcano" and the minor increase of the reward for claiming and repairing the dungeon coming to ten friggin' times the earlier one? Well, that was slightly concerning.

A better description was probably "brown trousering" but fuck it, I was in the zone now.

"Jack?" I muttered absently. There was absolutely no need to say it aloud, but I did it anyway. "Best if you clear out, mate. Get higher up and out of the direct area…then at least you can tell Kelly what a fuck-up I managed, all right?"

I got an amused refusal, and when I glanced over at him, I found him stretching out, watching me.

I narrowed my eyes, about to order him, and he lifted a wing, making sure I was watching, then dragged a claw down the middle of it, parting the membrane like silk.

"What the fu—" I started to snarl; then I choked out a laugh. He'd made his position clear—he was staying with me. And considering what a shitty master I'd been to him so far, that mere gesture brought tears to my eyes.

"All right, you big daft bugger," I whispered, as he reached over to another section of his wing, pausing to look at me challengingly. "I can take a hint. Just start the repairs or whatever. I'm gonna need you flying hard to reach the others once we fix this mess."

I got a mental image of me on his back, and I nodded.

"Together," I said, and he nodded in return, before starting to repair the wing.

I saw the way it sealed over in seconds. Clearly his damage repair systems were a different grade than before—if he'd even possessed them at all—but if I challenged him, I had no doubt what the result would be.

He was staying, and I didn't have the time to fuck around anymore.

I reached into the bag of holding and dragged out the core shard, standing and striding forward to look at the core where it wobbled on its axis in the badly hidden core room.

I took a deep breath and blew it out; then I shook my head and stabbed the core shard into the shivering core before me. The entire thing stopped its frantic spin; the light flared as it lashed out in uncontrolled energy waves; mana poured off it like a waterfall. I had a split second to wonder whether I'd just made sure my atoms were about to be rearranged across the planet, before the second effect of stabbing it into a damaged core made itself felt and known.

A fucking horrific pain raced down my hand from the shard. My fingers burned and blackened; my hand reduced to carbon. My wrist was next, then my forearm as pain overloaded my mind.

I panicked, trying to wrench my arm free. But even as I tried it, I realized that time had slipped into that "wonderfully" slowed arc that was generated by cores at the very edge of implosion.

I was going nowhere fast, and I did the last thing that I could think of, as my mind raced and the destruction of my body reached for my right shoulder.

I shifted my form into that of the avatar of the storm. For a fraction of a second, I felt relief.

Instead of freeing myself, I'd just opened myself to an even deeper bond.

I was now, depending on how you looked at it, pure lightning mana, with a memory overlay that thought of itself as Matt, the Dungeon Warmancer.

What it was, without a doubt, was energy, though. And in the current condition of the core, venting a very similar, and desperately needed, energy, it grabbed and dragged me inward, its semi-sentient processor recognizing a lifeline.

Fuck me, that made it hurt even more as I was torn into the core. I frantically reached out, screaming, pushing my identity at the core, even as I tried to hang onto the last fragments of my mind.

Time seemed to freeze, completely, as the core examined me, examined the energy, the mana, and the credentials, the links that I was capable of, that I had already hooked into my soul, and finally a long-dead dungeon fairy that was reduced to a fragment of scent as much as anything else.

That triggered a desperate need—an almost infant's desire for its comforter—for the one thing, the one being that should be there to protect and guide the rudimentary sentience.

I didn't know what had happened to the fairy, but this dungeon had always known that she should have been there, and wasn't.

It felt that loss and inside it, as I dipped deeper in to its memories, trying to figure out what the hell had happened, I saw why the core was so big, and yet so weak.

It'd been force-fed the lives of thousands.

Each and every one of the people who had been murdered, chopped up to feed the saurians, had been killed with those cleavers. And those chopping blocks I'd ignored? They were more than mere fuckin' wood and metal—they were linked to conduits.

Every death had fed the dungeon, as it'd fed the lizard folk, and my God.

The idiot hadn't even tried to get the majority of technologies on each level. He'd seen a chance for transformation, to grow into what he thought would be a dragon. I didn't know if it'd been true he could—the research was stalled, and now, when I reset the dungeon, would be forever lost—but it'd come at the cost that even if it had worked, the dungeon was so unstable it'd have failed before long even if I'd not come.

I saw it all in a flash, and that as a complex manaform myself, I had an option that I'd never known before.

I could access the lower levels of the core.

The outer shell wasn't keeping me out, not the way it had before. Although I'd have loved to explore that, to see what I could learn and do, I didn't have the time to fuck around.

The shard was already collapsing. The form that it had taken for transport, that of a needle-thin wedge that widened to that of two fingers at the "thick" end, was already half gone, sucked into the core that was using it for…shitfuck!

It was using it as highly compressed energy, and burning it to give me this time in the space between seconds!

The resource that I desperately needed to use on repairs was being wasted as I mulled over the fuckin' past!

I quickly reached into the bag of holding and pulled eight of the crystals out. I couldn't risk more—I might desperately need them, after all—but I judged I could risk these. I converted them into pure mana and fed that into the system, letting loose a breath of relief as it took it and momentarily stabilizing it.

That was when I dove in, splitting the stream of matter, dragging it around, feeling weak spots in the upper core's shell. Then, not knowing whether it'd work or not, I spun it. The matter twisted by my will alone to form an infinitesimal molecule-thick tip that began to eat into the core.

I spun it faster. It was costing more mass, and therefore mana, but I didn't dare to waste any time.

The outer shell began to spall; tiny fragments almost too small to see, things that made a hair seem huge, spun up and outward as the drill bit into the shell, slowly digging deeper.

If I'd had a lip, I'd have bitten through it by now, as what felt like an eternity passed before the drill sank deep enough to let me know it was really working.

Knowing that, and that it'd take longer than I wanted to in my subjective time to get in there, I now needed to make use of the mana that was streaming free.

The core needed that, or it'd fail.

Reaching out, I started sucking it into the only conduit I had available: the sections of me that hadn't been absorbed into the core yet.

My mind seemed to split. On one side, I was left directing the "drill," digging deeper and smoothing, guiding as it went. The other half saw my mana channels, but from a whole new perspective.

As a non-human, a fucking lightning avatar and who knew what else, my usual mana core was substantially different. The channels that led to it were simply sealed to my form, demanding nothing but lightning, and that couldn't be.

The mana that was pouring loose, fortunately, was pure. But I'd already fallen afoul of the fucker once, and I couldn't risk burning myself out by exposing myself to the pure form again.

I was a child of balance, I knew now instinctively, and that was where the mana wights came in: they were corrupted by the pure mana, no longer a balanced form, with one or more in ascendancy.

That meant I needed to corrupt the pure in turn.

Well, there was a nice easy place to start, and that was with the Air.

There was a shitload of Air mana around, and as I started spinning the two forms of mana through each other, I felt the other forms that were in large quantities in the area.

Blood, Nature, Death, and more were in reasonably high concentrations for obvious reasons. But the highest after Air? The one that was only slightly higher than the Water that hung heavy in the air, thanks to the location on the coast and in such a humid place because the dungeon suited itself to its inhabitants' needs?

Lightning.

I'd created a lightning storm—hell, I'd created three. And for most of the fight when I'd been down here, I'd been using lightning again.

Thought was as swift as action. The two blurred together as I reached out, using my mana to form a funnel, one that soared out of the room I was in, up through the holes in the roof and out into the wine-dark sky overhead.

Air, Water, and Lightning were dragged inward, compressed, forced to drag up the pure mana and spin it. I recreated my normal mana channels but huge, meters across and hundreds of meters long, soaring upward.

I spun the tube, extending tendrils into the streaming mana, dragging more and more up, even as I painstakingly carved out pure Lightning, Air, and Water forms in alternate tendrils.

As the pure interacted with them, without any force to demand the contrary, it was in turn corrupted, and that grew faster and faster.

I formed a funnel at the top and bottom, sucking in at ground level and blowing out overhead, and the stars began to vanish behind building clouds.

The storm that built overhead wasn't just big—it was primal. This wasn't the carefully controlled lightning storms I usually summoned; this was raw creation, the kind of atmospheric event that reshapes coastlines and spawns legends.

The funnel I'd created became a vortex, drawing in more mana than I'd ever handled before. Pure mana spiraled upward, hitting the corrupted forms I'd crafted and splitting into its component parts. Lightning, Air, and Water twisted together in a deadly dance, each feeding off the others in an accelerating cycle.

The clouds grew so dense they looked solid, a ceiling of roiling darkness that stretched from horizon to horizon. Lightning didn't just flash—fuck no. It wrote new constellations across the sky, branching patterns that lingered like afterimages burned into reality itself. Thunder became a constant physical presence, a wall of sound that made the very ground vibrate.

Below, in what remained of the throne room, Jack watched as my form began to blur, electricity arcing between what was left of me and the world around as I channeled more and more power. The core shard was almost half gone now, but it had served its purpose. A hole was almost through the topmost layer; the damaged dungeon core began to stabilize, drinking in the converted mana I fed it.

But the storm was becoming something more than just a power source. Each lightning strike carried a fragment of my consciousness, spreading my awareness across the entire area. I could feel every raindrop, taste every electric discharge, sense the way the air currents twisted and fought.

The nearby sea itself began to respond. Waves built as the atmospheric pressure dropped to unprecedented levels. Waterspouts formed along the coast, dancing like living things as they wove between the lightning bolts. The rain, when it finally fell, came down in sheets so dense it was like the sea itself had taken to the air.

Outside of the slowed time, the world saw the mother of all storms spinning up. And had there still been meteorologists out there, they'd have been sacrificing their firstborns—or you know, knowing the one guy I knew in that trade, someone else's firstborn, as Ray wasn't getting laid this side of the sun collapsing—just in the hope of watching what was coming.

Inside the core, time moved like treacle, but the storm outside was growing exponentially. Each lightning strike fed back into the system I'd created; the corrupted mana spun faster through my makeshift channels, growing stronger with every cycle.

The pure mana converted at a ridiculous rate now, and watching it, feeling it flow through me, I shuddered with the incredible power levels.

The storm was always there in some form—the nascent potential energy that existed out there…the humidity, the wind…all delicately balanced on the edge of tipping into hurricanes and more. This wasn't just power; this was fundamental force, the kind of energy that could reshape continents if you weren't careful.

Overhead, the storm had become something unprecedented. The clouds weren't just black anymore—they had taken on a metallic sheen, electricity coursing through them constantly. The rain fell in sheets so dense that the city below was barely visible, and where lightning struck, it left glowing scars in reality that took seconds to fade.

The Caspian was raging even more now, its waters rising in massive swells that defied natural law. Waterspouts danced and grew between the lightning strikes, each one powerful enough to lift ships…if there had been any left to lift. The air pressure had dropped so low that ears would pop for miles around, though the few left alive close enough to feel it were already running in all directions.

But something was happening with the core. It had been quiet, almost dormant as I worked. But now it stirred. The mana patterns I'd created affected it in ways I hadn't predicted. The pure energy wasn't just pouring out as it had been; now, thanks to the combination of the mana that was pouring through me and the shard that I was using to drill a hole into it while gripping the fucker, I was connected even more to the core.

A core that was glowing brighter and brighter.

"Oh shit," I muttered, feeling the changes beginning to cascade. "Jack? We might have a problem…"

The core's internal structure started to resonate with the storm above; each lightning strike sent vibrations through its damaged matrix. The hole I'd drilled finally burst all the way through but the energy patterns were becoming unstable. If I couldn't balance them soon…

"Right," I muttered to myself, "time to find out if I'm actually as clever as I think I am, or if I'm about to turn Azerbaijan into a new crater."

The shard was collapsing, no longer stable enough to be integrated in the usual manner. Instead, I was breaking it down molecularly—don't ask me how; I was going entirely on instinct—as I poured forth the energy of the storm, redirecting and rerouting it, even as the sky grew colder and blacker overhead.

Thunder rolled and lightning lit the heavens, as I split streams of matter, pouring them free to twist and slide, like the building blocks of reality, to form new connections here inside the core, linking the mid and upper levels.

These would never unlock technologies; they'd not grant new abilities—as far as I understood them—but they were forming pillars that would support the core.

As they linked between the upper and mid layers, they branched out, great supports shifting and forming fresh tectonic plates.

Where in a healthy core the entire thing should be solid—more or less, anyway—here, there wasn't that option.

The lowest level of the core was barely solid as a base. The next had a dozen sections that branched out, but they were unstable. And the third were grouped too close together as the Dungeon Lord had single-mindedly focused on his desires.

That meant that I could either try to reforge the entire core—which might take days of effort, even in here, and still come to nothing—or I could do what I did best and botch it together, hoping for the best.

In drilling through the upper layer and reforming that with the next, forming a much more solid and cohesive shell, I'd staved off the immediate failures and fractures.

The next level… I had possibly enough matter to drill my way through to the next layer, to save it and reform it, but I knew I didn't with the lowest, and I certainly didn't have the time.

That gave me only two options. And as one of them was "run like my ass was on fire," I'd started on the other before I'd had the time to consciously decide.

The storm above—it was no longer *a* storm, but *the* storm—was already rolling beyond my infant Storm Titan's ability to control.

Instead, I pulled the plug, no longer feeding it, and ripped the spires that extended into the funnel free. I reformed the funnel, twisting it around, sucking down rather than up, to form four tunnels that twisted and wove around one another.

First came the Lightning. I fed it through me, leading the way and pouring into the core.

I connected all that I could, shifting the core layers and forcing them from the semi-stable, semi-failing pattern it was locked into, and snapped the connections from the lower and upper layers free.

The shock and pain of that reverberated through the core and the light flared, then dimmed, and then flared again.

"Come on…you can do this!" I forced out from between gritted teeth as I fought to guide the mana in the right ways, through channels I was creating on the fly. "Keep it together!"

The next layer down, where there were only a few connections between the lower and upper cores, shook and trembled. Power flared and leaked, as entire sections of the core failed. Blackness spread, even as I slammed power into them, the lightning surging again and again.

The second funnel was forming inside the first. I'd delayed it as long as I could, arcing it around slowly, trying to contain it, to prevent the damage that I knew I was risking. But I couldn't delay it forever, not without losing the mana we needed.

Air was this one, and it was a tunnel inside the Lightning. Bleeding across was held to a minimum by spinning the outer layers of the funnels in opposite directions, forming a tube.

As that one slid inside the Lightning and through me, I slowly brought around the next—Water—and started its counter spin, with the fourth held back as long as I possibly could.

The mid-level of the core was flaring now, beating like a heart in panic. The lower levels were deteriorating, the upper had broken free, and it was only the constant pulsing of lightning into it that held it all together.

That was when I pulled.

The conduits ran from the smallest core up and out, leading from core layer to core layer, with more added as each layer grew.

So many of them were broken already that I needed to be careful…tugging, gently guiding instead of yanking. But as the core started to move, I made more changes, hoping that the power I was feeding the core would be enough for it to accept the changes and make them work.

On the upper to mid layers, I'd created a small section, at the north and south poles where all the conduits flowed in and out.

They were sealed into a section that adjusted for the slowly rising spin of the layer below, and then they fed it out.

My own core was like this—it was a spinning core suspended between two spikes—so I knew it was possible to do it, for the core to locate all the conduits and flood them through. But, for whatever reason, this one wasn't; it was scattered about with the connections, probably because the fucker was so unstable.

That meant that I needed the lower levels of the core to reform, to accept the input at the poles, because if the lowest levels failed and died entirely, then the dungeon was fucked.

Alternatively, the upper levels could never grow if the lower ones weren't at least semi-stable.

I'd formed a solid shell between the mid and upper levels, so that was fine, but the lower ones were barely a hairsbreadth from collapse. And I couldn't reach all the way through them all, not in the time I had.

That left me with one option as I saw it, and the Earth was my guide.

Tectonic plates moved slowly, sliding under each other and freeing more up, new sections; new continents rose and fell, and the world changed all the time.

For a planet-sized structure, it was impossible to see it happening in real-time, but here with the shell being the way that it was, and as small as I could grow to see the details, I knew that there was a chance.

As the lower levels began to spin, I did the only thing I could, and I started to feed it more power.

The Lightning was first, powering through me and into the core, slamming into it, like a cosmic-scale defibrillator, pulsing power—and life—into the core over and over again, providing the naked surges it needed.

Next, I connected the Air funnel, pouring more mana in and breathing across the shell. The upper layer to the mid drew it in, accepting it—with difficulty, but accepting it—as it was all that it had.

Next came the Water. Inside the shell, great oceans poured forth, rolling across continents formed by my will.

The lower levels began to accept the power being pulsed down to them, and they adjusted. The core no longer battled to stabilize the upper, mid, and lower segments. The lower snapped free, simply focused on that: reforming, adjusting, and following my lead.

Where I couldn't reach, the core itself—semi-sentient and designed to maintain itself—now took my guidance, presumably as it would have done from its fairy. The lowest level began to form and reform. The pillars that led from that level to hold the next, now broken, were reabsorbed into the lower core, and it began to pick up speed, spinning.

The magnetic field generated from the spinning of the lower levels, combined with the conduits linked at the north and south poles, shifted enough that the shell that surrounded it slowly realigned.

It no longer bobbed and weaved, on the verge of collapse. Instead, it evened out, the Lightning, Air, and Water mana all helping it to reform.

That was when the fourth funnel filtered through, and I unsealed the end.

The pure mana roared out in a heartbeat. All the lost pure mana that I could find filtered through. Constrained by the three counter-rotating funnels it was held inside of, the bleed-through into me was minimized.

Instead, it slammed into the core—its designed and most perfect form of energy input, its reason to exist…to purify and refine mana to reach this pinnacle—and the effect was instantaneous.

The core flared again, this time the blue-white suffused with gold. And then the heartbeat of the core stuttered, before slamming into a fast staccato rhythm.

Systems all around me flared then stabilized, rebooting. More and more of the core came online. The sensations of the dungeon spread, as numbed and phantom limbs reawakened; sensations like pins and needles in a sleepy set of fingers accompanied the reconnection of sections of the dungeon that had been barely operable at best.

Now they were restarting, conduits restoring, though it'd be days before they were solid and fully aware again.

For now, though, I didn't have to care about that. I stepped back, time having restarted at some point in the last few hours for me, and minutes for the rest of the world. I felt the steadying claw that Jack braced against my back, before helping me to the throne, where I slumped again, catching my breath.

"Fuck me, that was an experience…" I mumbled, reaching up and resting my head in my hands.

Long minutes passed as I lay there, half sitting, half slumped, before I became aware of a distant jingling sound.

I slowly raised my head, twisting to look over at the front of what had been the throne room. To my fucking great surprise, it was packed.

I blinked, totally taken aback. As in that way that the world can, when you rise from a deep sleep, the local sounds filtered in gently at first, then those of slightly farther away, then more and more until I found I was slumped in a bloody throne, in full, blood-covered armor, staring out over a sea of easily hundreds of people.

Front and center were the surviving three orcs. Behind them were several dozen of the saurians, and beyond them were, well, people.

Hundreds of people, mainly in absolutely tattered and filthy rags. Some in the remains of Western clothing, some wearing more Middle East and Asian outfits, some partially or even fully naked.

They came in every shape, nationality, and size. The one unifying feature was that they looked, with the best will in the world, like shit.

"What the fuck happened to you all?" I muttered, not thinking about it, as the orc Grokmar, their leader, stood proudly.

"We find." He clapped his first to his chest. "We win. Then dungeon change, and we know you lead us again here. All is right, so we bring your tribute."

With that, he gestured out across the gathered, clearly fucking terrified people and the confused saurians, and once again I face-palmed.

"Oh, for fuck's sake! I don't even know where to start with this shit, that's so wrong!" I moaned into my hand, before straightening slowly, at a thought. I reached out, feeling the connections that were forming. Although the link between the dungeons wasn't solid yet, there was one thing I could do that would fix it, tout suite.

I pulled up my notifications, flicking away the kills again from before as they tried to wave at me, and focused on the one that was actually helpful.

Sod all the rest—that class skill point was being spent, and there was no doubt as to what it was being spent on. As much as I'd have loved to look through and spend it on something that was more fun, I knew what had to be done.

> *Evolution: Gates!* No longer is the Dungeon a distant creation. This skill unlocks the creation of the Gates, transportals that can be built inside the Dungeon and activated at a remote location to provide a stable link between the two points.
>
> *This skill ranks in levels from 0 (Single Gate) to 5 (Unlimited)* (Current level: 2, Duodecad).

It wasn't as fun as I'd have liked; it wasn't a power surge that would let me topple high mountains or fuck more shit up. But damn, it was needed.

I puzzled over the word for a while, then shook my head and just checked the gates that the system now identified as "available" and worked backward.

"Huh," I muttered. Apparently "duodecad" was some posh, formal name for twelve. Who knew that kinda shit?

With the bonus gate that I'd received as a perk a while ago, this brought me to thirteen in total, which was definitely going to be unlucky for some. With the six in use, I now had seven spare.

Well, six actually, as the gate here was still coming back online now, and as soon as the connection stabilized, it was going to use a gate slot, or license or whatever it was classed as.

Fortunately, as the systems stabilized, even as I looked, I managed to make a solid connection, and nodded to myself as the number flickered from seven available to six.

"Gotcha." I smiled, then forced myself to my feet. I reached out into the dungeon sense; both my own home dungeon and this one suddenly merged, flows buffering against each other.

"Matt?" Kelly gasped into my mind. "Oh, thank fuck. You're okay?"

"I am," I said to her, smiling. "But I need you to send Ashley and her 'hearts and minds' team. There's a lot of people who need her help here."

"On it. But I need you to get to the next dungeon. The shit's hit the fan and we need to shore it up!"

"Explain on the way!" I agreed, before switching to speak to the confused residents of the throne room.

"I have help incoming for you all, and an explanation. But for now, rest, recover, and no fighting or fucking eating each other! I have to go, so…" I couldn't help it, as a long-buried memory fought its way up from my boots and out of my mouth before I could think better of it. "Be excellent to each other!"

Bill and fuckin' Ted strike back.

With that, I launched myself through the holes in the ceiling. Jack thundered after me, even as I locked the dungeon down to my command group, including Ashley, and allowed her primary authority here in the absence of Kelly, Aly, or myself to assign others access.

Then we spun, me landing atop Jack's back as he arced and aligned on the next dungeon, and started to beat his mighty wings.

CHAPTER FORTY-SEVEN

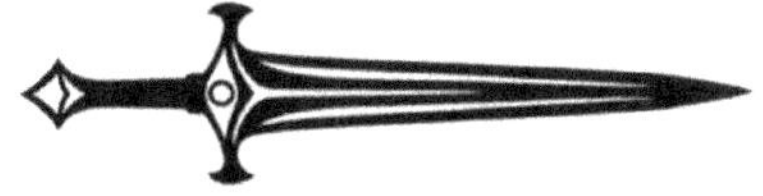

The miles were already flowing back under Jack's mighty body, his wings beating hard. I hunkered down, taking advantage of the establishing field around the dungeon and the Reach Out and Touch Me skill, to maintain contact with Kelly for a short while at least.

"Okay, fill me in." I shifted my mind into the dungeon as my body physically clung to the back of the dragon. In seconds, I stood before her, Clarissa, Aly, and Markus.

"You first," Kelly said. "Is the dungeon secure?"

I glanced up at the still swelling storm that spread across the area, now literally miles wide and thundering fit to break the sky.

"Secure, maybe. It's ours at least, and the control center is solid. I've designated you, Aly, and Ashley to have authority to fix it up—sorry Clarissa and Markus, I didn't think you'd be awake so didn't include you at that point."

"Well, the shit hit the fan…that's the way it is." Kelly sighed. "What happened?"

"Well, as I said, shit, basically." I settled into my mental projection before Kelly, Aly, and the others. "The lizard dungeon was worse than we thought. They weren't just hostile—they were using it as a slaughterhouse for humans. Literally a meat-processing facility."

I ran a hand through my hair, grimacing. "We took them down hard, but discovered a problem with our new armor. It's got some kind of berserker enchantment. I totally lost control, right up until a cannonball to the face broke me out of it. We need to warn everyone wearing the new sets, and scrap them until we can figure a way around it, or just replace them without the enchantment."

I paused for a second as a nearby boom of thunder and sheet lightning lit up the sky, with rain thundering down across a land that barely knew the concept under normal conditions.

"The core was completely fucked, missing its fairy and damaged from shitty upgrades. Instead of shattering it, I gambled on repairs. Used the core shard I'd been holding onto and channeled a massive storm through the damn thing to stabilize it. Had to reorganize the entire core structure using Lightning, Air, and Water mana. It worked, but it was close. And there's now an out-of-control super-storm in the area, so yeah, there's that too.

"The dungeon's secured now, though, and while it's still linking to our network, so long as the gate is active it's connecting both sides together. There's a few of the orcs left alive, a bunch of lizards that are going to need serious therapy to understand that people eating is a no-no—or, better yet, the headsman. And I found hundreds of prisoners who need help. That's why I wanted Ashley's team heading there to handle that situation. But Kelly says there's trouble at the next target, so Jack and I are en route. What's the situation there?"

I fixed Kelly with a stare, and she blinked, obviously processing that little info dump, before clearing her throat and nodding.

"There were heavy losses in the original dungeon-born assault, and then we lost contact with both teams shortly after they crossed over," she said. "The armor berserker mode is probably going to explain a lot of that. But is it going to be dangerous for you to deal with them if they're as confused as you say you were?"

"Maybe, maybe not," I disagreed. "I knew who Jack was, and maintained my contact with him the entire time I was there, even through the times that I had no clue what was going on. I think the enchantment is going to be a complex one, now that I've had the time to think about it a little. If you triggered something like that with any team, and didn't have an inbuilt friend-or-foe thing, you'd just lose everyone, so they should be able to recognize me still. For values of 'should,'" I said.

"Well, that's a relief." Kelly sighed. "Okay, that's one problem. And you're en route…how long?"

"A couple of hours," I admitted. "I'm about twelve thousand miles from there at the minute, so three or four hours at least."

"Well, the chances are the whole situation will be over by then. I'd hoped to get you there sooner, but…" She shook her head, looking frustrated, then covered her eyes and spoke up quickly.

"Shit, I'm sorry, Matt. I know you've been going as fast as you could…I'm just thinking aloud." She looked at me, clearly hoping I'd not been offended.

"It's fine," I assured her. "Look, Jack's pushing hard, and the connection behind me is still forming. Once the gate closes, I'll probably lose you. Anything else to report?"

"Yes!" She straightened up, taking a deep breath, and went on quickly. "We've got even more confusing information out of London."

"Oh, for fuck's sake, what now?" I growled.

"We've got a warning from the earl…" She paused. "He's asking us to reroute, because there's likely to be an attempt on the core, and asking us *not* to tell him where or how it's traveling."

"What?" I asked, now thoroughly confused. "I thought we knew that he was going to make an attempt on the damn thing!"

"He's said that he's gone ahead, as was agreed with us, with the setting up of the area ready for the core, but that he's heard internally that there's been a sudden unexplained movement of troops, one that's being hidden as much as possible. He thinks that his report on the core transportation is the only likely reason, and that if we don't divert or switch up the guard, then there's going to be an attack on it."

"What the fuck is going on!" I snarled. "I mean, seriously, are they all playing their games? This is worse than that fuckin' thrones series!"

"If I may?" Clarissa spoke up; I looked over at her and gestured to go ahead. "Do you think the earl can be trusted?"

"Possibly," I said slowly.

"No, Matt. Do you think you can trust the earl—not their confidants, not their companions or political affiliations. You and Kelly spent a substantial time with the earl and his wife, talking one-on-one. You've proved adept at seeking out people who are genuinely in the dungeon for the good of the many so far, in promoting those you have trust in. By and large, that's worked out well.

"Where we've had issues has been in others, in people you've frequently disliked outright straight from the start, and then in situations where we, and I mean *all* of us, have saddled you with the need to give people chances. There were some of the people I brought with me, who I felt I had to offer a chance to, and that you honored.

"There were your old neighbors, there were members of the army, and now the London delegation. Each and every time you've reacted badly to them, you've masked it as well as you could. This isn't to say you're perfect, but by and large, you've known. Do *you* believe we can trust the earl and his wife?" She fixed me with a patient gaze.

"I… I think so?" I said after a few seconds' thought. "I mean, I didn't get that 'snaky motherfucker' feeling from him or his wife. They've hidden shit, but…"

"But they're not close allies and friends, not yet," Clarissa said. "So before we jump to conclusions, let's consider the position we've put them in, and look at their actions with an eye to trusting them instead." She summoned a tea set and started to make herself and Markus one as she went on.

"First, they join the meeting as a third party that represents a faction in the government. They have power, but less than they'd like, and are trying to do the honest thing. Does this match with what you've seen?" She glanced at me, eyebrow arched.

"Yeah, pretty much. They hate Johnstone and Trust as well, which earns them extra points in my book," I admitted.

"And with that in mind, they appear to have pulled that pair's teeth, forcing them to step back, as you responded better to the earl, gaining them, and their faction, better standing in the government. Agreed?"

"Yeah?"

"Now, if we follow this logically, we expected them to raid us, so you set up the fake core, and gave them a warning about it, while setting it out as a target. What did you expect them to do with that information?"

"To report it."

"To whom?" the older lady said crisply, stirring a single sugar into the cup then tapping her spoon lightly on the rim, filling the air with a chime of good chinaware.

"To their faction, and from there to the other factions."

"Excellent. That was what we expected. And did they warn you they'd have to do this?"

"I think so." I shrugged, glancing at Kelly.

"They did," she agreed. "They said that they'd pass word on the clear path."

"Okay, so if they did this, and they are in turn entrusted with the rebuilding or changing of a section of London…you said that you gave them directions to do that?"

"Yeah. Then we saw them through the dungeon sense. Turned out that his wife is the field marshal, and she's basically leading all the soldiers around, making them clear out and fix up the area we recommended," I said slowly.

"So she and her husband the earl are busy sorting out the area you told them to, and then what?" Clarissa asked.

"We heard them setting up a fake core area to keep it hidden," I said softly. "I assumed it was to be hidden from us, when we go looking, because they've raided and stolen the core."

"What if instead they're acting with honor?" Markus interjected. "What if they trust their fellow factions as much as we do? If they gain access to the dungeon and set it up there, and then another faction tries to take it from them, the fake core makes sense."

"Then they've passed on the route, ordered it be left alone, and are now what? Being kept out of the way while the core raid goes on without them?" I asked.

"Probably." Aly snorted. "If they're anything like we think, let's say that they reported it; they find out the suspicious side of things, or they have a fit of conscience, and they decide it's not worth the risk?"

"Then they report it to us. That could be fucking their own side over, but if they think that the raid will be unsuccessful, or a trap, it's the smart thing to do. It keeps them in with a chance." I grunted. "That or they're playing a double bluff."

"Maybe, but again, benefit of the doubt—if they are truly being honest here, there's a possible ally to be recruited. At worst, they could have given us this warning too late. It's mere hours from the attack, from what we can tell."

"And they asked us *not* to tell them the changes," Kelly said. "If they knew there's a chance the report gets out…"

"You think they're actually on the level?" I blinked.

"I think there's a chance," she admitted. "And if they are, what do we do? If we let the other factions take control of the core, I mean, we know it's a fake, but they won't. If another faction has taken the core, and the group have no idea it's fake, they're going to set it up where it's best for them, not where we've recommended. London's a big place. We might not be able to work with it."

"There's a signal crawler there, right?" I asked Aly, who nodded.

"A seeker," she corrected. "There's one in the fake core so we can track it, but London is a big place—over five hundred square miles. And if it's even ten miles away from our site, it could take weeks to reach the new location."

"Then there's no choice," I said. "We need to deliver the core to the earl, because without it we lose our leverage and expose the setup, if nothing else."

"We'd be giving him, and London, a dungeon," Markus cautioned.

"Do we have a choice?" I glanced around.

"How would we even do it?" Kelly asked, and I saw looks ranging from disapproval to agreement on the others' faces.

"Honestly, I'm going to take advantage of the situation here." I grinned at her. "I'm on the back of a dragon, flying from one fight to the next, so I'm going to leave this entirely up to you to sort."

"You bastard." Kelly swore, but I saw the edge of a smile tugging at her lips. "You're fine with me giving the dungeon core to him, though?"

"The fake?" I asked. "Yeah. Not the real one…at least not yet."

"Glad we agree." She smiled clearly now.

"Wait, you fucker!" I gasped. "This was what you wanted me to say?" I realized as I replayed the half glances and the phrasing she'd used.

"It's what I think is the only viable move here," she admitted. "It makes getting the core to the location his problem, it makes the setup we've bled over still work, and it gives us access to their mana and tech base. But I want to add that if it looks like they won't get it, I want to have the sentinels destroy the core, and detonate their own."

"What kind of devastation are we looking at?" I asked.

"Substantial," Aly advised. "A few hundred meters in all directions will be toast, essentially. That could be a lot of deaths. We make it out that this was a test due to their actions before, and we can still deliver the core to the earl, but we ask for a reasonable price for it."

"And that would be?" I asked.

"Honestly, whatever I can come up with at this stage," Kelly admitted. "You want to deal with it?"

"Nope. On the back of a dragon, on my way to war, remember?" I pointed out.

"Then you'll be happy with whatever I manage to get us then," she suggested.

I nodded. "I will," I agreed. "Okay, just to reiterate, the shit's hitting the fan at both of the last dungeons, and— Wait, weren't you going to have the dickheads from London with you right now?"

"They're with me here in the arena," she agreed. "We went ahead with the meeting idea, and have a few people there still. Notably, the earl and his wife are part of it. And if he knew and he's playing us for a fool, then he's a better actor than I thought. A messenger arrived for him and he stepped out to take it—that's how he knew. His wife is good as well. She shut down everything beyond a bit of anger and cold 'let's deal with this.' But him? Furious," Kelly admitted. "Struggled with it for about thirty seconds, then just went for it…asked to speak to me privately and laid the whole thing out."

"And you're still there?" I asked.

"Next door to them. The others are mainly Dungeon Lords or their representatives, and they understand the whole 'we're under attack and we've gone into lockdown' story. They're not happy, but they know that the invading forces got absolutely slaughtered as soon as they arrived, and they're using it as an opportunity to forge some alliances. I think we've made a good impression on a few who weren't sure about us."

"Anything else I need to know?" I asked, feeling the connection wavering.

"Only that I love you," she said quickly, as Aly spoke up.

"Matt? Do your best?" she asked. Her silence so far spoke volumes about her self-control, considering Mike was currently in the farthest dungeon away.

"I will!" I assured them all, feeling the connection failing. "Tell Finn what I said and that…"

Then it was gone. I felt shaken to my core as I was slammed back into my body, now hunched over atop a dragon. I blinked at my hands where they gripped a spine ahead of me. The water-attenuated bloody mess that had covered me now streamed away across his side.

"Fuck," I snarled, before closing my eyes and mastering my emotions. There was nothing I could do from the back of Jack to help beyond what I was.

This time, it was down to everyone else.

CHAPTER FORTY-EIGHT

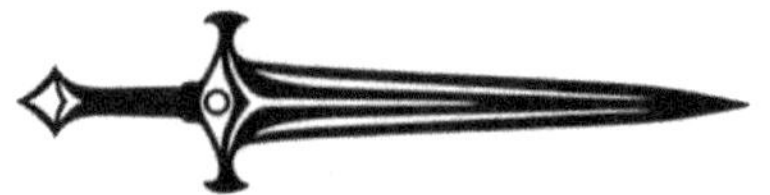

The flight was longer than I'd have liked it to be, that's for sure, but Jack managed it in about three hours, most of which was spent flying over devastation.

The miles blurred beneath us as Jack's wings beat steadily through the bitter night air. We crossed eastern Turkey in a blur. The devastated terrain told its own story: abandoned highways like broken spines across the land, occasional clusters of torchlight marking survivor outposts in the darkness.

The November wind chilled even my armor, making me shiver slightly. I hunched down closer to Jack, trying not to think about how many humans would be alive, come spring. This winter had come early and brutal. Snow already blanketed the higher elevations we passed, and considering that I was passing close by and soon to be over the Mediterranean Sea, snow wasn't exactly something everyone here accepted as part of life.

The Mediterranean slowly appeared and then stretched ahead, its waters rough and wild. We dipped low, scudding across the whitecaps, trying to keep as low a profile as possible, while still seeing what was going on.

Finally, in the distance, marked by sporadic gunfire, Mount Attavyros emerged through the pre-dawn gloom, its peak lost in storm clouds. The scattered lights of the city of Rhodes whipped past as we lifted on the wind, passing over it close enough I felt I could have reached out and touched the ancient city. Fresh scorch marks on the buildings below suggested we weren't the first to visit recently.

I didn't know what the hell had happened here, nor why the shitting fuck of a goddamn necromancer had chosen to set up here. But this was where the seeker had indicated for the necro base, and there sure as shit was plenty of indications that our people were here.

Namely, as Jack flared his wings, beating them hard to land atop the restored Temple of Zeus, it was bugger all like it'd been described to me.

The whole area had been a ruin, according to the dungeon-born who stepped through: a collection of smaller buildings that seemed rakish and barely holding together, along with passages that led downward into the main dungeon, was what she'd described.

When Jack landed, though, it was anything but that.

I'd seen pictures of the Temple of Zeus, and yeah, this was *a* temple of Zeus, not *the* temple, but damn someone had gone all out with the rebuild.

It was somewhat similar to the Parthenon, in that it was made of marble, massive, and surrounded by huge pillars that supported a peaked roof.

The spaces between the pillars—unlike in our version in bloody Newcastle—were open, and inside was a walled-in sanctuary, a second sort of building that was only for the righteous—read "rich" here—and it was beautiful.

That was clearly what they'd built recently, but how the hell they'd built it in such a short time, I had no clue. I was betting, considering that the entire area was defended—*was* being an important word here—and there was both snow and bodies strewn about, as well as dirt and the signs of wear and weather on the building, that what the dungeon-born had seen was some kind of an illusion.

Either way, though, what I saw right now was a clusterfuck. There looked to be three different groups represented in the bodies that lay cold below me.

First, and it broke my heart to see it, there were a lot of my dungeon-born: Scepiniir, kobolds, goblins, and yeah, humans…some of which I recognized. I jerked my gaze aside, refusing to look as I felt a responsive surge of anger.

The last thing I could afford was to lose myself to the bloody rage thanks to the armor, and although the crystal that powered it had cracked, I didn't dare risk it.

There were hundreds of dead, and more were fighting behind hastily formed barricades against what looked to have been waves of incoming forces.

The second group were, yeah, the undead. I'd expected to see them here, but what I'd not expected to see were the fairies and cyclops.

Well, I didn't know what the hell the singular was for a cyclops…cyclops? Were more than one cyclopeses? Fuck it, one-eyed non-trouser snake-looking mofos.

That was what I was seeing here. And they looked to have fallen in battle against both sides?

I tried to read the fight, but gave up after a few seconds. Whatever the story was, I had people down there now, and they were in danger. Everything else could be sorted out later.

"Looks like you're staying up here, buddy," I said softly to Jack, knowing he'd hear it. I stepped off his back and hopped down to land on the roof by a clawed foot. "Defend those of our people who are left and help them as best you can."

"*Overwatch*" was the best way to describe the thought that came from him—a combination of images, of feelings and understanding. Again, it wasn't quite words, but we understood each other instantly. He released the roof and leapt backward, wings beating, even as I twisted and leapt as well, plunging from the roof to do—yeah, I know it's cliched, but fuck it—a three-point superhero landing.

The next image from him—well, it had to be dragged from my memory, but clearly I'd been sharing too much with him, because it was a serious hot-looking female actress, the Widow one, in all the leathers, doing the same move.

Except with my face on her, looking bloody demented.

"I hate you!" I called up to him as I bounded to my feet and sprinted for the passage that led downward out of the night.

I'd seen gunfire in the distance when I'd been on approach. But by the time we arrived here, what looked to have been the most recent assault had been beaten off. So that was Jack's first mission: find where they were coming from and torch it.

As soon as I'd landed, a cheer had gone up from a few of our people. I felt a surprising surge of relief as Robin and Rathaharn strode over to me, along with one of the priest trainees, and a sergeant I didn't remember the name of.

"Robin, what's happened here?" I asked her, singling her out as my first Paladin.

She nodded, removing her helmet and saluting, fist to chest. "Dungeon Lord."

I smiled, waiting. No matter how many goddamn times I told her, she kept that bloody formality.

"The others are inside. We've lost a lot of good people, but we're holding the line now, though we're low on ammunition. I don't suppose you have any?"

"Not in amounts that would make a difference," I admitted, though I pulled out five magazines for the assault rifle and handgun, handing them over.

"Thank you." She sighed. "Anything is better than nothing at this stage. We knew there was likely to be a lot of them, but they just keep coming."

"Are they local to the area or being summoned?" I asked.

"Summoned. We keep seeing the surge of light," she said. "We can't hold all the areas they're using, though, so as soon as we capture one, they just move to another."

"Well, Jack's here now and—" I broke off as he raced past farther down the hill; his plasma breath carved a divot into the ancient hillside that reduced his targets to charred remnants even as they appeared. "Well, that, basically." I shrugged. "Jack should be able to help you for now. Where are the others…inside, you said?"

"Aye." She nodded. "Chris and the others are in there. I said we'd hold the line here, while they went for the kill."

"Okay, hold on…if you need to, fall back and we can have Jack reduce the fucking hill to cinders," I agreed. "I'll go back them up. Before I go…any problems with the armor?"

"Armor?" She frowned, glancing at her own. "No? It's great."

"The armor like mine," I clarified, knowing that she'd wanted to keep her current set that Rathaharn was training her and her teams in, but that Chris and a handful of the others had been in newer sets similar to my own.

"Well…" She hesitated, then saw the impatient look I was giving her. "There were a few incidents where people were pushing a lot harder than was safe, and they wouldn't listen, but that's it."

"That's a fucking relief then." I sighed. "Right, hold on, I'll be back as quick as I can."

My mission, as I thundered down the slanted passage out of the Greek night, passing marble slabs forming the walls, floor, and ceiling, torches that burned fitfully to try to dispel the gloom, and the remains of fighters, was to figure out what the fuck was going on, and save my people.

Chris, Captain Rhodes, and a team of her brightest stars had been put together for this assault. Although "brightest" wasn't exactly the word I'd usually use to describe Chris, the big bugger was that, and he was a powerhouse in his own right.

He'd also been joined by his girlfriend, Becky, which was unusual in itself.

Mainly because this was the first time in ages that Becky had been out on a mission. When she'd known that the target was the undead, she'd asked to be in on it.

I'd had no problem with that, generally, but she was seriously under-leveled and underpowered for a real fight, which had made me ask her directly, with Kelly by my side, what the hell was going on.

"I need to level my class, and well, the best way I can see to do it is the undead, all right?" she'd said, making me blink.

"Your class is a…" I prompted, having forgotten the name, but I damn well remembered the effects.

"Fey Wrangler." She sighed. "I don't know how to describe it, except that it's not what I thought when I took it, okay? It requires souls to grow, and I mean literally grow. The more souls I tear apart and feed the class on, the stronger I'll get. I understand this sounds creepy as all hell, and yeah, again, seriously not happy here about it, *but…*" She paused, her arms folded across her chest as she glanced from Kelly to me and back again, clearly thinking this was a better entreaty to make to her.

"I don't want to be weak, to be scared, or to be someone you can't rely on," she said softly. "I love Chris, I do, but I can't just be 'Chris's girlfriend' and someone he needs to protect if the shit hits the fan, all right? I'm my own person, and if my class needs souls, then I have to accept that, or abandon what could be a powerful gift. From what I understand, the longer a dungeon-born exists, the greater the chance of a soul developing, right?"

"Yeah?" I agreed, not liking where this was going.

"Then I want to be in on the dungeon attacks, because when we come across some boss-style monsters, some powerful, leveled undead, then I should—and I want to be clear…I *should*—be able to be a trump card. I can rip their soul free, and that's going to take a powerful enemy off the board, and give me a chance to level-up."

"But—and I'm not good at this, so fuck it, I'm just going to say it—you're both weak as shit right now to be doing this and undertrained, not to mention you just missed the perfect opportunity to test that, against the damn undead invasion!" I pointed out, getting a wince from both Kelly and Chris, who stood off to one side, leaning against the wall with his arms folded as well.

"I know, and I've been berating myself for it ever since!" she snapped. "I know I'm going to slow you down. I know I'm not as strong as I could be. But after last time, after the way that everyone looked at me? What the hell did you think I was going to do? It took weeks before people even spoke to me normally in the canteen after that!"

"You did rip someone's soul out," I pointed out.

"It was an asuras!"

"Which is what's left of a human soul that was carved up and used to animate a drone," I agreed. "But it's still a fucking soul."

"Look, either I can try to get stronger and try to make my life here with you all, or you can just tell me that you don't want me and I'll leave," she said hotly.

"What?" I blinked, surprised. "We do—"

"No!" She jabbed me in the chest with a finger, and I blinked. "Either you trust me and I'll stay, or you don't, in which case I'd rather go, seriously. Not out of the dungeon…I'm not stupid—and not out of your life. Don't give me that look." She twisted to rest a hand on Chris's shoulder as she said that, before looking back at me.

"But, if you don't trust me, if you don't want me here? Just say it and I'll back out of things more. You've expanded a lot from the way it was early on. There's plenty of places I can go, unless you want me gone properly?" She cocked her head at that, and I snorted.

"Becky, you know I'm shit at diplomacy, but I do care and I do try, so listen up because I'm no doubt going to fuck it up again," I said. "I like you, and he, that big lump of smelly madness, actually loves you, and if that was all I knew about you, that'd be enough. No, I don't want you gone. Yes, I am concerned about the class, mainly because by your own admission you don't understand it, and that whole 'rip your soul out and eat it' ability is fucking terrifying."

I nodded at her, and she had the good grace to nod back.

"But my concern was genuinely for you being under-leveled. If that big galoot gets hit by a truck these days, the truck is coming off worse. If you get shot or stabbed or eaten or fuck knows what? You're still a lot squishier. So here's the deal, all right?"

"Go." She readied herself.

"You want to go? You can go, but you do it with two caveats. First, if Rhodes says you do something, you do it—no backtalk, no thinking you know best. You do what she says, or you'll never go on a mission that she oversees again. As she's one of the only military leaders we currently have. That might mean no more missions period, okay?"

"And the second one?" She raised her chin.

"You keep that damn idiot under control." I nodded at Chris. "Fuck's sake, you know what he's like. I have to take a spray bottle and squirt him all the time to stop him pissing in the potted plants. See if you can't housebreak him, all right?"

That got a snort of amusement, and then a sigh and a nod. "Yeah, all right, I can try. But honestly? I blame the parents."

"Yeah, well, you know…some people." I shrugged. "You should have seen him at school…the teachers hated him."

"And the janitor, I bet." She grinned. "So, I'm good?"

"Until the next time I find a turd in a plant. Remember, he's your responsibility—train him better!" I fixed her with a mock serious glare.

"Just you wait," Chris said jovially. "I'm putting the next one in your pillowcase. You'll roll over in the middle of the night, and wa-pow! You'll know I visited you!"

"And I'll chemically castrate you," Kelly said seriously. "A tablet in your drink, like the opposite of one of those you use to fix your dick. I'll make sure it's forever floppy if you *ever* put something like that in *my* bed!"

"Oh, now there's a terrifying thought…" he muttered, apparently still considering it.

"Give it up, lover." Becky sighed, before kissing his cheek. "It's your only real talent. If that goes, you go."

That was the conversation we'd had, and it kept replaying in my mind as I raced along the passage, worried in case the next body I'd come across would be hers, or worse, one of our other people because she'd lost control.

The passage twisted downward, the marble walls scarred by weapons fire and magic alike: Patches of frost. Blackened stretches where it looked like the darkness itself had eaten the walls. And worse marked where fairy magic—presumably—had lashed out, while damaged streaks showed where return fire had found its mark. The occasional splatter of silvery fairy blood mixed with the dark, coagulated ichor of the undead told its own story.

"Subtle as a brick to the balls, Chris," I muttered, following the trail of destruction through passages and across buried intersections. I came across occasional frescos, many of which had been reduced to gravel; others showed signs of hasty attempts at defense, furniture piled against them as cover, but now blasted apart.

The sound of gunfire echoed up from below, accompanied by the high-pitched keening that only pissed-off fairies could manage. I spun, pausing to try to work out the direction the sounds were coming from. Then I set off thundering along another passage, augmenting my run with my flight ability, until I was literally gliding faster than Usain Bolt could have sprinted—landing, pushing off and gliding, then kicking off again, hurtling along as more screams rang out. Unlike the gentle tinkling of Ciara's voice, these sounds were like nails down the cosmic chalkboard.

I paused at a junction, finding a cyclops sprawled across the corridor. The massive fucker had taken enough rounds to drop a tank, but what caught my eye was the collar around its neck: black metal etched with symbols that practically radiated wrongness.

"Well, shit me sideways," I breathed, skidding to a halt and then kneeling to examine it closer. "You weren't exactly here by choice, were you, big guy?"

The corridors themselves were beautiful, or had been before Chris and company had redecorated with high explosives and spells. Scenes from Greek mythology were carved into the marble: Zeus hurling thunderbolts. Poseidon commanding the waves. Even what looked like Hades in his underworld…though if that was Persephone, well, maybe I could see the whole crush thing he'd had going on for her.

Pretty fucking ironic considering what the undead had done to the place.

More gunfire erupted from somewhere ahead and distantly below, followed by Chris's distinctive bellow: "PUSH THEM BACK! DON'T LET THE FUCKERS REGROUP!"

I started to run again, following the sounds of battle. The passage opened into what had probably been some kind of audience chamber, now converted into a killing ground.

The entrance came to a raised balcony that overlooked a great hall. Spiral staircases on either side led down, and a row of gently flickering candles ringed the entire room, bringing a gentle light to what had to have been a beautiful scene once.

Now, the dead were everywhere: fairies with their bodies and wings shredded, more cyclops with those same fucking collars, and scattered among them, the desiccated remains of the undead.

Below, I could see some of our people fighting against incoming undead and more that were streaming from passages on either side. At the far end of the room, a third passage led off between two large flaming braziers.

I ran up to the edge and leapt over, twisting in midair to land smoothly in the center of the room, and unleashed a channeled bolt of lightning into the passage to the right. It brought screams and the sound of bodies being blasted from their feet. Then I ducked under a bolt of utter blackness, and sprinted for the nearest pillar, summoning a shield of lightning barely in time.

"Matt!" Captain Rhodes's voice cracked out as I skidded to a halt, firing off another blast. She was directing fire from behind a fallen column, her team methodically pinning the enemy down and back, trying to keep them bottled up in the passages. "Where the fuck have you been!"

"Traffic was hell!" I called back, ducking as a bolt of fairy magic sizzled overhead, crashing into a section of rock that shifted. The stonework started to scream, a face rising out of it to writhe and shriek insanity. "What's the situation?"

"Clusterfuck with sprinkles!" she snapped. "We've got undead commanders forcing fairy troops to fight! Some kind of control collars. Chris is trying to break through to their core room, and half my fucking team is going mad! I keep having to heal them!"

I winced, looking over at the absolutely exhausted-looking healer sprawled on the floor behind the impromptu barrier, clearly trying to meditate.

"It's the armor!" I called back. "The armor is powering a berserker rage."

"What absolute fuck-nugget thought THAT was a good idea?!" she half screamed at me.

I grinned, nodding. "Oh yeah, Finn's going to be apologizing for a while, I think!"

"He'll be doing it around my fist when I rip his balls out through his mouth!" she shot back, before unleashing another blast of concentrated fire.

Clearly the group had been fighting for a while, but the combination of Rhodes's experience and the quick work of the healer had kept them more or less on track.

I'd not have thought that a berserker rage could be "healed," but if it had a physical component, like I'd found with the adrenaline surges, I guess it made sense that could be purged at least.

A massive explosion rocked the chamber suddenly, and Chris's voice boomed out again from the third exit at the far end: "GOT IT! PASSAGE IS CLEAR!"

"Your boy's subtle as ever!" I shouted to Becky, having spotted her near Rhodes.

Her hands glowed with an eerie light as she continued her chant. Arcane symbols and lines appeared in the air as she cast whatever mad fucking spell she was working on.

She glared at me, a smear of blood and rock dust coating the side of her face, and I grinned at her, knowing that for her, this was a terrifying encounter, even without her wearing our upgraded armor.

For the rest of us, this was an average Tuesday.

She suddenly straightened up and twisted around the pillar, shrieking something in a language that I really never wanted to hear again. The glowing lights that had been hovering all around her suddenly flexed, then flattened out, smoothing through the air to form a massive, two-ringed concentric circle that hung horizontally in the air, facing the enemy.

Six circles sprang to life, spinning faster and faster in the outer ring. The central ring split into six segments, then folded inward, opening a hole in reality.

The six circles then slammed to a halt; golden chains burst free like a nest of snakes to lash out, latching onto anything before her.

A single fairy was caught as the circles began to spin again, this time counterclockwise, and dragged forward, wailing in fear and panic. But the other five chains had fastened onto another undead, larger than the normal and less, well, boney.

This was more of a zombie, or hell, I didn't have the words to identify it, beyond "that fucker's not well." As soon as the chains hit it, the Examine spell wouldn't work anymore.

All I got were a series of question marks, right up until the soul was ripped out of the body, screaming through the air.

Both souls were dragged into the void, which promptly slammed shut, before the spell vanished in a crack of displaced air.

Becky collapsed to the floor, her eyes rolling back in her head, even as what I guessed had been an undead commander collapsed to the floor, very re-dead.

"You know what? I think she might be useful after all!" Rhodes called to me, grinning fiercely as dozens of the undead staggered to a halt. "Once we've got her trained up."

"Always good to hear!" I called back. "You got this? I'll go give Chris some backup!"

"This isn't what we thought, Matt!" Rhodes cut in, her voice tight. "The undead, they're not—"

Another explosion cut her off, and the marble floor beneath us trembled. Through the smoke and chaos ahead, I could see more of those control collars glinting on fallen fairy bodies. A dozen more streamed forward, hands glowing, spells building as a pair of cyclops roared in the distance, thundering into the room to act as more or less human shields.

"Yeah," I rumbled. The anger was building but I fought to keep it controlled. "I'm getting that picture. What the hell happened? Who are the fairies and how—"

"We think they turned this place into their fucking forward base. The undead aren't coming from here, and the fresh summoned ones are generic, totally unaware and weak as shit," she replied. "These collars look like they're forcing the fairies to serve, and the big fuckers as well. They're both cannon fodder and a distraction. And as near as I can tell, the place has been stripped to the bone, so whatever the others are facing with the slavers? That has to be connected to this shit!"

"Slave collars and a dungeon full of slavers…yeah, sounds likely," I growled. "You got this?"

"When do I not?" she called back. "Fuck off and sort that magic shit out. I'll deal with the real work."

I didn't bother to argue, just pushed off, unleashing a lightning bolt to both corridors, blasting a handful of what had to be freshly summoned fairies from the air.

I ran for the passage out, bouncing off one wall and picking up speed as I took a corner. Signs of battle were ahead, including shattered stone and fallen masonry.

Hurdling a slumped form, I skidded and took the next corner. A fresh chamber opened up ahead, and I swore viciously as I took in the contents of the core room all in one go.

"Chris, you mad bastard, get down from there!" I roared up at him, where he was being shook back and forth, stabbing at a vine that was shaking him like a terrier shakes a rat.

"Try…ing…urk!" he managed to get out.

I fired off an Incinerate, aiming it at the juncture of the vine where it grew out from the rest, even as I took in the overall room.

The core chamber was huge compared to mine, at least five meters square. And unlike the cores that I had, this one looked more organic rather than technological.

It hovered in the middle of a nest of reaching branches, clearly once surrounded by leaves and flowering plants. The room must have once been a garden of wondrous delight.

Now almost all of it was dead.

A handful of vines whipped back and forth. The "tree" that seemed to be the primary housing for the core was brown and grey, with diseased-looking sap leaking from a dozen places. The vines cracked even as they waved. And nailed to the trunk—and I mean *nailed*—were a dozen fairies.

They'd been pinned in place; a design, glowing bright red and beating like a heart, was carved around them. Questing black tendrils extended from the design and stabbed into the bodies, apparently sucking the life out of them directly, even as the fairies shrieked.

Chris tumbled to the floor nearby, and I shoved out, breaking his fall and bouncing him to the side, rolling to a halt before gasping out a single word.

"Twat!" he gasped up at me in greeting, his eyes bloodshot through the visor of the helm.

I nodded. What I'd done in shoving him would have looked terrible to anyone who didn't understand.

It was what we'd been taught when we'd started rock climbing together: if someone falls, don't get under them—you'll break their fall and break both of your bones.

Instead, get to the side and shove them sideways. You'd take a portion of the impact, but much reduced, and they'd be the same as the force was redirected into a roll instead of a, well, *splat.*

I'd done it on instinct, training taking over. Although I could have flown to catch him if it'd been higher up, it was about four meters, meaning it was an annoyance more than anything.

He coughed, then retched, before clicking his helmet free and spitting onto the floor, making it clear he'd not actually gone all the way with the vomiting, thankfully for him.

"About time you turned up, shitbag," he snarled. "Just in time to take the credit, eh?" He glared at me.

I nodded again, forcing a smile. He was going to be hopped up on adrenaline, and borderline berserker at the minute. Definitely time to watch my words.

"You know me, brother. I came as quick as I could." The opening there was unmissable, especially for a dick like Chris, and I breathed a sigh of relief when he was "him" enough to take it still.

"That's what she said about you…" He grunted. "You gonna fix this or what?"

"On it, mate," I assured him, striding forward. I pressed my hand to the tree and took a deep breath, trying not to look at the fairies and hear their cries.

I pulled up my notifications, finding the usual "you have entered a dungeon" one first, and then a new one for the specific situation.

Congratulations, Dungeon Warmancer!

You have discovered an actively hostile Dungeon! As the latest adventuring party to enter the Dungeon, in full knowledge of its potential and your own capability, you have received a Quest!

Whoever rules the Dungeon, rules the land!

As a rival Dungeon Warmancer, you have entered a hostile dungeon, triggering a maximum-level response…

The Hostile Dungeon, identified as Dungeon 076, and its Dungeon Lord are now fully aware of you and your identity—and will stop at nothing to terminate you. Should you make it through the Dungeon to the Core, however, and claim control, you would receive the following rewards!

- **1x Satellite Dungeon Facility**

OR

- **1x Dungeon Core Shard**
- **1x Additional Dungeon Core Upgrade Path**
- **1x Dungeon Perk**
- **1x Tech Upgrade (Random)**
- **1x Class Skill Point**
- **10,000 XP**

Yup, so far so standard.

Congratulations, Dungeon Warmancer!

You have found an unguarded Dungeon Core and have completed the first part of your Quest!

HOWEVER, this dungeon has been infected and claimed by another, one that has refused to take the chance of exposing themselves to the risk of personal exploration.

To enforce their will, without the presence of a Dungeon Lord, they have instead infected the Tree of Life with a necrotic plague!

What will you do?

Now is the time of choice. Should you be willing to lose the current dungeon, and its inhabitants, you may claim the core and rip it free of the Tree of Life. Such an act will surely doom those that were linked to it, including the resident Dungeon Fairy, who lingers on the cusp of death as it is.

Alternatively, you may choose to claim the dungeon as a vassal, placing it and its inhabitants under your direct command and that of those you select. WARNING: Should you fail to eliminate the source of this plague before the core shatters, the dungeon will be lost to your enemy.

Rewards:

- ***A Satellite Dungeon core***

OR

- ***1x Vassal Dungeon***
- ***1x Additional Dungeon Core Bonus Research***
- ***1x Dungeon Perk***
- ***1x Tech Upgrade (Random)***
- ***1x Class Skill Point***
- ***150,000 XP***

"Oh joy…"

CHAPTER FORTY-NINE

"Please…great lord…" came the whisper from my right.

I glanced up, seeing a bulbous protrusion that swelled out of the trunk almost a meter over my head.

Like the rest of the tree, it was grey and diseased-looking, but worst of all was the fairy that I could see half submerged into the weeping and cancerous mass.

She was clearly a dungeon fairy, the cybernetic parts of her looking rusted and failing. Flickering tiny sections sparked fitfully as she struggled to lift a hand toward me in supplication.

"Please…we beg…"

"Please…"

I turned, seeing the others nailed to the fucking tree on all sides, and the golden nails that did it, that shook with each beat of their tiny hearts.

"What do I have to do?" I asked, unthinking.

"Free us…"

"Let us…die…"

"Feed…"

A dozen voices rose, some twisted with feral need, others pleading, still more confused and making no sense.

Through them all, the dungeon fairy spoke up, forcing her voice through the cacophony. The bubbling of phlegm in her throat made it hard to understand, but I got it.

"The…nails. Free…me of…them, then…kill the sour….ce…"

"The enemy dungeon?" I asked. "The undead one?"

She couldn't speak, just nodded, her head sagging to bounce listlessly.

"If I claim that dungeon and clear it of the undead that control it currently, that'll save you?" I pressed, and she managed a weak nod.

"And you'll swear to serve me as a vassal dungeon, you and all your survivors?" I pushed harder; if I didn't have this in place before the end, then she might try to wriggle out later. "You will serve me faithfully, no attempting to take over the dungeon, or to try to subvert me?"

"Made to…serve," she managed to get out. "Built…will serve you!"

"Swear it!"

"I…" she mumbled.

I shook my head, dipping a hand into my bag and tugging the sphere free. "No, you swear it on this!" I lifted into the air, offering the oath stone.

She stared for a brief second then struggled, trying to drag a hand free of the creeping engulfment of the tree. When she couldn't, I instead pressed it to her. When the notification flared before me, I cursed, having gotten more than I bargained for.

Congratulations, Dungeon Warmancer!

You have received an oath of unconditional fealty from both Xen-Xara, the Dungeon Fairy of Dungeon [082], and from the Tree of Life, through which she is bonded, tying Dungeon [082] as a vassal.

You have [17 hours, 11 minutes, 14 seconds] until the failure of this dungeon, rendering your oath to protect and cleanse her dungeon moot. Should you fail in this Oath, you will lose a consummate level of power in forfeiture for each life lost, including that of the dungeon currently rated at [Iron].

Should you succeed, you will gain the following:

- ***1x Vassal Dungeon***
- ***1x Dungeon Fairy [Bound]***
- ***[Unknown]x Fairies***
- ***[Unknown]x Cyclops***
- ***1x Fairy Dungeon Core Research Path***
- ***1x Dungeon Perk***
- ***1x Class Skill Point***
- ***250,000 XP***

I looked from the notification to the last one, then sighed. It'd been replaced, the quest altered, so I wasn't getting the original ten, then the hundred and fifty, and then the two hundred and fifty XP coming to a total of four hundred and ten. I was just getting the one set of rewards that had been scaled up to compensate for the difficulty.

Behind me, I heard more spells going off and gunfire. I glared at the fairy, Xen-Xara. "What the hell?" I asked her.

"Can't…stop!" She gasped, foam flecked with green bubbling out of her mouth. "Nails!"

"Fuck!" I reached out, trying to find them. But they were buried in the tree and the now hardened mass that had grown over her. "Where's the dungeon?" I asked her. "Is it the slavers one?"

"No…" she mumbled. "Hidden…"

"Dammit!" I snarled, dragging a dagger free and cutting into the tree, doing my best not to cut into her, but it was hard. As I did, I reached out into the quests I'd received already, namely the declaration of war.

Since that had been made, I had access to the war screen, and through that…well, I grinned to myself as I mentally viewed a map of the earth. On it, blinking merrily, were the current locations of the dungeons and individuals I was at war with.

The dungeon I was currently in was marked as "contested," clearly because I was here and the dungeon core and its attendant fairy were trying to surrender to me.

Thanks to the symbols, the golden nails, and the corruption, they were having difficulty, but the thought was there.

There was that lunatic corsair pirate woman off in the Atlantic at the minute, approaching the island of Tenerife, but I dismissed her as a problem for another day.

Next was the third dungeon, blinking away in Cameroon.

That was the slavers' dungeon, where Mike and the rest of the team were busy fighting. As much as I wanted to, I had to accept that I couldn't help them.

I had to trust that they had this, because even with the best will in the world, it'd take at least another seven hours to get to Cameroon from here. And of course, because that was how this shit always worked out, the location I was getting for the undead bastards was nowhere near.

Instead, it flashed in a place I'd only ever heard described as the "Empty Quarter" and then only in passing on an archaeology show.

Fuck.

I pulled up the details, plotting them across in my mind, even as I dug and dug at the gold embedded in the wood.

It'd take maybe five hours from where I was currently, to get to there, and if I added on flight time to Cameroon, to help Mike and the others, then from there to the Empty Quarter…thirteen or so hours.

That'd give me four hours before the failure of this dungeon entirely, which wasn't going to work. The fight to take and fix the last dungeon had taken at least five or six hours, not counting the time spent in the slowed time segment and the traveling time.

No, I had to trust in Mike and the others to achieve their mission, and I needed to secure this as best I could, then go.

"Chris!" I called down.

"What do you want, you floating twat?" he shouted back up. "Unlike you, I've been busy all day!"

"Get your knife and make yourself useful!" I grunted back, levering out a section of wood and doing my best to ignore the wail of pained protest that came from both the Tree of Life and the dungeon fairy. "We need to get the nails out of them and get them free!"

"No!" the fairy before me burbled. "Life for the Tree!"

"What?" I glared at her. "I thought we needed to free you!"

"Life… Tree needs Life!" she managed to force out.

"Fuck!"

"What?" Chris shouted up.

"It wasn't an offer!" I barked instinctively as my mind whirled, trying to figure it all out. "You're saying that all the others need to remain here, to give their lives to keep the tree alive?" I asked her and she nodded, her head sagging again.

"And the summons?" I asked.

"Will…keep coming," she admitted. "They are bound…collars."

"The collars that they're being summoned with are binding them to attack?" I asked, and she nodded again.

"Okay, if we free them of the collars, could they help you?"

"Yes!" She panted; what I could see of her chest heaved as a fresh trickle of liquid ran from the corner of her tiny mouth. "Yes!"

"Okay, okay…how the hell do we do this?" I muttered. "Chris! Check with Rhodes—how much ammo and shit do you have? Can you survive like this for another seventeen hours?"

"Fuck no," he responded without pause. "I know I'm down to my last two mags. The others might have more, but not enough for that."

"Claim..." the dungeon fairy burbled. "Claim and summon!"

"Summon... But they're summoning from the dungeon already? Can I cut them off?"

"No."

"So how the hell?" I started.

She shook her head, clearly barely able to force the words out. "Will open...access channel."

"You can open a channel to access the dungeon, but they're going to be summoning more of your people all the time as well?" I asked. "Just nod."

She did.

"Okay, that's gonna drain you, though, and fast." I paused. "If we can claim the immediate area, though, we could give one of our people access, and they could harvest the bodies and rubble out there, keep you going a little longer?"

"Yes!"

I could see all sorts of possible problems with the plan, and it was clear that the enemy dungeon was breaking this one down to enable it to summon reinforcements already. But at least if we managed to open a channel into it, there were options.

"Do it," I ordered, before looking back at her injuries. "Do I free you or not?"

"Yes." Tears streamed from one eye, the other milky white and weeping pus. "My children must give their lives, though...they must feed the Tree."

"Got it." I growled, digging the knife in again. "Chris, what I need you to tell Rhodes is..."

Five minutes later, I managed to pull the last nail free. There'd been six of them—one through either thigh, each shoulder and each wing— keeping her pinned in place. The one that I'd thought at first was through her chest was simply off center and protruding more than the other shoulder and showed what an inexpert job had been done.

"You sure about this?" I called down to Rhodes, where she sat below me, cross-loading ammunition.

"Not even slightly," she admitted. "You sure you can spare the ammo?"

"I'm better with a blade and magic anyway." I was just glad that I'd thought to take the rifle in the first place, and wished I'd taken more ammo, now that I'd handed over what I had left.

As it was, since we'd gained access to the core and limited access to the local area, we'd started to push out. It'd not taken long to find that even though our people were out in the room that led up to this, there was no way we could spend the mana we'd need to expand our influence all the way along that corridor and out to cover the other end.

Instead, the decision was made that we'd drag all the bodies into here that we could; then we'd create barricades and start summoning fairies.

The dungeon had access to half a dozen varieties, and several were powerfully magical, so the hope was that they'd be able to subdue their kin, then we could strip the collars off.

Failing that, there was always the option of sealing the tunnel and damn well hoping that they could hold out longer than it took the other side to tunnel through.

I didn't like it.

I kept oscillating between saying "fuck it, not worth the risk" and knowing that it was, despite the danger to my friends.

This was a more or less intact dungeon in a new location that had access to different technologies than we did. Entire research opportunities were here, and would be folded into our dungeon once we took it. And, for the first time, we'd have access to a vassal dungeon fairy.

No more guessing and hoping. And because she'd sworn an oath, one that we both understood would not only kill her if she tried to betray me but would also kill her dungeon, the one reason that she had for existing?

It was too much of a possible benefit to lose. But I hated doing the math that took into account the possible loss of my oldest friend and his team.

The little fairy sagged in my hand, and I gently levered her out of the gap in the tree. The sap or pus or whatever that had been bubbling over her slid off as I lifted her and floated free, landing nearby. I doused her with a water bottle, washing away as much as I could.

She hissed; the substance bubbled and clearly burned into her on contact with the water. I cursed, laying her on the floor, atop a blanket that the healer thoughtfully put down.

The thought was kind, even though it, too, started to blister and smoke as soon as the messy, half-washed-off gloop touched it.

I doused her again in the water and the healer dragged the blanket over the little body, wiping as much as possible off, before hitting her with a heal, and then almost collapsing.

"Just rest." I tugged a weak healing potion free and pulled the cork out, offering it to the little fairy. She took a bare sip; then, coughing and hardly able to force the words out, asked that the other fairies be given the rest.

Rhodes took the potion and stood, moving from one to another, gently giving them a little sip. "You got more of this?" she asked me.

I nodded, pulling out three more. The way the fights had gone so far, I could at least afford to give those. Although we couldn't link this dungeon to ours until it was fully claimed, we did have access to its resources, one of which was a sight for sore eyes.

"Mana potions," I said softly. "We've finally got access to them."

"Oh, thank fuck," the healer whispered. "Gimmie."

"No," Rhodes snapped. "Unless we can replace that mana, we can't afford to spend it, and every summon we perform drains the fairies more."

"The other side—" the healer whined.

I cut her off. "We've claimed this area. That means we've cut them off from the mana and life energy that the fairies are producing, but it also means that the tree is cut off from anywhere else it can draw mana from for the core. Rhodes is right. We can produce a tiny amount in here, and it's mainly the bodies that we can steal and breakdown. But I don't know how the hell the other side are producing anything. Fuck it. As long as we can keep the fairies alive, the dungeon has a chance…it's them feeding it as if they were conduits and mana converters."

"Yes…" the dungeon fairy breathed. "Save them…"

"We will," I assured her, before standing and turning to Chris as he came along the corridor, pausing in the shattered doorway.

"Do you want me to come?" Chris asked me, even though the look in his eyes begged me not to say yes.

"No," I said sadly. "They need you here, brother." And it was true; they needed him. And as much as I wanted him with me, if I said yes, and we lost this dungeon? He'd be leaving Becky to die here. There was no way I could fly on my own as fast as Jack had managed so far, and if I did, I'd burn through all my mana on the way.

The space that he had on his back was limited, and there was no way that I could fit me and Chris there, let alone the three of us. And if I tried, what message would that send to the others? That they're expendable?

"Stay alive," I told Chris quietly, gripping his shoulder. "I mean it. If I come back and find you've gotten yourself and everyone else killed…"

"You'll what?" He tried to grin, but it came out strained. "Bring me back just to kill me again?"

"Something like that." I pulled him into a quick, fierce hug. We both knew this could be the last time we saw each other.

Stepping back, I turned to Rhodes. "I'm granting you authority over the local dungeon functions. You'll be able to direct the defenses and manage the mana flow." I pulled out a small pouch from my bag of holding; the crystals inside clicked softly. "Kelly gave me these for an emergency, and this definitely qualifies. Use them well."

Rhodes took the pouch, weighing it carefully. "How many?"

"There's twelve left, I think. Each one's worth about a thousand mana. Make them last."

She nodded sharply, tucking them away. "We'll hold."

"Good. Because if this works, this dungeon will be our foothold in the region. These fairies, this knowledge, it's worth protecting. You know I'd not risk you unless I had to." I turned to address everyone. "I need you all to keep this core safe until I can deal with the source of the infection. The undead assholes are going to throw everything they have at you, but you've got advantages—defensible positions, access to fairy summons, and most importantly, each other."

"And Rhodes." Chris forced a grin. "You know she'll kick the shit out of anyone who dies without her permission!"

"You're not wrong," I grunted, seeing the twinkle in Rhodes's eyes as she opened her mouth to speak.

The healer raised her hand. "The summons?" she asked, having not seen Rhodes start to speak.

"Right." I moved to the core interface, quickly navigating through the available options. "We need something to even the field as much as we can. And those out there? They're mass-producing the weakest ones, I bet, so let's see what we've got…"

I studied the available options. My eyes caught on two particular species. "These two. The lumina lure and…what they're calling a broken."

"A what?" Chris shifted his sight and stared into the dungeon interface. "Yeah, no, mate—that one looks fucked up."

"It is," I confirmed. "But look at the base template—it's a warrior sprite variant. The damage to the dungeon has corrupted it, but that might actually work in our favor. It's unpredictable, which means the enemy won't know what to expect either."

Rhodes moved closer, examining the descriptions. “And the lumina lure?”

“Perfect for what we need. They can navigate the dungeon instinctively, act as scouts, and…” I paused, selecting the first summon. “They’re excellent at misdirection. Use the lures to draw a fairy in or separate it in the fight, and the broken to subdue it, then get the collar off.”

The air shimmered as Rhodes held the little bag of mana crystals up, and I winced, draining it by half already, as the first fairy materialized. The lumina lure’s crystalline form caught what little light there was, sending rainbow refractions dancing across the walls. Its wings pulsed with a hypnotic rhythm that I had to force myself to look away from.

Six inches high and as much flowing, glowing colorful crystal as living being, it shone in the dim light, mesmerizing in its ethereal beauty.

“It’s…so beautiful,” the healer breathed, reaching out with one hand then jerking back as the second summon manifested.

The broken appeared as all summons did: a burst of firefly energy that shimmered into being, seeming to “print” into existence, before bursting to life in a burst of static-like energy. Its mottled gray form instantly darted to a shadowed corner. The patchwork armor it wore clinked softly as it moved; silver eyes scanned us all with an unsettling intensity. It flashed backward, bracing itself against the wall, more feral than anything I’d seen that wasn’t a damn goblin.

“They’ll work together,” I explained quickly. “The lure can draw enemies into prepared positions, while the broken can strike from the shadows. Use them sparingly, though. Each summon drains the core’s resources, and if you lose these, you’ll have to decide if the expense is worth replacing them.”

“And the exit?” Rhodes asked, already thinking ahead.

“We narrow it.” I moved to the doorway, examining the structure. “Once I’m clear, pull back your forces that are outside and narrow the tunnel down to just wide enough for single-file combat. The lure can help funnel them into killing zones, and the broken can pick off any that make it through.”

“As much as I’d like to focus on defenses as well, it’ll only take one bright spark on their side to consider closing off the entrance and sealing us in, so I need to start work on an alternative air supply as well, and that won’t be cheap,” Rhodes muttered, before shaking her head. “That’s my problem, though. We’ve nearly taken the dungeon, and I’d damned if I’m losing it now.”

Chris joined me at the doorway, his expression grim. “You’ll need to move fast. They’ve started a fresh attack out there, and our people are getting pushed back.”

Thanks to my increased Perception, even at this distance, if I focused, I could hear them: the distant shuffling of undead feet, the screams of the trapped fairies, the roars of cyclops, and the occasional scrape of metal on stone.

“I need a minute,” I told Rhodes. “Get everyone into position. When I go, it’s going to get messy.”

She nodded. “I need to be with my people. Once you’re gone, I’ll start closing up.” With that, she was off, already heading to better direct her people to defensive positions. The lumina lure drifted to her side, its ethereal beauty a stark contrast to the grim surroundings. The broken remained in its corner, but I could feel its attention fixed on me, waiting.

"Chris." I turned to my oldest friend one last time. "Remember what I said. Stay alive."

He gripped my arm briefly. "You too, brother. Now let's get you out of here."

I nodded, pausing and taking a deep breath, checking my mana reserves. The last few hours of solid flight had been kind to me—fifteen hundred mana an hour I'd gotten back—and the little incident with the storm back in Baku had actually cost me less than I'd thought, thanks to the nature of me being a Storm Titan wannabe.

As such, I had a little over ten thousand mana, now, and it was going to cost me five hours of flight time. With meditation, I could stretch out a few extra thousand mana as well, I was sure, but just in case, I kept a reserve of four thousand. The other six, I channeled into the tree, and I felt the sigh of relief that slid from each and every fairy at that gift.

"That's…all I can do," I apologized. I wanted to do more, but the risk was too great. Instead, I stood straight, looked around the remaining injured in the room, and nodded. "I'm proud of you all. Hold the line. I'll take the fight to the enemy, and in six hours, this should all be over."

"Three cheers for—" one of the soldiers started to call, and I cut him off with a leveled finger.

"Don't you fuckin' dare!" I growled. "I'm not that kinda dickhead. Now, watch each other's backs, listen to Rhodes, and for the love of God, if Chris tells you to pull his finger, send him as far away as you can. Hold the line. I'll be back." With that rousing speech, I headed for the way out.

The passage beyond was a mess of bodies and debris, the corpses that could be grabbed having presumably been dragged back in here at Rhodes's order for absorption. Ahead, there were signs of fighting clear in the scarred walls and scattered brass, and of course, thanks to the sound of movement ahead, lots more of it to come.

"Ready?" Chris called from behind me as we ran.

"Born that way." I flexed my fingers, feeling the lightning build. "Remember, narrow the passages leading in once I'm clear and Robin and the others are in here. Don't be a hero."

"Says the wanker about to solo an army."

"Yeah, well, do as I say, not as I do and all that shit," I called back at him, then turned serious. "Really though, hold this place. I need something to come back to."

The square chamber ahead was chaos. Our people had set up makeshift barriers across the eastern and western entrances where the enemy forces kept pouring in. Rhodes had positioned shooters to create overlapping fields of fire, but they were being slowly pushed back.

If we'd been able to expand out, to push the dungeon control, or our section of it out to here, they could have narrowed each of the passages and created better defensive measures. But the mana that we had just wasn't going to cut it.

Better that they focus on the passage leading to the core chamber and keep that secure as long as possible. If they could capture and then free fairies, as shitty as it was, they could then add to the life that was being given to the tree, and keep it going longer.

"Here they come!" Rhodes's voice rang out over the sounds of combat. "Everyone in position!"

I didn't wait. Instead, I burst forward into the chamber, leaping over the barriers and fallen pillars that we'd been using for cover, wreathed in crackling energy.

The first wave of undead and collared fairies was already pushing through the eastern entrance. Lightning exploded from my hands. Chain reactions bounced between targets as I carved through their ranks, spending mana like water to give our people a better chance.

"South exit!" Rhodes shouted from behind me. "We'll cover your retreat!"

A cyclops roared as it shoved its way free and into the room from the western entrance, swinging a massive club that I ducked under, throwing myself into a magic-assisted slide that took me past before blasting its knee out with a Storm-Strike. It screamed and toppled sideways, and I snorted as I popped to my feet again.

If not for the enemy constantly refreshing their forces here thanks to having partial control over the dungeon, there'd be no risk to our forces.

As it was, the waves that came in were dangerous in their composition. That was because ammo was running low, not due to their skill or individual lethality. They didn't last long enough to become sentient and the core wasn't powerful enough and neither were the templates high-leveled enough to produce them straight off the bat, as near as I could tell.

As such, it was dangerous, but now that our people could also summon and adjust the surrounding area, provided nobody massively fucked up, it was manageable.

Behind me, I could hear Rhodes coordinating short bursts of single-shot defensive fire, keeping the enemies contained while our people began their planned withdrawal toward the core chamber, dragging more bodies with them.

"Go!" I shouted, not slowing down. Another channeled lightning blast cleared the southern passage, leaving bodies smoking. I vaulted over them, then launched into the air, clearing the balcony and landing in the upper area, pausing for a brief look back down below—and getting a finger upraised in "salute" from Chris.

That fucker never changed.

I spun and started to sprint. The passage curved ahead, and I could hear more reinforcements coming from somewhere in front. Well, that was just perfect—it meant they were too busy trying to stop me rather than focusing on the others.

A small but solid group appeared, led by what looked like a more powerful undead fairy wearing some kind of armor. It raised its hands, dark energy gathering…

I didn't give it time to cast. A single blast of Incinerate to the head took the fucker out, then a channeled blast of lightning followed it up, just to make sure. I'd been building it since I started running and it detonated through the corridor, the confined space amplifying its effect. I slowed as I approached the impact site, the passage doglegging to the left as the smoke cleared.

Nothing moved in the corridor ahead.

"Matt!" Chris's voice echoed distantly from behind. "We're starting to fall back!"

"Go!" I shouted back, already moving forward again. He probably couldn't hear me, and I was far enough ahead that I'd never hear his reply anyway.

The sounds of combat faded as I raced through the devastated corridor. *They'd be okay; they had to be. Almost there. Just had to reach the surface, find Jack, and...*

A wall of absolute darkness sprang up ahead. I didn't slow down, instead channeling one final burst of lightning that carved straight through it blindly. I erupted from the temple entrance into the pre-dawn air, immediately banking hard right as spell fire from my right tracked my movement.

I'd exited into a fresh push from the other side. Between the sporadic gunfire and the shouts, screams, and spells, it took a second to spot Robin and her little leadership cadre. But as soon as I had, I sprinted off.

The glorious building that stood proud atop the mountain to my right looked considerably more burned and blackened now, and clearly the staggered reinforcements below were being delayed thanks to my automata's efforts up here and our people's mad tenacity.

"Jack, get ready to move out!" I roared, knowing he'd be watching, and yeah, I skidded into cover as sure enough, my draconic companion swooped around a few seconds later, bathing the side of the temple in plasma fire that left staggering, screaming bodies falling. Then he dropped from above, mechanical wings spreading as he swooped in close.

I skidded to a halt near Robin and Rathaharn, and spoke quickly. "We've taken the core but there's a lot of issues. Fall back inside, watch out for the bastards trying to cut you off, and help Chris and the others defend the core. I'm going to the next dungeon, but they can explain it all. You got that?"

"Fall back, aye. Catch up with Chris and hold the line, aye!" It was the sergeant who responded when Robin stared at me, open-mouthed, but she nodded a split second later, and I gave her a quick thumbs-up before crouching.

I launched myself upward and landed on his back in a practiced motion, already pulling up the map in my mind. He beat his wings again, soaring upward and ignoring a single parting shot of a shard of ice that was sent our way.

The impression I got from him of the spell was basically that it wasn't even worth avoiding, it was that pathetic compared to him.

An image flashed through my mind, a map overlaid with possible flight paths, accompanied by a sense of questioning eagerness.

"The Empty Quarter," I told him grimly. "Fast as you can manage." I shot him the information I had, limited as it was, combined with, that unlike the attack on the first dungeon, this time war had been declared, and if the enemy had discovered the setting, they'd be able to see we were coming.

We shot eastward as the sun began to rise, leaving Rhodes, Chris, and the others to hold the line. I didn't look back. Couldn't afford to.

They'd survive. They had to. I had a dungeon to conquer.

CHAPTER FIFTY

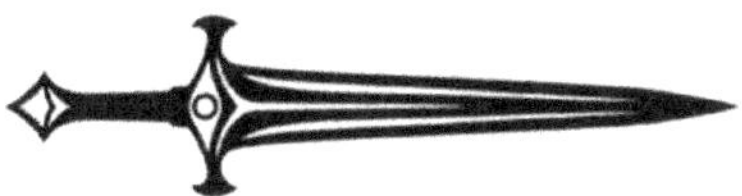

Five hours is a long damn time to think about how badly you've fucked up, it turns out.

I lay flat against Jack's back as we skimmed the clouds, trying to minimize our profile while still maintaining enough height to see any threats coming. The bastard seemed to be enjoying himself. Occasional images of him wishing he could have been around before the fall and doing this, with missiles trying to track him, flashed through my mind, along with an overwhelming sense of "bring it on."

"Just because you'd be basically immune to that crap doesn't mean I would," I muttered, getting the mental equivalent of a snort in return.

The meditation was helping, at least. I'd gotten my mana regeneration into a decent groove, focusing on pulling in ambient storm energy from the clouds around us. Doing it while moving was a bitch and a half, but needs must when the devil's throwing undead at you.

I'd considered using the ability that I'd gotten from hitting my century in Intelligence, but the area of control it required was fixed in place. As soon as it activated, it would be left behind us, costing instead of helping, and as much as I wanted to help the others back at the dungeon, had I cast it and then left? I'd be even lower on mana when I arrived for the next fight.

That meant I was back to the old way of meditating, cursing and determined that I'd try experimenting with that ability when I wasn't running like an idiot, and I devoted myself to it as much as possible, only occasionally rising out of the depths to look around and worry.

This whole situation stank worse than Chris's gym bag. The undead had already proved they were clever bastards. That business with the fairy dungeon's core showed planning and patience I should have considered, especially after meeting that bastard that claimed to be the Dungeon Lord's rep twice now. It just kept making me wonder what other surprises they had waiting, and whether he'd actually been the Dungeon Lord or not.

Last time I'd gone up against a dungeon that knew I was coming, it had been that clockwork nightmare. Yeah, Simon was an unhinged asshole, but his fixation on Marchioness was a massive help: he could have been upgrading his defenses and making better creatures, but he'd instead been working on versions of her to vent his anger—and who knew what else—on.

It'd been a relief, a massive one, because when I thought back to it, what I'd have done in his place? I'd have made tiny, tiny machines, or massive ones.

I'd have sealed corridors in steel, and then had the roof, floor, and walls close in with massive pistons, squish people to jam and be done with it. Or pour acid in.

Fuck, when my mind started thinking about what I'd have done to face us? I came up with so many ideas that it was plain terrifying.

Fighting humans instead of all the mad shit I normally had to was a lot easier—and a lot more vicious, because frankly although I was a borderline human still, I'd always fantasized about killing practically everyone around me.

That was what working in IT did for you. There was only so many times you could hear the same shit and the same excuses every day.

Yeah, I'd probably create tiny machines that could be poured out of a bucket as people walked overhead, or a pit that was filled with them, and have them built like tiny beetles or something? They get into your armor and bite and chew, too small to avoid, metal shells so you can't crush them…and just damn.

I'd have living humans eaten away to bones in seconds.

Now I was *shitting* myself about the dungeon to come.

I needed my damn team. Going in alone, as I was, was just bloody stupid, and I knew it. But the way that this had all fallen out? I'd set myself up for this, and I had to find a solution, and fast.

Once I'd done it though, that was it. I was determined that no more was I going to be the point of failure, the "feature" instead of the bug, as I cursed myself to be. I needed to develop my team more, instead of splitting them off to carry out the assaults on their own.

Hell, I'd even sent Beta and bloody Kilo off—and they, along with Chris, were my mental safety blankets these days. I got in the shit, and they came and backed me up!

No, this had to be the last "lone gunman" shit I pulled. In the pit of my stomach, I damn well knew I was living on borrowed time, and a single mistake was all it'd take.

The more I thought about the fight that was to come, the more I went around in circles.

That fight against Simon had been simpler than I had any right to expect, as machines were predictable in their way. They followed patterns, protocols…and once you knew what they were doing, you could exploit it. The undead, though? These ones, specifically? They'd shown more imagination than I was used to, and I didn't like that.

An image flashed from Jack—the corpse of a massive mechanical bull we'd fought, its build replaced with skeletal components as a suggestion—and I got his point.

"Yeah, they might combine approaches," I agreed. "But that's not what worries me. It's the fact they went after that fairy dungeon first, corrupted it slowly. Makes me think they're playing a longer game than we realized. I'm just hoping there aren't others they've done the same with."

The Empty Quarter stretched out ahead of us now. Saudi Arabia flashed past beneath, its endless rolling dunes under the morning sun. Perfect territory for an undead army: nothing living to get in their way, plenty of space to hide their operations underground.

I pulled up my mental map again, checking our course. The target was deep in the Rub' al Khali desert, which would normally be a defensive nightmare. But for undead who didn't need water, food, or shelter from the sun? It was fucking ideal.

I didn't know whether this was luck or planning, but for an undead dungeon? I couldn't think of a better location. Even in the ocean's depths, you'd have fish feeding on the corpses and the occasional leviathan or something.

Here?

There was a damn reason they'd called it the Empty Quarter.

"They'll have traps," I said aloud, more to organize my thoughts than for Jack's benefit. "Probably buried in the sand. And they'll be expecting me to come in hot and heavy with lightning, since that's what worked against their forces before. They'll have made adjustments after what they saw in the Rhodes dungeon, though obviously they've not had much time to do that…"

A fresh image appeared, one he'd clearly lifted straight from my mind where he showed me standing atop the exit from the trial dungeon, the cheering throngs in the seats on all sides, and specifically, that they'd sent a representative to watch.

"And yeah, great. I showed them all sorts of abilities there, didn't I? Fuck," I muttered, closing my eyes and reminding myself that it'd been for a good reason, and that we had a shitload of dungeons that wanted to play nice thanks to that bit of PR.

Another image from Jack: the plasma cannon he'd used on the temple steps, though this time it washed across a load of sand, and a sense that traps that were buried under six inches of solid glass didn't matter.

"Good point. They might not know about how much you can actually do, or even anything about you, really. You were in and out pretty fast at the last dungeon. They could think you're real…" I paused, then patted a metal panel. "I mean, you know, flesh and blood."

I got a sense of "whatever" from him, and surety that he didn't need to be "weak and fleshy" thanks to the images of people collapsing from hunger, exhaustion, and blood loss, while he kept flying on serenely.

I squinted into the distance, wondering what kinda clusterfuck this undead dungeon was going to be, considering the one goddamn thing that I'd really wanted to avoid until now was the bastard undead getting their claws on their own dungeon.

A glint of metal caught my eye, barely visible through the heat haze. Jack banked slightly, sending me an image enhanced by his much better eyes. It looked to be some sort of old ruin he'd spotted, a kind of fortified structure, mostly buried under centuries of sand. Only the highest points of what looked like defensive towers still breached the surface, though someone had apparently decided to say "fuck it" and put a single flag atop the tallest, snapping in the wind and gleaming with the rising sun.

It could have had a pattern on it, but from this distance, and the light we had, it was just a black streamer.

"Careful," I thought at him as he arced out to circle it. I checked my map and notifications to be sure, then nodded to myself. This was it, all right, and yeah.

This was exactly the kind of place the undead would choose: an abandoned fortress-city from the ancient Silk Road trade routes, I vaguely remembered being taught, its walls and chambers preserved beneath the desert. Perfect for their purposes, and absolutely the last place I wanted to face them if I was bringing conventional forces.

Jack sent back an image of his plasma breath melting the sand to glass, but I shook my head. "No, it'd just turn the sand to more armor. They'll be deeper underground, I'm betting." I studied the barely visible structures. "See how the sand's disturbed in patterns? They've been excavating, but trying to hide it."

The impression I got back was distinctly unimpressed, something about how they'd wasted their time. A half second later, he showed me a deeper scan of the area, revealing a sprawling complex of tunnels and chambers that ran here and there like a rabbit warren beneath the sand.

I couldn't help but grin at that. One point for the tech tree right there.

Okay, scanning over the image quickly, some of the architecture looked decidedly more recent than the ancient ruins. And in some places, there were both sections that were still showing as buried and collapsed, while others were clearly regular and solid, making me guess that they'd been expanded or reclaimed recently.

"Okay," I muttered. "They've been busy. How far down does it go?"

The answer made me curse again. The complex descended in layers, with the newest construction at the bottom of a third layer, or at least that was as far as he could sense. This wasn't just some hastily occupied ruin; they'd been developing this site for months, maybe longer.

That was also a relief, though, I realized. This wasn't new, which would have meant that they were actually set up somewhere else and using this place as a decoy again.

"We need to find a way in that isn't an obvious trap." I studied the layout Jack was sharing. "But first, can you show me any creatures or anything?"

The sensor sweep he did next revealed exactly what I'd been afraid of: hundreds of mana signatures—most of them undead, I was guessing—and mainly clustered in the upper levels. But it was the larger readings that worried me. Something big was down there, and it was waiting at the end of the…

Then I grinned—I couldn't help it. "Any Scepiniir?"

A half dozen points flashed into sight, one of which changed even as I watched, altering to give off a mana signature that radiated death.

"Oh, you stupid fucker," I breathed, relieved. "You actually fell for it."

Jack sent me a sense of confusion. Then, as I opened my mind to him, sharing the full trap, I sensed amusement, then a predatory glee as well as I shared my cunning plan.

There were three layers to the site. The uppermost entered into a long corridor that I just knew was going to be booby-trapped to shit, and the lack of any undead beyond a desultory one here and there made it even more obvious.

There was just enough to give me something to face, and not enough to slow me down, so I'd push hard and be straight into the middle of the trap before I knew it.

If not for Jack's radar or sensors or whatever, I'd have had little choice. But thanks to that?

"Okay, fuck the main entrance. You see this bit?" I highlighted a section, and sent him my evil plan.

There were two ways I could do this, and one of them was the sensible, calm, and collected method, which would result in the minimum of risk and collateral destruction. And the other was the way that I had already decided this was going to be done.

Jack was on board with it straightaway, and I had to admit, even if only to him, it was a stroke of genius.

The main entrance was a long, snaking corridor that led to and through a dozen smaller rooms. Here and there, dotted around, were sections that led off, concealed behind false walls.

Some held obvious collections of undead waiting patiently, and others…well, they held something. The sensors weren't infallible, and especially not at this distance through sand, rock, and whatever else.

The mana signatures were clear enough, but trying to make out what a probable liquid was, by reading mana signatures through a third party, even one as closely linked as Jack?

Nope, it was just a mélange of readings.

Then, after all the passages had been passed through, there was, right at the end, a massive triangular room. It was designed with the stairs down to the next level at the narrowest and farthest point. A dozen pillars held up the roof—but clearly served as shields for the waiting creatures hiding behind them.

Well, that was nice for them, I decided, because unlike their clear plan that I attack head-on and go through the meat grinder, it was time to even the odds a little.

Jack arched around, and I stepped off his back, lifting myself into the air as he took a path that was going to result in admittedly a little damage to him, but a lot to them, suddenly climbing for extra height.

He beat his wings faster and faster, ascending a few hundred meters higher, before flipping over and diving like a meteor.

Just before he landed, he drew his wings in, put his feet together, and focused all his weight into as small a point as possible, slamming into the sand.

A lot of the force was lost to the layers of sand—of course it was…no other way that could happen—but when a multi-ton dragon lands on anything, especially with a vengeance, there's damage.

The damage in this case was to shatter part of the roof and cave it in at a point three-quarters of the way down the main room. He registered several points of damage, including his right rear leg locking up, servos and sections on it failing. But the result was a hole that was at least a meter square and a dozen deep, and ten seconds of frantic digging later, let him put his head through to say hello.

Or, you know, "die, heathens, in the fire of cleansing plasma," as was more the case.

He lashed it around in a circle, though most of the focus was sent toward the far end and the largest concentration of the undead. Then he dragged his head back out, clearing the hole and making room for me, as I came screaming in from above.

I shoved down, hard, as I hit the gap, not physically pressing onto anything, but flaring my magic out and adjusting the air pressure, the caress of the mana, all of it.

Heat raced out of the hole already, as did smoke and a veritable wall of pressure. But that was part of the plan.

My impact blasted an area clear, forcing the air outward. Before it had a chance to rush back in, I was already moving, hoping that those minor laws of thermodynamics wouldn't mean my end.

I spun, fixed on the exit—or the entrance to the next level, depending on your point of view—and threw myself into the air, hurtling forward again.

Behind me, the entrance to this section was now fully ablaze. Jack was already working on the next section of the roof, breaking it loose and clearing away all that he could. That allowed the blaze to continue, and prevented any of the inhabitants of the first floor to come to the dungeon's aid.

The first floor was already down, and there were two left to go, though I knew it was never going to be as easy as this last section had been. The last floor especially was going to be a kick in the tits.

The stairwell leading down was intact, thankfully—another reason I'd ordered him to fire in the other direction—and although it was dark, I could see enough by the combination of the fires behind and the lightning that I lit in my right hand that I didn't have to slow.

I took the stairs with a combination of flight and leaping, touching down for a heartbeat, then off again. The connection to Jack and his sensors allowed me to move faster than was probably sensible.

I hit the bottom of the stairwell, felt the shift at almost the same time as my foot hit the ground and jumped into a forward flip, nearly ending it all as a spear came out of the wall at just the wrong angle.

The tip bounced off the top of my helmet, and I continued around, landing with a skid and then running forward, into the second hall.

The second floor opened into what had once been some kind of grand hall, now repurposed into a military staging ground. My stomach turned as I caught glimpses of uniforms from various eras through the darkness. Wehrmacht feldgrau mixed with British desert khaki and Ottoman olive. The undead soldiers moved with an unsettling precision that said "retained muscle memory" at the least, even if not consciousness.

Worst of all, as soon as I appeared, they lifted their weapons and took aim. Half dropped to one knee and the others skidded to a halt to aim.

Rifle butts slammed to shoulders, barrels tracked, and I swore, casting a Lightning Shield.

I dodged left, then dove right, rolling and coming to my feet behind a pillar. Dozens of shots ricocheted off the ancient stone; the edges of my shield that peeked out from behind the pillar suddenly flared as it was hit. I cursed, scrambled to my feet, and sprinted for the next pillar as a bloody grenade bounced off the wall nearby and landed next to me.

A handful more bullets spanged into my shield, then a handful of fragments from the grenade. I snarled, glaring around the pillar before bursting into the open once more, seeing another two hefting grenades again.

"Right, you fucker!" I snarled, adjusting my grip on the war hammer. "Let's see if lightning works as well on dead Nazis!"

I unleashed a Lightning Bolt, followed by two more into the nearest cluster of uniformed corpses. The spell arced between several of them and across their metal equipment, sending five to the ground, re-dead.

But these weren't mindless shamblers. The rest immediately took cover behind stone pillars, returning fire with old guns that were either meticulously maintained, or recently built.

Either way, though, the one thing they'd missed was that I'd not hit them with the three blasts at random. I cut the shield, the drain not worth the cost, and counted down, hoping that I'd not taken them too soon.

A bullet pinged off my pauldron as I dove behind a fallen column. WW2-era guns might be ancient by modern standards, but they could still punch holes in you just fine. I needed to keep moving; staying still would let them set up a proper firing line.

That was when the first grenade went off with a muffled *crump* buried beneath its owner. The second and third, though, went off in short order right after it. And where most of the blast was tamped down by the first one, there was no such cover for these.

Fragments and flaming debris roared out, undead staggering and shots going wide, and that was when I burst into motion.

I vaulted over my cover, using a brief burst of wind to carry me higher than they'd expect, then dropped and skidded. A field of air between the underside of my boots and the ground made it like ice, as I skated across the ancient stone, then darted sideways.

My hammer came down on an Ottoman officer's skull even as I unleashed another Lightning Bolt to clear my landing zone. The poorly preserved uniforms offered no protection against the electricity, and the neat rows of undead soldiers began to break up as they tried to adapt to an enemy that was nothing like they'd known in life.

I dragged a channeled bolt across four more, sending them crashing to the floor, even as I kicked the remains of the Ottoman officer free of my hammer.

I knew better than to get cocky, but honestly, sometimes?

I couldn't help but grin as I launched forward, dropping to my knees as bullets screamed past overhead. The ground again felt like an ice rink for me as I flashed across it; then I lifted into the air with another judicious use of my Air mana.

The fight with Kh'aan had taught me so much, and yet I'd barely touched on it since, unable to really train it, as to do so was impossible in this armor.

Still, the knowledge of that fight was with me, and although I couldn't fully let loose, I damn well could do more than any human before me had.

I threw my hammer at a figure that was hefting a grenade, hurled a lightning strike to my left, and launched myself into the middle of another group. Their bullets spanged off my armor and whizzed into the darkness as I started to laugh.

I grabbed a rotten skull in my right hand, squeezed hard, and yanked. The neck gave way at almost the same second that the temples fractured, and the skull collapsed in my hand.

The body dropped, the animating sentience gone, and I snapped out a backhand with my left, even as the rifles zeroed in.

I felt the impacts of a dozen bullets as I fought in close, and aside from a handful of sharp pains that barely lasted long enough to notice, that was it.

The armor was strong enough that they had to be incredibly lucky to get a joint or uncovered section, and those few that did make it through?

Well, what the hell—they were gnats pissing on my armor and telling me it was a thunderstorm!

Pathetic!

I spun through them all; kicks and punches lashed out, snap kicks shattered rib cages or reduced pelvises to dust.

That wasn't enough to put the undead down. They felt no pain, but the one thing they did feel was my goddamn foot when I'd stomp on their skulls a second later.

In less than a minute, I glared around, disappointed that it was over, and yet surging inside, ready for…

A sudden sense of warning flared in me, and I spun, searching the darkness, looking for the threat, before finally seeing the sending that Jack was maintaining, and cursing.

In the distance, I could hear more running feet, as reinforcements headed straight for me. I moved, stooping and ripping my hammer free of the unlucky catcher, before starting to run. Adrenaline surged and rolled inside me; the need to fight, to prove myself warred with the sure and certain knowledge that once again, the fucking armor was doing a number on me.

"Which way?" I snapped, before sending my apologies to Jack silently, getting a soothing reassurance from him, as a map appeared in the corner of my vision.

I followed Jack's guidance through the warren of corridors, his sensor data showing me clusters of enemies trying to converge on my position. Most I could evade. Time, after all, wasn't on my side and I needed to save my strength for whatever waited below.

A flash of warning from Jack had me diving back into a side passage as something big thundered past the intersection ahead. The image he sent showed me what I'd avoided: a makeshift battle wagon, basically a truck chassis with sheets of metal welded on and packed with a modified undead that was running it, Flintstones-style, in a ring that I'd have to pass a handful more times to get to the next floor at least. Crude but effective, especially in these tight corridors.

"Thanks for the heads-up," I muttered, getting a sense of smug satisfaction in return. The next image he sent showed me a more twisting route, but it avoided the majority of the undead that were gathering in larger numbers and went straight through what looked like residential quarters.

The mana signatures there were fewer, but stronger, more focused. These weren't mindless soldiers, I just knew…because why give undead living quarters and somewhere to relax? It wasn't like they needed to polish their fuckin' bones.

Or maybe they did. *Sex Lives of the Dead* would have been a reality show that the old world would have had on in a heartbeat, I had no doubt.

"Lovely. Because of course the shortcut goes through the VIP section," I muttered, adjusting and heading in that direction.

I burst from cover, hammer leading the way. I darted up the ring passage in the direction that cart had come from, then crashed through a barricade that sealed off a new passage. Oak splinters flew as I smashed furniture and debris in all directions.

The "living" quarters beyond were a jarring mix of modern comforts and ancient architecture: lights powered by mana crystals, preserved rugs over stone floors, and personal effects that made my skin crawl. These undead were trying to maintain a mockery of life.

A wraith emerged from one wall. Tendrils of darkness reached for me, but I was already moving. Lightning coursed through my hammer as I brought it around in an arc. The wraith shrieked as the lightning-wreathed metal smashed it from the air, bones reduced to fragments.

But the noise had drawn attention, and doors were slamming open all along the corridor.

An armored figure stepped out, wearing what looked like a bastardized mix of crusader plate and modern tactical gear. The red glow in its eye sockets fixed on me as it raised a sword crackling with corrupt magic.

"Intruder," it rasped. "You will serve our master in death."

"Really?" I glared at it. "That's the best you can do? No evil monologue about how inevitable your victory is?"

"I am Death!" the walking cliché before me howled. "The destroyer of worlds and—"

The first Incinerate went off in the skull a half second later. As the metal helmet glowed cherry red, the speech cut off abruptly, followed by my hammer smashing the sword free of its hand.

Then came a snap kick to the groin. Sure, it was dishonorable to kick another guy in the balls, but if this guy had used them for anything besides marbles in the last decade, I was the Queen of May. And besides, the important point here was the flexion area.

As the corpse doubled over, my hammer whistled around to take the helmet in the back of the head, and it launched off its shoulders—complete with the head still inside—as if it'd been fired by a catapult.

More came out of the various doors, and I snorted, lifting my left hand, ready to unleash a blast of lightning, when the sound hit me.

No matter how good the armor was, it couldn't stop everything, and in order for me to be able to hear anything, I had to be able to hear everything.

That wouldn't have been an issue, if it wasn't a goddamn banshee that attacked next.

The world seemed to shake apart as I staggered. Pain flared in my head as the walls, floor, and ceiling magnified the effect, channeling the blast into a horrific one. I crashed into a wall, swinging blindly at anything and everything as I tried to make sense of the world and the fucking horrific pain I was in.

For a handful of seconds, I floundered, stabbing; then there was a wet pop and the sound vanished.

That might have been a good thing—had it not been because a second banshee had joined in, and the combination of the pair shrieking at me had deafened me entirely.

The world was shaking, my eyes flaring with terrible pain as I tried to focus, but I saw nothing.

I reached out to Jack, knowing that I really fucking needed help…and right now. As my eyes failed, the shuddering images dying away to utter blackness, and the feeling of my organs, of the building headache—it all let me know that if I didn't come up with a counter and fucking fast, it was all over.

Jack delivered, though, sensing me and directing me. I spun around, aiming at the greatest concentration, and unleashed Atomic Furnace, turning a section of the corridor into the heart of a star for a brief burst. Then I collapsed to the floor, desperately pulling lightning out and through me.

I managed it for a few seconds, then cursed. I hauled my helmet free and tossed it aside, knowing what I had to do, and that Jack was watching over me.

The undead that had been caught in the area of effect were gone—the banshees thankfully among them. But this was a dungeon where the standard undead were being given self-awareness and upgrades to their powers, where they were being leveled like my own team and like the kobolds under me had been.

That was why I needed my armor off, and fast.

The heat in the corridor was horrific. The effect of that spell being used in here had shattered the ancient stonework. Glass was everywhere, glowing with heat—or it would be, according to Jack's sensors, which were all I could see with right now.

I yanked at my armor, falling sideways and rolling on the floor as I fumbled for catches and latches, desperately trying to get at them. A sudden wash of icy cold flooded the room, and I felt myself being picked up and hurled into the back wall.

I fell. My inner ear didn't help the situation as it made it seem to me like I was lying on my back, even as everything else—the feeling in my friggin' knees, for example—told me I was braced upright.

I forced out a breath, feeling the cold that seeped into me. I tried to undo another latch, but my fingers grew numb. I frantically aimed—thanks to Jack's ongoing sensor relay—a blast of lightning in the general direction of the gathering undead.

The only reason they weren't already on me was the superheated section of the corridor. But that was cooling rapidly, thanks to whatever magic was fucking chilling me as well.

I felt the motion of the air at almost the same time as the pain came. I rolled sideways, caught and dragged by it. This time, I lay there, trying to make sense of the world, and it took long seconds.

When I finally came back to myself—that I managed only because I was pulling lightning into and around myself—I was on my knees again, though this time I was being held in place.

Something gripped me by both shoulders. I muzzily tried to make sense of it, and the screamed warnings that were coming from Jack.

Something was wrong, very wrong, and I couldn't seem to make it all make sense. I couldn't see, either—or at least, not very well. Something was there—a change of color, not just the blackness—and a distant noise...the sound of something running full bore, of clattering, metal bouncing.

I was shifted, and I blinked. Dried and sticky blood moved enough on my eyes that something before me resolved, and I blinked again in confusion.

There was a corpse lord there, but instead of helping me, it was holding me? Its upper arms held my shoulders, and it was braced on one foot? The other was planted against my chest?

I frowned, trying to make sense of it, staring up along the polished bone. Jack continued to hurl impressions of threat and pain at me, so many that I couldn't make sense of any of them, until a single image resolved.

A dozen legs, all peeking out through the bottom of a metal cart, and a collection of arms that spun levers, each connected to wheels that enabled the cart to go even faster.

The whole thing had been seen in a blur, a snapshot as it flashed past, and that sound… The clattering roar, the slap of bones on the stone, the crashing of metal against metal and the echo of the cart…

I blinked as reality slammed back into me. The sudden realization of what was approaching came a half second behind the cruel smile that was reflected in the eyes of the corpse lord. It kicked out, hurling me into the corridor behind, as the cart roared around the corner and into view.

CHAPTER FIFTY-ONE

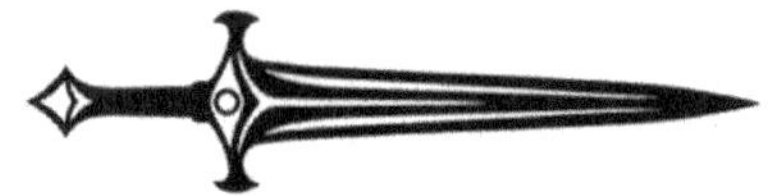

The cart hit like a freight train.

Metal screamed, stone shattered, and my world became a symphony of breaking things, including me. My armor, for all its enchanted strength, crumpled like tinfoil as countless tons of momentum transferred through it. The impact drove me back, then down; the floor actually cratered beneath me as the cart's momentum spent itself in a catastrophic eruption of debris.

Time stretched like toffee as my consciousness flickered. Through the haze of agony, I felt it…that familiar electric tingle, the storm stirring in my soul. The pressure crushing me should have been the end, but instead it was like squeezing a lightning bolt, as the armor that had been imprisoning me, slowing and containing me, failed.

You can't crush lightning.

"The intruder is dead!" one of the undead crowed in a voice like rustling parchment, picking through the wreckage. "See how his armor is shattered? None could survive such—"

I let go.

My physical form dissolved into pure energy, coursing through the metal debris as if it wasn't there. The sensation was incredible—no pain, no limitations…just pure power. I could feel every mote of electricity in the air, every static charge, every potential.

The undead gathered closer, their hollow celebration cut short as arcs of blue-white power began to dance between the pieces of my ruined armor. The light built rapidly, throwing their skeletal faces into sharp relief as they began to back away.

Too late.

I burst from the wreckage in a blinding flash, my form coalescing from lightning itself. No armor now. I didn't need it. Power crackled across my skin and sparked from my eyes as I straightened to my full height.

"That," I grinned, my voice carrying an electric undertone that made the very air vibrate, "was your one free shot."

The corpse lord's glowing eyes widened as its voice ground out slowly, "Im…poss…ible—"

"I am the Storm." I cut him off, lightning dancing between my fingers. "And now it's my turn!"

I moved like quicksilver, barely a blink of time, a hummingbird's heartbeat between me being in the middle of the wreckage, and then being by the side of a mage-looking fucker.

I instinctively knew that was the most dangerous of them. As I appeared by his side, I lashed out. My left fist punched through his chest and out the far side, ripping back, even as I grabbed his head in my other hand and pulsed a fast burst of lightning through my palm and between my fingers.

As that palm covered his skull, the effect was instantly fatal as I unleashed a taser of epic proportions directly into what was left of his brain.

I dropped the remains to the floor. Then, a split second later, I was on the far side. A creature dressed like a Saracen raider swung at me with a curved tulwar; I simply moved back, then back again, reforming my body in the flash of lightning until I stood, unharmed, as the blade swung past.

It tried to adjust, only to find I'd grabbed the blade. I wrenched it free like I was taking it from a sleeping toddler, barely a level of noticeable resistance.

I casually flipped the blade in the air, then rammed it through the thing's skull at the bridge of the nose, driving it back into the corpse lord behind and the blade through that as well. I left them pinned to the wall, ripping the corpse lord's skull free almost absently, and hurled it at another undead, sending the pair to the ground with a sound like coconuts knocking together.

That left one undead upright and more or less alive. He backed away quickly, hands raised; his eyes were rotting and desiccated, its fingers more bone than flesh. The clothing revealed it had once been an aviator.

"I didn't want to…" it gasped, before I was there, standing in front of it, and glaring down.

"Then run," I said coldly, before flashing past it and down the corridor, feeling the new freedom of my form, of the power of an ascendant Cyclone, a Storm Titan rising.

I felt it, and I *gloried* in it.

With the armor gone, I wasn't constantly battling my own adrenaline. My feelings and emotions seemed clearer, more accurate and honest. As I hurtled down the corridors, seeing the way my mana was steadily depleting, I grinned to myself and kept going.

I needed to make it to the final floor for the next stage in the plan, but that had just been made a fuckload easier.

I passed through more living quarters, and for the first time, these showed signs of living habitation. There were food and drink cartons, collections of rubbish and beds, living areas that were built around fires, with chimneys that presumably had been built when the design was older and then were replaced with gems that glowed with heat and light.

I paused, coalescing next to one of them, and grinned. I reached out and felt the mana contained in it, and that it was both a radiant device and an absorption one.

Mana was sucked in from the world around it, presumably tweaked to feed on Life and Unlife mana, from the signs I'd seen so far; then it put out Fire and Light mana, bringing heat and comfort to what I guessed were the few human inhabitants.

More fool them.

I laid a hand on the gemstone, feeling an uncomfortable heat that lasted all of a second, before I was offered the option of trying to capture it, by investing my mana in it.

I refused, and instead sucked the fucker *dry*.

It was only two thousand mana I got, but that was more than I'd lost in healing myself and in my little pyrotechnic display, so it was a win overall. Thirty seconds later, I'd jumped back and forth across the collection of living quarters, and I was nearly back to full mana. Grinning, I burst into light again, hurtling down the passage and into the final room on the floor, before passing through a hail of gunfire, grenades going off, and fragments that exploded in all directions.

I was seeing why Kh'aan's armor had been so unique now. The quicksilver adjusted and reformed as he used it, instead of trapping me like mine had. I made a mental note that such things were to be a massive focus moving forward.

Appearing in the middle of the enemy, I unleashed a pair of Atomic Furnaces, making damn sure they'd not be following me down to the next level. Then I vanished again, reaching the far end of the floor in seconds. Behind me, the sudden roar of fire and the air being sucked out of the world created devastation.

I dropped into my human form, glad that for whatever reason I'd finally managed to create something besides my flesh with my mana, in that I was clad again in my seamless under-armor gear: a stretchy, form-fitting, and yet comfortable outfit that had one massive bonus over anything else.

Namely that, with it covering me, the meat and two veg weren't bouncing out of control as I jogged down the stairs.

I pulled up the notifications I'd received until now, focusing specifically on the kill counts and grinning as I saw the most important bit.

Not that the entire notification had, at my will, restructured to show the ones from the saurian dungeon, the Temple of Zeus, and here as well. No, the best bit was that from the kills I'd managed so far, I'd leveled, and it was time to make the most of that.

Congratulations! You have killed the following:

Saurian Dungeon Combat:

- ***3x Kitchen Saurians [Common], Level 10, 300 XP***
- ***45x Warrior Saurians [Uncommon], Level 4-21, 9,218 XP***
- ***2x Magic Snakes [Elite], Level 25, 1,000 XP***
- ***1x Wannabe Dragon Lord [Elite Boss], Level 30, 5,000 XP***
- ***2x Shadow Guard Wyverns [Elite], Level 25, 2,000 XP***

Temple of Zeus Combat:

- ***25x Controlled Fairies [Uncommon], Level 4-17, 5,882 XP***
- ***4x Cyclops [Common], Level 1-7, 8,455 XP***
- ***30x Basic Undead [Common], Level 1-11, 3,404 XP***
- ***8x Elite Undead Guards [Elite], Level 2-22, 5,020 XP***

Undead Elite Combat:

- ***1x Crusader Death Knight [Elite], Level 25, 750 XP***
- ***1x Undead Mage [Elite], Level 25, 750 XP***
- ***1x Saracen Raider [Elite], Level 25, 500 XP***
- ***1x Corpse Lord [Elite], Level 27, 1,000 XP***
- ***2x Banshee [Elite], Level 25, 2,000 XP***
- ***1x Wraith [Elite], Level 25, 500 XP***

Military Undead Combat:

- ***42x Wehrmacht Soldiers [Uncommon], Level 6-20, 7,004 XP***
- ***1x Ottoman Officer [Elite], Level 25, 500 XP***
- ***18x Mixed Military Undead [Uncommon], Level 4-19, 2,478 XP***
- ***5x Elite Guards [Elite], Level 21-25, 2,889 XP***
- ***12x Lesser Undead [Common], Level 1-15, 1,005 XP***

Total XP awarded: 65,255 XP
Current XP to next level stands at: 146,410/135,000

Congratulations! You have reached Level 34. Current XP to next level stands at 11,410/150,000. You have 15 unspent Stat Points and 0 unspent Skill Points.

I couldn't help but grin at that. An extra level was damn nice—I thank you very much—but more than that was that I got fifteen damn points for hitting them!

I pulled up the stat sheet and rolled through quickly, reading over the points I'd earned in the latest few weeks, and grinned evilly.

You have gained additional Stat Points in the following areas through constant effort.

- **+1 Agility**
- **+1 Constitution**
- **+1 Wisdom**

Continue to work hard to increase these or other stats...

With the fifteen points I had, I dropped seven into Constitution, and six into Strength, as well as the last two points into Wisdom, taking the first two both over the barrier and into the century, boosting my health and Strength at the same time. I tried to read the results, before screaming and falling—tumbling the length of the goddamn stairs, mainly on my face—as my body went into shock and locked up, reforming and upgrading.

Congratulations! For the first time, you have surpassed the century mark in two key attributes at the same time: Strength and Constitution. This momentous achievement signifies a significant step in your ascension toward true godhood.

As the First Lord of the Storm, your physical form has undergone a profound transformation. The raw power of your strengthened body is now matched by an indomitable constitution, granting you unparalleled resilience.

In recognition of this milestone, you have gained the following abilities:

***Titanic Fortitude:** Your maximum health and stamina have increased exponentially. You now possess the constitution of a living fortress, shrugging off blows that would cripple lesser beings. Your wounds heal with uncanny speed, and your endurance in the face of fatigue is nigh-limitless. Note: This ability grants a 2x increase to your maximum health and stamina, as well as a 5x increase to your natural healing and stamina regeneration rates.*

***Crushing Strength:** The might of your unbreakable physique allows you to exert godlike force. Your strikes now possess the power to shatter stone and bend steel. Enemies that dare to stand against you will be crushed beneath the weight of your wrath. Note: This ability grants a 2x increase to your physical damage output, as well as the chance to stun or disrupt foes with your devastating blows.*

With these boons, your transformation into a true god is well underway. Continue your journey, First Lord, for the path to true divinity lies ahead.

Name: Matt, First Lord of the Storm				
Host Powers: 1 (Enhanced Regeneration)				
Species: Cyclone		**Bonus**: None		
Level: 34		**Progress to next level**: 11,410/150,000		
Stat	**Current Points**	**Description**	**Effect**	**Progress to Next Level**
Agility	101	Governs dodge and movement	Heightened chance to dodge attacks Level: Godling	4/100
Charisma	53	Governs likely success to charm, seduce, or threaten	More likely to succeed in events that require seduction, persuasion, or threats Level: Enhanced Humanoid	69/100
Constitution	100	Governs Health and Health Regeneration	HP: 100x200 = 20,000 Level: Godling	7/100
Dexterity	65	Governs ability with weapons and crafting	Increased chance of improved crafting result or increased melee damage Level: Enhanced Humanoid	62/100
Endurance	91	Governs Stamina and Stamina Regeneration	Stamina: 91x180 = 16,380 Level: Demigod	97/100
Intelligence	106	Governs base manapool,	Mana: 106x110 (x2) = 23,320	8/100

		standard intellectual capacity	Level: Godling	
Luck	65	Governs overall chance of bonuses and critical hits	Increased chance of positive outcome Level: Enhanced Humanoid	66/100
Perception	60	Governs ranged damage and chance to spot hidden items/traps	+50 to all ranged attacks Level: Enhanced Humanoid	51/100
Strength	100	Governs damage with melee weapons and carrying capacity	Enhanced damage with Melee weapons Level: Godling	98/100
Wisdom	78	Governs mana regeneration	1560 mana regenerated per hour *(Arcanist class 2 boost)*	4/100

By the time I finally forced myself to my hands and knees, and then back to my feet, I could hear the clatter of incoming feet, from above and behind me. But as I flexed my right hand and my left, feeling the power that flowed through me, I couldn't help but grin.

Yeah, I was already annoyed with myself for one thing—I'd left my fucking sword and other equipment back up there in the corridor, including my goddamn bag of holding, like a complete dick, excited by the power that was flowing through me. But as I looked ahead, seeing a heavily carved stone portal that stood silent at the end of the passage, I knew that it didn't matter.

The final round was all that lay waiting. And the fight that was to come? Well, my swordsmanship wasn't going to be the point in that fight.

I stood, stepping forward to the massive portal, and reached out with one hand, laying it flat and then pushing it open.

The door swung silently back. A rumbling noise as sand was ground to dust filled the air, and beyond the portal, the next passage lit slowly.

It was limestone, that much I knew, as I rested a hand on its battered surface. I stepped through the doorway; the distant sense of Jack wishing me well and good fortune cut off as the door closed again with a loud boom.

As I'd expected, I received an immediate notification, and I pulled it up.

Congratulations, Dungeon Warmancer!

You have entered the [Eleventh Steel Dungeon].

This dungeon is [Bound] and as such [cannot] be claimed.

Do you wish to continue?

*

Warning!

Crossing the boundary will signify that you are ready and accept the risk posed to you by the inhabitants of the dungeon.

*

WARNING!

This Dungeon is set to [Advanced] and will be a lethal challenge for the unwary…

I nodded, waiting. A red line appeared before me, just like before. A light flowed across the floor, running across and hovering like a terminator line between this world and the next.

I stepped across it, and read the next prompt. In here, at least, I was being protected from the rest of the dungeon, by its own rules.

Congratulations, Dungeon Warmancer!

You have chosen to continue! The dungeon has been set to provide a formidable challenge to all inhabitants, leveling as required and…

[Error]

This Trial Dungeon has been overridden by the resident Dungeon Lord, and the prior inhabitants of the dungeon have been artificially boosted to your current level…

[Error]

Current Dungeon inhabitants are unable to match power levels due to innate conditions. Entrant is identified as a [Cyclone]. Internal inhabitants cannot be artificially boosted to this point without additional resources dedicated to the dungeon.

Do you wish to surrender all items brought into the trial dungeon to permit exit?

[Error]

No items identified beyond Dungeon Warmancer unit …Reassessing…

Solution Found: [Trial] Dungeon will be upgraded to [Elimination] Dungeon, subject to all parties agreeing.

Dungeon Warmancer: To enable an accurate level of challenge for your current physical condition, all current residents of the trial dungeon must

be eliminated, their current XP, energy, and capabilities reset and channeled into a single opponent.

Do you agree?

Yes/No...

A second screen appeared over the top of the current one, making it clear that it was the text presented to my opponent, and that he'd already agreed.

Solution Found: [Trial] Dungeon will be upgraded to [Elimination] Dungeon, subject to all parties agreeing.

Lord Summoner: To enable an accurate level of challenge for your current physical condition, all current residents of the trial dungeon must be eliminated, their current XP, energy, and capabilities reset and channeled into a single opponent.

[AGREED]

I grinned to myself as I saw the flash that indicated he'd agreed. I really hoped that it meant as I was betting, that he'd not read the conditions and details.

Just to make sure, and to maintain both the illusion *and* the trap, I agreed as well, watching as the screen vanished, and a final one popped up.

Excellent!

As a Dungeon Warmancer, you have entered an opposing Dungeon, that you are currently in a declared war with. This Elimination dungeon is activating, and all requests to exit have been offered and refused. Are you prepared to fight against Elimination?

Yes/No

> ***Note:*** *Although the rewards for surviving a full elimination Dungeon are significant (including possible core level upgrades), the risk is also commensurately higher.*

Prepare yourself for Elimination...

I kept grinning to myself as the dungeon around me suddenly twisted, the entire thing shaking like a shitting dog. I crouched, resting the palm of one hand on the floor as I watched the ceiling, wondering whether I'd made a massive fuck-up and was about to be wiped out by my own hubris. Then the second change rang out—or, more accurately, the scream rang out.

It hung in the air for long after it should have, echoing over and over as if it came from a dozen throats. But despite it all, I knew it was from one, really. Ahead of me, a second door opened slowly, hanging open invitingly, as the dungeon shifted, even as I watched.

I rose to my feet, noting that the screamer had taken a fresh lungful and then had gone again, the sound seemingly full of unexpected agony. I started forward, wondering whether I even needed to use the ace up my sleeve now.

The corridor that had ran ahead of me when I'd checked Jack's oh-so-convenient map had changed, no longer weaving back and forth. Instead, it opened into a dozen different sections…an ancient, buried bazaar or marketplace, I'd have guessed, repopulated by the dead.

Instead, now, those sections sat empty. The far end seemed to slide closer; the rumbling of the ground made it clear that it was no optical illusion.

"POWER!" I heard a distant strangled voice screech. "SUCH POWER!"

"Sounds like my opponent is getting over the shock," I muttered to myself. Regardless of anything else, the stupid fucker setting up to offer a trial dungeon, clearly thinking to weaken me inside it, had provided me with a wonderful opportunity.

All his dungeon-born forces, no matter how many there had been, had been killed, and their levels, their life force, magic, and whatever else animated them, had been ripped free to artificially increase the level of the dickbag I was about to face.

That was a good thing; it freed up the rest of my people in the Zeus Temple dungeon, for example. Any undead that had been fighting there, I was betting, had been consumed as well, *but*… I wasn't going into this with the advantage of godhood over a much weaker foe as I had been.

That was fine, though, because that had never been something I'd been relying on.

I strode down the passage, stepping out into the bazaar and seeing the dimly lit vaulted ceilings, the dusty walls, the shattered stone, and ancient graffiti as idiots dead a thousand years declared that they'd once been there.

I snorted in disgust, knowing that humans were humans no matter where you were, and remembering seeing the names carved into the goddamn sphynx in Egypt once.

Glancing from side to side, I went on, seeing the curled-up bodies, drained of everything by their lord, the summoner, as I racked my brains over what I was about to face.

That undead lich dick had said that he was a summoner—and yeah, the prompt had made that clear…not a necromancer, a summoner.

That he'd then taken over an undead dungeon, one that again, had no fairy? That was a bit stranger, but not important currently.

He'd said that they'd been somewhere far from any others, and although I'd thought he'd been referring to somewhere high in the mountains, this was honestly a much better location.

How he'd come across it, I had no idea, but here and there, I saw technological and modern remnants. Magazines, glossy ones that had once been full of meaningless celebrity shite, stood in neat rows in a small booth, making me pause in confusion.

Worse still was that the figure that was holding one, collapsed on the floor and curled up, fingers having torn pages free, was an obviously long-dead creature.

It looked human, but between the long eyeteeth, the sallow features—where they could be made out—and the jewelry, not to mention the long legs and clawed fingers, I could see that it hadn't been.

It was also undead, or re-dead, or unlife or—you know what? Fuck it.

It was *dead.*

It was dead, and it'd clearly been reading a fucking magazine when its imitation life had been ripped free.

What that said about the reality all around us that even the monsters at the bottom of a buried dungeon in the middle of the fucking desert wanted to keep up with the mostly no-longer-living fucking lunatic celebrities didn't bear thinking of.

I kept going. My footsteps raised small puffs of dust, every noise amplified by the unnatural silence. Reaching the far end of the bazaar, passing dozens of bodies, including many that were armed with antique weapons, I stepped out and into another corridor.

Torches burned fitfully in sconces in the walls. The flickering light danced as I passed, the pop and crackle the only sound beyond my breathing. Until, at last, I came to a carved entrance that had clearly never been part of the original structure.

It was made of polished amber glass. My side was dusty, but the far one? I could dimly see rivulets of condensation running down it. I laid a hand on it and pushed, and it opened easily. I stepped through it, and I couldn't help but pause, staring out over the underground cavern that was revealed.

Aboveground, there was nothing for hundreds of miles but shifting quartz sands and ruins. But below it? I had no clue whether this was a creation of the dungeon—I could feel the magic in the area, after all—but the cavern was a rich oasis of life. If this had been here all along?

The civilizations that had once called this inhospitable dust ball home could have still been here.

More to the point, though, as I stood atop the amber glass balcony, staring out over lush tropical vegetation, wild flowering plants, and dozens of different kinds of fruit-bearing trees that together formed an orchard, I had to admit I was impressed, even as the door slid slowly shut behind me, sealing the moisture in.

That was when the portal to hell opened below my feet, of course.

CHAPTER FIFTY-TWO

I launched into the air, even as a hand the size of an excavator reached out. Claw-tipped fingers, black and wizened, snapped closed inches from me, then slowly retreated.

A voice rang out from the distance. "You dodged it? You surprise me, but very well. Well done."

"Well done?" I called back, shifting around in the air as I floated into the cavern, only now seeing the patterns that had been carved into the glass of the balcony. As I looked, I could see the mana leeching away from them, and the portal slid shut. "Was that supposed to be a welcome mat? Fuckin' rude greeting, if you ask me!"

"You invaded my home, and you expected different?" the voice called.

I moved through the air, heading for it. "You declared war on *me*, dickbag," I pointed out. "Don't go acting all butt-hurt because I didn't let you win."

"Ah, well, yes, there is that." The figure ahead sighed.

I squinted, seeing them as they came out of the mist.

It was a human—male, I guessed by the voice, though the long robes that trailed in the air behind them and hid their face, as well as the golden-tipped fingers, the jewels, and the inlaid ornamental getup could have been hiding three kobolds for all I cared.

"All threats aside, had I realized that leap in power that awaited me simply for declaring war, I'd have done it long ago," he admitted.

I stared at him, wondering whether he understood what he'd done. "You killed all your people—you get that, right?" I asked.

"Minions," he replied airily, waving a hand negligently.

"Little yellow fuckers?"

"No, but their value was limited to their value to me…hence, minions." He glared at me. Gleaming black eyes stared out of a mask that had more gold on it than was reasonable for anyone to possess, and I blinked as I recognized it.

"Wait, isn't that a knockoff of King Tut's mask?" I asked.

"No, it's the original!" he declared proudly.

"You what?"

"The original mask, worn by the boy-king and—"

"That thing sat on his moldering face for thousands of years, and you thought it was a good idea to drill eyeholes and put it on?" I interrupted him. "Fuck's sake, I bet you've got a nasty case of the ancient Egyptian clap."

"SILENCE!" he screamed.

I noticed the way that there was a section of the lips cut away to allow him to speak and breathe.

"Fuck me, you're literally licking where his bandages were. Damn, you're brave. I'd not even use my ex's Chap Stick, and I knew where her lips had been," I said, unable to help myself even though I saw how much it infuriated him.

"Infidel!" he declared stridently.

"Dickhead," I replied conversationally.

"Surrender!" he demanded.

"That's not how this works, and you know it," I pointed out. "I mean, you *can* surrender if you want and I'll make it quick, but—and this is a bit of a spoiler—today is going to end badly for you."

"I have never been defeated!" he screamed.

"Seriously? What, are you some kind of prodigy? Or wait, have you never been in a fight?" I asked curiously. "I mean, it's easy to never be defeated if you never fight. I've lost a lot, though mainly when I was a kid, and got my teeth handed to me for backtalking."

That was apparently a sore spot, as that was when the fight started.

He slapped both palms together. A golden disc appeared on each that he twisted to point at me, even as they revolved and spun.

In the center of each disc, there were a pair of glowing triangles, all composed of light. They spun faster and faster, their points passing through one another, before slamming to a halt, as the air in the middle suddenly vanished and a gout of water roared free of the middle of each.

Apparently, I was supposed to stay still for this, possibly being all shocked and awed, or maybe tossing a coin and clapping, before asking him whether he could produce a pigeon from his pants next.

Needless to say, I'd launched myself forward, summoning a pair of Incinerate spells aimed at his forehead and crotch, deciding that if either got through, the fight was over.

Unfortunately, that was when I found the shield.

It flared into life and the spell's mana was torn from me, made worse because I'd been attempting to channel them to make sure they got through.

Four hundred mana for each spell was bodily ripped out, and a pair of undead kobolds—uncommon, I guessed, from the style—appeared, looking highly confused before stabbing at me with long spears.

I almost burst out laughing. The spell wasn't a bad one—a hidden shield that took your opponent's mana and used it to summon a new creature for you was damn inventive.

The issue?

We were both hovering thirty feet up at this point, as I'd not bothered to head to the ground, and he'd risen to meet me.

That meant that as the kobolds had been summoned on a level with us, they stabbed out, missed, then fell, passing trees and rocks at increasing speeds before they crashed into the ground in an explosion of broken bones.

I would have laughed, and possibly pointed at the same time to add insult to injury, but the water that he'd summoned hit me then, and fuck me, it wasn't nice.

One stream was icy cold, literally at the point of being a solid. The taste of saltwater told me that it was taken from an ocean. The second was hot enough that it'd have boiled a lobster. And the pair combining was enough to shock me momentarily.

Worse still, as I transitioned from my more or less mortal form into the avatar of the storm, instead of flashing forward, as I'd planned, pulsing through the water, I was instead pushed back.

I shifted, bursting upward, forcing myself free of the water momentarily. It followed me, steam and ice radiating off me, and that was when I got the second shock, as he came back into sight.

I'd seen those multi-limbed Indian deities in images, but damn, as I twisted around to face him, I saw the multitude of arms moving for the first time in reality.

A fresh shield appeared behind and towered over me. A second appeared ahead, and two more floating discs materialized to either side. This time, though, chains shot out of them. The tips ended in a spike of gold that twisted and stabbed, hunting me through the air like serpents.

I slid sideways. My own lightning shields flared into life as both chains crashed into them. I fired off a pair of lightning bolts, crashing into the shields as they slid inward, aiming to crush me between them.

The surface of each lit with roiling flames, swirling in complicated patterns that then produced additional discs scattered across the face of the shield. Each sent a fresh spear tip, followed by a chain—this time created of fire—to crash into my own shield.

I blinked, stunned by the onslaught. More and more of the discs flared to life, and I realized finally that the longer this fight went on, the more it favored the goddamn summoner on his home turf.

I fired off four more Incinerates, not wanting to waste a more powerful spell. I cursed when the spells failed and instead four more creatures appeared.

Again, they were kobolds, and I twisted, flashing left and right, trying to get some room, before unleashing a Lightning Storm, determined to see what damage I could do.

All I needed was a few seconds in close, but his shields flared again and again, and I had no clue how the hell he had so much mana.

I hit a shield, Ice mana this time, and I felt the heat being ripped from me. I flashed from my normal form into that of the lightning avatar; I darted to the left twenty meters in a heartbeat, before pausing and glaring at him as he shifted his shields around and continued with the summoning.

The air above him blackened. Storm clouds rolled out of nowhere, as the humidity changed. The air became charged as I slammed a second and third casting of Lightning Storm into the air around us.

Every time I shifted into the avatar form, I found that as I reformed myself afterward, I did it by will alone.

That meant that the injuries that I'd had before, unless I wanted to take them with me, were healed, which was incredible.

I launched forward, hoping to distract him. I slammed into the shield, this one flaming—again—and instead of trying to avoid it, I smashed both fists into it as hard as I could.

Lightning cascaded off, even as flames burned into me. Blue-white light flared and pulsed out into the shield, draining it. I hammered my fists in again and again, as I tried to drain his mana, by overextending his shield.

Another shield flared as it slammed into me from behind. This one crackled with a sickly green energy that tried to leech my strength. Crackling streamers of fire lifted from the shield before me to lock onto the one behind, even as green lightning flared and popped, reaching for me.

I shoved off, transforming again, and flashed out of the gap between the shields, covering a hundred meters in a second, before reforming and hovering there, panting.

My body was healed again. The burning agony that had been consuming my arms was gone, and even my nerves tingled, fresh and perfect. But the ghostly memory of the pain remained, dying away.

The shields, though?

They were perfect—not a single sign of failure yet—and if anything, they were *growing*.

More were forming, sliding into reality on all sides as the fucker began to make a cube of power. Elemental forms that should have been battling each other appeared, then slid into place.

The edges of the shields, of the containment cube he was making, were crackling zones of explosive contamination. But the fucker was somehow managing to keep them intact, and that spoke to a much more skilled mage than me.

My lightning storms flared, the discharge beginning with three times the normal power. They unleashed lightning that could have powered a city back before the end of the world. As the strikes hit his shield, he fucking *laughed.*

Dozens of creatures appeared, all undead, erupting into the air, before plunging to the ground far below. The majority shattered on impact: kobolds, goblins, some kind of snake-man, and—joy—Scepiniir, before more standard humanoid undead fell with a crash.

I blasted backward. My lightning form flickered as I darted back into it and flashed across to the far side, searching for a way out of the box and bouncing back, before surveying the battlefield again. Something wasn't adding up.

"Getting tired?" The summoner's voice held that smug tone that made me want to punch him in his shiny borrowed face. "Your attacks grow weaker."

He wasn't wrong, which was the annoying part. My mana wasn't regenerating as fast as it should. And every spell I threw at him seemed to feed into his shields, and then power his summons even more.

Most of them were dead—heh—or at least rendered un-functional by the fall, though a few down there were dragging themselves across the floor.

That's when I noticed it. As I hovered there, letting my mana vision adjust to my storm form, I could see the patterns of energy flowing through the cavern. They weren't random. The tropical plants, the carved amber glass, even the scattered chunks of ruins…they were all part of a massive magical circuit.

"Son of a bitch," I muttered. "You've been planning this for a while, haven't you?"

The summoner spread his arms—all fucking six of them—in a grandiose gesture. "For months! This entire chamber is my masterwork. Every Dungeon Lord who thought to challenge me would find themselves here, their power feeding my ascension, and that was before I knew that I could simply power-level myself by permitting a godling in here!"

I dodged another set of those golden chains, noting how they seemed to draw power from specific points in the cavern. "That's why you kept pushing other dungeons until they declared war. You wanted them to come here at full strength."

"The more power they brought, the more I could take!" He laughed, the sound echoing unnaturally. "And you, oh mighty Storm Lord, you've brought more power than all the others combined!"

Three more shields materialized around me as I tried to blast him with a concentrated lightning storm. The electricity just fed into his network, powering up another wave of those damn discs.

My lightning avatar form flickered again. I was burning through mana faster than I could regenerate it, and every attack I launched just seemed to make him stronger. Even my usual trick of overwhelming opponents with sheer power wasn't working. The bastard had built himself a perfect energy recycling system.

"I have to admit," I caught my breath as I hovered in the middle of what was now a rapidly shrinking clear area, "this is a pretty impressive setup. Must have taken ages to build."

"Indeed! And now"—he raised his hands, magical circles forming around each one—"you'll see its true potential!"

The air literally crackled with power now, making me nod to myself. The mana that I'd been unleashing was being sucked in, but only slowly. The conversion from my spells to his summons wasn't perfect, and neither was it instantaneous, despite the impression it gave.

There was a lot being lost. The kobolds were basic fuckers, judging from the way they shattered on impact. That meant that as near as I could remember, they were coming in at about forty mana a pop in costs.

Ten percent or so of the overall mana I was unleashing was all that he was spending, meaning that the rest of the mana was still gathering around us. And the shields he was casting had to be leaking a fuckload of mana as well.

I didn't know how he'd lasted this long. Summoning things that fucking big would have bottomed me out pretty quickly, especially after I started whaling on them as I had. But, again, that was fine.

As a summoner, I guessed that he was big on magic—certainly, that made sense. But the important bit of the upgrade notification wasn't about magic.

It was about upgrading him to be my "physical match." Although he might have been that before all of this—though I doubted it—if he had, then I was hoping he'd been mainly focused on magic as his weapon of choice, and not physical training.

That meant two things as far as I was concerned.

First, with the sheer levels of mana he'd been throwing around, either he was about to run out of mana, or he was draining it from the dungeon and into himself to keep himself going.

Secondly, unless he was used to the body, he was going to be very uncoordinated, graceless, and, I bet, distracted by glorying over the enhancements he'd just gotten.

If he was able to keep this much mana going for spells, then there was no way that he'd been investing in his body the way I had before all of this, so I bet he was going to turn out to be a shitty close combat fighter.

It was definitely time for my trump card.

I took a deep breath and reached out to the dungeon. I could feel it refusing me as an enemy Dungeon Lord, but it couldn't block me entirely—and that was important, because I only needed a slight connection to a Cinthian-created system for this.

"Are those Scepiniir bodies down there?" I shouted at him, pushing mana into the dungeon, making damn sure that I was connected to it, just in case that mattered.

"Yes!" he boomed. "You fool—you even gave me their patterns!"

"How did they die?" I called out, my voice echoing through the chamber.

"What does it matter?" he sneered, golden mask glinting as he gestured with multiple arms. "They were mine to use as I pleased!"

"Humor me." I dodged another chain. "Did you provide them with proper quarters? Sacred spaces for meditation? Dramatic declaration stands? Or did you just throw them in some hole when you weren't using them?"

The summoner scoffed. "They were tools, nothing more. I summoned them, sacrificed them, and raised their corpses. What difference could such trivialities make now?"

"Trivialities?" I couldn't help but grin, feeling the dungeon's connection pulse through the air in sudden response to his words. "You know, when the Scepiniir agreed to be part of the dungeon system, they came with this massive rule book. Most dungeons probably never read past the first page. I'm curious…did you? We sent you the rules, even printed them out to make it easier."

"Your point?" The shields slid closer, the air crackling with energy.

"My point is that even beyond that rule book, there are three absolute rules when dealing with Scepiniir, and you had to have seen them in your dungeon system regardless of the massive fuck-off tome of other rules you had. You stupidly broke or ignored all of them. First: no Scepiniir may be forced into a bonded pairing against its will. Second: no Scepiniir may be sacrificed to another species, nor consumed by any through any bond or partnership with the dungeon. And last? No Scepiniir can be forced into servitude, nor arenas for the purpose of entertainment."

He stared at me, then sneered. "I have broken none of those rules!"

"Really?" I asked. "You sure about that? So you didn't sacrifice them, when you killed, then consumed them to raise as undead versions?"

There was a pause, then he snorted. "So what if I did? You think I care what some minion on the far side of the galaxy thinks? I don't! I'll do what I want, and—"

I raised my voice, letting it carry. "I call upon the judgment of Warmaster Kh'aan! This one has violated the Sacred Accords!"

The summoner's laughter rose, then cut short. His hands rose and he stared at them, as if confused, then at the dungeon around him.

"What…what is this?" he demanded. His extra arms wavered as his carefully constructed matrix of power began to flicker.

"This," I said, "is what happens when you piss off a race of warrior-cats who've spent millennia perfecting the art of magical contracts."

The air grew thick with heavy power—not his recycled mana, but something far older and more primal. A sudden thunder of drums began to reverberate through the air. The golden mask turned sharply, scanning the chamber. The very walls began to vibrate as the drums rose in volume, building steadily.

Seconds passed; I backed away slowly, eyes fixed on him as he apparently tried to interface with the dungeon. A deep resonant boom echoed through the chamber, and for a moment, reality itself seemed to shudder.

The carefully constructed magical circuits in the walls began to crack, golden light seeping through like molten metal.

The shields that had paused in their inexorable slide toward me, along with dozens of golden chains that had been frozen in the act of trying to catch me, suddenly vanished as their mana was ripped free, and I grinned in satisfaction.

"No!" The summoner's voice cracked as his shields started to dissolve. "This is my domain! My power!"

"Not anymore." I watched as the elaborate tropical plants withered and the amber glass walls began to lose their luster. "You know what the best part about those contracts is? The Scepiniir made sure they were linked directly to the dungeon system itself. That was a condition of the premier fuckin' warrior race in the galaxy allowing themselves to be used in it. No override possible, not even for a Dungeon Lord."

The air split with a sound like thunder, and a figure materialized between us: Kh'aan, the Scepiniir warmaster. His silvery quicksilver metal armor gleamed with internal light. He didn't waste time with words. His presence alone was enough to start the transformation.

The chamber's walls exploded outward—not in a shower of debris, but in a controlled dissolution. The accumulated mana from the summoner's recycling system…all that power he'd been so proud of, all the mana that had been in use by the spells that had been about to kick my fuckin' arse—all of it was drawn into Kh'aan's ritual.

The elaborate tropical paradise crumbled away, replaced by towering stone walls weathered by centuries of combat as the arena, the final floor of the trial dungeon, burst from the ground below. Sand poured across the formerly lush vegetation as pillars rocketed up on all sides around us.

"Wait!" The summoner's extra arms began to fade as his enhanced form was stripped away. "You can't do this! I am the master here!"

"You were warned." I floated down to stand on the sand of the newly formed arena floor. Thousands of seats rose around us, carved from living rock, each marked with ancient runes of judgment. "The Scepiniir don't joke about their traditions."

Kh'aan's voice rolled across the arena like distant thunder: "The pact has been broken, and by the laws of immutable reality, restitution is demanded. The Scepiniir name a champion to defend their claim, and the challenge is set. Two enter, one leaves. No magic but what flows in your blood. No weapons but those you hold. The Sands of Judgment await."

A pressure slammed down atop me, nearly driving me to the ground. I hissed in pain, feeling the intense buzz of a thousand, thousand strands of individual mana, as they tore into my skin, weaving a tapestry across it.

I banished the covering that I'd been summoning from the top half; the under-armor top section vanished into the ether as the mana was released.

I stood naked to the waist, staring at the tribal markings that swirled and arced, the black that covered and marked my skin, patterns that appeared by the hundreds. Each was separate, and yet touched and blended into the others. I knew them on sight, as if I'd been born to the culture.

They were the tribal marks of the Scepiniir. Each tribe had its own proud heritage, its own reason for being who and what they were—the Greyskins, the Mountains of the Moon, the Vibrant Wheel to name but a few of the thousand tribes—and each and every one had just magically marked me, claiming me as their own.

I stared up at Kh'aan as he stared down at me, and I wondered whether I'd been manipulated into this, or gifted with it. Blood ran from what must have been tens of thousands of tiny wounds across my skin. Only my face was left untouched, and almost there the tattoos rose, reaching like fingers of smoke along my neck to end in lines that hinted.

The summoner staggered as his ornate robes hung loose and powerless around him. The mask of Tutankhamun now looked absurdly out of place and incredibly heavy as he staggered. "This…this is impossible! My mana networks…my power…"

I could heal myself, I knew; at any time, I could simply reform. But if I did that now? If I reformed myself without the tattoos? I'd be pissing on the honor of the Scepiniir in a way that no Dungeon Lord could have before me.

Instead, I forced myself to straighten, to ignore the feeling that every inch of me had been flayed alive, and I faced my opponent, who barely stood, staring at his shaking hands in shock.

"Yeah," I said. The lightning that flowed in my blood suddenly danced across my knuckles. "Turns out there's a reason the Scepiniir are so particular about arena combat."

Kh'aan raised his hand, and twelve figures materialized on platforms around the arena's perimeter—his personal honor guard, each in armor that seemed to ripple with contained power. They began a rhythmic beating of weapons against shields that echoed through the vast space.

The summoner's eyes darted between me and Kh'aan, then to the exits that no longer existed. His borrowed mask gleamed dully in the strange light that seemed to come from everywhere and nowhere.

"You think this changes anything?" he snarled, but there was an edge of desperation in his voice now. "I am still a Dungeon Lord! I still have power!"

"True," I agreed, settling into a fighting stance. "But now you have to use your *own* power, not your tricks and toys. Ready to find out if you're actually as badass as you pretend to be?"

He responded by launching himself at me with a scream of rage. Golden light blazed around his hands as he formed them into claws. But something was different now: his attacks were slower, less certain. Without his enhanced form and mana networks, he was just another fool who'd relied too heavily on his magic tricks, and not enough on his tools.

The summoner's hands blazed with mingled fire and frost as he charged, but his movements were sluggish compared to before. The pain of my newly acquired tribal markings burned across my skin, but with each pulse of agony, I knew that I was doing something that mattered.

I wasn't just fighting against another asshole human. I was earning a place with the Scepiniir, and hopefully, earning Kh'aan's respect.

"Even stripped of my networks, I still command the elements!" the dickhead roared, hurling a wave of necromantic energy that would have reduced a normal man to ash.

I met it with a lightning-wreathed fist. Storm-Strike converted my punch into a spear of pure electrical force that shattered the rolling wall of necromantic energy. The collision sent sparks cascading across the arena floor, the sand beneath our feet turning to glass as it ground out.

He staggered back, clearly shocked by the counter. His borrowed mask tilted as he shook his head, clearly struggling with its weight now that his enhanced strength was gone. "Impossible! Lightning cannot—"

"What?" I cut him off. Electricity arced between the tribal markings that now covered my torso. Each pattern seemed to resonate with the storm energy, amplifying it as it raced across my skin. "You still don't get it, do you? You think that a dead body should grant you fuckin' power? It's MANA—all of it is, or none of it is! If you can create a fuckin' wall with it, I can too. If I can punch it out, so can you. Or you could, anyway, if you understood what the hell you were doing."

To demonstrate, I unleashed a blast that combined Lightning and pure Storm mana twisted into a bolt, but I unleashed it through a shadow-boxing jab. The air itself seemed to shred around the blast as it struck his hastily raised barrier. The shield—now powered only by his innate abilities and internal mana—shattered like glass.

He leapt aside. His mask came partially loose, obscuring his vision. He frantically ripped it free, hurling the priceless artifact to the sand as he screamed in rage. His second and a fucking third shield all shimmered into place, making it clear that the stupid fucker was committed to draining his mana even quicker than I'd thought he would.

His hands were already moving, summoning spirits and minor undead in desperation. He was down to four arms as well, rather than the eight or ten he'd commanded before. Elemental blasts appeared, erupting into the air and hurtling forward...but they were pale shadows of what he'd commanded before.

I summoned my own shield, lunging forward and using it as a battering ram as I ran after him. A vortex in the fabric of reality appeared, a void beyond filled with screaming souls that tried to escape. I hit it with the leading edge of the shield before anything could escape. The lightning poured into the void, draining my shield but disrupting the spell as well.

It snapped shut. A grey-green form that had been halfway free of it—eyeless and all teeth and ethereal bones—shrieked as it was caught and cut in two.

It burst into vapor, and next it was the turn of skeletal hands that ripped free of the sand, desperately grasping, snatching at me, only to be trampled beneath my feet.

I launched myself across the gap between us, not daring to transform into my lightning avatar form, to change my skin again. So, instead, I did it the old-fashioned way.

He tried to back up, then snarled and lashed out with a punch that was so poorly concealed and aimed that he might as well have sent me a love note in the mail.

I slapped it aside, deflecting to the right, and slammed a punch into his stomach with my left, feeling the heavy golden armor take the blow and wincing as my knuckles and fingers nearly broke.

The effect on him was worse, though. He staggered, gasping, and swung wildly, clearly hoping to drive me back. I took the blow on my left forearm, lifting it into place just in time and grunting with the power of the impact. Then I snapped out a punch that rocked his head back and left him spitting blood.

I grinned as I followed up—a left cross to the chin, a blow aimed straight at the plates of gold over his left bicep. He grunted, and damn me, it hurt; the raised patterns that covered the golden armor he'd worn under the robes were ornate and clearly ancient.

He'd probably stolen it from some long-forgotten tomb. The patterning was clearly well made, and in quantities that you just didn't get in the modern world, or at least not before the fall.

The important point that I was seeing, though, as he reeled and staggered?

It was *ornamental*.

CHAPTER FIFTY-THREE: THE LAST CHAPTER

Good armor was supposed to defend you. It was supposed to stop the injuries transferring through to fuck you up. But the golden shit that he wore?

It had to be the remains of a dozen dead kings and pharaohs. None of it had been intended for anything so prosaic as defense, and the way he shook his arm made that clear.

I grinned.

He stumbled backward, his remaining arms flailing as he tried to maintain his balance. The golden armor that had looked so impressive was working against him now, each piece a dead weight that dragged at his movements.

"What's wrong?" I taunted, pressing forward. "Those ancient kings not helping much now? Maybe you should've spent more time training and less time grave robbing!"

He snarled; dark energy crackled around his hands as he tried to form another spell. "You dare mock me? I have harvested power from the greatest rulers of—"

I cut him off with another lightning-enhanced strike, this one catching him in the chest. The ornate breastplate—probably worth millions to some museum—crumpled like tinfoil. Lightning arced across the golden surface, finding every decorative ridge and flowing through the elaborate patterns.

He screamed, more in rage than pain, and unleashed everything he had left. Fire and ice, death and decay—all of them and more poured out in a desperate wave. But without his networks, without his enhanced mana and the fucking dungeon all around him, it was unfocused, wild.

I met it head-on, storm energy coursing through the tribal markings that covered my skin. The lightning that erupted from my strikes wasn't just countering his spells—it was shattering them, sending their component mana scattering to the winds.

"You don't get it, do you?" I roared as I advanced through his failing barrage. "All that stolen power, all those borrowed artifacts…they were just crutches. You never learned what real power is."

He answered with another barrage of spells, this time summoning a wall of ice between us. I shattered it with a lightning-charged punch, following through as shards exploded outward. His eyes widened as I cleared the debris faster than he'd expected.

Two of his arms hurled death magic while the others tried to form another shield. I ducked under the necrotic blasts, feeling them sizzle past my head, and slammed my shoulder into his hastily formed barrier. It cracked, then shattered as I channeled lightning through the point of impact.

The collision sent him staggering. I pressed the advantage, landing three rapid strikes before he could recover: left ribs, right shoulder, solar plexus. Each impact left spiderweb cracks in the ornate golden armor. Lightning followed the decorative patterns, turning them into channels for my power.

He tried to counter with a desperate swing, but his form was sloppy. I caught his arm, twisted, and used his own momentum to slam him face-first into the arena floor. The impact left an impression in the sand, and more pieces of golden armor broke free.

"Impossible," he gasped, rolling away from my follow-up strike. "I am the Dungeon Lord! I command—"

"You command shit." I caught his next wild swing and drove my knee into his stomach. "You're just another idiot who thought stealing power made him strong."

Pain radiated through me now—through my fists, through my knees. But instead of channeling my mana and shifting my form, then reforming from the lightning avatar, back to normal, I dragged the lightning up from my core and around.

Gods, it felt slow, healing like this now, actually taking entire *seconds* to heal instead of just reforming myself and being healed.

His response was to release a pulse of pure mana, raw and unfocused. It would have killed most opponents through sheer force. I met it with my own blast of lightning. The collision turned the air between us into plasma and we both staggered. Then I launched myself through it, grabbing onto his armor and dragging him toward me as we both fell.

We hit the ground. I headbutted him, then shifted my grip, locking my hands around the tops of his biceps, where the golden armor was already battered and beaten.

Crushing Strength, as it turned out, was well named. I bore down, squeezing with all my might, bending and crushing the armor, sealing it in, damaging his muscles beneath and forcing the blood to pass imperfectly.

We might have been magically altered to be equals, but I'd spent months on the sharp end of the stick, fighting day by day and being hurt over and over.

I was conditioned and trained. I was experienced in the fight, able to ignore pain to a degree and fight through…while he had no such experience and training.

His squeal as the metal bent inward was high-pitched. The combination of the sudden nerve impulses that were misfiring thanks to the bent metal and the numbness meant that "T. rex arms" were suddenly a real thing for him. Then add in the bloody face from the headbutt, and the terror and confusion as I dragged myself up to kneel over him…it all added up to one thing beyond anything else.

The stupid fucker had bought into his own hype, and had actually never considered that he could lose.

Despite all my determination, despite all the things that could go wrong, I knew it when the time was right, and I activated 'Aegis of Recovery'. All around me, the light of a new dome flared, golden and blue-white in rolling waves. It bathed the pair of us in a magical light that sped my mana recovery up to double, before I activated my final century ability: Temporal Momentum.

The world around me slowed to half its speed. My mana flared and started to drop steadily. But its decline was slowed, again by half, thanks to the doubled regeneration.

I made the most of it, punching him across the face with a right cross, then a left.

His face rippled with each blow, slow motion shifts in the pouchy fat from each impact. I saw the way he tried to speak, even as he flailed weakly at me.

I smacked both hands aside, then slammed a fist into his throat; his eyes widened in pain and terror. The changes that I'd manifested with each century were incredible. The sheer physical power had made it clear that I was literally approaching godlike in reality, but whatever abilities he'd been gifted as he was artificially boosted obviously weren't working out for him, beyond having a much higher constitution than any human deserved.

Blows that should have cracked his skull and left his brain as pink porridge were instead stunning him, but that was fine.

I punched him in the nose, as hard as I could. His head rocked back to bounce off the sand as he tried to cover his throat and face with his arms.

Then I grabbed his wrist, twisted it out and yanked the arm to full extension, leaned back and lifted my foot, bringing it up to rest against the outside of his elbow before he could realize what I was doing and toss me off him.

Then I pulled as hard as I could with both hands and pushed with my leg.

The scream that escaped him as the flexion joint shattered and opened the wrong way was incredible. As I released the arm to flop weakly loose, his other arm came across to grab at it, uncovering his throat.

Big mistake.

My knuckles came down as hard as I could, crushing his larynx. He frantically tried to spit words out…to beg, to curse, to surrender—I didn't know. But I knew one thing for sure.

This wasn't a fight to first blood, and it wasn't one that the Scepiniir would permit to end with a shake of the hand and us going our own separate ways.

Neither would this fucker have ever allowed that if he had the advantage.

I had no clue how many deaths he was responsible for, but I didn't doubt there were many. And to win here, to save Chris and my friends, to claim the Temple of Zeus dungeon and this one, he had to die.

I punched down hard. His fingers scrabbled at his throat, and the distraction of him being unable to breathe made the last few blows almost trivial. There was a desultory attempt at a block, a few twists and thrusts as he tried to topple me off. But time was on my side—quite literally—and I saw the blows coming, angled my responses around them, and continued to beat him to death.

By the time I pushed off him, standing slowly and turning my back on the body that lay twitching, its skull shattered and claret draining into the sands, I was heaving for breath, but I knew it was done.

I looked up at the silent figure of Warmaster Kh'aan standing, silently observing, and I raised my fists into the air, blood and cranial fluids dripping from them as I called out.

"Warmaster Kh'aan!" I bellowed. "It is done. The honor of the Scepiniir has been defended!"

Silence reined for long seconds. He made a single gesture to the guard, and they began to make noises, random and discordant as before, and in the silence of my mind, I heard him.

"Well done, young cub. Perhaps what I seek is finally within my grasp after all. Three times. Three times I will permit you to summon me as a reward for this.

But be warned. The third time, you and I shall fight, and truly. If you would have my service, you must prove yourself. No more will I pull my blows…no more will I teach. Instead, in that final fight, you will ascend, or die."

With that, he lifted his arms, and he, and all the watchers around the outside of the arena, all Scepiniir in his honor guard, burst into flames, standing proud and silent as they literally burned to death, giving off not a sign of pain or fear.

"Fuck me, you crazy bastards," I whispered to myself, staring wide-eyed at them as the bodies fell, before finally, the notifications started coming in.

Congratulations! You have killed the following:

- ***1x Lord Summoner Valkos, Dungeon Lord #56 [Elite], Level 34, 25,000 XP***

Total XP awarded: 25,000 XP
Current XP to next level stands at: 36,410/165,000

Congratulations, Dungeon Warmancer! You have completed a Quest!

Quest: Whoever rules the Dungeon, rules the land!

Valkos, Lord Summoner of Dungeon #56, has fallen in honorable combat. As this was the result of an [Elimination] bout, all rewards go to the victor; congratulations, Dungeon Warmancer!

Please note, Dungeon Core #56 has sustained significant damage and requires internal strengthening and repairs before higher-tier functions can be restored.

Unlocking Dungeon Access in 3…2…1…

I grunted as the world around me spun viciously. A sudden need to vomit built and a lump filled my throat, before I managed to choke it down, staring at the floor and panting.

By the time I'd managed to get full control of myself again, the air before me was filled with more boxes.

Most were simple ones to deal with. Two dungeons had been identified as seeking primary access and bond with me. I had to pick one—no surprises that I picked my own Newcastle dungeon—and made that the primary, with this as a secondary vassal.

Then it became a case of approving access to others, and unlocking the mana systems. The stupid bastard Valkos—I glanced at the cooling corpse in disgust—had somehow locked all the dungeon's mana routing systems to himself. For the entirety of the fight, and for the creation of the elimination trial, all the mana that the damn dungeon needed, including the basic shit to just maintain itself, was all being siphoned off to him.

That meant that the dungeon had been literally cannibalizing itself to try to maintain the core.

It took long minutes to reroute and unlock those changes, to correct the conduits and to change the fuckers to actually feed the dungeon rather than that dickhead of a Dungeon Lord.

In the process, though, I found a few new things.

A "Corruption Twin Generator" was the tech that the bastard had been using to claim the Temple of Zeus's dungeon, by somehow making its entire internal properties identical, at a molecular level, to this one.

I found that, and thankfully the fucker had already failed as soon as I'd entered the dungeon and the mana had been rerouted.

That meant that when I tried to access the distant dungeon, I was rebuffed, but that was fine; I could feel more notifications waiting. The fairy Xen-Xara hadn't gone back on her word, I saw as I pulled the relevant notification up to check; it was just that she was trying to reestablish the network and link to the gate. As soon as the connection to here had gone down, that dungeon had been freed and she'd offered a link to me.

I approved it. The system told me that I was now linked to that dungeon as its lord—again, my Newcastle dungeon was challenged for primacy, and I slapped that fucker down, hard.

No clue why I was able to see all of this through the system but I couldn't access them remotely yet. I just accepted that as a part of the whole Reach Out and Touch Me limitation on my skills. I'd be upgrading that again soon.

Next was the surprise that the Temple of Zeus dungeon wasn't the only subservient and compelled dungeon that this fucker had taken over.

There was another in a set of mountains of Sinai, but when I checked, whoever was there had locked down, *hard*. As soon as they'd been freed by this idiot's death, they'd cut off any communication and links. I bet, after meeting this asshole as I had, that they'd be keeping it that way.

The next few notifications were all about the upgrades. And as much as they were important, seeing that I'd gained access to the previous rewards and research tasks that this dungeon and Zeus had managed, they weren't enough to keep me reading.

I had new fairies and fey creatures, undead and spirits, as well as elemental technologies and sand-based stuff that I just knew Alison was going to lose her shit over when she saw it all.

I pulled up the next notification in line and nodded to myself, seeing the rewards. It basically repeated that the quest had been completed, but as this one came with bonuses, it was good to see.

Congratulations, Dungeon Warmancer!

You have completed your quest and have been declared Dungeon Lord by both Xen-Xara, the Dungeon Fairy of Dungeon [076], and from the Tree of Life, through which she is bonded, tying Dungeon [076] as a vassal as well.

For your success, you receive the following:

- ***1x Vassal Dungeon***
- ***1x Dungeon Fairy [Bound]***

- ***19x Fairies***
- ***1x Cyclops***
- ***1x Fairy Dungeon Core Research Path***
- ***1x Dungeon Perk***
- ***1x Class Skill Point***
- ***250,000 XP***

Congratulations! You have reached Level 36. Current XP to next level stands at 121,410/165,000. You have 15 unspent Stat Points and 1 unspent Skill Point.

Again, I sighed in relief. It was done. And as the last barriers came down, Jack reestablished his link to me, the roar of the dragon overhead ringing out in triumph.

EPILOGUE

"Fuck me, that's a relief," I whispered as I took Kelly in my arms, holding her tight and squeezing her for a few seconds as everything was made right again.

The reactivation of the dungeon had taken two hours. And in that time, I'd marched back and forth across the dungeon over and over, desperate to be moving, hating that I was wasting time that every instinct screamed at me should be spent flying to help my friends.

I'd known better, though.

In staying where I was, in allowing the dungeon to reactivate and heal the damage that had been done, I'd gained access to the nexus gates again. And as soon as they were up and running?

I'd simply stepped across thousands of miles, emerging at Newcastle to find a dungeon in full party mode.

Unable to help myself, and regardless of the potential waste of the point, the first thing I'd done when I'd gotten access to it was to pull up my class skills and flick through them until I came to what I needed, the choice being a very clear one as I spent the point and unlocked the next level.

<u>Reach Out and Touch Me:</u> *Your Dungeon is no longer only controllable when you are within its own environs. Now you can interact with it at increasing distances. This skill ranks in levels from 0 (Local) to 5 (Interstellar). (Current level: 3, Domain of the WorldSinger)*

As soon as I'd done that, I'd reached out to Kelly and confirmed that the fight against the slavers was still ongoing. That'd driven me wild with a need to be moving, to be doing *something* to help Mike and his team.

I knew, though—I just knew—that should I set off flying now? I'd be actively wasting time, rather than waiting until the dungeon connected back to the network and I could use the gates instead.

Ten minutes before the portal was able to be reactivated, though, the big mad bastard came through for us all, and the notifications started to stream in. He'd won, and although the fight hadn't been an easy one, the slavers were mainly dead, he was in control of the dungeon, and the war was over.

At last, peace reigned across all our sites. And by the time I got home, well, it was all that I could do to not crush Kelly in the sheer bloody relief that I felt.

"You're home," she whispered into my chest, and I nodded, agreeing wholeheartedly.

"Wherever *you* are, is home," I replied, meaning every word.

The others arrived over the next few hours. The portals opened in dribs and drabs to let in a few at a time; then silence, then a rush of people; then nothing, again and again.

Mike was in a state when he got back, the signs of a dozen wounds clear. His armor—what was left of it—was burned, blackened, and generally smashed to shit.

His team weren't much better, and although most had survived, it was down to a lot of luck, and to Mike spending the lives of dungeon-born like water.

Chris was pretty battered as well, though he'd had a lot more time to recover. Once the dungeon lost its connection to the undead lot, Xen-Xara had been good about summoning more fairies, specifically ones skilled at healing, as well as special fruits that boosted mana regeneration.

It seemed that a lot of the issues we'd had with potions and fumbling our way forward were going to be dealt with by the inclusion of fairy magics and their fascination with growing herbs.

Robin, who Rhodes had now firmly taken under her wing and had been trying to teach tactics to…well, she'd learned some valuable lessons as well.

I'd not even noticed in all the stress and strain of my own fights that she'd been drawing on my divine core, but she'd apparently gone all "I shall smite thee, oh smitey mofo," several times, mainly thanks to the armor's effect.

Finn was so apologetic, it had gone through the stage of anger and annoyance into that special level of abuse that only close friends could manage.

Fortunately, as much as everyone had agreed on the whole "never again" side of the armor, they were all—and I mean *all*—impressed with just how durable the armor had proved.

People had taken direct hits from high-powered weapons and they'd survived, solely thanks to how incredible it was. And as such, although he was getting a lot of gentle—and some not so gentle—ribbing, it was clear that he'd not actually lost our people's respect and trust.

The benefits of prototyping and multiple test subjects had been made clear, though.

Robin had gained a new class—Thunderclast, which was apparently something to do with bringing the storm. That had been overjoying for her at first, though less so for those around her.

At the minute, all she'd been able to manage was a heavy rain, and it was centered on her, even when she went indoors.

Dante had made some great strides in magical theory, and where my own Warmancer class combined with the Dungeon Lord class to create specific bonuses, so did his Avatar of Flame.

His evolution—he'd been with Mike—had brought an AOE attack named Rains of Gehenna that really was a crowd-pleaser. Provided the crowd was into seeing its enemies made into deep-fried-crispy-people-McNuggets, anyway.

It essentially let him designate an area and bring the rain. But instead of water, in this case it was oil that had been superheated to three hundred degrees.

There were a lot of people who vomited at the results, but when you took its nastiness into account, it was actually an insanely effective way of breaking an enemy.

Five seconds into its fifteen-second effect and the entire enemy force were begging to surrender—all it'd taken was letting a few of those enemies to escape to spread the word. That apparently resulted in the entire next enemy group surrendering en masse when he started to chant.

Like I said, *effective*.

It wasn't all good news, unfortunately.

As much as I'd hoped that he could be saved, and Jo and the others had fought an insanely hard fight to make sure he would, Griffiths had succumbed to his wounds.

There were just too many injuries. Despite the magical healing that we had at hand, there was only so much that could be healed, when the body was as broken as his had been.

Personally, when I'd gone to his side to say goodbye, I was sure it was because although many of his people had now been reunited with their families, he'd been one of the unlucky ones who hadn't.

Kelly had pointed out that there was no way for the brave soldier to have known, but I knew, and I chose to believe that no matter what he was doing now, he was with his family again.

Others had fallen in the fight; hundreds had been lost. And one that had died in a completely unrelated way had been Drak.

The little kobold adventurer had finally begun pulling his weight after Ciara laid into him about his addiction and the likelihood of him winding up in jail.

As such, when we'd been off at war, he'd been on a routine scouting mission with another dungeon-born kobold, and had fallen foul of a group of raiders.

His burned corpse was identifiable only from his armor, it was that bad, and his companion had vanished as well. I felt guilty as hell, and Ciara apologized to me a dozen times over, offering to serve a penance for having pushed him to his death in such a manner. But in the end, that was the way the world was. Shit happened, and there was nothing we could do about it.

The deal with London had been made, and the fake core handed over, though it'd taken some scrambling to arrange, and a lot of panicked running by their army to get it all fixed up.

Kelly had given me a brief once-over with it, and I had to admit, it'd gone well.

She'd told them that we'd been moving the core close to London deliberately as a test after all the shit they'd pulled, and it was one that the earl and his wife had passed. Then she'd explained that there were significant forces held in reserve, hidden and ready to eliminate any attackers, had they tried that, and had finally warned that had it looked like we were going to lose the core, then it would have been detonated. An action that would have sterilized the surrounding area for about a mile on all sides, leaving only a crater.

Then she'd asked sweetly whether the earl wanted to deal with the London forces that were closing on the core or whether she should.

The bluff had worked, or the earl wasn't letting on that it hadn't either way. She'd provided enough in the way of details on the nearby hidden troops that it was clear we did know about them and knew more about the London lot than they knew about us, and they'd backed the fuck off, sharpish.

The deal that she'd struck with the earl was that he and his wife were to be the designated controllers of the dungeon core, and that they were to provide ten percent of all technological materials collected as a ten-year tithe to us.

We were to be given access to any and all technology they researched, and to the museums at will. She'd explained away the museums as a religious thing for the kobolds primarily with the dinosaurs, and that had been waved off as unimportant.

Chris was already drawing up a list of the dinos and random extinct crap he wanted resurrecting.

In reality, the core had been guided to the area we'd recommended by our transporters, and then they'd shut down, their bodies being consumed by the "new core" as it activated.

It was all smoke and mirrors, but fuck it. The important detail was that London thought they had a core, it was in place where we wanted it, and Emma, Jenn, Jimmy, and Andre were having a whale of a time hiding beneath their feet, expanding the dungeon out and basically recovering from all the shit they'd been through.

I'd wanted to send them on the assaults, but in the end, the London dungeon was incredibly valuable—or I hoped it would become so—and the decision had been made to base them out of there for now.

They had, unsurprisingly, made the effort to come back for the party though.

Free drinks were free drinks.

Akuba and Kaatachi had come, and had persuaded Lelani to visit as well, and she and "Engineer Zheng" were touring the party, making deals every time I looked around.

Kai was apparently much happier back at the dungeon, but had sent his regards, as well as a request that I visit them to discuss the pantheon and its possible expansion with him.

I'd told Robin she needed to get her least batshit cultist to speak with Ashley, and that the three of them would be responsible for spreading the "good word" and then I'd left them to plan, feeling only slightly guilty over the glare that Ashley had given me.

Chris and Becky had apparently sorted out any issues between them, though a lot of it had something to do with her seeing him go absolutely nuclear when he thought she was injured, and beating an undead cyclops—not exactly a physically weak opponent at the best of times—into a pile of broken bones.

He'd done that using a token—I'd sort of forgotten that he could transform his body, boosting it with parts of various creatures—that he'd grabbed out of his collection at random.

It'd turned out to be a massive tooth—not from a tiger as he'd planned, but from a silverback gorilla. He'd swelled to twice his size, and had beaten it and a dozen other enemies into paste, before doing the whole chest-beating routine.

She'd done a really embarrassing demonstration of that part three times since I'd gotten back now, and he was mortified, which provided us all with free entertainment.

By the time that Earl Morris and his lady, Field Marshal Macmillan, Sara-Ann, Countess of Stockport arrived, General Blackstone and Hawk had come too. I'd mellowed to the point that as much as I distrusted them all on instinct, I agreed it was right to invite them, and managed to keep my disapproval to a minimum.

They hadn't been so stupid as to bring Johnstone and Trust, after all.

"Thank you for the invitation." The earl stared around, clearly impressed. "I have to admit, my last visit to Newcastle was under less pleasant circumstances, and the request that we bring bathing suits now makes a lot more sense."

The group had joined Kelly and me, and the majority of our command and leadership cadre, in the massive outdoor pool. I forced a smile onto my face. I had to admit, either they were insanely skilled at faking this shit, or they were genuinely impressed.

"Well, Kelly told me about the deal with the dungeon core that she struck while I was at war, and the warning that you gave, so it seemed only fair to take you off the shit list, and instead invite you to the party," I admitted.

"It's an impressive one." Sara-Ann smiled widely. "I especially enjoy the drinks available."

She should, I had to admit. As part of the deal with Kelly giving them the dungeon core—the fake one, not a real one—she'd taken one of every bottle and form of stored food that the earl had access to.

That had turned out to be a massive storehouse of top-tier booze, not to mention preserves and weird-ass shit like caviar and pickled shark.

We'd absorbed it into the dungeon, and now, on all sides, she could see my people—human, goblin, Scepiniir, kobold, and more—staggering around, quaffing from bottles that a week ago were among the last of their kind in the world, and were arguably worth more than a king's ransom…although admittedly only to a very small number of very weird people.

Personally, I was happy with my rum and Coke—dark rum, of course; I wasn't a heathen—and I lay back, half submerged in the water as I watched the southerners, my eyes heavy-lidded. I opened my mouth to make a point that probably wasn't about to be as subtle as I wanted it to be.

That was when the notification overrode everything for me and for everyone around me, as a new kind of prompt appeared.

Unlike the others I'd seen, it was neither ornate and impressive, nor simple and measured like most system notifications that subtly hinted that you were barely worth the effort of its acknowledgment.

No, this was entirely new. As I sat up in the water, my drink spilling, I swore. My voice joined hundreds on all sides, and probably tens of thousands if not more around the world.

The new notification was a deep and angry red, each word picked out on a black background and lined in yellow. Even the border around the outside pulsed and shivered, as if desperate to drive the point home.

—BEWARE, BEWARE, BEWARE—

Approaching Orakai Swarmship detected

Tentative identification: Halcyon Scout class—advance assault and system interdiction vessel.

Incoming vessel has breached the outermost sensor ring, and is decelerating inward. Time to arrival:

37 solar cycles, 19 sections, 4 briefs.

—BEWARE, BEWARE, BEWARE—

"Oh, for fuck's sake!" I roared, dumping my drink and glaring at the notification. "Fuck right off!"

THE END OF BOOK 8

THANKS!

Hi everyone, well, I hope you enjoyed that? As I said at the beginning of the book, I'm going to be jumping across to UnderVerse next, so by the time you read this, I'll hopefully have most of book 8 done, and depending on when you do, I may even have 9 or more finished!

If you want to follow me on social media, have a look for my author page on Facebook, reach out on Reddit, or join my discord, my author pages have all the relevant links!

They also have a regular link to Patreon, should you decide that you want to read ahead!

My plan for the next year is that UnderVerse 8 will launch on eBook and paperback around June/July, with UnderVerse 9 around September/October, and then Rise of Mankind roughly three months after that for each book.

To warn you now though, audio can be a little out from that, usually 3-6 months, depending on availability, so please take these dates with a pinch of salt. After all, incredible narrators are worth waiting for.

Lastly, if you're looking to grab a beer, and shoot the shit, I'll be at JordanCon in Atlanta around April this year, LitRPG Con in Denver around July and DragonCon in Atlanta around September again. Hope to see you there, and as always, thank you so much for your support.

You have no idea of the difference it makes.

-Jez
10/02/2025

PATREON

Hi everyone! Okay, when this launches in February all of my Patreon supporters will have already read it, and some will have already finished the next book I've been working on as well, which is UnderVerse 8! The highest tiers will also have access to a secret project, and will be busily reading the end of UnderVerse 8, and possibly even book 9. So, if you want to read them perhaps 4-6 months ahead of release? Come join us on the dark side!

HOWEVER: I do want to point out one thing everyone, the app stores on apple and android platforms have enforced that a 30% mandatory percentage goes to them for any purchasing done through the apps. So the app store Patreon subscription has increased by that amount automatically, PLEASE sign up through the website instead, it's still Patreon's website, and the increase doesn't apply there.

There's several of those wonderful supporters out there that I have to thank personally as well; ASeaInStorm, Mischa, Niall, Kevin, Lex, and Steve thank you all!

TO REPLACE WITH CURRENT MEMBERS

https://www.patreon.com/Jezcajiao

UNDERVERSE 8: TOWER OF GAIJ

By Jez Cajiao

Stranded thousands of miles form their companions, Jax, Oracle and Sehran are alone, cut off from all support, and the only thing they have in plenty, are enemies.

Stranded on a hostile continent with only his companions, Jax faces a stark reality: all the power of his newfound crown means nothing in a land where no one knows his name—and wouldn't care if they did. With time running out and shadows gathering, he needs to carve out more than just survival from this foreign soil.

The Tower of Gaij looms on the horizon, an ancient fortress of power that could be their salvation. But in these lands, nothing worth taking comes without blood. As rival claimants gather and forgotten powers stir in the darkness, Jax will have to embrace the ruthless lessons the UnderVerse has taught him—or lose everything he's fought to protect.

It turns out building an empire was the easy part. Keeping alive long enough to return to it? That's going to take something darker than mere leadership.

In a land where every shadow hides a blade, even a prince must remember: crowns make excellent targets.

Note: This is a Dark Fantasy Epic LitRPG. Expect graphic violence, strong language, and morally complex themes. Reader discretion is advised.

THEFT OF DECKS

By Lars Machmuller

When the deck is stacked against you? Change the game!

In the frontier town of Isarn, Chase will never be more than the lowly Darkborn thief he is. Banned from training, banned from acquiring better cards, if the Lightborn had their way, he'd be banned from life itself.

He's not alone though, and the one thing he and his friends have is determination. Losing a hand to a brutal punishment only fueled his obsession to get access to his own amazing, reality-bending cards.

That is the path to power and a future for them all. Nobody cares where you came from when you're rich enough. For now, though, they're facing both established powers, churches and age-old prejudices. It's time to get to work, and if the Lightborn won't share and play nice?

Sometimes the only way to get dealt a better hand is to steal the whole damn deck!

QUEST ACADEMY

By Brian J. Nordon

A world infested by demons.
An Academy designed to train Heroes to save humanity from annihilation.
A new student's power could make all the difference.

Humans have been pushed to the brink of extinction by an ever-evolving demonic threat. Portals are opening faster than ever, Towers bursting into the skies and Dungeons being mined below the last safe havens of society. The demons are winning.

Quest Academy stands defiantly against them, as a place to train the next generation of Heroes. The Guild Association is holding the line, but are in dire need of new blood and the powerful abilities they could bring to the battlefront. To be the saviors that humanity needs, they need to surpass the limits of those that came before them.

In a war with everything on the line, every power matters. With an adaptive enemy, comes the need for a constant shift in tactics. A new age of strategy is emerging, with even the unlikeliest of Heroes making an impact.

Salvatore Argento has never seen a demon.
He has never aspired to become a Hero.
Yet his power might be the one to tip the odds in humanity's favor.

WANDERING WARRIOR

By Michael Head

A divine quest to deliver justice.
One year to accomplish his mission.
After nineteen planets, there's something different about this one.

James Holden has reached the maximum level there is for a human. That's perfect, since he's the only one of his kind. A wandering warrior, without control of his destination, tossed between universes by gods who've failed to tell him why. James is the lone Judge on a new world in need of someone to balance the scales. He isn't afraid to do so with extreme prejudice. As the Chief Justice, he has to right the wrongs the innocent can't fix themselves.

As James quickly discovers, the roots of corruption run deep. Guilds choose to protect themselves rather than the people. Monsters roam the wilderness unchecked. Judgment is usually a decision between right and wrong, but nothing is ever that simple. This time, being the strongest human won't be enough to punish the guilty. James might have to recruit some new blood, even if he prefers to work alone.

On his twentieth world, he is going to win, no matter the cost. James will have to find a way to break past the limits of the system if he's going to have a chance at making a difference.

KNIGHTS OF ETERNITY

By Rachel Ní Chuirc

When Zara awoke in chains she thought she'd gone mad.

She was Zara the Fury - mistress of flame and fear. Her name was whispered across the land, from ramshackle taverns to the royal court. Even the heroic Gilded Knights thought twice before crossing her path.

She was feared—*respected.*

Now she was curled up on a dirt floor on her fiancé's orders. Valerius, leader of the Gilded, mocks her cries for help. And the kingdom is on the brink of war over the missing Lady Eternity…

But that wasn't why Zara thought she had gone mad.

The reason why is that the last thing she remembered was blood, an arcade screen, and the gun that changed everything.

But no chains can hold the Fury, and when she gets out?
The world is going to *burn.*

SCARLET CITADEL

By Jack Fields

Gormon Hughes is 19, thin as a broom, and has—not for the first time in his life—been swept into the path of trouble. Poor, recently heartbroken, and indebted to the sort of people who file their teeth into needle points and devour wriggling bloated spiders for fun, Hughes sets his sights on salvation.

That salvation is the Scarlet Citadel, a wealthy organization of pageant fighters, monster hunters, and secret keepers. With the aid of strange oracles, rare good fortune, and a unique power that bubbles like champagne in the core of Hughes' being, he must join the Citadel and advance himself.

But the ladder of progression is harsh and dark. The rungs are slippery.

And falling means disaster...

A FOREST OF VANITY AND VALOUR

By Adam Beswick

An aggressive debt collector banished from the kingdom. Now his life depends on his ability to help the less fortunate...

Vireo Reinhold relishes collecting his monarch's proper dues. Working hard to prolong and fund the king's never-ending war, the self-centered official revels in the perks of luxury that come with his unorthodox role. But his world upends when he unearths an ancient spellbook that promises to unlock a shadowy, forgotten magic.

Embroiled in a secret affair with a fellow noble's wife, Vireo is mortified when he's forced to commit an unthinkable act. Driven into exile, no longer able to coerce the vulnerable, and with the powerful tome in his enemy's hands, the fallen agent's only shot at survival hangs on his skills at saving others.

Can Vireo redeem himself as the people's champion before they all fall to a sinister fate?

A Forest of Vanity and Valour is the dark first book in the Tales of Levanthria fantasy-retelling series. If you like fast-paced action, evil-to-good transformations, and classic stories with a twist, then you'll love A.P Beswick's ominous tale.

FACEBOOK AND SOCIAL MEDIA

If you want to reach out, chat or shoot the shit, you can always find me on either my author page here:

www.facebook.com/JezCajiaoAuthor

OR

We've recently set up a new Facebook group to spread the word about cool LitRPG books. It's dedicated to two very simple rules;

1: Let's spread the word about new and old brilliant LitRPG books.

2: Don't be a Dick!

They sound like really simple rules, but you'd be amazed…

Come join us!

https://www.facebook.com/groups/LITRPGLegion

I'm also on Discord here: https://discord.gg/u5JYHscCEH

Or I'm reaching out on other forms of social media atm, I'm just spread a little thin that's all!

You're most likely to find me on Discord, but please, don't be offended when I don't approve friend requests on my personal Facebook pages. I did originally, and several people abused that, sending messages to my family and being generally unpleasant, hence, the author page:

www.facebook.com/JezCajiaoAuthor

I hope you understand.

LEGION

Okay everybody, if you've not yet seen or heard, well, the secret is out! My wife Chrissy, and our friend Geneva and I have launched the Legion Publishers!

We're taking on new authors, as well as experienced ones, focusing primarily on the LitRPG side of things, but we're open to anything really, with one very clear rule that guides our company:

Don't be a dick.

That's it. Our contracts aren't hidden behind layers of legalese, you can find them here:

https://www.legionpublishers.com/legioncontract

If you want to reach out and ask any questions, get an idea of the support we offer, and possibly become part of the family? We'd love to hear from you, just tap the link and fill in the form:

https://www.legionpublishers.com/contact-and-submissions

Hope you're having a good one!

-Jez, Chrissy and Geneva

LITRPG!

To learn more about LitRPG, talk to other authors including myself, and to just have an awesome time, please join the LitRPG Group

www.facebook.com/groups/LitRPGGroup

FACEBOOK

There's also a few really active Facebook groups I'd recommend you join, as you'll get to hear about great new books, new releases and interact with all your (new) favorite authors! (I may also be there, skulking at the back and enjoying the memes…)

https://www.facebook.com/groups/LitRPGlegion/

https://www.facebook.com/groups/GamelitSociety

https://www.facebook.com/groups/LitRPG.books

https://www.facebook.com/groups/LitRPGforum/

www.ingramcontent.com/pod-product-compliance
Lightning Source LLC
Chambersburg PA
CBHW060753210726
48292CB00013B/69

* 9 7 8 1 9 1 5 6 1 7 3 0 9 *